THE GRANTA BOOK OF THE AMERICAN
SHORT STORY

THE GRANTA BOOK OF THE
AMERICAN SHORT STORY

EDITED BY RICHARD FORD

GRANTA BOOKS
LONDON
in association with
PENGUIN BOOKS

GRANTA BOOKS

2/3 Hanover Yard, Noel Road, Islington, London N1 8BE

Published in association with the Penguin Group
Penguin Books Ltd, 27 Wrights Lane, London W8 5TZ, England
Viking Penguin, a division of Penguin Books USA Inc.,
375 Hudson Street, New York NY 10014, USA
Penguin Books Australia Ltd, Ringwood, Victoria, Australia
Penguin Books Canada Ltd, 2801 John Street, Markham,
Ontario, Canada L3R 1B4
Penguin Books (NZ) Ltd, 182–190 Wairau Road,
Auckland 10, New Zealand

Penguin Books Ltd, Registered Offices: Harmondsworth, Middlesex, England

First published by Granta Books 1992

1 3 5 7 9 10 8 6 4 2

Introduction copyright © Richard Ford 1992
For other copyrights see Acknowledgments

Printed in Great Britain by Butler & Tanner Ltd, Frome and London

A CIP catalogue record for this book is available from the British Library

ISBN 0 14 014220 7

CONTENTS

INTRODUCTION

I've always supposed that Frank O'Connor, the great and beloved Irish story writer, was only taunting us back in 1962—the year I wrote *my* first short story—when he said that we Americans have handled the short story so wonderfully, one could say that it is our national art form.

Why, I've thought, would as good a story writer as there ever was from a country where the short story was *already* the national art form decide to cut us in unless it was to make fun with fulsome praise.

Over the decades Americans, of course, *have* written short stories wonderfully, even though I'm not ready to claim them as our national art form, and in fact I can't even see in the great variety of American moods, hues, tones, effects, forms, and narrative strategies much difference between our short stories and, say, Irish ones, or ours and the Italian, or the French, or even ours and the English. Place names. A few Giuseppes and Nigels where ours turn out to be Lukes and Cindys. But that's all. Nothing especially fundamental; each nationality producing a sufficient rainbow of stories that O'Connor's rather generic and, for him, liberal definition of a short story as being simply a piece of artistic organization made of words, seems to suit.

The Lonely Voice, O'Connor's little book of essays on the short story, is certainly the most provocative and attentive there is on the form, and is probably where anyone, including me, who has an overview of the short story—American and European both—got it. Published in America in 1962, and containing a dozen affectionate, rather quirky but lucid essays on Turgenev, Lawrence, Babel, Hemingway, Mary Lavin and others, *The Lonely Voice* sets forth what have become famous postulates of the 'traditional' short story: that stories have no essential or natural forms, but are made-up things that aren't even always short; that they should be plausible, have exposition, development and drama; that good stories are almost always about 'outlawed figures' hoping to escape from 'submerged population groups,' rather than about 'normal' characters who fit into society as a whole—a concern O'Connor reserved for novels; that stories are natively romantic, individualistic and intransigent; and that America is a brutal place full of dislocated people who sometimes fool you and act nice, thereby making the US a natural place for short stories to flourish.

Europeans have always liked typifying American literature as being primarily about brooding male figures alone on a vast, windy continent, wishing hopelessly and romantically to keep in check some awful brutality we secretly love. Stephen Spender, in his unctuous and chin-pulling essay on the American writer *circa* 1949, delivered the judgment that 'Intense loneliness gives all great American literature something in common, the sense of a lonely animal howling in the dark, like wolves in a story of Jack London.' I can only guess that a certain kind of person gets giddy fantasizing about such a primordial (and non-existent) place he doesn't have to live in but can read about in private.

Frank O'Connor's favorite American writer back in 1962 seems to have been Sherwood Anderson (dead, by then, twenty years), and his favorite book of stories Anderson's classic, *Winesburg, Ohio*, full in fact of all those lonely, brooding, quasi-loonies. But to read *Winesburg*, published in 1919, as being typical of American short fiction, then or now, is like being an explorer who arrives in Australia today, sees a kangaroo, and concludes kangaroos probably run everything. One needs to go farther toward the interior.

The Lonely Voice in fact came along just as the latest phase of formal experiment and re-visioning in American short story writing was creating a tumult among writers and readers, and O'Connor can certainly be excused for not being on the cutting edge of another country's newest writing, particularly when that writing seemed so different from what he liked. Many of O'Connor's firmest convictions, though—about plausibility and character, exposition, development— were, at the beginning of the sixties, being uprooted and turned upside down by Americans writing what came to be called 'anti-stories' or 'metafiction,' and later on in the seventies, 'postmodernist fiction' or just plain 'fictions.'

This was new work with uncertain settings, stories often without characters *at all*, much less lonely, outlawed ones; stories without linear developments or events or closures, stories that goaded conventional plausibility, and in which words were imagined not first as windows to meaning or even to the factual world, as had been the case since slightly before Cervantes, but as narrative *objets* with arbitrary, sometimes ironically-assigned references, palpable shapes, audible sounds, rhythms—all of whose intricacies and ironies produced aesthetic as well as ordinary cognitive pleasures. These were often outrageous, loudly-funny, declamatory, brainy, biting, self-referring stories, if in fact they were 'stories' at all (much more chin-pulling went on about this). They defied the mimetic-realistic unities Frank O'Connor loved so much, and many of us who were beginning to be writers in the sixties loved them and were shocked by them, even if we loved O'Connor's unities, too, and couldn't write in the new way.

This was new writing affected by the Latin American literature arriving then in the States, in particular stories by Jorge Luis Borges and novels by Carlos Fuentes and, later, Gabriel García Márquez; by the aesthetics of Gruppo 63 in Italy and the *Nouveau Roman* in France; even by the decline of the New Criticism, an analytical protocol popular in American university pedagogy since the thirties, and the slick way of anatomizing literature by isolating its formal features for close study.

Otherwise, as with experiment at any time, whatever fractious and dislocating business was in the American air became an influence: the commencement of the Viet Nam war simultaneous to the brief, halcyon, Kennedy days; new writing by Africans and Native Americans; a generation of war babies heading off to college where upsetting books were waiting.

Experiment wasn't new in American writing, though it had remained something of an acquired taste among readers. But because of the wider publication of non-traditional stories (Donald Barthelme became a fixture in the *New Yorker*), and because of the increased numbers of university writing programs where teachers who were writers took the liberty to teach what they liked and wrote themselves, the 'conversation' over what was a good story became public and even almost popular.

These new 'fictions' implied an ungracious opinion held by many American writers and readers: that the prior generations' work was dull and sleepy and worse; it was irrelevant and compromised and complacent about its own forms, as if these previous writers—America's best ones—considered a story's form to be a template rather than what the new writers thought it was, an infinitely mutable and variegated process that had constantly to be kept fluid and lively. 'Process' was a word on many lips in the sixties and seventies. Truth was a process of collaborative myth. Education was a process of boundary-less disciplines. Marriage was a process of evolving harmonies. *Life* was certainly a process of many shocking and ill-fitting things, little of which was being truthfully or even interestingly referred to by such ham-handedly normative conceits as plots, settings, characters, sequential narrative time or knowable point of view—the traditional forms of story-ness.

A much-thumbed collection of short fiction from the sixties, *The Anti-Story Anthology*, containing work by Borges and other foreigners as well as by Americans (Gass, Barth, Barthelme), too, complained in its introduction that American fiction of the fifties was 'perhaps the most conservative of mid-century, probably the single mode of artistic expression most self-imitative.' Unpretty words: predictable, bland, even formless were used to unseat the old in favor of what the editor thought was the *now* stuff then.

I remember reading a column by Gordon Lish in a 1971 *Esquire*, relishing his new captaincy of the magazine's fiction duties—a change in command I remember as producing considerable, fidgety curiosity among us American short story wanna-bes, since *Esquire* had published a great deal of the best American fiction since the thirties, and we all wished it would publish ours. 'Fiction has now become a vehicle for conveying a feeling,' Lish wrote, ' . . . the principal elements in a piece become tone, mood, atmosphere, style, color, form—the aesthetic elements—as against the narrative elements on which were established the great stories of the fifties.'

That all sounded fine to me, although 'aesthetic elements' hadn't seemed exactly lacking in the work of earlier generations I knew about, nor in writing going on at the time. Work I liked—by John Updike, Joyce Carol Oates, Leonard Michaels—was neither predictable *nor* conservative, even if it went on representing people as people and the dialog made a kind of usual sense. In any case, Eudora Welty knew plenty about mood and atmosphere, color and style as long ago as 1941, as did Paul Bowles whom I was then reading. And there was Flannery O'Connor and James Baldwin. They wrote about feeling. And then there was Faulkner, who seemed to do everything all at once and had no equal.

To me, the new work all around was thrilling, but so was the old, and as a reader I didn't see a need to choose, though my tendencies as a writer were toward the traditional. There were extremes of form—I understood that. But if in stories yet to be written, these extremes could be made by writers to accommodate one another—contrary formal features joined, language's 'poetic qualities' re-certified for wider use—then change, even *refinement* would occur. And probably, I thought, they would occur in the context of traditional convictions proving resilient. That, I thought, would be the short story's future.

And it was. Many of these newly-surprising and perplexing 'fictions' were, in fact, read by Americans drilled in rather traditional narrative expectations, readers who were willing to impose their presumptions on stories that didn't like their presumptions. Anti-stories *were*, however, usually written in sentences one could read as well as 'experience' like tone poems. They had beginnings and middles if not always exactly endings. 'Images' seemed abundant. Readers often came to terms with such stories by seizing whatever evidence of narrative cohesion was available, postulating 'characters' where there were only voices, seeking correspondences and repetitions, noting things linear which might signal that stories referred outwards toward a plausible world instead of inwards to themselves or to some other, 'magical' realm. These readers may ultimately have appreciated this new work as being only ingenious permutations upon an older and already perfectly good method. But it's worth saying as a base principle that no matter how any story is 'understood,' its artistic intention is considerably rewarded if someone will simply read it. And these were read, even if among writers and readers they didn't supplant the practice of more traditional forms, a fact that may owe as much to comfort and habit as to the absolute excellence of any particular aesthetic.

What's important, though, for this nearly fifty years in American story writing—since 1944, the year I was born—is that these were and still are provoking issues among people who read and would write literature. The torque between so-called representational and non-representational writing has prolonged a feeling of unsettlement among writers as well as a preoccupation with invigorating the story's form as a way of creating effects in stories which would transcend form altogether. Maybe this is not altogether so strange in a country widely perceived to have no literary life, howling around in the dark as we all seem to be. Like wolves.

Not long ago, a young Italian academic, a university professor of American culture, remarked to me rather bemusedly at a cocktail party that one couldn't tell much about the American character—its people, its Gestalt—from reading its 'imaginative literature.' Novels, I supposed he meant, and short stories—since he was talking to me. Journalism, in his judgment, produced a clearer view. But before I could ask him a clearer view of what, precisely—cowboys? frontier wives? robber barons? And by the way, which journalism (*The National Enquirer, Mother Jones, Foreign Affairs, The Sporting News? The Bergen Record?*) and oh yes, which novels and stories (I hoped not mine), he'd floated off toward the carpaccio out of earshot, so that I was left with only a quandary. How could this be true? Should we even expect to find our national character expressed in our fiction?

The matter of imaginative literature as somehow being a report on or a distillation of one's national character had, in fact, been on my mind since reading the Canadian novelist Robertson Davies's interview in the *Paris Review*. There, Mr Davies said that Canadians might reasonably expect a sense of *their* national character from their national literature, and that they would find that sense in 'works that cause the reader to be visited dimly, briefly, by revelations such as cannot be produced by rational thinking. Works in which you can see not yourself but, for a second, the Inaccessible.' I took this to mean that at least part of one's national character, the part which imaginative literature can give evidence of is—as is true of much that great literature turns up—unrecognized or even nonexistent before its literary existence dawns.

Nearly the first thing that came to my mind, though, on hearing the doubts of my Italian friend, was to defend American literature against implied wishes that it produce as clear a picture as journalism.

What journalism means to provide, and fiction mostly doesn't (though sometimes it may), is what the American political columnist, Walter Lippmann, called 'a picture of reality on which the citizen can act.' Not how a citizen *ought* to act, or how she *might* act, but how he *can*. Put in its simplest terms: where are the streets safe so that I can go there? Where's a town I can get a job in? Whom can I vote for who'll represent my beliefs? Journalism means to tell us these things and tell us clearly. And there's no doubt that figuring out how we *can act* in our own country is a figuring which eventually reveals facets of our national character; just as there's no doubt that the line of journalism's mission and that of imaginative literature come continually to intersect and diverge.

Imaginative literature, at least initially, means to tell us something different, something made-up and for which we may have to suspend our disbelief, something whose existence is specific to a piece of writing and can't be accurately paraphrased, and which often deals with those consequences of our acts which we are likely to overlook because they're small, or buried in our interior selves, or both; or because language turns out to be an ambiguous thing which doesn't always announce what it seems to be announcing so that we are forced to act out of confusion. This may be one good reason that literature's relationship to our national character didn't seem clear to my Italian friend: because it's frequently about things that *aren't* clear but that need clearing up so that we can lead more morally responsible or even pleasurable lives—things we may not want to do because they're difficult.

Short stories in particular often seem to be about just such complicatedly difficult things: what final difference does it make if you act one way or another; what's your whole future worth once a deed's been done; is what I did good, bad or somewhere in the middle; based on what I read in this short story, how *should* a person act in other such situations? How do people actually feel in comparison with how convention tells us they feel? And more. Donald Barthelme's splendidly looney story, 'The Indian Uprising,' has at stake nothing more or less than the continued vitality of the short story itself, gone all out of whack and breaking apart, yet still seeming to hang together as an object of aesthetic pleasure and intuition. Even this stirs our moral imagination by appealing to our faith that an enlivened art is somehow necessary to our survival.

We come to literature—the stories in this anthology will bear me out—for, among other things, a view of morality in action, one of morality's main tenets being how we assess those human choices made as a consequence of no choice being clearly the right one. This, I believe, is the otherwise inaccessible data Mr Davies spoke of— inaccessible for being small or internalized in us or simply forbidding. Though in these tiny aperçus, these made-up stories, we can see our national character not so much reported on as actually *formed*, formed in the way Stephen Daedelus hoped to form the uncreated conscience of his race, just beneath the surface of its public one.

Oh sure, you can sometimes stumble into useful info while reading a dreamed-up short story. Recently in an obituary of the Irish writer Sean O'Faolain, I read that his stories were a chronicle of the Irish Troubles of 1916. So, maybe we learn some cultural history there, though maybe not. Flannery O'Connor's famous story, 'A Good Man Is Hard To Find', might seem to be a caution against taking your next vacation in the south of Georgia. And Tobias Wolff's wonderful short story, 'The Rich Brother', included here, might be said to comment wryly upon the disintegration of the American family, post 1960s.

Of course my Italian friend from the hors d'oeuvres table might simply prefer to ignore what short stories tell, even though they be as prettied up as language and form can make them, and as such attest, if to nothing else, to the American character's fondness for just such things as pretty stories. Being ignored is always literature's nemesis. And any country's national oeuvre, mine included, will often not have at its core the headline stuff, the easily noticed. Rather it will contain what a nation in its heart of hearts and represented by its writers feels should be paid attention to more closely but for reasons of difficulty or obscurity or human frailty or simple inaccessibility is in danger of being lost.

So, ultimately, how is the American character represented in these stories? Not generally, and perhaps not at all, since there's no rule which says that's their duty. Still, unless it's tainted by ideology or prejudice or hindsight or ignorance, national character as portrayed by any nation's best writing is never going to be generalizable, so that the effect of a reader's 'finding' it should be as Ford Madox Ford wrote, the same complicated effect life has on mankind.

And here, while we're at least near the subject, is as good a place as any to mention what I'm sure will be the freighted question of just what *is* an American story. Is it a story in which America's the setting? Is it one written by a writer born in America—which is the way we restrict our presidents to an elite pool of possibles. Is it a story published first in America, so that V. S. Pritchett and William Trevor would now and then qualify? And Canadians. Are they Americans or just North Americans? As national identities fall, get refabricated and fall again, a more generous definition would certainly seem best, one which doesn't attempt, as Salman Rushdie wrote, 'to contain writers inside passports,' and one which is forgettable the moment its provisional needs are met.

Therefore—and notwithstanding the fact that you can please almost no one with a statement of limits—my definition allows an American to be anyone who persuasively claims to be one, and an American short story to be a story written in English by an American. Nothing more complicated or adversarial seems right. I'm also prepared to allow that American short stories be written in Lakota Sioux, Spanish, Viet Namese, Hungarian or some other American language. But as most people calling themselves Americans can't read these languages, I've ruled them out for purposes of this anthology (though for other purposes they probably qualify).

English for all its restrictive, complicated, colonial aspects, is a remarkably adaptable and accepting literary language, full of nuance, flexibility, minute coloration as well as the possibility of growth from without. I never hear regarding English what I do of French in France, that he or she 'knows perfect English.' Except in the minds of fifth grade teachers and members of usage panels, there *is* no perfect English—not in America anyway, and certainly not for the purposes of imaginative writing There is only interesting and not interesting English, vivid and boring English. So, while it's admittedly an imperfect scheme, restricting the American short story provisionally to English is not quite the evil linguacentrism it might appear at first, but only a concession to the fact that English is still the lingua franca over here.

Once over the sheer betwaddlement of selecting all these excellent stories, and setting aside any concern with whether they're traditional or metafictional, and whether or not they spell out our national Zeitgeist in capital letters, I find it comforting also not to have to make claims for one ten-year period's ascendancy over another's—that the eighties were 'better' than the seventies, for instance—the kind of claims, as I've noted, anthologists cook up to flatter their own taste or to line out their turf or position their books within the marketplace, claims that by and large simply aren't true.

A doubter, of course, will always come cringingly forward to say, 'Well, you can always find a *few* good stories in any decade.' But that's all I *ever* want! Anyway, good stories aren't good because plenty of less good ones were written at the same time. 'When poetry's good,' Randall Jarrell once wrote to Allen Tate, 'It *is* good.' Likewise with stories. Good stories are good absolutely. It's why they appeal to us so.

Only in such intellectual dead zones as the marketplace or a course syllabus can decade-delimited claims be taken seriously, anyway. And except for periods when half a population is preoccupied by fighting a war or suffering some natural disaster—which has not been the case in America since I've been alive, Viet Nam notwithstanding—much good work of all sorts and styles has occurred all the time. Maybe a literary statistician in some low-wattage graduate program could tabulate more good stories in a given year than another (I'm sure someone's beavering away at it now). But I doubt the differentials would be great, or that I could decide what they proved. Some people will of course disagree with me. But still it's my best advice that you harbor only individual opinions about individual stories, since that way a truly good story will have its best chance of winning you.

There is a companion argument to be made against the issue of periodicity—or maybe I should say historicity—in the American short story's life. Norman Mailer wrote in *Existential Errands* the now famous-if-ponderous, 'Probably we will never be able to determine the psychic havoc of the concentration camps and the atom bomb upon the unconscious mind of almost everyone alive in those years.' And about that he wasn't wrong. Though let's not suppose everybody writing in the fifties wrote from squarely beneath that burden, or that their work needs to be or can be 'traced' to it; no more than did all American writers of the sixties 'reflect' the Viet Nam experience or the sexual and drug revolutions, or all of us in the lamentable eighties interpret the rise in the junk bond market or the disintegration of the family farm or 'chronicle' our nation in the grip of moral decline.

Tracing a story back to its supposed milieu is tricky business. And such a thing can always be done and be made to prove almost anything. Though at the very least, doing so depends heavily on the tracer's view of history, which might after all be composed of little lit-crit modules like, 'The Jazz Age,' or 'The Lost Generation,' or something even more numbing. These 'conveniences' invite us to think about history by not thinking about it very carefully, and along the way they distort complex pieces of writing into being oversimplified 'documents' in support of somebody's dismal belief in a 'theme.' Back in 1947, Eudora Welty published a story in an anthology entitled *Fiction Illuminating the Neuroses of Our Time*. But were the forties an especially neurotic time? I guess they were. But, still, wouldn't the forties be *Stories of the War*? Or *Stories After the War*?

Beyond that, making short stories into exponents for history certainly isn't the most interesting thing we can do with them, even though I understand that to do so may be irresistible to some readers as a way of lingering in a story, or of co-authoring it in the way Sartre describes. I myself prefer to think that long before stories can be reflections of life—windows, mirrors, exponents, commentaries upon an age—they are, again as O'Connor put it, pieces of artistic organization. Or they are, as the novelist William Gass wrote, 'wonderful devices for controlling the speed of the mind, for resting it after a hard climb.' In other words they're words—and pauses and noises and rhythms and more. 'Once language exists only to convey information it is dying,' the poet Richard Hugo wrote. And some part of me would like, in that spirit, to set aside my own grouchy traditionalism and haul stories back from morbid historical 'utilization' and keep them lively. Some part of me as well would like to reacquaint the act of reading with the makeshift act of writing, caught up as the latter is in words and silences and flux and contingency on the way to achieving form, even eventually to making meanings, painting word-pictures of mountains and sunsets and women's breasts. When Faulkner, in *As I Lay Dying*, wrote that Dewy Dell Bundren's breasts were 'mammalian ludicrosities,' he had something more in mind than a good pair of lungs. He had words in mind, sonorous, riotous words clinging to their referents like exotic drapery.

'Some people . . . run to conceits or wisdom . . . , ' Barthelme's oracular Miss R. states in 'The Indian Uprising,' 'but I hold to the hard, brown, nutlike word. I might point out that there is enough aesthetic excitement here to satisfy anyone but a damned fool.'

And *I* might point out that there's giddy pleasure, illumination and solace too, not only in the word but in its dynamic relations to the ones all around it. As we read, we can sense the precarious nature of any literary construction, its barely containable excitation of words which mimics our own suffusion in experience, and whose eventual style, like a ballerina's *line*, is an expression of the manner by which chaos is conditionally and beautifully held at bay.

I don't know why people write stories. Raymond Carver said he wrote them because he was drunk a lot and his kids were driving him crazy, and a short story was all he had concentration for. Sometimes, he said, he wrote them in a parked car.

Perhaps, on the slightly more majestic other hand, there's a rage for order in certain of us, a fury which nothing but a nice, compact little short-course bundle like a story can satisfy.

Or maybe story writers—more so than novelists—are moralists at heart, and the form lends itself to acceptable expressions of caution: You! You're not paying enough attention to your life, parcelled out as it is in increments smaller and more significant than you seem aware of. Here's a form which invites more detailed notice—displaying life not as it is, admittedly, but in flashbacks, in hyper-reality, with epiphanies and without, with closures, time foreshortenings, beauties of all sorts to please you and keep you interested.

Certainly short stories are inherited things. As imprecise as they may be in purely technical-formal terms, we write them now largely because other people wrote them before. American writers usually can't sit still until we've expressed our indebtedness to prior all-stars of the form (Chekhov, Turgenev, de Maupassant being some of our favorites), trying to unite our efforts to the grand tradition. Maybe there's simply an urge in us to imitate something excellent which, when we do it, makes us feel good.

The late book critic Anatole Broyard once wrote of the poet Randall Jarrell that 'a poet is a man, who, having nothing to do, finds something to do.' And of all these speculations I guess I like that one most. Extended to writing short stories, Broyard's notion of moral languor on a cruise for moral consequence, eventually finding it in a pretty 'glancing' form like a short story, satisfies my appreciation of any art's basic gratuitousness, as well as art's being arbitrary and utterly optional for all involved. Broyard's dictum also, incidentally, rings true to my understanding of contemporary mankind's sense of mission upon the planet, as well as to my experience of other writers, and to my experience of being one myself.

My own first effort at the form was an inept little piece of melancholy I called 'Saturday' (as yet unpublished). It was written when I was seventeen, about a boy, surprisingly enough, also seventeen, who kills a Saturday morning dodging chores and brooding over some feeling of Sartrian loss in life—a feeling he has no apparent right to nor public words for, but to which the privileged language of my story gave logic and expression. What I think about that story and about most of those I've written since then is that I wrote them because lived life somehow wasn't enough, in some way didn't hit the last note convincingly and was too quickly gone. Not at all that the stuff of my story was especially autobiographical. It may or may not have been; though that doesn't interest me since raw material for stories comes from all corners of experience, and in any case I'm talking about why stories get written, not whether my personal glass is half full or half empty.

Yet, consequence, or at least that feeling of greater consequence, possible *final* consequence—the feeling which literature can confer upon the lives of both writers and readers—was something I either felt a need for or saw an opportunity to create. And I wrote my story as an attempt to bring it into existence, and perhaps to certify something—

my own worth, maybe. God only knows what I might've needed to certify. Maybe this is just another one of those neuroses of our time.

Or maybe all these reasons are solid ones, and there are legions more I know nothing about—like broomsticks in *The Sorcerer's Apprentice*, that garish phantasm of an imagination gone out of control, attesting therein to: a rage for order.

In two breaths, Flannery O'Connor said about short stories that they were 'one of the most natural and fundamental ways of human expression;' and later that, 'The more I write, the more mysterious I find the process.' Short stories indeed feel as though they arise out of *some* fierce schism which they by their very existence mean to reconcile. And fascination edging on to mystery does exist in the discrepancy between great stories' ingenious capacity to penetrate us, and our ineludible awareness of their brevity. 'They cast a spell,' William Trevor said, speaking of the great ones. Though when they fail they seem to us merely small.

The condition of the American short story from 1944 to last Thursday is here displayed rather idiosyncratically, I admit. The stories I've included are finally simply ones I like—stories that have altered my appreciation of what a short story might surprisingly contain or be about; stories that by their brilliance have seemed to sanction the entire endeavor of being a writer; others that have shined like beacons out of my memory and upon rereading shine still.

They are for the most part *literary* stories, by which I mean not necessarily that they will send you away thinking, but that they aspire to the condition of literature: that they are made as well as they can be; that they're imbued with a confident awareness of their own forms and effects (they know that we know they're stories); that they please by 'operating' in some sensible even if antagonistic relation to St Beuve's famous requirement of the very best writing—that it enrich the human mind, increase its treasure, cause it to advance a step, reveal some eternal passion in the heart where all seemed known and discovered. These requirements can, of course, be met variously. 'There are dozens of ways of expressing verisimilitude,' Frank O'Connor wrote in *The Lonely Voice*, and in the stories that follow you will, indeed, see several.

My own until-recently-private standards for what comprises a good story written by somebody other than me should be, I think, mentioned here, along with two or three gate-keeping remarks: that standards almost always come after the fact and by themselves neither predict nor produce great short stories; that the very best stories observe standards all their own, discovered unpredictably in the private rigors of writing; that toward short stories I feel vulnerable to any conception of form that inspires invention and discovery; and that I'm willing to call a piece of writing a short story if that's what the writer says it is. Ultimately, it's a good thing that American short stories remain as dissimilar and as formally underdefined as they are.

As for me, I've always liked stories that strain my credulity, rather than ones that affirm what I know, and in payment for that strain make me aware of something I didn't know—the otherwise inaccessible. These are stories that prove, for example, the connection between bliss and bale, or the discrepancy between conventional wisdom and the truth, or that reveal affection residing where before it had seemed absent. Such stories concede what I believe—that literature is a privileged speaking which readers come to hungry for what lived life cannot usually provide.

I've always liked stories that make proportionately ample rather than slender use of language, feeling as I do that exposure to a writer's special language is a rare and consoling pleasure. I think of stories as objects made of language, not just as reports on or illustrations of life, and within that definition, a writer's decision to represent life 'realistically' is only one of a number of possibilities for the use of his or her words.

Forgive me, but I like stories that I finally come to feel I understand; that is, whose *purport* I become confident about because of some gesture in the story itself—this, even though the story may not make a lick of ordinary sense. I don't consider stories to be documents for analysis or texts for study. But since as a willing reader I know stories are *made things* and without a natural form, I like them to have contemplated all the important curiosities they arouse in me, or at least create the illusion that they've contemplated them.

I like stories that end rather than merely stop, stories that somehow assure me that their stopping point is the best moment for all progress to cease.

In broader terms, I like stories I don't feel I could have written myself, and that are at least smarter than I am about their own subject matters. Otherwise, why bother reading them if you don't have to?

Beyond that, even though I prefer stories in which the goings-on inside seem to matter in the way life and death seem to matter, if that is not the intention, then I like the story's effects to compensate for that preference of mine. I like stories whose ends you can't predict when you've read to the middle. Often mid-way of a story I make just such a silent prediction and am always disappointed when I'm right. Though whatever's there at the end needs, for greatest power, to arise *somehow* (plausibly?) out of the story's terms.

Finally I do like best of all stories whose necessity is in the implied recognition that someplace *out there* there exists an urgency—a chaos, an insanity, a misrule of some dire sort which can end life as we know it but for the fact that this very story is written, this order found, this style determined, the worst averted, and we are beneficiaries of that order by being readers.*

The nearly fifty years bridged by this anthology do not, I hope I've made it clear, constitute a 'literary period.' Nor is this book a teaching anthology with 'notes for further study' at the ends of entries. Readers at all familiar with American stories will see there are several 'standards' included, as well as some stories that I think will be new, especially to British eyes. Among my few disappointments is the fact that I have not been allowed by the author to include work by J. D. Salinger, particularly his story, 'A Perfect Day for Bananafish,' published in 1953. And there were several quite wonderful stories I regretfully did not include for reasons of the book's becoming too unwieldy to carry around. At the end I made myself at least half satisfied not by including every story I completely admired, but by putting in every one I felt I could not leave out. What follows then is not the full circle of American stories since the war squared and complete, but a collection from which to make a good start on the rest. Better to do that, I think, than nothing.

No attempt has been made to be fair to anyone but the chooser in choosing these stories; no effort taken to represent regions or ethnic groups or writers of 'special orientation,' or to spend much time pinpointing movements or renaissances or schools of writing, if such things can be said to exist in a country as disorganized as mine. The apparent shift in writerly values which occurred in America in the 1960s occurred just as I was beginning to be not only a more practiced and purposeful reader but also a writer. And it is possible that I was

*Any of these standards I am of course immediately willing to abandon if a story can make itself essential to me by some other means.

then and am now more seized by those changes and their putative importance than would be a reader who'd begun another line of work then. In any case, categories which distinguish among 'types of writing' seem to me now just needless envelopes for life and literature the effect of which is to make both life and literature seem simpler, more submissive to reason than they are, and less interesting.

Surely now I've said enough about the American short story. Even the kindest, most forbearing of appreciations eventually threatens to worry its subject out of existence. Whereas I have meant to do only the most generous, high-minded and opposite, what any writer would like to do if he could: clear out the clutter, shove aside the impediments between readers and stories—including even the achy old impediment of Americanness. These are wondrous stories that follow. They treat us to language. They stir our moral imaginations. They take our minds off our woes, and give order to the previously unordered for the purpose of making beauty and clarity anew. They do the best for us that fiction can do.

Now, read.

Richard Ford, 1992

THE GRANTA BOOK OF THE AMERICAN
SHORT STORY

A Day in the Open

Jane Bowles

In the outskirts of the capital there was a low white house, very much like the other houses around it. The street on which it stood was not paved, as this was a poor section of the city. The door of this particular house, very new and studded with nails, was bolted inside and out. A large room, furnished with some modern chromium chairs, a bar, and an electric record machine, opened onto the empty patio. A fat little Indian boy was seated in one of the chairs, listening to the tune *Good Night, Sweetheart*, which he had just chosen. It was playing at full volume and the little boy was staring very seriously ahead of him at the machine. This was one of the houses owned and run by Señor Kurten, who was half Spanish and half German.

It was a gray afternoon. In one of the bedrooms Julia and Inez had just awakened. Julia was small and monkey-like. She was appealing only because of her extraordinarily large and luminous eyes. Inez was tall and high-breasted. Her head was a bit too small for her body and her eyes were too close together. She wore her hair in stiff waves.

Julia was moaning on her bed.

'My stomach is worse today,' she said to Inez. 'Come over and feel it. The lump on the right side is bigger.' She twisted her head on the pillow and sighed. Inez was staring sternly into space.

'No,' she said to Julia. 'I cannot bear to feel that lump. *Santa Maria!* With something like that inside me I should go wild.' She made a wry face and shuddered.

'You must not feel it if you do not want to,' said Julia drowsily. Inez poured herself some *guaro*. She was a heavy drinker but her vitality remained unimpaired, although her skin often broke out in pimples. She ate violet lozenges to cover the smell of liquor on her breath and often popped six or seven of them into her mouth at once. Being full of enterprise she often made more money outside the whorehouse then she did at her regular job.

Julia was Mexican and a great favorite with the men, who enjoyed feeling that they were endangering her very life by going to bed with her.

1

'Well,' said Inez, 'I think that this afternoon I will go to the movies, if you will lend me a pair of your stockings. You had better lie here in your bed. I would sit here with you but it makes me feel very strange now to stay in this room. It is peculiar because, you know, I am a very calm woman and have suffered a great deal since I was born. You should go to a doctor,' she added.

'I cannot bear to be out in the street,' said Julia. 'The sun is too hot and the wind is too cold. The smell of the market makes me feel sick, although I have known it all my life. No sooner have I walked a few blocks than I must find some park to sit in, I am so tired. Then somebody comes and tries to sell me orchids and I buy them. I have been out three times this week and each time I have bought some flowers. Now you know I can't afford to do this, but I am so weak and ill that I am becoming more like my grandmother every day. She had a feeling that she was not wanted here on this earth, either by God or by other people, so she never felt that she could refuse anyone anything.'

'Well, if you are going to become like your grandmother,' said Inez, 'it will be a sad mistake. I should forget this sort of thing. You'll get to the doctor. Meanwhile, sit in the sun more. I don't want to be unkind . . .'

'No, no. You are not unkind,' Julia protested.

'You sit in this dark room all day long even when there is sun and you do not feel so sick.'

Julia was feeling more desperately lonely than she had ever felt before in her life. She patted her heart. Suddenly the door pushed open and Señor Kurten came into the room. He was a slight man with a low forehead and a long nose.

'Julia and Inez,' he said. 'Señor Ramirez just telephoned that he is coming over this afternoon with a friend. He is going to take you both out to the country on a picnic and you are to hurry up and be ready. Try to bring them back to the bar in the evening.'

'Hans,' said Julia. 'I am sick. I can't see Señor Ramirez or anyone else.'

'Well, you know I can't do anything if he wants to see you. If he was angry he could make too much trouble. I am sorry.' Señor Kurten left the room, closing the door slowly behind him.

'He is so important,' said Inez, rubbing some eau de cologne over Julia's forehead. 'So important, poor child. You must go.' Her hand was hard and dry.

'Inez—' Julia clutched at Inez's kimono just as she was walking away. She struggled out of bed and threw herself into the arms of her friend. Inez was obliged to brace herself against the foot of the bed to keep from being knocked over.

'Don't make yourself crazy,' said Inez to Julia, but then Inez began to cry; the sound was high like the squeal of a pig.

'Inez,' said Julia. 'Get dressed and don't cry. I feel better, my little baby.'

They went into the bar and sat down to await the arrival of Señor Ramirez and his friend. Julia's arm was flung over the side of the chair, and her purse was swinging from her hand on an unusually long strap. She had put a little red dot in the corner of each eye, and rouged her cheeks very highly.

'You don't look very good,' said Inez. 'I'm afraid in my heart for you.'

Julia opened her eyes wide and stared fixedly ahead of her at the wall. The Indian boy was polishing a very large alarm clock with care.

Soon Señor Ramirez stuck his head through the doorway. He had a German face but there was something very Spanish in the angle of his slouched fedora hat. His mustaches were blond and abundant. He had just shaved, and the talcum powder was visible on his chin and on his cheeks. He wore a pink shirt and a light tweed jacket, and on the fourth finger of each hand a heavy gold ring studded with a jewel.

'Come on, daughters,' he said. 'The car is waiting outside, with my friend. Move along.'

Señor Ramirez drove very quickly. Julia and Inez sat uncomfortably on the edge of the back seat, hanging onto the straps at the side.

'We are going on a picnic,' shouted Señor Ramirez. 'I've brought with me five bottles of champagne. They are in the back of the car and they were all packed in ice by my cook. There is no reason why we should not have everything we want with us. They are inside a basket in the back. She wrapped the ice in a towel. That way it doesn't melt so quickly, but still we have to get there in a pretty short time. I drink nothing but American whiskey, so I brought along a quart of it for myself. What do you think of that?'

'Oh, how nice,' said Julia.

'I think we shall have a wonderful time,' said Inez.

3

Señor Ramirez's friend Alfredo looked ill and disgruntled. He did not say anything himself, nor did the angle of his head indicate that he was listening to a word that anyone else was saying.

It was a cold day and the parasols under which the policemen stood were flapping in the wind. They passed a new yellow brick building, high at the top of six or seven flights of yellow brick steps.

'That is going to be a new museum,' said Señor Ramirez. 'When it opens we are all going to have a big dinner there together. Everyone there will be an old friend of mine. That's nothing. I can have dinner with fifty people every night of my life.'

'A life of fiesta,' put in Inez.

'Even more than that. They are more than just fiestas,' he said, without quite knowing what he meant himself.

The sun was shining into Julia's lap. She felt lightheaded and feverish. Señor Ramirez turned the radio on as loud as he could. They were broadcasting *Madame Butterfly* as the car reached the outskirts of the city.

'I have three radios at home,' said Señor Ramirez.

'Ah,' said Inez. 'One for the morning, one for the night and one for the afternoon.' Julia listened to Inez with interest and wonder. They were on the edge of a deep ravine, going round a curve in the road. The mountainside across the ravine was in the shade, and some Indians were climbing toward the summit.

'Walk, walk, walk . . . ' said Julia mournfully. 'Oh, how tired it makes me feel to watch them.'

Inez pinched her friend's arm. 'Listen,' she whispered to her. 'You are not in your room. You daren't say things like that. You must not speak of being tired. It's no fun for them. They wouldn't like it.'

'We'll be coming to that picnic spot in a minute,' said Señor Ramirez. 'Nobody knows where it is but me. I like to have a spot, you know, where all my friends won't come and disturb me. Alfredo,' he added, 'are you hungry?'

'I don't think this Alfredo is very nice, do you?' Inez asked very softly of Julia.

'Oh, yes,' said Julia, for she was not quick to detect a mean nature in anybody, being altogether kind and charitable herself. At last, after driving through a path wide enough for only one car, they arrived at the picnic spot. It was a fair-sized clearing in a little forest. Not far from it, at the bottom of a hill, was a little river and a waterfall. They got out and listened to the noise of the water. Both of the women were delighted with the sound.

'Since it is so sunny out, ladies,' said Señor Ramirez, 'I am going to walk around in my underpants. I hope that my friend will do the same if he wants to.'

'What a lucky thing for us,' said Inez in a strident voice. 'The day begins right.' Señor Ramirez undressed and slipped on a pair of tennis shoes. His legs were very white and freckled.

'Now I will give you some champagne right away,' he said to them, a little out of breath because he had struggled so quickly out of his clothes. He went over to where he had laid the basket and took from it a champagne bottle. On his way back he stumbled over a rock; the bottle fell from his hand and was smashed in many pieces. For a moment his face clouded over and he looked as though he were about to lose his temper; instead, seizing another bottle from the basket, he flung it high into the air, almost over the tops of the trees. He returned elated to his friends.

'A gentleman,' he said, 'always knows how to make fun. I am one of the richest businessmen in this country. I am also the craziest. Like an American. When I am out I always have a wonderful time, and so does everyone who is with me, because they know that while I am around there is always plenty. Plenty to eat, plenty to drink, and plenty of beautiful women to make love to. Once you have been out with me,' he pointed his finger at Julia and Inez, 'any other man will seem to you like an old-lady schoolteacher.'

He turned to Alfredo. 'Tell me, my friend, have you not had the time of your life with me?'

'Yes, I have,' said Alfredo. He was thinking very noticeably of other things.

'His mind is always on business,' Señor Ramirez explained to Julia. 'He is also very clever. I have gotten him this job with a German concern. They are manufacturing planes.' Alfredo said something to Señor Ramirez in German, and they spoke no longer on the subject. They spread out their picnic lunch and sat down to eat.

Señor Ramirez insisted on feeding Julia with his own fingers. This rather vexed Inez, so she devoted herself to eating copiously. Señor Ramirez drank quantities of whiskey out of a tin folding cup. At the end of fifteen or twenty minutes he was already quite drunk.

'Now, isn't it wonderful to be all together like this, friends? Alfredo, aren't these two women the finest, sweetest women in the world? I do not understand why in the eyes of God they should be condemned to the fires of hell for what they are. Do you?'

Julia moaned and rose to her feet.

'No, no!' she said, looking up helplessly at the branches overhead.

'Come on,' said Señor Ramirez. 'We're not going to worry about this today, are we?' He took hold of her wrist and pulled her down to the ground beside him. Julia hid her face in her hands and leaned her head against his shoulder. Soon she was smiling up at him and stroking his face.

'You won't leave me alone?' she asked, laughing a little in an effort to bring him to terms with her. If anyone were to be pitted successfully against the Divine, she thought, it would certainly be someone like Señor Ramirez. The presence of such men is often enough to dispel fear from the hearts of certain people for whom God is more of an enemy than a friend. Señor Ramirez's principal struggle in life was one of pride rather than of conscience; and because his successes were numerous each day, replenishing his energy and his taste for life, his strength was easily felt by those around him. Now that he was near her, Julia felt that she was safe from hell, and she was quite happy even though her side still hurt her very badly.

'Now,' said Inez, 'I think that we should all play a game, to chase gloomy thoughts out of this girl's head.'

She rose to her feet and snatched Señor Ramirez's hat from where it lay beside him on the ground, placing it a few feet away upside down on the grass. Then she gathered some acorns in the picnic basket.

'Now,' she said. 'We will see who can throw these acorns into the hat. He will win.'

'I think,' said Señor Ramirez, 'that the two women should be naked while we are playing this; otherwise it will be just a foolish children's game.'

'And we are not children at all,' said Inez, winking at him. The two women turned and looked at Alfredo questioningly.

'Oh, don't mind him,' said Señor Ramirez. 'He sees nothing but numbers in his head.'

The two girls went behind some bushes and undressed. When they returned, Alfredo was bending over a ledger and trying to explain something to Señor Ramirez, who looked up, delighted that they had returned so quickly, so that he would not be obliged to listen.

'Ah,' he said. 'Now this looks much more like friends together, doesn't it, Alfredo?'

'Come on,' said Inez. 'We will all get into line here with this basket and each one will try to throw the acorn into the hat.'

Señor Ramirez grew quite excited playing the game; then he began to get angry because he never managed to get the acorn into the hat. Inez screeched with laughter and threw her acorn wider and wider of the mark, each time purposely, in order to soothe, if possible, the hurt pride of Señor Ramirez. Alfredo refused to play at all.

'Games don't interest me,' said Señor Ramirez suddenly. 'I'd like to play longer with you, daughters, but I can't honestly keep my mind on the game.'

'It is of no importance at all, really,' said Inez, busily trying to think up something to do next.

'How are your wife and children?' Julia asked him.

Inez bit her lip and shook her head.

'They are well taken care of. I have sent them to a little town where they are staying in a pension. Quiet women—all three of them—the little girls and the mother. I am going to sleep.' He stretched out under a tree and put his hat over his face. Alfredo was absorbed in his ledger. Inez and Julia sat side by side and waited.

'You have the brain of a baby chicken,' Inez said to Julia. 'I must think for both of us. If I had not had a great deal of practice when I had to keep count of all the hundreds of tortillas that I sold for my mother, I don't know where we would be.'

'Dead, probably,' said Julia. They began to feel cold.

'Come,' said Inez. 'Sing with me.' They sang a song about leaving and never returning, four or five times through. When Señor Ramirez awakened he suggested to Julia that they go for a walk. She accepted sweetly, and so they started off through the woods. Soon they reached a good-sized field where Señor Ramirez suggested that they sit for a while.

'The first time I went to bed with a woman,' he said, 'it was in the country like this. The land belonged to my father. Three or four times a day we would come out into the fields and make love. She loved it, and would have come more often if I had asked her to. Some years later I went to her wedding and I had a terrible fight there. I don't even remember who the man was, but in the end he was badly hurt. I can tell you that.'

'If you put your arms around me,' said Julia, 'I will feel less cold. You don't mind my asking you to do this, but I love you very much and I feel very contented with you.'

'That's good,' said Señor Ramirez, looking off at the mountains and shielding his eyes from the sun. He was listening to the sound of the waterfall, which was louder here. Julia was laughing and touching various parts of his body.

'Ah,' she said. 'I don't mind my side hurting me so badly if I can only be happy the way I am now with you. You are so sweet and so wonderful.'

He gave her a quick loud kiss on the mouth and rose to his feet.

'Listen,' he said. 'Wouldn't you like to come into the water with me?'

'I am too sick a woman to go into the water, and I am a little bit afraid.'

'In my arms you don't have to be afraid. I will carry you. The current would be too strong for you to manage anyway.' Señor Ramirez was now as gay as a lark, although he had been bored but a moment before. He liked nothing better than performing little feats that were assured of success from the beginning. He carried her down to the river, singing at the top of his voice.

The noise of the falls was very loud here, and Julia clung tightly to her escort.

'Don't let go, now,' she said. But her voice seemed to fly away behind her like a ribbon caught in the wind. They were in the water and Señor Ramirez began to walk in the direction of the falls.

'I will hold tight, all right,' he said. 'Because the water runs pretty swiftly near the falls.' He seemed to enjoy stepping precariously from one stone to another with Julia in his arms.

'This is not so easy, you know. This is damned hard. The stones are slippery.' Julia tightened her grip around his neck and kissed him quickly all over his face.

'If I let you go,' he said, 'the current would carry you along like a leaf over the falls, and then one of those big rocks would make a hole in your head. That would be the end, of course.' Julia's eyes widened with horror, and she yelled with the suddenness of an animal just wounded.

'But why do you scream like that, Julia? I love you, sweetheart.' He had had enough of struggling through the water, and so he turned around and started back.

'Are we going away from the waterfall?'

'Yes. It was wonderful, wasn't it?'

'Very nice,' she said.

He grew increasingly careless as the current slackened, with the result that he miscalculated and his foot slipped between two stones. This threw him off his balance and he fell. He was unhurt, but the back of Julia's head had hit a stone. It started to bleed profusely. He struggled to his feet and carried her to the riverbank. She was not sure that she was not dying, and hugged him all the more closely. Pulling her along, he walked quickly up the hill and back through the woods to where Inez and Alfredo were still sitting.

'It will be all right, won't it?' she asked him a bit weakly.

'Those damn rocks were slippery,' he growled. He was sulky, and eager to be on his way home.

'Oh, God of mine!' lamented Inez, when she saw what had happened. 'What a sad ending for a walk! Terrible things always happen to Julia. She is a daughter of misfortune. It's a lucky thing that I am just the contrary.'

Señor Ramirez was in such a hurry to leave the picnic spot that he did not even want to bother to collect the various baskets and plates he had brought with him. They dressed, and he yelled for them all to get into the car. Julia wrapped a shawl around her bleeding head. Inez went around snatching up all the things, like an enraged person.

'Can I have these things?' she asked her host. He nodded his head impatiently. Julia was by now crying rhythmically like a baby that has almost fallen asleep.

The two women sat huddled together in the back of the car. Inez explained to Julia that she was going to make presents of the plates and baskets to her family. She shed a tear or two herself. When they arrived at the house, Señor Ramirez handed some banknotes to Inez from where he was sitting.

'Adios,' he said. The two women got out of the car and stood in the street.

'Will you come back again?' Julia asked him tenderly, ceasing to cry for a moment.

'Yes. I'm coming back again,' he said. 'Adios.' He pressed his foot on the accelerator and drove off.

The bar was packed with men. Inez led Julia around through the patio to their room. When she had shut the door, she slipped the banknotes into her pocket and put the baskets on the floor.

'Do you want any of these baskets?' she asked.

Julia was sitting on the edge of her bed, looking into space. 'No, thank you,' she said. Inez looked at her, and saw that she was far away.

'Señor Ramirez gave me four drinking cups made out of plastic,' said Inez. 'Do you want one of them for yourself?'

Julia did not answer right away. Then she said: 'Will he come back?'

'I don't know,' Inez said. 'I'm going to the movies. I'll come and see you afterwards, before I go into the bar.'

'All right,' said Julia. But Inez knew that she did not care. She shrugged her shoulders and went out through the door, closing it behind her.

1945

A Distant Episode

Paul Bowles

The September sunsets were at their reddest the week the Professor decided to visit Aïn Tadouirt, which is in the warm country. He came down out of the high, flat region in the evening by bus, with two small overnight bags full of maps, sun lotions and medicines. Ten years ago he had been in the village for three days; long enough, however, to establish a fairly firm friendship with a café-keeper, who had written him several times during the first year after his visit, if never since. 'Hassan Ramani,' the Professor said over and over, as the bus bumped downward through ever warmer layers of air. Now facing the flaming sky in the west, and now facing the sharp mountains, the car followed the dusty trail down the canyons into air which began to smell of other things besides the endless ozone of the heights: orange blossoms, pepper, sun-baked excrement, burning olive oil, rotten fruit. He closed his eyes happily and lived for an instant in a purely olfactory world. The distant past returned—what part of it, he could not decide.

The chauffeur, whose seat the Professor shared, spoke to him without taking his eyes from the road. *'Vous êtes géologue?'*

'A geologist? Ah, no! I'm a linguist.'

'There are no languages here. Only dialects.'

'Exactly. I'm making a survey of variations on Moghrebi.'

The chauffeur was scornful. 'Keep on going south,' he said. 'You'll find some languages you never heard of before.'

As they drove through the town gate, the usual swarm of urchins rose up out of the dust and ran screaming beside the bus. The Professor folded his dark glasses, put them in his pocket; and as soon as the vehicle had come to a standstill he jumped out, pushing his way through the indignant boys who clutched at his luggage in vain, and walked quickly into the Grand Hotel Saharien. Out of its eight rooms there were two available—one facing the market and the other, a smaller and cheaper one, giving onto a tiny yard full of refuse and barrels, where two gazelles wandered about. He took the smaller room, and pouring the entire pitcher of water into the tin

11

basin, began to wash the grit from his face and ears. The afterglow was nearly gone from the sky, and the pinkness in objects was disappearing, almost as he watched. He lit the carbide lamp and winced at its odor.

After dinner the Professor walked slowly through the streets to Hassan Ramani's café, whose back room hung hazardously out above the river. The entrance was very low, and he had to bend down slightly to get in. A man was tending the fire. There was one guest sipping tea. The *qaouaji* tried to make him take a seat at the other table in the front room, but the Professor walked airily ahead into the back room and sat down. The moon was shining through the reed latticework and there was not a sound outside but the occasional distant bark of a dog. He changed tables so he could see the river. It was dry, but there was a pool here and there that reflected the bright night sky. The *qaouaji* came in and wiped off the table.

'Does this café still belong to Hassan Ramani?' he asked him in the Moghrebi he had taken four years to learn.

The man replied in bad French: 'He is deceased.'

'Deceased?' repeated the Professor, without noticing the absurdity of the word. 'Really? When?'

'I don't know,' said the *qaouaji*. 'One tea?'

'Yes. But I don't understand . . . '

The man was already out of the room, fanning the fire. The Professor sat still, feeling lonely, and arguing with himself that to do so was ridiculous. Soon the *qaouaji* returned with the tea. He paid him and gave him an enormous tip, for which he received a grave bow.

'Tell me,' he said, as the other started away. 'Can one still get those little boxes made from camel udders?'

The man looked angry. 'Sometimes the Reguibat bring in those things. We do not buy them here.' Then insolently, in Arabic: 'And why a camel-udder box?'

'Because I like them,' retorted the Professor. And then because he was feeling a little exalted, he added, 'I like them so much I want to make a collection of them, and I will pay you ten francs for every one you can get me.'

'*Khamstache*,' said the *qaouaji*, opening his left hand rapidly three times in succession.

'Never. Ten.'

'Not possible. But wait until later and come with me. You can give me what you like. And you will get camel-udder boxes if there are any.'

He went into the front room, leaving the Professor to drink his tea and listen to the growing chorus of dogs that barked and howled as the moon rose higher into the sky. A group of customers came into the front room and sat talking for an hour or so. When they had left, the *qaouaji* put out the fire and stood in the doorway putting on his burnous. 'Come,' he said.

Outside in the street there was very little movement. The booths were all closed and the only light came from the moon. An occasional pedestrian passed, and grunted a brief greeting to the *qaouaji*.

'Everyone knows you,' said the Professor, to cut the silence between them.

'Yes.'

'I wish everyone knew me,' said the Professor, before he realized how infantile such a remark must sound.

'*No* one knows you,' said his companion gruffly.

They had come to the other side of the town, on the promontory above the desert, and through a great rift in the wall the Professor saw the white endlessness, broken in the foreground by dark spots of oasis. They walked through the opening and followed a winding road between rocks, downward toward the nearest small forest of palms. The Professor thought. 'He may cut my throat. But his café— he would surely be found out.'

'Is it far?' he asked, casually.

'Are you tired?' countered the *qaouaji*.

'They are expecting me back at the Hotel Saharien,' he lied.

'You can't be there and here,' said the *qaouaji*.

The Professor laughed. He wondered if it sounded uneasy to the other.

'Have you owned Ramani's café long?'

'I work there for a friend.' The reply made the Professor more unhappy than he had imagined it would.

'Oh. Will you work tomorrow?'

'That is impossible to say.'

The Professor stumbled on a stone, and fell, scraping his hand. The *qaouaji* said: 'Be careful.'

The sweet black odor of rotten meat hung in the air suddenly.

'Agh!' said the Professor, choking. 'What is it?'

The *qaouaji* had covered his face with his burnous and did not answer. Soon the stench had been left behind. They were on flat ground. Ahead the path was bordered on each side by a high mud

13

wall. There was no breeze and the palms were quite still, but behind the walls was the sound of running water. Also, the odor of human excrement was almost constant as they walked between the walls.

The Professor waited until he thought it seemed logical for him to ask with a certain degree of annoyance: 'But where are we going?'

'Soon,' said the guide, pausing to gather some stones in the ditch.

'Pick up some stones,' he advised. 'Here are bad dogs.'

'Where?' asked the Professor, but he stooped and got three large ones with pointed edges.

They continued very quietly. The walls came to an end and the bright desert lay ahead. Nearby was a ruined marabout, with its tiny dome only half standing, and the front wall entirely destroyed. Behind it were clumps of stunted, useless palms. A dog came running crazily toward them on three legs. Not until it got quite close did the Professor hear its steady low growl. The *qaouaji* let fly a large stone at it, striking it square in the muzzle. There was a strange snapping of jaws and the dog ran sideways in another direction, falling blindly against rocks and scrambling haphazardly about like an injured insect.

Turning off the road, they walked across the earth strewn with sharp stones, past the little ruin, through the trees, until they came to a place where the ground dropped abruptly away in front of them.

'It looks like a quarry,' said the Professor, resorting to French for the word 'quarry,' whose Arabic equivalent he could not call to mind at the moment. The *qaouaji* did not answer. Instead he stood still and turned his head, as if listening. And indeed, from somewhere down below, but very far below, came the faint sound of a low flute. The *qaouaji* nodded his head slowly several times. Then he said: 'The path begins here. You can see it well all the way. The rock is white and the moon is strong. So you can see well. I am going back now and sleep. It is late. You can give me what you like.'

Standing there at the edge of the abyss which at each moment looked deeper, with the dark face of the *qaouaji* framed in its moonlit burnous close to his own face, the Professor asked himself exactly what he felt. Indignation, curiosity, fear, perhaps, but most of all relief and the hope that this was not a trick, the hope that the *qaouaji* would really leave him alone and turn back without him.

He stepped back a little from the edge, and fumbled in his pocket for a loose note, because he did not want to show his wallet. Fortunately there was a fifty-franc bill there, which he took out and handed to the man. He knew the *qaouaji* was pleased, and so he paid no attention when he heard him saying: 'It is not enough. I have to walk a long way home and there are dogs . . . '

'Thank you and good night,' said the Professor, sitting down with his legs drawn up under him, and lighting a cigarette. He felt almost happy.

'Give me only one cigarette,' pleaded the man.

'Of course,' he said, a bit curtly, and he held up the pack.

The *qaouaji* squatted close beside him. His face was not pleasant to see. 'What is it?' thought the Professor, terrified again, as he held out his lighted cigarette toward him.

The man's eyes were almost closed. It was the most obvious registering of concentrated scheming the Professor had ever seen. When the second cigarette was burning, he ventured to say to the still-squatting Arab: 'What are you thinking about?'

The other drew on his cigarette deliberately, and seemed about to speak. Then his expression changed to one of satisfaction, but he did not speak. A cool wind had risen in the air, and the Professor shivered. The sound of the flute came up from the depths below at intervals, sometimes mingled with the scraping of nearby palm fonds one against the other. 'These people are not primitives,' the Professor found himself saying in his mind.

'Good,' said the *qaouaji*, rising slowly. 'Keep your money. Fifty francs is enough. It is an honor.' Then he went back into French: *'Ti n'as qu'à discendre, to' droit.'* He spat, chuckled (or was the Professor hysterical?), and strode away quickly.

The Professor was in a state of nerves. He lit another cigarette, and found his lips moving automatically. They were saying: 'Is this a situation or a predicament? This is ridiculous.' He sat very still for several minutes, waiting for a sense of reality to come to him. He stretched out on the hard, cold ground and looked up at the moon. It was almost like looking straight at the sun. If he shifted his gaze a little at a time, he could make a string of weaker moons across the sky. 'Incredible,' he whispered. Then he sat up quickly and looked about. There was no guarantee that the *qaouaji* really had gone back to town. He got to his feet and looked over the edge of the precipice. In the moonlight the bottom seemed miles away. And there was nothing to give it scale; not a tree, not a house, not a person . . . He listened for the flute, and heard only the wind going by his ears. A sudden violent desire to run back to the road seized him, and he turned and looked in the direction the *qaouaji* had taken. At the same time he felt softly for his wallet in his breast pocket. Then he spat over the edge of the cliff. Then he made water over it, and listened intently, like a child. This gave him the impetus to start down the path into the abyss. Curiously enough, he was not dizzy. But prudently he kept from peering to his right, over the edge. It was a steady and steep downward climb. The monotony of it put him into a frame of mind not unlike that which had been induced by the bus ride. He was murmuring 'Hassan Ramani' again, repeatedly and in rhythm. He stopped, furious with himself for the sinister overtones the name now suggested to him. He decided he was exhausted from the trip. 'And the walk,' he added.

He was now well down the gigantic cliff, but the moon, being directly overhead, gave as much light as ever. Only the wind was left behind, above, to wander among the trees, to blow through the dusty streets of Aïn Tadouirt, into the hall of the Grand Hotel Saharien, and under the door of his little room.

It occurred to him that he ought to ask himself why he was doing this irrational thing, but he was intelligent enough to know that since he was doing it, it was not so important to probe for explanations at that moment.

Suddenly the earth was flat beneath his feet. He had reached the bottom sooner than he expected. He stepped ahead distrustfully still, as if he expected another treacherous drop. It was so hard to know in this uniform, dim brightness. Before he knew what had happened the dog was upon him, a heavy mass of fur trying to push him backwards, a sharp nail rubbing down his chest, a straining of muscles against him to get the teeth into his neck. The Professor thought: 'I refuse to die this way.' The dog fell back; it looked like an Eskimo dog. As it sprang again, he called out, very loud; 'Ay!' It fell against him, there was a confusion of sensations and a pain somewhere. There was also the sound of voices very near to him, and he could not understand what they were saying. Something cold and metallic was pushed brutally against his spine as the dog still hung for a second by his teeth from a mass of clothing and perhaps flesh. The Professor knew it was a gun, and he raised his hands, shouting in Moghrebi: 'Take away the dog!' But the gun merely pushed him forward, and since the dog, once it was back on the ground, did not leap again, he took a step ahead. The gun kept pushing; he kept taking steps. Again he heard voices, but the person directly behind him said nothing. People seemed to be running about; it sounded that way, at least. For his eyes, he discovered, were still shut tight against the dog's attack. He opened them. A group of men was advancing toward him. They were dressed in the black clothes of the Reguibat. 'The Reguiba is a cloud across the face of the sun.' 'When the Reguiba appears the righteous man turns away.' In how many shops and market-places he had heard these maxims uttered banteringly among friends. Never to a Reguiba, to be sure, for these men do not frequent towns. They send a representative in disguise, to arrange with shady elements there for the disposal of captured goods. 'An opportunity,' he thought quickly, 'of testing the accuracy of such statements.' He did not doubt for a moment that the adventure would prove to be a kind of warning against such foolishness on his part—a warning which in retrospect would be half sinister, half farcical.

Two snarling dogs came running from behind the oncoming men and threw themselves at his legs. He was scandalized to note that no one paid any attention to this breach of etiquette. The gun pushed him harder as he tried to sidestep the animals' noisy assault. Again he cried: 'The dogs! Take them away!' The gun shoved him forward with great force and he fell, almost at the feet of the crowd of men facing him. The dogs were wrenching at his hands and arms. A boot kicked them aside, yelping, and then with increased vigor it kicked the Professor in the hip. Then came a chorus of kicks from different sides, and he was rolled violently about on the earth for a while. During this time he was conscious of hands reaching into his pockets and removing everything from them. He tried to say: 'You have all my money; stop kicking me!' But his bruised facial muscles would not work; he felt himself pouting, and that was all. Someone dealt him a terrific blow on the head, and he thought: 'Now at least I shall lose consciousness, thank Heaven.' Still he went on being aware of the guttural voices he could not understand, and of being bound tightly about the ankles and chest. Then there was black silence that opened like a wound from time to time, to let in the soft, deep notes of the flute playing the same succession of notes again and again. Suddenly he felt excruciating pain everywhere—pain and cold. 'So I have been unconscious, after all,' he thought. In spite of that, the present seemed only like a direct continuation of what had gone before.

It was growing faintly light. There were camels near where he was lying; he could hear their gurgling and their heavy breathing. He could not bring himself to attempt opening his eyes, just in case it should turn out to be impossible. However, when he heard someone approaching, he found that he had no difficulty in seeing.

The man looked at him dispassionately in the gray morning light. With one hand he pinched together the Professor's nostrils. When the Professor opened his mouth to breathe, the man swiftly seized his tongue and pulled on it with all his might. The Professor was gagging and catching his breath; he did not see what was happening. He could not distinguish the pain of the brutal yanking from that of the sharp knife. Then there was an endless choking and spitting that went on automatically, as though he were scarcely a part of it. The word 'operation' kept going through his mind; it calmed his terror somewhat as he sank back into darkness.

The caravan left sometime toward midmorning. The Professor, not unconscious, but in a state of utter stupor, still gagging and drooling blood, was dumped doubled-up in a sack and tied at one side of a camel. The lower end of the enormous amphitheater contained a natural gate in the rocks. The camels, swift *mehara*, were lightly laden on this trip. They passed through single file, and slowly mounted the gentle slope that led up into the beginning of the desert. That night, at a stop behind some low hills, the men took him out, still in a state which permitted no thought, and over the dusty rags that remained of his clothing they fastened a series of curious belts made of the bottoms of tin cans strung together. One after another of these bright girdles was wired about his torso, his arms and legs, even across his face, until he was entirely within a suit of armor that covered him with its circular metal scales. There was a good deal of merriment during this decking-out of the Professor. One man brought out a flute and a younger one did a not ungraceful caricature of an Ouled Naïl executing a cane dance. The Professor was no longer conscious; to be exact, existed in the middle of the movements made by these other men. When they had finished dressing him the way they wished him to look, they stuffed some food under the tin bangles hanging over his face. Even though he chewed mechanically, most of it eventually fell out onto the ground. They put him back into the sack and left him there.

Two days later they arrived at one of their own encampments. There were women and children here in the tents, and the men had to drive away the snarling dogs they had left there to guard them. When they emptied the Professor out of his sack, there were screams of fright, and it took several hours to convince the last woman that he was harmless, although there had been no doubt from the start that he was a valuable possession. After a few days they began to move on again, taking everything with them, and traveling only at night as the terrain grew warmer.

Even when all his wounds had healed and he felt no more pain, the Professor did not begin to think again, he ate and defecated, and he danced when he was bidden, a senseless hopping up and down that delighted the children, principally because of the wonderful jangling racket it made. And he generally slept through the heat of the day, in among the camels.

Wending its way southeast, the caravan avoided all stationary civilization. In a few weeks they reached a new plateau, wholly wild and with a sparse vegetation. Here they pitched camp and remained, while the *mehara* were turned loose to graze. Everyone was happy here; the weather was cooler and there was a well only a few hours away on a seldom-frequented trail. It was here they conceived the idea of taking the Professor to Fogara and selling him to the Touareg.

It was a full year before they carried out this project. By this time the Professor was much better trained. He could do a handspring, make a series of fearful growling noises which had, nevertheless, a certain element of humor; and when the Reguibat removed the tin from his face they discovered he could grimace admirably while he danced. They also taught him a few basic obscene gestures which never failed to elicit delighted shrieks from the women. He was now brought forth only after especially abundant meals, when there was music and festivity. He easily fell in with their sense of ritual, and evolved an elementary sort of 'program' to present when he was called for: dancing, rolling on the ground, imitating certain animals, and finally rushing toward the group in feigned anger, to see the resultant confusion and hilarity.

When three of the men set out for Fogara with him, they took four *mehara* with them, and he rode astride his quite naturally. No precautions were taken to guard him, save that he was kept among them, one man always staying at the rear of the party. They came within sight of the walls at dawn, and they waited among the rocks all day. At dusk the youngest started out, and in three hours he returned with a friend who carried a stout cane. They tried to put the Professor through his routine then and there, but the man from Fogara was in a hurry to get back to town, so they all set out on the *mehara*.

In the town they went directly to the villager's home, where they had coffee in the courtyard sitting among the camels. Here the Professor went into his act again, and this time there was prolonged merriment and much rubbing together of hands. An agreement was reached, a sum of money paid, and the Reguibat withdrew, leaving the Professor in the house of the man with the cane, who did not delay in locking him into a tiny enclosure off the courtyard.

The next day was an important one in the Professor's life, for it was then that pain began to stir again in his being. A group of men came to the house, among whom was a venerable gentleman, better clothed than those others who spent their time flattering him, setting fervent kisses upon his hands and the edges of his garments. This person made a point of going into classical Arabic from time to time, to impress the others, who had not learned a word of the Koran. Thus his conversation would run more or less as follows: 'Perhaps at In Salah. The French there are stupid. Celestial vengeance is approaching. Let us not hasten it. Praise the highest and cast thine anathema against idols. With paint on his face. In case the police wish to look close.' The others listened and agreed, nodding their heads slowly and solemnly. And the Professor in his stall beside them listened, too. That is, he was *conscious* of the sound of the old man's Arabic. The words penetrated for the first time in many months. Noises, then: 'Celestial vengeance is approaching.' Then: 'It is an honor. Fifty francs is enough. Keep your money. Good.' And the *qaouaji* squatting near him at the edge of the precipice. Then 'anathema against idols' and more gibberish. He turned over panting on the sand and forgot about it. But the pain had begun. It operated in a kind of delirium, because he had begun to enter into consciousness again. When the man opened the door and prodded him with his cane, he cried out in a rage, and everyone laughed.

They got him onto his feet, but he would not dance. He stood before them, staring at the ground, stubbornly refusing to move. The owner was furious, and so annoyed by the laughter of the others that he felt obliged to send them away, saying that he would await a more propitious time for exhibiting his property, because he dared not show his anger before the elder. However, when they had left he dealt the Professor a violent blow on the shoulder with his cane, called him various obscene things, and went out into the street, slamming the gate behind him. He walked straight to the street of the Ouled Naïl, because he was sure of finding the Reguibat there among the girls, spending the money. And there in a tent he found one of them still abed, while an Ouled Naïl washed the tea glasses. He walked in and almost decapitated the man before the latter had even attempted to sit up. Then he threw his razor on the bed and ran out.

The Ouled Naïl saw the blood, screamed, ran out of her tent into the next, and soon emerged from that with four girls who rushed together into the coffeehouse and told the qaouaji who had killed the Reguiba. It was only a matter of an hour before the French military police had caught him at a friend's house, and dragged him off to the barracks. That night the Professor had nothing to eat, and the next afternoon, in the slow sharpening of his consciousness caused by increasing hunger, he walked aimlessly about the courtyard and the rooms that gave onto it. There was no one. In one room a calendar hung on the wall. The Professor watched nervously, like a dog watching a fly in front of its nose. On the white paper were black objects that made sounds in his head. He heard them: 'Grande Epicerie du Sahel. Juin. Lundi, Mardi, Mercredi . . . '

The tiny ink marks of which a symphony consists may have been made long ago, but when they are fulfilled in sound they become imminent and mighty. So a kind of music of feeling began to play in the Professor's head, increasing in volume as he looked at the mud wall, and he had the feeling that he was performing what had been written for him long ago. He felt like weeping; he felt like roaring through the little house, upsetting and smashing the few breakable objects. His emotion got no further than this one overwhelming desire. So, bellowing as loud as he could, he attacked the house and its belongings. Then he attacked the door into the street, which resisted for a while and finally broke. He climbed through the opening made by the boards he had ripped apart, and still bellowing and shaking his arms in the air to make as loud a jangling as possible, he began to gallop along the quiet street toward the gateway of the town. A few people looked at him with great curiosity. As he passed the garage, the last building before the high mud archway that framed the desert beyond, a French soldier saw him. 'Tiens,' he said to himself, 'a holy maniac.'

Again it was sunset time. The Professor ran beneath the arched gate, turned his face toward the red sky, and began to trot along the Piste d'In Salah, straight into the setting sun. Behind him, from the garage, the soldier took a potshot at him for good luck. The bullet whistled dangerously near the Professor's head, and his yelling rose into an indignant lament as he waved his arms more wildly, and hopped high into the air at every few steps, in an access of terror.

The soldier watched a while, smiling, as the cavorting figure grew smaller in the oncoming evening darkness, and the rattling of the tin became a part of the great silence out there beyond the gate. The wall of the garage as he leaned against it still gave forth heat, left there by the sun, but even then the lunar chill was growing in the air.

1947

BLACKBERRY WINTER
Robert Penn Warren

It was getting into June and past eight o'clock in the morning, but there was a fire—even if it wasn't a big fire, just a fire of chunks—on the hearth of the big stone fireplace in the living room. I was standing on the hearth, almost into the chimney, hunched over the fire, working my bare toes slowly on the warm stone. I relished the heat which made the skin of my bare legs warp and creep and tingle, even as I called to my mother, who was somewhere back in the dining room or kitchen, and said: 'But it's June, I don't have to put them on!'

'You put them on if you are going out,' she called.

I tried to assess the degree of authority and conviction in the tone, but at that distance it was hard to decide. I tried to analyze the tone, and then I thought what a fool I had been to start out the back door and let her see that I was barefoot. If I had gone out the front door or the side door she would never have known, not till dinner time anyway, and by then the day would have been half gone and I would have been all over the farm to see what the storm had done and down to the creek to see the flood. But it had never crossed my mind that they would try to stop you from going barefoot in June, no matter if there had been a gully-washer and a cold spell.

Nobody had ever tried to stop me in June as long as I could remember, and when you are nine years old, what you remember seems forever; for you remember everything and everything is important and stands big and full and fills up Time and is so solid that you can walk around and around it like a tree and look at it. You are aware that time passes, that there is a movement in time, but that is not what Time is. Time is not a movement, a flowing, a wind then, but it is, rather, a kind of climate in which things are, and when a thing happens it begins to live and keeps on living and stands solid in Time like the tree that you can walk around. And if there is a movement, the movement is not Time itself, any more than a breeze is climate, and all the breeze does is to shake a little the leaves on the tree which is alive and solid. When you are nine, you know that there

23

are things that you don't know, but you know that when you know something you know it. You know how a thing has been and you know that you can go barefoot in June. You do not understand that voice from back in the kitchen which says that you cannot go barefoot outdoors and run to see what has happened and rub your feet over the wet shivery grass and make the perfect mark of your foot in the smooth, creamy, red mud and then muse upon it as though you had suddenly come upon that single mark on the glistening auroral beach of the world. You have never seen a beach, but you have read the book and how the footprint was there.

The voice had said what it had said, and I looked savagely at the black stockings and the strong, scuffed brown shoes which I had brought from my closet as far as the hearth rug. I called once more, 'But it's June,' and waited.

'It's June,' the voice replied from far away, 'but it's blackberry winter.'

I had lifted my head to reply to that, to make one more test of what was in that tone, when I happened to see the man.

The fireplace in the living room was at the end; for the stone chimney was built, as in so many of the farmhouses in Tennessee, at the end of a gable, and there was a window on each side of the chimney. Out of the window on the north side of the fireplace I could see the man. When I saw the man I did not call out what I had intended, but, engrossed by the strangeness of the sight, watched him, still far off, come along the path by the edge of the woods.

What was strange was that there should be a man there at all. That path went along the yard fence, between the fence and the woods which came right down to the yard, and then on back past the chicken runs and on by the woods until it was lost to sight where the woods bulged out and cut off the back field. There the path disappeared into the woods. It led on back, I knew, through the woods and to the swamp, skirted the swamp where the big trees gave way to sycamores and water oaks and willows and tangled cane, and then led on to the river. Nobody ever went back there except people who wanted to gig frogs in the swamp or to fish in the river or to hunt in the woods, and those people, if they didn't have a standing permission from my father, always stopped to ask permission to cross the farm. But the man whom I now saw wasn't, I could tell even at that distance, a sportsman. And what would a sportsman have been doing down there after a storm? Besides, he was coming from the river, and nobody had gone down there that morning. I knew that for a fact, because if anybody had passed, certainly if a stranger had passed, the dogs would have made a racket and would have been out on him. But this man was coming up from the river and had come up through the woods. I suddenly had a vision of him moving up the grassy path in the woods, in the green twilight under the big trees, not making any sound on the path, while now and then, like drops off the eaves, a big drop of water would fall from a leaf or bough and strike a stiff oak leaf lower down with a small, hollow sound like a drop of water hitting tin. That sound, in the silence of the woods, would be very significant.

When you are a boy and stand in the stillness of the woods, which can be so still that your heart almost stops beating and makes you want to stand there in the green twilight until you feel your very feet sinking into and clutching the earth like roots and your body breathing slow through its pores like the leaves—when you stand there and wait for the next drop to drop with its small, flat sound to a lower leaf, that sound seems to measure out something, to put an end to something, to begin something, and you cannot wait for it to happen and are afraid it will not happen, and then when it has happened, you are waiting again, almost afraid.

But the man whom I saw coming through the woods in my mind's eye did not pause and wait, growing into the ground and breathing with the enormous, soundless breathing of the leaves. Instead, I saw him moving in the green twilight inside my head as he was moving at that very moment along the path by the edge of the woods, coming toward the house. He was moving steadily, but not fast, with his shoulders hunched a little and his head thrust forward, like a man who has come a long way and has a long way to go. I shut my eyes for a couple of seconds, thinking that when I opened them he would not be there at all. There was no place for him to have come from, and there was no reason for him to come where he was coming, toward our house. But I opened my eyes, and there he was, and he was coming steadily along the side of the woods. He was not yet even with the back chicken yard.

'Mama,' I called.

'You put them on,' the voice said.

'There's a man coming,' I called, 'out back.'

She did not reply to that, and I guessed that she had gone to the kitchen window to look. She would be looking at the man and wondering who he was and what he wanted, the way you always do in the country, and if I went back there now she would not notice right off whether or not I was barefoot. So I went back to the kitchen.

She was standing by the window. 'I don't recognize him,' she said, not looking around at me.

'Where could he be coming from?' I asked.

'I don't know,' she said.

'What would he be doing down at the river? At night? In the storm?'

She studied the figure out the window, then said, 'Oh, I reckon maybe he cut across from the Dunbar place.'

That was, I realized, a perfectly rational explanation. He had not been down at the river in the storm, at night. He had come over this morning. You could cut across from the Dunbar place if you didn't mind breaking through a lot of elder and sassafras and blackberry bushes which had about taken over the old cross path, which nobody ever used any more. That satisfied me for a moment, but only for a moment. 'Mamma,' I asked, 'what would he be doing over at the Dunbar place last night?'

Then she looked at me, and I knew I had made a mistake, for she was looking at my bare feet. 'You haven't got your shoes on,' she said.

But I was saved by the dogs. That instant there was a bark which I recognized as Sam, the collie, and then a heavier, churning kind of bark which was Bully, and I saw a streak of white as Bully tore round the corner of the back porch and headed out for the man. Bully was a big, bone-white bull dog, the kind of dog that they used to call a farm bull dog but that you don't see any more, heavy chested and heavy headed, but with pretty long legs. He could take a fence as light as a hound. He had just cleared the white paling fence toward the woods when my mother ran out to the back porch and began calling, 'Here you, Bully! Here you!'

Bully stopped in the path, waiting for the man, but he gave a few more of those deep, gargling, savage barks that reminded you of something down a stone-lined well. The red clay mud, I saw, was splashed up over his white chest and looked exciting, like blood.

The man, however, had not stopped walking even when Bully took the fence and started at him. He had kept right on coming. All he had done was to switch a little paper parcel which he carried from the right hand to the left, and then reach into his pants pocket to get something. Then I saw the glitter and knew that he had a knife in his hand, probably the kind of mean knife just made for devilment and nothing else, with a blade as long as the blade of a frog sticker, which will snap out ready when you press a button in the handle. That knife must have had a button in the handle, or else, how could he have had the blade out glittering so quick and with just one hand?

Pulling his knife against the dogs was a funny thing to do, for Bully was a big, powerful brute and fast, and Sam was all right. If those dogs had meant business, they might have knocked him down and ripped him before he got a stroke in. He ought to have picked up a heavy stick, something to take a swipe at them with and something which they could see and respect when they came at him. But he apparently did not know much about dogs. He just held the knife blade close against the right leg, low down, and kept on moving down the path.

Then my mother had called, and Bully had stopped. So the man let the blade of the knife snap back into the handle, and dropped it into his pocket, and kept on coming. Many women would have been afraid with the strange man who they knew had that knife in his pocket. That is, if they were alone in the house with nobody but a nine-year-old boy. And my mother was alone, for my father had gone off, and Dellie, the cook, was down at her cabin because she wasn't feeling well. But my mother wasn't afraid. She wasn't a big woman, but she was clear and brisk about everything she did and looked everybody and everything right in the eye from her own blue eyes in her tanned face. She had been the first woman in the county to ride a horse astride (that was back when she was a girl and long before I was born), and I have seen her snatch up a pump gun and go out and knock a chicken hawk out of the air like a busted skeet when he came over her chicken yard. She was a steady and self-reliant woman, and when I think of her now after all the years she has been dead, I think of her brown hands, not big, but somewhat square for a woman's hands, with square-cut nails. They looked, as a matter of fact, more like a young boy's hands than a grown woman's. But back then it never crossed my mind that she would ever be dead.

She stood on the back porch and watched the man enter the back gate, where the dogs (Bully had leaped back into the yard) were dancing and muttering and giving sidelong glances back to my mother to see if she meant what she had said. The man walked right by the dogs, almost brushing them, and didn't pay them any attention. I could see now that he wore old khaki pants, and a dark wool coat with stripes in it, and a gray felt hat. He had on a gray shirt with blue stripes in it, and no tie. But I could see a tie, blue and reddish, sticking in his side coat-pocket. Everything was wrong about what he wore. He ought to have been wearing blue jeans or overalls, and a straw hat or an old black felt hat, and the coat, granting that he might have been wearing a wool coat and not a jumper, ought not to have had those stripes. Those clothes, despite the fact that they were old enough and dirty enough for any tramp, didn't belong there in our back yard, coming down the path, in Middle Tennessee, miles away from any big town, and even a mile off the pike.

When he got almost to the steps, without having said anything, my mother, very matter-of-factly, said, 'Good morning.'

'Good morning,' he said, and stopped and looked her over. He did not take off his hat, and under the brim you could see the perfectly unmemorable face, which wasn't old and wasn't young, or thick or thin. It was grayish and covered with about three days of stubble. The eyes were a kind of nondescript, muddy hazel, or something like that, rather bloodshot. His teeth, when he opened his mouth, showed yellow and uneven. A couple of them had been knocked out. You knew that they had been knocked out, because there was a scar, not very old, there on the lower lip just beneath the gap.

'Are you hunting work?' my mother asked him.

'Yes,' he said—not 'yes, mam'—and still did not take off his hat.

'I don't know about my husband, for he isn't here,' she said, and didn't mind a bit telling the tramp, or whoever he was, with the mean knife in his pocket, that no man was around, 'but I can give you a few things to do. The storm has drowned a lot of my chicks. Three coops of them. You can gather them up and bury them. Bury them deep so the dogs won't get at them. In the woods. And fix the coops the wind blew over. And down yonder beyond that pen by the edge of the woods are some drowned poults. They got out and I couldn't get them in. Even after it started to rain hard: poults haven't got any sense.'

'What are them things—poults?' he demanded, and spat on the brick walk. He rubbed his foot over the spot, and I saw that he wore a black, pointed-toe low shoe, all cracked and broken. It was a crazy kind of shoe to be wearing in the country.

'Oh, they're young turkeys,' my mother was saying. 'And they haven't got any sense. I oughtn't to try to raise them around here

28

with so many chickens, anyway. They don't thrive near chickens, even in separate pens. And I won't give up my chickens.' Then she stopped herself and resumed briskly on the note of business. 'When you finish that, you can fix my flower beds. A lot of trash and mud and gravel has washed down. Maybe you can save some of my flowers if you are careful.

'Flowers,' the man said, in a low, impersonal voice which seemed to have a wealth of meaning, but a meaning which I could not fathom. As I think back on it, it probably was not pure contempt. Rather, it was a kind of impersonal and distant marveling that he should be on the verge of grubbing in a flower bed. He said the word, and then looked off across the yard.

'Yes, flowers,' my mother replied with some asperity, as though she would have nothing said or implied against flowers. 'And they were very fine this year.' Then she stopped and looked at the man. 'Are you hungry?' she demanded.

'Yeah,' he said.

'I'll fix you something,' she said, 'before you get started.' She turned to me. 'Show him where he can wash up,' she commanded, and went into the house.

I took the man to the end of the porch where a pump was and where a couple of wash pans sat on a low shelf for people to use before they went into the house. I stood there while he laid down his little parcel wrapped in newspaper and took off his hat and looked around for a nail to hang it on. He poured the water and plunged his hands into it. They were big hands, and strong looking, but they did not have the creases and the earth-color of the hands of men who work outdoors. But they were dirty, with black dirt ground into the skin and under the nails. After he had washed his hands, he poured another basin of water and washed his face. He dried his face, and with the towel still dangling in his grasp, stepped over to the mirror on the house wall. He rubbed one hand over the stubble on his face. Then he carefully inspected his face, turning first one side and then the other, and stepped back and settled his striped coat down on his shoulders. He had the movements of a man who has just dressed up to go to church or a party—the way he settled his coat and smoothed it and scanned himself in the mirror.

Then he caught my glance on him. He glared at me for an instant out of the bloodshot eyes, then demanded in a low, harsh voice, 'What are you looking at?'

'Nothing,' I managed to say, and stepped back a step from him.

He flung the towel down, crumpled, on the shelf, and went toward the kitchen door and entered without knocking.

My mother said something to him which I could not catch. I started to go in again, then thought about my bare feet, and decided to go back of the chicken yard, where the man would have to come to pick up the dead chicks. I hung around behind the chicken house until he came out.

He moved across the chicken yard with a fastidious, not quite finicking motion, looking down at the curdled mud flecked with bits of chicken-droppings. The mud curled up over the soles of his black shoes. I stood back from him some six feet and watched him pick up the first of the drowned chicks. He held it up by one foot and inspected it.

There is nothing deader looking than a drowned chick. The feet curl in that feeble, empty way which back when I was a boy, even if I was a country boy who did not mind hog-killing or frog-gigging, made me feel hollow in the stomach. Instead of looking plump and fluffy, the body is stringy and limp with the fluff plastered to it, and the neck is long and loose like a little string of rag. And the eyes have that bluish membrane over them which makes you think of a very old man who is sick about to die.

The man stood there and inspected the chick. Then he looked all around as though he didn't know what to do with it.

'There's a great big old basket in the shed,' I said, and pointed in the shed attached to the chicken house.

He inspected me as though he had just discovered my presence, and moved toward the shed.

'There's a spade there, too,' I added.

He got the basket and began to pick up the other chicks, picking each one up slowly by a foot and then flinging it into the basket with a nasty, snapping motion. Now and then he would look at me out of the bloodshot eyes. Every time he seemed on the verge of saying something, but he did not. Perhaps he was building up to say something to me, but I did not wait that long. His way of looking at me made me so uncomfortable that I left the chicken yard.

Besides, I had just remembered that the creek was in flood, over the bridge, and that people were down there watching it. So I cut across the farm toward the creek. When I got to the big tobacco field I saw that it had not suffered much. The land lay right and not many tobacco plants had washed out of the ground. But I knew that a lot of tobacco round the country had been washed right out. My father had said so at breakfast.

My father was down at the bridge. When I came out of the gap in the osage hedge into the road, I saw him sitting on his mare over the heads of the other men who were standing around, admiring the flood. The creek was big here, even in low water; for only a couple of miles away it ran into the river, and when a real flood came, the red water got over the pike where it dipped down to the bridge, which was an iron bridge, and high over the floor and even the side railings of the bridge. Only the upper iron work would show, with the water boiling and frothing red and white around it. That creek rose so fast and so heavy because a few miles back it came down out of the hills, where the gorges filled up with water in no time when a rain came. The creek ran in a deep bed with limestone bluffs along both sides until it got within three quarters of a mile of the bridge, and when it came out from between those bluffs in flood it was boiling and hissing and steaming like water from a fire hose.

Whenever there was a flood, people from half the county would come down to see the sight. After a gully-washer there would not be any work to do anyway. If it didn't ruin your crop, you couldn't plow and you felt like taking a holiday to celebrate. If it did ruin your crop, there wasn't anything to do except to try to take your mind off the mortgage, if you were rich enough to have a mortgage, and if you couldn't afford a mortgage you needed something to take your mind off how hungry you would be by Christmas. So people would come down to the bridge and look at the flood. It made something different from the run of days.

There would not be much talking after the first few minutes of trying to guess how high the water was this time. The men and kids just stood around, or sat their horses or mules, as the case might be, or stood up in the wagon beds. They looked at the strangeness of the flood for an hour or two, and then somebody would say that he had better be getting on home to dinner and would start walking down the gray, puddled limestone pike, or would touch heel to his mount and start off. Everybody always knew what it would be like when he got down to the bridge, but people always came. It was like church or a funeral. They always came, that is, if it was a summer and the flood unexpected. Nobody ever came down in winter to see high water.

When I came out of the gap in the bodock hedge, I saw the crowd, perhaps fifteen or twenty men and a lot of kids, and saw my father sitting his mare, Nellie Gray. He was a tall, limber man and carried himself well. I was always proud to see him sit a horse, he was so quiet and straight, and when I stepped through the gap of the hedge that morning, the first thing that happened was, I remember, the warm feeling I always had when I saw him up on a horse, just sitting. I did not go toward him, but skirted the crowd on the far side, to get a look at the creek. For one thing, I was not sure what he would say about the fact that I was barefoot. But the first thing I knew, I heard his voice calling, 'Seth!'

I went toward him, moving apologetically past the men, who bent their large, red or thin, sallow faces above me. I knew some of the men, and knew their names, but because those I knew were there in a crowd, mixed with the strange faces, they seemed foreign to me, and not friendly. I did not look up at my father until I was almost within touching distance of his heel. Then I looked up and tried to read his face, to see if he was angry about my being barefoot. Before I could decide anything from that impassive, high-boned face, he had leaned over and reached a hand to me. 'Grab on,' he commanded.

I grabbed on and gave a little jump, and he said, 'Up-see-daisy!' and whisked me, light as a feather, up to the pommel of his McClellan saddle.

'You can see better up here,' he said, slid back on the cantle a little to make me more comfortable, and then, looking over my head at the swollen, tumbling water, seemed to forget all about me. But his right hand was laid on my side, just above my thigh, to steady me.

I was sitting there as quiet as I could, feeling the faint stir of my father's chest against my shoulders as it rose and fell with his breath, when I saw the cow. At first, looking up the creek, I thought it was just another big piece of driftwood steaming down the creek in the ruck of water, but all at once a pretty good-size boy who had climbed part way up a telephone by the pike so that he could see better yelled out, 'Golly-damn, look at that-air cow!'

Everybody looked. It was a cow all right, but it might just as well have been driftwood; for it was dead as a chunk, rolling and roiling down the creek, appearing and disappearing feet up or head up, it didn't matter which.

The cow started up the talk again. Somebody wondered whether it would hit one of the clear places under the top girder of the bridge and get through or whether it would get tangled in the drift and trash that had piled against the upright girders and braces. Somebody remembered how about ten years before so much driftwood had piled up on the bridge that it was knocked off its foundations. Then the cow hit. It hit the edge of the drift against one of the girders, and hung there. For a few seconds it seemed as though it might tear loose, but then we saw that it was really caught. It bobbed and heaved on its side there in a slow, grinding, uneasy fashion. It had a yoke around its neck, the kind made out of a forked limb to keep a jumper behind fence.

'She shore jumped one fence,' one of the men said.

And another: 'Well, she done jumped her last one, fer a fack.'

Then they began to wonder about whose cow it might be. They decided it must belong to Milt Alley. They said that he had a cow that was a jumper, and kept her in a fenced-in piece of ground up the creek. I had never seen Milt Alley, but I knew who he was. He was a squatter and lived up the hills a way, on a shirt-tail patch of set-on-edge land, in a cabin. He was pore white trash. He had lots of children. I had seen the children at school, when they came. They were thin-faced, with straight, sticky-looking, dough-colored hair, and they smelled something like old sour buttermilk, not because they drank so much buttermilk but because that is the sort of smell which children out of those cabins tend to have. The big Alley boy drew dirty pictures and showed them to the little boys at school.

That was Milt Alley's cow. It looked like the kind of cow he would have, a scrawny, old, sway-backed cow, with a yoke around her neck. I wondered if Milt Alley had another cow.

'Poppa,' I said, 'do you think Milt Alley has got another cow?'

'You say "Mr Alley,"' my father said quietly.

'Do you think he has?'

'No telling,' my father said.

Then a big gangly boy, about fifteen, who was sitting on a scraggly little old mule with a piece of croker sack thrown across the saw-tooth spine, and who had been staring at the cow, suddenly said to nobody in particular, 'Reckin anybody ever et drownt cow?'

He was the kind of boy who might just as well as not have been the son of Milt Alley, with his faded and patched overalls ragged at the bottom of the pants and the mud-stiff brogans hanging off his skinny, bare ankles at the level of the mule's belly. He had said what he did, and then looked embarrassed and sullen when all the eyes swung at him. He hadn't meant to say it, I am pretty sure now. He would have been too proud to say it, just as Milt Alley would have been too proud. He had just been thinking out loud, and the words had popped out.

There was an old man standing there on the pike, an old man with a white beard. 'Son,' he said to the embarrassed and sullen boy on the mule, 'you live long enough and you'll find a man will eat anything when the time comes.'

'Time gonna come fer some folks this year,' another man said.

'Son,' the old man said, 'in my time I et things a man don't like to think on. I was a sojer and I rode with Gin'l Forrest, and them things we et when the time come. I tell you. I et meat what got up and run when you taken out yore knife to cut a slice to put on the fire. You had to knock it down with a carbene butt, it was so active. That-air meat would jump like a bullfrog, it was so full of skippers.'

But nobody was listening to the old man. The boy on the mule turned his sullen sharp face from him, dug a heel into the side of the mule and went off up the pike with a motion which made you think that any second you would hear mule bones clashing inside that lank and scrofulous hide.

'Cy Dundee's boy,' a man said, and nodded toward the figure going up the pike on the mule.

'Reckin Cy Dundee's young-uns seen times they'd settle fer drownt cow,' another man said.

The old man with the beard peered at them both from his weak, slow eyes, first at one and then at the other. 'Live long enough,' he said, 'and a man will settle for what he kin git.'

Then there was silence again, with the people looking at the red, foam-flecked water.

My father lifted the bridle rein in his left hand, and the mare turned and walked around the group and up the pike. We rode on up to our big gate, where my father dismounted to open it and let me myself ride Nellie Gray through. When he got to the lane that led off from the drive about two hundred yards from our house, my father said, 'Grab on.' I grabbed on, and he let me down to the ground. 'I'm going to ride down and look at my corn,' he said. 'You go on.' He took the lane, and I stood there on the drive and watched him ride off. He was wearing cowhide boots and an old hunting coat, and I thought that that made him look very military, like a picture. That and the way he rode.

I did not go to the house. Instead, I went by the vegetable garden and crossed behind the stables, and headed down for Dellie's cabin. I wanted to go down and play with Jebb, who was Dellie's little boy about two years older than I was. Besides, I was cold. I shivered as I walked, and I had gooseflesh. The mud which crawled up between my toes with every step I took was like ice. Dellie would have a fire, but she wouldn't make me put on shoes and stockings.

Dellie's cabin was of logs, with one side, because it was on a slope, set on limestone chunks, with a little porch attached to it, and had a little white-washed fence around it and a gate with plow-points on a wire to clink when somebody came in, and had two big white oaks in the yard and some flowers and a nice privy in the back with some honeysuckle growing over it. Dellie and Old Jebb, who was Jebb's father and who lived with Dellie and had lived with her for twenty-five years even if they never had got married, were careful to keep everything nice around their cabin. They had the name all over the community for being clean and clever Negroes. Dellie and Jebb were what they used to call 'white-folks' niggers.' There was a big difference between their cabin and the other two cabins farther down where the other tenants lived. My father kept the other cabins weatherproof, but he couldn't undertake to go down and pick up after the litter they strewed. They didn't take the trouble to have a vegetable patch like Dellie and Jebb or to make preserves from wild plum, and jelly from crab apple the way Dellie did. They were shiftless, and my father was always threatening to get shed of them. But he never did. When they finally left, they just got up and left on their own, for no reason, to go and be shiftless somewhere else. Then some more came. But meanwhile they lived down there, Matt Rawson and his family, and Sid Turner and his, and I played with their children all over the farm when they weren't working. But when I wasn't around they were mean sometimes to Little Jebb. That was because the other tenants down there were jealous of Dellie and Jebb.

I was so cold that I ran the last fifty yards to Dellie's gate. As soon as I had entered the yard, I saw that the storm had been hard on Dellie's flowers. The yard was, as I have said, on a slight slope, and the water running across had gutted the flower beds and washed out all the good black woods-earth which Dellie had brought in. What little grass there was in the yard was plastered sparsely down on the ground, the way the drainage water had left it. It reminded me of the way the fluff was plastered down on the skin of the drowned chicks that the strange man had been picking up, up in my mother's chicken yard.

I took a few steps up the path to the cabin and then I saw that the drainage water had washed a lot of trash and filth out from under Dellie's house. Up toward the porch, the ground was not clean any more. Old pieces of rag, two or three rusted cans, pieces of rotten rope, some hunks of old dog dung, broken glass, old paper, and all sorts of things like that had washed out from under Dellie's house to foul her clean yard. It looked just as bad as the yards of the other cabins, or worse. It was worse, as a matter of fact, because it was a surprise. I had never thought of all that filth being under Dellie's house. It was not anything against Dellie that the stuff had been under the cabin. Trash will get under any house. But I did not think of that when I saw the foulness which had washed out on the ground which Dellie sometimes used to sweep with a twig broom to make nice and clean.

I picked my way past the filth, being careful not to get my bare feet on it, and mounted to Dellie's door. When I knocked, I heard her voice telling me to come in.

It was dark inside the cabin, after the daylight, but I could make out Dellie piled up in bed under a quilt, and Little Jebb crouched by the hearth, where a low fire simmered. 'Howdy,' I said to Dellie, 'how you feeling?'

Her big eyes, the whites surprising and glaring in the black face, fixed on me as I stood there, but she did not reply. It did not look like Dellie, or act like Dellie, who would grumble and bustle around our kitchen, talking to herself, scolding me or Little Jebb, clanking pans, making all sorts of unnecessary noises and mutterings like an old-fashioned black steam thrasher engine when it has got up an extra head of steam and keeps popping the governor and rumbling and shaking on its wheels. But now Dellie just lay up there on the bed, under the patch-work quilt, and turned the black face, which I scarcely recognized, and the glaring white eyes to me.

'How you feeling?' I repeated.

'I'se sick,' the voice said croakingly out of the strange black face which was not attached to Dellie's big, squat body, but stuck out from under a pile of tangled bedclothes. Then the voice added: 'Mighty sick.'

'I'm sorry,' I managed to say.

The eyes remained fixed on me for a moment, then they left me and the head rolled back on the pillow. 'Sorry,' the voice said, in a flat way which wasn't question or statement of anything. It was just the empty word put into the air with no meaning or expression, to float off like a feather or a puff of smoke, while the big eyes, with the whites like the peeled white of hard-boiled eggs, stared at the ceiling.

'Dellie,' I said after a minute, 'there's a tramp up at the house. He's got a knife.'

She was not listening. She closed her eyes.

I tiptoed over to the hearth where Jebb was and crouched beside him. We began to talk in low voices. I was asking him to get out his train and play train. Old Jebb had put spool wheels on three cigar boxes and put wire links between the boxes to make a train for Jebb. The box that was the locomotive had the top closed and a length of broom stick for a smoke stack. Jebb didn't want to get the train out, but I told him I would go home if he didn't. So he got out the train, and the colored rocks, and fossils of crinoid stems, and other junk he used for the load, and we began to push it around, talking the way we thought trainmen talked, making a chuck-chucking sound under the breath for the noise of the locomotive and now and then uttering low, cautious toots for the whistle. We got so interested in playing train that the toots got louder. Then, before he thought, Jebb gave a good, loud *toot-toot*, blowing for a crossing.

'Come here,' the voice said from the bed.

Jebb got up slow from his hands and knees, giving me a sudden, naked, inimical look.

'Come here!' the voice said.

Jebb went to the bed. Dellie propped herself weakly up on one arm, muttering, 'Come closer.'

Jebb stood closer.

'Last thing I do, I'm gonna do it,' Dellie said. 'Done tole you to be quiet.'

Then she slapped him. It was an awful slap, more awful for the kind of weakness which it came from and brought to focus. I had seen her slap Jebb before, but the slapping had always been the kind of easy slap you would expect from a good-natured, grumbling Negro woman like Dellie. But this was different. It was awful. It was so awful that Jebb didn't make a sound. The tears just popped out and ran down his face, and his breath came sharp, like gasps.

Dellie fell back. 'Cain't even be sick,' she said to the ceiling. 'Git sick and they won't even let you lay. They tromp all over you. Cain't even be sick.' Then she closed her eyes.

I went out of the room. I almost ran getting to the door, and I did run across the porch and down the steps and across the yard, not caring whether or not I stepped on the filth which had washed out from under the cabin. I ran almost all the way home. Then I thought about my mother catching me with the bare feet. So I went down to the stables.

I heard a noise in the crib, and opened the door. There was Big Jebb, sitting on an old nail keg, shelling corn into a bushel basket. I went in, pulling the door shut behind me, and crouched on the floor near him. I crouched there for a couple of minutes before either of us spoke, and watched him shelling the corn.

He had very big hands, knotted and grayish at the joints, with calloused palms which seemed to be streaked with rust with the rust coming up between the fingers to show from the back. His hands were so strong and tough that he could take a big ear of corn and rip the grains right off the cob with the palm of his hand, all in one motion, like a machine. 'Work long as me,' he would say, 'and the good Lawd'll give you a hand lak cass-ion won't nuthin' hurt.' And his hands did look like cast iron, old cast iron streaked with rust.

He was an old man, up in his seventies, thirty years or more older than Dellie, but he was strong as a bull. He was a squat sort of man, heavy in the shoulders, with remarkably long arms, the kind of build they say the river natives have on the Congo from paddling so much in their boats. He had a round bullet-head, set on powerful shoulders. His skin was very black, and the thin hair on his head was now grizzled like tufts of old cotton batting. He had small eyes and a flat nose, not big, and the kindest and wisest old face in the world, the blunt, sad, wise face of an old animal peering tolerantly out on the goings-on of the merely human creatures before him. He was a good man, and I loved him next to my mother and father. I crouched there on the floor of the crib and watched him shell corn with the rusty cast-iron hands, while he looked down at me out of the little eyes set in the blunt face.

'Dellie says she's mighty sick,' I said.

'Yeah,' he said.

'What's she sick from?'

'Woman-mizry,' he said.

'What's woman-mizry?'

'Hit comes on 'em,' he said. 'Hit just comes on 'em when the time

38

comes.'

'What is it?'

'Hit is the change,' he said. 'Hit is the change of life and time.'

'What changes?'

'You too young to know.'

'Tell me.'

'Time come and you find out everything.'

I knew that there was no use in asking him any more. When I asked him things and he said that, I always knew that he would not tell me. So I continued to crouch there and watch him. Now that I had sat there a little while, I was cold again.

'What you shiver fer?' he asked me.

'I'm cold. I'm cold because it's blackberry winter,' I said.

'Maybe 'tis and maybe 'tain't,' he said.

'My mother says it is.'

'Ain't sayen Miss Sallie doan know and ain't sayen she do. But folks doan know everything.'

'Why isn't it blackberry winter?'

'Too late fer blackberry winter. Blackberries done bloomed.'

'She said it was.'

'Blackberry winter just a leetle cold spell. Hit come and then hit go away, and hit is growed summer of a sudden lak a gunshot. Ain't no tellen hit will go way this time.'

'It's June,' I said.

'June,' he replied with great contempt. 'That what folks say. What June mean? Maybe hit is come cold to stay.'

'Why?'

'Cause this-here old yearth is tahrd. Hit is tahrd and ain't gonna perduce. Lawd let hit come rain one time forty days and forty nights, 'cause He was tahrd of sinful folks. Maybe this-here old yearth say to the Lawd, Lawd, I done plum tahrd, Lawd, lemme rest. And Lawd say, Yearth, you done yore best, you give 'em cawn and you give 'em taters, and all they think on is they gut, and, Yearth, you kin take a rest.'

'What will happen?'

'Folks will eat up everything. The yearth won't perduce no more. Folks cut down all the trees and burn 'em 'cause they cold, and the yearth won't grow no more. I been tellen 'em. I been tellen folks. Sayen, maybe this year, hit is the time. But they doan listen to me, how the yearth is tahrd. Maybe this year they find out.'

'Will everything die?'

'Everything and everybody, hit will be so.'

'This year?'

'Ain't no tellen. Maybe this year.'

'My mother said it is blackberry winter,' I said confidently, and got up.

'Ain't sayen nuthin' agin Miss Sallie,' he said.

I went to the door of the crib. I was really cold now. Running, I had got up a sweat and now I was worse.

I hung on the door, looking at Jebb, who was shelling corn again.

'There's a tramp came to the house,' I said. I had almost forgotten the tramp.

'Yeah.'

'He came by the back way. What was he doing down there in the storm?'

'They comes and they goes,' he said, 'and ain't no tellen.'

'He had a mean knife.'

'The good ones and the bad ones, they comes and they goes. Storm or sun, light or dark. They is folks and they comes and they goes lak folks.'

I hung on the door, shivering.

He studied me a moment, then said, 'You git on to the house. You ketch yore death. Then what yore mammy say?'

I hesitated.

'You git,' he said.

When I came to the back yard, I saw that my father was standing by the back porch and the tramp was walking toward him. They began talking before I reached them, but I got there just as my father was saying, 'I'm sorry, but I haven't got any work. I got all the hands on the place I need now. I won't need any extra until wheat thrashing.'

The stranger made no reply, just looked at my father.

My father took out his leather coin purse, and got out a half-dollar. He held it toward the man. 'This is for half a day,' he said.

The man looked at the coin, and then at my father, making no motion to take the money. But that was the right amount. A dollar a day was what you paid them back in 1910. And the man hadn't even worked half a day.

Then the man reached out and took the coin. He dropped it into the right side pocket of his coat. Then he said, very slowly and without feeling: 'I didn't want to work on your ____ farm.'

40

He used the word which they would have frailed me to death for using.

I looked at my father's face and it was streaked white under the sunburn. Then he said, 'Get off this place. Get off this place or I won't be responsible.'

The man dropped his right hand into his pants pocket. It was the pocket where he kept the knife. I was just about to yell to my father about the knife when the hand came back out with nothing in it. The man gave a kind of twisted grin, showing where the teeth had been knocked out above the new scar. I thought that instant how maybe he had tried before to pull a knife on somebody else and had got his teeth knocked out.

So now he just gave that twisted, sickish grin out of the unmemorable, grayish face, and then spat on the brick path. The glob landed just about six inches from the toe of my father's right boot. My father looked down at it, and so did I. I thought that if the glob had hit my father's boot something would have happened. I looked down and saw the bright glob, and on one side of it my father's strong cowhide boots, with the brass eyelets and the leather thongs, heavy boots splashed with good red mud and set solid on the bricks, and on the other side the pointed-toe, broken, black shoes, on which the mud looked so sad and out of place. Then I saw one of the black shoes move a little, just a twitch first, then a real step backward.

The man moved in a quarter circle to the end of the porch, with my father's steady gaze upon him all the while. At the end of the porch, the man reached up to the shelf where the wash pans were to get his little newspaper-wrapped parcel. Then he disappeared around the corner of the house and my father mounted the porch and went into the kitchen without a word.

I followed around the house to see what the man would do. I wasn't afraid of him now, no matter if he did have the knife. When I got around in front, I saw him going out the yard gate and starting up the drive toward the pike. So I ran to catch up with him. He was sixty yards or so up the drive before I caught up.

I did not walk right up even with him at first, but trailed him, the way a kid will, about seven or eight feet behind, now and then running two or three steps in order to hold my place against his longer stride. When I first came up behind him, he turned to give me a look, just a meaningless look, and then fixed his eyes up the drive and kept on walking.

When we had got around the bend in the drive which cut the house from sight, and were going along by the edge of the woods, I decided to come up even with him. I ran a few steps, and was by his side, or almost, but some feet off to the right. I walked along in this position for a while, and he never noticed me. I walked along until we got within sight of the big gate that let on the pike.

Then I said: 'Where did you come from?'

He looked at me then with a look which seemed almost surprised that I was there. Then he said, 'It ain't none of yore business.'

We went on another fifty feet.

Then I said, 'Where are you going?'

He stopped, studied me dispassionately for a moment, then suddenly took a step toward me and leaned his face down at me. The lips jerked back, but not in any grin, to show where the teeth were knocked out and to make the scar on the lower lip come white with the tension.

He said: 'Stop following me. You don't stop following me and I cut yore throat, you little son-of-a-bitch.'

Then he went on to the gate, and up the pike.

That was thirty-five years ago. Since that time my father and mother have died. I was still a boy, but a big boy, when my father got cut on the blade of a mowing machine and died of lockjaw. My mother sold the place and went to town to live with her sister. But she never took hold after my father's death and she died within three years, right in middle life. My aunt always said, 'Sallie just died of a broken heart, she was so devoted.' Dellie is dead, too, but she died, I heard, quite a long time after we sold the farm.

As for Little Jebb, he grew up to be a mean and ficey Negro. He killed another Negro in a fight and got sent to the penitentiary, where he is yet, the last I heard tell. He probably grew up to be mean and ficey from just being picked on so much by the children of the other tenants, who were jealous of Jebb and Dellie for being thrifty and clever and being white-folks' niggers.

Old Jebb lived forever. I saw him ten years ago and he was about a hundred then, and not looking much different. He was living in town then, on relief—that was back in the Depression—when I went to see him. He said to me: 'Too strong to die. When I was a young feller just comen on and seen how things wuz, I prayed the Lawd. I said, O, Lawd, gimme strength and meke me strong fer to do and to in-dure.

42

The Lawd hearkened to my prayer. He give me strength. I was induren proud fer being strong and me much man. The Lawd give me my prayer and my strength. But now He done gone off and fergot me and left me alone with my strength. A man doan know what to pray fer, and him mortal.'

Jebb is probably living yet, as far as I know.

That is what has happened since the morning when the tramp leaned his face down at me and showed his teeth and said: 'Stop following me. You don't stop following me and I cut yore throat, you little son-of-a-bitch.' That was what he said, for me not to follow him. But I did follow him, all the years.

1947

O City of Broken Dreams

John Cheever

When the train from Chicago left Albany and began to pound down the river valley toward New York, the Malloys, who had already experienced many phases of excitement, felt their breathing quicken, as if there were not enough air in the coach. They straightened their backs and raised their heads, searching for oxygen, like the crew of a doomed submarine. Their daughter, Mildred-Rose, took an enviable way out of the agitation. She fell asleep. Evarts Malloy wanted to get the suitcases down from the rack, but Alice, his wife, studied the timetable and said that it was too soon. She stared out of the window and saw the noble Hudson.

'Why do they call it the rind of America?' she asked her husband.

'The Rhine,' Evarts said. 'Not the rind.'

'Oh.'

They had left their home in Wentworth, Indiana, the day before, and in spite of the excitements of travel and their brilliant destination, they both wondered, now and then, if they had remembered to turn off the gas and extinguish the rubbish fire behind the barn. They were dressed, like the people you sometimes see in Times Square on Saturday nights, in clothing that had been saved for their flight. His light shoes had perhaps not been out of the back of the closet since his father's funeral or his brother's wedding. She was wearing her new gloves for the first time—the gloves she had been given for Christmas ten years ago. His tarnished collar pin and his initialled tie clip, with its gilt chain, his fancy socks, the rayon handkerchief in his breast pocket, and the carnation made of feathers in his lapel had all been husbanded in the top drawer of his bureau for years in the firm conviction that life would someday call him from Wentworth.

Alice Malloy had dark, stringy hair, and even her husband, who loved her more than he knew, was sometimes reminded by her lean face of a tenement doorway on a rainy day, for her countenance was long, vacant, and weakly lighted, a passage for the gentle transports and miseries of the poor. Evarts Malloy was very thin. He had worked as a bus driver and he stooped a little. Their child slept with her thumb in her mouth. Her hair was dark and her dirty face was lean, like her mother's. When a violent movement of the train roused her, she drew noisily at the thumb until she lost consciousness again. She had been unable to store up as much finery as her parents, since she was only five years old, but she wore a white fur coat. The matching hat and muff had been lost generations before; the skins of the coat were sere and worn, but as she slept, she stroked them, as if they had remarkable properties that assured her that all was well, all was well.

The conductor who came through the car taking tickets after Albany noticed the Malloys, and something about their appearance worried him. As he came back through the car, he stopped at their seat and talked with them, first about Mildred-Rose and then about their destination.

'You people going to New York for the first time?' he asked.

'Yes,' Evarts said.

'Going down to see the sights?'

'Oh, no,' Alice said. 'We're going on business.'

'Looking for a job?' the conductor asked.

'Oh, no,' Alice said. 'Tell him, Evarts.'

'Well, it really isn't a job,' Evarts said. 'I'm not looking for a job, I mean. I mean I sort of have a job.' His manner was friendly and simple and he told his story enthusiastically, for the conductor was the first stranger to ask for it. 'I was in the Army, you see, and then, when I got out of the Army, I went back home and began driving the bus again. I'm a night bus driver. But I didn't like it. I kept getting stomach aches, and it hurt my eyes, driving at night, so in my spare time, during the afternoons, I began to write this play. Now, out on Route 7, near Wentworth, where we live, there's this old woman named Mama Finelli, who has a gas station and a snake farm. She's a very salty and haunting old character, and so I decided to write this play about her. She has all these salty and haunting sayings. Well, I wrote this first act—and then Tracey Murchison, the producer, comes out from New York to give a lecture at the Women's Club about the problems of the theatre. Well, Alice went to this lecture, and when he was complaining, when Murchison was complaining about the lack of young playwrights, Alice raises her hand and she tells Murchison that her husband is a young playwright and will he read his play. Didn't you Alice?'

'Yes,' Alice said.

'Well, he hems and haws,' Evarts said, 'Murchison hems and haws, but Alice pins him down, because all these other people are listening, and when he finished his lecture, she goes right up on the platform and she gives him the play—she's got it in her pocketbook. Well, then she goes back to his hotel with him and she sits right beside him until he's read the play—the first act, that is. That's all I've written. Well in this play there's a part he wants for his wife, Madge Beatty, right off. I guess you know who Madge Beatty is. So you know what he does then? He sits right down and he writes out a check for thirty-five dollars and he says for me and Alice to come to New York! So we take all our money out of the savings bank and we burn our bridges and here we are.'

'Well, I guess there's lots of money in it,' the conductor said. Then he wished the Malloys luck and walked away.

Evarts wanted to take the suitcases down at Poughkeepsie and again at Harmon, but Alice checked each place against the timetable and made him wait. Neither of them had seen New York before, and they watched its approaches greedily, for Wentworth was a dismal town and even the slums of Manhattan looked wonderful to them that afternoon. When the train plunged into the darkness beneath Park Avenue, Alice felt that she was surrounded by the inventions of giants, and she roused Mildred-Rose and tied the little girl's bonnet with trembling fingers.

As the Malloys stepped from the train, Alice noticed that the paving, deep in the station, had a frosty glitter, and she wondered if diamonds had been ground into the concrete. She forbade Evarts to ask directions. 'If they find out we're green, they'll fleece us,' she whispered. They wandered through the marble waiting room, following the noise of traffic and klaxons as if it were the bidding of life. Alice had studied a map of New York, and when they left the station, she knew which direction to take. They walked along Forty-second Street to Fifth Avenue. The faces that passed them seemed purposeful and intent, as if they all belonged to people who were pursuing the destinies of great industries. Evarts had never seen so many beautiful women, so many pleasant, young faces, promising an easy conquest. It was a winter afternoon, and the light in the city was clear and shaded with violet, just like the light on the fields around Wentworth.

Their destination, the Hotel Mentone, was on a side street west of Sixth Avenue. It was a dark place, with malodorous chambers, miserable food, and a lobby ceiling decorated with as much gilt and gesso as the Vatican chapels. It was a popular hotel among the old, it was attractive to the disreputable, and the Malloys had found the way there because the Mentone advertised on railroad-station hoardings all through the West. Many innocents had been there before them, and their sweetness and humility had triumphed over the apparent atmosphere of ruined splendor and petty vice and had left in all the public rooms a humble odor that reminded one of a country feed store on a winter afternoon. A bellboy took them to their room. As soon as he had gone, Alice examined the bath and pulled aside the window curtains. The window looked onto a brick wall, but when she raised it, she could hear the noise of traffic, and it sounded, as it had sounded in the station, like the irresistible and titanic voice of life itself.

The Malloys found their way, that afternoon, to the Broadway Automat. They shouted with pleasure at the magical coffee spigots and the glass doors that sprang open. 'Tomorrow, I'm going to have the baked beans,' Alice cried, 'and the chicken pie the day after that and the fish cakes after that.' When they had finished their supper, they went out into the street. Mildred-Rose walked between her parents, holding their calloused hands. It was getting dark, and the lights of Broadway answered all their simple prayers. High in the air were large, brightly lighted pictures of bloody heroes, criminal lovers, monsters, and armed desperadoes. The names of movies and soft drinks, restaurants and cigarettes were written in a jumble of light, and in the distance they could see the pitiless winter afterglow beyond the Hudson River. The tall buildings in the East were lighted and seemed to burn, as if fire had fallen onto their dark shapes. The air was full of music, and the light was brighter than day. They drifted with the crowd for hours.

Mildred-Rose got tired and began to cry, so at last her parents took her back to the Mentone. Alice had begun to undress her when someone knocked softly on the door.

'Come in,' Evarts called.

A bellboy stood in the doorway. He had the figure of a boy, but his face was gray and lined. 'I just wanted to see if you people were all right,' he said. 'I just wanted to see if maybe you wanted a little ginger ale or some ice water.'

'Oh, no, thank you kindly,' Alice said. 'It was very nice of you to

47

ask, though.'

'You people just come to New York for the first time?' the bellboy asked. He closed the door behind him and sat on the arm of a chair.

'Yes,' Evarts said. 'We left Wentworth—that's in Indiana—yesterday on the nine-fifteen for South Bend. Then we went to Chicago. We had dinner in Chicago.'

'I had the chicken pie,' Alice said. 'It was delicious.' She slipped Mildred-Rose's nightgown over her head.

'Then we came to New York,' Evarts said.

'What are you doing here?' the bellboy asked. 'Anniversary?' He helped himself to a cigarette from a package on the bureau and slipped into the chair.

'Oh, no,' Evarts said. 'We hit the jackpot.'

'Our ship's come in,' Alice said.

'A contest?' the bellboy asked. 'Something like that?'

'Oh, no,' Evarts said.

'You tell him, Evarts,' Alice said.

'Yes,' the bellboy said. 'Tell me, Evarts.'

'Well, you see,' Evarts said, 'it began like this.' He sat down on the bed and lighted a cigarette. 'I was in the Army, you see, and then when I got out of the Army, I went back to Wentworth . . . ' He repeated to the bellboy the story he had told the conductor.

'Oh, you lucky, lucky kids!' the bellboy exclaimed when Evarts had finished. 'Tracey Murchison! Madge Beatty! You lucky, lucky kids.' He looked at the poorly furnished room. Alice was arranging Mildred-Rose on the sofa, where she would sleep. Evarts was sitting on the edge of the bed swinging his legs. 'What you need now is a good agent,' the bellboy said. He wrote a name and address on a piece of paper and gave it to Evarts. 'The Hauser Agency is the biggest agency in the world,' he said, 'and Charlie Leavitt is the best man in the Hauser Agency. I want you to feel free to take your problems to Charlie, and if he asks who sent you, tell him Bitsey sent you.' He went toward the door. 'Good night, you lucky, lucky kids,' he said. 'Good night. Sweet sleep. Sweet dreams.'

The Malloys were the hard working children of an industrious generation and they were up at half past six the next morning. They scrubbed their faces and their ears and brushed their teeth with soap. At seven o'clock, they started for the Automat. Evarts had not slept that night. The noise of traffic had kept him awake, and he had spent the small hours sitting at the window. His mouth felt scorched with tobacco smoke, and the loss of sleep had left him nervous. They were all surprised to find New York still sleeping. They were shocked. They had their breakfast and returned to the Mentone. Evarts called Tracey Murchison's office, but no one answered. He telephoned the office several times after that. At ten o'clock, a girl answered the phone. 'Mr Murchison will see you at three,' she said. She hung up. Since there was nothing to do but wait, Evarts took his wife and daughter up Fifth Avenue. They stared in the store windows. At eleven o'clock, when the doors of Radio City Music Hall opened, they went there.

This was a happy choice. They prowled the lounges and toilets for an hour before they took their seats, and when, during the stage show, an enormous samovar rose up out of the orchestra pit and debouched forty men in Cossack uniform singing 'Dark Eyes,' Alice and Mildred-Rose shouted with joy. The stage show, beneath its grandeur, seemed to conceal a simple and familiar intelligence, as if the drafts that stirred the miles of golden curtain had blown straight from Indiana. The performance left Alice and Mildred-Rose distracted with pleasure, and on the way back to the Mentone, Evarts had to lead them along the sidewalk to keep them from walking into hydrants. It was a quarter of three when they got back to the hotel. Evarts kissed his wife and child goodbye and started for Murchison's.

He got lost. He was afraid he would be late. He began to run. He asked directions of a couple of policemen and finally reached the office building.

The front room of Murchison's office was dingy—intentionally dingy, Evarts hoped—but it was not inglorious, for there were many beautiful men and women there, waiting to see Mr Murchison. None of them were sitting down, and they chatted together as if delighted by the delay that held them there. The receptionist led Evarts into a further office. This office was also crowded but the atmosphere was of haste and trouble, as if the place were being besieged. Murchison was there and he greeted Evarts strenuously. 'I've got your contracts right here,' he said, and he handed Evarts a pen and pushed a stack of contracts toward him. 'Now I want you to rush over and see Madge,' Murchison said as soon as Evarts had signed the contracts. He looked at Evarts, plucked the feather carnation out of his lapel, and tossed it into a wastebasket. 'Hurry, hurry, hurry,' he said. 'She's at 400 Park Avenue. She's crazy to see you. She's waiting now. I'll see you later tonight—I think Madge has something planned—but hurry.'

Evarts rushed into the hall and rang impatiently for the elevator. As soon as he had left the building, he got lost and wandered into the fur district. A policeman directed him back to the Mentone. Alice and Mildred-Rose were waiting in the lobby, and he told them what had happened. 'I'm on my way to see Madge Beatty now,' he said. 'I've got to hurry!' Bitsey, the bellboy, overheard this conversation. He dropped some bags he was carrying and joined the group. He told Evarts how to get to Park Avenue. Evarts kissed Alice and Mildred-Rose again. They waved goodbye as he ran out the door.

Evarts had seen so many movies of Park Avenue that he observed its breadth and bleakness with a sense of familiarity. He took an elevator to the Murchisons' apartment and was led by a maid into a pretty living room. A fire was burning, and there were flowers on the mantel. He sprang to his feet when Madge Beatty came in. She was frail, animated, and golden, and her hoarse and accomplished voice made him feel naked. 'I read your play, Evarts,' she said, 'and I loved it, I loved it, I loved it.' She moved lightly around the room, talking now directly at him, now over her shoulder. She was not as young as she had first appeared to be, and in the light from the windows she looked almost wizened. 'You're going to do more with my part when you write the second act, I hope,' she said. 'You're going to build it up and build it up and build it up.'

'I'll do anything you want, Miss Beatty,' Evarts said.

She sat down and folded her beautiful hands. Her feet were very big, Evarts noticed. Her shins were thin, and this made her feet seem very big. 'Oh, we love your play, Evarts,' she said. 'We love it, we want it, we need it. Do you know how much we need it? We're in debt, Evarts, we're dreadfully in debt.' She laid a hand on her breast and spoke in a whisper. 'We owe one million nine hundred and sixty-five thousand dollars.' She let the precious light flood her voice again. 'But now I'm keeping you from writing your beautiful play,' she said. 'I'm keeping you from work, and I want you to go back and write and write and write, and I want you and your wife to come here any time after nine tonight and meet a few of our warmest friends.'

Evarts asked the doorman how to get back to the Mentone, but he misunderstood the directions and got lost again. He walked around the East Side until he found a policeman, who directed him back to the hotel. It was so late when he returned that Mildred-Rose was crying with hunger. The three of them washed and went to the Automat and walked up and down Broadway until nearly nine. Then they went back to the hotel. Alice put on her evening dress, and she and Evarts kissed Mildred-Rose good night. In the lobby, they met Bitsey and told him where they were going. He promised to keep an eye on Mildred-Rose.

The walk over to the Murchison's was longer than Evarts remembered. Alice's wrap was light. She was blue with cold when they reached the apartment building. They could hear in the distance, as they left the elevator, someone playing a piano and a woman singing 'A kiss is but a kiss, a sigh is but a sigh . . . ' A maid took their wraps, and Mr Murchison greeted them from a farther door. Alice ruffled and arranged the cloth peony that hung from the front of her dress, and they went in.

The room was crowded, the lights were dim, the singer was ending her song. There was a heady smell of animal skins and astringent perfume in the air. Mr Murchison introduced the Malloys to a couple who stood near the door, and abandoned them. The couple turned their backs on the Malloys. Evarts was shy and quiet, but Alice was excited and began to speculate, in a whisper, about the identities of the people around the piano. She felt sure that they were all movie stars, and she was right.

The singer finished her song, got up from the piano, and walked away. There was a little applause and then a curious silence. Mr Murchison asked another woman to sing. 'I'm not going to go on after *her*,' the woman said. The situation, whatever it was, had stopped conversation. Mr Murchison asked several people to perform, but they all refused. 'Perhaps Mrs Malloy will sing for us,' he said bitterly.

'All right,' Alice said. She walked to the center of the room. She took a position and, folding her hands and holding them breast-high, began to sing.

Alice's mother had taught her to sing whenever her host asked, and Alice had never violated any of her mother's teachings. As a child, she had taken singing lessons from Mrs Bachman, an elderly widow who lived in Wentworth. She had sung in grammar-school assemblies and in high-school assemblies. On family holidays, there had always come a time, in the late afternoon, when she would be asked to sing; then she would rise from her place on the hard sofa near the stove or come from the kitchen, where she had been washing dishes, to sing the songs Mrs Bachman had taught her.

The invitation that night had been so unexpected that Evarts had not had a chance to stop his wife. He had felt the bitterness in Murchison's voice, and he would have stopped her, but as soon as she began to sing, he didn't care. Her voice was well pitched, her figure was stern and touching, and she sang for those people in obedience to her mannerly heart. When he had overcome his own bewilderment, he noticed the respect and attention the Murchison's guests were giving her music. Many of them had come from towns as small as Wentworth; they were goodhearted people, and the simple air, rendered in Alice's fearless voice, reminded them of their beginnings. None of them were whispering or smiling. Many of them had lowered their heads, and he saw a woman touch her eyes with a handkerchief. Alice had triumphed, he thought, and then he recognized the song as 'Annie Laurie.'

Years ago, when Mrs Bachman had taught Alice the song, she had taught her to close it with a piece of business that brought her success as a child, as a girl, as a high-school senior, but that, even in the stuffy living room in Wentworth, with its inexorable smells of poverty and cooking, had begun to tire and worry her family. She had been taught on the closing line, 'Lay me doun and dee,' to fall in a heap on the floor. She fell less precipitously now that she had got older, but she still fell, and Evarts could see that night, by her serene face, that a fall was in her plans. He considered going to her, embracing her, and whispering to her that the hotel was burning or that Mildred-Rose was sick. Instead, he turned his back.

Alice took a quick breath and attacked the last verse. Evarts had begun to sweat so freely that the brine got into his eyes. 'I'll lay me doun and dee,' he heard her sing; he heard the loud crash as she hit the floor; he heard the screams of helpless laughter, the tobacco coughs, and the oaths of a woman who laughed so hard she broke her pearl bib. The Murchisons' guests seemed bewitched. They wept, they shook, they stooped, they slapped one another on the back, and walked, like the demented, in circles. When Evarts faced the scene, Alice was sitting on the floor. He helped her to her feet. 'Come, darling,' he said. 'Come.' With his arm around her, he led her into the hall.

'Didn't they like my song?' she asked. She began to cry.

'It doesn't matter, my darling,' Evarts said, 'it doesn't matter, it doesn't matter.' They got their wraps and walked back through the cold to the Mentone.

Bitsey was waiting for them in the corridor outside their room. He wanted to hear all about the party. Evarts sent Alice into the room and talked with the bellboy alone. He didn't feel like describing the party. 'I don't think I want to have anything more to do with the Murchison's,' he said. 'I'm going to get a new producer.'

'That's the boy, that's the boy,' Bitsey said. 'Now you're talking. But, first, I want you to go up to the Hauser Agency and see Charlie Leavitt.'

'All right,' Evarts said. 'All right, I'll go and see Charlie Leavitt.'

Alice cried herself to sleep that night. Again, Evarts couldn't sleep. He sat in a chair by the window. He fell into a doze, a little before dawn, but not for long. At seven o'clock, he led his family off to the Automat.

Bitsey came up to the Malloys' room after breakfast. He was very excited. A columnist in one of the four-cent newspapers had reported Evarts' arrival in New York. A Cabinet member and a Balkan king were mentioned in the same paragraph. Then the telephone began to ring. First, it was a man who wanted to sell Evarts a second-hand mink coat. Then a lawyer and a dry-cleaner called, a dressmaker, a nursery school, several agencies, and a man who said he could get them a good apartment. Evarts said no to all these importunities, but in each case he had to argue before he could hang up. Bitsey had made a noon appointment for him with Charlie Leavitt, and when it was time, he kissed Alice and Mildred-Rose and went down to the street.

The Hauser Agency was located in one of the buildings in Radio City. Now Evarts' business took him through the building's formidable doors as legitimately, he told himself, as anyone else. The Hauser offices were on the twenty-sixth floor. He didn't call his floor until the elevator had begun its ascent. 'It's too late now,' the operator said. 'You got to tell me the number of the floor when you get in.' This branded him as green to all the other people in the car, Evarts knew, and he blushed. He rode to the sixtieth floor and then back to the twenty-sixth. As he left the car, the elevator operator sneered.

At the end of a long corridor, there was a pair of bronze doors, fastened by a bifurcated eagle. Evarts turned the wings of the imperial bird and stepped into a lofty manor hall. The panelling on its walls was worm-pitted and white with rot. In the distance, behind a small glass window, he saw a woman wearing earphones. He walked over to her, told her his business, and was asked to sit down. He sat on a leather sofa and lighted a cigarette. The richness of the hall impressed him profoundly. Then he noticed that the sofa was covered with dust. So were the table, the magazines on it, the lamp, the bronze cast of Rodin's 'Le Baiser'—everything in the vast room was covered with dust. He noticed at the same time the peculiar stillness of the hall. All the usual noises of an office were lacking. Into this stillness, from the distant earth, rose the recorded music from the skating rink, where a carillon played 'Joy to the World! The Lord Is Come!' The magazines on the table beside the sofa were all five years old.

After a while, the receptionist pointed to a double door at the end of the hall, and Evarts walked there, timidly. The office on the other side of the door was smaller than the room he had just left but dimmer, richer, and more imposing, and in the distance he could still hear the music of the skating rink. A man was sitting at an antique desk. He stood as soon as he saw Evarts. 'Welcome, Evarts, welcome to the Hauser Agency!' he shouted. 'I hear you've got a hot property there, and Bitsey tells me you're through with Tracey Murchison. I haven't read your play, of course, but if Tracey wants it, I want it, and so does Sam Farley. I've got a producer for you, and I think I've got a pre-production deal lined up. One hundred thou' on a four-hundred-thou' ceiling. Sit down, sit down.'

Mr Leavitt seemed either to be eating something or to be having trouble with his teeth, for at the end of every sentence he worked his lips noisily and thoughtfully, like a gourmet. He might have been eating something, since there were crumbs around his mouth. Or he might have been having trouble with his teeth, because the labial noises continued all through the interview. Mr Leavitt wore a lot of gold. He had several rings, a gold identification bracelet, and a gold bracelet watch, and he carried a heavy gold cigarette case, set with jewels. The case was empty, and Evarts furnished him with cigarettes as they talked.

'Now, I want you to go back to your hotel, Evarts,' Mr Leavitt shouted, 'and I want you to take it easy. Charlie Leavitt is taking care of your property. I want you to promise me you won't worry. Now, I understand that you've signed a contract with Murchison. I'm going to declare that contract null and void, and my lawyer is going to declare that contract null and void, and if Murchison contests it, we'll drag him into court and have the judge declare that contract null and void. Before we go any further, though,' he said, softening his voice, 'I want you to sign these papers, which will give me authority to represent you.' He pressed some papers and a gold fountain pen on Evarts. 'Just sign these papers,' he said sadly, 'and you'll make four hundred thousand dollars. Oh, you authors!' he exclaimed. 'You lucky authors!'

As soon as Evarts had signed the papers, Mr Leavitt's manner changed and he began to shout again. 'The producer I've got for you is Sam Farley. The star is Susan Hewitt. Sam Farley is Tom Farley's brother. He's married to Clarissa Douglas and he's George Howland's uncle. Pat Levy's his brother-in-law and Mitch Kababian and Howie Brown are related to him on his mother's side. She was Lottie Mayes. They're a very close family. They're a great little team. When your show opens in Wilmington, Sam Farley, Tom Farley, Clarissa Douglas, George Howland, Pat Levy, Mitch Kababian, and Howie Brown are all right down there in that hotel writing your third act. When your show goes up to Baltimore, Sam Farley, Tom Farley, Clarissa Douglas, George Howland, Pat Levy, Mitch Kababian, and Howie Brown, they go up to Baltimore with it. And when your show opens up on Broadway with a high-class production who's down there in the front row, rooting for you?' Mr Leavitt had strained his voice, and he ended in a hoarse whisper, 'Sam Farley, Tom Farley, Clarissa Douglas, George Howland, Pat Levy, Mitch Kababian, and Howie Brown.

'Now, I want you to go back to your hotel and have a good time,' he shouted after he had cleared his throat. 'I'll call you tomorrow and tell you when Sam Farley and Susan Hewitt can see you, and I'll telephone Hollywood now and tell Max Rayburn that he can have it for one hundred thou' on a four-hundred-thou' ceiling, and not one iota less.' He patted Evarts on the back and steered him gently toward the door. 'Have a good time, Evarts,' he said.

As Evarts walked back through the hall, he noticed that the receptionist was eating a sandwich. She beckoned to him.

'You want to take a chance on a new Buick convertible?' she whispered. 'Ten cents a chance.'

'Oh, no, thank you,' Evarts said.

'Fresh eggs?' she asked. 'I bring them in from Jersey every morning.'

'No, thank you,' Evarts said.

Evarts hurried back through the crowds to the Mentone, where Alice, Mildred-Rose, and Bitsey were waiting. He described his interview with Leavitt to them. 'When I get that four hundred thou',' he said, 'I'm going to send some money to Mama Finelli.' Then Alice remembered a lot of other people in Wentworth who needed money. By way of a celebration, they went to a spaghetti house that night instead of the Automat. After dinner, they went to Radio City Music Hall. Again, that night, Evarts was unable to sleep.

In Wentworth, Alice had been known as the practical member of the family. There was a good deal of jocularity on this score. She drew up the budget and managed the egg money, and it was often said that Evarts would have misplaced his head if it hadn't been for Alice. This businesslike strain in her character led her to remind Evarts on the following day that he had not been working on his play. She took the situation in hand. 'You just sit in the room,' she said, 'and write the play, and Mildred-Rose and I will walk up and down Fifth Avenue, so you can be alone.'

Evarts tried to work, but the telephone began to ring again and he was interrupted regularly by jewelry salesmen, theatrical lawyers, and laundry services. At about eleven, he picked up the phone and heard a familiar and angry voice. It was Murchison. 'I brought you from Wentworth,' he shouted, 'and I made you what you are today. Now they tell me you breached my contract and double-crossed me with Sam Farley. I'm going to break you, I'm going to ruin you, I'm going to sue you, I'm—' Evarts hung up, and when the phone rang a minute later, he didn't answer it. He left a note for Alice, put on his hat, and walked up Fifth Avenue to the Hauser offices.

When he turned the bifurcated eagle of the double doors and stepped into the manor hall that morning, he found Mr Leavitt there, in his shirtsleeves, sweeping the carpet. 'Oh, good morning,' Leavitt said. 'Occupational therapy.' He hid the broom and dustpan behind a velvet drape. 'Come in, come in,' he said, slipping into his jacket and leading Evarts toward the inner office. 'This afternoon, you're going to meet Sam Farley and Susan Hewitt. You're one of the luckiest men in New York. Some men never see Sam Farley. Not even once in a lifetime—never hear his wit, never feel the force of his unique personality. And as for Susan Hewitt . . . ' He was speechless for a moment. He said the appointment was for three. 'You're going to meet them in Sam Farley's lovely home,' he said, and he gave Evarts the address.

Evarts tried to describe the telephone conversation with Murchison, but Leavitt cut him off. 'I asked you one thing,' he shouted. 'I asked you not to worry. Is that too much? I ask you to talk with Sam Farley and take a look at Susan Hewitt and see if you think she's right for the part. Is that too much? Now, have a good time. Take in a newsreel. Go to the zoo. Go see Sam Farley at three o'clock.' He patted Evarts on the back and pushed him toward the door.

Evarts ate lunch at the Mentone with Alice and Mildred-Rose. He had a headache. After lunch, they walked up and down Fifth Avenue, and when it got close to three, Alice and Mildred-Rose walked with him to Sam Farley's house. It was an impressive building, faced with rough stone, like a Spanish prison. He kissed Mildred-Rose and Alice goodbye and rang the bell. A butler opened the door. Evarts could tell he was a butler because he wore striped pants. The butler led him upstairs to a drawing room.

'I'm here to see Mr Farley,' Evarts said.

'I know,' the butler said. 'You're Evarts Malloy. You've got an appointment. But he won't keep it. He's stuck in a floating crap game in the Acme Garage, at a Hundred and Sixty-fourth Street and he won't be back until tomorrow. Susan Hewitt's coming, though. You're supposed to see her. Oh, if you only knew what goes on in this place!' He lowered his voice to a whisper and brought his face closer to Evarts'. 'If these walls could only talk! There hasn't been any heat in this house since we came back from Hollywood and he hasn't paid me since the twenty-first of June. I wouldn't mind so much, but the son of a bitch has never learned to let the water out of his bathtub. He takes a bath and leaves the dirty water standing there. To stagnate. On top of everything else, I cut my finger washing dishes yesterday.' There was a dirty bandage on the butler's forefinger, and he began, hurriedly, to unwrap layer after layer of bloody gauze. 'Look,' he said, holding the wound to Evarts' face. 'Cut right through to the bone. Yesterday you could see the bone. Blood. Blood all over everything. Took me half an hour to clean up. It's a miracle I didn't get an infection.' He shook his head at this miracle. 'When the mouse comes, I'll send her up.' He wandered out of the room, trailing the length of bloody bandage after him.

Evarts' eyes were burning with fatigue. He was so tired that if he had rested his head against anything, he would have fallen asleep.

He heard the doorbell ring and the butler greet Susan Hewitt. She ran up the stairs and into the drawing room.

She was young, and she came into the room as if it were her home and she had just come back from school. She was light, her features were delicate and very small, and her fair hair was brushed simply and had begun to darken, of its own course, and was streaked softly with brown, like the grain in pine wood. 'I'm so happy to meet you, Evarts,' she said. 'I want to tell you that I love your play.' How she could have read his play, Evarts did not know, but he was too confused by her beauty to worry or to speak. His mouth was dry. It might have been the antic pace of the last days, it might have been his loss of sleep—he didn't know—but he felt as though he had fallen in love.

'You remind me of a girl I used to know,' he said. 'She worked in a lunch wagon outside South Bend. Never worked in a lunch wagon outside South Bend, did you?'

'No,' she said.

'It isn't only that,' he said. 'You remind me of all of it. I mean the night drives. I used to be a night bus driver. That's what you remind me of. The stars, I mean, and the grade crossings, and the cattle lined up along the fences. And the girls in the lunch counters. They always looked so pretty. But you never worked in a lunch counter.'

'No,' she said.

'You can have my play,' he said. 'I mean I think you're right for the part. Sam Farley can have the play. Everything.'

'Thank you, Evarts,' she said.

'Will you do me a favor?' he asked.

'What?'

'Oh, I know it's foolish,' he said. He got up and walked around the room. 'but there's nobody here, nobody will know about it. I hate to ask you.'

'What do you want?'

'Will you let me lift you?' he said. 'Just let me lift you. Just let me see how light you are.'

'All right,' she said. 'Do you want me to take off my coat?'

'Yes, yes, yes,' he said. 'Take off your coat.'

She stood. She let her coat fall to the sofa.

'Can I do it now?' he said.

'Yes.'

He put his hands under her arms. He raised her off the floor and then put her down gently. 'Oh, you're so light!' he shouted. 'You're so light, you're so fragile, you don't weigh any more than a suitcase. Why, I could carry you, I could carry you anywhere, I could carry you from one end of New York to the other.' He got his hat and coat and ran out of the house.

Evarts felt bewildered and exhausted when he returned to the Mentone. Bitsey was in the room with Mildred-Rose and Alice. He kept asking questions about Mama Finelli. He wanted to know where she lived and what her telephone number was. Evarts lost his temper at the bellboy and told him to go away. He lay down on the bed and fell asleep while Alice and Mildred-Rose were asking him questions. When he woke, an hour later, he felt much better. They went to the Automat and then to Radio City Music Hall, and they got to bed early, so that Evarts could work on his play in the morning. He couldn't sleep.

After breakfast, Alice and Mildred-Rose left Evarts alone in the room and he tried to work. He couldn't work, but it wasn't the telephone that troubled him that day. The difficulty that blocked his play was deep, and as he smoked and stared at the brick wall, he recognized it. He was in love with Susan Hewitt. This might have been an incentive to work, but he had left his creative strength in Indiana. He shut his eyes and tried to recall the strong, dissolute voice of Mama Finelli, but before he could realize a word, it would be lost in the noise from the street.

If there had been anything to set his memory free—a train whistle, a moment of silence, the smells of a barn—he might have been inspired. He paced the room, he smoked, he sniffed the sooty window curtains and stuffed his ears with toilet paper, but there seemed to be no way of recalling Indiana at the Mentone. He stayed near the desk all that day. He went without lunch. When his wife and child returned from Radio City Music Hall, where they had spent the afternoon, he told them he was going to take a walk. Oh, he thought as he left the hotel, if I could only hear the noise of a crow!

He strode up Fifth Avenue, holding his head high, trying to divine in the confusion of sound a voice that might lead him. He walked rapidly until he reached Radio City and could hear, in the distance, the music from the skating rink. Something stopped him. He lighted a cigarette. Then he heard someone calling him. 'Behold the lordly moose, Evarts,' a woman shouted. It was the hoarse, dissolute voice of Mama Finelli, and he thought that desire had deranged him until he turned and saw her, sitting on one of the benches, by a dry pool. 'Behold the lordly moose, Evarts,' she called, and she put her hands, spread like antlers, above her head. This was the way she greeted everyone in Wentworth.

'Behold the lordly moose, Mama Finelli,' Evarts shouted. He ran to her side and sat down. 'Oh, Mama Finelli, I'm so glad to see you,' he said. 'You won't believe it, but I've been thinking about you all day. I've been wishing all day that I could talk with you.' He turned to drink in her vulpine features and her whiskery chin. 'How did you ever get to New York, Mama Finelli?'

'Come up on a flying machine,' she cried. 'Come up on a flying machine today. Have a sandwich.' She was eating some sandwiches from a paper bag.

'No, thanks,' he said. 'What do you think of New York?' he asked. 'What do you think of that high building?'

'Well, I don't know,' she said, but he could see that she did know and he could see her working her face into shape for a retort. 'I guess there's just but the one, for if there hada been two, they'd of pollinated and bore!' She whooped with laughter and struck herself on the legs.

'What are you doing in New York, Mama Finelli? How did you happen to come here?'

'Well,' she said, 'man named Tracey Murchison calls me on the telephone long distance and says for me to come up to New York and sue you for libel. Says you wrote a play about me and I can sue you for libel and git a lot of money and split it with him, fairly, he says, and then I don't have to run the gas station no more. So he wires me money for the flying-machine ticket and I come up here and I talk with him and I'm going to sue you for libel and split it with him, sixty–forty. That's what I'm going to do,' she said.

Later that night, the Malloys returned to the marble waiting room of Grand Central and Evarts began to search for a Chicago train. He found a Chicago train, bought some tickets, and they boarded a coach. It was a rainy night, and the dark, wet paving, deep in the station, did not glitter, but it was still Alice's belief that diamonds had been ground into it, and that was the way she would tell the story. They had picked up the lessons of travel rapidly, and they arranged themselves adroitly over several seats. After the train started, Alice made friends with a plain-spoken couple across the aisle, who were travelling with a baby to Los Angeles. The woman had a brother there, who had written to her enthusiastically about the climate and the opportunities.

'Let's go to Los Angeles,' Alice said to Evarts. 'We still have a little money and we can buy tickets in Chicago and you can sell your play in Hollywood, where nobody's ever heard of Mama Finelli or any of the others.'

Evarts said that he would make his decision in Chicago. He was weary and he fell asleep. Mildred-Rose put her thumb into her mouth, and soon both she and her mother had lost consciousness, too. Mildred-Rose stroked the sere skins of her coat and they told her that all was well, all was well.

The Malloys may have left the train in Chicago and gone back to Wentworth. It is not hard to imagine their homecoming, for they would be welcomed by their friends and relations, although their stories might not be believed. Or they may have changed, at Chicago, for a train to the West, and this, to tell the truth, is easier to imagine. One can see them playing hearts in the lounge car and eating cheese sandwiches in the railroad stations as they travelled through Kansas and Nebraska—over the mountains and on to the Coast.

1948

THE LOTTERY
Shirley Jackson

The morning of June 27th was clear and sunny, with the fresh warmth of a full-summer day; the flowers were blossoming profusely and the grass was richly green. The people of the village began to gather in the square, between the post office and the bank, around ten o'clock; in some towns there were so many people that the lottery took two days and had to be started on June 26th, but in this village, where there were only about three hundred people, the whole lottery took less than two hours, so it could begin at ten o'clock in the morning and still be through in time to allow the villagers to get home for noon dinner.

The children assembled first, of course. School was recently over for the summer, and the feeling of liberty sat uneasily on most of them; they tended to gather together quietly for a while before they broke into boisterous play, and their talk was still of the classroom and the teacher, of books and reprimands. Bobby Martin had already stuffed his pockets full of stones, and the other boys soon followed his example, selecting the smoothest and roundest stones; Bobby and Harry Jones and Dickie Delacroix—the villagers pronounced this name 'Dellacroy'—eventually made a great pile of stones in one corner of the square and guarded it against the raids of the other boys. The girls stood aside, talking among themselves, looking over their shoulders at the boys, and the very small children rolled in the dust or clung to the hands of their older brothers or sisters.

Soon the men began to gather, surveying their own children, speaking of planting and rain, tractors and taxes. They stood together, away from the pile of stones in the corner, and their jokes were quiet and they smiled rather than laughed. The women, wearing faded house dresses and sweaters, came shortly after their men-folk. They greeted one another and exchanged bits of gossip as they went to join their husbands. Soon the women, standing by their husbands, began to call to their children, and the children came reluctantly, having to be called four or five times. Bobby Martin ducked under his mother's grasping hand and ran, laughing, back to the pile of stones. His father spoke up sharply, and Bobby came quickly and took his place between his father and his oldest brother.

The lottery was conducted—as were the square dances, the teenage club, the Halloween program—by Mr Summers, who had time and energy to devote to civic activities. He was a round-faced, jovial man and he ran the coal business, and people were sorry for him, because he had no children and his wife was a scold. When he arrived in the square, carrying the black wooden box, there was a murmur of conversation among the villagers, and he waved and called, 'Little later today, folks.' The postmaster, Mr Graves, followed him, carrying a three-legged stool, and the stool was put in the center of the square and Mr Summers set the black box down on it. The villagers kept their distance, leaving a space between themselves and the stool, and when Mr Summers said, 'Some of you fellows want to give me a hand?' there was a hesitation before two men, Mr Martin and his oldest son, Baxter, came forward to hold the box steady on the stool while Mr Summers stirred up the papers inside it.

The original paraphernalia for the lottery had been lost long ago, and the black box now resting on the stool had been put into use even before Old Man Warner, the oldest man in town, was born. Mr Summers spoke frequently to the villagers about making a new box, but no one liked to upset even as much tradition as was represented by the black box. There was a story that the present box had been made with some pieces of the box that had preceded it, the one that had been constructed when the first people settled down to make a village here. Every year, after the lottery, Mr Summers began talking again about a new box, but every year the subject was allowed to fade off without anything's being done. The black box grew shabbier each year; by now it was no longer completely black but splintered badly along one side to show the original wood color, and in some places faded or stained.

Mr Martin and his oldest son, Baxter, held the black box securely on the stool until Mr Summers had stirred the papers thoroughly with his hand. Because so much of the ritual had been forgotten or discarded, Mr Summers had been successful in having slips of paper substituted for the chips of wood that had been used for generations. Chips of wood, Mr Summers had argued, had been all very well when the village was tiny, but now that the population was more than three hundred and likely to keep on growing, it was necessary to use something that would fit more easily into the black box. The night before the lottery, Mr Summers and Mr Graves made up the slips of paper and put them in the box, and it was then taken to the safe of Mr Summers' coal company and locked up until Mr Summers was ready to take it to the square next morning. The rest of the year, the box was put away, sometimes one place, sometimes another; it had spent one year in Mr Graves's barn and another year underfoot in the post office, and sometimes it was set on a shelf in the Martin grocery and left there.

There was a great deal of fussing to be done before Mr Summers declared the lottery open. There were the lists to make up—of heads of families, heads of households in each family, members of each household in each family. There was the proper swearing-in of Mr Summers by the postmaster, as the official of the lottery; at one time, some people remembered, there had been a recital of some sort, performed by the official of the lottery, a perfunctory, tuneless chant that had been rattled off duly each year; some people believed that the official of the lottery used to stand just so when he said or sang it, others believed that he was supposed to walk among the people, but years and years ago this part of the ritual had been allowed to lapse. There had been, also, a ritual salute, which the official of the lottery had had to use in addressing each person who came up to draw from the box, but this also had changed with time, until now it was felt necessary only for the official to speak to each person approaching. Mr Summers was very good at all this; in his clean white shirt and blue jeans, with one hand resting carelessly on the black box, he seemed very proper and important as he talked interminably to Mr Graves and the Martins.

Just as Mr Summers finally left off talking and turned to the assembled villagers, Mrs Hutchinson came hurriedly along the path to the square, her sweater thrown over her shoulders, and slid into place in the back of the crowd. 'Clean forgot what day it was,' she said to Mrs Delacroix, who stood next to her, and they both laughed softly. 'Thought my old man was out back stacking wood,' Mrs Hutchinson went on, 'and then I remembered it was the twenty-seventh and came a-running.' She dried her hands on her apron, and Mrs Delacroix said, 'You're in time, though. They're still talking away up there.'

Mrs Hutchinson craned her neck to see through the crowd and found her husband and children standing near the front. She tapped Mrs Delacroix on the arm as a farewell and began to make her way through the crowd. The people separated good-humoredly to let her through; two or three people said, in voices just loud enough to be heard across the crowd, 'Here comes your Missus, Hutchinson,' and 'Bill, she made it after all.' Mrs Hutchinson reached her husband, and Mr Summers, who had been waiting, said cheerfully, 'Thought we were going to have to get on without you, Tessie.' Mrs Hutchinson said, grinning, 'Wouldn't have me leave m'dishes in the sink, now, would you, Joe?' and soft laughter ran through the crowd as the people stirred back into position after Mrs Hutchinson's arrival.

'Well, now,' Mr Summers said soberly, 'guess we better get started, get this over with, so's we can go back to work. Anybody ain't here?'

'Dunbar,' several people said. 'Dunbar, Dunbar.'

Mr Summers consulted his list. 'Clyde Dunbar,' he said. That's right. He's broke his leg, hasn't he? Who's drawing for him?'

'Me, I guess,' a woman said, and Mr Summers turned to look at her. 'Wife draws for her husband,' Mr Summers said. 'Don't you have a grown boy to do it for you, Janey?' Although Mr Summers and everyone else in the village knew the answer perfectly well, it was the business of the official of the lottery to ask such questions formally. Mr Summers waited with an expression of polite interest while Mrs Dunbar answered.

'Horace's not but sixteen yet,' Mrs Dunbar said regretfully. 'Guess I gotta fill in for the old man this year.'

'Right,' Mr Summers said. He made a note on the list he was holding. Then he asked, 'Watson boy drawing this year?'

A tall boy in the crowd raised his hand. 'Here,' he said. 'I'm drawing for m'mother and me.' He blinked his eyes nervously and ducked his head as several voices in the crowd said things like 'Good fellow, Jack,' and 'Glad to see your mother's got a man to do it.'

'Well,' Mr Summers said, 'guess that's everyone. Old Man Warner make it?'

'Here,' a voice said, and Mr Summers nodded.

A sudden hush fell on the crowd as Mr Summers cleared his throat and looked at the list. 'All ready?' he called. 'Now, I'll read the names—heads of families first—and the men come up and take a paper out of the box. Keep the paper folded in your hand without looking at it until everyone has had a turn. Everything clear?'

The people had done it so many times that they only half listened to the directions; most of them were quiet, wetting their lips, not looking around. Then Mr Summers raised one hand high and said, 'Adams.' A man disengaged himself from the crowd and came forward. 'Hi, Steve,' Mr Summers said, and Mr Adams said, 'Hi, Joe.' They grinned at one another humorlessly and nervously. Then Mr Adams reached into the black box and took out a folded paper. He held it firmly by one corner as he turned and went hastily back to his place in the crowd, where he stood a little apart from his family, not looking down at his hand.

'Allen,' Mr Summers said. 'Anderson . . . Bentham.'

'Seems like there's no time at all between lotteries any more,' Mrs Delacroix said to Mrs Graves in the back row. 'Seems like we got through with the last one only last week.'

'Time sure goes fast,' Mrs Graves said.

'Clark . . . Delacroix.'

'There goes my old man,' Mrs Delacroix said. She held her breath while her husband went forward. 'Dunbar,' Mr Summers said, and Mrs Dunbar went steadily to the box while one of the women said, 'Go on, Janey,' and another said, 'There she goes.'

'We're next,' Mrs Graves said. She watched while Mr Graves came around from the side of the box, greeted Mr Summers gravely, and selected a slip of paper from the box. By now, all through the crowd there were men holding the small folded papers in their large hands, turning them over and over nervously. Mrs Dunbar and her two sons stood together, Mrs Dunbar holding the slip of paper.

'Harburt . . . Hutchinson.'

'Get up there, Bill,' Mrs Hutchinson said, and the people near her laughed.

'Jones.'

'They do say,' Mr Adams said to Old Man Warner, who stood next to him, 'that over in the north village they're talking of giving up the lottery.'

Old Man Warner snorted. 'Pack of crazy fools,' he said. 'Listening to the young folks, nothing's good enough for *them*. Next thing you know, they'll be wanting to go back to living in caves, nobody work any more, live *that* way for a while. Used to be a saying about "Lottery in June, corn be heavy soon." First thing you know, we'd all be eating stewed chickweed and acorns. There's *always* been a lottery,' he added petulantly. 'Bad enough to see young Joe Summers up there joking with everybody.'

'Some places have already quit lotteries,' Mrs Adams said.

'Nothing but trouble in *that*,' Old Man Warner said stoutly. 'Pack of young fools.'

'Martin.' And Bobby Martin watched his father go forward. 'Overdyke . . . Percy.'

'I wish they'd hurry,' Mrs Dunbar said to her older son. 'I wish they'd hurry.'

'They're almost through,' her son said.

'You get ready to run tell Dad,' Mrs Dunbar said.

Mr Summers called his own name and then stepped forward precisely and selected a slip from the box. Then he called, 'Warner.'

'Seventy-seventh year I been in the lottery,' Old Man Warner said as he went through the crowd. 'Seventy-seventh time.'

'Watson.' The tall boy came awkwardly through the crowd. Someone said, 'Don't be nervous, Jack,' and Mr Summers said, 'Take your time, son.'

'Zanini.'

After that, there was a long pause, a breathless pause, until Mr Summers, holding his slip of paper in the air, said, 'All right, fellows.' For a minute, no one moved, and then all the slips of paper were opened. Suddenly, all the women began to speak at once, saying 'Who is it?', 'Who's got it?', 'Is it the Dunbars?', 'Is it the Watsons?' Then the voices began to say, 'It's Hutchinson. It's Bill,' 'Bill Hutchinson got it.'

'Go tell your father,' Mrs Dunbar said to her older son.

People began to look around to see the Hutchinsons. Bill Hutchinson was standing quiet staring down at the paper in his hand. Suddenly, Tessie Hutchinson shouted to Mr Summers, 'You didn't give him time enough to take any paper he wanted. I saw you. It wasn't fair.'

'Be a good sport, Tessie,' Mrs Delacroix called, and Mrs Graves said, 'All of us took the same chance.'

'Shut up, Tessie,' Bill Hutchinson said.

'Well, everyone,' Mr Summers said, 'that was done pretty fast, and now we've got to be hurrying a little more to get done in time.' He consulted his next list. 'Bill,' he said, 'you draw for the Hutchinson family. You got any other households in the Hutchinsons?'

'There's Don and Eva,' Mrs Hutchinson yelled. 'Make *them* take their chance!'

'Daughters draw with their husbands' families, Tessie.' Mr

Summers said gently. 'You know that as well as anyone else.'

'It wasn't *fair*,' Tessie said.

'I guess not, Joe,' Bill Hutchinson said regretfully. 'My daughter draws with her husband's family, that's only fair. And I've got no other family except the kids.'

'Then, as far as drawing for families is concerned, it's you,' Mr Summers said in explanation, 'and as far as drawing for households is concerned, that's you, too. Right?'

'Right,' Bill Hutchinson said.

'How many kids, Bill?' Mr Summers asked formally.

'Three,' Bill Hutchinson said. 'There's Bill, Jr, and Nancy, and little Dave. And Tessie and me.'

'All right, then,' Mr Summers said. 'Harry, you got their tickets back?'

Mr Graves nodded and held up the slips of paper. 'Put them in the box, then.' Mr Summers directed. 'Take Bill's and put it in.'

'I think we ought to start over,' Mrs Hutchinson said, as quietly as she could. 'I tell you it wasn't *fair*. You didn't give him time enough to choose. *Every*body saw that.'

Mr Graves had selected the five slips and put them in the box, and he dropped all the papers but those onto the ground, where the breeze caught them and lifted them off.

'Listen, everybody,' Mrs Hutchinson was saying to the people around her.

'Ready, Bill?' Mr Summers asked, and Bill Hutchinson, with one quick glance around at his wife and children, nodded.

'Remember,' Mr Summers said, 'take the slips and keep them folded until each person has taken one. Harry, you help little Dave.' Mr Graves took the hand of the little boy, who came willingly with him up to the box. 'Take a paper out of the box, Davy,' Mr Summers said. Davy put his hand into the box and laughed. 'Take just *one* paper,' Mr Summers said. 'Harry, you hold it for him.' Mr Graves took the child's hand and removed the folded paper from the tight fist and held it while little Dave stood next to him and looked up at him wonderingly.

'Nancy next,' Mr Summers said. Nancy was twelve, and her school friends breathed heavily as she went forward, switching her skirt, and took a slip daintily from the box. 'Bill, Jr,' Mr Summers said, and Billy, his face red and his feet over-large, nearly knocked the box over as he got a paper out. 'Tessie,' Mr Summers said. She hesitated for a minute, looking around defiantly, and then set her lips and went up to the box. She snatched a paper out and held it behind her.

'Bill,' Mr Summers said, and Bill Hutchinson reached into the box and felt around, bringing his hand out at last with the slip of paper in it.

The crowd was quiet. A girl whispered, 'I hope it's not Nancy,' and the sound of the whisper reached the edges of the crowd.

'It's not the way it used to be,' Old Man Warner said clearly. 'People ain't the way they used to be.'

'All right,' Mr Summers said. 'Open the papers. Harry, you open little Dave's.'

Mr Graves opened the slip of paper and there was a general sigh through the crowd as he held it up and everyone could see that it was blank. Nancy and Bill, Jr, opened theirs at the same time, and both beamed and laughed, turning around to the crowd and holding their slips of paper above their heads.

'Tessie,' Mr Summers said. There was a pause, and then Mr Summers looked at Bill Hutchinson, and Bill unfolded his paper and showed it. It was blank.

'It's Tessie,' Mr Summers said, and his voice was hushed. 'Show us her paper, Bill.'

Bill Hutchinson went over to his wife and forced the slip of paper out of her hand. It had a black spot on it, the black spot Mr Summers had made the night before with the heavy pencil in the coal-company office. Bill Hutchinson held it up, and there was a stir in the crowd.

'All right folks,' Mr Summers said. 'Let's finish quickly.'

Although the villagers had forgotten the ritual and lost the original black box, they still remembered to use stones. The pile of stones the boys had made earlier was ready; there were stones on the ground with the blowing scraps of paper that had come out of the box. Mrs Delacroix selected a stone so large she had to pick it up with both hands and turned to Mrs Dunbar. 'Come on,' she said. 'Hurry up.'

Mrs Dunbar had small stones in both hands, and she said, gasping for breath, 'I can't run at all. You'll have to go ahead and I'll catch up with you.'

The children had stones already, and someone gave little Davy Hutchinson a few pebbles.

Tessie Hutchinson was in the center of a cleared space by now, and she held her hands out desperately as the villagers moved in on her. 'It isn't fair,' she said. A stone hit her on the side of the head.

Old Man Warner was saying, 'Come on, come on, everyone.' Steve Adams was in the front of the crowd of villagers, with Mrs Graves beside him.

'It isn't fair, it isn't right,' Mrs Hutchinson screamed, and then they were upon her.

1948

THE VIEW FROM THE BALCONY

Wallace Stegner

The fraternity house where they lived that summer was a good deal like a barracks, with its dormitory cut up into eight little plywood cells each with one dormer window, and its two shower rooms divided between the men and the women. They communized their cooking in the one big kitchen and ate together at a refectory table forty feet long. But the men were all young, all veterans, all serious students, and most of the wives worked part time in the university, so that their home life was a thing that constantly disintegrated and reformed, and they got along with a minimum of friction.

The lounge, as big as a basketball court, they hardly used. What they did use, daytime and nighttime, the thing that converted the austere barracks life into something sumptuous and country-clubbish, was the rooftop deck that stretched out from the lounge over the ten-car garage.

Directly under the bluff to which the house clung ran the transcontinental highway, but the deck was hidden and protected above it. At night the air was murmurous with insects, and sitting there, they would be bumped by blundering June bugs and feel the velvet kiss of moths. By standing up they could see the centerline of the highway palely emergent in the glow of the street lamp at the end of the drive. Beyond the highway, flowing with it in the same smooth curve, low-banked and smooth and dark and touched only with sparks and glimmers of light, was the Wawasee River.

More than a mile of the far shore was kept wild as a city park, and across those deep woods on insect-haunted nights, when traffic noise died for a moment and the night hung still around them, they could hear the lions roar.

The lions were in the zoo at the other side of the park. At first it was a shock to the students in the fraternity house to hear that heavy-chested, coughing, snarling roar, a more dangerous and ominous sound than should be heard in any American night, and for a moment any of them could have believed that the midland heat of

71

the night was tropical heat and that real and wild lions of an ancient incorrigible ferocity roamed the black woods beyond the river. But after a week or two the nightly roaring had become as commonplace as the sound of traffic along the highway, and they rarely noticed it.

Altogether the fraternity house was a good place, in spite of the tasteless ostentation of the big echoing lounge and the Turkish-bath heat of the sleeping cubicles. They were lucky to be in it. They felt how lucky they were, and people who came out to drink beer on weekends kept telling them how lucky they were. So many less lucky ones were crammed into backstairs rooms or regimented into converted barracks. Out here there was a fine spaciousness, a view, a freedom. They were terribly lucky.

Deep in a sun-struck daydream, drowning in light and heat, the sun like a weight on her back and her body slippery with perspiration and her mouth pushed wetly out of shape against her wrist, Lucy Graham lay alone on the deck in the sultry paralysis of afternoon. Her eyes looked into an empty red darkness; in her mind the vague voluptuous uncoiling of memory and fantasy was slowed almost to a stop, stunned almost to sleep.

All around her the afternoon was thick, humid, stirring with the slow fecundities of Midwestern summer—locust-shrill and bird-cheep and fly-buzz, child-shout and the distant chime of four o'clock from the university's clock tower. Cars on the highway grew from hum to buzz-saw whine and slapped past and diminished, coning away to a point of sound, a humming speck. Deep inside the house a door banged, and she heard the scratch of her own eyelashes against her wrist as she blinked, thinking groggily that it was time to get up and shower. Everyone would be coming home soon; Tommy Probst would be through with his exams by four-thirty, and tonight there would be a celebration and a keg of beer.

For a while longer she lay thinking of Tommy, wishing Charley were as far along as that, with his thesis done and nothing but the formalities left. Then it struck her as odd, the life they all lived: this sheltered, protected present tipping ever so slightly toward the assured future. After what they had been, navigator and bombardier, Signal Corps major, artillery captain, Navy lieutenant and yeoman and signalman first class, herself a WAAF and two or three of the other wives WACS or WAVES—after being these things it was almost comic of them to be so seriously and deeply involved in becoming psychologists, professors, pharmacists, historians.

She sat up, her head swimming and the whole world a sheeted glare. Lifting the hair from her neck, she let the cooling air in and shook her head at the absurdity of lying in the sun until her brains were addled and her eyes almost fried from her head. But in England there had never been the time, rarely the place, seldom the sun. She was piggy about the sun as she had been at first about the food. From here England seemed very scrawny and very dear, but very far away. Looking at her arm, she could not believe the pagan color of her own skin.

Quick steps came across the terrazzo floor of the lounge, and Phyllis Probst stepped out, hesitating in the door. 'Have you seen anything of Tommy?'

'No,' Lucy said. 'Is he through his exams already?'

'An extraordinarily complex look came over Phyllis' face. She looked hot, her hair was stringy, she seemed half out of breath. Her brows frowned and her mouth smiled a quick weak smile and her eyes jumped from Lucy out across the highway and back again.

Lucy stood up. 'Is something wrong?'

'No,' Phyllis said. 'No, it's just . . . You haven't seen him at all?'

'Nobody's been home. I did hear a door bang just a minute ago, though.'

'That was me,' Phyllis said. 'I thought he might have come home and gone to bed.'

'Phyllis, is he sick?' Lucy said, and took Phyllis' arm. She felt the arm tremble. Still with the terrified, anxious, distressed expression on her face, Phyllis began to cry.

'I've got to find him,' she said, and tried to pull away.

'We'll find him,' Lucy said. 'What happened? Tell me.'

'He . . . I don't know. Helen Fast called me from the Graduate School office about two. I don't know whether he got sick, or whether the questions were too hard, or what. Helen said he came out once and asked for a typewriter, because he's left-handed and he smudges so when he writes, and she gave him a portable. But in a few minutes he came out again and put the portable on her desk and gave her a queer desperate look and walked out.'

'Oh, what a shame,' Lucy said, and with her arm around Phyllis sought for something else to say.

'But where *is* he?' Phyllis asked. 'I called the police and the hospital and I went to every beer joint in town.'

'Don't worry,' Lucy said, and pushed her gently inside. 'You come and take a cool shower and relax. We'll send the boys hunting when they come.'

They came, half a household of them, before the two girls were halfway up the stairs, and they brought Tommy with them. He walked through the door like a prisoner among deputies, quietly, his dark smooth head bent a little as if in thought. Lucy saw his eyes lift and meet his wife's in an indescribable look. 'Thanks for the lift,' Tommy said to Charley Graham, and went up the stairs and took his wife's arm, and together they went down the corridor.

Lucy came back down to where her husband stood. 'What on earth happened?'

He pursed up his lips, lifting his shoulders delicately, looked at the others, who were dispersing toward dormitory and shower room. 'We cruised the park on a hunch and found him over there tossing sticks in the river,' Charley said.

'Why didn't he take the exams?'

Her husband lifted his shoulders again.

'But it's so absurd!' she said. 'He could have written the Lord's Prayer backward and they would have passed him. It was just a ritual, like an initiation. Everyone said so.'

'Of course,' he said. 'It was a cinch.' He put an arm across her shoulders, made a face as if disgusted by the coco-butter gooiness, and kissed her from a great distance. 'Kind of dampens the party.'

'We'd better not have it.'

'Why not? I'm going to ask Richards and Latour to come over. They can straighten Tommy out.'

'Will they give him another chance, do you think?'

'*Give* him?' Charley said. 'They'll force it on him.'

In the lounge after dinner the atmosphere was weighted and awkward. Lucy had a feeling that somehow, without in any way agreeing on it, the whole lot of them had arrived at a policy of elaborately ignoring what had happened to Tommy. Faced with the uncomfortable alternatives of ignoring it or of slapping him on the back, encouraging him, they had chosen the passive way. It was still too hot on the deck for sitting; in the lounge they were too aware of each other. Some hunted up corners and dove into books. The others lounged and waited. Watching them, Lucy saw how the eyes strayed to Tommy when his back was turned, judging him. She saw that look even in Charley's face, the contempt that narrowed the eyes and fluttered the nostrils. As if geared up to play a part, Tommy stayed, looking self-consciously tragic. His wife was around him like an anxious hen.

Donna Earp stood up suddenly into a silence. 'Lord, it's sultry,' she said. 'I wish it would rain.'

She went out on the deck, and Lucy and Charley followed her. The sun was dazzling and immense behind the maple tree that overhung the corner. Shadows stretched almost across the quiet river. The roof was warm through Lucy's shoes, and the railing was hot to her hand.

'Has anyone talked to him at all?' she said.

Charley shook his head, shrugged in that Frenchy little way he had.

'Won't it look queer?'

'Richards and Latour are coming. They'll talk to him.'

'What about getting the beer, then? It's like a funeral in there.'

'Funeral!' Charley said, and snorted. 'That's another thing that happened today. Quite a day.' He looked at the sun, disintegrating behind the trees.

'Whose funeral?'

'Kay Cedarquist's.'

'Who's she?'

'She's a girl,' he said. 'Maybe I'd better get the beer, I'll tell you later about the funeral. It's a howl.'

'Sounds like a peculiar funeral.'

'Peculiar is a small word for it,' he said. In the doorway he met Art Morris, and haled him along to get the beer.

After the glare, the shade of the tree was wonderful. Lucy sat on the railing looking over the river, and a car pulled into the drive and parked with its nose against the bluff. Paul Latour, the psychology professor, and Clark Richards, head of the department of social science, got out and held assisting hands for Myra, Richards' young wife. For several seconds the three stood looking up, smiling. They seemed struck by something; none of them spoke until Professor Richards with his hand in his bosom took a stance and said:

> O! she doth teach the torches to burn bright.
> It seems she hangs upon the cheek of night
> Like a rich jewel in an Ethiop's ear . . .

He was a rather chesty man, neat in a white suit; in the violet shadow of the court his close-clipped mustache smudged his mouth.

Latour's grim and difficult smile was upturned beside him, Myra Richards' schoolgirl face swam below there like a lily on a pond. 'Hi, lucky people,' Myra said. 'What repulsively romantic surroundings!'

'Come up,' Lucy said. 'It's cooler at this altitude.'

They made her feel pretty, they took away the gloom that Tommy Probst's failure had dropped upon them all. When you were all working through the assured present to the assured future, it was more than a personal matter when someone failed. Ever since dinner they had been acting as if the foundations were shaken, and she knew why. She was glad Richards and Latour were here, outsiders, older, with better perspective.

As she sat waiting for them the lion roared, harsh and heavy across the twilight river. 'Down, Bruno!' Henry Earp said automatically, and there was a laugh. The door banged open, and Charley and Art staggered the keg through, to set it up on a table. The talk lifted suddenly in tempo. The guests stepped out onto the deck in a chorus of greeting; the lounge emptied itself, lugubrious Probsts and all, into the open air. Gloom dissolved in the promise of festivity. Charley drew the first soapy glasses from the keg. Far across several wooded bends the university's clock tower, lacy and soaring, was pinned suddenly against the sky by the floodlights.

She saw them working on Tommy during the evening. Within the first half-hour, Clark Richards took him over in the corner, and Lucy saw them talking there, an attractive picture of *magister* and *studens*, Tommy with his dark head bent and his face smoothed perfectly expressionless, Richards solid and confident and reassuring. She saw him leave Tommy with a clap on the shoulder, and saw Tommy's smile that was like spoken thanks, and then Phyllis came slipping over to where Tommy stood, wanting to be told of the second chance. Some time later, when the whole party had been loosened by beer and a carful of other students had arrived, and the twilight was so far gone into dusk that the river was only a faint metallic shine along the foot of the woods, Paul Latour hooked his arm into Tommy's and unsmiling, looking glum as a detective, led him inside. By that time the party was loud.

Lucy stayed on the fringes of it, alert to her duties as hostess, knowing that the other girls forgot any such responsibilities as soon as they had a couple of drinks. She rescued glasses for people who set them down, kept edging through the crowd around the keg to get glasses filled, talked with new arrivals; circulated quietly, seeing that no bashful student got shoved off into a corner, making sure that Myra Richards didn't get stranded anywhere. But after a half-hour she quit worrying about Myra; Myra was drinking a good deal and having a fine gay time.

It did not cool off much with the dark. The deck was breathless and sticky, and they drank their beer fast because it warmed so rapidly in the glass. Inside, as she paused by the keg, Lucy saw Latour and Tommy still talking head to head in the lighted lounge. Cocking her head a little, she listened to the sound of the party, appraising it. She heard Myra's laugh and a series of groans and hoots from the boys, apparently at someone's joke.

She moved away from the brittle concentration of noise and out toward the rail, and as she passed through the crowd she heard Art Morris say, '. . . got the Westminster Choir and a full symphony orchestra to do singing commercials. That's what Hollywood is, one big assembled empty Technique. They hunt mosquitoes with .155's.'

No one was constrained any more; everything was loose and bibulous. As she leaned on the rail a voice spoke at her shoulder, and she turned to see Professor Richards with a glass of beer in his hand and his coat off. But he still looked dignified because he had kept his tie on and his sleeves rolled down. Most of the boys were down to T-shirts, and a girl who had come with the carload of students was in a halter that was hardly more than a bra. She was out in an open space now, twirling, showing the full ballerina skirt she had made out of an India print bedspread.

'Find any breeze?' Richards said.

'No, just looking at the river.'

'It's very peaceful,' he said. 'You're lucky to have this place.'

'I know.' She brushed an insect from her sticky cheek. It was pleasant to her to be near this man, with his confidence and his rich resonant voice, and a privilege that they could all know him on such informal terms. Until six months ago he had been something big and important in the American Military Government in Germany.

He was saying, 'How do you like it by now? It's a good bit different from England.'

'I'm liking it wonderfully,' she said. 'People have been lovely.'

'Thoroughly acclimated?'

'Not quite to this heat.'

'This just makes the corn grow,' he said, and she heard in his voice, with forgiving amusement that it should be there in the voice of this

77

so-distinguished man, the thing she had heard in so many American voices—the confidence they had that everything American was bigger and better and taller and colder and hotter and wider and deeper than anything else. 'I've seen it a hundred degrees at two in the morning,' Richards said. 'Inside a house, of course.'

'It must be frightful.'

He shrugged, smiling with his smudged mouth in the semidarkness. 'Myra and I slept three nights on the golf course last time we had that kind of weather.'

'We've already slept out here a night or two,' Lucy said. She looked across the shadowy, crowded, noisy deck. 'Where is Myra? I haven't had a chance to talk to her at all.'

'A while ago she was arguing Zionism with a bunch of the boys,' Richards said. He chuckled with his full-chested laugh, indulgent and avuncular. 'She knows nothing whatever about Zionism.'

Lucy had a brief moment of wondering how a professor really looked upon his students. Could he feel completely at ease among men and women of so much less experience and learning, or did he always have a bit of the paternal in his attitude? And when he married a girl out of one of his classes, as Professor Richards had, did he ever— and did *she* ever—get over feeling that he was God omnipotent?

'I imagine you must feel a little as I did when I got back from Germany,' he was saying. 'After living under such a cloud of fear and shortages and loss, suddenly to come out into the sun.'

'Yes,' she said. 'I've felt it. I take the sun like medicine.'

'It's too bad we can't sweep that cloud away for the whole world,' Richards said. He looked out over the river, and she thought his voice had a stern, austere ring. 'England particularly. England looked straight in the face of disaster and recognized it for what it was and fought on. It's a pity the cloud is still there. They've earned something better.'

'Yes,' she said again, for some reason vaguely embarrassed. Talk about England's grit always bothered her. You didn't talk about it when you were in any of it. Why should it be talked about outside? To dispel the slight pompous silence she said, 'I saw you talking to Tommy Probst.'

Richards laughed. 'Momentary funk,' he said. 'It's preposterous. He's one of the best students we've had in years. He'll come up and take it again tomorrow and pass it like a shot.'

He touched her shoulder with a pat that was almost fatherly, almost courtly, and lifted his empty glass in explanation and drifted away.

In the corner by the beer keg, people were jammed in a tight group. A yell of laughter went up, hoots, wolf calls. As the lounge door let a brief beam of light across the deck Lucy saw Myra in the middle of the crowd. Her blond hair glinted silver white, her eyes had a sparkle, her mouth laughed. A vivid face. No wonder Professor Richards had picked her out of a whole class.

Charley broke out of the crowd, shaking his head and grinning, bony-shouldered in the T-shirt. He put a damp arm around her and held his glass for her to sip. 'How's my Limey bride?'

'Steamed like a pudding,' she said. 'It sounds like a good party over here.'

He gave her a sidelong down-mouthed look. 'Doak was just telling the saga of the funeral.'

Laughter broke out again, and Myra's voice said, 'Doak, I think that's the most awful thing I've ever . . . '

'Tell me,' Lucy said, 'what's so screamingly funny about a girl's funeral?'

'Didn't you ever hear about Kay Cedarquist?'

'No.'

'She was an institution. Schoenkampf's lab assistant, over in Biology. She had cancer. That's what she died of, day before yesterday.'

Lucy waited. 'Is it just that I'm British?'

Wiping beer from his lips with his knuckles, Charley grinned at her in the shadow. 'Nothing is so funny to Americans as a corpse,' he said. 'Unless it's a decaying corpse, or one that falls out of the coffin. Read Faulkner, read Caldwell. Kay sort of fell out of the coffin.'

'Oh, my God,' Lucy said, appalled.

'Oh, not really. See, she was Schoenkampf's mistress as well as his assistant. He's got a wife and four kids and they're all nudists. I'll tell you about them too some time. But Schoenkampf also had Kay, and he set her up in an apartment.'

He drank again, raised a long admonishing finger. 'But,' he said. 'When Schoenkampf was home with Mrs Schoenkampf and the four nudist children, Kay had a painter from Terre Haute. He spent a lot of time in our town and painted murals all over Kay's walls . . . haven't I ever told you about those murals?'

'No.'

'Gentle Wawasee River scenes,' Charley said. 'Happy farm children in wood lot and pasture, quiet creeks, steepled towns. Kay told Schoenkampf she had it done because art rested her nerves. She had this double feature going right up to the time she died, practically.'

'You're making this all up,' Lucy said.

He put his hands around her waist and lifted her to the rail. 'Sit up here.' Confidential and grinning, he leaned over her, letting her in on the inside. It was a pose she had loved in him when they walked all over Salisbury talking and talking and talking, when they were both in uniform.

'But if she had cancer,' she said, 'wasn't she ill, in bed?'

'Not till the last month.' He knocked the bottom of his glass lightly against the stone and seemed to brood, half amused. 'She was a good deal of a mess,' he said. 'Also, she had dozens of short subjects besides her double feature. Graduate students, married or single, she wasn't fussy. Nobody took her cancer very seriously. Then all of a sudden she up and died.'

Lucy stirred almost angrily, moving her arm away from his sticky bare skin. 'I don't think all that's funny, Charley.'

'Maybe not. But Kay had no relatives at all, so Schoenkampf had to arrange the funeral. To keep himself out of it as much as possible, he got a bunch of students to act as pallbearers. Every one of them had passed his qualifying exams. That was what got the snickers.'

'Graduate students?' Lucy said. 'What have their qualifying exams to do . . . ?' Then she saw, and giggled involuntarily, and was angry at herself for giggling. Over the heads of the crowd she saw the group of students still clustered in the corner. They had linked arms in a circle and were singing 'I Wanted Wings.' Myra was still among them, between Doak and the girl in the bra and the India print bedspread.

'Who?' she said. 'Doak and Jackson and that crowd?'

'They led the parade,' Charley said, and snorted like a horse into his glass. 'I guess there were three or four unfortunates who couldn't find an empty handle on the coffin.'

Sitting quietly, the stone still faintly warm through her dress, she felt as if a greasy film had spread over her mind. It was such a nasty little sordid story from beginning to end, sneaking and betrayal and double betrayal and fear and that awful waiting, and finally death and heartless grins. 'Well,' Charley said, 'I see you don't like my tale.'

She turned toward him, vaguely and impulsively wanting reassurance. 'Charley, was she pretty?'

'No,' he said. 'Not pretty at all, just easy.'

What she wanted, the understanding, wasn't there. 'I think it's wry,' she said. 'Just wry and awful.'

'It ought to be,' he said, 'but somehow it isn't. Not if you knew Kay. You didn't.'

With a kind of dismay she heard herself say, not knowing until she said it that there was that much distress and that much venom in her, the thing that leaped abruptly and unfairly to her mind. 'Did *you*?'

He stared at her, frowned, looked amazed, and then grinned, and the moment he grinned it was all right again, she could laugh and they were together and not apart. But when he waved his glass and suggested that they go see how the beer was holding out she shook her head and stayed behind on the railing. As he worked his way tall through the jam of shadowy people she had an impulse to jump down and follow him so that not even twenty feet of separation could come desperately between, but the bray of talk and laughter from the deck was like a current that pinned her back against the faintly warm stone, threatening to push her off, and she looked behind her once into the dark pit of the court and tightened her hands on the railing.

She disliked everyone there for being strangers, aliens to her and to her ways of feeling, unable from the vast plateau of security to see or understand the desperation and fear down below. And even while she hated them for it, she felt a pang of black and bitter envy of that untroubled assurance they all had, that way of shrugging off trouble because no trouble that could not be cured had ever come within their experience. Even the war—a temporary unpleasantness. *Their* homes hadn't leaped into unquenchable flame or shaken down in rubble and dust. *They* had known no families in Coventry. Fighting the war, they could still feel not desperate but magnanimous, like good friends who reached out to help an acquaintance in a scuffle.

She hated them, and as she saw Paul Latour approaching her and knew she could not get away, she hated him worst of all. His face was like the face of a predatory bird, beaked, grim-lipped; because of some eye trouble he always wore dark glasses, and his prying, intent, hidden stare was an agony to encounter. His mouth was hooked back in a constant sardonic smile. He not merely undressed her with his eyes; he dissected her most intimate organs, and she knew he was a cruel man, no matter how consistently and amazingly kind he had been to Charley, almost like a father, all the way through school. Charley said he had a mind like a fine watch. But she wished he would not come over, and she trembled, unaccountably emotional, feeling trapped.

Then he was in front of her, big-shouldered for his height, not burly but somehow giving the impression of great strength, and his face like the cold face of a great bird thrust toward her and the hidden stare stabbed into her and the thin smile tightened. 'Nobody to play with?' he asked. There was every unpleasant and cutting suggestion in the remark. A wallflower. Maybe halitosis. Perhaps B.O.

She came back quickly enough. 'Too hot to play.' To steer the talk away from her she said, 'You've been conferring with Tommy.'

'Yes,' he said, and a spasm of what seemed almost contempt twisted across his mouth. 'I've been conferring with Tommy.'

'Is he all right now?'

'What do you mean, all right?'

'Is he over his . . . trouble?'

'He is if he can make up his mind to grow up.'

Now it was her turn. 'What do you mean?'

The dark circles of his glasses stared at her blankly, and then she realized that Latour was laughing. 'I thought you were an intelligent woman.'

'I'm not,' she said half bitterly, 'I'm stupid.'

His laugh was still there, an almost soundless chuckle. Beyond him the circle of singers had widened to include almost everyone on the deck, and thirty people were bellowing, 'We were sailing a-lo-o-o-ng, on Moonlight Bay . . .'

Latour came closer, to be heard. 'You mean to tell me you haven't even yet got wise to Tommy?'

'I don't know what you mean. He's a very good student—'

'Oh, student!' Latour said. 'Sure, he's a student. There's nothing wrong with his brains. He's just a child, that's all, he never grew up.'

A counterattraction to the singing had started in the lounge. A few of the energetic had turned on the radio and were dancing on the smooth terrazzo floor. Lucy saw figures float by the lighted door: Donna and Henry Earp, the Kinseys, Doak and Myra Richards, Tommy and Phyllis. The radio cut quick and active across the dragging tempo of the singing.

'But he was in the air force three years,' she said. 'He's a grown man, he's been through a lot. I never saw anything childish in him.'

He turned his head; his profile was cruel and iron against the light. 'You're disgustingly obtuse,' his mocking voice said. 'What did *you* make of that show he put on today?'

'I don't know,' she said, hesitating. 'That he was afraid, I suppose.'

'Afraid of what?'

'Of what? That he'd fail, that he wouldn't make it after all.'

'Go to the foot of the class.'

'Pardon?'

'Go to the foot of the class,' Latour said. 'Look at the record. Only child, doting mother. I knew him as an undergraduate, and he's been trying for five or six years to break loose. Or he thought he was. If it hadn't been for the war he'd have found out sooner that he wasn't. The war came just as he graduated, just right so he could hide in it. He could even make a show like a hero, like a flyboy. But not as a pilot, notice. He busted out in pilot training. Somebody else would have the real responsibility. After the war, back to school where he's still safe, with GI benefits and no real decisions to make. And then all of a sudden he wakes up and he's pretty near through. In about three hours he'll be out in the bright light all by himself with a Ph.D in his hand and a career to make and no mother, no Army, no university, to cuddle him. He wasn't afraid of that exam, he was afraid of passing it.'

Lucy was silent. She believed him completely, the pattern matched at every edge, but she rebelled at the triumph and contempt in his voice. Suppose he was completely right: Tommy Probst was still his student and presumably his friend, somebody to like and help, not someone to triumph over. Sticky with the slow ooze of perspiration, feeling the hot night dense and smothering around her, she moved restlessly on the rail. Latour reached into the pocket of his seersucker jacket and brought out a pint bottle.

'Drink? I've been avoiding the bellywash everyone else is drinking.'

'No, thank you,' Lucy said. 'Couldn't I get you a glass and some ice?'

'I like it warm,' he said. 'Keeps me reminded that it's poison.'

She saw then what she had not seen before, that he was quite drunk, but out of her vague rebelliousness she said, 'Mr Latour, all the boys are in Tommy's position almost exactly, aren't they? They're right at that edge where they have to be fully responsible adults. They all work much too hard. Any of them could crack just the way Tommy did. Charley could do it. It isn't a disgrace.'

Latour's head went back, the bottle to his lips, and for a moment he was a bird drinking, his iron beak in the air, at once terrible and ridiculous. 'You needn't worry about Charley,' he said when he had brought the bottle down. 'Charley's another breed of rat. He's the kind that wants to wear the old man's breeches even before they're off the old man's legs. Tommy's never got over calling me "Sir." Charley'd eat me tomorrow if he thought he could get away with it.'

'Who'd do what?' Charley said. He had appeared behind Latour with two glasses in his hands. He passed one to Lucy with a quick lift of the eyebrows and she loved him again for having seen that she was trapped.

'You, you ungrateful whelp,' Latour said. He dropped the bottle in his pocket; his blank stare and forward-thrusting face seemed to challenge Charley. 'I'll tell you what you think. You think you're younger than I am. That's right. You think you're better-looking than I am. Maybe that's right too. You think you could put me down. That's a foolish mistake. You think you're as smart as I am, and that's even more foolish.'

His thumb jerked up under Charley's wishbone like a disemboweling knife, and Charley grunted. 'Given half a chance,' Latour said, 'you'd open your wolfish jaws and swallow me. You're like the cannibals who think it gives them virtue to eat their enemy's heart. You'd eat mine.'

'He's distraught,' Charley said to Lucy. 'Maybe we should get him into a tepid bath.'

'You and who else?' Latour said, like a belligerent kid. His sardonic fixed grin turned on Lucy. 'You can see how it goes in his mind. I develop a lot of apparatus for testing perception, and I fight the whole damn university till I get a lab equipped with sound equipment and Phonelescopes and oscillographs and electronic microscopes, and then punks like this one come along and pick my brains and think they know as much as the old man. I give them the equipment and provide them with ideas and supervise their work and let them add their names to mine on scholarly articles, and they think they're all ready to put on the old man's breeches.'

'Why, Paul,' Charley said, 'you've got an absolute anxiety neurosis.

You should see a psychiatrist. You'll brood yourself into paranoia and begin to have persecution complexes. You've got one now. Here I've been holding you up all year, and you think I'm secretly plotting to eat you. You really should talk to a good psychologist.'

'Like who?' Latour said, grinning. 'Some punk like you whose soft spot hasn't hardened yet?'

'There are one or two others almost as good,' Charley said, 'but Graham is the best.'

Latour took the bottle from his pocket and drank again and screwed on the cap and dropped the bottle back in the pocket. His stare never left Charley's face; his soundless chuckle broke out into a snort.

'A punk,' he said. 'A callow juvenile, a pubescent boy, a beardless youth. You're still in the spanking stage.'

Winking at Lucy, Charley said, 'Takes a good man.'

'Oh, not so good,' Latour said. 'Any *man* could do it.'

His hand shot out for Charley's wrist, and Charley jerked back, slopping his beer. It seemed to Lucy that something bright and alert had leaped up in both of them, and she wanted to tell them to drop it, but the noise of singing and the moan of dance music from the lounge made such a current of noise that she didn't trust her voice against it. But Latour's edged foolery bothered her; she didn't think he was entirely joking, and she didn't think Charley thought so either. She watched them scuffle and shove each other, assuming exaggeratedly the starting pose for a wrestling match. Latour reached in his pocket and handed her the almost empty whisky bottle; he removed his glasses and passed them to her, and she saw his eyes like dark holes with a glint of light at the bottom.

'For heaven's sake,' she said, 'you're not going to . . .'

Latour exploded into violent movement, reached and leaned and jerked in a flash, and suddenly Charley's length was across his shoulder, held by crotch and neck, and Latour with braced legs was staggering forward. He was headed directly for the rail. Charley's legs kicked frantically, his arm whipped around Latour's neck in a headlock, but Latour was brutally strong. Face twisted under Charley's arm, he staggered ahead.

Lucy screamed, certain for a moment that Latour was going to throw Charley over. But her husband's legs kicked free, and he swung sideward to get his feet on the floor. Latour let go his neck hold, and his palms slapped against Charley's body as he shifted.

Charley was clinging to his headlock, twisting the blockier Latour into a crouch. Then somehow Latour dove under him, and they crashed.

The whole crowd was around them, shutting off the light from the lounge so that the contestants grunted and struggled in almost total darkness. Lucy bent over them, screaming at Charley to quit it, let go. Someone moved in the crowd, and in a brief streak of light she saw Latour's hands, iron strong, tearing Charley's locked fingers apart, and the veins ridged on Charley's neck as he clung to his hold.

'Stop it!' she screamed at them. 'You'll get all dirty, you'll get hurt, stop it, please, Charley!'

Latour broke free and spun Charley like a straw man, trying to get a hold for a slam. But as they went to the floor again Charley's legs caught him in a head scissors and bent him harshly back.

'Great God,' Henry Earp said beside Lucy. 'What is this, fun or fight?'

'I don't know,' she said. 'Fun. But make them stop.' She grabbed the arm of Clark Richards. 'Make them stop, please!'

Richards bent over the wrestlers, quiet now, Latour's head forced back and Charley lying still, just keeping the pressure on. 'Come on,' Richards said. He slapped them both on the back. 'Bout's a draw. Let go, Charley.'

'Okay with me,' Charley said. 'You satisfied with a draw, Paul?'

Latour said nothing. 'All right,' Richards said. 'Let's call it off, Paul. Someone might get hurt.'

As Charley unlocked his legs and rolled free, Latour was up and after him like a wolf, but Richards and Henry and several others held him back. He put a hand to his neck and stood panting. 'That was a dirty hold, Graham.'

'Not so dirty as getting dumped twenty feet into a courtyard,' Charley said. His T-shirt was ripped half off him. He grinned fixedly at Latour. Sick and fluttery at what had happened, Lucy took his hand, knowing that it was over now, the support was gone, the rest of the way was against difficulties all the way. 'You foolish people,' she said. 'You'll spoil a good party.'

Somehow, by the time she had got herself together after her scare, the party had disintegrated. The unmarried graduate students who had been noisily there all evening had vanished, several of the house couples had gone quietly to bed. The keg was empty, and a half-bottle of whisky stood unwanted on the table. A whole carful of people had gone out the Terre Haute road for sandwiches, taking Paul Latour with them. The court below the rail was empty except for Charley's jeep and Clark Richards' sedan, and the deck was almost deserted, when Richards stepped out of the lounge with his white coat on, ready to go home.

He came from light into darkness, so that for a moment he stood turning his head, peering. 'Myra?' he said. 'We should be getting on.'

'She isn't out here,' Lucy said, and jumped down from the railing where she had been sitting talking to Charley. 'Isn't she in the lounge?'

'I just looked,' Richards said. 'Maybe she's gone up to the ladies' room.'

He came out to lean against the rail near them, looking out across the darkness to the floodlighted clock tower floating in the sky. 'It's a little like the spire of Salisbury Cathedral, isn't it?' he said. 'Salisbury Cathedral across the Avon.' He turned his face toward Lucy. 'Isn't that where you're from, Salisbury?'

'Yes,' she said, 'it is rather like.'

Then an odd thing happened. The southwest horizon leaped up suddenly, black and jagged, hill and tree and floating tower, with the green glow of heat lightning behind it, and when the lightning winked out, the tower went with it, leaving only the unbroken dark. 'Wasn't that queer?' she said. 'They must have turned off the floodlights just at that instant. It was almost as if the lightning wiped it out.'

They were all tired, yawning, languid with the late hour and the beer and the unremitting, oozing heat. Richards looked at his watch, holding it so that light from the lounge fell on it. 'Where can Myra be?' he said. 'It's one o'clock.'

Slowly Charley slid off the rail, groaning. 'Could she be sick? Did she have too much, you think?'

'I don't know,' Richards said. His voice was faintly snappish, irritated. 'I don't think so, but she could have, I suppose.'

'Let me just look up in the shower room,' Lucy said, and slipped away from them, through the immense hot lounge. Art Morris was asleep on the big sofa, looking greasy with sweat under the bluish light. Down the long wide hall she felt like a tiny lost figure in a nightmare and thought what a really queer place this was to live in, after all. So big it forgot about you. She pushed the door, felt for the switch. Light leaped on the water-beaded tile, the silence opened to the lonely drip of a tap. No one was in the shower room, no shoes showed under the row of toilet doors.

When she got back to the deck, someone had turned on the powerful light above the door, and the party lay in wreckage there, a surly shambles of slopped beer and glasses and wadded napkins and trampled cigarette butts. In that light the Earps and Charley and Richards were looking at each other abashed.

'It's almost a cinch she went with the others out to the Casino,' Charley was saying. 'There was a whole swarm of them went together.'

'You'd think she would have said something,' Richards said. His voice was so harsh that Lucy looked at him in surprise and saw his mouth tight and thin, his face drawn with inordinate anxiety. 'She wasn't upstairs?'

Lucy shook her head. For an instant Richards stood with his hands opening and closing at his sides. Abruptly he strode to the rail and looked over it, following it around to the corner and peering over into the tangle of weeds and rubbish at the side. He spun around as if he feared guns were pointed at his back. 'Who saw her last? What was she doing? Who was she with?'

No one spoke for a moment, until Henry Earp said cautiously, 'She was dancing a while ago, a whole bunch of us were. But that was a half-hour ago, at least.'

'Who with?' Richards said, and then slapped at the air with his hand and said, 'No, that wouldn't tell us anything. She must have gone for a sandwich.'

'We can go see,' Charley said. 'Matter of fact, I'd like a sandwich myself. Why don't we run up the road and see if she's at the Casino? She probably didn't notice what time it was.'

'No,' Richards said grimly. Lucy found it hard to look at him, she was so troubled with sympathy and embarrassment. 'Probably she didn't.' He looked at Charley almost vaguely, and sweat was up on his forehead. 'Would you mind?' he said. 'Perhaps I ought to stay here, in case she . . .'

'I'll stay here,' Lucy said. The distraught vague eyes touched her.

'You'll want something to eat too. You go along.'

'No,' she said. 'I'd rather stay. I would anyway.' To Charley she said, 'Why don't you and Henry and Donna go? You could look in at the Casino and the Tavern and all those places along there.'

With his arm around her he walked her to the lounge door, and everything that had passed that evening was in their look just before he kissed her. When she turned around Richards was watching. In the bald light, swarming with insects that crawled and leaped and fluttered toward the globe above the doors, his eyes seemed to glare. Lucy clicked off the light and dropped them back into darkness.

'Should you like a drink?' she said into the black.

After a moment he answered, 'No, thank you.'

Gradually his white-suited figure emerged again as her eyes adjusted. He was on the rail looking out across the river and woods. Heat lightning flared fitfully again along the staring black horizon. The jeep started down below them; the lights jumped against the bluff, turned twisting the shadows, and were gone with the diminishing motor.

'Don't worry,' Lucy said. 'I'm sure she just forgot about the time and went for something to eat. We should have had something here, but somehow with so many to plan things, nothing ever gets planned.'

'I don't like that river,' Richards said. 'It's so absolutely black down there . . .' He swung around at her. 'Have you got a flashlight?'

'I think so,' she said, 'but don't you suppose—'

'Could I borrow it, please?' he said. 'I'm going down along the bank to look. If you'd stay here—if she should come back . . .'

She slipped in and past the still-sleeping Art Morris and found a flashlight in the kitchen drawer, and now suddenly it was as if she were five years back in time, the cool tube in her hand, the intense blackout darkness around, the sense of oppression, the waiting, the search. That sense was even stronger a few minutes later as she sat on the rail and saw the thin slash of the light down along the riverbank, moving slowly, cutting on and off, eventually disappearing in the trees.

It was very still. Perched on the rail, she looked out from the deck they were so lucky to have, over the night-obliterated view that gave them such a sense of freedom and space, and in all the dark there was no sound louder than the brush of a moth's wings or the tick of an armored bug against the driveway light. Then far up the highway a point of sound bored into the silence and grew and rounded, boring through layers of dark and soundless air, until it was a rush and a threat and a roar, and headlights burst violently around the corner of the bluff and reached across the shine of water and picked out, casual and instantaneous, a canoe with a couple in it.

It was there, starkly white, for only a split instant, and then the road swung, the curtain came down. She found it hard to believe that it had been there at all; she even felt a little knife-prick of terror that it could have been there—so silent, so secret, so swallowed in the black, as unseen and unfelt and unsuspected as a crocodile at a jungle ford.

The heat lightning flared again like the flare of distant explosions or the light of buning towns. Instinctively, out of a habit long outgrown, and even while her eyes remained fixed on the place where the canoe had been, she waited for the sound of the blast, but nothing came; she found herself waiting almost ridiculously, with held breath, and that was the time when the lion chose to roar again.

That challenge, coming immediately after the shock of seeing the silent and somehow stealthy canoe, brought a thought that stopped her pulse: 'What if he should be loose?' She felt the adrenaline pump into her blood as she might have felt an electric shock. Her heart pounded and her breath came fast through her open mouth. What if he should be loose?

What if, in these Indiana woods by this quiet river where all of them lived and worked for a future full of casual expectation, far from the jungles and the velds where lions could be expected and where darkness was full of danger, what if here too fear prowled on quiet pads and made its snarling noise in the night? This fraternity house where they lived amicably was ringed with dark water and darker woods where the threat lay in wait. This elevated balcony which she could flood with light at the flip of a finger, this fellowship of youth and study and common experience and common hopes, this common belief in the future, were as friable as walls of cane, as vulnerable as grass huts, and she did not need the things that had happened that evening, or the sight of Clark Richards' tiny light flicking and darting back toward her along the riverbank, to know that what she had lived through for six years was not over and would perhaps never be over for any of them, that in their hearts they were alone, terrified, and at bay, each with his ears attuned to some roar across the woods, some ripple of the water, some whisper of a footstep in the dark.

1948

NO PLACE FOR YOU, MY LOVE

Eudora Welty

They were strangers to each other, both fairly well strangers to the place, now seated side by side at luncheon—a party combined in a free-and-easy way when the friends he and she were with recognized each other across Galatoire's. The time was a Sunday in summer— those hours of afternoon that seem Time Out in New Orleans.

The moment he saw her little blunt, fair face, he thought that here was a woman who was having an affair. It was one of those odd meetings when such an impact is felt that it has to be translated at once into some sort of speculation.

With a married man, most likely, he supposed, slipping quickly into a groove—he was long married—and feeling more conventional, then, in his curiosity as she sat there, leaning her cheek on her hand, looking no further before her than the flowers on the table, and wearing that hat.

He did not like her hat, any more than he liked tropical flowers. It was the wrong hat for her, thought this Eastern businessman who had no interest whatever in women's clothes and no eye for them; he thought the unaccustomed thing crossly.

It must stick out all over me, she thought, so people think they can love me or hate me just by looking at me. How did it leave us—the old, safe, slow way people used to know of learning how one another feels, and the privilege that went with it of shying away if it seemed best? People in love like me, I suppose, give away the short cuts to everybody's secrets.

Something, though, he decided, had been settled about her predicament—for the time being, anyway; the parties to it were all still alive, no doubt. Nevertheless, her predicament was the only one he felt so sure of here, like the only recognizable shadow in that restaurant, where mirrors and fans were busy agitating the light, as the very local talk drawled across and agitated the peace. The shadow lay between her fingers, between her little square hand and her cheek, like something always best carried about the person. Then suddenly, as she took her hand down, the secret fact was still there—

91

it lighted her. It was a bold and full light, shot up under the brim of that hat, as close to them all as the flowers in the center of the table.

Did he dream of making her disloyal to that hopelessness that he saw very well she's been cultivating down here? He knew very well that he did not. What they amounted to was two Northerners keeping each other company. She glanced up at the big gold clock on the wall and smiled. He didn't smile back. She had that naïve face that he associated, for no good reason, with the Middle West—because it said 'Show me,' perhaps. It was a serious, now-watch-out-everybody face, which orphaned her entirely in the company of these Southerners. He guessed her age, as he could not guess theirs: thirty-two. He himself was further along.

Of all human moods, deliberate imperviousness may be the most quickly communicated—it may be the most successful, most fatal signal of all. And two people can indulge in imperviousness as well as in anything else. 'You're not very hungry either,' he said.

The blades of fan shadows came down over their two heads, as he saw inadvertently in the mirror, with himself smiling at her now like a villain. His remark sounded dominant and rude enough for everybody present to listen back a moment; it even sounded like an answer to a question she might have just asked him. The other women glanced at him. The Southern look—Southern mask—of life-is-a-dream irony, which could turn to pure challenge at the drop of a hat, he could wish well away. He liked naïveté better.

'I find the heat down here depressing,' she said, with the heart of Ohio in her voice.

'Well—I'm in somewhat of a temper about it, too,' he said.

They looked with grateful dignity at each other.

'I have a car here, just down the street,' he said to her as the luncheon party was rising to leave, all the others wanting to get back to their houses and sleep. 'If it's all right with—Have you ever driven down south of here?'

Out on Bourbon Street, in the bath of July, she asked at his shoulder, 'South of New Orleans? I didn't know there was any south to *here*. Does it just go on and on?' She laughed, and adjusted the exasperating hat to her head in a different way. It was more than frivolous, it was conspicuous, with some sort of glitter or flitter tied in a band around the straw and hanging down.

'That's what I'm going to show you.'

'Oh, you've been there?'

'No!'

His voice rang out over the uneven, narrow sidewalk and dropped back from the walls. The flaked-off, colored houses were spotted like the hides of beasts faded and shy, and were hot as a wall of growth that seemed to breathe flower-like down onto them as they walked to the car parked there.

'It's just that it couldn't be any worse—we'll see.'

'All right, then,' she said. 'We will.'

So, their actions reduced to amiability, they settled into the car—a faded-red Ford convertible with a rather threadbare canvas top, which had been standing in the sun for all those lunch hours.

'It's rented,' he explained. 'I asked to have the top put down, and was told I'd lost my mind.'

'It's out of this world. *Degrading* heat,' she said and added, 'Doesn't matter.'

The stranger in New Orleans always sets out to leave it as though following the clue in a maze. They were threading through the narrow and one-way streets, past the pale violet bloom of tired squares, the brown steeples and statues, the balcony with the live and probably famous black monkey dipping along the railing as over a ballroom floor, past the grillework and the lattice-work to all the iron swans painted flesh color on the front steps of bungalows outlying.

Driving, he spread his new map and put his finger down on it. At the intersection marked Arabi, where their road led out of the tangle and he took it, a small Negro seated beneath a black umbrella astride a box chalked 'Shou Shine' lifted his pink-and-black hand and waved them languidly good-by. She didn't miss it, and waved back.

Below New Orleans there was a raging of insects from both sides of the concrete highway, not quite together, like the playing of separated marching bands. The river and the levee were still on her side, waste and jungle and some occasional settlements on his—poor houses. Families bigger than housefuls thronged the yards. His nodding, driving head would veer from side to side, looking and almost lowering. As time passed and the distance from New Orleans grew, girls ever darker and younger were disposing themselves over the porches and the porch steps, with jet-black hair pulled high, and ragged palm-leaf fans rising and falling like rafts of butterflies. The children running forth were nearly always naked ones.

She watched the road. Crayfish constantly crossed in front of the wheels, looking grim and bonneted, in a great hurry.

'How the Old Woman Got Home,' she murmured to herself.

He pointed, as it flew by, at a saucepan full of cut zinnias which stood waiting on the open lid of a mailbox at the roadside, with a little note tied onto the handle.

They rode mostly in silence. The sun bore down. They met fishermen and other men bent on some local pursuits, some in sulphur-colored pants, walking and riding; met wagons, trucks, boats in trucks, autos, boats on top of autos—all coming to meet them, as though something of high moment were doing back where the car came from, and he and she were determined to miss it. There was nearly always a man lying with his shoes off in the bed of any truck otherwise empty—with the raw, red look of a man sleeping in the daytime, being jolted about as he slept. Then there was a sort of dead man's land, where nobody came. He loosened his collar and tie. By rushing through the heat at high speed, they brought themselves the effect of fans turned onto their cheeks. Clearing alternated with jungle and canebrake like something tried, tried again. Little shell roads led off on both sides; now and then a road of planks led into the yellow-green.

'Like a dance floor in there.' She pointed.

He informed her, 'In there's your oil, I think.'

There were thousands, millions of mosquitoes and gnats—a universe of them, and on the increase.

A family of eight or nine people on foot strung along the road in the same direction the car was going, beating themselves with the wild palmettos. Heels, shoulders, knees, breasts, back of the heads, elbows, hands, were touched in turn—like some game, each playing it with himself.

He struck himself on the forehead, and increased their speed. (His wife would not be at her most charitable if he came bringing malaria home to the family.)

More and more crayfish and other shell creatures littered their path, scuttling or dragging. These little samples, little jokes of creation, persisted and sometimes perished, the more of them the deeper down the road went. Terrapins and turtles came up steadily over the horizons of the ditches.

Back there in the margins were worse—crawling hides you could not penetrate with bullets or quite believe, grins that had come down from the primeval mud.

'Wake up.' Her Northern nudge was very timely on his arm. They had veered toward the side of the road. Still driving fast, he spread his map.

Like a misplaced sunrise, the light of the river flowed up; they were mounting the levee on a little shell road.

'Shall we cross here?' he asked politely.

He might have been keeping track over years and miles of how long they could keep that tiny ferry waiting. Now skidding down the levee's flank, they were the last-minute car, the last possible car that could squeeze on. Under the sparse shade of one willow tree, the small, amateurish-looking boat slapped the water, as, expertly, he wedged on board.

'Tell him we put him on hub cap!' shouted one of the numerous olive-skinned, dark-eyed young boys standing dressed up in bright shirts at the railing, hugging each other with delight that that last straw was on board. Another boy drew his affectionate initials in the dust of the door on her side.

She opened the door and stepped out, and, after only a moment's standing at bay, started up a little iron stairway. She appeared above the car, on the tiny bridge beneath the captain's window and the whistle.

From there, while the boat still delayed in what seemed a trance—as if it were too full to attempt the start—she could see the panlike deck below, separated by its rusty rim from the tilting, polished water.

The passengers walking and jostling about there appeared oddly amateurish, too—amateur travelers. They were having such a good time. They all knew each other. Beer was being passed around in cans, bets were being loudly settled and new bets made, about local and special subjects on which they all doted. One red-haired man in a burst of wildness even tried to give away his truckload of shrimp to a man on the other side of the boat—nearly all the trucks were full of shrimp—causing taunts and then protests of 'They good! They good!' from the giver. The young boys leaned on each other thinking of what next, rolling their eyes absently.

A radio pricked the air behind her. Looking like a great tomcat just above her head, the captain was digesting the news of a fine stolen automobile.

At last a tremendous explosion burst—the whistle. Everything

95

shuddered in outline from the sound, everybody said something—everybody else.

They started with no perceptible motion, but her hat blew off. It went spiraling to the deck below, where he, thank heaven, sprang out of the car and picked it up. Everybody looked frankly up at her now, holding her hands to her head.

The little willow tree receded as its shade was taken away. The heat was like something falling on her head. She held the hot rail before her. It was like riding a stove. Her shoulders dropping, her hair flying, her skirt buffeted by the sudden strong wind, she stood there, thinking they all must see that with her entire self all she did was wait. Her set hands, with the bag that hung from her wrist and rocked back and forth—all three seemed objects bleaching there, belonging to no one; she could not feel a thing in the skin of her face; perhaps she was crying, and not knowing it. She could look down and see him just below her, his black shadow, her hat, and his black hair. His hair in the wind looked unreasonably long and rippling. Little did he know that from here it had a red undergleam like an animal's. When she looked up and outward, a vortex of light drove through and over the brown waves like a star in the water.

He did after all bring the retrieved hat up the stairs to her. She took it back—useless—and held it to her skirt. What they were saying below was more polite than their searchlight faces.

'Where you think he come from, that man?'

'I bet he come from Lafitte.'

'Lafitte? What you bet, eh?'—all crouched in the shade of trucks, squatting and laughing.

Now his shadow fell partly across her; the boat had jolted into some other strand of current. Her shaded arm and shaded hand felt pulled out from the blaze of light and water, and she hoped humbly for more shade for her head. It had seemed so natural to climb up and stand in the sun.

The boys had a surprise—an alligator on board. One of them pulled it by a chain around the deck, between the cars and trucks, like a toy—a hide that could walk. He thought, Well they had to catch one sometime. It's Sunday afternoon. So they have him on board now, riding him across the Mississippi River . . . The playfulness of it beset everybody on the ferry. The hoarseness of the boat whistle, commenting briefly, seemed part of the general appreciation.

'Who wants to rassle him? Who want to, eh?' two boys cried,

looking up. A boy with shrimp-colored arms capered from side to side, pretending to have been bitten.

What was there so hilarious about jaws that could bite? And what danger was there once in this repulsiveness—so that the last worldly evidence of some old heroic horror of the dragon had to be paraded in capture before the eyes of country clowns?

He noticed that she looked at the alligator without flinching at all. Her distance was set—the number of feet and inches between herself and it mattered to her.

Perhaps her measuring coolness was to him what his bodily shade was to her, while they stood pat up there riding the river, which felt like the sea and looked like the earth under them—full of the red-brown earth, charged with it. Ahead of the boat it was like an exposed vein of ore. The river seemed to swell in the vast middle with the curve of the earth. The sun rolled under them. As if in memory of the size of things, uprooted trees were drawn across their path, sawing at the air and tumbling one over the other.

When they reached the other side, they felt that they had been racing around an arena in their chariot, among lions. The whistle took and shook the stairs as they went down. The young boys, looking taller, had taken out colored combs and were combing their wet hair back in solemn pompadour above their radiant foreheads. They had been bathing in the river themselves not long before.

The cars and trucks, then the foot passengers and the alligator, waddling like a child to school, all disembarked and wound up the weed-sprung levee.

Both respectable and merciful, their hides, she thought, forcing herself to dwell on the alligator as she looked back. Deliver us all from the naked in heart. (As she had been told.)

When they regained their paved road, he heard her give a little sigh and saw her turn her straw-colored head to look back once more. Now that she rode with her hat in her lap, her earrings were conspicuous too. A little metal ball set with small pale stones danced beside each square, faintly downy cheek.

Had she felt a wish for someone else to be riding with them? He thought it was more likely that she would wish for her husband if she had one (his wife's voice) than for the lover in whom he believed. Whatever people liked to think, situations (if not scenes) were usually three-way—there was somebody else always. The one who didn't—couldn't—understand the two made the formidable third.

97

He glanced down at the map flapping on the seat between them, up at his wristwatch, out at the road. Out there was the incredible brightness of four o'clock.

On this side of the river, the road ran beneath the brow of the levee and followed it. Here was a heat that ran deeper and brighter and more intense than all the rest—its nerve. The road grew one with the heat as it was one with the unseen river. Dead snakes stretched across the concrete like markers—inlaid mosaic bands, dry as feathers, which their tires licked at intervals that began to seem clocklike.

No, the heat faced them—it was ahead. They could see it waving at them, shaken in the air above the white of the road, always at a certain distance ahead, shimmering finely as a cloth, with running edges of green and gold, fire and azure.

'It's never anything like this in Syracuse,' he said.

'Or in Toledo, either,' she replied with dry lips.

They were driving through greater waste down here, through fewer and even more insignificant towns. There was water under everything. Even where a screen of jungle had been left to stand, splashes could be heard from under the trees. In the vast open, sometimes boats moved inch by inch through what appeared endless meadows of rubbery flowers.

Her eyes overcome with brightness and size, she felt a panic rise, as sudden as nausea. Just how far below questions and answers, concealment and revelation, they were running now—that was still a new question, with a power of its own, waiting. How dear—how costly—could this ride be?

'It looks to me like your road can't go much further,' she remarked cheerfully. 'Just over there, it's all water.'

'Time out,' he said, and with that he turned the car into a sudden road of white shells that rushed at them narrowly out of the left.

They bolted over a cattle guard, where some rayed and crested purple flowers burst out of the vines in the ditch, and rolled onto a long, narrow, green, mowed clearing: a churchyard. A paved track ran between two short rows of raised tombs, all neatly white-washed and now brilliant as faces against the vast flushed sky.

The track was the width of the car with a few inches to spare. He passed between the tombs slowly but in the manner of a feat. Names took their places on the walls slowly at a level with the eye, names as near as the eyes of a person stopping in conversation, and as far away in origin, and in all their music and dead longing, as Spain. At intervals were set packed bouquets of zinnias, oleanders, and some kind of purple flowers, all quite fresh, in fruit jars, like nice welcomes on bureaus.

They moved on into an open plot beyond, of violent-green grass, spread before the green-and-white frame church with worked flower beds around it, flowerless poinsettias growing up to the windowsills. Beyond was a house, and left on the doorstep of the house a fresh-caught catfish the size of a baby—a fish wearing whiskers and bleeding. On a clothesline in the yard, a priest's black gown on a hanger hung airing, swaying at man's height, in a vague, trainlike, ladylike sweep along an evening breath that might otherwise have seemed imaginary from the unseen, felt river.

With the motor cut off, with the raging of the insects about them, they sat looking out at the green and white and black and red and pink as they leaned against the sides of the car.

'What is your wife like?' she asked. His right hand came up and spread—iron, wooden, manicured. She lifted her eyes to his face. He looked at her like that hand.

Then he lit a cigarette, and the portrait, and the right-hand testimonial it made, were blown away. She smiled, herself as unaffected as by some stage performance; and he was annoyed in the cemetery. They did not risk going on to her husband—if she had one.

Under the supporting posts of the priest's house, where a boat was, solid ground ended and palmettos and water hyacinths could not wait to begin; suddenly the rays of the sun, from behind the car, reached that lowness and struck the flowers. The priest came out onto the porch in his underwear, stared at the car a moment as if he wondered what time it was, then collected his robe off the line and his fish off the doorstep and returned inside. Vespers was next, for him.

After backing out between the tombs he drove on still south, in the sunset. They caught up with an old man walking in a sprightly way in their direction, all by himself, wearing a clean bright shirt printed with a pair of palm trees fanning green over his chest. It might better be a big colored woman's shirt, but she didn't have it. He flagged the car with gestures like hoops.

'You're coming to the end of the road,' the old man told them. He pointed ahead, tipped his hat to the lady, and pointed again. 'End of the road.' They didn't understand that he meant, 'Take me.'

They drove on. 'If we do go any further, it'll have to be by water—is that it?' he asked her, hesitating at this odd point.

'You know better than I do,' she replied politely.

The road had for some time ceased to be paved; it was made of shells. It was leading into a small, sparse settlement like the others a few miles back, but with even more of the camp about it. On the lip of the clearing, directly before a green willow blaze with the sunset gone behind it, the row of houses and shacks faced out on broad, colored, moving water that stretched to reach the horizon and looked like an arm of the sea. The houses on their shaggy posts, patchily built, some with plank runways instead of steps, were flimsy and alike, and not much bigger than the boats tied up at the landing.

'Venice,' she heard him announce, and he dropped the crackling map in her lap.

They coasted down the brief remainder. The end of the road—she could not remember ever seeing a road simply end—was a spoon shape, with a tree stump in the bowl to turn around by.

Around it, he stopped the car, and they stepped out, feeling put down in the midst of a sudden vast pause or subduement that was like a yawn. They made their way on foot toward the water, where at an idle-looking landing men in twos and threes stood with their backs to them.

The nearness of darkness, the still uncut trees, bright water partly under a sheet of flowers, shacks, silence, dark shapes of boats tied up, then the first sounds of people just on the other side of thin walls—all this reached them. Mounds of shells like day-old snow, pink-tinted, lay around a central shack with a beer sign on it. An old man up on the porch there sat holding an open newspaper, with a fat white goose sitting opposite him on the floor. Below, in the now shadowless and sunless open, another old man, with a colored pencil bright under his hat brim, was late mending a sail.

When she looked clear around, thinking they had a fire burning somewhere now, out of the heat had risen the full moon. Just beyond the trees, enormous, tangerine-colored, it was going solidly up. Other lights just striking into view, looking farther distant, showed moss shapes hanging, or slipped and broke matchlike on the water that so encroached upon the rim of ground they were standing on.

There was a touch at her arm—his, accidental.

'We're at the jumping-off place,' he said.

She laughed, having thought his hand was a bat, while her eyes rushed downward toward a great pale drift of water hyacinths—still partly open, flushed and yet moonlit, level with her feet—through which paths of water for the boats had been hacked. She drew her hands up to her face under the brim of her hat; her own cheeks felt like the hyacinths to her, all her skin still full of too much light and sky, exposed. The harsh vesper bell was ringing.

'I believe there must be something wrong with me, that I came on this excursion to begin with,' she said, as if he had already said this and she were merely in hopeful, willing, maddening agreement with him.

He took hold of her arm, and said, 'Oh, come on—I see we can get something to drink here, at least.'

But there was a beating, muffled sound from over the darkening water. One more boat was coming in, making its way through the tenacious, tough, dark flower traps, by the shaken light of what first appeared to be torches. He and she waited for the boat, as if on each other's patience. As if borne in on a mist of twilight or a breath, a horde of mosquitoes and gnats came singing and striking at them first. The boat bumped, men laughed. Somebody was offering somebody else some shrimp.

Then he might have cocked his dark city head down at her; she did not look up at him, only turned when he did. Now the shell mounds, like the shacks and trees, were solid purple. Lights had appeared in the not-quite-true window squares. A narrow neon sign, the lone sign, had come out in bright blush on the beer shack's roof: 'Baba's Place.' A light was on on the porch.

The barnlike interior was brightly lit and unpainted, looking not quite finished, with a partition dividing this room from what lay behind. One of the four cardplayers at a table in the middle of the floor was the newspaper reader; the paper was in his pants pocket. Midway along the partition was a bar, in the form of a pass-through to the other room, with a varnished, second-hand fretwork overhang. They crossed the floor and sat, alone there, on wooden stools. An eruption of humorous signs, newspaper cutouts and cartoons, razor-blade cards, and personal messages of significance to the owner or his friends decorated the overhang, framing where Baba should have been but wasn't.

Through there came a smell of garlic and cloves and red pepper, a blast of hot cloud escaped from a cauldron they could see now on a stove at the back of the other room. A massive back, presumably

101

female, with a twist of gray hair on top, stood with a ladle akimbo. A young man joined her and with his fingers stole something out of the pot and ate it. At Baba's they were boiling shrimp.

When he got ready to wait on them, Baba strolled out to the counter, young, black-headed, and in very good humor.

'Coldest beer you've got. And food—What will you have?'

'Nothing for me, thank you,' she said. 'I'm not sure I could eat, after all.'

'Well, I could,' he said, shoving his jaw out. Baba smiled. 'I want a good solid ham sandwich.'

'I could have asked him for some water,' she said, after he had gone.

While they sat waiting, it seemed very quiet. The bubbling of the shrimp, the distant laughing of Baba, and the slap of cards, like the beating of moths on the screens, seemed to come in fits and starts. The steady breathing they heard came from a big rough dog asleep in the corner. But it was bright. Electric lights were strung riotously over the room from a kind of spider web of old wires in the rafters. One of the written messages tacked before them read, 'Joe! At the boyy!!' It looked very yellow, older than Baba's Place. Outside, the world was pure dark.

Two little boys, almost alike, almost the same size, and just cleaned up, dived into the room with a double bang of the screen door, and circled around the card game. They ran their hands into the men's pockets.

'Nickel for some pop!'

'Nickel for some pop!'

'Go 'way and let me play, you!'

They circled around and shrieked at the dog, ran under the lid of the counter and raced through the kitchen and back, and hung over the stools at the bar. One child had a live lizard on his shirt, clinging like a breast pin—like lapis lazuli.

Bringing in a strong odor of geranium talcum, some men had come in now—all in bright shirts. They drew near the counter, or stood and watched the game.

When Baba came out bringing the beer and sandwich, 'Could I have some water?' she greeted him.

Baba laughed at everybody. She decided the woman back there must be Baba's mother.

Beside her, he was drinking his beer and eating his sandwich—

ham, cheese, tomato, pickle, and mustard. Before he finished, one of the men who had come in beckoned from across the room. It was the old man in the palm-tree shirt.

She lifted her head to watch him leave her, and was looked at, from all over the room. As a minute passed, no cards were laid down. In a far-off way, like accepting the light from Arcturus, she accepted it that she was more beautiful or perhaps more fragile than the women they saw every day of their lives. It was just this thought coming into a woman's face, and at this hour, that seemed familiar to them.

Baba was smiling. He had set an opened, frosted brown bottle before her on the counter, and a thick sandwich, and stood looking at her. Baba made her eat some supper, for what she was.

'What the old fellow wanted,' said he when he came back at last, 'was to have a friend of his apologize. Seems church is just out. Seems the friend made a remark coming in just now. His pals told him there was a lady present.'

'I see you bought him a beer,' she said.

'Well, the old man looked like he wanted *something*.'

All at once the juke box interrupted from back in the corner, with the same old song as anywhere. The half-dozen slot machines along the wall were suddenly all run to like Maypoles, and thrown into action—taken over by further battalions of little boys.

There were three little boys to each slot machine. The local custom appeared to be that one pulled the lever for the friend he was holding up to put the nickel in, while the third covered the pictures with the flat of his hand as they fell into place, so as to surprise them all if anything happened.

The dog lay sleeping on in front of the raging juke box, his ribs working fast as a concertina's. At the side of the room a man with a cap on his white thatch was trying his best to open a side screen door, but it was stuck fast. It was he who had come in with the remark considered ribald; now he was trying to get out the other way. Moths as thick as ingots were trying to get in. The cardplayers broke into shouts of derision, then joy, then tired derision among themselves; they might have been here all afternoon—they were the only ones not cleaned up and shaved. The original pair of little boys ran in once more, with the hyphenated bang. They got nickels this time, then were brushed away from the table like mosquitoes, and they rushed under the counter and on to the cauldron behind,

103

clinging to Baba's mother there. The evening was at the threshold.

They were quite unnoticed now. He was eating another sandwich, and she, having finished part of hers, was fanning her face with her hat. Baba had lifted the flap of the counter and come out into the room. Behind his head there was a sign lettered in orange crayon: 'Shrimp Dance Sun. PM.' That was tonight, still to be.

And suddenly she made a move to slide down from her stool, maybe wishing to walk out into that nowhere down the front steps to be cool a moment. But he had hold of her hand. He got down from his stool, and, patiently, reversing her hand in his own—just as she had had the look of being about to give up, faint—began moving her, leading her. They were dancing.

'I get to thinking this is what we get—what you and I deserve,' she whispered, looking past his shoulder into the room. 'And all the time, it's real. It's a real place—away off down here . . . '

They danced gratefully, formally, to some song carried on in what must be the local patois, while no one paid any attention as long as they were together, and the children poured the family nickels steadily into the slot machines, walloping the handles down with regular crashes and troubling nobody with winning.

She said rapidly, as they began moving together too well, 'One of those clippings was an account of a shooting right here. I guess they're proud of it. And that awful knife Baba was carrying . . . I wonder what he called me,' she whispered in his ear.

'Who?'

'The one who apologized to you.'

If they had ever been going to overstep themselves, it would be now as he held her closer and turned her, when she became aware that he could not help but see the bruise at her temple. It would not be six inches from his eyes. She felt it come out like an evil star. (Let it pay him back, then, for the hand he had stuck in her face when she'd tried once to be sympathetic, when she'd asked about his wife.) They danced on still as the record changed, after standing wordless and motionless, linked together in the middle of the room, for the moment between.

Then, they were like a matched team—like professional, Spanish dancers wearing masks—while the slow piece was playing.

Surely even those immune from the world, for the time being, need the touch of one another, or all is lost. Their arms encircling each other, their bodies circling the odorous, just-nailed-down floor, they were, at last, imperviousness in motion. They had found it, and had almost missed it: they had had to dance. They were what their separate hearts desired that day, for themselves and each other.

They were so good together that once she looked up and half smiled. 'For whose benefit did we have to show off?'

Like people in love, they had a superstition about themselves almost as soon as they came out on the floor, and dared not think the words 'happy' or 'unhappy,' which might strike them, one or the other, like lightning.

In the thickening heat they danced on while Baba himself sang with the mosquito-voiced singer in the chorus of '*Moi pas l'aimez ça,*' enumerating the *ça*'s with a hot shrimp between his fingers. He was counting over the platters the old woman now set out on the counter, each heaped with shrimp in their shells boiled to iridescence, like mounds of honeysuckle flowers.

The goose wandered in from the back room under the lid of the counter and hitched itself around the floor among the table legs and people's legs, never seeing that it was neatly avoided by two dancers—who nevertheless vaguely thought of this goose as learned, having earlier heard an old man read to it. The children called it Mimi, and lured it away. The old thatched man was again drunkenly trying to get out by the stuck side door; now he gave it a kick, but was prevailed on to remain. The sleeping dog shuddered and snored.

It was left up to the dancers to provide nickels for the juke box; Baba kept a drawerful for every use. They had grown fond of all the selections by now. This was the music you heard out of the distance at night—out of the roadside taverns you fled past, around the late corners in cities half asleep, drifting up from the carnival over the hill, with one odd little strain always managing to repeat itself. This seemed a homey place.

Bathed in sweat, and feeling the false coolness that brings, they stood finally on the porch in the lapping night air for a moment before leaving. The first arrivals of the girls were coming up the steps under the porch light—all flowered fronts, their black pompadours giving out breathlike feelers from sheer abundance. Where they'd resprinkled it since church, the talcum shone like mica on their downy arms. Smelling solidly of geranium, they filed across the porch with short steps and fingers joined, just timed to turn their smiles loose inside the room. He held the door open for them.

'Ready to go?' he asked her.

Going back, the ride was wordless, quiet except for the motor and the insects driving themselves against the car. The windshield was soon blinded. The headlights pulled in two other spinning storms, cones of flying things that, it seemed, might ignite at the last minute. He stopped the car and got out to clean the windshield thoroughly with his brisk, angry motions of driving. Dust lay thick and cratered on the roadside scrub. Under the now ash-white moon, the world traveled through very faint stars—very many slow stars, very high, very low.

It was a strange land, amphibious—and whether water-covered or grown with jungle or robbed entirely of water and trees, as now, it had the same loneliness. He regarded the great sweep—like steppes, like moors, like deserts (all of which were imaginary to him); but more than it was like any likeness, it was South. The vast, thin, wide-thrown pale, unfocused star-sky, with its veils of lightning adrift, hung over this land as it hung over the open sea. Standing out in the night alone, he was struck as powerfully with recognition of the extremity of this place as if all other bearings had vanished—as if snow had suddenly started to fall.

He climbed back inside and drove. When he moved to slap furiously at his shirtsleeves, she shivered in the hot, licking night wind that their speed was making. Once the car lights picked out two people—a Negro couple, sitting on two facing chairs in the yard outside their lonely cabin—half undressed, each battling for self against the hot night, with long white rags in endless, scarflike motions.

In peopleless open places there were lakes of dust, smudge fires burning at their hearts. Cows stood in untended rings around them, motionless in the heat, in the night—their horns standing up sharp against that glow.

At length, he stopped the car again, and this time he put his arm under her shoulder and kissed her—not knowing ever whether gently or harshly. It was the loss of that distinction that told him this was now. Then their faces touched unkissing, unmoving, dark, for a length of time. The heat came inside the car and wrapped them still, and the mosquitoes had begun to coat their arms and even their eyelids.

Later, crossing a large open distance, he saw at the same time two fires. He had the feeling that they had been riding for a long time across a face—great, wide, and upturned. In its eyes and open mouth were those fires they had had glimpses of, where the cattle had drawn together: a face, a head, far down here in the South—south of South, below it. A whole giant body sprawled downward then, on and on, always, constant as a constellation or an angel. Flaming and perhaps falling, he thought.

She appeared to be sound asleep, lying back flat as a child, with her hat in her lap. He drove on with her profile beside his, behind his, for he bent forward to drive faster. The earrings she wore twinkled with their rushing motion in an almost regular beat. They might have spoken like tongues. He looked straight before him and drove on, at a speed that, for the rented, overheated, not at all new Ford car, was demoniac.

It seemed often now that a barnlike shape flashed by, roof and all outlined in lonely neon—a movie house at a crossroads. The long white flat road itself, since they had followed it to the end and turned around to come back, seemed able, this far up, to pull them home.

A thing is incredible, if ever, only after it is told—returned to the world it came out of. For their different reasons, he thought, neither of them would tell this (unless something was dragged out of them): that, strangers, they had ridden down into a strange land together and were getting safely back—by a slight margin, perhaps, but margin enough. Over the levee wall now, like an aurora borealis, the sky of New Orleans, across the river, was flickering gently. This time they crossed by bridge, high above everything, merging into a long light-stream of cars turned cityward.

For a long time afterward he was lost in the streets, turning almost at random with the noisy traffic until he found his bearings. When he stopped the car at the next sign and leaned forward frowning to make it out, she sat up straight on her side. It was Arabi. He turned the car right round.

'We're all right now,' he muttered, allowing himself a cigarette.

Something that must have been with them all along suddenly, then, was not. In a moment, tall as panic, it rose, cried like a human, and dropped back.

'I never got my water,' she said.

She gave him the name of her hotel, he drove her there, and he said good night on the sidewalk. They shook hands.

'Forgive . . . ' For, just in time, he saw she expected it of him.

And that was just what she did, forgive him. Indeed, had she waked in time from a deep sleep, she would have told him her story.

She disappeared through the revolving door, with a gesture of smoothing her hair, and he thought a figure in the lobby strolled to meet her. He got back in the car and sat there.

He was not leaving for Syracuse until early in the morning. At length, he recalled the reason; his wife had recommended that he stay where he was this extra day so that she could entertain some old, unmarried college friends without him underfoot.

As he started up the car, he recognized in the smell of exhausted, body-warm air in the streets, in which the flow of drink was an inextricable part, the signal that the New Orleans evening was just beginning. In Dickie Grogan's, as he passed, the well-known Josefina at her organ was charging up and down with '*Claire de Lune.*' As he drove the little Ford safely to its garage, he remembered for the first time in years when he was young and brash, a student in New York, and the shriek and horror and unholy smother of the subway had its original meaning for him as the lilt and expectation of love.

1952

THE STATE OF GRACE

Harold Brodkey

There is a certain shade of red brick—a dark, almost melodious red, sombre and riddled with blue—that is my childhood in St Louis. Not the real childhood, but the false one that extends from the dawning of consciousness until the day that one leaves home for college. That one shade of red brick and green foliage is St Louis in the summer (the winter is just a gray sky and a crowded school bus and the wet footprints on the brown linoleum floor at school), and that brick and a pale sky is spring. It's also loneliness and the queer, self-pitying wonder that children whose families are having catastrophes feel.

I can remember that brick best on the back of our apartment house; it was on all the apartment houses on that block, and also on the apartment house where Edward lived—Edward was a small boy I took care of on the evenings when his parents went out. As I came up the street from school, past the boulevard and its ugliness (the vista of shoe-repair shops, dime stores, hairdressers', pet shops, the Tivoli Theatre, and the closed Piggly Wiggly, about to be converted into a Kroger's), past the place where I could see the masonic Temple, built in the shape of some Egyptian relic, and the two huge concrete pedestals flanking the boulevard (what they supported I can't remember, but on both of them, in a brown paint, was a large heart and the information that someone named Erica loved someone named Peter), past the post office, built in WPA days of yellow brick and chrome, I hurried toward the moment when at last, on the other side, past the driveway of the garage of the Castlereagh Apartments, I would be at the place where the trees began, the apartment houses of dark-red brick, and the empty stillness.

In the middle of that stillness and red brick was my neighborhood, the terribly familiar place where I was more comfortably an exile than anywhere else. There were two locust trees that were beautiful to me—I think because they were small and I could encompass them (not only with my mind and heart but with my hands as well). Then came an apartment house of red brick (but not quite the true shade)

109

where a boy I knew lived, and two amazingly handsome brothers, who were also strong and kind, but much older than I and totally uninterested in me. Then came an alley of black macadam and another vista, which I found shameful but drearily comfortable, of garages and ashpits and telephone poles and the backs of apartment houses—including ours—on one side, the backs of houses on the other. I knew many people in the apartments but none in the houses, and this was the ultimate proof, of course, to me of how miserably degraded I was and how far sunken beneath the surface of the sea. I was on the bottom, looking up through the waters, through the shifting bands of light—through, oh, innumerably more complexities than I could stand—at a sailboat driven by the wind, some boy who had a family and a home like other people.

I was thirteen, and six feet tall, and I weighed a hundred and twenty-five pounds. Though I fretted wildly about my looks (my ears stuck out and my hair was like wire), I also knew I was attractive; girls had smiled at me, but none whom I might love and certainly none of the seven or eight goddesses in the junior high school I attended. Starting in about second grade, I always had the highest grades—higher than anybody who had ever attended the schools I went to—and I terrified my classmates. What terrified them was that so far as they could see, it never took any effort; it was like legerdemain. I was never teased, I was never tormented; I was merely isolated. But I was known as 'the walking encyclopedia,' and the only way I could deal with this was to withdraw. Looking back, I'm almost certain I could have had friends if I'd made the right overtures, and that it was not my situation but my forbidding pride that kept them off; I'm not sure. I had very few clothes, and all that I had had been passed to me from an elder cousin. I never was able to wear what the other boys wore.

Our apartment was on the third floor. I usually walked up the back stairs, which were mounted outside the building in a steel framework. I preferred the back stairs—it was a form of rubbing at a hurt to make sure it was still there—because they were steep and ugly and had garbage cans on the landings and wash hanging out, while the front door opened off a court where rosebushes grew, and the front stairs were made of some faintly yellow local marble that was cool and pleasant to the touch and to the eye. When I came to our back door, I would open the screen and call out to see if my mother was home. If she was not home, it usually meant that she was visiting my father, who had been dying in the hospital for four years and would linger two more before he would come to terms with death. As far as I know, that was the only sign of character he ever showed in his entire life, and I suppose it was considerable, but I hoped, and even sometimes prayed, that he would die—not only because I wouldn't have to visit the hospital again, where the white-walled rooms were filled with odors and sick old men (and a tangible fear that made me feel a falling away inside, like the plunge into the unconscious when the anesthetic is given), but because my mother might marry again and make us all rich and happy once more. She was still lovely then, still alight with the curious incandescence of physical beauty, and there was a man who had loved her for twenty years and who loved her yet and wanted to marry her. I wished so hard my father would die, but he just wouldn't. If my mother was home, I braced myself for unpleasantness, because she didn't like me to sit and read; she hated me to read. She wanted to drive me outdoors, where I would become an athlete and be like other boys and be popular. It filled her with rage when I ignored her advice and opened a book; once, she rushed up to me, her face suffused with anger, took the book (I think it was *Pride and Prejudice*), and hurled it out the third-story window. At the time, I sat and tried to sneer, thinking she was half mad, with her exaggerated rage, and so foolish not to realize that I could be none of the things she thought I ought to be. But now I think—perhaps wistfully—that she was merely desperate, driven to extremes in her anxiety to save me. She felt—she knew, in fact—that there was going to come a moment when, like an acrobat, I would have to climb on her shoulders and on the shoulders of all the things she had done for me, and leap out into a life she couldn't imagine (and which I am leading now), and if she wanted to send me out wrapped in platitudes, in an athletic body, with a respect for money, it was because she thought that was the warmest covering.

But when I was thirteen, I only wondered how anyone so lovely could be so impossible. She somehow managed it so that I hated her far more than I loved her, even though in the moments before sleep I would think of her face, letting my memory begin with the curving gentleness of her eyelids and circle through all the subtle interplay of shadows and hollows and bones, and the half-remembered warmth of her chest, and it would seem to me that this vision of her, always standing in half light (as probably I had seen her once when I was younger, and sick, perhaps, though I don't really remember), was only as beautiful to me as the pattern in an immeasurably ancient and faded Persian rug. In the vision, as in the rug, I could trace the lines in and out and experience some unnamed pleasure, but it had almost no meaning, numbed as I was by the problems of being her son.

Being Jewish also disturbed me, because it meant I could never be one of the golden people—the blond athletes, with their easy charm. If my family had been well off, I might have felt otherwise, but I doubt it.

My mother had a cousin whom I called Aunt Rachel, and we used to go and see her three or four times a year. I hated it. She lived in what was called the Ghetto, which was a section of old houses in downtown St Louis with tiny front porches and two doors, one to the upstairs and one to the downstairs. Most people lived in them only until they could move to something better; no one had ever liked living there. And because of that, the neighborhood had the quality of being blurred; the grass was never neat, the window frames were never painted, no one cared about or loved the place. It was where the immigrants lived when they arrived by train from New York and before they could move uptown to the apartments near Delmar Boulevard, and eventually to the suburbs—to Clayton, Laclede, and Ladue. Aunt Rachel lived downstairs. Her living room was very small and had dark-yellow wallpaper, which she never changed. She never cleaned it, either, because once I made a mark on it, to see if she would, and she didn't. The furniture was alive and frightening; it was like that part of the nightmare where it gets so bad that you decide to wake up. I always had to sit on it. It bulged in great curves of horsehair and mohair, and it was dark purple and maroon and dark green, and the room had no light in it anywhere. Somewhere on the other side of the old, threadbare satin draperies that had been bought out of an old house was fresh air and sunshine, but you'd never know it. It was as much like a peasant's hut as Aunt Rachel could manage, buying furniture in cut-rate furniture stores. And always there were the smells—the smell of onion soup and garlic and beets. It was the only place where I was ever rude to my mother in public. It was always full of people whom I hardly ever knew, but who knew me, and I had to perform. My mother would say, 'Tell the people what your last report card was,' or 'Recite them the poem that Miss Huntington liked so well.' That was when the feeling of unreality was strongest. Looking back now, I think that what frightened me was their fierce urgency; I was to be rich and famous and make all their tribulations worth while. But I didn't want that responsibility. Anyway, if I were going to be what they wanted me to be, and if I had to be what I was, then it was too much to expect me to take them as they were. I had to go beyond them and despise them, but first I had to be with them—and it wasn't fair.

It was as if my eyelids had been propped open, and I had to see these things I didn't want to see. I felt as if I had taken part in something shameful, and therefore I wasn't a nice person. It was like my first sexual experiences: What if anyone knew? What if everyone found out? . . . How in hell could I ever be gallant and carefree?

I had read too many books by Englishmen and New Englanders to want to know anything but graceful things and erudite things and the look of white frame houses on green lawns. I could always console myself by thinking my brains would make me famous (brains were good for something, weren't they?) but then my children would have good childhoods—not me. I was irrevocably deprived, and it was the irrevocableness that hurt, that finally drove me away from any sensible adjustment with life to the position that dreams had to come true or there was no point in living at all. If dreams came true, then I would have my childhood in one form or another, someday.

If my mother was home when I came in from school, she might say that Mrs Leinberg had called and wanted me to baby-sit, and I would be plunged into yet another of the dilemmas of those years. I had to baby-sit to earn money to buy my lunch at school, and there were times, considering the dilemma I faced at the Leinbergs', when I preferred not eating, or eating very little, to baby-sitting. But there wasn't any choice; Mother would have accepted for me, and made Mrs Leinberg promise not to stay out too late and deprive me of my sleep. She would have a sandwich ready for me to eat, so that I could rush over in time to let Mr and Mrs Leinberg go out to dinner. Anyway, I would eat my sandwich reading a book, to get my own back, and then I would set out. As I walked down the back stairs on my way to the Leinbergs', usually swinging on the railings by my arms to build up my muscles, I would think forlornly of what it was to be me, and wish things were otherwise, and I did not understand myself or my loneliness or the cruel deprivation the vista down the alley meant.

There was a short cut across the back yards to the apartment house where the Leinbergs lived, but I always walked by my two locust trees and spent a few moments loving them; so far as I knew, I loved nothing else.

Then I turned right and crossed the street and walked past an apartment house that had been built at right angles to the street, facing a strange declivity that had once been an excavation for still another apartment house, which had never been built, because of the depression. On the other side of the declivity was a block of three apartment houses, and the third was the Leinbergs'. Every apartment in it had at least eight rooms, and the back staircase was enclosed, and the building had its own garages. All this made it special and expensive, and a landmark in the neighborhood.

Mr Leinberg was a drug manufacturer and very successful. I thought he was a smart man, but I don't remember him at all well (I never looked at men closely in those days but always averted my head in shyness and embarrassment; they might guess how fiercely I wanted to belong to them) and I could have been wrong. Certainly the atmosphere then, during the war years—it was 1943—was that everyone was getting rich; everyone who could work, that is. At any rate, he was getting rich, and it was only a matter of time before the Leinbergs moved from that apartment house to Laclede or Ladue and had a forty-thousand-dollar house with an acre or so of grounds.

Mrs Leinberg was very pretty; she was dark, like my mother, but not as beautiful. For one thing, she was too small; she was barely five feet tall, and I towered over her. For another, she was not at all regal. But her lipstick was never on her teeth, and her dresses were usually new, and her eyes were kind. (My mother's eyes were incomprehensible; they were dark stages where dimly seen mob scenes were staged and all one ever sensed was tumult and drama, and no matter how long one waited, the lights never went up and the scene never was explained.) Mrs Leinberg would invite me to help myself in the icebox, and then she would write down the telephone number of the place where she was going to be. 'Keep Edward in the back of the apartment, where he won't disturb the baby,' she would tell me. 'If the baby does wake up, pick her up right away. That's very important. I didn't pick Edward up, and I'll always regret it.' She said that every time, even though I could see Edward lurking in the back hallway, waiting for his parents to leave so he could run out and jump on me and our world could come alive again. He would listen, his small face—he was seven—quite blank with hurt and the effort to pierce the hurt with understanding.

Mrs Leinberg would say, 'Call me if she wakes up.' And then, placatingly, to her husband, 'I'll just come home to put her back to sleep, and then I'll go right back to the party—' Then, to me, 'But she almost always sleeps, so don't worry about it.'

'Come on, Greta. He knows what to do,' Mr Leinberg would say impatiently.

I always heard contempt in his voice—contempt for his wife, for Edward, and for me. I would be standing by the icebox looking down on the two little married people. Edward's father had a jealous and petulant mouth. 'Come on, Greta,' it would say impatiently. 'We'll be back by eleven,' it would say to me.

'Edward goes to bed at nine,' Mrs Leinberg would say, her voice high and birdlike, but tremulous with confusion and vagueness. Then she would be swept out the front door, so much prettily dressed matchwood, in her husband's wake. When the door closed, Edward would come hurtling down the hall and tackle my knees if I was staring after his parents, or, if I was facing him, leap onto my chest and into my arms.

'What shall we play tonight?'

He would ask that and I would have to think. He trembled with excitement, because I could make up games wonderful to him—like his daydreams, in fact. Because he was a child, he trusted me almost totally, and I could do anything with him. I had that power with children until I was in college and began at last to be like other people.

In Edward's bedroom was a large closet; it had a rack for clothes, a washstand, a built-in table, and fifteen or twenty shelves. The table and shelves were crowded with toys and games and sports equipment. I owned a Monopoly board I had inherited from my older sister, an old baseball glove (which was so cheap I never dared use it in front of my classmates, who had real gloves signed by real players), and a collection of postcards. The first time I saw that closet, I practically exploded with pleasure; I took down each of the games and toys and played with them, one after another, with Edward. Edward loved the fact that we never played a game to its conclusion but would leap from game to game after only a few moves, until the leaping became the real game and the atmosphere of laughter the real sport.

It was comfortable for me in the back room, alone in the apartment with Edward, because at last I was chief; and not only that, I was not being seen. There was no one there who could see through me, or think of what I should be or how I should behave; and I have always been terrified of what people thought of me, as if what they thought was a hulking creature that would confront me if I should turn a wrong corner.

There were no corners. Edward and I would take his toy pistols and stalk each other around the bed. Other times, we were on the bed, the front gun turret of a battleship sailing to battle the Japanese fleet in the Indian Ocean. Edward would close his eyes and roll with pleasure when I went 'Boom! Boom! BOOOOM!'

'It's sinking! It's sinking, isn't it?'

'No, stupid. We only hit its funnel. We have to shoot again. Boom, Boom—'

Edward's fingers would press his eyelids in a spasm of ecstasy; his delirious, taut, little boy's body would fall backward on the soft pillows and bounce, and his back would curve; the excited breathy laughter would pour out like so many leaves spilling into spring, so many lilacs thrusting into bloom.

Under the bed, in a foxhole (Edward had a Cub Scout hat and I had his plastic soldier helmet), we turned back the yellow hordes from Guadalcanal. Edward dearly loved to be wounded. 'I'm hit!' he'd shriek. 'I'm hit!' He'd press his hand against his stomach and writhe on the wooden floor. 'They shot me in the guts—'

I didn't approve of his getting wounded so soon, because then the scene was over; both his and my sense of verisimilitude didn't allow someone to be wounded and then get up. I remember how pleased he was when I invented the idea that after he got wounded, he could be someone else; so, when we crawled under the bed, we would decide to be eight or twelve or twenty Marines, ten each to get wounded, killed, or maimed as we saw fit, provided enough survived so that when we crawled out from under the bed we could charge the Japanese position under the dining-room table and leave it strewn with corpses.

Edward was particularly good at the detective game, which was a lot more involved and difficult. In that, we would walk into the kitchen, and I would tell him that we had received a call about a murder. Except when we played Tarzan, we never found it necessary to be characters. However, we always had names. In the detective game, we were usually Sam and Fred. We'd get a call telling us who was murdered, and then we'd go back to the bedroom and examine

116

the corpse and question the suspects. I'd fire questions at an empty chair. Sometimes Edward would get tired of being my sidekick and he'd slip into the chair and be the quaking suspect. Other times, he would prowl around the room on his hands and knees with a magnifying glass while I stormed and shouted at the perpetually shifty suspect: 'Where were you, Mrs Eggnogghead [giggles from Edward], at ten o'clock, when Mr Eggnogghead [laughter, helpless with pleasure, from Edward] was slain with the cake knife?'

'Hey, Fred! *I found bloodstains.*' Edward's voice would quiver with a creditable imitation of the excitement of radio detectives.

'Bloodstains! Where, Sam? Where? This may be the clue that breaks the case.'

Edward could sustain the *commedia dell' arte* for hours if I wanted him to. He was a precocious and delicate little boy, quivering with the malaise of being unloved. When we played, his child's heart would come into its own, and the troubled world where his vague hungers went unfed and mothers and fathers were dim and far away—too far away ever to reach in and touch the sore place and make it heal—would disappear, along with the world where I was not sufficiently muscled or sufficiently gallant to earn my own regard. (What ever had induced my mother to marry that silly man, who'd been unable to hang on to his money? I could remember when we'd had a larger house and I'd been happy; why had she let it get away?) It angered me that Edward's mother had so little love for him and so much for her daughter, and that Edward's father should not appreciate the boy's intelligence—he thought Edward was a queer duck, and effeminate. I could have taught Edward the manly postures. But his father didn't think highly of me: I was only a baby-sitter, and a queer duck too. Why, then, should Edward be more highly regarded by his father than I myself was? I wouldn't love him or explain to him.

That, of course, was my terrible dilemma. His apartment house, though larger than mine, was made of the same dark-red brick, and I wouldn't love him. It was shameful for a boy my age to love a child anyway. And who was Edward? He wasn't as smart as I'd been at his age, or as fierce. At his age, I'd already seen the evil in people's eyes, and I'd begun the construction of my defenses even then. But Edward's family was more prosperous, and the cold winds of insecurity (*Where will the money come from?*) hadn't shredded the dreamy chrysalis of his childhood. He was still immersed in the dim, wet wonder of the folded wings that might open if someone loved

117

him; he still hoped, probably, in a butterfly's unthinking way, for spring and warmth. How the wings ache, folded so, waiting; that is, they ache until they atrophy.

So I was thirteen and Edward was seven and he wanted me to love him, but he was not old enough or strong enough to help me. He could not make his parents share their wealth and comfort with me, or force them to give me a place in their home. He was like most of the people I knew—eager and needful of my love; for I was quite remarkable and made incredible games, which were better than movies or than the heart could hope for. I was a dream come true. I was smart and virtuous (no one knew that I occasionally stole from the dime store) and fairly attractive, maybe even very attractive. I was often funny and always interesting. I had read everything and knew everything and got unbelievable grades. Of course I was someone whose love was desired. Mother, my teachers, my sister, girls at school, other boys—they all wanted me to love them.

But I wanted them to love me first.

None of them did. I was fierce and solitary and acrid, marching off the little mile from school, past the post office, all yellow brick and chrome, and my two locust trees (water, water everywhere and not a drop to drink), and there was no one who loved me first. I could see a hundred cravennesses in the people I knew, a thousand flaws, a million weaknesses. If I had to love first, I would love only perfection. Of course, I could help heal the people I knew if I loved them. No, I said to myself, why should I give them everything when they give me nothing? How many hurts and shynesses and times of walking up the back stairs had made me that way? I don't know. All I know is that Edward needed my love and I wouldn't give it to him. I was only thirteen. There isn't much you can blame a boy of thirteen for, but I'm not thinking of the blame; I'm thinking of all the years that might have been—if I'd only known then what I know now. The waste, the God-awful waste.

Really, that's all there is to this story. The boy I was, the child Edward was. That and the terrible desire to suddenly turn and run shouting back through the corridors of time, screaming at the boy I was, searching him out, and pounding on his chest: Love him, you damn fool, love him.

1954

THE MAGIC BARREL

Bernard Malamud

Not long ago there lived in uptown New York, in a small, almost meager room, though crowded with books, Leon Finkle, a rabbinical student in the Yeshivah University. Finkle, after six years of study, was to be ordained in June and had been advised by an acquaintance that he might find it easier to win himself a congregation if he were married. Since he had no present prospects of marriage, after two tormented days of turning it over in his mind, he called in Pinye Salzman, a marriage broker, whose two-line advertisement he had read in the *Forward*.

The matchmaker appeared one night out of the dark fourth-floor hallway of the graystone rooming house, grasping a black, strapped portfolio that had been worn thin with use. Salzman, who had been long in the business, was of slight but dignified build, wearing an old hat and an overcoat too short and tight for him. He smelled frankly of fish, which he loved to eat, and although he was missing a few teeth, his presence was not displeasing, because of an amiable manner curiously contrasted by mournful eyes. His voice, his lips, his wisp of beard, his bony fingers were animated, but give him a moment of repose, and his mild blue eyes soon revealed a depth of sadness, a characteristic that put Leo a little at ease although the situation, for him, was inherently tense.

He at once informed Salzman why he had asked him to come, explaining that his home was in Cleveland, and that but for his parents, who had married comparatively late in life, he was alone in the world. He had for six years devoted himself entirely to his studies, as a result of which, quite understandably, he had found himself without time for a social life and the company of young women. Therefore he thought it the better part of trial and error—of embarrassing fumbling—to call in an experienced person to advise him in these matters. He remarked in passing that the function of the marriage broker was ancient and honorable, highly approved in the Jewish community, because it made practical the necessary without hindering joy. Moreover, his own parents had been brought together by a matchmaker. They had made, if not a financially profitable marriage—since neither had possessed any worldly goods to speak of—at least a successful one in the sense of their everlasting devotion to one another. Salzman listened in embarrassed surprise, sensing a sort of apology. Later, however, he experienced a glow of pride in his work, an emotion that had left him years ago, and he heartily approved of Finkle.

The two men went to their business. Leo had led Salzman to the only clear place in the room, a table near a window that overlooked the lamplit city. He seated himself at the matchmaker's side but facing him, attempting by an act of will to suppress the unpleasant tickle in his throat. Salzman eagerly unstrapped his portfolio and removed a loose rubber band from a thin packet of much-handled cards. As he flipped through them, a gesture and sound that physically hurt Leo, the student pretended not to see and gazed steadfastly out the window. Although it was still February, winter was on its last legs, signs of which he had for the first time in years begun to notice. He now observed the round white moon, moving high in the sky through a cloud-menagerie, and watched with half-open mouth as it penetrated a huge hen and dropped out of her like an egg laying itself. Salzman, though pretending through eyeglasses he had just slipped on, to be engaged in scanning the writing on the cards, stole occasional glances at the young man's distinguished face, noting with pleasure the long, severe scholar's nose, brown eyes heavy with learning, sensitive yet ascetic lips, and a certain almost hollow quality of the dark cheeks. He gazed around at shelves upon shelves of books and let out a soft but happy sigh.

When Leo's eyes fell upon the cards, he counted six spread out in Salzman's hand.

'So few?' he said in disappointment.

'You wouldn't believe me how much cards I got in my office,' Salzman replied. 'The drawers are already filled to the top, so I keep them now in a barrel, but is every girl good for a new rabbi?'

Leo blushed at this, regretting all he had revealed of himself in a curriculum vitae he had sent to Salzman. He had thought it best to acquaint him with his strict standards and specifications, but in having done so now felt he had told the marriage broker more than was absolutely necessary.

He hesitantly inquired, 'Do you keep photographs of your clients on file?'

'First comes family, amount of dowry, also what kind promises,' Salzman replied, unbuttoning his tight coat and settling himself in the chair. 'After comes pictures, rabbi.'

'Call me Mr Finkle. I'm not a rabbi yet.'

Salzman said he would, but instead called him doctor, which he changed to rabbi when Leo was not listening too attentively.

Salzman adjusted his horn-rimmed spectacles, gently cleared his throat and read in an eager voice the contents of the top card:

'Sophie P. Twenty-four years. Widow for one year. No children. Educated high school and two years college. Father promises eight thousand dollars. Has wonderful wholesale business. Also real estate. On mother's side comes teachers, also one actor. Well known on Second Avenue.'

Leo gazed up in surprise. 'Did you say a widow?'

'A widow don't mean spoiled, rabbi. She lived with her husband maybe four months. He was a sick boy, she made a mistake to marry him.'

'Marrying a widow has never entered my mind.'

'This is because you have no experience. A widow, specially if she is young and healthy like this girl, is a wonderful person to marry. She will be thankful to you the rest of her life. Believe me, if I was looking now for a bride, I would marry a widow.'

Leo reflected, then shook his head.

Salzman hunched his shoulders in an almost imperceptible gesture of disappointment. He placed the card down on the wooden table and began to read another:

'Lily H. High-school teacher. Regular. Not a substitute. Has savings and new Dodge car. Lived in Paris one year. Father is a successful dentist thirty-five years. Interested in professional man. Well Americanized family. Wonderful opportunity.'

'I know her personally,' said Salzman. 'I wish you could see this girl. She is a doll. Also very intelligent. All day you could talk to her about books and theater and what not. She also knows current events.'

'I don't believe you mentioned her age?'

'Her age?' Salzman said, raising his brows in surprise. 'Her age is thirty-two years.'

Leo said after a while, 'I'm afraid that seems a little too old.'

Salzman let out a laugh. 'So how old are you, rabbi?'

'Twenty-seven.'

'So what is the difference, tell me, between twenty-seven and thirty-two? My own wife is seven years older than me. So what did I suffer?—Nothing. If Rothschild's daughter wants to marry you, would you say on account of her age, no?'

'Yes,' Leo said dryly.

Salzman shook off the no in the yes. 'Five years don't mean a thing. I give you my word that when you will live with her for one week, you will forget her age. What does it mean five years—that she lived more and knows more than somebody who is younger? On this girl, God bless her, years are not wasted. Each one that it comes makes better the bargain.'

'What subject does she teach in high school?'

'Languages. If you heard the way she reads French, you will think it is music. I am in the business twenty-five years, and I recommend her with my whole heart. Believe me, I know what I'm talking, rabbi.'

'What's on the next card?' Leo said abruptly.

Salzman reluctantly turned up the third card:

'Ruth K. Nineteen years. Honor student. Father offers thirteen thousand dollars cash to the right bridegroom. He is a medical doctor. Stomach specialist with marvelous practice. Brother-in-law owns own garment business. Particular people.'

Salzman looked up as if he had read his trump card.

'Did you say nineteen?' Leo asked with interest.

'On the dot.'

'Is she attractive?' He blushed. 'Pretty?'

Salzman kissed his fingertips. 'A little doll. On this I give you my word. Let me call the father tonight and you will see what means pretty.'

But Leo was troubled. 'You're sure she's that young?'

'This I am positive. The father will show you the birth certificate.'

'Are you positive there isn't something wrong with her?' Leo insisted.

'Who says there is wrong?'

'I don't understand why an American girl her age should go to a marriage broker.'

A smile spread over Salzman's face.

'So for the same reason you went, she comes.'

Leo flushed. 'I am pressed for time.'

Salzman, realizing he had been tactless, quickly explained. 'The father came, not her. He wants she should have the best, so he looks around himself. When we will locate the right boy, he will introduce him and encourage. This makes a better marriage than if a young girl without experience takes for herself. I don't have to tell you this.'

'But don't you think this young girl believes in love?' Leo spoke uneasily.

Salzman was about to guffaw, but caught himself and said soberly, 'Love comes with the right person, not before.'

Leo parted dry lips but did not speak. Noticing that Salzman had snatched a quick glance at the next card, he cleverly asked, 'How is her health?'

'Perfect,' Salzman said, breathing with difficulty. 'Of course, she is a little lame on her right foot from an auto accident that it happened to her when she was twelve years, but nobody notices on account she is so brilliant and also beautiful.'

Leo got up heavily and went to the window. He felt curiously bitter and upbraided himself for having called in the marriage broker. Finally, he shook his head.

'Why not?' Salzman persisted, the pitch of his voice rising.

'Because I hate stomach specialists.'

'So what do you care what is his business? After you marry her, do you need him? Who says he must come every Friday night to your house?'

Ashamed of the way the talk was going, Leo dismissed Salzman, who went home with melancholy eyes.

Though he had felt only relief at the marriage broker's departure, Leo was in low spirits the next day. He explained it as arising from Salzman's failure to produce a suitable bride for him. He did not care for his type of clientele. But when Leo found himself hesitating over whether to seek out another matchmaker, one more polished than Pinye, he wondered if it could be—his protestations to the contrary, and although he honored his father and mother—that he did not, in essence, care for the matchmaking institution? This thought he quickly put out of his mind yet found himself still upset. All day he ran around in a fog—missed an important appointment, forgot to give out his laundry, walked out of a Broadway cafeteria without paying and had to run back with the ticket in his hand; had even not recognized his landlady in the street when she passed with a friend and courteously called out, 'A good evening to you, Doctor Finkle.' By nightfall, however, he had regained sufficient calm to sink his nose into a book and there found peace from his thoughts.

Almost at once there came a knock on the door. Before Leo could say enter, Salzman, commercial cupid, was standing in the room. His face was gray and meager, his expression hungry, and he looked as if he would expire on his feet. Yet the marriage broker managed, by some trick of the muscles, to display a broad smile.

'So good evening. I am invited?'

Leo nodded, disturbed to see him again, yet unwilling to ask him to leave.

Beaming still, Salzman laid his portfolio on the table. 'Rabbi, I got for you tonight good news.'

'I've asked you not to call me rabbi. I'm still a student.'

'Your worries are finished. I have for you a first-class bride.'

'Leave me in peace concerning this subject.' Leo pretended lack of interest.

'The world will dance at your wedding.'

'Please, Mr Salzman, no more.'

'But first must come back my strength,' Salzman said weakly. He fumbled with the portfolio straps and took out of the leather case an oily paper bag, from which he extracted a hard seeded roll and a small smoked whitefish. With one motion of his hand he stripped the fish out of its skin and began ravenously to chew. 'All day in a rush,' he muttered.

Leo watched him eat.

'A sliced tomato you have maybe?' Salzman hesitantly inquired.

'No.'

The marriage broker shut his eyes and ate. When he had finished, he carefully cleaned up the crumbs and rolled up the remains of the fish in the paper bag. His spectacled eyes roamed the room until he discovered, amid some piles of books, a one-burner gas stove. Lifting his hat, he humbly asked, 'A glass of tea you got, rabbi?'

Conscience-stricken, Leo rose and brewed the tea. He served it with a chunk of lemon and two cubes of lump sugar, delighting Salzman.

After he had drunk his tea, Salzman's strength and good spirits were restored.

'So tell me, rabbi,' he said amiably, 'you considered any more the three clients I mentioned yesterday?'

'There was no need to consider.'

'Why not?'

'None of them suits me.'

'What, then, suits you?'

Leo let it pass because he could give only a confused answer.

Without waiting for a reply, Salzman asked, 'You remember this girl I talked to you—the high-school teacher?'

'Age thirty-two?'

But, surprisingly, Salzman's face lit in a smile. 'Age twenty-nine.'

Leo shot him a look. 'Reduced from thirty-two?'

'A mistake,' Salzman avowed. 'I talked today with the dentist. He took me to his safety deposit box and showed me the birth certificate. She was twenty-nine last August. They made her a party in the mountains where she went for her vacation. When her father spoke to me the first time, I forgot to write the age and I told you thirty-two, but now I remember this was a different client, a widow.'

'The same one you told me about? I thought she was twenty four?'

'A different. Am I responsible that the world is filled with widows?'

'No, but I'm not interested in them, nor for that matter, in schoolteachers.'

Salzman passionately pulled his clasped hands to his breast. Looking at the ceiling he exclaimed, 'Jewish children, what can I say to somebody that he is not interested in high-school teachers? So what then you are interested?'

Leo flushed but controlled himself.

'In who else you will be interested,' Salzman went on, 'if you not interested in this fine girl that she speaks four languages and has personally in the bank ten thousand dollars? Also her father guarantees further twelve thousand. Also she has a new car, wonderful clothes, talks on all subjects, and she will give you a first-class home and children. How near do we come in our life to paradise?'

'If she's so wonderful, why wasn't she married ten years ago?'

'Why,' said Salzman with a heavy laugh. '—Why? Because she is *partikler*. This is why. She wants only the *best*.'

Leo was silent, amused at how he had trapped himself. But Salzman had aroused his interest in Lily H., and he began seriously to consider calling on her. When the marriage broker observed how intently Leo's mind was at work on the facts he had supplied, he felt positive they would soon come to an agreement.

Late Saturday afternoon, conscious of Salzman, Leo Finkle walked with Lily Hirschorn along Riverside Drive. He walked briskly and erectly, wearing with distinction the black fedora he had that morning taken with trepidation out of the dusty hatbox on his closet shelf, and the heavy black Saturday coat he had thoroughly whisked clean. Leo also owned a walking stick, a present from a distant relative, but had decided not to use it. Lily, petite and not unpretty, had on something signifying the approach of spring. She was *au courant*, animatedly, with all subjects, and he weighed her words and found her surprisingly sound—score another for Salzman, whom he uneasily sensed to be somewhere around, hiding perhaps high in a tree along the street, flashing the lady signals; or perhaps a cloven-hoofed Pan, piping nuptial ditties as he danced his invisible way before them, strewing wild buds on the walk and purple summer grapes in their path, symbolizing fruit of a union, of which there was yet none.

Lily startled Leo by remarking, 'I was thinking of Mr Salzman, a curious figure, wouldn't you say?'

Not certain what to answer, he nodded.

She bravely went on, blushing, 'I for one am grateful for his introducing us. Aren't you?'

He courteously replied, 'I am.'

'I mean,' she said with a little laugh—and it was all in good taste, or at least gave the effect of being not in bad—'do you mind that we came together so?'

He was not afraid of her honesty, recognizing that she meant to set the relationship aright, and understanding that it took a certain amount of experience in life, and courage, to want to do it quite that way. One had to have some sort of past to make that kind of beginning.

He said that he did not mind. Salzman's function was traditional and honorable—valuable for what it might achieve, which, he pointed out, was frequently nothing.

Lily agreed with a sigh. They walked on for a while, and she said after a long silence, again with a nervous laugh, 'Would you mind if I asked you something a little bit personal? Frankly, I find the subject fascinating.' Although Leo shrugged, she want on half embarrassedly, 'How was it that you came to your calling? I mean, was it a sudden passionate inspiration?'

Leo, after a time, slowly replied, 'I was always interested in the Law.'

'You saw it revealed in it the presence of the Highest?'

He nodded and changed the subject. 'I understand you spent a little time in Paris, Miss Hirschorn?'

'Oh, did Mr Salzman tell you, Rabbi Finkle?' Leo winced, but she went on, 'It was ages and ages ago and almost forgotten. I remember I had to return for my sister's wedding.'

But Lily would not be put off. 'When,' she asked in a trembly voice, 'did you become enamored of God?'

He stared at her. Then it came to him that she was talking not about Leo Finkle, but a total stranger, some mystical figure, perhaps even passionate prophet that Salzman had conjured up for her—no relation to the living or dead. Leo trembled with rage and weakness. The trickster had obviously sold her a bill of goods, just as he had him, who'd expected to become acquainted with a young lady of twenty-nine, only to behold, the moment he laid eyes upon her strained and anxious face, a woman past thirty-five and aging very rapidly. Only his self-control, he thought, had kept him this long in her presence.

'I am not,' he said gravely, 'a talented religious person,' and in seeking words to go on, found himself possessed by fear and shame. 'I think,' he said in a strained manner, 'that I came to God not because I love Him, but because I did not.'

This confession he spoke harshly because its unexpectedness shook him.

Lily wilted. Leo saw a profusion of loaves of bread sailing like ducks high over his head, not unlike the loaves by which he had counted himself to sleep last night. Mercifully, then, it snowed, which he would not put past Salzman's machinations.

He was infuriated with the marriage broker and swore he would throw him out of the room the moment he reappeared. But Salzman did not come that night, and when Leo's anger had subsided, an unaccountable despair grew in its place. At first he thought this was caused by his disappointment in Lily, but before long it became evident that he had involved himself with Salzman without a true knowledge of his own intent. He gradually realized—with an emptiness that seized him with six hands—that he had called in the broker to find him a bride because he was incapable of doing it himself. This terrifying insight he had derived as a result of his meeting and conversation with Lily Hirschorn. Her probing questions had somehow irritated him into revealing—to himself more than her—the true nature of his relationship with God, and from that it had come upon him, with shocking force, that apart from his parents, he had never loved anyone. Or perhaps it went the other way, that he did not love God so well as he might, because he had not loved man. It seemed to Leo that his whole life stood starkly revealed and he saw himself, for the first time, as he truly was—unloved and loveless. This bitter but somehow not fully unexpected revelation brought him to a point of panic controlled only by extraordinary effort. He covered his face with his hands and wept.

The week that followed was the worst of his life. He did not eat, and lost weight. His beard darkened and grew ragged. He stopped attending lectures and seminars and almost never opened a book. He seriously considered leaving the Yeshivah, although he was deeply troubled at the thought of the loss of all his years of study—saw them like pages from a book strewn over the city—and at the devastating effect of this decision upon his parents. But he had lived without knowledge of himself, and never in the Five Books and all the Commentaries—*mea culpa*—had the truth been revealed to him. He did not know where to turn, and in all this desolating loneliness there was no *to whom*, although he often thought of Lily but not once could bring himself to go downstairs and make the call. He became touchy and irritable, especially with his landlady, who asked him all manner of questions; on the other hand, sensing his own disagreeableness, he waylaid her on the stairs and apologized abjectly until, mortified, she ran from him. Out of this, however, he drew the consolation that he was yet a Jew and that a Jew suffered. But gradually, as the long and terrible week drew to a close, he regained his composure and some idea of purpose in life: to go on as planned. Although he was imperfect, the ideal was not. As for his quest of a bride, the thought of continuing afflicted him with anxiety and heartburn, yet perhaps with this new knowledge of himself he would be more successful than in the past. Perhaps love would now come to him and a bride to that love. And for this sanctified seeking who needed a Salzman?

The marriage broker, a skeleton with haunted eyes, returned that very night. He looked, withal, the picture of frustrated expectancy— as if he had steadfastly waited the week at Miss Lily Hirschorn's side for a telephone call that never came.

Casually coughing, Salzman came immediately to the point: 'So how did you like her?'

Leo's anger rose and he could not refrain from chiding the matchmaker: 'Why did you lie to me, Salzman?'

Salzman's pale face went dead white, as if the world had snowed on him.

'Did you not state that she was twenty-nine?' Leo insisted.

'I give you my word—'

'She was thirty-five. *At least* thirty-five.'

'Of this I would not be too sure. Her father told me—'

'Never mind. The worst of it was that you lied to her.'

'How did I lie to her, tell me?'

'You told her things about me that weren't true. You made me out to be more, consequently less than I am. She had in mind a totally different person, a sort of semimystical Wonder Rabbi.'

'All I said, you was a religious man.'

'I can imagine.'

Salzman sighed. 'This is my weakness that I have,' he confessed. 'My wife says to me I shouldn't be a salesman, but when I have two fine people that they would be wonderful to be married, I am so happy that I talk too much.' He smiled wanly. 'This is why Salzman is a poor man.'

Leo's anger went. 'Well, Salzman, I'm afraid that's all.'

The marriage broker fastened hungry eyes on him.

'You don't want any more a bride?'

'I do,' said Leo, 'but I have decided to seek her in a different way. I am no longer interested in an arranged marriage. To be frank, I now admit the necessity of premarital love. That is, I want to be in love with the one I marry.'

'Love?' said Salzman, astounded. After a moment he said, 'For us, our love is our life, not for the ladies. In the ghetto they—'

'I know, I know,' said Leo. 'I've thought of it often. Love, I have said to myself, should be a by-product of living and worship rather than its own end. Yet for myself I find it necessary to establish the level of my need and to fulfill it.'

Salzman shrugged but answered, 'Listen, rabbi, if you want love, this I can find for you also. I have such beautiful clients that you will love them the minute your eyes will see them.'

Leo smiled unhappily. 'I'm afraid you don't understand.'

But Salzman hastily unstrapped his portfolio and withdrew a manila packet from it.

'Pictures,' he said, quickly laying the envelope on the table.

Leo called after him to take the pictures away, but as if on the wings of the wind, Salzman had disappeared.

March came. Leo had returned to his regular routine. Although he felt not quite himself yet—lacked energy—he was making plans for a more active social life. Of course it would cost something, but he was an expert in cutting corners; and when there were no corners left he could make circles rounder. All the while Salzman's pictures had lain on the table, gathering dust. Occasionally as Leo sat studying, or enjoying a cup of tea, his eyes fell on the manila envelope, but he never opened it.

The days went by, and no social life to speak of developed with a member of the opposite sex—it was difficult, given the circumstances of his situation. One morning Leo toiled up the stairs to his room and stared out the window at the city. Although the day was bright, his view of it was dark. For some time he watched the people in the street below hurrying along and then turned with a heavy heart to his little room. On the table was the packet. With a sudden relentless gesture he tore it open. For a half-hour he stood there, in a state of excitement, examining the photographs of the ladies Salzman had included. Finally, with a deep sigh he put them down. There were six, of varying degrees of attractiveness, but look at them long enough and they all became Lily Hirschorn: all past their prime, all starved behind bright smiles, not a true personality in the lot. Life, despite their anguished struggles and frantic yoohooings, had passed them by; they were photographs in a brief case that stank of fish. After a while, however, as Leo attempted to return the pictures into the envelope, he found another in it, a small snapshot of the type taken by a machine for a quarter. He gazed at it a moment and let out a cry.

Her face deeply moved him. Why, he could at first not say. It gave him the impression of youth—all spring flowers—yet age—a sense of having been used to the bone, wasted; this all came from the eyes, which were hauntingly familiar, yet absolutely strange. He had a strong impression that he had met her before, but try as he might he could not place her, although he could almost recall her name, as if he had read it written in her own handwriting. No, this couldn't be; he would have remembered her. It was not, he affirmed, that she had an extraordinary beauty—no, although her face was attractive enough; it was that *something* about her moved him. Feature for feature, even some of the ladies of the photographs could do better; but she leaped forth to the heart—had lived, or wanted to—more than just wanted, perhaps regretted it—had somehow deeply suffered: it could be seen in the depths of those reluctant eyes, and from the way the light enclosed and shone from her, and within her, opening whole realms of possibility: this was her own. Her he desired. His head ached and eyes narrowed with the intensity of his gazing, then, as if a black fog had blown up in the mind, he experienced fear of her and was aware that he had received an impression, somehow, of filth. He shuddered, saying softly, it is thus with us all. Leo brewed some tea in a small pot and sat sipping it, without sugar, to calm himself. But before he had finished drinking, again with excitement he examined the face and found it good: good for him. Only such a one could truly understand Leo Finkle and help him to seek whatever he was seeking. How she had come to be among the discards in Salzman's barrel he could never guess, but he knew he must urgently go find her.

Leo rushed downstairs, grabbed up the Bronx telephone book, and searched for Salzman's home address. He was not listed, nor was his office. Neither was he in the Manhattan book. But Leo remembered having written down the address on a slip of paper after he had read Salzman's advertisement in the 'personals' column of the *Forward*. He ran up to his room and tore through his papers, without luck. It was exasperating. Just when he needed the matchmaker he was nowhere to be found. Fortunately Leo remembered to look in his wallet. There on a card he found his name written and a Bronx address. No phone number was listed, which, Leo now recalled, was the reason he had originally communicated with Salzman by letter. He got on his coat, put a hat on over his skull cap and hurried to the subway station. All the way to the far end of the Bronx he sat on the edge of his seat. He was more than once tempted to take out the picture and see if the girl's face was as he remembered it, but he refrained, allowing the snapshot to remain in his inside coat pocket, content to have her so close. When the train pulled into the station, he was waiting at the door and bolted out. He quickly located the street Salzman had advertised.

The building he sought was less than a block from the subway, but it was not an office building, nor even a loft, nor a store in which one could rent office space. It was an old and grimy tenement. Leo found Salzman's name in pencil on a soiled tag under the bell and climbed three dark flights to his apartment. When he knocked, the door was opened by a thin, asthmatic, gray-haired woman, in felt slippers.

'Yes?' she said, expecting nothing. She listened without listening. He could have sworn he had seen her somewhere before but knew it was an illusion.

'Salzman—does he live here? Pinye Salzman,' he said, 'the matchmaker?'

She stared at him a long time. 'Of course.'

He felt embarrassed. 'Is he in?'

'No.' Her mouth was open, but she offered nothing more.

'This is urgent. Can you tell me where his office is?'

'In the air.' She pointed upward.

'You mean he has no office?' Leo said.

'In his socks.'

He peered into the apartment. It was sunless and dingy, one large room divided by a half-open curtain, beyond which he could see a sagging metal bed. The nearer side of the room was crowded with rickety chairs, old bureaus, a three-legged table, racks of cooking utensils, and all the apparatus of a kitchen. But there was no sign of Salzman or his magic barrel, probably also a figment of his imagination. An odor of frying fish made Leo weak to the knees.

'Where is he?' he insisted. 'I've got to see your husband.'

At length she answered, 'So who knows where he is? Every time he thinks a new thought he runs to a different place. Go home, he will find you.'

'Tell him Leo Finkle.'

She gave no sign that she had heard.

He went downstairs, deeply depressed.

But Salzman, breathless, stood waiting at his door.

Leo was overjoyed and astounded. 'How did you get here before me?'

'I rushed.'

'Come inside.'

They entered. Leo fixed tea and a sardine sandwich for Salzman.

As they were drinking, he reached behind him for the packet of pictures and handed them to the marriage broker.

Salzman put down his glass and said expectantly, 'You found maybe somebody you like?'

'Not among these.'

The marriage broker turned sad eyes away.

'Here's the one I like.' Leo held forth the snapshot.

Salzman slipped on his glasses and took the picture into his trembling hand. He turned ghastly and let out a miserable groan.

'What's the matter?' cried Leo.

'Excuse me. Was an accident this picture. She is not for you.'

Salzman frantically shoved the manila packet into his portfolio. He thrust the snapshot into his pocket and fled down the stairs.

Leo, after momentary paralysis, gave chase and cornered the marriage broker in the vestibule. The landlady made hysterical outcries, but neither of them listened.

'Give me back the picture, Salzman.'

'No.' The pain in his eyes was terrible.

'Tell me where she is then.'

'This I can't tell you. Excuse me.'

He made to depart, but Leo, forgetting himself, seized the matchmaker by his tight coat and shook him frenziedly.

'Please,' sighed Salzman. '*Please*.'

Leo ashamedly let him go. 'Tell me who she is,' he begged. 'It's very important for me to know.'

'She is not for you. She is a wild one—wild, without shame. This is not a bride for a rabbi.'

'What do you mean wild?'

'Like an animal. Like a dog. For her to be poor was a sin. This is why she is dead now.'

'In God's name, what do you mean?'

'Her I can't introduce to you,' Salzman cried.

'Why are you so excited?'

'Why he asks,' Salzman said, bursting into tears. 'This is my baby, my Stella, she should burn in hell.'

Leo hurried up to bed and hid under the covers. Under the covers he thought his whole life through. Although he soon fell asleep he could not sleep her out of his mind. He woke, beating his breast. Though he prayed to be rid of her, his prayers went unanswered. Through days of torment he struggled endlessly not to love her; fearing success, he escaped it. He then concluded to convert her to goodness, himself to God. The idea alternately nauseated and exalted him.

He perhaps did not know that he had come to a final decision until he encountered Salzman in a Broadway cafeteria. He was sitting alone at a rear table, sucking the bony remains of a fish. The marriage broker appeared haggard, and transparent to the point of vanishing.

Salzman looked up at first without recognizing him. Leo had

grown a pointed beard, and his eyes were weighted with wisdom.

'Salzman,' he said, 'love has at last come to my heart.'

'Who can love from a picture?' mocked the marriage broker.

'It is not impossible.'

'If you can love her, then you can love anybody. Let me show you some new clients that they just sent me their photographs. One is a little doll.'

'Just her I want,' Leo murmured.

'Don't be a fool, doctor. Don't bother with her.'

'Put me in touch with her, Salzman,' Leo said humbly. 'Perhaps I can do her a service.'

Salzman had stopped chewing, and Leo understood with emotion that it was now arranged.

Leaving the cafeteria, he was, however, afflicted by a tormenting suspicion that Salzman had planned it all to happen this way.

Leo was informed by letter that she would meet him on a certain corner, and she was there one spring night, waiting under a street lamp. He appeared, carrying a small bouquet of violets and rosebuds. Stella stood by the lamppost, smoking. She wore white with red shoes, which fitted his expectations, although in a troubled moment he had imagined the dress red, and only the shoes white. She waited uneasily and shyly. From afar he saw that her eyes—clearly her father's—were filled with desperate innocence. He pictured, in hers, his own redemption. Violins and lit candles revolved in the sky. Leo ran forward with the flowers outthrust.

Around the corner, Salzman, leaning against a wall, chanted prayers for the dead.

1954

GOOD COUNTRY PEOPLE
Flannery O'Connor

Besides the neutral expression that she wore when she was alone, Mrs Freeman had two others, forward and reverse, that she used for all her human dealings. Her forward expression was steady and driving like the advance of a heavy truck. Her eyes never swerved to left or right but turned as the story turned as if they followed a yellow line down the center of it. She seldom used the other expression because it was not often necessary for her to retract a statement, but when she did, her face came to a complete stop, there was an almost imperceptible movement of her black eyes, during which they seemed to be receding, and then the observer would see that Mrs Freeman, though she might stand there as real as several grain sacks thrown on top of each other, was no longer there in spirit. As for getting anything across to her when this was the case, Mrs Hopewell had given it up. She might talk her head off. Mrs Freeman could never be brought to admit herself wrong on any point. She would stand there and if she could be brought to say anything, it was something like, 'Well, I wouldn't of said it was and I wouldn't of said it wasn't,' or letting her gaze range over the top kitchen shelf where there was an assortment of dusty bottles, she might remark, 'I see you ain't ate many of them figs you put up last summer.'

They carried on their most important business in the kitchen at breakfast. Every morning Mrs Hopewell got up at seven o'clock and lit her gas heater and Joy's. Joy was her daughter, a large blonde girl who had an artificial leg. Mrs Hopewell thought of her as a child though she was thirty-two years old and highly educated. Joy would get up while her mother was eating and lumber into the bathroom and slam the door, and before long, Mrs Freeman would arrive at the back door. Joy would hear her mother call, 'Come on in,' and then they would talk for a while in low voices that were indistinguishable in the bathroom. By the time Joy came in, they had usually finished the weather report and were on one or the other of Mrs Freeman's daughters, Glynese or Carramae, Joy called them Glycerin and Caramel. Glynese, a redhead, was eighteen and had many admirers;

Carramae, a blonde, was only fifteen but already married and pregnant. She could not keep anything in her stomach. Every morning Mrs Freeman told Mrs Hopewell how many times she had vomited since the last report.

Mrs Hopewell liked to tell people that Glynese and Carramae were two of the finest girls she knew and that Mrs Freeman was a *lady* and that she was never ashamed to take her anywhere or introduce her to anybody they might meet. Then she would tell how she had happened to hire the Freemans in the first place and how they were a godsend to her and how she had had them four years. The reason for her keeping them so long was that they were not trash. They were good country people. She had telephoned the man whose name they had given as a reference and he had told her that Mr Freeman was a good farmer but that his wife was the nosiest woman ever to walk the earth. 'She's got to be into everything,' the man said. 'If she don't get there before the dust settles, you can bet she's dead, that's all. She'll want to know all your business. I can stand him real good,' he had said, 'but me nor my wife neither could have stood that woman one more minute on this place.' That had put Mrs Hopewell off for a few days.

She had hired them in the end because there were no other applicants but she had made up her mind beforehand exactly how she would handle the woman. Since she was the type who had to be into everything, then, Mrs Hopewell had decided, she would not only let her be into everything, she would *see to it* that she was into everything—she would give her the responsibility of everything, she would put her in charge. Mrs Hopewell had no bad qualities of her own but she was able to use other people's in such a constructive way that she never felt the lack. She had hired the Freemans and she had kept them four years.

Nothing is perfect. This was one of Mrs Hopewell's favorite sayings. Another was: that is life! And still another, the most important, was: well, other people have their opinions too. She would make these statements, usually at the table, in a tone of gentle insistence as if no one held them but her, and the large hulking Joy, whose constant outrage had obliterated every expression from her face, would stare just a little to the side of her, her eyes icy blue, with the look of someone who has achieved blindness by an act of will and means to keep it.

When Mrs Hopewell said to Mrs Freeman that life was like that,

Mrs Freeman would say, 'I always said so myself.' Nothing had been arrived at by anyone that had not first been arrived at by her. She was quicker than Mr Freeman. When Mrs Hopewell said to her after they had been on the place a while, 'You know, you're the wheel behind the wheel,' and winked, Mrs Freeman had said, 'I know it. I've always been quick. It's some that are quicker than others.'

'Everybody is different,' Mrs Hopewell said.

'Yes, most people is,' Mrs Freeman said.

'It takes all kinds to make the world.'

'I always said it did myself.'

The girl was used to this kind of dialogue for breakfast and more of it for dinner; sometimes they had it for supper too. When they had no guest they ate in the kitchen because that was easier. Mrs Freeman always managed to arrive at some point during the meal and to watch them finish it. She would stand in the doorway if it were summer but in the winter she would stand with one elbow on top of the refrigerator and look down on them, or she would stand by the gas heater, lifting the back of her skirt slightly. Occasionally she would stand against the wall and roll her head from side to side. At no time was she in any hurry to leave. All this was very trying on Mrs Hopewell but she was a woman of great patience. She realized that nothing is perfect and that in the Freemans she had good country people and that if, in this day and age, you get good country people, you had better hang onto them.

She had had plenty of experience with trash. Before the Freemans she had averaged one tenant family a year. The wives of these farmers were not the kind you would want to be around you for very long. Mrs Hopewell, who had divorced her husband long ago, needed someone to walk over the fields with her; and when Joy had to be impressed for these services, her remarks were usually so ugly and her face so glum that Mrs Hopewell would say, 'If you can't come pleasantly, I don't want you at all,' to which the girl, standing square and rigid-shouldered with her neck thrust slightly forward, would reply, 'If you want me, here I am—LIKE I AM.'

Mrs Hopewell excused this attitude because of the leg (which had been shot off in a hunting accident when Joy was ten). It was hard for Mrs Hopewell to realize that her child was thirty-two now and that for more than twenty years she had had only one leg. She thought of her still as a child because it tore her heart to think instead of the poor stout girl in her thirties who had never danced a step or had any *normal* good times. Her name was really Joy but as soon as she was twenty-one and away from home, she had had it legally changed. Mrs Hopewell was certain that she had thought and thought until she had hit upon the ugliest name in any language. Then she had gone and had the beautiful name, Joy, changed without telling her mother until after she had done it. Her legal name was Hulga.

When Mrs Hopewell thought the name, Hulga, she thought of the broad blank hull of a battleship. She would not use it. She continued to call her Joy to which the girl responded but in a purely mechanical way.

Hulga had learned to tolerate Mrs Freeman who saved her from taking walks with her mother. Even Glynese and Carramae were useful when they occupied attention that might otherwise have been directed at her. At first she had thought she could not stand Mrs Freeman for she had found that it was not possible to be rude to her. Mrs Freeman would take on strange resentments and for days together she would be sullen but the source of her displeasure was always obscure; a direct attack, a positive leer, blatant ugliness to her face—these never touched her. And without warning one day, she began calling her Hulga.

She did not call her that in front of Mrs Hopewell who would have been incensed but when she and the girl happened to be out of the house together, she would say something and add the name Hulga to the end of it, and the big spectacled Joy-Hulga would scowl and redden as if her privacy had been intruded upon. She considered the name her personal affair. She had arrived at it first purely on the basis of its ugly sound and then the full genius of its fitness had struck her. She had a vision of the name working like the ugly sweating Vulcan who stayed in the furnace and to whom, presumably, the goddess had to come when called. She saw it as the name of her highest creative act. One of her major triumphs was that her mother had not been able to turn her dust into Joy, but the greater one was that she had been able to turn it herself into Hulga. However, Mrs Freeman's relish for using the name only irritated her. It was as if Mrs Freeman's beady steel-pointed eyes had penetrated far enough behind her face to reach some secret fact. Something about her seemed to fascinate Mrs Freeman and then one day Hulga realized that it was the artificial leg. Mrs Freeman had a special fondness for the details of secret infections, hidden deformities, assaults upon children. Of diseases, she preferred the lingering or incurable. Hulga had heard

Mrs Hopewell give her the details of the hunting accident, how the leg had been literally blasted off, how she had never lost consciousness. Mrs Freeman could listen to it any time as if it had happened an hour ago.

When Hulga stumped into the kitchen in the morning (she could walk without making the awful noise but she made it—Mrs Hopewell was certain—because it was ugly-sounding), she glanced at them and did not speak. Mrs Hopewell would be in her red kimono with her hair tied around her head in rags. She would be sitting at the table, finishing her breakfast and Mrs Freeman would be hanging by her elbow outward from the refrigerator, looking down at the table. Hulga always put her eggs on the stove to boil and then stood over them with her arms folded, and Mrs Hopewell would look at her—a kind of indirect gaze divided between her and Mrs Freeman—and would think that if she would only keep herself up a little, she wouldn't be so bad looking. There was nothing wrong with her face that a pleasant expression wouldn't help. Mrs Hopewell said that people who looked on the bright side of things would be beautiful even if they were not.

Whenever she looked at Joy this way she could not help but feel that it would have been better if the child had not taken the Ph.D. It had certainly not brought her out any and now that she had it, there was no more excuse for her to go to school again. Mrs Hopewell thought it was nice for girls to go to school to have a good time but Joy had 'gone through.' Anyhow, she would not have been strong enough to go again. The doctors had told Mrs Hopewell that with the best of care, Joy might see forty-five. She had a weak heart. Joy had made it plain that if it had not been for this condition, she would be far from these red hills and good country people. She would be in a university lecturing to people who knew what she was talking about. And Mrs Hopewell could very well picture her there, looking like a scarecrow and lecturing to more of the same. Here she went about all day in a six-year-old skirt and a yellow sweat shirt with a faded cowboy on a horse embossed on it. She thought this was funny; Mrs Hopewell thought it was idiotic and showed simply that she was still a child. She was brilliant but she didn't have a grain of sense. It seemed to Mrs Hopewell that every year she grew less like other people and more like herself—bloated, rude, and squint-eyed. And she said such strange things! To her own mother she had said—without warning, without excuse, standing up in the middle of a meal with her face purple and her mouth half full—'Woman! do you ever look inside? Do you ever look inside and see what you are *not*? God!' she had cried sinking down again and staring at her plate, 'Malebranche was right: we are not our own light. We are not our own light!' Mrs Hopewell had no idea to this day what brought that on. She had only made the remark, hoping Joy would take it in, that a smile never hurt anyone.

The girl had taken the Ph.D. in philosophy and this left Mrs Hopewell at a complete loss. You could say, 'My daughter is a nurse,' or 'My daughter is a schoolteacher,' or even, 'My daughter is a chemical engineer.' You could not say, 'My daughter is a philosopher.' That was something that had ended with the Greeks and Romans. All day Joy sat on her neck in a deep chair, reading. Sometimes she went for walks but she didn't like dogs or cats or birds or flowers or nature or nice young men. She looked at nice young men as if she could smell their stupidity.

One day Mrs Hopewell had picked up one of the books the girl had just put down and opening it at random, she read, 'Science, on the other hand, has to assert its soberness and seriousness afresh and declare that it is concerned solely with what-is. Nothing—how can it be for science anything but a horror and a phantasm? If science is right, then one thing stands firm: science wishes to know nothing of nothing. Such is after all the strictly scientific approach to Nothing. We know it by wishing to know nothing of Nothing.' These words had been underlined with a blue pencil and they worked on Mrs Hopewell like some evil incantation in gibberish. She shut the book quickly and went out of the room as if she were having a chill.

This morning when the girl came in, Mrs Freeman was on Carramae. 'She thrown up four times after supper,' she said, 'and was up twict in the night after three o'clock. Yesterday she didn't do nothing but ramble in the bureau drawer. All she did. Stand up there and see what she could run up on.'

'She's got to eat,' Mrs Hopewell muttered, sipping her coffee, while she watched Joy's back at the stove. She was wondering what the child had said to the Bible salesman. She could not imagine what kind of a conversation she could possibly have had with him.

He was a tall gaunt hatless youth who had called yesterday to sell them a Bible. He had appeared at the door, carrying a large black suitcase that weighted him so heavily on one side that he had to brace himself against the door facing. He seemed on the point of collapse but he said in a cheerful voice, 'Good morning, Mrs Cedars!' and set the suitcase down on the mat. He was not a bad-looking young man though he had on a bright blue suit and yellow socks that were not pulled up far enough. He had prominent face bones and a streak of sticky-looking brown hair falling across his forehead.

'I'm Mrs Hopewell,' she said.

'Oh!' he said, pretending to look puzzled but with his eyes sparkling, 'I saw it said "The Cedars" on the mailbox so I thought you was Mrs Cedars!' and he burst out in a pleasant laugh. He picked up the satchel and under cover of a pant, he fell forward into her hall. It was rather as if the suitcase had moved first, jerking him after it. 'Mrs Hopewell!' he said and grabbed her hand. 'I hope you are well!' and he laughed again and then all at once his face sobered completely. He paused and gave her a straight earnest look and said, 'Lady, I've come to speak of serious things.'

'Well, come in,' she muttered, none too pleased because her dinner was almost ready. He came into the parlor and sat down on the edge of a straight chair and put the suitcase between his feet and glanced around the room as if he were sizing her up by it. Her silver gleamed on the two sideboards; she decided he had never been in a room as elegant as this.

'Mrs Hopewell,' he began, using her name in a way that sounded almost intimate, 'I know you believe in Chrustian service.'

'Well yes,' she murmured.

'I know,' he said and paused, looking very wise with his head cocked on one side, 'that you're a good woman. Friends have told me.'

Mrs Hopewell never liked to be taken for a fool. 'What are you selling?' she asked.

'Bibles,' the young man said and his eye raced around the room before he added, 'I see you have no family Bible in your parlor, I see that is the one lack you got!'

Mrs Hopewell could not say, 'My daughter is an atheist and won't let me keep the Bible in the parlor.' She said, stiffening slightly, 'I keep my Bible by my bedside.' This was not the truth. It was in the attic somewhere.

'Lady,' he said, 'the word of God ought to be in the parlor.'

'Well, I think that's a matter of taste,' she began. 'I think . . . '

'Lady,' he said, 'for a Chrustian, the word of God ought to be in every room in the house besides in his heart. I know you're a

Chrustian because I can see it in every line of your face.'

She stood up and said, 'Well, young man, I don't want to buy a Bible and I smell my dinner burning.'

He didn't get up. He began to twist his hands and looking down at them, he said softly, 'Well lady, I'll tell you the truth—not many people want to buy one nowadays and besides, I know I'm real simple. I don't know how to say a thing but to say it. I'm just a country boy.' He glanced up into her unfriendly face. 'People like you don't like to fool with country people like me!'

'Why!' she cried, 'good country people are the salt of the earth! Besides, we all have different ways of doing, it takes all kinds to make the world go 'round. That's life!'

'You said a mouthful,' he said.

'Why, I think there aren't enough good country people in the world!' she said, stirred. 'I think that's what's wrong with it!'

His face had brightened. 'I didn't inraduce myself,' he said. 'I'm Manley Pointer from out in the country around Willohobie, not even from a place, just from near a place.'

'You wait a minute,' she said. 'I have to see about my dinner.' She went out to the kitchen and found Joy standing near the door where she had been listening.

'Get rid of the salt of the earth,' she said, 'and let's eat.'

Mrs Hopewell gave her a pained look and turned the heat down under the vegetables. '*I* can't be rude to anybody,' she murmured and went back into the parlor.

He had opened the suitcase and was sitting with a Bible on each knee.

'You might as well put those up,' she told him. 'I don't want one.'

'I appreciate your honesty,' he said. 'You don't see any more real honest people unless you go way out in the country.'

'I know,' she said, 'real genuine folks!' Through the crack in the door she heard a groan.

'I guess a lot of boys come telling you they're working their way through college,' he said, 'but I'm not going to tell you that. Somehow,' he said, 'I don't want to go to college. I want to devote my life to Chrustian service. See,' he said, lowering his voice, 'I got this heart condition. I may not live long. When you know it's something wrong with you and you may not live long, well then, lady . . . ' He paused, with his mouth open, and stared at her.

He and Joy had the same condition! She knew that her eyes were filling with tears but she collected herself quickly and murmured, 'Won't you stay for dinner? We'd love to have you!' and was sorry the instant she heard herself say it.

'Yes mam,' he said in an abashed voice, 'I would sher love to do that!'

Joy had given him one look on being introduced to him and then throughout the meal had not glanced at him again. He had addressed several remarks to her, which she had pretended not to hear. Mrs Hopewell could not understand deliberate rudeness, although she lived with it, and she felt she had always to overflow with hospitality to make up for Joy's lack of courtesy. She urged him to talk about himself and he did. He said he was the seventh child of twelve and that his father had been crushed under a tree when he himself was eight year old. He had been crushed very badly, in fact, almost cut in two and was practically not recognizable. His mother had got along the best she could by hard working and she had always seen that her children went to Sunday School and that they read the Bible every evening. He was now nineteen year old and he had been selling Bibles for four months. In that time he had sold seventy-seven Bibles and had the promise of two more sales. He wanted to become a missionary because he thought that was the way you could do most for people. 'He who losest his life shall find it,' he said simply and he was so sincere, so genuine and earnest that Mrs Hopewell would not for the world have smiled. He prevented his peas from sliding onto the table by blocking them with a piece of bread which he later cleaned his plate with. She could see Joy observing sidewise how he handled his knife and fork and she saw too that every few minutes, the boy would dart a keen appraising glance at the girl as if he were trying to attract her attention.

After dinner Joy cleared the dishes off the table and disappeared and Mrs Hopewell was left to talk with him. He told her again about his childhood and his father's accident and about various things that had happened to him. Every five minutes or so she would stifle a yawn. He sat for two hours until finally she told him she must go because she had an appointment in town. He packed his Bibles and thanked her and prepared to leave, but in the doorway he stopped and wrung her hand and said that not on any of his trips had he met a lady as nice as her and he asked if he could come again. She had said she would always be happy to see him.

Joy had been standing in the road, apparently looking at

something in the distance, when he came down the steps toward her, bent to the side with his heavy valise. He stopped where she was standing and confronted her directly. Mrs Hopewell could not hear what he said but she trembled to think what Joy would say to him. She could see that after a minute Joy said something and that then the boy began to speak again, making an excited gesture with his free hand. After a minute Joy said something else at which the boy began to speak once more. Then to her amazement, Mrs Hopewell saw the two of them walk off together, toward the gate. Joy had walked all the way to the gate with him and Mrs Hopewell could not imagine what they had said to each other, and she had not yet dared to ask.

Mrs Freeman was insisting upon her attention. She had moved from the refrigerator to the heater so that Mrs Hopewell had to turn and face her in order to seem to be listening. 'Glynese gone out with Harvey Hill again last night,' she said. 'She had this sty.'

'Hill,' Mrs Hopewell said absently, 'is that the one who works in the garage?'

'Nome, he's the one that goes to chiropracter school,' Mrs Freeman said. 'She had this sty. Been had it two days. So she says when he brought her in the other night he says, "Lemme get rid of that sty for you," and she says, "How?" and he says, "You just lay yourself down acrost the seat of that car and I'll show you." So she done it and he popped her neck. Kept on a-popping it several times until she made him quit. This morning,' Mrs Freeman said, 'she ain't got no sty. She ain't got no traces of a sty.'

'I never heard of that before,' Mrs Hopewell said.

'He ast her to marry him before the Ordinary,' Mrs Freeman went on, 'and she told him she wasn't going to be married in no *office*.'

'Well, Glynese is a fine girl,' Mrs Hopewell said. 'Glynese and Carramae are both fine girls.'

'Carramae said when her and Lyman was married Lyman said it sure felt sacred to him. She said he said he wouldn't take five hundred dollars for being married by a preacher.'

'How much would he take?' the girl asked from the stove.

'He said he wouldn't take five hundred dollars,' Mrs Freeman repeated.

'Well we all have work to do,' Mrs Hopewell said.

'Lyman said it just felt more sacred to him,' Mrs Freeman said. 'The doctor wants Carramae to eat prunes. Says instead of medicine. Says them cramps is coming from pressure. You know where I think it is?'

'She'll be better in a few weeks,' Mrs Hopewell said.

'In the tube,' Mrs Freeman said. 'Else she wouldn't be as sick as she is.'

Hulga had cracked her two eggs into a saucer and was bringing them to the table along with a cup of coffee that she had filled too full. She sat down carefully and began to eat, meaning to keep Mrs Freeman there by questions if for any reason she showed an inclination to leave. She could perceive her mother's eye on her. The first round-about question would be about the Bible salesman and she did not wish to bring it on. 'How did he pop her neck?' she asked.

Mrs Freeman went into a description of how he had popped her neck. She said he owned a '55 Mercury but that Glynese said she would rather marry a man with only a '36 Plymouth who would be married by a preacher. The girl asked what if he had a '32 Plymouth and Mrs Freeman said what Glynese had said was a '36 Plymouth.

Mrs Hopewell said there were not many girls with Glynese's common sense. She said what she admired in those girls was their common sense. She said that reminded her that they had had a nice visitor yesterday, a young man selling Bibles. 'Lord,' she said, 'he bored me to death but he was so sincere and genuine I couldn't be rude to him. He was just good country people, you know,' she said, '—just the salt of the earth.'

'I seen him walk up,' Mrs Freeman said, 'and then later—I seen him walk off,' and Hulga could feel the slight shift in her voice, the slight insinuation, that he had not walked off alone, had he? Her face remained expressionless but the color rose into her neck and she seemed to swallow it down with the next spoonful of egg. Mrs Freeman was looking at her as if they had a secret together.

'Well, it takes all kinds of people to make the world go 'round,' Mrs Hopewell said. 'It's very good we aren't all alike.'

'Some people are more alike than others,' Mrs Freeman said.

Hulga got up and stumped, with about twice the noise that was necessary, into her room and locked the door. She was to meet the Bible salesman at ten o'clock at the gate. She had thought about it half the night. She had started thinking of it as a great joke and then she had begun to see profound implications in it. She had lain in bed imagining dialogues for them that were insane on the surface but that reached below to depths that no Bible salesman would be aware of. Their conversation yesterday had been of this kind.

He had stopped in front of her and had simply stood there. His face was bony and sweaty and bright, with a little pointed nose in the center of it, and his look was different from what it had been at the dinner table. He was gazing at her with open curiosity, with fascination, like a child watching a new fantastic animal at the zoo, and he was breathing as if he had run a great distance to reach her. His gaze seemed somehow familiar but she could not think where she had been regarded with it before. For almost a minute he didn't say anything. Then on what seemed an insuck of breath, he whispered, 'You ever ate a chicken that was two days old?'

The girl looked at him stonily. He might have just put this question up for consideration at the meeting of a philosophical association. 'Yes,' she presently replied as if she had considered it from all angles.

'It must have been mighty small!' he said triumphantly and shook all over with little nervous giggles, getting very red in the face, and subsiding finally into his gaze of complete admiration, while the girl's expression remained exactly the same.

'How old are you?' he asked softly.

She waited some time before she answered. Then in a flat voice she said, 'Seventeen.'

His smiles came in succession like waves breaking on the surface of a little lake. 'I see you got a wooden leg,' he said. 'I think you're brave. I think you're real sweet.'

The girl stood blank and solid and silent.

'Walk to the gate with me,' he said. 'You're a brave sweet little thing and I liked you the minute I seen you walk in the door.'

Hulga began to move forward.

'What's your name?' he asked, smiling down on the top of her head.

'Hulga,' she said.

'Hulga,' he murmured, 'Hulga. Hulga. I never heard of anybody name Hulga before. You're shy, aren't you, Hulga?' he asked.

She nodded, watching his large red hand on the handle of the giant valise.

'I like girls that wear glasses,' he said. 'I think a lot. I'm not like these people that a serious thought don't ever enter their heads. It's because I may die.'

'I may die too,' she said suddenly and looked up at him. His eyes were very small and brown, glittering feverishly.

'Listen,' he said, 'don't you think some people was meant to meet on account of what all they got in common and all? Like they both think serious thoughts and all?' He shifted the valise to his other hand so that the hand nearest her was free. He caught hold of her elbow and shook it a little. 'I don't work on Saturday,' he said. 'I like to walk in the woods and see what Mother Nature is wearing. O'er the hills and far away. Pic-nics and things. Couldn't we go on a picnic tomorrow? Say yes, Hulga,' he said and gave her a dying look as if he felt his insides about to drop out of him. He had even seemed to sway slightly toward her.

During the night she imagined that she seduced him. She imagined that the two of them walked on the place until they came to the storage barn beyond the two back fields and there, she imagined, that things came to such a pass that she very easily seduced him and that then, of course, she had to reckon with his remorse. True genius can get an idea across even to an inferior mind. She imagined that she took his remorse in hand and changed it into a deeper understanding of life. She took all his shame away and turned it into something useful.

She set off for the gate at exactly ten o'clock, escaping without drawing Mrs Hopewell's attention. She didn't take anything to eat, forgetting that food is usually taken on a picnic. She wore a pair of slacks and a dirty white shirt, and as an afterthought, she had put some Vapex on the collar of it since she did not own any perfume. When she reached the gate no one was there.

She looked up and down the empty highway and had the furious feeling that she had been tricked, that he had only meant to make her walk to the gate after the idea of him. Then suddenly he stood up, very tall, from behind a bush on the opposite embankment. Smiling, he lifted his hat which was new and wide-brimmed. He had not worn it yesterday and she wondered if he had bought it for the occasion. It was toast-colored with a red and white band around it and was slightly too large for him. He stepped from behind the bush still carrying the black valise. He had on the same suit and the same yellow socks sucked down in his shoes from walking. He crossed the highway and said, 'I knew you'd come!'

The girl wondered acidly how he had known this. She pointed to the valise and asked, 'Why did you bring your Bibles?'

He took her elbow, smiling down on her as if he could not stop. 'You can never tell when you'll need the word of God, Hulga,' he said. She had a moment in which she doubted that this was actually happening and then they began to climb the embankment. They went down into the pasture toward the woods. The boy walked lightly by her side, bouncing on his toes. The valise did not seem to be heavy today; he even swung it. They crossed half the pasture without saying anything and then, putting his hand easily on the small of her back, he asked softly, 'Where does your wooden leg join on?'

She turned an ugly red and glared at him and for an instant the boy looked abashed. 'I didn't mean you no harm,' he said, 'I only meant you're so brave and all. I guess God takes care of you.'

'No,' she said, looking forward and walking fast, 'I don't even believe in God.'

At this he stopped and whistled. 'No!' he exclaimed as if he were too astonished to say anything else.

They walked on and in a second he was bouncing at her side, fanning with his hat. 'That's very unusual for a girl,' he remarked, watching her out of the corner of his eye. When they reached the edge of the wood, he put his hand on her back again and drew her against him without a word and kissed her heavily.

The kiss, which had more pressure than feeling behind it, produced that extra surge of adrenalin in the girl that enables one to carry a packed trunk out of a burning house, but in her, the power went at once to the brain. Even before he released her, her mind, clear and detached and ironic anyway, was regarding him from a great distance, with amusement but with pity. She had never been kissed before and she was pleased to discover that it was an unexceptional experience and all a matter of the mind's control. Some people might enjoy drain water if they were told it was vodka. When the boy, looking expectant but uncertain, pushed her gently away, she turned and walked on, saying nothing as if such business, for her, were common enough.

He came along panting at her side, trying to help her when he saw a root that she might trip over. He caught and held back the long swaying blades of thorn vine until she had passed beyond them. She led the way and he came breathing heavily behind her. Then they came out on a sunlit hillside, sloping softly into another one a little smaller. Beyond, they could see the rusted top of the old barn where the extra hay was stored.

The hill was sprinkled with small pink weeds. 'Then you ain't saved?' he asked suddenly, stopping.

The girl smiled. It was the first time she had smiled at him at all. 'In my economy,' she said, 'I'm saved and you are damned but I told you I don't believe in God.'

Nothing seemed to destroy the boy's look of admiration. He gazed at her now as if the fantastic animal at the zoo had put its paw through the bars and given him a loving poke. She thought he looked as if he wanted to kiss her again and she walked on before he had the chance.

'Ain't there somewheres we can sit down sometime?' he murmured, his voice softening toward the end of the sentence.

'In that barn,' she said.

They made for it rapidly as if it might slide away like a train. It was a large two-story barn, cool and dark inside. The boy pointed up the ladder that led into the loft and said, 'It's too bad we can't go up there.'

'Why can't we?' she asked.

'Yer leg,' he said reverently.

The girl gave him a contemptuous look and putting both hands on the ladder, she climbed it while he stood below, apparently awestruck. She pulled herself expertly through the opening and then looked down at him and said, 'Well, come on if you're coming,' and he began to climb the ladder, awkwardly bringing the suitcase with him.

'We won't need the Bible,' she observed.

'You never can tell,' he said, panting. After he had got into the loft, he was a few seconds catching his breath. She had sat down in a pile of straw. A wide sheath of sunlight, filled with dust particles, slanted over her. She lay back against a bale, her face turned away, looking out the front opening of the barn where hay was thrown from a wagon into the loft. The two pink-speckled hillsides lay back against a dark ridge of woods. The sky was cloudless and cold blue. The boy dropped down by her side and put one arm under her and the other over her and began methodically kissing her face, making little noises like a fish. He did not remove his hat but it was pushed far enough back not to interfere. When her glasses got in his way, he took them off and slipped them into his pocket.

The girl at first did not return any of the kisses but presently she began to and after she had put several on his cheek, she reached his lips and remained there, kissing him again and again as if she were trying to draw all the breath out of him. His breath was clear and sweet like a child's and the kisses were sticky like a child's. He mumbled about loving her and about knowing when he first seen her that he loved her, but the mumbling was like the sleepy fretting of a child being put to sleep by his mother. Her mind, throughout this, never stopped or lost itself for a second to her feelings. 'You ain't said you loved me none,' he whispered finally, pulling back from her. 'You got to say that.'

She looked away from him off into the hollow sky and then down at a black ridge and then down farther into what appeared to be two green swelling lakes. She didn't realize he had taken her glasses but this landscape could not seem exceptional to her for she seldom paid any close attention to her surroundings.

'You got to say it,' he repeated. 'You got to say you love me.'

She was always careful how she committed herself. 'In a sense,' she began, 'if you use the word loosely, you might say that. But it's not a word I use. I don't have illusions. I'm one of those people who see *through* to nothing.'

The boy was frowning. 'You got to say it. I said it and you got to say it,' he said.

The girl looked at him almost tenderly. 'You poor baby,' she murmured. 'It's just as well you don't understand,' and she pulled him by the neck, face-down, against her. 'We are all damned,' she said, 'but some of us have taken off our blindfolds and see that there's nothing to see. It's a kind of salvation.'

The boy's astonished eyes looked blankly through the ends of her hair. 'OK,' he almost whined, 'but do you love me or don'tcher?'

'Yes,' she said and added, 'in a sense. But I must tell you something. There mustn't be anything dishonest between us.' She lifted his head and looked him in the eye. 'I am thirty years old,' she said. 'I have a number of degrees.'

The boy's look was irritated but dogged. 'I don't care,' he said. 'I don't care a thing about what all you done. I just want to know if you love me or don'tcher?' and he caught her to him and wildly planted her face with kisses until she said, 'Yes, yes.'

'OK then,' he said, letting her go. 'Prove it.'

She smiled, looking dreamily out on the shifty landscape. She had seduced him without even making up her mind to try. 'How?' she asked, feeling that he should be delayed a little.

He leaned over and put his lips to her ear. 'Show me where your wooden leg joins on,' he whispered.

The girl uttered a sharp little cry and her face instantly drained of color. The obscenity of the suggestion was not what shocked her. As a child she had sometimes been subject to feelings of shame but education had removed the last traces of that as a good surgeon scrapes for cancer; she would no more have felt it over what he was asking than she would have believed in his Bible. But she was as sensitive about the artificial leg as a peacock about his tail. No one ever touched it but her. She took care of it as someone else would his soul, in private and almost with her own eyes turned away. 'No,' she said

'I known it,' he muttered, sitting up. 'You're just playing me for a sucker.'

'Oh no no!' she cried. 'It joins on at the knee. Only at the knee. Why do you want to see it?'

The boy gave her a long penetrating look. 'Because,' he said, 'it's what makes you different. You ain't like anybody else.'

She sat staring at him. There was nothing about her face or her round freezing-blue eyes to indicate that this had moved her; but she felt as if her heart had stopped and left her mind to pump her blood. She decided that for the first time in her life she was face to face with real innocence. This boy, with an instinct that came from beyond wisdom, had touched the truth about her. When after a minute, she said in a hoarse high voice, 'All right,' it was like surrendering to him completely. It was like losing her own life and finding it again, miraculously, in his.

Very gently he began to roll the slack leg up. The artificial limb, in a white sock and brown flat shoe, was bound in a heavy material like canvas and ended in an ugly jointure where it was attached to the stump. The boy's face and his voice were entirely reverent as he uncovered it and said, 'Now show me how to take it off and on.'

She took it off for him and put it back on again and then he took it off himself, handling it as tenderly as if it were a real one. 'See!' he said with a delighted child's face. 'Now I can do it myself!'

'Put it back on,' she said. She was thinking that she would run away with him and that every night he would take the leg off and every morning put it back on again. 'Put it back on,' she said.

'Not yet,' he murmured, setting it on its foot out of her reach. 'Leave it off for a while. You got me instead.'

She gave a little cry of alarm but he pushed her down and began to kiss her again. Without the leg she felt entirely dependent on him. Her brain seemed to have stopped thinking altogether and to be about some other function it was not very good at. Different expressions raced back and forth over her face. Every now and then the boy, his eyes like two steel spikes, would glance behind him where the leg stood. Finally she pushed him off and said, 'Put it back on me now.'

'Wait,' he said. He leaned the other way and pulled the valise toward him and opened it. It had a pale blue spotted lining and there were only two Bibles in it. He took one of these out and opened the cover of it. It was hollow and contained a pocket flask of whiskey, a pack of cards, and a small blue box with printing on it. He laid these out in front of her one at a time in an evenly-spaced row, like one presenting offerings at the shrine of a goddess. He put the blue box in her hand. THIS PRODUCT TO BE USED ONLY FOR THE PREVENTION OF DISEASE, she read, and dropped it. The boy was unscrewing the top of the flask. He stopped and pointed, with a smile, to the deck of cards. It was not an ordinary deck but one with an obscene picture on the back of each card. 'Take a swig,' he said, offering her the bottle first. He held it in front of her, but like one mesmerized, she did not move.

Her voice when she spoke had an almost pleading sound. 'Aren't you,' she murmured, 'aren't you just good country people?'

The boy cocked his head. He looked as if he were just beginning to understand that she might be trying to insult him. 'Yeah,' he said, curling his lip slightly, 'but it ain't held me back none. I'm as good as you any day in the week.'

'Give me my leg,' she said.

He pushed it farther away with his foot. 'Come on now, let's begin to have us a good time,' he said coaxingly. 'We ain't got to know one another good yet.'

'Give me my leg!' she screamed and tried to lunge for it but he pushed her down easily.

'What's the matter with you all of a sudden?' he asked, frowning as he screwed the top on the flask and put it quickly back inside the Bible. 'You just a while ago said you didn't believe in nothing. I thought you was some girl!'

Her face was almost purple. 'You're a Christian!' she hissed. 'You're a fine Christian! You're just like them all—say one thing and do another. You're a perfect Christian, you're . . . '

The boy's mouth was set angrily. 'I hope you don't think,' he said in a lofty indignant tone, 'that I believe in that crap! I may sell Bibles but I know which end is up and I wasn't born yesterday and I know

152

where I'm going!'

'Give me my leg!' she screeched. He jumped up so quickly that she barely saw him sweep the cards and the blue box into the Bible and throw the Bible into the valise. She saw him grab the leg and then she saw it for an instant slanted forlornly across the inside of the suitcase with a Bible at either side of its opposite ends. He slammed the lid shut and snatched up the valise and swung it down the hold and then stepped through himself.

When all of him had passed but his head, he turned and regarded her with a look that no longer had any admiration in it. 'I've gotten a lot of interesting things,' he said. 'One time I got a woman's glass eye this way. And you needn't to think you'll catch me because Pointer ain't really my name. I use a different name at every house I call at and don't stay nowhere long. And I'll tell you another thing, Hulga,' he said, using the name as if he didn't think much of it, 'you ain't so smart. I been believing in nothing ever since I was born!' and then the toast-colored hat disappeared down the hole and the girl was left, sitting on the straw in the dusty sunlight. When she turned her churning face toward the opening, she saw his blue figure struggling successfully over the green speckled lake.

Mrs Hopewell and Mrs Freeman, who were in the back pasture, digging up onions, saw him emerge a little later from the woods and head across the meadow toward the highway. 'Why, that looks like that nice dull young man that tried to sell me a Bible yesterday,' Mrs Hopewell said, squinting. 'He must have been selling them to the Negroes back in there. He was so simple,' she said, 'but I guess the world would be better off if we were all that simple.'

Mrs Freeman's gaze drove forward and just touched him before he disappeared under the hill. Then she returned her attention to the evil-smelling onion shoot she was lifting from the ground. 'Some can't be that simple,' she said. 'I know I never could.'

1955

IN TIME WHICH MADE A
MONKEY OF US ALL

Grace Paley

No doubt that is Eddie Teitelbaum on the topmost step of 1434, a dark-jawed, bossy youth in need of repair. He is dredging a cavity with a Fudgsicle stick. He is twitching the cotton in his ear. He is sniffing and snarling and swallowing spit because of rotten drainage. But he does not give a damn. Physicalities aside, he is only knee-deep so far in man's inhumanity; he is reconciled to his father's hair-shirted Jacob, Itzik Halbfunt; he is resigned to his place in this brick-lined Utrillo which runs east and west, flat in the sun, a couple of thousand stoop steps. On each step there is probably someone he knows. For the present, no names.

Now look at the little kids that came in those days to buzz at his feet. That is what they did, they gathered in this canyon pass, rumbling at the knee of his glowering personality. Some days he heeded them a long and wiggily line which they followed up and down the street, around the corner, and back to 1434.

On dark days he made elephants, dogs, rabbits, and long-tailed mice for them out of pipe cleaners. 'You can also make a neat ass cleaner this way,' he told them for a laugh, which turned their mothers entirely against him. Well, he was a poor sloppy bastard then, worked Saturdays, Sundays, summers, and holidays, no union contract in his father's pet shop. But penny-wise as regards the kids, he was bubble-gum foolish, for bubble gum strengthens the jaw. He never worried about teeth but approved of dentures and, for that matter, all prostheses.

In the end, man will probably peel his skin (said Eddie) to favor durable plastics, at which time, kaput the race problem. A man will be any color he chooses or translucent too, if the shape and hue of intestines can be made fashionable. Eddie had lots of advance information which did not turn a hair of his head, for he talked of the ineluctable future; but all his buddies, square or queer, clever and sentimental, pricked their ears in tears.

He also warned them of the spies who peeked from windows or plopped like stones on the street which was the kids' by all unentailed rights. Mrs Goredinsky, head spy the consistency of fresh putty, sat on an orange crate every morning, her eye on the door of 1434. Also Mrs Green, Republican poll watcher in November—the rest of the year she waited in her off-the-street doorway, her hand trembling, her head turning one way, then the other.

'Tennis, anyone?' asked Carl Clop, the super's son.

'Let her live,' said Eddie, marking time.

Then one day old Clop, the super, rose from the cellar, scrambling the kids before him with the clatter of bottle tops. He took a stance five steps below Eddie, leaned on his broom, and pretended to make conversation.

'What's the matter, son?' he asked. 'Where's your pals?'

'Under the kitchen table,' said Eddie. 'They got juiced on apricot nectar.'

'Go on, Eddie; you got an in. Who's the bum leaves Kleenex in the halls?'

'I don't know. Goredinsky has a cold for months.'

'Aah, her, what you got against her, a old pot of cabbage soup? You always make a remark on her.'

Out of a dark window in second-floor front a tiny voice sang to the tune of 'My Country, 'tis of Thee':

> *Mrs Goredinsky was a spy*
> *Caught by the FBI.*
> *Tomorrow she will die—*
> *Won't that be good?*

'Get a load of that, Clop,' said Eddie. 'Nobody has any privacy around here, you notice? Listen to me, Clop, in the country in superbia, every sonofabitch has a garage to tinker in. On account of that, great ideas, brilliant inventions come from out of town. Why the hell shouldn't we produce as fine minds as anybody else?'

Now Eddie was just helping Clop out, talkwise, maintaining relations with authority, so to speak. He would have ended the conversation right then and there, since at that moment he was in the mental act of inventing a cockroach segregator, a device which would kill only that cockroach which emigrated out of its pitchy crack into the corn flakes of people. If properly conceived and delicately contrived, all the other cockroaches would be left alone to gum up the lathes and multiply and finally inherit the entire congressional district. Why not?

'Not so dumb,' said Mr Clop. 'Privacy.' Then he let Eddie have a bewhiskered, dead-eye, sideways leer. 'What you need privacy for, you? To stick it into girls?'

No reply.

Clop retrieved the conversation. 'So that's how it goes, that's how they get ahead of us, the farmers. What do you know? How come someone don't figure it out, to educate you kids up a little, especially in summer? The city's the one pays the most taxes. Anyway, what the hell you do on the stoop all day? How come Carl hangs out in front of Michailovitch, morning noon night, every time I look up? Come on, get the hell off the stoop here, you Teitelbaum,' he yelled. 'Stupids. Stick the Kleenex in your pocket.' He gave Eddie a splintery whisk with the broom. He turned away, frowning, thinking. 'Go 'way, bums,' he mumbled at two loitering infants, maybe four years old.

Nevertheless, Clop was a man of grave instinct, a serious man. Three days later he offered Eddie the key to the bicycle and carriage room of 1436, the corner and strategic building.

'For thinking up inventions,' said Clop. 'What are we, animals?' He went on to tell that he was proud to be associated with scientific research. So many boys were out bumming, on the tramp, tramp, tramp. Carl, his own son, looked bad, played poker day and night under the stairs with Shmul, the rabbi's son, a Yankee in a skullcap. Therefore, Clop begged Eddie to persuade Carl to do a little something in his line of thinking and follow-through. He really liked science very much, Mr Clop said, but needed a little encouragement, since he had no mother.

'OK, OK.' Eddie was willing. 'He can help me figure out a rocket to the moon.'

'The moon?' Mr Clop asked. He peeked out the cellar window at a piece of noonday sky.

Right before Eddie's mirage-making eyes for his immediate use was a sink, electricity, gas outlets, and assorted plumbing pipes. What else is basic to any laboratory? Do you think that the Institute for Advanced Studies started out any stronger than that, or all the little padlocked cyclotron houses? The beginning of everything is damp and small, but wide-armed oaks—according to myth, legend, and the folk tales of the people—from solitary acorns grow.

Eddie's first chore was the perfection of the cockroach segregator. At cost plus 6 per cent, he trailed some low-voltage wire all around local kitchen baseboards, which immediately returned to its gummy environment under the linoleum the cockroach which could take a hint. It electrocuted the stubborn fools not meant by Darwin anyway to survive.

There was nothing particularly original in this work. Eddie would be the first to concede that he had been thinking about the country and cows all summer, as well as barbed wire, and had simply applied recollected knowledge to the peculiar conditions of his environment.

'What a hell of a summer this is turning into,' said Carl, plucking a bug off the lab's wire. 'I mean, we ought to have some fun too, Eddie. How about it? I mean, if we were a club, we would be more well rounded.'

'Everyone wants fun,' said Eddie.

'I don't mean real fun,' said Carl. 'We could be a science club. But just you and me—No, I'm sick of that crap. Get some more guys in. Make it an organization, Eddie.'

'Why not?' said Eddie, anxious to get to work.

'Great. I've been thinking of some names. How's ... Advanseers ... Get it?'

'Stinks.'

'I thought of a funny one . . . like on those little cards. How about the Thimkers?'

'Very funny.'

Carl didn't press it. 'All right. but we have to get some more members.'

'Two,' said Eddie, thinking a short laugh.

'Well, OK. But, Eddie, what about girls? I mean, after all, women have the vote a long time. They're doctors and . . . What about Madame Curie? There's others.'

'Please, Carl, lay off. We got about thirteen miles of wire left. I got to figure out something.'

Carl couldn't stop. He liked girls all around him, he said. They made him a sunny, cheerful guy. He could think of wonderful witticisms when they were present. Especially Rita Niskov and Stella Rosenzweig.

He would like to go on, describing, as an example, the Spitz twins, how they were so top-heavy but with hips like boys. Hadn't Eddie seen them afloat at they Seymour Street Pool, water-winged by their airtight tits?

Also darling little Stella Rosenzweig, like a Vassar girl despite being only in third-term high. When you danced with her, you could feel something like pinpricks, because although she was little she was extremely pointed.

Eddie was absolutely flipped by a ground swell of lust just before lunch. To save himself, he coldly said, 'No, no. No girls. Saturday nights they can come over for a little dancing, a little petting. Fix up the place. No girls in the middle of the week.'

He promised, however, to maintain an open line between Carl and the Spitz twins by recruiting for immediate membership their brother Arnold. That was a lucky, quiet choice. Arnold needed a corner in which to paint. He stated that daylight would eventually disappear and with it the myths about northlight. He founded in that dark cellar a school of painters called the Light Breakers, who still work together in a loft on East Twenty-ninth Street under two 25-watt bulbs.

On Carl's recommendation Shmul Klein was ingathered, a great fourth hand, but Eddie said no card tables. Shmul had the face of an unentrammeled guy. Did he make book after school? No, no, he said, rumors multiplied: the truth was single.

He was a journalist of life, as Eddie was a journeyman in knowledge. When questioned about his future, he would guess that he was destined to trip over grants, carrying a fearsome load of scholarships on his way to a soft job in advertising, using a fraction of his potential.

Well, there were others, of course, who glinted around, seeking membership under the impression that a neighborhood cat house was being established. Eddie laughed and pointed to a market glutted by individual initiative, not to mention the way the bottom has fallen out of the virgin as moral counterweight.

It took time out of Eddie to be a club. Whole afternoons and weekends were lost for public reasons. The boys asked him to hold open meetings so that the club's actual disposition would be appreciated by the parents of girls. Eddie talked then on 'The Dispersal of the Galaxies and the Conservation of Matter.' Carl applauded twice, in an anarchy of enthusiasm. Mr Clop listened, was impressed, asked what he could do for them, and then tied their wattage into Mrs Goredinsky's meter.

Eddie offered political lectures, too, as these are times which, if man were human, could titillate his soul. From the four-by-six room which Eddie shared with Itzik Halbfunt, his father's monkey, he saw configurations of disaster revise the sky before anyone even smelled smoke.

'Who was the enemy?' he asked, to needle a little historicity into his clubmates. 'Was it the People of the Sea? Troy? Rome? The Saracens? The Huns? The Russians? The colonies in Africa, the stinking proletariat? The hot owners of capital?'

Typically he did not answer. He let them weave these broad questions on poor pinheaded looms while he slipped into Michailovitch's for a celery tonic.

He shared his profits from the cockroach segregator with the others. This way they took an interest and were courteous enough to heed his philosophic approach, as did the clients to whom he pointed out a human duty to interfere with nature as little as possible except for food-getting (survival), a seminal tragedy which obtains in the wild forests as well.

Reading, thinking on matters beyond the scope of the physical and chemical sciences carried his work from the idealistic cockroach segregator to a telephone dial system for people on relief within a ten-block radius—and finally to the well-known War Attenuator, which activated all his novitiate lab assistants but featured his own lonely patience.

'Eddie, Eddie, you take too much time,' said his father. 'What about us?

'You,' said Eddie.

How could he forget his responsibilities at the Teitelbaum Zoo, a pet shop where three or four mutts, scabby with sawdust, slept in the window? A hundred gallons of goldfish were glassed inside, four canaries singing tu-wit-tu-wu—all waited for him to dump the seeds, the hash, the mash into their dinner buckets. Poor Itzik Halbfunt, the monkey from Paris, France, waited too, nibbling his beret. Itzik looked like Mr Teitelbaum's uncle who had died of Jewishness in the epidemics of '40, '41. For this reason he would never be sold. 'Too bad,' is an outsider's comment, as a certain local Italian would have paid maybe $45 for that monkey.

In sorrow Mr Teitelbaum had turned away forever from his neighbor, man, and for life, then, he squinted like a cat and hopped like a bird and drooped like a dog. Like a parrot, all he could say and repeat when Eddie made his evening break was, 'Eddie, don't leave the door open, me and the birds will fly away.'

'If you got wings, Papa, fly,' said Eddie. And that was Eddie's life for years and years, from childhood on: he shoveled dog shit and birdseed, watching the goldfish float and feed and die in a big glass of water far away from China.

One Monday morning in July, bright and hot and early, Eddie called the boys together for assignments in reconnaissance and mapping. Carl knew the basement extremely well, but Eddie wanted a special listing of doors and windows, their conditions established. There were three buildings involved in this series, 1432, 1434, 1436. He requested that they keep a diary in order to arrive at viable statistics on how many ladies used the laundry facilities at what hours, how hot the hot water generally was at certain specific times.

'Because we are going to work with gases now. Gas expands, compresses, diffuses, and may be liquefied. If there is any danger involved at any point, I will handle it and be responsible. Just don't act like damn fools. I promise you,' he added bitterly, 'a lot of fun.'

He asked them to develop a little competence with tools. Carl as the son of Clop, plumber, electrician, and repairman, was a happy, aggressive teacher. In the noisy washing-machine hours of morning, under Carl's supervision, they drilled barely visible holes in the basement walls and pipe-fitted long-wear rubber tubes. The first series of tests required a network of delicate ducts.

'I am the vena cava and the aorta,' Eddie paraphrased. 'Whatever goes from me must return to me. You be the engineers. Figure out the best way to nourish all outlying areas.'

By 'nourish,' Shmul pointed out, he really meant 'suffocate.'

On the twenty-ninth of July they were ready. At 8.13 a.m. the first small-scale, small-area test took place. At 8.12 a.m., just before the moment of pff, all the business of the cellars was being transacted— garbage transferred from small cans into large ones; early wide-awake grandmas, rocky with insomnia, dumped wash into the big tubs; boys in swimming trunks rolled baby carriages out into the cool morning. A coal truck arrived, shifted, backed up across the sidewalk, stopped, shoved its black ramp into one sooty cellar window, and commenced to roar.

Mr Clop's radio was loud. As he worked, rolling the cans, hoisting them with Carl's help up the wooden cellar steps, arguing with the coalmen about the right of way, he listened to the news. He wanted to know if the sun would roll out, flashy as ever; if there was a chance for rain, as his brother grew tomatoes in Jersey.

At 8.13 a.m. the alarm clock in the laboratory gave the ringing word. Eddie touched a button in the substructure of an ordinary glass coffeepot, from whose spout two tubes proceeded into the wall. A soft hiss followed: the coffeepot steamed and clouded and cleared.

Forty seconds later Mr Clop howled, 'Jesus, who farted?' although the smell was not quite like that at all, Eddie the concoctor knew. It was at least *meant* to be greener, skunkier, closer to the deterrents built into animals and flowers, but stronger. He was informed immediately of a certain success by the bellows of the coal delivery men, the high cries of the old ladies.

Satisfied, Eddie touched another button, this at the base of Mrs Spitz's reconstructed vacuum cleaner. The reverse process used no more than two minutes. The glass clouded, the spout was stoppered, the genie returned.

Eddie knew it would take the boys a little longer to get free of their observation posts and the people who were observing them. During that speck of time his heart sank as hearts may do after a great act of love. He suffered a migraine from acceding desolation. When Carl brought excited news, he listened sadly, for what is life? he thought.

'God, great!' cried Carl. 'History-making! Crazee! Eddie, Eddie, a mystery! No one knows how what where . . .'

'Yet,' Eddie said. 'You better quiet down, Carl.'

'But listen, Eddie, nobody can figure it out,' said Carl. 'How long did it last? It ended before that fat dope, Goredinsky, got out of our toilet. She was hollering and pulling up her bloomers and pulling down her dress. I watched from the door. It laid me sidewise. She's not even supposed to use that toilet. It's ours.'

'Yeh,' said Eddie.

'Wait a minute, wait a minute, listen. My father kept saying, "Jesus dear, did I forget to open an exhaust someplace? Jesus dear, what did I do? Did I wreck up the flues? Tell me, tell me, give me a hint!"'

'Your father's a very nice old guy,' Eddie said coldly.

'Oh, I know that,' said Carl.

'Wonderful head,' said Arnold, who had just entered.

'Look at my father,' Eddie said, taking the dim and agitated view. 'Look at him, he sits in that store, he doesn't shave, maybe twice a week. Sometimes he doesn't move an hour or two. His nose drips, so the birds know he's living. That lousy sonofabitch, he used to be a whole expert on world history, he supports a stinking zoo and that filthy monkey that can't even piss straight.' . . . Bitterness for his cramped style and secondhand pants took his breath away. So he laughed and let them have the facts. 'You know, my old man was so hard up just before he got married and he got such terrific respect for women (he respects women, let me tell you) that you know what he did? He snuck into the Bronx Zoo and he rammed it up a chimpanzee there. You're surprised, aren't you! Listen to me, they shipped that baby away to France. If my father'd've owned up, we'd've been rich. It makes me sore to think about. He'd've been the greatest buggerer in recorded history. He'd be wanted in pigsties and stud farms. They'd telegraph him a note from Irkutsk to get in on those crazy cross-pollination experiments. What he could do to winter wheat! That cocksucker tells everyone he went over to Paris to see if his cousins were alive. He went over to get my big brother Itzik. To bring him home. To aggravate my mother and me.'

'Aw . . . ' said Carl.

'So that's it,' said Shmul, a late reporter, playing alongside Eddie. 'That's how you got so smart. Constant competition with an oddball sibling . . . Aha . . . '

'Please,' said Arnold, his sketch pad wobbly on his knee. 'Please Eddie, raise your arms like that again, like you just did when you were mad. It gives me an idea.'

'Jerks,' said Eddie, and spat on the spotless laboratory floor. 'A bunch of jerks.'

Still and all, the nineteenth-century idea that progress is immanent is absolutely correct. For his sadness dwindled and early August was a time of hard work and glorious conviviality. The mystery of the powerful nontoxic gas from an unknowable source remained. The boys kept their secret. Outsiders wondered. They knew. They swilled Coke like a regiment which has captured all the enemy pinball machines without registering a single tilt.

Saturday nights at the lab were happy, ringing with 45 r.p.m.'s, surrounded by wonderful women. All kinds of whistling adventures were recorded by Shmul . . . He had it all written down: how one night Mr Clop wandered in looking for fuses and found Arnold doing life sketches of Rita Niskov. She held a retort over one breast in order to make technical complications for Arnold, who was ambitious. 'Keep it up, keep it up, son,' mumbled Clop, to whom it was all a misunderstanding.

And another night Blanchie Spitz took off everything but her drawers and her brassière and because of a teaspoon of rum in a quart and a half of Coke decided to do setting-up exercises to the tune of the 'Nutcracker Suite.' 'Ah, Blanchie,' said Carl, nearly nauseous with love, 'do me a belly dance, baby.' 'I don't know what a belly dance is, Carl,' she said, and to the count of eight went into a deep knee bend. Arnold lassoed her with Rita's skirt, which he happened to have in his hand. He dragged Blanchie off to a corner, where he slapped her, dressed her, asked her what her fee was and did it include relatives, and before she could answer he slapped her again, then took her home, Rita's skirt flung over one shoulder. This kind of event will turn an entire neighborhood against the most intense chronology of good works. Rita's skirt, hung by a buttonhole, fluttered for two days from the iron cellar railing and was unclaimed. Girls, Shmul editorialized in his little book, live a stone-age life in a blown-glass cave.

Eddie had to receive most of this chattery matter from Shmul. The truth is that Eddie did not take frequent part in the festivities, as Saturday was his father's movie night. Mr Teitelbaum would have closed the shop, but the manager of the Loew's refused to sell Itzik a ticket. 'Show me,' said Mr Teitelbaum, 'where it says no monkeys.' 'Please,' said the manager, 'this is my busy night.' Itzik had never been alone, for although he was a brilliant monkey, in the world of men he is dumb. 'Ach,' said Mr Teitelbaum, 'you know what it's like to have a monkey for a pet? It's like raising up a moron. You get very attached, no matter what, and very tied down.'

'Still and all, things are picking up around here,' said Carl.

About a week after the unpleasant incident with the girls (which eventually drove the entire Niskov family about six blocks uptown where they were unknown), Eddie asked for an off-schedule meeting. School was due to begin in three weeks, and he was determined to complete the series which would prove his War Attenuator marketable among the nations.

'Don't exaggerate,' said Shmul. 'What we have here is a big smell.'

'Non-toxic,' Eddie pointed out. 'No matter how concentrated, non-toxic. Don't forget that, Klein, because that's the beauty of it. An instrument of war that will not kill. Imagine that.'

'OK,' he said. 'I concede. So?'

'Shmul, you got an eye. What did the people do during the late test? Did they choke? Did their eyes run? What happened?'

'I already told you, Eddie. Nothing happened. They only ran. They ran like hell. They held their noses and they tore out the door and a couple of kids crawled up the coal ramp. Everybody gave a yelp and then ran.'

'What about your father, Carl?'

'Oh, for Christ's sake, if I told you once, I told you twenty times, he got out fast. Then he stood on the steps, holding his nose and figuring out who to pass the buck to.'

'Well, that's what I mean, boys. It's the lesson of the cockroach segregator. The peaceful guy who listens to the warning of his senses will survive generations of defeat. Who needs the inheritance of the louse with all that miserable virulence in his nucleic acid? Who? I haven't worked out the political strategy altogether, but our job here, anyway, is just to figure out the technology.

'OK, now the rubber tubes have to be extended up to the first and second floor of 1432, 1434, 1436—the three attached buildings. Do not drill into Michailovitch on the corner, as this could seep into the ice cream containers and fudge and stuff, and I haven't tested out all comestibles. If you work today and tomorrow, we should be done by Thursday. On Friday the test goes forward; by noon we ought have all reports and know what we have. Any questions? Carl, get the tools, you're in charge. I have to fix this goddamn percolater and see what the motor's like. We'll meet on Friday morning. Same time— 7.30 a.m.'

Then Eddie hurried back to the shop to clean the bird cages which he had forgotten about for days because of the excitement in his mind. Itzik offered him a banana. He accepted. Itzik peeled it for him, then got a banana for himself. He threw the peels into the trash can, for which Eddie kissed him on his foolish face. He jumped to Eddie's shoulder to tease the birds. Eddie did not like him to do this, for those birds will give you psittacosis (said Eddie) if you aggravate them too much. This is an untested hypothesis, but it makes sense; as you know, people who loathe you will sneeze in your face when their mucous membranes are most swollen or when their throat is host to all kinds of cocci.

'Don't, Itzikel,' he said gently, and put the monkey down. Then Itzik hung from Eddie's shoulder by one long arm, eating the banana behind his back. 'That's how I like to see you,' said Mr Teitelbaum when he looked into the shop. 'Once in a while anyway.'

Eddie was near the end of a long summer's labor. He could bear being peaceful and happy.

On Friday morning Carl, Arnold, and Shmul waited outside. They had plenty of bubble gum and lollipops in which Eddie had personally invested. They were responsible for maintaining equilibrium among the little children who might panic. They also had notebooks, and in these reports each boy was expected to cover only one building.

Inside, Eddie played a staccato note on the button under the percolator. After that it was very simple. People poured from the three buildings. Tenants on the upper floors, which were not involved, poked their heads out the windows because of the commotion. The controls were so fine that they had gotten only the barest whiff and had assumed it to be the normal smell of morning rising from the cracked back of the fish market three blocks east.

Eddie had agreed not to leave the laboratory until reports came in from the other boys. He was perplexed when half an hour had passed and they did not appear. There wasn't even a book to read. So he busied himself disconnecting his home-constructed appliances, funneling the residue powder into a paper envelope which he kept in his back pocket. Suddenly he worried about everyone. What could happen to Itsy Bitsy Michailovitch, who sat outside his father's store spinning a yo-yo and singing a no-song to himself all day? He was in fact a goddamn helpless idiot. What about Mrs Spitz, who would surely stop to put her corset on and would faint away and maybe crack her skull on a piece of rococo mahogany? What about heart failure in people over forty? What about the little Susskind kids? They were so wild, so baffled out of sense, they might jump into the dumb-waiter shaft.

He was scrubbing the sink, trying to uproot his miserable notions, when the door opened. Two policemen came in and put their hands on him. Eddie looked up and saw his father. Their eyes met and because of irrevocable pain held. That was the moment (said Shmul, later on after that and other facts) that Eddie fell headfirst into the black heart of a deep depression. This despair required all his personal attention for years.

No one could make proper contact with him again, to tell him the news. Did he know that he had caused the death of all his father's stock? Even the three turtles, damn it, every last minnow, even the worms that were the fishes' Sunday dinner had wriggled their last. The birds were dead at the bottom of their clean cages.

Itzik Halbfunt lay in a coma from which he would not recover. He lay in Eddie's bed on Eddie's new mattress, between Eddie's sheets. 'Let him die at home,' said Mr Teitelbaum, 'not with a bunch of poodles at Speyer's.'

He caressed his scrawny shoulder that was itchy and furry and cried, 'Halbfunt, Halbfunt, you were my little friend.'

No matter how lovingly a person or a doctor rapped at the door to Eddie's mind, Eddie refused to say 'come in.' Carl Clop called loudly, taking a long distance, local stop, suburban train several times to tell Eddie that it was really he who had thought it would be wonderful to see old Teitelbaum run screaming with hysterical Itzik. For the pleasure this sight would give, Carl had connected the rubber tubes to a small vent between the basement of 1436 and the rear of the pet shop. He had waited at the corner and, sure enough, they had come at last, Mr Teitelbaum running and Itzik gasping for breath. Clop's bad luck, said Clop, to have a son who wasn't serious.

Eddie was remanded to the custody of Dr Scott Tully, director of A Home For Boys, in something less than three weeks. The police impounded Shmul's notebooks but learned only literary things about faces and the sex habits of adolescent boys. Also found was an outline of a paper Eddie had planned for the anti-vivisectionist press, describing his adventures as a self-prepared subject for the gas tolerance experiments. It was entitled NO GUINEA PIG FRONTS FOR ME. As any outsider can judge, this is an insane idea.

Eddie was cared for at A Home For Boys by a white-frocked attendant, cross-eyed and muscle-bound, with strong canines oppressing his lower lip, a nose neatly broken and sloppily joined. This was Jim Sunn and he was kind to Eddie. 'Because he's no trouble to me, Mr Teitelbaum, he's a good boy. If he opens his eyes wide, I know he wants to go to the bathroom. He ain't crazy, Mr Teitelbaum, he just got nothing to say right now, is all. I seen a lot of cases, don't you worry.'

Mr Teitelbaum didn't have too much to say himself, and this made him feel united with Eddie. He came every Sunday and sat with him in silence on a bench in the garden behind A Home; in bad weather they met in the parlor, a jolly rectangle scattered with small hooked rugs. They sat for one hour opposite one another in comfortable chairs, peaceful people, then Eddie opened his eyes wide and Jim Sunn said, 'OK. Let's go, buddy. Shut-eye don't hurt the kings of the jungle. Bears hibernate.' Mr Teitelbaum stood on his tiptoes and enfolded Eddie in his arms. 'Sonny, don't worry so much,' he said, then went home.

This situation prevailed for two years. One cold winter day Mr Teitelbaum had the flu and couldn't visit. 'Where the hell's my father?' Eddie growled.

That was the opener. After that Eddie said other things. Before the week had ended, Eddie said, 'I'm sick of peppers, Jim. They give me gas.'

A week later he said, 'What's the news? Long Island sink yet?'

Dr Tully had never anticipated Eddie's return. ('Once they go up this road, they're gone,' he had confided to the newspapermen.) He invited a consultant from a competing but friendly establishment. He was at last able to give Eddie a Rorschach, which restored his confidence in his original pessimism.

'Let him have more responsibility,' the consultant suggested, which they did at once, allowing him because of his background to visit the A Home For Boys' Zoo. He was permitted to fondle a rabbit and tease two box turtles. There was a fawn, caged and sick. Also a swinging monkey, but Eddie didn't bat an eyelash. That night he vomited. 'What's with the peppers, Jimmy? Can't that dope cook? Only with peppers?'

Dr Tully explained that Eddie was now a helper. As soon as there was a vacancy, he would be given sole responsibility for one animal. 'Thank God,' Mr Teitelbaum said. 'A dumb animal is a good friend.'

At last a boy was cured, sent home to his mother; a vacancy existed. Dr Tully considered this a fortunate vacancy, for the cured boy had been in charge of the most popular snake in the zoo. The popularity of the snake had made the boy very popular. The popularity of the boy had increased his self-confidence; he had become vice-president of the Boys' Assembly; he had acquired friends and sycophants, he had become happy, cured, and had been returned to society.

On the very first day Eddie proved his mettle. He cleaned the cage with his right hand, holding the snake way out with his left. He had many admirers immediately.

'When you go home, could I have the job?' asked a very pleasant small boy who was only mildly retarded, but some father was willing to lay out a fortune because he was ashamed. 'I'm not going anywhere, sonny,' said Eddie. 'I like it here.'

On certain afternoons, shortly after milk and cookies, Eddie had to bring a little white mouse to his snake. He slipped the mouse into the cage, and that is why this snake was so popular: the snake did not eat

167

the mouse immediately. At four o'clock the boys began to gather. They watched the mouse cowering in the corner. They watched the lazy snake wait for his hungry feelings to tickle him all along his curly interior. Every now and then he hiked his spine and raised his head, and the boys breathed hard. Sometime between four-thirty and six o'clock he would begin to slither aimlessly around the cage. The boys laid small bets on the time, winning and losing chunks of chocolate cake or a handful of raisins. Suddenly, but without fuss (and one had to be really watching), the snake stretched his long body, opened his big mouth, and gulped the little live mouse, who always went down squeaking.

Eddie could not disapprove, because this was truly the nature of the snake. But he pulled his cap down over his eyes and turned away.

Jimmy Sunn told him at supper one night, 'Guess what I heard. I heard you're acquiring back your identity. Not bad.'

'My identity?' asked Eddie.

A week later Eddie handed in a letter of resignation. He sent a copy to his father. The letter said: 'Thank you, Dr Tully. I know who I am. I am no mouse killer. I am Eddie Teitelbaum, the Father of the Stink Bomb, and I am known for my Dedication to Cause and my Fearlessness in the Face of Effect. Do not bother me any more. I have nothing to say. Sincerely.'

Dr Tully wrote a report in which he pointed with pride to his consistent pessimism in the case of Eddie Teitelbaum. This was considered remarkable, in the face of so much hope, and it was remembered by his peers.

While Eddie was making the decision to go out of his mind as soon as possible, other decisions were being made elsewhere. Mr Teitelbaum, for instance, decided to die of grief and old age—which frequently overlap—and that was the final decision for all Teitelbaums. Shmul sat down to think and was disowned by his father.

Arnold ran away to East Twenty-ninth Street, where he built up a lovely bordello of naked oils at considerable effort and expense.

But Carl, the son of Clop, had tasted with Eddie's tongue. He went to school and stayed for years in order to become an atomic physicist for the Navy. Nowadays on the 8.07 Carl sails out into the hophead currents of our time, fights the undertow with little beep-beep signals. He has retained his cheerful disposition and for this service to the world has just received a wife who was washed out of the

Rockettes for being too beautiful.

The War Attenuator has been bottled weak under pressure. It is sometimes called Teitelbaum's Mixture, and its ingredients have been translated into Spanish on the label. It is one of the greatest bug killers of all time. Unfortunately it is sometimes hard on philodendrons and old family rubber plants.

Mrs Goredinsky still prefers to have her kitchen protected by the Segregator. An old-fashioned lady, she drops in bulk to her knees to scrub the floor. She cannot help seeing the cockroach caught and broiled in his own juice by the busy A.C. She flicks the cockroach off the wall. She smiles and praises Eddie.

1956

SONNY'S BLUES

James Baldwin

I read about it in the paper, in the subway, on my way to work. I read it, and I couldn't believe it, and I read it again. Then perhaps I just stared at it, at the newsprint spelling out his name, spelling out the story. I stared at it in the swinging lights of the subway car, and in the faces and bodies of the people, and in my own face, trapped in the darkness which roared outside.

It was not to be believed and I kept telling myself that, as I walked from the subway station to the high school. And at the same time I couldn't doubt it. I was scared, scared for Sonny. He became real to me again. A great block of ice got settled in my belly and kept melting there slowly all day long, while I taught my classes algebra. It was a special kind of ice. It kept melting, sending trickles of ice water all up and down my veins, but it never got less. Sometimes it hardened and seemed to expand until I felt my guts were going to come spilling out or that I was going to choke or scream. This would always be at a moment when I was remembering some specific thing Sonny had once said or done.

When he was about as old as the boys in my classes his face had been bright and open, there was a lot of copper in it; and he'd had wonderfully direct brown eyes, and great gentleness and privacy. I wondered what he looked like now. He had been picked up, the evening before, in a raid on an apartment downtown, for peddling and using heroin.

I couldn't believe it: but what I mean by that is that I couldn't find any room for it anywhere inside me. I had kept it outside me for a long time. I hadn't wanted to know. I had had suspicions, but I didn't name them, I kept putting them away. I told myself that Sonny was wild, but he wasn't crazy. And he'd always been a good boy, he hadn't ever turned hard or evil or disrespectful, the way kids can, so quick, so quick, especially in Harlem. I didn't want to believe that I'd ever see my brother going down, coming to nothing, all that light in his face gone out, in the condition I'd already seen so many others. Yet it had happened and here I was, talking about algebra to a lot of

170

boys who might, every one of them for all I knew, be popping off needles every time they went to the head. Maybe it did more for them than algebra could.

I was sure that the first time Sonny had ever had horse, he couldn't have been much older than these boys were now. These boys, now, were living as we'd been living then, they were growing up with a rush and their heads bumped abruptly against the low ceiling of their actual possibilities. They were filled with rage. All they really knew were two darknesses, the darkness of their lives, which was now closing in on them, and the darkness of the movies, which had blinded them to that other darkness, and in which they now, vindictively, dreamed, at once more together than they were at any other time, and more alone.

When the last bell rang, the last class ended, I let out my breath. It seemed I'd been holding it for all that time. My clothes were wet—I may have looked as though I'd been sitting in a steam bath, all dressed up, all afternoon. I sat alone in the classroom a long time. I listened to the boys outside, downstairs, shouting and cursing and laughing. Their laughter struck me for perhaps the first time. It was not the joyous laughter which—God knows why—one associates with children. It was mocking and insular, its intent was to denigrate. It was disenchanted, and in this, also, lay the authority of their curses. Perhaps I was listening to them because I was thinking about my brother and in them I heard my brother. And myself.

One boy was whistling a tune, at once very complicated and very simple, it seemed to be pouring out of him as though he were a bird, and it sounded very cool and moving through all that harsh, bright air, only just holding its own through all those other sounds.

I stood up and walked over to the window and looked down into the courtyard. It was the beginning of the spring and the sap was rising in the boys. A teacher passed through them every now and again, quickly, as though he or she couldn't wait to get out of that courtyard, to get those boys out of their sight and off their minds. I started collecting my stuff. I thought I'd better get home and talk to Isabel.

The courtyard was almost deserted by the time I got downstairs. I saw this boy standing in the shadow of a doorway, looking just like Sonny. I almost called his name. Then I saw that it wasn't Sonny, but somebody we used to know, a boy from around our block. He'd been Sonny's friend. He'd never been mine, having been too young for me, and, anyway, I'd never liked him. And now, even though he was a grown-up man, he still hung around that block, still spent hours on the street corners, was always high and raggy. I used to run into him from time to time and he'd often work around to asking me for a quarter or fifty cents. He always had some real good excuse, too, and I always gave it to him. I don't know why.

But now, abruptly, I hated him. I couldn't stand the way he looked at me, partly like a dog, partly like a cunning child. I wanted to ask him what the hell he was doing in the school courtyard.

He sort of shuffled over to me, and he said, 'I see you got the papers. So you already know about it.'

'You mean about Sonny? Yes, I already know about it. How come they didn't get you?'

He grinned. It made him repulsive and it also brought to mind what he'd looked like as a kid. 'I wasn't there. I stay away from them people.'

'Good for you.' I offered him a cigarette and I watched him through the smoke. 'You come all the way down here just to tell me about Sonny?'

'That's right.' He was sort of shaking his head and his eyes looked strange, as though they were about to cross. The bright sun deadened his damp dark brown skin and it made his eyes look yellow and showed up the dirt in his kinked hair. He smelled funky. I moved a little away from him and I said, 'Well, thanks. But I already know about it and I got to get home.'

'I'll walk you a little ways,' he said. We started walking. There were a couple of kids still loitering in the courtyard and one of them said goodnight to me and looked strangely at the boy beside me.

'What're you going to do?' he asked me. 'I mean, about Sonny?'

'Look. I haven't seen Sonny for over a year, I'm not sure I'm going to do anything. Anyway, what the hell *can* I do?'

'That's right,' he said quickly, 'ain't nothing you can do. Can't much help old Sonny no more, I guess.'

It was what I was thinking and so it seemed to me he had no right to say it.

'I'm surprised at Sonny, though,' he went on—he had a funny way of talking, he looked straight ahead as though he were talking to himself—'I thought Sonny was a smart boy, I thought he was too smart to get hung.'

'I guess he thought so too,' I said sharply, 'and that's how he got

172

hung. And how about you? You're pretty goddamn smart, I bet.'

Then he looked directly at me, just for minute. 'I ain't smart,' he said. 'If I was smart, I'd have reached for a pistol a long time ago.'

'Look. Don't tell *me* your sad story, if it was up to me, I'd give you one.' Then I felt guilty—guilty, probably for never having supposed that the poor bastard *had* a story of his own, much less a sad one, and I asked, quickly, 'What's going to happen to him now?'

He didn't answer this. He was off by himself some place.

'Funny thing,' he said, and from his tone we might have been discussing the quickest way to get to Brooklyn, 'when I saw the papers this morning, the first thing I asked myself was if I had anything to do with it. I felt sort of responsible.'

I began to listen more carefully. The subway station was on the corner, just before us, and I stopped. He stopped, too. We were in front of a bar and he ducked slightly, peering in, but whoever he was looking for didn't seem to be there. The juke box was blasting away with something black and bouncy and I half watched the barmaid as she danced her way from the juke box to her place behind the bar. And I watched her face as she laughingly responded to something someone said to her, still keeping time to the music. When she smiled one saw the little girl, one sensed the doomed, still-struggling woman beneath the battered face of the semi-whore.

'I never *give* Sonny nothing,' the boy said finally, 'but a long time ago I come to school high and Sonny asked me how it felt.' He paused, I couldn't bear to watch him, I watched the barmaid, and I listened to the music which seemed to be causing the pavement to shake. 'I told him it felt great.' The music stopped, the barmaid paused and watched the juke box until the music began again. 'It did.'

All this was carrying me some place I didn't want to go. I certainly didn't want to know how it felt. It filled everything, the people, the houses, the music, the dark, quicksilver barmaid, with menace; and this menace was their reality.

'What's going to happen to him now?' I asked again.

'They'll send him away some place and they'll try to cure him.' He shook his head. 'Maybe he'll even think he's kicked the habit. Then they'll let him loose'—he gestured, throwing his cigarette into the gutter. 'That's all.'

'What do you mean, that's *all*?'

But I knew what he meant.

'I *mean*, that's *all*.' He turned his head and looked at me, pulling down the corners of his mouth. 'Don't you know what I mean?' he asked, softly.

'How the hell *would* I know what you mean?' I almost whispered it, I don't know why.

'That's right,' he said to the air, 'how would *he* know what I mean?' He turned toward me again, patient and calm, and yet I somehow felt him shaking, shaking as though he were going to fall apart. I felt that ice in my guts again, the dread I'd felt all afternoon; and again I watched the barmaid, moving about the bar, washing glasses, and singing. 'Listen. They'll let him out and then it'll just start all over again. That's what I mean.'

'You mean—they'll let him out. And then he'll just start working his way back in again. You mean he'll never kick the habit. Is that what you mean?'

'That's right,' he said, cheerfully. '*You* see what I mean.'

'Tell me,' I said at last, 'why does he want to die? He must want to die, he's killing himself, why does he want to die?'

He looked at me in surprise. He licked his lips. 'He don't want to die. He wants to live. Don't nobody want to die, ever.'

Then I wanted to ask him—too many things. He could not have answered, or if he had, I could not have borne the answers. I started walking. 'Well, I guess it's none of my business.'

'It's going to be rough on old Sonny,' he said. We reached the subway station. 'This is your station?' he asked. I nodded. I took one step down. 'Damn!' he said, suddenly. I looked up at him. He grinned again. 'Damn it if I didn't leave all my money home. You ain't got a dollar on you, have you? Just for a couple of days, is all.'

All at once something inside gave and threatened to come pouring out of me. I didn't hate him any more. I felt that in another moment I'd start crying like a child.

'Sure,' I said. 'Don't sweat,' I looked in my wallet and didn't have a dollar, I only had a five. 'Here,' I said. 'That hold you?'

He didn't look at it—he didn't want to look at it. A terrible closed look came over his face, as though he were keeping the number on the bill a secret from him and me. 'Thanks,' he said, and now he was dying to see me go. 'Don't worry about Sonny. Maybe I'll write him or something.'

'Sure,' I said. 'You do that. So long.'

'Be seeing you,' he said. I went on down the steps.

And I didn't write Sonny or send him anything for a long time. When I finally did, it was just after my little girl died, and he wrote me back a letter which made me feel like a bastard.

Here's what he said:

Dear brother,

You don't know how much I needed to hear from you. I wanted to write you many a time but I dug how much I must have hurt you and so I didn't write. But now I feel like a man who's been trying to climb up out of some deep, real deep and funky hole and just saw the sun up there, outside. I got to get outside.

I can't tell you much about how I got here. I mean I don't know how to tell you. I guess I was afraid of something or I was trying to escape from something and you know I have never been very strong in the head (smile). I'm glad Mama and Daddy are dead and can't see what's happened to their son and I swear if I'd known what I was doing I would never have hurt you so, you and a lot of other fine people who were nice to me and who believed in me.

I don't want you to think it had anything to do with me being a musician. It's more than that. Or maybe less than that. I can't get anything straight in my head down here and I try not to think about what's going to happen to me when I get outside again. Sometime I think I'm going to flip and *never* get outside and sometime I think I'll come straight back. I tell you one thing, though, I'd rather blow my brains out than go through this again. But that's what they all say, so they tell me. If I tell you when I'm coming to New York and if you could meet me, I sure would appreciate it. Give my love to Isabel and the kids and I was sure sorry to hear about little Gracie. I wish I could be like Mama and say the Lord's will be done, but I don't know it seems to me that trouble is the one thing that never does get stopped and I don't know what good it does to blame it on the Lord. But maybe it does some good if you believe it.

Your brother,
Sonny

Then I kept in constant touch with him and I sent him whatever I could and I went to meet him when he came back to New York. When I saw him many things I thought I had forgotten came flooding back to me. This was because I had begun, finally, to wonder about Sonny, about the life that Sonny lived inside. This life, whatever it was, had made him older and thinner and it had deepened the distant stillness in which he had always moved. He looked very unlike my baby brother. Yet, when he smiled, when we shook hands, the baby brother I'd never known looked out from the depths of his private life, like an animal waiting to be coaxed into the light.

'How you been keeping?' he asked me.

'All right. And you?'

'Just fine.' He was smiling all over his face. 'It's good to see you again.'

'It's good to see you.'

The seven years' difference in our ages lay between us like a chasm: I wondered if these years would ever operate between us as a bridge. I was remembering, and it made it hard to catch my breath, that I had been there when he was born; and I had heard the first words he had ever spoken. When he started to walk, he walked from our mother straight to me. I caught him just before he fell when he took the first steps he ever took in this world.

'How's Isabel?'

'Just fine. She's dying to see you.'

'And the boys?'

'They're fine, too. They're anxious to see their uncle.'

'Oh, come on. You know they don't remember me.'

'Are you kidding? Of course they remember you.'

He grinned again. We got into a taxi. We had a lot to say to each other, far too much to know how to begin.

As the taxi began to move, I asked, 'You still want to go to India?'

He laughed. 'You still remember that. Hell, no. This place is Indian enough for me.'

'It used to belong to them,' I said.

And he laughed again. 'They damn sure knew what they were doing when they got rid of it.'

Years ago, when he was around fourteen, he'd been all hipped on the idea of going to India. He read books about people sitting on rocks, naked, in all kinds of weather, but mostly bad, naturally, and walking barefoot through hot coals and arriving at wisdom. I used to say that it sounded to me as though they were getting away from wisdom as fast as they could. I think he sort of looked down on me for that.

'Do you mind,' he asked, 'if we have the driver drive alongside the park? On the west side—I haven't seen the city in so long.'

'Of course not,' I said. I was afraid that I might sound as though I were humoring him, but I hoped he wouldn't take it that way.

So we drove along, between the green of the park and the stony, lifeless elegance of hotels and apartment buildings, toward the vivid, killing streets of our childhood. These streets hadn't changed, though housing projects jutted up out of them now like rocks in the middle of a boiling sea. Most of the houses in which we had grown up had vanished, as had the stores from which we had stolen, the basements in which we had first tried sex, the rooftops from which we had hurled tin cans and bricks. But houses exactly like the houses of our past yet dominated the landscape, boys exactly like the boys we once had been found themselves smothering in these houses, came down into the streets for light and air and found themselves encircled by disaster. Some escaped the trap, most didn't. Those who got out always left something of themselves behind, as some animals amputate a leg and leave it in the trap. It might be said, perhaps, that I had escaped, after all, I was a school teacher; or that Sonny had, he hadn't lived in Harlem for years. Yet, as the cab moved uptown through streets which seemed, with a rush, to darken with dark people, and as I covertly studied Sonny's face, it came to me that what we both were seeking through our separate cab windows was that part of ourselves which had been left behind. It's always at the hour of trouble and confrontation that the missing member aches.

We hit 110th Street and started rolling up Lenox Avenue. And I'd known this avenue all my life, but it seemed to me again, as it had seemed on the day I'd first heard about Sonny's trouble, filled with a hidden menace which was its very breath of life.

'We almost there,' said Sonny.

'Almost.' We were both too nervous to say anything more.

We live in a housing project. It hasn't been up long. A few days after it was up it seemed uninhabitably new, now, of course, it's already rundown. It looks like a parody of the good, clean, faceless life—God knows the people who live in it do their best to make it a parody. The beat-looking grass lying around isn't enough to make their lives green, the hedges will never hold out the streets, and they know it. The big windows fool no one, they aren't big enough to make space out of no space. They don't bother with the windows, they watch the TV screen instead. The playground is most popular with the children who don't play at jacks, or skip rope, or roller skate, or swing, and they can be found in it after dark. We moved in partly because it's not too far from where I teach, and partly for the kids;

177

but it's really just like the houses in which Sonny and I grew up. The same things happen, they'll have the same things to remember. The moment Sonny and I started into the house I had the feeling that I was simply bringing him back into the danger he had almost died trying to escape.

Sonny has never been talkative. So I don't know why I was sure he'd be dying to talk to me when supper was over the first night. Everything went fine, the oldest boy remembered him, and the youngest boy liked him, and Sonny had remembered to bring something for each of them; and Isabel, who is really much nicer than I am, more open and giving, had gone to a lot of trouble about dinner and was genuinely glad to see him. And she's always been able to tease Sonny in a way that I haven't. It was nice to see her face so vivid again and to hear her laugh and watch her make Sonny laugh. She wasn't, or, anyway, she didn't seem to be, at all uneasy or embarrassed. She chatted as though there were no subject which had to be avoided and she got Sonny past his first, faint stiffness. And thank God she was there, for I was filled with that icy dread again. Everything I did seemed awkward to me, and everything I said sounded freighted with hidden meaning. I was trying to remember everything I'd heard about dope addiction and I couldn't help watching Sonny for signs. I wasn't doing it out of malice. I was trying to find out something about my brother. I was dying to hear him tell me he was safe.

'Safe!' my father grunted, whenever Mama suggested trying to move to a neighborhood which might be safer for children. 'Safe, hell! Ain't no place safe for kids, nor nobody.'

He always went on like this, but he wasn't, ever, really as bad as he sounded, not even on weekends, when he got drunk. As a matter of fact, he was always on the lookout for 'something a little better,' but he died before he found it. He died suddenly, during a drunken weekend in the middle of the war, when Sonny was fifteen. He and Sonny hadn't ever got on too well. And this was partly because Sonny was the apple of his father's eye. It was because he loved Sonny so much and was frightened for him, that he was always fighting with him. It doesn't do any good to fight with Sonny. Sonny just moves back, inside himself, where he can't be reached. But the principal reason that they never hit it off is that they were so much alike. Daddy was big and rough and loud-talking, just the opposite of

Sonny, but they both had—that same privacy.

Mama tried to tell me something about this, just after Daddy died. I was home on leave from the army.

This was the last time I ever saw my mother alive. Just the same, this picture gets all mixed up in my mind with pictures I had of her when she was younger. The way I always see her is the way she used to be on a Sunday afternoon, say, when the old folks were talking after the big Sunday dinner. I always see her wearing pale blue. She'd be sitting on the sofa. And my father would be sitting in the easy chair, not far from her. And the living room would be full of church folks and relatives. There they sit, in chairs all around the living room, and the night is creeping up outside, but nobody knows it yet. You can see the darkness growing against the windowpanes and you hear the street noises every now and again, or maybe the jangling beat of a tambourine from one of the churches close by, but it's real quiet in the room. For a moment nobody's talking, but every face looks darkening, like the sky outside. And my mother rocks a little from the waist, and my father's eyes are closed. Everyone is looking at something a child can't see. For a minute they've forgotten the children. Maybe a kid is lying on the rug, half asleep. Maybe somebody's got a kid in his lap and is absent-mindedly stroking the kid's head. Maybe there's a kid, quiet and big-eyed, curled up in a big chair in the corner. The silence, the darkness coming, and the darkness in the faces frighten the child obscurely. He hopes that the hand which strokes his forehead will never stop—will never die. He hopes that there will never come a time when the old folks won't be sitting around the living room, talking about where they've come from, and what they've seen, and what's happened to them and their kinfolk.

But something deep and watchful in the child knows that this is bound to end, is already ending. In a moment someone will get up and turn on the light. Then the old folks will remember the children and they won't talk any more that day. And when light fills the room, the child is filled with darkness. He knows that every time this happens he's moved just a little closer to that darkness outside. The darkness outside is what the old folks have been talking about. It's what they've come from. It's what they endure. The child knows that they won't talk any more because if he knows too much about what's happened to *them*, he'll know too much too soon, about what's going to happen to *him*.

The last time I talked to my mother, I remember I was restless. I wanted to get out and see Isabel. We weren't married then and we had a lot to straighten out between us.

There Mama sat, in black, by the window. She was humming an old church song, *Lord, you brought me from a long ways off.* Sonny was out somewhere. Mama kept watching the streets.

'I don't know,' she said, 'if I'll ever see you again, after you go off from here. But I hope you'll remember the things I tried to teach you.'

'Don't talk like that,' I said, and smiled. 'You'll be here a long time yet.'

She smiled, too, but she said nothing. She was quiet for a long time. And I said, 'Mama, don't you worry about nothing. I'll be writing all the time, and you be getting the checks . . .'

'I want to talk to you about your brother,' she said, suddenly. 'If anything happens to me he ain't going to have nobody to look out for him.'

'Mama,' I said, 'ain't nothing going to happen to you *or* Sonny. Sonny's all right. He's a good boy and he's got good sense.'

'It ain't a question of his being a good boy,' Mama said, 'nor of his having good sense. It ain't only the bad ones, nor yet the dumb ones that gets sucked under.' She stopped, looking at me. 'Your Daddy once had a brother,' she said, and she smiled in a way that made me feel she was in pain. 'You didn't never know that, did you?'

'No,' I said, 'I never knew that,' and I watched her face.

'Oh, yes,' she said, 'your Daddy had a brother.' she looked out of the window again. 'I know you never saw your Daddy cry. But *I* did—many a time, through all these years.'

I asked her, 'What happened to his brother? How come nobody's ever talked about him?'

This was the first time I ever saw my mother look old.

'His brother got killed,' she said, 'when he was just a little younger than you are now. I knew him. He was a fine boy. He was maybe a little full of the devil, but he didn't mean nobody no harm.'

Then she stopped and the room was silent, exactly as it had sometimes been on those Sunday afternoons. Mama kept looking out into the streets.

'He used to have a job in the mill,' she said, 'and, like all young folks, he just liked to perform on Saturday nights. Saturday nights, him and your father would drift around to different places, go to dances and things like that, or just sit around with people they knew, and your father's brother would sing, he had a fine voice, and play along with himself on his guitar. Well, this particular Saturday night, him and your father was coming home from some place, and they were both a little drunk and there was a moon that night, it was bright like day. Your father's brother was feeling kind of good, and he was whistling to himself, and he had his guitar slung over his shoulder. They was coming down a hill and beneath them was a road that turned off from the highway. Well, your father's brother, being always kind of frisky, decided to run down this hill, and he did, with that guitar banging and clanging behind him, and he ran across the road, and he was making water behind a tree. And your father was sort of amused at him and he was still coming down the hill, kind of slow. Then he heard a car motor and that same minute his brother stepped from behind the tree, into the road, in the moonlight. And he started to cross the road. And your father started to run down the hill, he says he don't know why. This car was full of white men. They was all drunk, and when they seen your father's brother they let out a great whoop and holler and they aimed the car straight at him. They was having fun, they just wanted to scare him, the way they do sometimes, you know. But they was drunk. And I guess the boy, being drunk, too, and scared, kind of lost his head. By the time he jumped it was too late. Your father says he heard his brother scream when the car rolled over him, and he heard the wood of that guitar when it give, and he heard them strings go flying, and he heard them white men shouting, and the car kept on a-going and it ain't stopped till this day. And, time your father got down the hill, his brother weren't nothing but blood and pulp.'

Tears were gleaming on my mother's face. There wasn't anything I could say.

'He never mentioned it,' she said, 'because I never let him mention it before you children. Your Daddy was like a crazy man that night and for many a night thereafter. He says he never in his life seen anything as dark as that road after the lights of that car had gone away. Weren't nothing, weren't nobody on that road, just your Daddy and his brother and that busted guitar. Oh, yes. Your Daddy never did really get right again. Till the day he died he weren't sure but that every white man he saw was the man that killed his brother.'

She stopped and took out her handkerchief and dried her eyes and looked at me.

'I ain't telling you all this,' she said, 'to make you scared or bitter or to make you hate nobody. I'm telling you this because you got a brother. And the world ain't changed.'

I guess I didn't want to believe this. I guess she saw this in my face. She turned away from me, toward the window again, searching those streets.

'But I praise my Redeemer,' she said at last, 'that He called your Daddy home before me. I ain't saying it to throw no flowers at myself, but, I declare, it keeps me from feeling too cast down to know I helped your father get safely through this world. Your father always acted like he was the roughest, strongest man on earth. And everybody took him to be like that. But if he hadn't had me there—to see his tears!'

She was crying again. Still, I couldn't move. I said, 'Lord, Lord, Mama, I didn't know it was like that.'

'Oh, honey,' she said, 'there's a lot that you don't know. But you are going to find out.' She stood up from the window and came over to me. 'You got to hold on to your brother,' she said, 'and don't let him fall, no matter what it looks like is happening to him and no matter how evil you gets with him. You going to be evil with him many a time. But don't you forget what I told you, you hear?'

'I won't forget,' I said. 'Don't you worry, I won't forget. I won't let nothing happen to Sonny.'

My mother smiled as though she were amused at something she saw in my face. Then, 'You may not be able to stop nothing from happening. But you got to let him know you's *there*.'

Two days later I was married, and then I was gone. And I had a lot of things on my mind and I pretty well forgot my promise to Mama until I got shipped home on a special furlough for her funeral.

And, after the funeral, with just Sonny and me alone in the empty kitchen, I tried to find out something about him.

'What do you want to do?' I asked him.

'I'm going to be a musician,' he said.

For he had graduated, in the time I had been away, from dancing to the juke box to finding out who was playing what, and what they were doing with it, and he had bought himself a set of drums.

'You mean, you want to be a drummer?' I somehow had the feeling that being a drummer might be all right for other people but not for my brother Sonny.

'I don't think,' he said, looking at me very gravely, 'that I'll ever be a good drummer. But I think I can play piano.'

I frowned. I'd never played the role of the older brother quite so

seriously before, had scarcely ever, in fact, *asked* Sonny a damn thing.
I sensed myself in the presence of something I didn't really know
how to handle, didn't understand. So I made my frown a little deeper
as I asked: 'What kind of musician do you want to be?'

He grinned. 'How many kinds do you think there are?'

'Be *serious*,' I said.

He laughed, throwing his head back, and then looked at me. 'I *am*
serious.'

'Well, then, for Christ's sake, stop kidding around and answer a
serious question. I mean, do you want to be a concert pianist, you
want to play classical music and all that, or—or what?' Long before I
finished he was laughing again. 'For Christ's *sake*, Sonny!'

He sobered, but with difficulty. 'I'm sorry. But you sound so—
scared!' and he was off again.

'Well, you may think it's funny now, baby, but it's not going to be
so funny when you have to make your living at it, let me tell you
that.' I was furious because I knew he was laughing at me and I
didn't know why.

'No,' he said, very sober now, and afraid, perhaps, that he'd hurt
me, 'I don't want to be a classical pianist. That isn't what interests
me. I mean'—he paused, looking hard at me, as though his eyes
would help me to understand, and then gestured helplessly, as
though perhaps his hand would help—'I mean, I'll have a lot of
studying to do, and I'll have to study *everything*, but, I mean, I want
to play *with*—jazz musicians.' He stopped. 'I want to play jazz,' he
said.

Well, the word had never before sounded as heavy, as real, as it
sounded that afternoon in Sonny's mouth. I just looked at him and I
was probably frowning a real frown by this time. I simply couldn't
see why on earth he'd want to spend his time hanging around
nightclubs, clowning around on bandstands, while people pushed
each other around a dance floor. It seemed—beneath him, somehow.
I had never thought about it before, had never been forced to, but I
suppose I had always put jazz musicians in a class with what Daddy
called 'good-time people.'

'Are you *serious*?'

'Hell, *yes*, I'm serious.'

He looked more helpless than ever, and annoyed, and deeply hurt.

I suggested, helpfully: 'You mean—like Louis Armstrong?'

His face closed as though I'd struck him. 'No. I'm not talking about none of that old-time, down home crap.'

'Well, look, Sonny, I'm sorry, don't get mad. I just don't altogether get it, that's all. Name somebody—you know, a jazz musician you admire.'

'Bird.'

'Who?'

'Bird! Charlie Parker! Don't they teach you nothing in the goddamn army?'

I lit a cigarette. I was surprised and then a little amused to discover that I was trembling. 'I've been out of touch,' I said. 'You'll have to be patient with me. Now. Who's this Parker character?'

'He's just one of the greatest jazz musicians alive,' said Sonny, sullenly, his hands in his pockets, his back to me. 'Maybe *the* greatest,' he added, bitterly, 'that's probably why *you* never heard of him.'

'All right,' I said, 'I'm ignorant. I'm sorry. I'll go out and buy all the cat's records right away, all right?'

'It don't,' said Sonny, with dignity, 'make any difference to me. I don't care what you listen to. Don't do me no favors.'

I was beginning to realize that I'd never seen him so upset before. With another part of my mind I was thinking that this would probably turn out to be one of those things kids go through and that I shouldn't make it seem important by pushing it too hard. Still, I didn't think it would do any harm to ask: 'Doesn't all this take a lot of time? Can you make a living at it?'

He turned back to me and half leaned, half sat, on the kitchen table. 'Everything takes time,' he said, 'and—well, yes, sure, I can make a living at it. But what I don't seem to be able to make you understand is that it's the only thing I want to do.'

'Well, Sonny,' I said, gently, 'you know people can't always do exactly what they *want* to do—'

'*No*, I don't know that,' said Sonny, surprising me. 'I think people *ought* to do what they want to do, what else are they alive for?'

'You getting to be a big boy,' I said desperately, 'it's time you started thinking about your future.'

'I'm thinking about my future,' said Sonny, grimly. 'I think about it all the time.'

I gave up. I decided, if he didn't change his mind, that we could always talk about it later. 'In the meantime,' I said, 'you got to finish school.' We had already decided that he'd have to move in with Isabel and her folks. I knew this wasn't the ideal arrangement because

Isabel's folks are inclined to be dicty and they hadn't especially wanted Isabel to marry me. But I didn't know what else to do. 'And we have to get you fixed up at Isabel's.'

There was a long silence. He moved from the kitchen table to the window. 'That's a terrible idea. You know it yourself.'

'Do you have a *better* idea?'

He just walked up and down the kitchen for a minute. He was as tall as I was. He had started to shave. I suddenly had the feeling that I didn't know him at all.

He stopped at the kitchen table and picked up my cigarettes. Looking at me with a kind of mocking, amused defiance, he put one between his lips. 'You mind?'

'You smoking already?'

He lit the cigarette and nodded, watching me through the smoke. 'I just wanted to see if I'd have the courage to smoke in front of you.' He grinned and blew a great cloud of smoke to the ceiling. 'It was easy.' He looked at my face. 'Come on, now. I bet you was smoking at my age, tell the truth.'

I didn't say anything but the truth was on my face, and he laughed. But now there was something very strained in his laugh. 'Sure. And I bet that ain't all you was doing.'

He was frightening me a little. 'Cut the crap,' I said. 'We already decided that you was going to go and live at Isabel's. Now what's got into you all of a sudden?'

'*You* decided it,' he pointed out. '*I* didn't decide nothing.' He stopped in front of me, leaning against the stove, arms loosely folded. 'Look, brother. I don't want to stay in Harlem no more, I really don't.' He was very earnest. He looked at me, then over toward the kitchen window. There was something in his eyes I'd never seen before, some thoughtfulness, some worry all his own. He rubbed the muscle of one arm. 'It's time I was getting out of here.'

'Where do you want to *go*, Sonny?'

'I want to join the army. Or the navy, I don't care. If I say I'm old enough, they'll believe me.'

Then I got mad. It was because I was so scared. 'You must be crazy. You goddamn fool, what the hell do you want to go and join the *army* for?'

'I just told you. To get out of Harlem.'

'Sonny, you haven't even finished *school*. And if you really want to be a musician, how do you expect to study if you're in the *army*?'

He looked at me, trapped, and in anguish. 'There's ways. I might be able to work out some kind of deal. Anyway, I'll have the GI Bill when I come out.'

'*If* you come out.' We stared at each other. 'Sonny, please. Be reasonable. I know the setup is far from perfect. But we got to do the best we can.'

'I ain't learning nothing in school,' he said. 'Even when I go.' He turned away from me and opened the window and threw his cigarette out into the narrow alley. I watched his back. 'At least, I ain't learning nothing you'd want me to learn.' He slammed the window so hard I thought the glass would fly out, and turned back to me. 'And I'm sick of the stink of these garbage cans!'

'Sonny,' I said, 'I know how you feel. But if you don't finish school now, you're going to be sorry later that you didn't.' I grabbed him by the shoulders. 'And you only got another year. It ain't so bad. And I'll come back and I swear I'll help you do *whatever* you want to do. Just try to put up with it till I come back. Will you please do that? For me?'

He didn't answer and he wouldn't look at me.

'Sonny. You hear me?'

He pulled away. 'I hear you. But you never hear anything *I* say.'

I didn't know what to say to that. He looked out of the window and then back at me. 'OK,' he said, and sighed. 'I'll try.'

Then I said, trying to cheer him up a little, 'They got a piano at Isabel's. You can practice on it.'

And as a matter of fact, it did cheer him up for a minute. 'That's right,' he said to himself. 'I forgot that.' His face relaxed a little. But the worry, the thoughtfulness, played on it still, the way shadows play on a face which is staring into the fire.

But I thought I'd never hear the end of that piano. At first, Isabel would write me, saying how nice it was that Sonny was so serious about his music and how, as soon as he came in from school, or wherever he had been when he was supposed to be at school, he went straight to that piano and stayed there until suppertime. And, after supper, he went back to that piano and stayed there until everybody went to bed. He was at the piano all day Saturday and all day Sunday. Then he bought a record player and started playing records. He'd play one record over and over again, all day long sometimes, and he'd improvise along with it on the piano. Or he'd play one section of the record, one chord, one change, one progression, then he'd do it on the piano. Then back to the record. Then back to the piano.

Well, I really don't know how they stood it. Isabel finally confessed that it wasn't like living with a person at all, it was like living with sound. And the sound didn't make any sense to her, didn't make any sense to any of them—naturally. They began, in a way, to be afflicted by this presence that was living in their home. It was as though Sonny were some sort of god, or monster. He moved in an atmosphere which wasn't like theirs at all. They fed him and he ate, he washed himself, he walked in and out of their door; he certainly wasn't nasty or unpleasant or rude, Sonny isn't any of those things; but it was as though he were all wrapped up in some cloud, some fire, some vision all his own; and there wasn't any way to reach him.

At the same time, he wasn't really a man yet, he was still a child, and they had to watch out for him in all kinds of ways. They certainly couldn't throw him out. Neither did they dare to make a great scene about that piano because even they dimly sensed, as I sensed, from so many thousands of miles away, that Sonny was at that piano playing for his life.

But he hadn't been going to school. One day a letter came from the school board and Isabel's mother got it—there had, apparently, been other letters but Sonny had torn them up. This day, when Sonny came in, Isabel's mother showed him the letter and asked where he'd been spending his time. And she finally got it out of him that he'd been down in Greenwich Village, with musicians and other characters, in a white girl's apartment. And this scared her and she started to scream at him and what came up, once she began—though she denies it to this day—was what sacrifices they were making to give Sonny a decent home and how little he appreciated it.

Sonny didn't play the piano that day. By evening, Isabel's mother had calmed down but then there was the old man to deal with, and Isabel herself. Isabel says she did her best to be calm but she broke down and started crying. She says she just watched Sonny's face. She could tell, by watching him, what was happening with him. And what was happening was that they penetrated his cloud, they had reached him. Even if their fingers had been a thousand times more gentle than human fingers ever are, he could hardly help feeling that they had stripped him naked and were spitting on that nakedness. For he also had to see that his presence, that music, which was life or death to him, had been torture for them and that they had endured it, not at all for his sake, but only for mine. And Sonny couldn't take that. He can take it a little better today than he could then but he's still not very good at it and, frankly, I don't know anybody who is.

The silence of the next few days must have been louder than the sound of all the music every played since time began. One morning, before she went to work, Isabel was in his room for something and she suddenly realized that all of his records were gone. And she knew for certain that he was gone. And he was. He went as far as the navy would carry him. He finally sent me a postcard from some place in Greece and that was the first I knew that Sonny was still alive. I didn't see him any more until we were both back in New York and the war had long been over.

He was a man by then, of course, but I wasn't willing to see it. He came by the house from time to time, but we fought almost every time we met. I didn't like the way he carried himself, loose and dreamlike all the time, and I didn't like his friends, and his music seemed to be merely an excuse for the life he led. It sounded just that weird and disordered.

Then we had a fight, a pretty awful fight, and I didn't see him for months. By and by I looked him up, where he was living, in a furnished room in the Village, and I tried to make it up. But there were lots of other people in the room and Sonny just lay on his bed, and he wouldn't come downstairs with me, and he treated these other people as though they were his family and I weren't. So I got mad and then he got mad, and then I told him that he might just as well be dead as live the way he was living. Then he stood up and he told me not to worry about him any more in life, that he *was* dead as far as I was concerned. Then he pushed me to the door and the other people looked on as though nothing were happening, and he slammed the door behind me. I stood in the hallway, staring at the door. I heard somebody laugh in the room and then the tears came to my eyes. I started down the steps, whistling to keep from crying. I kept whistling to myself, *You going to need me, baby, one of these cold, rainy days.*

I read about Sonny's trouble in the spring. Little Grace died in the fall. She was a beautiful little girl. But she only lived a little over two years. She died of polio and she suffered. She had a slight fever for a couple of days, but it didn't seem like anything and we just kept her in bed. And we would certainly have called the doctor, but the fever dropped, she seemed to be all right. So we thought it had just been a cold. Then, one day, she was up, playing, Isabel was in the kitchen fixing lunch for the two boys when they'd come in from school, and she heard Grace fall down in the living room. When you have a lot of children you don't always start running when one of them falls, unless they start screaming or something. And, this time, Gracie was quiet. Yet, Isabel says that when she heard that *thump* and then that silence, something happened to her to make her afraid. And she ran to the living room and there was little Grace on the floor, all twisted up, and the reason she hadn't screamed was that she couldn't get her breath. And when she did scream, it was the worst sound, Isabel says, that she'd ever heard in all her life, and she still hears it sometimes in her dreams. Isabel will sometimes wake me up with a low, moaning, strangling sound and I have to be quick to awaken her and hold her to me and where Isabel is weeping against me seems a mortal wound.

I think I may have written Sonny the very day that little Grace was buried. I was sitting in the living room in the dark, by myself, and I suddenly thought of Sonny. My trouble made his real.

One Saturday afternoon, when Sonny had been living with us, or anyway, been in our house, for nearly two weeks, I found myself wandering aimlessly about the living room, drinking from a can of beer, and trying to work up courage to search Sonny's room. He was out, he was usually out whenever I was home, and Isabel had taken the children to see their grandparents. Suddenly I was standing still in front of the living room window, watching Seventh Avenue. The idea of searching Sonny's room made me still. I scarcely dared to admit to myself what I'd be searching for. I didn't know what I'd do if I found it. Or if I didn't.

On the sidewalk across from me, near the entrance to a barbecue joint, some people were holding an old-fashioned revival meeting. The barbecue cook, wearing a dirty white apron, his conked hair reddish and metallic in the pale sun, and a cigarette between his lips, stood in the doorway, watching them. Kids and older people paused in their errands and stood there, along with some older men and a couple of very tough-looking women who watched everything that happened on the avenue, as though they owned it, or were maybe owned by it. Well, they were watching this, too. The revival was being carried on by three sisters in black, and a brother. All they had were their voices and their Bibles and a tambourine. The brother was testifying and while he testified two of the sisters stood together, seeming to say, amen, and the third sister walked around with the tambourine outstretched and a couple of people dropped coins into it. Then the brother's testimony ended and the sister who had been taking up the collection dumped the coins into her palm and transferred them to the pocket of her long black robe. Then she raised both hands, striking the tambourine against the air, and then against one hand, and she started to sing. And the two other sisters and the brother joined in.

It was strange, suddenly, to watch, though I had been seeing these meetings all my life. So, of course, had everybody else down there. Yet, they paused and watched and listened and I stood still at the widow. *' Tis the old ship of Zion,'* they sang, and the sister with the tambourine kept a steady, jangling beat, *'it has rescued many a thousand!'* Not a soul under the sound of their voices was hearing this song for the first time, not one of them had been rescued. Nor had they seen much in the way of rescue work being done around them. Neither did they especially believe in the holiness of the three sisters and the brother, they knew too much about them, knew where they lived, and how. The woman with the tambourine, whose voice dominated the air, whose face was bright with joy, was divided by very little from the woman who stood watching her, a cigarette between her heavy, chapped lips, her hair a cuckoo's nest, her face scarred and swollen from many beatings, and her black eyes glittering like coal. Perhaps they both knew this, which was why, when, as rarely, they addressed each other, they addressed each other as Sister. As the singing filled the air the watching, listening faces underwent a change, the eyes focusing on something within; the music seemed to soothe a poison out of them; and time seemed, nearly, to fall away from the sullen, belligerent, battered faces, as though they were fleeing back to their first condition, while dreaming of their last. The barbecue cook half shook his head and smiled, and dropped his cigarette and disappeared into his joint. A man fumbled in his pockets for change and stood holding it in his hand impatiently, as though he had just remembered a pressing appointment further up the avenue. He looked furious. Then I saw Sonny, standing on the edge of the crowd. He was carrying a wide, flat notebook with a green cover, and it made him look, from where I was standing, almost like a schoolboy. The coppery sun brought out the copper in his skin, he was very faintly smiling, standing very still.

Then the singing stopped, the tambourine turned into a collection plate again. The furious man dropped in his coins and vanished, so did a couple of the women, and Sonny dropped some change in the plate, looking directly at the woman with a little smile. He started across the avenue, toward the house. He has a slow, loping walk, something like the way Harlem hipsters walk, only he's imposed on this his own half-beat. I had never really noticed it before.

I stayed at the window, both relieved and apprehensive. As Sonny disappeared from my sight, they began singing again. And they were still singing when his key turned in the lock.

'Hey,' he said.

'Hey, yourself. You want some beer?'

'No. Well, maybe.' But he came up to the window and stood beside me, looking out. 'What a warm voice,' he said.

They were singing *If I could only hear my mother pray again!*

'Yes,' I said, 'and she can sure beat that tambourine.'

'But what a terrible song,' he said, and laughed. He dropped his notebook on the sofa and disappeared into the kitchen. 'Where's Isabel and the kids?'

'I think they want to see their grandparents. You hungry?'

'No.' He came back into the living room with his can of beer. 'You want to come some place with me tonight?'

I sensed, I don't know how, that I couldn't possibly say no. 'Sure. Where?'

He sat down on the sofa and picked up his notebook and started leafing through it. 'I'm going to sit in with some fellows in a joint in the Village.'

'You mean, you're going to play, tonight?'

'That's right.' He took a swallow of his beer and moved back to the window. He gave me a sidelong look. 'If you can stand it.'

'I'll try,' I said.

He smiled to himself and we both watched as the meeting across the way broke up. The three sisters and the brother, heads bowed, were singing *God be with you till we meet again*. The faces around them were very quiet. Then the song ended. The small crowd dispersed. We watched the three women and the lone man walk slowly up the avenue.

'When she was singing before,' said Sonny, abruptly, 'her voice reminded me for a minute of what heroin feels like sometimes— when it's in your veins. It makes you feel sort of warm and cool at the same time. And distant. And—and sure.' He sipped his beer, very deliberately not looking at me. I watched his face. 'It makes you feel—in control. Sometimes you've got to have that feeling.'

'Do you?' I sat down slowly in the easy chair.

'Sometimes.' He went to the sofa and picked up his notebook again. 'Some people do.'

'In order,' I asked, 'to play?' And my voice was very ugly, full of contempt and anger.

'Well'—he looked at me with great, troubled eyes, as though, in fact, he hoped his eyes would tell me things he could never otherwise say—'they *think* so. And *if* they think so—!'

'And what do *you* think?' I asked.

He sat on the sofa and put his can of beer on the floor. 'I don't know,' he said, and I couldn't be sure if he were answering my question or pursuing his thoughts. His face didn't tell me. 'It's not so much to *play*. It's to *stand* it, to be able to make it at all. On any level.' He frowned and smiled: 'In order to keep from shaking to pieces.'

'But these friends of yours,' I said, 'they seem to shake themselves to pieces pretty goddamn fast.'

'Maybe.' He played with his notebook. And something told me that I should curb my tongue, that Sonny was doing his best to talk, that I should listen. 'But of course you only know the ones that've gone to pieces. Some don't—or at least they haven't *yet* and that's just about all *any* of us can say.' He paused. 'And then there are some who just live, really, in hell, and they know it and they see what's happening and they go right on. I don't know.' He sighed, dropped the notebook, folded his arms. 'Some guys, you can tell from the way they play, they on something *all* the time. And you can see that, well, it makes something real for them. But of course,' he picked up his beer from the floor and sipped it and put the can down again, 'they *want* to, too, you've got to see that. Even some of them that say they don't—*some*, not all.'

'And what about you?' I asked—I couldn't help it. 'What about you? Do *you* want to?'

He stood up and walked to the window and I remained silent for a long time. Then he sighed. 'Me,' he said. Then: 'While I was downstairs before, on my way here, listening to that woman sing, it struck me all of a sudden how much suffering she must have had to go through—to sing like that. It's *repulsive* to think you have to suffer that much.'

I said: 'But there's no way not to suffer—is there, Sonny?'

'I believe not,' he said and smiled, 'but that's never stopped anyone from trying.' He looked at me. 'Has it?' I realized, with this mocking look, that there stood between us, forever, beyond the power of time or forgiveness, the fact that I had held silence—so long!—when he had needed human speech to help him. He turned back to the window. 'No, there's no way not to suffer. But you try all kinds of ways to keep from drowning in it, to keep on top of it, and to make it seem—well, like *you*. Like you did something, all right, and now you're suffering for it. You know?' I said nothing. 'Well you know,' he said, impatiently, 'why *do* people suffer? Maybe it's better to do something to give it a reason, *any* reason.'

'But we just agreed,' I said, 'that there's no way not to suffer. Isn't it better, then, just to—take it?'

'But nobody just takes it,' Sonny cried, 'that's what I'm telling you! *Everybody* tries not to. You're just hung up on the *way* some people try—it's not *your* way!'

The hair on my face began to itch, my face felt wet. 'That's not true,' I said, 'that's not true. I don't give a damn what other people do, I don't even care how they suffer. I just care how *you* suffer.' And he looked at me. 'Please believe me,' I said, 'I don't want to see you— die—trying not to suffer.'

'I won't,' he said flatly, 'die trying not to suffer. At least, not any faster than anybody else.'

'But there's no need,' I said, trying to laugh, 'is there? in killing yourself.'

I wanted to say more, but I couldn't. I wanted to talk about will power and how life could be—well, beautiful. I wanted to say that it was all within; but was it? or, rather, wasn't that exactly the trouble? And I wanted to promise that I would never fail him again. But it would all have sounded—empty words and lies.

So I made the promise to myself and prayed that I would keep it.

'It's terrible sometimes, inside,' he said, 'that's what's the trouble. You walk these streets, black and funky and cold, and there's not really a living ass to talk to, and there's nothing shaking, and there's no way of getting it out—that storm inside. You can't talk it and you can't make love with it, and when you finally try to get with it and play it, you realize *nobody's* listening. So *you've* got to listen. You got to find a way to listen.'

And then he walked away from the window and sat on the sofa

again, as though all the wind had suddenly been knocked out of him. 'Sometimes you'll do *anything* to play, even cut your mother's throat.' He laughed and looked at me. 'Or your brother's.' Then he sobered. 'Or your own.' Then: 'Don't worry. I'm all right now and I think I'll *be* all right. But I can't forget—where I've been. I don't mean just the physical place I've been, I mean where I've *been*. And *what* I've been.'

'What have you been, Sonny?' I asked.

He smiled—but sat sideways on the sofa, his elbow resting on the back, his fingers playing with his mouth and chin, not looking at me. 'I've been something I didn't recognize, didn't know I could be. Didn't know anybody could be.' He stopped, looking inward, looking helplessly young, looking old. 'I'm not talking about it now because I feel *guilty* or anything like that—maybe it would be better if I did, I don't know. Anyway, I can't really talk about it. Not to you, not to anybody,' and now he turned and faced me. 'Sometimes, you know, and it was actually when I was most *out* of the world, I felt that I was in it, that I was *with* it, really, and I could play or I didn't really have to *play*, it just came out of me, it was there. And I don't know how I played, thinking about it now, but I know I did awful things, those times, sometimes, to people. Or it wasn't that I *did* anything to them— it was that they weren't real.' He picked up the beer can; it was empty; he rolled it between his palms: 'And other times—well, I needed a fix, I needed to find a place to lean, I needed to clear a space to *listen*—and I couldn't find it, and I—went crazy, I did terrible things to *me*, I was terrible *for* me.' He began pressing the beer can between his hands, I watched the metal begin to give. It glittered, as he played with it like a knife, and I was afraid he would cut himself, but I said nothing. 'Oh well. I can never tell you. I was all by myself at the bottom of something, stinking and sweating and crying and shaking, and I smelled it, you know? *my* stink, and I thought I'd die if I couldn't get away from it and yet, all the same, I knew that everything I was doing was just locking me in with it. And I didn't know,' he paused, still flattening the beer can, 'I didn't know, I still *don't* know, something kept telling me that maybe it was good to smell your own stink, but I didn't think that *that* was what I'd been trying to do—and—who can stand it?' and he abruptly dropped the ruined beer can, looking at me with a small, still smile, and then rose, walking to the window as though it were the lodestone rock. I watched his face, he watched the avenue. 'I couldn't tell you when Mama died—but the reason I wanted to leave Harlem so bad was to get away from drugs. And then, when I ran away, that's what I was running from—really. When I came back, nothing had changed, I hadn't changed, I was just—older.' And he stopped, drumming with his fingers on the windowpane. The sun had vanished, soon darkness would fall. I watched his face. 'It can come again,' he said, almost as though speaking to himself. Then he turned to me. 'It can come again,' he repeated. 'I just want you to know that.'

'All right,' I said, at last. 'So it can come again. All right.'

He smiled, but the smile was sorrowful. 'I had to try to tell you,' he said.

'Yes,' I said. 'I understand that.'

'You're my brother,' he said, looking straight at me, and not smiling at all.

'Yes,' I repeated, 'yes. I understand that.'

He turned back to the window, looking out. 'All that hatred down there,' he said, 'all that hatred and misery and love. It's a wonder it doesn't blow the avenue apart.'

We went to the only nightclub on a short, dark street, downtown. We squeezed through the the narrow, chattering, jampacked bar to the entrance of the big room, where the bandstand was. And we stood there for a moment, for the lights were very dim in this room and we couldn't see. Then, 'Hello, boy,' said the voice and an enormous black man, much older than Sonny or myself, erupted out of all that atmospheric lighting and put an arm around Sonny's shoulder. 'I been sitting right here,' he said, 'waiting for you.'

He had a big voice, too, and heads in the darkness turned toward us.

Sonny grinned and pulled a little away, and said, 'Creole, this is my brother. I told you about him.'

Creole shook my hand. 'I'm glad to meet you, son,' he said, and it was clear that he was glad to meet me *there*, for Sonny's sake. And he smiled, 'You got a real musician in *your* family,' and he took his arm from Sonny's shoulder and slapped him, lightly, affectionately, with the back of his hand.

'Well. Now I've heard it all,' said a voice behind us. This was another musician, and a friend of Sonny's, a coal-black, cheerful-looking man, built close to the ground. He immediately began confiding to me, at the top of his lungs, the most terrible things about Sonny, his teeth gleaming like a lighthouse and his laugh coming up out of him like the beginning of an earthquake. And it turned out that everyone at the bar knew Sonny, or almost everyone; some were musicians, working there, or nearby, or not working, some were simply hangers-on, and some were there to hear Sonny play. I was introduced to all of them and they were all very polite to me. Yet, it was clear that, for them, I was only Sonny's brother. Here, I was in Sonny's world. Or, rather: his kingdom. Here, it was not even a question that his veins bore royal blood.

They were going to play soon and Creole installed me, by myself, at a table in a dark corner. Then I watched them, Creole, and the little black man, and Sonny, and the others, while they horsed around, standing just below the bandstand. The light from the bandstand spilled just a little short of them and, watching them laughing and gesturing and moving about, I had the feeling that they, nevertheless, were being most careful not to step into that circle of light too suddenly: that if they moved into the light too suddenly, without thinking, they would perish in flame. Then, while I watched, one of them, the small black man, moved into the light and crossed the bandstand and started fooling around with his drums. Then—being funny and being, also, extremely ceremonious—Creole took Sonny by the arm and led him to the piano. A woman's voice called Sonny's name and a few hands started clapping. And Sonny, also being funny and being ceremonious, and so touched, I think, that he could have cried, but neither hiding it nor showing it, riding it like a man, grinned, and put both hands to his heart and bowed from the waist.

Creole then went to the bass fiddle and a lean, very bright-skinned brown man jumped up on the bandstand and picked up his horn. So there they were, and the atmosphere on the bandstand and in the room began to change and tighten. Someone stepped up to the microphone and announced them. Then there were all kinds of murmurs. Some people at the bar shushed others. The waitress ran around, frantically getting in the last orders, guys and chicks got closer to each other, and the lights on the bandstand, on the quartet, turned to a kind of indigo. Then they all looked different there. Creole looked about him for the last time, as though he were making certain that all his chickens were in the coop, and then he—jumped and struck the fiddle. And there they were.

All I know about music is that not many people ever really hear it. And even then, on the rare occasions when something opens within, and the music enters, what we mainly hear, or hear corroborated, are personal, private, vanishing evocations. But the man who creates the music is hearing something else, is dealing with the roar rising from the void and imposing order on it as it hits the air. What is evoked in him, then, is of another order, more terrible because it has no words, and triumphant, too, for that same reason. And his triumph, when he triumphs, is ours. I just watched Sonny's face. His face was troubled, he was working hard, but he wasn't with it. And I had the feeling that, in a way, everyone on the bandstand was waiting for him, both waiting for him and pushing him along. But as I began to watch Creole, I realized that it was Creole who held them all back. He had them on a short rein. Up there, keeping the beat with his whole body, wailing on the fiddle, with his eyes half closed, he was listening to everything, but he was listening to Sonny. He was having a dialogue with Sonny. He wanted Sonny to leave the shoreline and strike out for the deep water. He was Sonny's witness that deep water and drowning were not the same thing—he had been there, and he knew. And he wanted Sonny to know. He was waiting for Sonny to do the things on the keys which would let Creole know that Sonny was in the water.

And, while Creole listened, Sonny moved, deep within, exactly like someone in torment. I had never before thought of how awful the relationship must be between the musician and his instrument. He has to fill it, this instrument, with the breath of life, his own. He has to make it do what he wants it to do. And a piano is just a piano. It's made out of so much wood and wires and little hammers and big ones, and ivory. While there's only so much you can do with it, the only way to find this out is to try; to try and make it do everything.

And Sonny hadn't been near a piano for over a year. And he wasn't on much better terms with his life, not the life that stretched before him now. He and the piano stammered, started one way, got scared, stopped; started another way, panicked, marked time, started again; then seemed to have found a direction, panicked again, got stuck. And the face I saw on Sonny I'd never seen before. Everything had been burned out of it, and, at the same time, things usually hidden were being burned in, by the fire and fury of the battle which was occurring in him up there.

Yet, watching Creole's face as they neared the end of the first set, I had the feeling that something had happened, something I hadn't heard. Then they finished, there was scattered applause, and then, without an instant's warning, Creole started into something else, it was almost sardonic, it was *Am I Blue*. And, as though he commanded, Sonny began to play. Something began to happen. And Creole let out the reins. The dry, low, black man said something awful on the drums, Creole answered, and the drums talked back. Then the horn insisted, sweet and high, slightly detached perhaps, and Creole listened, commenting now and then, dry, and driving, beautiful and calm and old. Then they all came together again, and Sonny was part of the family again. I could tell this from his face. He seemed to have found, right there beneath his fingers, a damn brand-new piano. It seemed that he couldn't get over it. Then, for a while, just being happy with Sonny, they seemed to be agreeing with him that brand-new pianos certainly were a gas.

Then Creole stepped forward to remind them that what they were playing was the blues. He hit something in all of them, he hit something in me, myself, and the music tightened and deepened, apprehension began to beat the air. Creole began to tell us what the blues were all about. They were not about anything very new. He and his boys up there were keeping it new, at the risk of ruin, destruction, madness, and death, in order to find new ways to make us listen. For, while the tale of how we suffer, and how we are delighted, and how we may triumph is never new, it always must be heard. There isn't any other tale to tell, it's the only light we've got in all this darkness.

And this tale, according to that face, that body, those strong hands on those strings, has another aspect in every country, and a new depth in every generation. Listen, Creole seemed to be saying, listen. Now these are Sonny's blues. He made the little black man on the drums know it, and the bright, brown man on the horn. Creole wasn't trying any longer to get Sonny in the water. He was wishing him Godspeed. Then he stepped back, very slowly, filling the air with the immense suggestion that Sonny speak for himself.

Then they all gathered around Sonny and Sonny played. Every now and again one of them seemed to say, amen. Sonny's fingers filled the air with life, his life. But that life contained so many others. And Sonny went all the way back, he really began with the spare, flat statement of the opening phrase of the song. Then he began to make it his. It was very beautiful because it wasn't hurried and it was no longer a lament. I seemed to hear with what burning he had made it his, with what burning we had yet to make it ours, how we could cease lamenting. Freedom lurked around us and I understood, at last, that he could help us to be free if we would listen, that he would never be free until we did. Yet, there was no battle in his face now, I heard what he had gone through, and would continue to go through until he came to rest in earth. He had made it his: that long line, of which we knew only Mama and Daddy. And he was giving it back, as everything must be given back, so that, passing through death, it can live forever. I saw my mother's face again, and felt, for the first time, how the stones of the road she had walked on must have bruised her feet. I saw the moonlit road where my father's brother died. And it brought something else back to me, and carried me past it, I saw my little girl again and felt Isabel's tears again, and I felt my own tears begin to rise. And I was yet aware that this was only a moment, that the world waited outside, as hungry as a tiger, and that trouble stretched above us, longer than the sky.

Then it was over. Creole and Sonny let out their breath, both soaking wet, and grinning. There was a lot of applause and some of it was real. In the dark, the girl came by and I asked her to take drinks to the bandstand. There was a long pause, while they talked up there in the indigo light and after a while I saw the girl put a Scotch and milk on top of the piano for Sonny. He didn't seem to notice it, but just before they started playing again, he sipped from it and looked toward me, and nodded. Then he put it back on top of the piano. For me, then, as they began to play again, it glowed and shook above my brother's head like the very cup of trembling.

1957

VENUS, CUPID, FOLLY AND TIME

Peter Taylor

Their house alone would not have made you think there was anything so awfully wrong with Mr Dorset or his old-maid sister. But certain things about the way both of them dressed had, for a long time, annoyed and disturbed everyone. We used to see them together at the grocery store, for instance, or even in one of the big department stores downtown, wearing their bedroom slippers. Looking more closely, we would sometimes see the cuff of a pajama top or the hem of a hitched-up nightgown showing from underneath their ordinary daytime clothes. Such slovenliness in one's neighbors is so unpleasant that even husbands and wives in West Vesey Place, which was the street where the Dorsets lived, had got so they didn't like to joke about it with each other. Were the Dorsets, poor old things, losing their minds? If so, what was to be done about it? Some neighbors got so they would not even admit to themselves what they saw. And a child coming home with an ugly report on the Dorsets was apt to be told that it was time he learned to curb his imagination.

Mr Dorset wore tweed caps and sleeveless sweaters. Usually he had his sweater stuffed down inside his trousers with his shirt tails. To the women and young girls in West Vesey Place this was extremely distasteful. It made them feel as though Mr Dorset had just come from the bathroom and had got his sweater inside his trousers by mistake. There was, in fact, nothing about Mr Dorset that was not offensive to the women. Even the old touring car he drove was regarded by most of them as a disgrace to the neighborhood. Parked out in front of his house, as it usually was, it seemed a worse violation of West Vesey's zoning than the house itself. And worst of all was seeing Mr Dorset wash the car.

Mr Dorset washed his own car! He washed it not back in the alley or in his driveway but out there in the street of West Vesey Place. This would usually be on the day of one of the parties which he and his sister liked to give for young people or on a day when they were going to make deliveries of the paper flowers or the homegrown figs which they sold to their friends. Mr Dorset would appear in the street

200

carrying two buckets of warm water and wearing a pair of skin-tight coveralls. The skin-tight coveralls, of khaki material but faded almost to flesh color, were still more offensive to the women and young girls than his way of wearing his sweaters. With sponges and chamois cloths and a large scrub brush (for use on the canvas top) the old fellow would fall to and scrub away, gently at first on the canvas top and more vigorously as he progressed to the hood and body, just as though the car were something alive. Neighbor children felt that he went after the headlights exactly as if he were scrubbing the poor car's ears. There was an element of brutality in the way he did it and yet an element of tenderness too. An old lady visiting in the neighborhood once said that it was like the cleansing of a sacrificial animal. I suppose it was some such feeling as this that made all women want to turn away their eyes whenever the spectacle of Mr Dorset washing his car presented itself.

As for Mr Dorset's sister, her behavior was in its way just as offensive as his. To the men and boys in the neighborhood it was she who seemed quite beyond the pale. She would come out on her front terrace at midday clad in a faded flannel bathrobe and with her dyed black hair all undone and hanging down her back like the hair of an Indian squaw. To us whose wives and mothers did not even come downstairs in their negligees, this was very unsettling. It was hard to excuse it even on the grounds that the Dorsets were too old and lonely and hard-pressed to care about appearances any more.

Moreover, there was a boy who had gone to Miss Dorset's house one morning in the early fall to collect for his paper route and saw this very Miss Louisa Dorset pushing a carpet sweeper about one of the downstairs rooms without a stitch of clothes on. He saw her through one of the little lancet windows that opened on the front loggia of the house, and he watched her for quite a long while. She was cleaning the house in preparation for a party they were giving for young people that night, and the boy said that when she finally got hot and tired she dropped down in an easy chair and crossed her spindly, blue-veined, old legs and sat there completely naked, with her legs crossed and shaking one scrawny little foot, just as unconcerned as if she didn't care that somebody was likely to walk in on her at any moment. After a little bit the boy saw her get up again and go and lean across a table to arrange some paper flowers in a vase. Fortunately he was a nice boy, though he lived only on the edge of the West Vesey Place neighborhood, and he went away without

201

ringing the doorbell or collecting for his paper that week. But he could not resist telling his friends about what he had seen. He said it was a sight he would never forget! And she an old lady more than sixty years old who, had she not been so foolish and self-willed, might have had a house full of servants to push that carpet sweeper for her!

This foolish pair of old people had given up almost everything in life for each other's sake. And it was not at all necessary. When they were young they could have come into a decent inheritance, or now that they were old they might have been provided for by a host of rich relatives. It was only a matter of their being a little tolerant—or even civil—toward their kinspeople. But this was something that old Mr Dorset and his sister could never consent to do. Almost all their lives they had spoken of their father's kin as 'Mama's in-laws' and of their mother's kin as 'Papa's in-laws.' Their family name was Dorset, not on one side but on both sides. Their parents had been distant cousins. As a matter of fact, the Dorset family in the city of Chatham had once been so large and was so long established there that it would have been hard to estimate how distant the kinship might be. But still it was something that the old couple never liked to have mentioned. Most of their mother's close kin had, by the time I am speaking of, moved off to California, and most of their father's people lived somewhere up East. But Miss Dorset and her old bachelor brother found any contact, correspondence, even an exchange of Christmas cards with these in-laws intolerable. It was a case, so they said, of the in-laws respecting the value of the dollar above all else, whereas they, Miss Louisa and Mr Alfred Dorset, placed importance on other things.

They lived in a dilapidated and curiously mutilated house on a street which, except for their own house, was the most splendid street in the entire city. Their house was one that you or I would have been ashamed to live in—even in the lean years of the early thirties. In order to reduce taxes the Dorsets had had the third story of the house torn away, leaving an ugly, flat-topped effect without any trim or ornamentation. Also, they had had the south wing pulled down and had sealed the scars not with matching brick but with a speckled stucco that looked raw and naked. All this the old couple did in violation of the strict zoning laws of West Vesey Place, and for doing so they would most certainly have been prosecuted except that they were the Dorsets and except that this was during the Depression when zoning laws weren't easy to enforce in a city like Chatham.

To the young people whom she and her brother entertained at their house once each year Miss Louisa Dorset liked to say: 'We have given up everything for each other. Our only income is from our paper flowers and our figs.' The old lady, though without showing any great skill or talent for it, made paper flowers. During the winter months, her brother took her in that fifteen-year-old touring car of theirs, with its steering wheel on the wrong side and with isinglass side curtains that were never taken down, to deliver these flowers to her customers. The flowers looked more like sprays of tinted potato chips than like any real flowers. Nobody could possibly have wanted to buy them except that she charged next to nothing for them and except that to people with children it seemed important to be on the Dorsets' list of worthwhile people. Nobody could really have wanted Mr Dorset's figs either. He cultivated a dozen little bushes along the back wall of their house, covering them in the wintertime with some odd-looking boxes which he had had constructed for the purpose. The bushes were very productive, but the figs they produced were dried up little things without much taste. During the summer months he and his sister went about in their car, with the side curtains still up, delivering the figs to the same customers who bought the paper flowers. The money they made could hardly have paid for the gas it took to run the car. It was a great waste and it was very foolish of them.

And yet, despite everything, this foolish pair of old people, this same Miss Louisa and Mr Alfred Dorset, had become social arbiters of a kind in our city. They had attained this position entirely through their fondness for giving an annual dancing party for young people. To *young* people—to *very* young people—the Dorsets' hearts went out. I don't mean to suggest that their hearts went out to orphans or to the children of the poor, for they were not foolish in that way. The guests at their little dancing parties were the thirteen- and fourteen-year-olds from families like the one they had long ago set themselves against, young people from the very houses to which, in season, they delivered their figs and their paper flowers. And when the night of one of their parties came round, it was in fact the custom for Mr Alfred to go in the same old car and fetch all the invited guests to his house. His sister might explain to reluctant parents that this saved the children the embarrassment of being taken to their first dance by

Mommy or Daddy. But the parents knew well enough that for twenty years the Dorsets had permitted no adult person, besides themselves, to put foot inside their house.

At those little dancing parties which the Dorsets gave, peculiar things went on—unsettling things to the boys and girls who had been fetched round in the old car. Sensible parents wished to keep their children away. Yet what could they do? For a Chatham girl to have to explain, a few years later, why she never went to a party at the Dorsets' was like having to explain why she had never been a debutante. For a boy it was like having to explain why he had not gone up East to school or even why his father hadn't belonged to the Chatham Racquet Club. If when you were thirteen or fourteen you got invited to the Dorsets' house, you went; it was the way of letting people know from the outset who you were. In a busy, modern city like Chatham you cannot afford to let people forget who you are—not for a moment, not at any age. Even the Dorsets knew that.

Many a little girl, after one of those evenings at the Dorsets', was heard to cry out in her sleep. When waked, or half waked, her only explanation might be: 'It was just the fragrance from the paper flowers.' Or: 'I dreamed I could really smell the paper flowers.' Many a boy was observed by his parents to seem 'different' afterward. He became 'secretive.' The parents of the generation that had to attend those parties never pretended to understand what went on at the Dorsets' house. And even to those of us who were in that unlucky generation, it seemed we were half a lifetime learning what really took place during our one evening under the Dorsets' roof. Before our turn to go ever came round, we had for years been hearing about what it was like from older boys and girls. Afterward, we continued to hear about it from those who followed us. And, looking back on it, nothing about the one evening when you were actually there ever seemed quite so real as the glimpses and snatches which you got from those people before and after you—the second-hand impressions of the Dorsets' behavior, of things they said, of looks that passed between them.

Since Miss Dorset kept no servants, she always opened her own door. I suspect that for the guests at her parties the sight of her opening her door, in her astonishing attire, came as the most violent shock of the whole evening. On these occasions, she and her brother got themselves up as we had never seen them before and never would again. The old lady invariably wore a modish white evening gown, a garment perfectly fitted to her spare and scrawny figure and cut in such high fashion that it must necessarily have been new that year. And never to be worn but that one night! Her hair, long and thick and newly dyed for the occasion, would be swept upward and forward in a billowy mass which was topped by a corsage of yellow and coral paper flowers. Her cheeks and lips would be darkly rouged. On her long bony arms and her bare shoulders she would have applied some kind of suntan powder. Whatever else you had been led to expect of the evening, no one had ever warned you sufficiently about the radical change to be noted in her appearance— or in that of her brother, either. By the end of the party Miss Louisa might look as dowdy as ever, and Mr Alfred a little worse than usual. But at the outset, when the party was assembling in their drawing room, even Mr Alfred appeared resplendent in a nattily tailored tuxedo, with exactly the shirt, the collar, and the tie which fashion prescribed that year. His gray hair was nicely trimmed, his puffy old face freshly shaven. He was powdered with the same dark powder that his sister used. One felt even that his cheeks had been lightly touched with rouge.

A strange perfume pervaded the atmosphere of the house. The moment you set foot inside, this awful fragrance engulfed you. It was like a mixture of spicy incense and sweet attar of roses. And always, too, there was the profusion of paper flowers. The flowers were everywhere—on every cabinet and console, every inlaid table and carved chest, on every high, marble mantelpiece, on the bookshelves. In the entrance hall special tiers must have been set up to hold the flowers, because they were there in overpowering masses. They were in such abundance that it seemed hardly possible that Miss Dorset could have made them all. She must have spent weeks and weeks preparing them, even months, perhaps even the whole year between parties. When she went about delivering them to her customers, in the months following, they were apt to be somewhat faded and dusty; but on the night of the party, the colors of the flowers seemed even more impressive and more unlikely than their number. They were fuchsia, they were chartreuse, they were coral, aquamarine, brown, they were even black.

Everywhere in the Dorsets' house too were certain curious illuminations and lighting effects. The source of the light was usually hidden and its purpose was never obvious at once. The lighting was a subtler element than either the perfume or the paper flowers, and ultimately it was more disconcerting. A shaft of lavender light would catch a young visitor's eye and lead it, seemingly without purpose, in among the flowers. Then just beyond the point where the strength of the light would begin to diminish, the eye would discover something. In a small aperture in the mass of flowers, or sometimes in a larger grotto-like opening, there would be a piece of sculpture—in the hall a plaster replica of Rodin's 'The Kiss,' in the library an antique plaque of Leda and the Swan. Or just above the flowers would be hung a picture, usually a black and white print but sometimes a reproduction in color. On the landing of the stairway leading down to the basement ballroom was the only picture that one was likely to learn the title of at the time. It was a tiny color print of Bronzino's 'Venus, Cupid, Folly and Time.' This picture was not even framed. It was simply tacked on the wall, and it had obviously been torn—rather carelessly, perhaps hurriedly—from a book or magazine. The title and the name of the painter were printed in the white margin underneath.

About these works of art most of us had been warned by older boys and girls; and we stood in painful dread of that moment when Miss Dorset or her brother might catch us staring at any one of their pictures or sculptures. We had been warned, time and again, that during the course of the evening moments would come when she or he would reach out and touch the other's elbow and indicate, with a nod or just the trace of a smile, some guest whose glance had strayed among the flowers.

To some extent the dread which all of us felt that evening at the Dorsets' cast a shadow over the whole of our childhood. Yet for nearly twenty years the Dorsets continued to give their annual party. And even the most sensible of parents were not willing to keep their children away.

But a thing happened finally which could almost have been predicted. Young people, even in West Vesey Place, will not submit forever to the prudent counsel of their parents. Or some of them won't. There was a boy named Ned Meriwether and his sister Emily Meriwether, who lived with their parents in West Vesey Place just one block away from the Dorsets' house. In November, Ned and Emily were invited to the Dorsets' party, and because they dreaded it they decided to play a trick on everyone concerned—even on themselves, as it turned out . . . They got up a plan for smuggling an uninvited guest into the Dorsets' party.

The parents of this Emily and Ned sensed that their children were concealing something from them and suspected that the two were up to mischief of some kind. But they managed to deceive themselves with the thought that it was only natural for young people—'mere children'—to be nervous about going to the Dorsets' house. And so instead of questioning them during the last hour before they left for the party, these sensible parents tried to do everything in their power to calm their two children. The boy and the girl, seeing this was the case, took advantage of it.

'You must not go down to the front door with us when we leave,' the daughter insisted to her mother. And she persuaded both Mr and Mrs Meriwether that after she and her brother were dressed for the party they should all wait together in the upstairs sitting room until Mr Dorset came to fetch the two young people in his car.

When, at eight o'clock, the lights of the automobile appeared in the street below, the brother and sister were still upstairs—watching from the bay window of the family sitting room. They kissed Mother and Daddy goodbye and then they flew down the stairs and across the wide, carpeted entrance hall to a certain dark recess where a boy named Tom Bascomb was hidden. This boy was the uninvited guest whom Ned and Emily were going to smuggle into the party. They had left the front door unlatched for Tom, and from the upstairs window just a few minutes ago they had watched him come across their front lawn. Now in the little recess of the hall there was a quick exchange of overcoats and hats between Ned Meriwether and Tom Bascomb; for it was a feature of the plan that Tom should attend the party as Ned and that Ned should go as the uninvited guest.

In the darkness of the recess, Ned fidgeted and dropped Tom Bascomb's coat on the floor. But the boy, Tom Bascomb, did not fidget. He stepped out into the light of the hall and began methodically getting into the overcoat which he would wear tonight. He was not a boy who lived in the West Vesey Place neighborhood (he was in fact the very boy who had once watched Miss Dorset cleaning house without any clothes on), and he did not share Emily's and Ned's nervous excitement about the evening. The sound of Mr Dorset's footsteps outside did not disturb him. When both Ned and Emily stood frozen by that sound, he continued buttoning the unfamiliar coat and even amused himself by stretching forth one arm to observe how high the sleeve came on his wrist.

The doorbell rang, and from his dark corner Ned Meriwether whispered to his sister and to Tom: 'Don't worry. I'll be at the Dorsets' in plenty of time.'

Tom Bascomb only shrugged his shoulders at this reassurance. Presently when he looked at Emily's flushed face and saw her batting her eyes like a nervous monkey, a crooked smile played upon his lips. Then, at a sign form Emily, Tom followed her to the entrance door and permitted her to introduce him to old Mr Dorset as her brother.

From the window of the upstairs sitting room the Meriwether parents watched Mr Dorset and this boy and this girl walking across the lawn toward Mr Dorset's peculiar-looking car. A light shone bravely and protectively from above the entrance of the house, and in its rays the parents were able to detect the strange angle at which Brother was carrying his head tonight and how his new fedora already seemed too small for him. They even noticed that he seemed a bit taller tonight.

'I hope it's all right,' said the mother.

'What do you mean "all right"?' the father asked petulantly.

'I mean—' the mother began, and then she hesitated. She did not want to mention that the boy out there did not look like their own Ned. It would have seemed to give away her feelings too much. 'I mean that I wonder if I should have put Sister in that long dress at this age and let her wear my cape. I'm afraid the cape is really inappropriate. She's still young for that sort of thing.'

'Oh,' said the father, 'I thought you meant something else.'

'Whatever else did you think I meant, Edwin?' the mother said, suddenly breathless.

'I thought you meant the business we've discussed before,' he said, although this was of course not what he had thought she meant. He had thought she meant that the boy out there did not look like their Ned. To him it had seemed even that the boy's step was different from Ned's. 'The Dorsets' parties,' he said, 'are not very nice affairs to be sending your children to, Muriel. That's all I thought you meant.'

'But we *can't* keep them away,' the mother said defensively.

'Oh, it's just that they are growing up faster than we realize,' said the father, glancing at his wife out of the corner of his eye.

By this time Mr Dorset's car had pulled out of sight, and from downstairs Muriel Meriwether thought she heard another door closing. 'What was that?' she said, putting one hand on her husband's.

'Don't be so jumpy,' her husband said irritably, snatching away his hand. 'It's the servants closing up in the kitchen.'

Both of them knew that the servants had closed up in the kitchen long before this. Both of them had heard quite distinctly the sound of the side door closing as Ned went out. But they went on talking and deceiving themselves in this fashion during most of the evening.

Even before she opened the door to Mr Dorset, little Emily Meriwether had known that there would be no difficulty about passing Tom Bascomb off as her brother. In the first place, she knew that without his spectacles Mr Dorset could hardly see his hand before his face and knew that due to some silly pride he had he never put on his spectacles except when he was behind the wheel of his automobile. This much was common knowledge. In the second place, Emily knew from experience that neither he nor his sister ever made any real pretense of knowing one child in their general acquaintance from another. And so, standing in the doorway and speaking almost in a whisper, Emily had merely to introduce first herself and then her pretended brother to Mr Dorset. After that the three of them walked in silence from their father's house to the waiting car.

Emily was wearing her mother's second-best evening wrap, a white lapin cape which, on Emily, swept the ground. As she walked between the boy and the man, the touch of the cape's soft silk lining on her bare arms and on her shoulders spoke to her silently of a strange girl she had seen in her looking glass upstairs tonight. And with her every step toward the car the skirt of her long taffeta gown whispered her own name to her: *Emily . . . Emily*. She heard it distinctly, and yet the name sounded unfamiliar. Once during this unreal walk from house to car she glanced at the mysterious boy, Tom Bascomb, longing to ask him—if only with her eyes—for some reassurance that she was really she. But Tom Bascomb was absorbed in his own irrelevant observations. With his head tilted back he was gazing upward at the nondescript winter sky where, among drifting clouds, a few pale stars were shedding their dull light alike on West Vesey Place and on the rest of the world. Emily drew her wrap tightly about her, and when presently Mr Dorset held open the door to the back seat of his car she shut her eyes and plunged into the pitch blackness of the car's interior.

Tom Bascomb was a year older than Ned Meriwether and he was nearly two years older than Emily. He had been Ned's friend first. He and Ned had played baseball together on Saturdays before Emily ever set eyes on him. Yet according to Tom Bascomb himself, with whom several of us older boys talked just a few weeks after the night he went to the Dorsets', Emily always insisted that it was she who had known him first. On what she based this false claim Tom could not say. And on the two or three other occasions when we got Tom to talk about that night, he kept saying that he didn't understand what it was that had made Emily and Ned quarrel over which of them knew him first and knew him better.

We could have told him what it was, I think. But we didn't. It would have been too hard to say to him that at one time or another all of us in West Vesey had had our Tom Bascombs. Tom lived with his parents in an apartment house on a wide thoroughfare known as Division Boulevard, and his only real connection with West Vesey Place was that that street was included in his paper route. During the early morning hours he rode his bicycle along West Vesey and along other quiet streets like it, carefully aiming a neatly rolled paper at the dark loggia, at the colonnaded porch, or at the ornamented doorway of each of the palazzi and châteaux and manor houses that glowered at him in the dawn. He was well thought of as a paper boy. If by mistake one of his papers went astray and lit on an upstairs balcony or on the roof of a porch, Tom would always take more careful aim and throw another. Even if the paper only went into the shrubbery, Tom got off his bicycle and fished it out. He wasn't the kind of boy to whom it would have occurred that the old fogies and the rich kids in West Vesey could very well get out and scramble for their own papers.

Actually, a party at the Dorsets' house was more a grand tour of the house than a real party. There was a half hour spent over very light refreshments (fruit Jello, English tea biscuits, lime punch). There was another half hour ostensibly given to general dancing in the basement ballroom (to the accompaniment of victrola music). But mainly there was the tour. As the party passed through the house, stopping sometimes to sit down in the principal rooms, the host and hostess provided entertainment in the form of an almost continuous dialogue between themselves. This dialogue was famous and was full of interest, being all about how much the Dorsets had given up for each other's sake and about how much higher the tone of Chatham society used to be than it was nowadays. They would invariably speak of their parents, who had died within a year of each other when Miss Louisa and Mr Alfred were still in their teens; they even spoke of their wicked in-laws. When their parents died, the wicked in-laws had first tried to make them sell the house, then had tried to separate them and send them away to boarding schools, and had ended by trying to marry them off to 'just anyone.' Their two grandfathers had still been alive in those days and each had had a hand in the machinations, after the failure of which each grandfather had disinherited them. Mr Alfred and Miss Louisa spoke also of how, a few years later, a procession of 'young nobodies' had come of their own accord trying to steal the two of them away from each other. Both he and she would scowl at the very recollection of those 'just anybodies' and those 'nobodies,' those 'would-be suitors' who always turned out to be misguided fortune hunters and had to be driven away.

The Dorsets' dialogue usually began in the living room the moment Mr Dorset returned with his last collection of guests. (He sometimes had to make five or six trips in the car.) There, as in other rooms afterward, they were likely to begin with a reference to the room itself or perhaps to some piece of furniture in the room. For instance, the extraordinary length of the drawing room—or reception room, as the Dorsets called it—would lead them to speak of an even longer room which they had had torn away from the house. 'It grieved us, we wept,' Miss Dorset would say, 'to have Mama's French drawing room torn away from us.'

'But we tore it away from ourselves,' her brother would add, 'as we tore away our in-laws—because we could not afford them.' Both of them spoke in a fine declamatory style, but they frequently interrupted themselves with a sad little laugh which expressed something quite different from what they were saying and which seemed to serve them as an aside not meant for our ears.

'That was one of our greatest sacrifices,' Miss Dorset would say, referring still to her mother's French drawing room.

And her brother would say: 'But we knew the day had passed in Chatham for entertainments worthy of that room.'

'It was the room which Mama and Papa loved best, but we gave it up because we knew, from our upbringing, which things to give up.'

From this they might go on to anecdotes about their childhood. Sometimes their parents had left them for months or even a whole year at a time with only the housekeeper or with trusted servants to see after them. 'You could trust servants then,' they explained. And: 'In those days parents could do that sort of thing, because in those days there was a responsible body of people within which your young people could always find proper companionship.'

In the library, to which the party always moved from the drawing room, Mr Dorset was fond of exhibiting snapshots of the house taken before the south wing was pulled down. As the pictures were passed around, the dialogue continued. It was often there that they told the story of how the in-laws had tried to force them to sell the house. 'For the sake of economy!' Mr Dorset would exclaim, adding an ironic 'Ha ha!'

'As though money—' he would begin.

'As though money ever took the place,' his sister would come in, 'of living with your own kind.'

'Or of being well born,' said Mr Dorset.

After the billiard room, where everyone who wanted it was permitted one turn with the only cue that there seemed to be in the house, and after the dining room, where it was promised refreshments would be served later, the guests would be taken down to the ballroom—purportedly for dancing. Instead of everyone's being urged to dance, however, once they were assembled in the ballroom, Miss Dorset would announce that she and her brother understood the timidity which young people felt about dancing and that all that she and he intended to do was to set the party a good example . . . It was only Miss Louisa and Mr Alfred who danced. For perhaps thirty minutes, in a room without light excepting that from a few weak bulbs concealed among the flowers, the old couple danced; and they danced with such grace and there was such perfect harmony in all their movements that the guests stood about in stunned silence, as if hypnotized. The Dorsets waltzed, they two-stepped, they even fox-trotted, stopping only long enough between dances for Mr Dorset, amid general applause, to change the victrola record.

But it was when their dance was ended that all the effects of the Dorsets' careful grooming that night would have vanished. And, alas, they made no effort to restore themselves. During the remainder of the evening Mr Dorset went about with his bow tie hanging limply on his damp shirtfront, a gold collar button shining above it. A strand of gray hair, which normally covered his bald spot on top, now would have fallen on the wrong side of his part and hung like fringe about his ear. On his face and neck the thick layer of powder was streaked with perspiration. Miss Dorset was usually in an even more disheveled state, depending somewhat upon the fashion of her dress

212

that year. But always her powder was streaked, her lipstick entirely gone, her hair falling down on all sides, and her corsage dangling somewhere about the nape of her neck. In this condition they led the party upstairs again, not stopping until they had reached the second floor of the house.

On the second floor we—the guests—were shown the rooms which the Dorsets' parents had once occupied (the Dorsets' own rooms were never shown). We saw, in glass museum cases along the hallway, the dresses and suits and hats and even the shoes which Miss Louisa and Mr Alfred had worn to parties when they were very young. And now the dialogue, which had been left off while the Dorsets danced, was resumed. 'Ah, the happy time,' one of them would say, 'was when we were *your* age!' And then, exhorting us to be happy and gay while we were still safe in the bosom of our own kind and before the world came crowding in on us with its ugly demands, the Dorsets would recall the happiness they had known when they were very young. This was their *pièce de résistance*. With many a wink and blush and giggle and shake of the forefinger—and of course standing before the whole party—they each would remind the other of his or her naughty behavior in some old-fashioned parlor game or of certain silly little flirtations which they had long ago caught each other in.

They were on their way downstairs again now, and by the time they had finished with this favorite subject they would be downstairs. They would be in the dark, flower-bedecked downstairs hall and just before entering the dining room for the promised refreshments: the fruit Jello, the English tea biscuits, the lime punch.

And now for a moment Mr Dorset bars the way to the dining room and prevents his sister from opening the closed door. 'Now, my good friends,' he says, 'let us eat, drink, and be merry!'

'For the night is yet young,' says his sister.

'Tonight you must be gay and carefree,' Mr Dorset enjoins.

'Because in this house we are all friends,' Miss Dorset says. 'We are all young, we all love one another.'

'And love can make us all young forever,' her brother says.

'Remember!'

'Remember this evening always, sweet young people!'

'Remember!'

'Remember what our life is like here!'

And now Miss Dorset, with one hand on the knob of the great

213

door which she is about to throw open, leans a little toward the guests and whispers hoarsely: 'This is what it is like to be young forever!'

Ned Meriwether was waiting behind a big japonica shrub near the sidewalk when, about twenty minutes after he had last seen Emily, the queer old touring car drew up in front of the Dorsets' house. During the interval, the car had gone from the Meriwether house to gather a number of other guests, and so it was not only Emily and Tom who alighted on the sidewalk before the Dorsets' house. The group was just large enough to make it easy for Ned to slip out from his dark hiding place and join them without being noticed by Mr Dorset. And now the group was escorted rather unceremoniously up to the door of the house, and Mr Dorset departed to fetch more guests.

They were received at the door by Miss Dorset. Her eyesight was no doubt better than her brother's, but still there was really no danger of her detecting an uninvited guest. Those of us who had gone to that house in the years just before Ned and Emily came along could remember that, during a whole evening, when their house was full of young people, the Dorsets made no introductions and made no effort to distinguish which of their guests was which. They did not even make a count of heads. Perhaps they did vaguely recognize some of the faces, because sometimes when they had come delivering figs or paper flowers to a house they had of necessity encountered a young child there, and always they smiled sweetly at it, asked its age, and calculated on their old fingers how many years must pass before the child would be eligible for an invitation. Yet at those moments something in the way they had held up their fingers and in the way they had gazed *at* the little face instead of into it had revealed their lack of interest in the individual child. And later, when the child was finally old enough to receive their invitation, he found it was still no different with the Dorsets. Even in their own house it was evidently to the young people as a group that the Dorsets' hearts went out; while they had the boys and girls under their roof they herded them about like so many little thoroughbred calves. Even when Miss Dorset opened the front door she did so exactly as though she were opening a gate. She pulled it open very slowly, standing half behind it to keep out of harm's way. And the children, all huddled together, surged in.

How meticulously this Ned and Emily Meriwether must have laid their plans for that evening! And the whole business might have come out all right if only they could have foreseen the effect which one part of their plan—rather a last-minute embellishment of it— would produce upon Ned himself. Barely ten minutes after they entered the house, Ned was watching Tom as he took his seat on the piano bench beside Emily. Ned probably watched Tom closely, because certainly he knew what the next move was going to be. The moment Miss Louisa Dorset's back was turned Tom Bascomb slipped his arm gently about Emily's little waist and commenced kissing her all over her pretty face. It was almost as if her were kissing away tears.

This spectacle on the piano bench, and others like it which followed, had been an inspiration of the last day or so before the party. Or so Ned and Emily maintained afterward when defending themselves to their parents. But no matter when it was conceived, a part of their plan it was, and Ned must have believed himself fully prepared for it. Probably he expected to join in the round of giggling which it produced from the other guests. But now that the time had come—it is easy to imagine—the boy Ned Meriwether found himself not quite able to join in the fun. He watched with the others, but he was not quite infected by their laughter. He stood a little apart, and possibly he was hoping that Emily and Tom would not notice his failure to appreciate the success of their comedy. He was no doubt baffled by his own feelings, by the failure of his own enthusiasm, and by a growing desire to withdraw himself from the plot and from the party itself.

It is easy to imagine Ned's uneasiness and confusion that night. And I believe the account which I have given of Emily's impressions and her delicate little sensations while on the way to the party has a ring of truth about it, though actually the account was supplied by girls who knew her only slightly, who were not at the party, who could not possibly have seen her afterward. It may, after all, represent only what other girls imagined she would have felt. As for the account of how Mr and Mrs Meriwether spent the evening, it is their very own. And they did not hesitate to give it to anyone who would listen.

It was a long time, though, before many of us had a clear picture of the main events of the evening. We heard very soon that the parties for young people were to be no more, that there had been a wild scramble and chase through the Dorsets' house, and that it had ended by the Dorsets locking some boy—whether Ned or Tom was not easy to determine at first—in a queer sort of bathroom in which the plumbing had been disconnected, and even the fixtures removed, I believe. (Later I learned that there was nothing literally sinister about the bathroom itself. By having the pipes disconnected to this, and perhaps other bathrooms, the Dorsets had obtained further reductions in their taxes.) But a clear picture of the whole evening wasn't to be had—not without considerable searching. For one thing, the Meriwether parents immediately, within a week after the party, packed their son and daughter off to boarding schools. Accounts from the other children were contradictory and vague—perversely so, it seemed. Parents reported to each other that the little girls had nightmares which were worse even than those which their older sisters had had. And the boys were secretive and elusive, even with us older boys when we questioned them about what had gone on.

One sketchy account of events leading up to the chase, however, did go the rounds almost at once. Ned must have written it back to some older boy in a letter, because it contained information which no one but Ned could have had. The account went like this: When Mr Dorset returned from his last roundup of guests, he came hurrying into the drawing room where the others were waiting and said in a voice trembling with excitement: 'Now, let us all be seated, my young friends, and let us warm ourselves with some good talk.'

At that moment everyone who was not already seated made a dash for a place on one of the divans or love seats or even in one of the broad window seats. (There were no individual chairs in the room.) Everyone made a dash, that is, except Ned. Ned did not move. He remained standing beside a little table rubbing his fingers over its polished surface. And from this moment he was clearly an object of suspicion in the eyes of his host and hostess. Soon the party moved from the drawing room to the library, but in whatever room they stopped Ned managed to isolate himself from the rest. He would sit or stand looking down at his hands until once again an explosion of giggles filled the room. Then he would look up just in time to see Tom Bascomb's cheek against Emily's or his arm about her waist.

For nearly two hours Ned didn't speak a word to anyone. He endured the Dorsets' dialogue, the paper flowers, the perfumed air, the works of art. Whenever a burst of giggling forced him to raise his eyes, he would look up at Tom and Emily and then turn his eyes away. Before looking down at his hands again, he would let his eyes travel slowly about the room until they came to rest on the figures of the two Dorsets. That, it seems, was how he happened to discover that the Dorsets understood, or thought they understood, what the giggles meant. In the great mirror mounted over the library mantel he saw them exchanging half-suppressed smiles. Their smiles lasted precisely as long as the giggling continued, and then, in the mirror, Ned saw their faces change and grow solemn when their eyes—their identical, tiny, dull, amber-colored eyes—focused upon himself.

From the library the party continued on the regular tour of the house. At last when they had been to the ballroom and watched the Dorsets dance, had been upstairs to gaze upon the faded party clothes in the museum cases, they descended into the the downstairs hall and were just before being turned into the dining room. The guests had already heard the Dorsets teasing each other about the silly little flirtations and about their naughtiness in parlor games when they were young and had listened to their exhortations to be gay and happy and carefree. Then just when Miss Dorset leaned toward them and whispered, 'This is what it is like to be young forever,' there rose a chorus of laughter, breathless and shrill, yet loud and intensely penetrating.

Ned Meriwether, standing on the bottom step of the stairway, lifted his eyes and looked over the heads of the party to see Tom and Emily half hidden in a bower of paper flowers and caught directly in a ray of mauve light. The two had squeezed themselves into a little niche there and stood squarely in front of the Rodin statuary. Tom had one arm placed about Emily's shoulders and he was kissing her lightly first on the lobe of one ear and then on the tip of her nose. Emily stood as rigid and pale as the plaster sculpture behind her and with just the faintest smile on her lips. Ned looked at the two of them and then turned his glance at once on the Dorsets.

He found Miss Louisa and Mr Alfred gazing quite openly at Tom and Emily and frankly grinning at the spectacle. It was more than Ned could endure. 'Don't you *know*?' he wailed, as if in great physical pain. 'Can't you *tell*? Can't you see who they *are*? They're *brother* and *sister!*'

From the other guests came one concerted gasp. And then an instant later, mistaking Ned's outcry to be something he had planned all along and probably intended—as they imagined—for the very cream of the jest, the whole company burst once again into

217

laughter—not a chorus of laughter this time but a volley of loud guffaws from the boys, and from the girls a cacophony of separately articulated shrieks and trills.

None of the guests present that night could—or would—give a satisfactory account of what happened next. Everyone insisted that he had not even looked at the Dorsets, that he, or she, didn't know how Miss Louisa and Mr Alfred reacted at first. Yet this was precisely what those of us who had gone there in the past *had* to know. And when finally we did manage to get an account of it, we knew that it was a very truthful and accurate one. Because we got it, of course, from Tom Bascomb.

Since Ned's outburst came after the dancing exhibition, the Dorsets were in their most disheveled state. Miss Louisa's hair was fallen half over her face, and that long, limp strand of Mr Alfred's was dangling about his left ear. Like that, they stood at the doorway to the dining room grinning at Tom Bascomb's antics. And when Tom Bascomb, hearing Ned's wail, whirled about, the grins were still on the Dorsets' faces even though the guffaws and the shrieks of laughter were now silenced. Tom said that for several moments they continued to wear their grins like masks and that you couldn't really tell how they were taking it all until presently Miss Louisa's face, still wearing the grin, began turning all the queer colors of her paper flowers. Then the grin vanished from her lips and her mouth fell open and every bit of color went out of her face. She took a step backward and leaned against the doorjamb with her mouth still open and her eyes closed. If she hadn't been on her feet, Tom said he would have thought she was dead. Her brother didn't look at her, but his own grin had vanished just as hers did, and his face, all drawn and wrinkled, momentarily turned a dull copperish green.

Presently, though, he too went white, not white in faintness but in anger. His little brown eyes now shone like resin. And he took several steps toward Ned Meriwether. 'What we know is that you are not one of us,' he croaked. 'We have perceived that from the beginning! We don't know how you got here or who you are. But the important question is, What are you doing here among these nice children?'

The question seemed to restore life to Miss Louisa. Her amber eyes popped wide open. She stepped away from the door and began pinning up her hair which had fallen down on her shoulders, and at the same time addressing the guests who were huddled together in

218

the center of the hall. 'Who is he, children? He is an intruder, that we know. If you know who he is, you must tell us.'

'Who *am* I? Why, I am Tom Bascomb!' shouted Ned, still from the bottom step of the stairway. 'I am Tom Bascomb, your paper boy.'

Then he turned and fled up the stairs toward the second floor. In a moment Mr Dorset was after him.

To the real Tom Bascomb it had seemed that Ned honestly believed what he had been saying; and his own first impulse was to shout a denial. But being a level-headed boy and seeing how bad things were, Tom went instead to Miss Dorset and whispered to her that Tom Bascomb was a pretty tough guy and that she had better let *him* call the police for her. She told him where the telephone was in the side hall, and he started away.

But Miss Dorset changed her mind. She ran after Tom telling him not to call. Some of the guests mistook this for the beginning of another chase. Before the old lady could overtake Tom, however, Ned himself had appeared in the doorway toward which she and Tom were moving. He had come down the back stairway and he was calling out to Emily, 'We're going *home*, Sis!'

A cheer went up from the whole party. Maybe it was this that caused Ned to lose his head, or maybe it was simply the sight of Miss Dorset rushing at him that did it. At any rate, the next moment he was running up the front stairs again, this time with Miss Dorset in pursuit.

When Tom returned from the telephone, all was quiet in the hall. The guests—everybody except Emily—had moved to the foot of the stairs and they were looking up and listening. From upstairs Tom could hear Ned saying, 'All right. All right. All right.' The old couple had him cornered.

Emily was standing in the little niche among the flowers. And it is the image of Emily Meriwether standing among the paper flowers that tantalizes me whenever I think or hear someone speak of that evening. That, more than anything else, can make me wish that I had been there. I shall never cease to wonder what kind of thoughts were in her head to make her seem so oblivious to all that was going on while she stood there, and, for that matter, what had been in her mind all evening while she endured Tom Bascomb's caresses. When, in years since, I have had reason to wonder what some girl or woman is thinking—some Emily grown older—my mind nearly always returns to the image of that girl among the paper flowers. Tom said that when he returned from the telephone she looked very solemn and pale still but that her mind didn't seem to be on any of the present excitement. Immediately he went to her and said, 'Your dad is on his way over, Emily.' For it was the Meriwether parents he had telephoned, of course, and not the police.

It seemed to Tom that so far as he was concerned the party was now over. There was nothing more he could do. Mr Dorset was upstairs guarding the door to the strange little room in which Ned was locked up. Miss Dorset was serving lime punch to the other guests in the dining room, all the while listening with one ear for the arrival of the police whom Tom pretended he had called. When the doorbell finally rang and Miss Dorset hurried to answer it, Tom slipped quietly out through the pantry and through the kitchen and left the house by the back door as the Meriwether parents entered by the front.

There was no difficulty in getting Edwin and Muriel Meriwether, the children's parents, to talk about what happened after they arrived that night. Both of them were sensible and clear-headed people, and they were not so conservative as some of our other neighbors in West Vesey. Being fond of gossip of any kind and fond of reasonably funny stories on themselves, they told how their children had deceived them earlier in the evening and how they had deceived themselves later. They tended to blame themselves more than the children for what had happened. They tried to protect the children from any harm or embarrassment that might result from it by sending them off to boarding school. In their talk they never referred directly to Tom's reprehensible conduct or to the possible motives that the children might have had for getting up their plan. They tried to spare their children and they tried to spare Tom, but unfortunately it didn't occur to them to try to spare the poor old Dorsets.

When Miss Louisa opened the door, Mr Meriwether said, 'I'm Edwin Meriwether, Miss Dorset. I've come for my son Ned.'

'And for your daughter Emily, I hope,' his wife whispered to him.

'And for my daughter Emily.'

Before Miss Dorset could answer him, Edwin Meriwether spied Mr Dorset descending the stairs. With his wife, Muriel, sticking close to his side Edwin now strode over to the foot of the stairs. 'Mr Dorset,' he began, 'my son Ned—'

From behind them, Edwin and Muriel now heard Miss Dorset saying, 'All the invited guests are gathered in the dining room.' From where they were standing the two parents could see into the dining room. Suddenly they turned and hurried in there. Mr Dorset and his sister of course followed them.

Muriel Meriwether went directly to Emily who was standing in a group of girls. 'Emily, where is your brother?'

Emily said nothing, but one of the boys answered: 'I think they've got him locked up upstairs somewhere.'

'Oh, no!' said Miss Louisa, a hairpin in her mouth—for she was still rather absent-mindedly working at her hair. 'It is an intruder that my brother has upstairs.'

Mr Dorset began speaking in a confidential tone to Edwin. 'My dear neighbor,' he said, 'our paper boy saw fit to intrude himself upon our company tonight. But we recognized him as an outsider from the start.'

Muriel Meriwether asked: 'Where *is* the paper boy? Where is the paper boy, Emily?'

Again one of the boys volunteered: 'He went out through the back door, Mrs Meriwether.'

The eyes of Mr Alfred and Miss Louisa searched the room for Tom. Finally their eyes met and they smiled coyly. '*All* the children are being mischievous tonight,' said Miss Louisa, and it was quite as though she had said, 'all *we* children.' Then, still smiling, she said, 'Your tie has come undone, Brother. Mr and Mrs Meriwether will hardly know what to think.'

Mr Alfred fumbled for a moment with his tie but soon gave it up. Now with a bashful glance at the Meriwether parents, and giving a nod in the direction of the children, he actually said, 'I'm afraid we've all decided to play a trick on Mr and Mrs Meriwether.'

Miss Louisa said to Emily: 'We've hidden our brother somewhere, haven't we?'

Emily's mother said firmly: 'Emily, tell me where Ned is.'

'He's upstairs, Mother,' said Emily in a whisper.

Emily's father said: 'I wish you to take me to the boy upstairs, Mr Dorset.'

The coy, bashful expressions vanished from the faces of the two Dorsets. Their eyes were little dark pools of incredulity, growing narrower by the second. And both of them were now trying to put their hair in order. 'Why, *we* know nice children when we see them,' Miss Louisa said peevishly. There was a pleading quality in her voice, too. 'We knew from the beginning that that boy upstairs didn't

221

belong amongst us,' she said. 'Dear neighbors, it isn't just the money, you know, that makes the difference.' All at once she sounded like a little girl about to burst into tears.

'It isn't just the money?' Edwin Meriwether repeated.

'Miss Dorset,' said Muriel with new gentleness in her tone, as though she had just recognized that it was a little girl she was talking to, 'there has been some kind of mistake—a misunderstanding.'

Mr Alfred Dorset said: 'Oh, we wouldn't make a mistake of that kind! People *are* different. It isn't something you can put your finger on, but it isn't the money.'

'I don't know what you're talking about,' Edwin said, exasperated. 'But I'm going upstairs and find that boy.' He left the room with Mr Dorset following him with quick little steps—steps like those of a small boy trying to keep up with a man.

Miss Louisa now sat down in one of the high-backed dining chairs which were lined up along the oak wainscot. She was trembling, and Muriel came and stood beside her. Neither of them spoke, and in almost no time Edwin Meriwether came downstairs again with Ned. Miss Louisa looked at Ned, and tears came into her eyes. 'Where is my brother?' she asked accusingly, as though she thought possibly Ned and his father had locked Mr Dorset in the bathroom.

'I believe he has retired,' said Edwin. 'He left us and disappeared into one of the rooms upstairs.'

'Then I must go up to him,' said Miss Louisa. For a moment she seemed unable to rise. At last she pushed herself up from the chair and walked from the room with the slow, steady gait of a somnambulist. Muriel Meriwether followed her into the hall and as she watched the old woman ascending the steps, leaning heavily on the rail, her impulse was to go and offer to assist her. But something made her turn back into the dining room. Perhaps she imagined that her daughter, Emily, might need her now.

The Dorsets did not reappear that night. After Miss Louisa went upstairs, Muriel promptly got on the telephone and called the parents of some of the other boys and girls. Within a quarter of an hour, half a dozen parents had assembled. It was the first time in many years that any adult had set foot inside the Dorset house. It was the first time that any parent had ever inhaled the perfumed air or seen the masses of paper flowers and the illuminations and the statuary. In the guise of holding consultations over whether or not they should put out the lights and lock up the house, the parents lingered much longer than was necessary before taking the young people home. Some of them even tasted the lime punch. But in the presence of their children they made no comment on what had happened and gave no indication of what their own impressions were—not even their impressions of the punch. At last it was decided that two of the men should see to putting out the lights everywhere on the first floor and down in the ballroom. They were a long time in finding the switches for the indirect lighting. In most cases, they simply resorted to unscrewing the bulbs. Meanwhile the children went to the large cloak closet behind the stairway and got their wraps. When Ned and Emily Meriwether rejoined their parents at the front door to leave the house, Ned was wearing his own overcoat and held his own fedora in his hand.

Miss Louisa and Mr Alfred Dorset lived on for nearly ten years after that night, but they gave up selling their figs and paper flowers and of course they never entertained young people again. I often wonder if growing up in Chatham can ever have seemed quite the same since. Some of the terror must have gone out of it. Half the dread of coming of age must have vanished with the dread of the Dorsets' parties.

After that night, their old car would sometimes be observed creeping about town, but it was never parked in front of their house any more. It stood usually at the side entrance where the Dorsets could climb in and out of it without being seen. They began keeping a servant too—mainly to run their errands for them, I imagine. Sometimes it would be a man, sometimes a woman, never the same one for more than a few months at a time. Both of the Dorsets died during the Second World War while many of us who had gone to their parties were away from Chatham. But the story went round— and I am inclined to believe it—that after they were dead and the house was sold, Tom Bascomb's coat and hat were found still hanging in the cloak closet behind the stairs.

Tom himself was a pilot in the war and was a considerable hero. He was such a success and made such a name for himself that he never came back to Chatham to live. He found bigger opportunities elsewhere I suppose, and I don't suppose he ever felt the ties to Chatham that people with Ned's kind of upbringing do. Ned was in the war too, of course. He was in the navy and after the war he did return to Chatham to live, though actually it was not until then that he had spent much time here since his parents bundled him off to boarding school. Emily came home and made her debut just two or three years before the war, but she was already engaged to some boy in the East; she never comes back any more except to bring her children to see their grandparents for a few days during Christmas or at Easter.

I understand that Emily and Ned are pretty indifferent to each other's existence nowadays. I have been told this by Ned Meriwether's own wife. Ned's wife maintains that the night Ned and Emily went to the Dorsets' party marked the beginning of this indifference, that it marked the end of their childhood intimacy and the beginning of a shyness, a reserve, even an animosity between them that was destined to be a sorrow forever to the two sensible parents who had sat in the upstairs sitting room that night waiting until the telephone call came from Tom Bascomb.

Ned's wife is a girl he met while he was in the navy. She was a Wave, and her background isn't the same as his. Apparently, she isn't too happy with life in what she refers to as 'Chatham proper.' She and Ned have recently moved out into a suburban development, which she doesn't like either and which she refers to as 'greater Chatham.' She asked me at a party one night how Chatham got its name (she was just making conversation and appealing to my interest in such things) and when I told her that it was named for the Earl of Chatham and pointed out that the city is located in Pitt County, she burst out laughing. 'How very elegant,' she said. 'Why has nobody ever told me that before?' But what interests me most about Ned's wife is that after a few drinks she likes to talk about Ned and Emily and Tom Bascomb and the Dorsets. Tom Bascomb has become a kind of hero—and I don't mean a wartime hero—in her eyes, though of course not having grown up in Chatham she has never seen him in her life. But she is a clever girl, and there are times when she will say to me, 'Tell me about Chatham. Tell me about the Dorsets.' And I try to tell her. I tell her to remember that Chatham looks upon itself as a rather old city. I tell her to remember that it was one of the first English-speaking settlements west of the Alleghenies and that by the end of the American Revolution, when veterans began pouring westward over the Wilderness Road or down the Ohio River, Chatham was often referred to as a thriving village. Then she tells me that I am being dull, because it is hard for her to concentrate on any aspect of the story that doesn't center around Tom Bascomb and that night at the Dorsets'.

But I make her listen. Or at least one time I did. The Dorset family, I insisted on saying, was in Chatham even in those earliest times right after the Revolution, but they had come here under somewhat different circumstances from those of the other early settlers. How could that really matter, Ned's wife asked, after a hundred and fifty years? How could distinctions between the first settlers matter after the Irish had come to Chatham, after the Germans, after the Italians? Well, in West Vesey Place it could matter. It had to. If the distinction was false, it mattered all the more and it was all the more necessary to make it.

But let me interject here that Chatham is located in a state about whose history most Chatham citizens—not newcomers like Ned's wife, but old-timers—have little interest and less knowledge. Most of us, for instance, are never even quite sure whether during the 1860s our state did secede or didn't secede. As for the city itself, some of us hold that it is geographically Northern and culturally Southern. Others say the reverse is true. We are all apt to want to feel misplaced in Chatham, and so we are not content merely to say that it is a border city. How you stand on this important question is apt to depend entirely on whether your family is one of those with a good Southern name or one that had its origin in New England, because those are the two main categories of old society families in Chatham.

But truly—I told Ned's wife—the Dorset family was never in either of those categories. The first Dorset had come, with his family and his possessions and even a little capital, direct from a city in the English Midlands to Chatham. The Dorsets came not as pioneers, but paying their way all the way. They had not bothered to stop for a generation or two to put down roots in Pennsylvania or Virginia or Massachusetts. And this was the distinction which some people wished always to make. Apparently those early Dorsets had cared no more for putting down roots in the soil of the New World than they had cared for whatever they had left behind in the Old. They were an obscure mercantile family who came to invest in a new Western city. Within two generations the business—no, the industry!—which they established made them rich beyond any dreams they could have had in the beginning. For half a century they were looked upon, if any family ever was, as our first family.

And then the Dorsets left Chatham—practically all of them except the one old bachelor and the one old maid—left it just as they had

225

come, not caring much about what they were leaving or where they were going. They were city people, and they were Americans. They knew that what they had in Chatham they could buy more of in other places. For them Chatham was an investment that had paid off. They went to live in Santa Barbara and Laguna Beach, in Newport and on Long Island. And the truth which it was so hard for the rest of us to admit was that, despite our families of Massachusetts and Virginia, we were all more like the Dorsets—those Dorsets who left Chatham —than we were *un*like them. Their spirit was just a little closer to being the very essence of Chatham than ours was. The obvious difference was that we had to stay on here and pretend that our life had a meaning which it did not. And if it was only by a sort of chance that Miss Louisa and Mr Alfred played the role of social arbiters among the young people for a number of years, still no one could honestly question their divine right to do so.

'It may have been their right,' Ned's wife said at this point, 'but just think what might have happened.'

'It's not a matter of what might have happened,' I said. 'It is a matter of what did happen. Otherwise, what have you and I been talking about?'

'Otherwise,' she said with an irrepressible shudder, 'I would not be forever getting you off in a corner at these parties to talk about my husband and my husband's sister and how it is they care so little for each other's company nowadays.'

And I could think of nothing to say to that except that probably we had now pretty well covered our subject.

1959

WELCOME TO THE MONKEY HOUSE

Kurt Vonnegut, Jr

So Pete Crocker, the sheriff of Barnstable County, which was the whole of Cape Cod, came into the Federal Ethical Suicide Parlor in Hyannis one May afternoon—and he told the two six-foot Hostesses there that they weren't to be alarmed, but that a notorious nothinghead named Billy the Poet was believed headed for the Cape.

A nothinghead was a person who refused to take his ethical birth-control pills three times a day. The penalty for that was $10,000 and ten years in jail.

This was at a time when the population on Earth was 17 billion human beings. That was far too many mammals that big for a planet that small. The people were virtually packed together like drupelets.

Drupelets are the pulpy little knobs that compose the outside of a raspberry.

So the World Government was making a two-pronged attack on overpopulation. One pronging was the encouragement of ethical suicide, which consisted of going to the nearest Suicide Parlor and asking a Hostess to kill you painlessly while you lay on a Barcalounger. The other pronging was compulsory ethical birth control.

The sheriff told the Hostesses, who were pretty, tough-minded, highly intelligent girls, that roadblocks were being set up and house-to-house searches were being conducted to catch Billy the Poet. The main difficulty was that the police didn't know what he looked like. The few people who had seen him and known him for what he was were women—and they disagreed fantastically as to his height, his hair color, his voice, his weight, the color of his skin.

'I don't need to remind you girls,' the sheriff went on, 'that a nothinghead is very sensitive from the waist down. If Billy the Poet somehow slips in here and starts making trouble, one good kick in the right place will do wonders.'

He was referring to the fact that ethical birth-control pills, the only legal form of birth control, made people numb from the waist down.

Most men said their bottom halves felt like cold iron or balsawood.

227

Most women said their bottom halves felt like wet cotton or stale ginger ale. The pills were so effective that you could blindfold a man who had taken one, tell him to recite the Gettysburg Address, kick him in the balls while he was doing it, and he wouldn't miss a syllable.

The pills were ethical because they didn't interfere with a person's ability to reproduce, which would have been unnatural and immoral. All the pills did was take every bit of pleasure out of sex.

Thus did science and morals go hand in hand.

The two Hostesses there in Hyannis were Nancy McLuhan and Mary Kraft. Nancy was a strawberry blonde. Mary was a glossy brunette. Their uniforms were white lipstick, heavy eye makeup, purple body stockings with nothing underneath, and black-leather boots. They ran a small operation—with only six suicide booths. In a really good week, say the one before Christmas, they might put sixty people to sleep. It was done with a hypodermic syringe.

'My main message to you girls,' said Sheriff Crocker, 'is that everything's well under control. You can just go about your business here.'

'Didn't you leave out part of your main message?' Nancy asked him.

'I don't get you.'

'I didn't hear you say he was probably headed straight for us.'

He shrugged in clumsy innocence. 'We don't know that for sure.'

'I thought that was all anybody *did* know about Billy the Poet: that he specializes in deflowering Hostesses in Ethical Suicide Parlors.' Nancy was a virgin. All Hostesses were virgins. They also had to hold advanced degrees in psychology and nursing. They also had to be plump and rosy, and at least six feet tall.

America had changed in many ways, but it had yet to adopt the metric system.

Nancy McLuhan was burned up that the sheriff would try to protect her and Mary from the full truth about Billy the Poet—as though they might panic if they heard it. She told the sheriff so.

'How long do you think a girl would last in the ESS,' she said, meaning the Ethical Suicide Service, 'if she scared that easy?'

The sheriff took a step backward, pulled in his chin. 'Not very long, I guess.'

'That's very true,' said Nancy, closing the distance between them

228

and offering him a sniff of the edge of her hand, which was poised for a karate chop. All Hostesses were experts at judo and karate. 'If you'd like to find out how helpless we are, just come toward me, pretending you're Billy the Poet.'

The sheriff shook his head, gave her a glassy smile. 'I'd rather not.'

'That's the smartest thing you've said today,' said Nancy, turning her back on him while Mary laughed. 'We're not scared—we're *angry*. Or we're not even *that*. He isn't *worth* that. We're *bored*. How boring that he should come a great distance, should cause all this fuss, in order to—' She let the sentence die there. 'It's just too absurd.'

'I'm not as mad at *him* as I am at the women who let him do it to them without a struggle'—said Mary—'who let him do it and then couldn't tell the police what he looked like. Suicide Hostesses at that!'

'Somebody hasn't been keeping up with her karate,' said Nancy.

It wasn't just Billy the Poet who was attracted to Hostesses in Ethical Suicide Parlors. All nothingheads were. Bombed out of their skulls with the sex madness that came from taking nothing, they thought the white lips and big eyes and body stocking and boots of a Hostess spelled *sex, sex, sex*.

The truth was, of course that sex was the last thing any Hostess ever had in mind. 'If Billy follows his usual MO,' said the sheriff, 'he'll study your habits and the neighborhood. And then he'll pick one or other of you and he'll send her a dirty poem in the mail.'

'Charming,' said Nancy.

'He has also been known to use the telephone.'

'How brave,' said Nancy. Over the sheriff's shoulder, she could see the mailman coming.

A blue light went on over the door of a booth for which Nancy was responsible. The person in there wanted something. It was the only booth in use at the time.

The sheriff asked her if there was a possibility that the person in there was Billy the Poet, and Nancy said, 'Well, if it is, I can break his neck with my thumb and forefinger.'

'Foxy Grandpa,' said Mary, who'd seen him, too. A Foxy Grandpa was any old man, cute and senile, who quibbled and joked and reminisced for hours before he let a Hostess put him to sleep.

Nancy groaned. 'We've spent the past two hours trying to decide on a last meal.'

And then the mailman came in with just one letter. It was

addressed to Nancy in smeary pencil. She was splendid with anger and disgust as she opened it, knowing it would be a piece of filth from Billy.

She was right. Inside the envelope was a poem. It wasn't an original poem. It was a song from olden days that had taken on new meanings since the numbness of ethical birth control had become universal. It went like this, in smeary pencil again:

> *We were walking through the park,*
> *A-goosing statues in the dark.*
> *If Sherman's horse can take it,*
> *So can you.*

When Nancy came into the suicide booth to see what he wanted, the Foxy Grandpa was lying on the mint-green Barcalounger, where hundreds had died so peacefully over the years. He was studying the menu from the Howard Johnson's next door and beating time to the Muzak coming from the loudspeaker on the lemon-yellow wall. The room was painted cinder block. There was one barred window with a Venetian blind.

There was a Howard Johnson's next door to every Ethical Suicide Parlor, and vice versa. The Howard Johnson's had an orange roof and the Suicide Parlor had a purple roof, but they were both the Government. Practically everything was the Government.

Practically everything was automated, too. Nancy and Mary and the sheriff were lucky to have jobs. Most people didn't. The average citizen moped around home and watched television, which was the Government. Every fifteen minutes his television would urge him to vote intelligently or consume intelligently, or worship in the church of his choice, or love his fellow men, or obey the laws—or pay a call to the nearest Ethical Suicide Parlor and find out how friendly and understanding a Hostess could be.

The Foxy Grandpa was something of a rarity, since he was marked by old age, was bald, was shaky, had spots on his hands. Most people looked twenty-two, thanks to anti-aging shots they took twice a year. That the old man looked old was proof that the shots had been discovered after his sweet bird of youth had flown.

'Have we decided on a last supper yet?' Nancy asked him. She heard peevishness in her own voice, heard herself betray her exasperation with Billy the Poet, her boredom with the old man. She was ashamed, for this was unprofessional of her. 'The breaded veal

230

cutlet is very good.'

The old man cocked his head. With the greedy cunning of second childhood, he had caught her being unprofessional, unkind, and he was going to punish her for it. 'You don't sound very friendly. I thought you were all supposed to be friendly. I thought this was supposed to be a pleasant place to come.'

'I beg your pardon,' she said. 'If I seem unfriendly, it has nothing to do with you.'

'I thought maybe I bored you.'

'No, no,' she said gamely, 'not at all. You certainly know some very interesting history.' Among other things, the Foxy Grandpa claimed to have known J. Edgar Nation, the Grand Rapids druggist who was the father of ethical birth control.

'Then *look* like you're interested,' he told her. He could get away with that sort of impudence. The thing was, he could leave any time he wanted to, right up to the moment he asked for the needle—and he had to *ask* for the needle. That was the law.

Nancy's art, and the art of every Hostess, was to see that volunteers didn't leave, to coax and wheedle and flatter them patiently, every step of the way.

So Nancy had to sit down there in the booth, to pretend to marvel at the freshness of the yarn the old man told, a story everybody knew, about how J. Edgar Nation happened to experiment with ethical birth control

He didn't have the slightest idea his pills would be taken by human beings someday,' said the Foxy Grandpa. 'His dream was to introduce morality into the monkey house at the Grand Rapids Zoo. Did you realize that?' he inquired severely.

'No. No, I didn't. That's very interesting.'

'He and his eleven kids went to church one Easter. And the day was so nice and the Easter service had been so beautiful and pure that they decided to take a walk through the zoo, and they were just walking on clouds.'

'Um.' The scene described was lifted from a play that was performed on television every Easter.

The Foxy Grandpa shoehorned himself into the scene, had himself chat with the Nations just before they got to the monkey house. '"Good morning, Mr Nation," I said to him. "It certainly is a nice morning." "And a good morning to *you*, Mr Howard," he said to me. "There is nothing like an Easter morning to make a man feel clean and reborn and at one with God's intentions."'

'Um.' Nancy could hear the telephone ringing faintly, naggingly, through the nearly soundproof door.

'So we went on to the monkey house together, and what do you think we saw?'

'I can't imagine.' Somebody had answered the phone.

'We saw a monkey playing with his private parts!'

'No!'

'Yes! And J. Edgar Nation was so upset he went straight home and he started developing a pill that would make monkeys in the springtime fit things for a Christian family to see.'

There was a knock on the door.

'Yes—?' said Nancy.

'Nancy,' said Mary, 'telephone for you.'

When Nancy came out of the booth, she found the sheriff choking on little squeals of law-enforcement delight. The telephone was tapped by agents hidden in the Howard Johnson's. Billy the Poet was believed to be on the line. His call had been traced. Police were already on their way to grab him.

'Keep him on, keep him on,' the sheriff whispered to Nancy, and he gave her the telephone as though it were solid gold.

'Yes—?' said Nancy.

'Nancy McLuhan?' said a man. His voice was disguised. He might have been speaking through a kazoo. 'I'm calling for a mutual friend.'

'Oh?'

'He asked me to deliver a message.'

'I see.'

'It's a poem.'

'All right.'

'Ready?'

'Ready.' Nancy could hear sirens screaming in the background of the call.

The caller must have heard the sirens, too, but he recited the poem without any emotion. It went like this:

'Soak yourself in Jergen's Lotion.
Here comes the one-man population explosion.'

They got him. Nancy heard it all—the thumping and clumping, the argle-bargle and cries.

The depression she felt when she hung up was glandular. Her

232

brave body had prepared for a fight that was not to be.

The sheriff bounded out of the Suicide Parlor, in such a hurry to see the famous criminal he'd helped catch that a sheaf of papers fell from the pocket of his trench coat.

Mary picked them up, called after the sheriff. He halted for a moment, said the papers didn't matter any more, asked her if maybe she wouldn't like to come along. There was a flurry between the two girls, with Nancy persuading Mary to go, declaring that she had no curiosity about Billy. So Mary left, irrelevantly handing the sheaf to Nancy.

The sheaf proved to be photocopies of poems Billy had sent to Hostesses in other places. Nancy read the top one. It made much of a peculiar side effect of ethical birth-control pills: They not only made people numb—they also made people piss blue. The poem was called *What the Somethinghead said to the Suicide Hostess*, and it went like this:

> *I did not sow, I did not spin,*
> *And thanks to pills I did not sin.*
> *I loved the crowds, the stink, the noise.*
> *And when I peed, I peed turquoise.*
>
> *I ate beneath a roof of orange;*
> *Swung with progress like a door hinge.*
> *'Neath purple roof I've come today*
> *To piss my azure life away.*
>
> *Virgin hostess, death's recruiter,*
> *Life is cute, but you are cuter.*
> *Mourn my pecker, purple daughter—*
> *All it passed was sky-blue water.*

'You never heard that story before—about how J. Edgar Nation came to invent ethical birth control?' the Foxy Grandpa wanted to know. His voice cracked.

'Never did,' lied Nancy.

'I though everybody knew that.'

'It was news to me.'

'When he got through with the monkey house, you couldn't tell it from the Michigan Supreme Court. Meanwhile, there was this crisis going on in the United Nations. The people who understood science said people had to quit reproducing so much, and the people who understood morals said society would collapse if people used sex for nothing but pleasure.'

The Foxy Grandpa got off his Barcalounger, went over to the window, pried two slats of the blind apart. There wasn't much to see out there. The view was blocked by the backside of a mocked-up thermometer twenty feet high, which faced the street. It was calibrated in billions of people on Earth, from zero to twenty. The make-believe column of liquid was a strip of translucent red plastic. It showed how many people there were on Earth. Very close to the bottom was a black arrow that showed what the scientists thought the population ought to be.

The Foxy Grandpa was looking at the setting sun through that red plastic, and through the blind, too, so that his face was banded with shadows and red.

'Tell me—' he said, 'when I die, how much will that thermometer go down? A foot?'

'No.'

'An inch?'

'Not quite.'

'You know what the answer is, don't you?' he said, and he faced her. The senility had vanished from his voice and eyes. 'One inch on that thing equals 83,333 people. You knew that, didn't you?'

'That—that might be true,' said Nancy, 'but that isn't the right way to look at it, in my opinion.'

He didn't ask her what the right way was, in her opinion. He completed a thought of his own, instead. 'I'll tell you something else that's true: I'm Billy the Poet, and you're a very good-looking woman.'

With one hand he drew a snub-nosed revolver from his belt. With the other, he peeled off his bald dome and wrinkled forehead, which proved to be rubber. Now he looked twenty-two.

'The police will want to know exactly what I look like when this is all over,' he told Nancy with a malicious grin. 'In case you're not good at describing people, and it's surprising how many women aren't:

I'm five foot two,
With eyes of blue,
With brown hair to my shoulders—
A manly elf
So full of self
The ladies say he smolders.'

Billy was ten inches shorter than Nancy was. She had about forty pounds on him. She told him he didn't have a chance, but Nancy was much mistaken. He had unbolted the bars on the window the night before and he made her go out the window and then down a manhole that was hidden from the street by the big thermometer.

He took her down into the sewers of Hyannis. He knew where he was going. He had a flashlight and a map. Nancy had to go before him along the narrow catwalk, her own shadow dancing mockingly in the lead. She tried to guess where they were, relative to the real world above. She guessed correctly when they passed under the Howard Johnson's, guessed from noises she heard. The machinery that processed and served the food there was silent. But, so people wouldn't feel too lonesome when eating there, the designers had provided sound effects for the kitchen. It was these Nancy heard—a tape recording of the clashing of silverware and the laughter of Negroes and Puerto Ricans.

After that she was lost. Billy had very little to say to her other than 'Right,' or, 'Left,' or 'Don't try anything funny, Juno, or I'll blow your great big fucking head off.'

Only once did they have anything resembling a conversation. Billy began it, and ended it, too. 'What in hell is a girl with hips like yours doing selling death?' he asked her from behind.

She dared to stop. 'I can answer that,' she told him. She was confident that she could give him an answer that would shrivel him like napalm.

But he gave her a shove, offered to blow her fucking head off again.

'You don't even want to hear my answer,' she taunted him. 'You're afraid to hear it.'

'I never listen to a woman till the pills wear off,' sneered Billy. That was his plan, then—to keep her a prisoner for at least eight hours. That was how long it took for the pills to wear off.

'That's a silly rule.'

'A woman's not a woman till the pills wear off.'

'You certainly manage to make a woman feel like an object rather than a person.'

'Thank the pills for that,' said Billy.

There were 80 miles of sewers under Greater Hyannis, which had a population of 400,000 drupelets, 400,000 souls. Nancy lost track of the time down there. When Billy announced that they had at last reached their destination, it was possible for Nancy to imagine that a year had passed.

She tested this spooky impression by pinching her own thigh, by feeling what the chemical clock of her body said. Her thigh was still numb.

Billy ordered her to climb iron rungs that were set in wet masonry. There was a circle of sickly light above. It proved to be moonlight filtered through the plastic polygons of an enormous geodesic dome. Nancy didn't have to ask the traditional victim's question, 'Where am I?' There was only one dome like that on Cape Cod. It was in Hyannis Port and it sheltered the ancient Kennedy Compound.

It was a museum of how life had been lived in more expansive times. The museum was closed. It was open only in the summertime.

The manhole from which Nancy and then Billy emerged was set in an expanse of green cement, which showed where the Kennedy lawn had been. On the green cement, in front of the ancient frame houses, were statues representing the fourteen Kennedys who had been Presidents of the United States or the World. They were playing touch football.

The President of the World at the time of Nancy's abduction, incidentally, was an ex-Suicide Hostess named 'Ma' Kennedy. Her statue would never join this particular touch-football game. Her name was Kennedy, all right, but she wasn't the real thing. People complained of her lack of style, found her vulgar. On the wall of her office was a sign that said, YOU DON'T HAVE TO BE CRAZY TO WORK HERE, BUT IT SURE HELPS, and another one that said THIMK!, and another one that said, SOME DAY WE'RE GOING TO HAVE TO GET ORGANIZED AROUND HERE.

Her office was in the Taj Mahal.

Until she arrived in the Kennedy Museum, Nancy McLuhan was confident that she would sooner or later get a chance to break every bone in Billy's little body, maybe even shoot him with his own gun. She wouldn't have minded doing those things. She thought he was more disgusting than a blood-filled tick.

It wasn't compassion that changed her mind. It was the discovery that Billy had a gang. There were at least eight people around the manhole, men and women in equal numbers, with stockings pulled over their heads. It was the women who laid firm hands on Nancy, told her to keep calm. They were all at least as tall as Nancy and they held her in places where they could hurt her like hell if they had to.

Nancy closed her eyes, but this didn't protect her from the obvious conclusion: These perverted women were sisters from the Ethical Suicide Service. This upset her so much that she asked loudly and bitterly, 'How can you violate your oaths like this?'

She was promptly hurt so badly that she doubled up and burst into tears.

When she straightened up again, there was plenty more she wanted to say, but she kept her mouth shut. She speculated silently as to what on Earth could make Suicide Hostesses turn against every concept of human decency. Nothingheadedness alone couldn't begin to explain it. They had to be drugged besides.

Nancy went over in her mind all the terrible drugs she'd learned about in school, persuaded herself that the women had taken the worst one of all. That drug was so powerful, Nancy's teachers had told her, that even a person numb from the waist down would copulate repeatedly and enthusiastically after just one glass. That had to be the answer: The women, and probably the men, too, had been drinking gin.

They hastened Nancy into the middle frame house, which was dark like all the rest, and Nancy heard the men giving Billy the news. It was in this news that Nancy perceived a glint of hope. Help might be on its way.

The gang member who had phoned Nancy obscenely had fooled the police into believing that they had captured Billy the Poet, which was bad for Nancy. The police didn't know yet that Nancy was missing, two men told Billy, and a telegram had been sent to Mary Kraft in Nancy's name, declaring that Nancy had been called to New York City on urgent family business.

That was where Nancy saw the glint of hope: Mary wouldn't believe that telegram. Mary knew Nancy had no family in New York. Not one of the 63,000,000 people living there was a relative of Nancy's.

The gang had deactivated the burglar-alarm system of the museum. They had also cut through a lot of the chains and ropes that were meant to keep visitors from touching anything of value. There was no mystery as to who and what had done the cutting. One of the men was armed with brutal lopping shears.

They marched Nancy into a servant's bedroom upstairs. The man with the shears cut the ropes that fenced off the narrow bed. They put Nancy into the bed and two men held Nancy while a woman gave her a knockout shot.

Billy the Poet had disappeared.

As Nancy was going under, the woman who had given her the shot asked her how old she was.

Nancy was determined not to answer, but discovered that the drug had made her powerless not to answer. 'Sixty-three,' she murmured.

'How does it feel to be a virgin at sixty-three?'

Nancy heard her own answer through a velvet fog. She was amazed by the answer, wanted to protest that it couldn't possibly be hers. 'Pointless,' she'd said.

Moments later, she asked the woman thickly, 'What was in that needle?'

'What was in the needle, honey bunch? Why, honey bunch, they call that "truth serum."'

The moon was down when Nancy woke up—but the night was still out there. The shades were drawn and there was candlelight. Nancy had never seen a lit candle before.

What awakened Nancy was a dream of mosquitoes and bees. Mosquitoes and bees were extinct. So were birds. But Nancy dreamed that millions of insects were swarming about her from the waist down. They didn't sting. They fanned her. Nancy was a nothinghead.

She went to sleep again. When she awoke next time, she was being led into a bathroom by three women, still with stockings over their heads. The bathroom was already filled with steam from somebody else's bath. There were somebody else's wet footprints crisscrossing the floor and the air reeked of pine-needle perfume.

Her will and intelligence returned as she was bathed and perfumed and dressed in a white nightgown. When the women stepped back to admire her, she said to them quietly, 'I may be a nothinghead now. But that doesn't mean I have to think like one or act like one.'

Nobody argued with her.

Nancy was taken downstairs and out of the house. She fully expected to be sent down a manhole again. It would be the perfect setting for her violation by Billy, she was thinking—down in a sewer.

But they took her across the green cement, where the grass used to be, and then across the yellow cement, where the beach used to be, and then out onto the blue cement, where the harbor used to be. There were twenty-six yachts that had belonged to various Kennedys, sunk up to their water lines in blue cement. It was to the most ancient of these yachts, the Marlin, once the property of Joseph P. Kennedy, that they delivered Nancy.

It was dawn. Because of the high-rise apartments all around the Kennedy Museum, it would be an hour before any direct sunlight would reach the microcosm under the geodesic dome.

Nancy was escorted as far as the companionway to the forward cabin of the Marlin. The women pantomimed that she was expected to go down the five steps alone.

Nancy froze for the moment and so did the women. And there were two actual statues in the tableau on the bridge. Standing at the wheel was a statue of Frank Wirtanen, once skipper of the Marlin. And next to him was his son and first mate, Carly. They weren't paying any attention to poor Nancy. They were staring out through the windshield at the blue cement.

Nancy, barefoot and wearing a thin white nightgown, descended bravely into the forward cabin, which was a pool of candlelight and pine-needle perfume. The companionway hatch was closed and locked behind her.

Nancy's emotions and the antique furnishings of the cabin were so complex that Nancy could not at first separate Billy the Poet from his surroundings, from all the mahogany and leaded glass. And then she saw him at the far end of the cabin, with his back against the door to the forward cockpit. He was wearing purple silk pajamas with a Russian collar. They were piped in red, and writhing across Billy's silken breast was a golden dragon. It was belching fire.

Anticlimactically, Billy was wearing glasses. He was holding a book.

Nancy poised herself on the next-to-the-bottom step, took a firm grip on the handholds in the companionway. She bared her teeth, calculated that it would take ten men Billy's size to dislodge her.

Between them was a great table. Nancy had expected the cabin to be dominated by a bed, possibly in the shape of a swan, but the Marlin was a day boat. The cabin was anything but a seraglio. It was about as voluptuous as a lower-middle-class dining room in Akron, Ohio, around 1910.

A candle was on the table. So were an ice bucket and two glasses and a quart of champagne. Champagne was as illegal as heroin.

Billy took off his glasses, gave her a shy, embarrassed smile, said, 'Welcome.'

'This is as far as I come.'

He accepted that. 'You're very beautiful there.'

'And what am I supposed to say—that you're stunningly handsome? That I feel an overwhelming desire to throw myself into your manly arms?'

'If you wanted to make me happy, that would certainly be the way to do it.' He said that humbly.

'And what about *my* happiness?'

The question seemed to puzzle him. 'Nancy—that's what this is all about.'

'What if my idea of happiness doesn't coincide with yours?'

'And what do you think my idea of happiness is?'

'I'm not going to throw myself into your arms, and I'm not going to drink that poison, and I'm not going to budge from here unless somebody makes me,' said Nancy. 'So I think your idea of happiness is going to turn out to be eight people holding me down on that table, while you bravely hold a cocked pistol to my head—and do what you want. That's the way it's going to have to be, so call your friends and get it over with!'

Which he did.

He didn't hurt her. He deflowered her with a clinical skill she found ghastly. When it was all over, he didn't seem cocky or proud. On the contrary, he was terribly depressed, and he said to Nancy, 'Believe me, if there'd been any other way—'

Her reply to this was a face like stone—and silent tears of humiliation.

His helpers let down a folding bunk from the wall. It was scarcely wider than a bookshelf and hung on chains. Nancy allowed herself to be put to bed in it, and she was left alone with Billy the Poet again. Big as she was, like a double bass wedged on that narrow shelf, she felt like a pitiful little thing. A scratchy, war-surplus blanket had been tucked in around her. It was her own idea to pull up a corner of the blanket to hide her face.

Nancy sensed from sounds what Billy was doing, which wasn't much. He was sitting at the table, sighing occasionally, sniffing occasionally, turning the pages of a book. He lit a cigar and the stink of it seeped under the blanket. Billy inhaled the cigar, then coughed and coughed and coughed.

When the coughing died down, Nancy said loathingly through the blanket, 'You're so strong, so masterful, so healthy. It must be wonderful to be so manly.'

Billy only sighed at this.

'I'm not a very typical nothinghead,' she said. 'I hated it—hated everything about it.'

Billy sniffed, turned a page.

'I suppose all the other women just loved it—couldn't get enough of it.'

'Nope.'

She uncovered her face. 'What do you mean, "Nope"?'

'They've all been like you.'

This was enough to make Nancy sit up and stare at him. 'The women who helped you tonight—'

'What about them?'

'You've done to them what you did to me?'

He didn't look up from his book. 'That's right.'

'Then why don't they kill you instead of helping you?'

'Because they understand.' And then he added mildly, 'They're *grateful*.'

Nancy got out of bed, came to the table, gripped the edge of the table, leaned close to him. And she said to him tautly, 'I am not grateful.'

'You will be.'

'And what could possibly bring about that miracle?'

'Time,' said Billy.

Billy closed his book, stood up. Nancy was confused by his magnetism. Somehow he was very much in charge again.

'What you've been through, Nancy,' he said, 'is a typical wedding night for a strait-laced girl of a hundred years ago, when everybody was a nothinghead. The groom did without helpers, because the bride wasn't customarily ready to kill him. Otherwise, the spirit of the occasion was much the same. These are the pajamas my great-great-grandfather wore on his wedding night in Niagara Falls.

'According to his diary, his bride cried all that night, and threw up twice. But, with the passage of time, she became a sexual enthusiast.'

It was Nancy's turn to reply by not replying. She understood the tale. It frightened her to understand so easily that, from gruesome

241

beginnings, sexual enthusiasm could grow and grow.

'You're a very typical nothinghead,' said Billy. 'If you dare to think about it now, you'll realize that you're angry because I'm such a bad lover, and a funny-looking shrimp besides. And what you can't help dreaming about from now on is a really suitable mate for a Juno like yourself.

'You'll find him, too—tall and strong and gentle. The nothinghead movement is growing by leaps and bounds.'

'But—' said Nancy, and she stopped there. She looked out a porthole at the rising sun.

'But what?'

'The world is in the mess it is today because of the nothingheadedness of olden times. Don't you see?' She was pleading weakly. 'The world can't afford sex anymore.'

'Of course it can afford sex,' said Billy. 'All it can't afford anymore is reproduction.'

'Then why the laws?'

'They're bad laws,' said Billy. 'If you go back through history, you'll find that the people who have been most eager to rule, to make the laws, to enforce the laws and to tell everybody exactly how God Almighty wants things here on Earth—those people have forgiven themselves and their friends for anything and everything. But they have been absolutely disgusted and terrified by the natural sexuality of common men and women.

'Why this is, I do not know. That is one of the many questions I wish somebody would ask the machines. I do know this: The triumph of that sort of disgust and terror is now complete. Almost every man and woman looks and feels like something the cat dragged in. The only sexual beauty that an ordinary human being can see today is in the woman who will kill him. Sex is death. There's a short and nasty equation for you: "Sex is death. QED."

'So you see, Nancy,' said Billy, 'I have spent this night, and many others like it, attempting to restore a certain amount of innocent pleasure to the world, which is poorer in pleasure than it needs to be.'

Nancy sat down and quietly bowed her head.

'I'll tell you what my grandfather did on the dawn of his wedding night,' said Billy.

'I don't think I want to hear it.'

'It isn't violent. It's—it's meant to be tender.'

'Maybe that's why I don't want to hear it.'

'He read his bride a poem.' Billy took the book from the table, opened it. 'His diary tells which poem it was. While we aren't bride and groom, and while we may not meet again for many years, I'd like to read this poem to you, to have you know I've loved you.'

'Please—no. I couldn't stand it.'

'All right, I'll leave the book here, with the place marked, in case you want to read it later. It's the poem beginning:

> *How do I love thee? Let me count the ways.*
> *I love thee to the depth and breadth and height*
> *My soul can reach, when feeling out of sight*
> *For the ends of Being and ideal Grace.*

Billy put a small bottle on top of the book. 'I am also leaving you these pills. If you take one a month, you will never have children. And still you'll be a nothinghead.'

And he left. And they all left but Nancy.

When Nancy raised her eyes at last to the book and bottle, she saw that there was a label on the bottle. What the label said was this: WELCOME TO THE MONKEY HOUSE.

1961

IN THE ZOO

Jean Stafford

Keening harshly in his senility, the blind polar bear slowly and ceaselessly shakes his head in the stark heat of the July and mountain noon. His open eyes are blue. No one stops to look at him; an old farmer, in passing, sums up the old bear's situation by observing, with a ruthless chuckle, that he is a 'back number.' Patient and despairing, he sits on his yellowed haunches on the central rock of his pool, his huge toy paws wearing short boots of mud.

The grizzlies to the right of him, a conventional family of father and mother and two spring cubs, alternately play the clown and sleep. There is a blustery, scoundrelly, half-likable bravado in the manner of the black bear on the polar's left; his name, according to the legend on his cage, is Clancy, and he is a rough-and-tumble, brawling blowhard, thundering continually as he paces back and forth, or pauses to face his audience of children and mothers and release from his great gray-tongued mouth a perfectly Vesuvian roar. If he were to be reincarnated in human form, he would be a man of action, possibly a football coach, probably a politician. One expects to see his black hat hanging from a branch of one of his trees; at any moment he will light a cigar.

The polar bear's next-door neighbors are not the only ones who offer so sharp and sad a contrast to him. Across a reach of scrappy grass and litter is the convocation of conceited monkeys, burrowing into each other's necks and chests for fleas, picking their noses with their long, black, finicky fingers, swinging by their gifted tails on the flying trapeze, screaming bloody murder. Even when they mourn— one would think the male orangutan was on the very brink of suicide—they are comedians; they only fake depression, for they are firmly secure in their rambunctious tribalism and in their appalling insight and contempt. Their flibbertigibbet gamboling is a sham, and, stealthily and shiftily, they are really watching the pitiful polar bear ('Back number,' they quote the farmer. 'That's *his* number all right,' they snigger), and the windy black bear ('Life of the party. Gasbag. Low IQ,' they note scornfully on his dossier), and the stupid, bourgeois grizzlies ('It's feed the face and hit the sack for them,' the monkeys say). And they are watching my sister and me, two middle-aged women, as we sit on a bench between the exhibits, eating popcorn, growing thirsty. We are thoughtful.

A chance remark of Daisy's a few minutes before has turned us to memory and meditation. 'I don't know why,' she said, 'but that poor blind bear reminds me of Mr Murphy.' The name 'Mr Murphy' at once returned us both to childhood, and we were floated far and fast, our later lives diminished. So now we eat our popcorn in silence with the ritualistic appetite of childhood, which has little to do with hunger; it is not so much food as a sacrament, and in tribute to our sisterliness and our friendliness I break the silence to say that this is the best popcorn I have ever eaten in my life. The extravagance of my statement instantly makes me feel self-indulgent, and for some time I uneasily avoid looking at the blind bear. My sister does not agree or disagree; she simply says that popcorn is the only food she has ever really liked. For a long time, then, we eat without a word, but I know, because I know her well and know her similarity to me, that Daisy is thinking what I am thinking; both of us are mournfully remembering Mr Murphy, who, at one time in our lives, was our only friend.

This zoo is in Denver, a city that means nothing to my sister and me except as a place to take or meet trains. Daisy lives two hundred miles farther west, and it is her custom, when my every-other-year visit with her is over, to come across the mountains to see me off on my eastbound train. We know almost no one here, and because our stays are short, we have never bothered to learn the town in more than the most desultory way. We know the Burlington uptown office and the respectable hotels, a restaurant or two, the Union Station, and, beginning today, the zoo in the city park.

But since the moment that Daisy named Mr Murphy by name our situation in Denver has been only corporeal; our minds and our hearts are in Adams, fifty miles north, and we are seeing, under the white sun at its pitiless meridian, the streets of that ugly town, its parks and trees and bridges, the bandstand in its dreary park, the roads that lead away from it, west to the mountains and east to the plains, its mongrel and multitudinous churches, its high school shaped like a loaf of bread, the campus of its college, an oasis of which we had no experience except to walk through it now and then, eyeing the woodbine on the impressive buildings. These things are engraved forever on our minds with a legibility so insistent that you have only to say the name of the town aloud to us to rip the rinds from our nerves and leave us exposed in terror and humiliation.

We have supposed in later years that Adams was not so bad as all that, and we know that we magnified its ugliness because we looked upon it as the extension of the possessive, unloving, scornful, complacent foster mother, Mrs Placer, to whom, at the death of our parents within a month of each other, we were sent like Dickensian grotesqueries—cowardly, weak-stomached, given to tears, backward in school. Daisy was ten and I was eight when, unaccompanied, we made the long trip from Marblehead to our benefactress, whom we had never seen and, indeed, never heard of until the pastor of our church came to tell us of the arrangement our father had made on his deathbed, seconded by our mother on hers. This man, whose name and face I have forgotten and whose parting speeches to us I have not forgiven, tried to dry our tears with talk of Indians and of buffaloes; he spoke, however, at much greater length, and in preaching cadences, of the Christian goodness of Mrs Placer. She was he said, childless and fond of children, and for many years she had been a widow, after the lingering demise of her tubercular husband, for whose sake she had moved to the Rocky Mountains. For his support and costly medical care, she had run a boarding house, and after his death, since he had left her nothing, she was obliged to continue running it. She had been a girlhood friend of our paternal grandmother, and our father, in the absence of responsible relatives, had made her the beneficiary of his life insurance on the condition that she lodge and rear us. The pastor, with a frankness remarkable considering that he was talking to children, explained to us that our father had left little more than a drop in the bucket for our care, and he enjoined us to give Mrs Placer, in return for her hospitality and sacrifice, courteous help and eternal thanks. 'Sacrifice' was a word we were never allowed to forget.

And thus it was, in grief for our parents, that we came cringing to the dry Western town and to the house where Mrs Placer lived, a house in which the square, uncushioned furniture was cruel and the pictures on the walls were either dour or dire and the lodgers, who lived on the upper floors among shadowy wardrobes and chiffoniers, had come through the years to resemble their landlady in appearance as well as in deportment.

After their ugly-colored evening meal, Gran—as she bade us call her—and her paying guests would sit, rangy and aquiline, rocking on the front porch on spring and summer and autumn nights, tasting their delicious grievances: those slights delivered by ungrateful sons and daughters, those impudences committed by trolley-car conductors and uppity salesgirls in the ready-to-wear, all those slurs and calculated elbow-jostlings that were their daily crucifixion and their staff of life. We little girls, washing the dishes in the cavernous kitchen, listened to their even, martyred voices, fixed like leeches to their solitary subject and their solitary creed—that life was essentially a matter of being done in, let down, and swindled.

At regular intervals, Mrs Placer, chairwoman of the victims, would say, 'Of course, I don't care; I just have to laugh,' and then would tell a shocking tale of an intricate piece of skulduggery perpetrated against her by someone she did not even know. Sometimes, with her avid, partial jury sitting there on the porch behind the bitter hopvines in the heady mountain air, the cases she tried involved Daisy and me, and, listening, we travailed, hugging each other, whispering, 'I wish she wouldn't! Oh, how did she find out?' How *did* she? Certainly we never told her when we were snubbed or chosen last on teams, never admitted to a teacher's scolding or to the hoots of laughter that greeted us when we bit on silly, unfair jokes. But she knew. She knew about the slumber parties we were not invited to, the beefsteak fries at which we were pointedly left out; she knew that the singing teacher had said in so many words that I could not carry a tune in a basket and that the sewing superintendent had said that Daisy's fingers were all thumbs. With our teeth chattering in the cold of our isolation, we would hear her protestant, litigious voice defending our right to be orphans, paupers, wholly dependent on her—except for the really ridiculous pittance from our father's life insurance—when it was all she could do to make ends meet. She did not care, but she had to laugh that people in general were so small-minded that they looked down on fatherless, motherless waifs like us and, by association, looked down on her. It seemed funny to her that people gave her no credit for taking on these sickly youngsters who were not even kin but only the grandchildren of a friend.

If a child with braces on her teeth came to play with us, she was, according to Gran, slyly lording it over us because our teeth were crooked but there was no money to have them straightened. And what could be the meaning of our being asked to come for supper at the doctor's house? Were the doctor and his la-di-la New York wife and those pert girls with their solid-gold barrettes and their Shetland

247

pony going to shame her poor darlings? Or shame their poor Gran by making them sorry to come home to the plain but honest life that was all she could provide for them?

There was no stratum of society not reeking with the effluvium of fraud and pettifoggery. And the school system was almost the worst of all: if we could not understand fractions, was that not our teacher's fault? And therefore what right had she to give us F? It was as plain as a pikestaff to Gran that the teacher was only covering up her own inability to teach. It was unlikely, too—highly unlikely—that it was by accident that time and time again the free medical clinic was closed for the day just as our names were about to be called out, so that nothing was done about our bad tonsils, which meant that we were repeatedly sick in the winter, with Gran fetching and carrying for us, climbing those stairs a jillion times a day with her game leg and her heart that was none too strong.

Steeped in these mists of accusation and hidden plots and double meanings, Daisy and I grew up like worms. I think no one could have withstood the atmosphere in that house where everyone trod on eggs that a little bird had told them were bad. They spied on one another, whispered behind doors, conjectured, drew parallels beginning 'With all due respect . . .' or 'It is a matter of indifference to *me* but . . . ' The vigilantes patrolled our town by day, and by night returned to lay their goodies at their priestess's feet and wait for her oracular interpretation of the innards of the butcher, the baker, the candlestick maker, the soda jerk's girl, and the barber's unnatural deaf white cat.

Consequently, Daisy and I also became suspicious. But it was suspicion of ourselves that made us mope and weep and grimace with self-judgment. Why were we not happy when Gran had sacrificed herself to the bone for us? Why did we not cut dead the paper boy who had called her a filthy name? Why did we persist in our willful friendliness with the grocer who had tried, unsuccessfully, to overcharge her on a case of pork and beans?

Our friendships were nervous and surreptitious; we sneaked and lied, and as our hungers sharpened, our debasement deepened; we were pitied; we were shifty-eyed, always on the lookout for Mrs Placer or one of her tattletale lodgers; we were hypocrites.

Nevertheless, one filament of instinct survived, and Daisy and I in time found asylum in a small menagerie down by the railroad tracks. It belonged to a gentle alcoholic ne'er-do-well, who did nothing all day long but drink bathtub gin in rickeys and play solitaire and smile to himself and talk to his animals. He had a little, stunted red vixen and a deodorized skunk, a parrot from Tahiti that spoke Parisian French, a woebegone coyote, and two capuchin monkeys, so serious and humanized, so small and sad and sweet, and so religious-looking with their tonsured heads that it was impossible not to think their gibberish was really an ordered language with a grammar that some day some philologist would understand.

Gran knew about our visits to Mr Murphy and she did not object, for it gave her keen pleasure to excoriate him when we came home. His vice was not a matter of guesswork; it was an established fact that he was half-seas over from dawn till midnight. 'With the black Irish,' said Gran, 'the taste for drink is taken in with the mother's milk and is never mastered. Oh, I know all about those promises to join the temperance movement and not to touch another drop. The way to hell is paved with good intentions.'

We were still little girls when we discovered Mr Murphy, before the shattering disease of adolescence was to make our bones and brains ache even more painfully than before, and we loved him and we hoped to marry him when we grew up. We loved him, and we loved his monkeys to exactly the same degree and in exactly the same way; they were husbands and fathers and brothers, these three little, ugly, dark, secret men who minded their own business and let us mind ours. If we stuck our fingers through the bars of the cage, the monkeys would sometimes take them in their tight, tiny hands and look into our faces with a tentative, somehow absent-minded sorrow, as if they terribly regretted that they could not place us but were glad to see us all the same. Mr Murphy, playing a solitaire game of cards called 'once in a blue moon' on a kitchen table in his back yard beside the pens, would occasionally look up and blink his beautiful blue eyes and say, 'You're peaches to make over my wee friends. I love you for it.' There was nothing demanding in his voice, and nothing sticky; on his lips the word 'love' was jocose and forthright, it had no strings attached. We would sit on either side of him and watch him regiment his ranks of cards and stop to drink as deeply as if he were dying of thirst and wave to his animals and say to them, 'Yes, lads, you're dandies.'

Because Mr Murphy was as reserved with us as the capuchins were, as courteously noncommittal, we were surprised one spring day when he told us that he had a present for us, which he hoped

Mrs Placer would let us keep; it was a puppy, for whom the owner had asked him to find a home—half collie and half Labrador retriever, blue-blooded on both sides.

'You might tell Mrs Placer—' he said, smiling at the name, for Gran was famous in the town. 'You might tell Mrs Placer,' said Mr Murphy, 'that this lad will make a fine watchdog. She'll never have to fear for her spoons again. Or her honor.' The last he said to himself, not laughing but tucking his chin into his collar; lines sprang to the corners of his eyes. He would not let us see the dog, whom we could hear yipping and squealing inside his shanty, for he said that our disappointment would weigh on his conscience if we lost our hearts to the fellow and then could not have him for our own.

That evening at supper, we told Gran about Mr Murphy's present. A dog? In the first place, why a dog? Was it possible that the news had reached Mr Murphy's ears that Gran had just this very day finished planting her spring garden, the very thing that a rampageous dog would have in his mind to destroy? What sex was it? A male! Females, she had heard, were more trustworthy; males roved and came home smelling of skunk; such a consideration of this, of course, would not have crossed Mr Murphy's fuddled mind. Was this young male dog housebroken? We had not asked? That was the limit!

Gran appealed to her followers, too raptly fascinated by Mr Murphy's machinations to eat their Harvard beets. 'Am I being farfetched or does it strike you as decidedly queer that Mr Murphy is trying to fob off on my little girls a young cur that has not been trained?' she asked them. 'If it were housebroken, he would have said so, so I feel it is safe to assume that it is not. Perhaps cannot *be* housebroken. I've heard of such cases.'

The fantasy spun on, richly and rapidly, with all the skilled helping hands at work at once. The dog was tangibly in the room with us, shedding his hair, scratching his fleas, shaking rain off himself to splatter the walls, dragging some dreadful carcass across the floor, chewing up slippers, knocking over chairs with his tail, gobbling the chops from the platter, barking, biting, fathering, fighting, smelling to high heaven of carrion, staining the rug with his muddy feet, scratching the floor with his claws. He developed rabies; he bit a child, two children! Three! Everyone in town! And Gran and her poor darlings went to jail for harboring this murderous, odoriferous, drunk, Roman Catholic dog.

And yet, astoundingly enough, she came around to agreeing to let us have the dog. It was, as Mr Murphy had predicted, the word 'watchdog' that deflected the course of the trial. The moment Daisy uttered it, Gran halted, marshaling her reverse march; while she rallied and tacked and reconnoitered, she sent us to the kitchen for the dessert. And by the time this course was under way, the uses of a dog, the enormous potentialities for investigation and law enforcement in a dog trained by Mrs Placer were being minutely and passionately scrutinized by the eight upright bloodhounds sitting at the table wolfing their brown Betty as if it were fresh-killed rabbit. The dog now sat at attention beside his mistress, fiercely alert, ears cocked, nose aquiver, the protector of widows, of orphans, of lonely people who had no homes. He made short shrift of burglars, homicidal maniacs, Peeping Toms, gypsies, bogus missionaries, Fuller Brush men with a risqué spiel. He went to the store and brought back groceries, retrieved the evening paper from the awkward place the boy had meanly thrown it, rescued cripples from burning houses, saved children from drowning, heeled at command, begged, lay down, stood up, sat, jumped through a hoop, ratted.

Both times—when he was a ruffian of the blackest delinquency and then a pillar of society—he was full-grown in his prefiguration, and when Laddy appeared on the following day, small, unsteady, and whimpering lonesomely, Gran and her lodgers were taken aback; his infant, clumsy paws embarrassed them, his melting eyes were unapropos. But it could never be said of Mrs Placer, as Mrs Placer her own self said, that she was a woman who went back on her word, and her darlings were going to have their dog, softheaded and feckless as he might be. All the first night, in his carton in the kitchen, he wailed for his mother, and in the morning, it was true, he had made a shambles of the room—fouled the floor, and pulled off the tablecloth together with a ketchup bottle, so that thick gore lay everywhere. At breakfast, the lodgers confessed they had had a most amusing night, for it had actually been funny the way the dog had been determined not to let anyone get a wink of sleep. After that first night, Laddy slept in our room, receiving from us, all through our delighted, sleepless nights, pats and embraces and kisses and whispers. He was our baby, our best friend, the smartest, prettiest, nicest dog in the entire world. Our soft and rapid blandishments excited him to yelp at us in pleased bewilderment, and then we would playfully grasp his muzzle, so that he would snarl, deep in his throat like an adult dog, and shake his head violently, and, when we

251

freed him, nip us smartly with great good will.

He was an intelligent and genial dog and we trained him quickly. He steered clear of Gran's radishes and lettuce after she had several times given him a brisk comeuppance with a strap across the rump, and he soon left off chewing shoes and the laundry on the line, and he outgrew his babyish whining. He grew like a weed; he lost his spherical softness, and his coat, which had been sooty fluff, came in stiff and rusty black; his nose grew aristocratically long, and his clever, pointed ears stood at attention. He was all bronzy, lustrous black except for an Elizabethan ruff of white and a tip of white at the end of his perky tail. No one could deny that he was exceptionally handsome and that he had, as well, great personal charm and style. He escorted Daisy and me to school in the morning, laughing interiorly out of the enormous pleasure of his life as he gracefully cantered ahead of us, distracted occasionally by his private interest in smells or unfamiliar beings in the grass but, on the whole, engrossed in his role of chaperon. He made friends easily with other dogs, and sometimes he went for a long hunting weekend into the mountains with a huge and bossy old red hound named Mess, who had been on the county most of his life and had made a good thing of it, particularly at the fire station.

It was after one of these three-day excursions into the high country that Gran took Laddy in hand. He had come back spent and filthy, his coat a mass of cockleburs and ticks, his eyes bloodshot, loud *râles* in his chest; for half a day he lay motionless before the front door like someone in a hangover; his groaning eyes explicitly saying 'Oh, for God's sake, leave me be' when we offered him food or bowls of water. Gran was disapproving, then affronted, and finally furious. Not, of course, with Laddy, since all inmates of her house enjoyed immunity, but with Mess, whose caddish character, together with that of his nominal masters, the firemen, she examined closely under a strong light, with an air of detachment, with her not caring but her having, all the same, to laugh. A lodger who occupied the back west room had something to say about the fire chief and his nocturnal visits to a certain house occupied by a certain group of young women, too near the same age to be sisters and too old to be the daughters of the woman who claimed to be their mother. What a story! The exophthalmic librarian—she lived in one of the front rooms—had some interesting insinuations to make about the deputy marshal, who had borrowed, significantly, she thought, a book on hypnotism. She also knew—she was, of course, in a most useful position in the town, and from her authoritative pen in the middle of the library her mammiform and azure eyes and her eager ears missed nothing—that the fire chief's wife was not as scrupulous as she might be when she was keeping score on bridge night at the Sorosis.

There was little at the moment that Mrs Placer and her disciples could do to save the souls of the Fire Department and their families, and therefore save the town from holocaust (a very timid boarder—a Mr Beaver, a newcomer who was not to linger long—had sniffed throughout this recitative as if he were smelling burning flesh), but at least the unwholesome bond between Mess and Laddy could and would be severed once and for all. Gran looked across the porch at Laddy, who lay stretched at full length in the darkest corner, shuddering and baying abortively in his throat as he chased jack rabbits in his dreams, and she said, 'A dog can have morals like a human.' With this declaration Laddy's randy, manly holidays were finished. It may have been telepathy that woke him; he lifted his heavy head from his paws, laboriously got up, hesitated for a moment, and then padded languidly across the porch to Gran. He stood docilely beside her chair, head down, tail drooping as if to say, 'OK, Mrs Placer, show me how and I'll walk the straight and narrow.'

The very next day, Gran changed Laddy's name to Caesar, as being more dignified, and a joke was made at the supper table that he had come, seen, and conquered Mrs Placer's heart—for within her circle, where the magnanimity she lavished upon her orphans was daily demonstrated, Mrs Placer's heart was highly thought of. On that day also, although we did not know it yet, Laddy ceased to be our dog. Before many weeks passed, indeed, he ceased to be anyone we had ever known. A week or so after he became Caesar, he took up residence in her room, sleeping alongside her bed. She broke him of the habit of taking us to school (temptation to low living was rife along those streets; there was a chow—well, never mind) by the simple expedient of chaining him to a tree as soon as she got up in the morning. This discipline, together with the stamina-building cuffs she gave his sensitive ears from time to time, gradually but certainly remade his character. From a sanguine, affectionate, easygoing Gael (with the fits of melancholy that alternated with the larkiness), he turned into an overbearing, military, efficient, loud-voiced Teuton. His bark, once wide of range, narrowed to one dark, glottal tone.

Soon the paper boy flatly refused to serve our house after Caesar efficiently removed the bicycle clip from his pants leg; the skin was not broken, or even bruised, but it was a matter of principle with the boy. The milkman approached the back door in a seizure of shakes like St Vitus's dance. The metermen, the coal men, and the garbage collector crossed themselves if they were Catholics and, if they were not, tried whistling in the dark. 'Good boy, good Caesar,' they caroled, and, unctuously lying, they said they knew his bark was worse than his bite, knowing full well that it was not, considering the very nasty nip, requiring stitches, he had given a representative of the Olson Rug company, who had had the folly to pat him on the head. Caesar did not molest the lodgers, but he disdained them and he did not brook being personally addressed by anyone except Gran. One night, he wandered into the dining room, appearing to be in search of something he had mislaid, and, for some reason that no one was ever able to divine, suddenly stood stock-still and gave the easily upset Mr Beaver a long and penetrating look. Mr Beaver, trembling from head to toe, stammered, 'Why—er, hello there, Caesar, old boy, old boy,' and Caesar charged. For a moment, it was touch and go, but Gran saved Mr Beaver, only to lose him an hour later when he departed, bag and baggage, for the YMCA. This rout and the consequent loss of revenue would more than likely have meant Caesar's downfall and his deportation to the pound if it had not been that a newly widowed druggist, very irascible and very much Gran's style, had applied for a room in her house a week or so before, and now he moved in delightedly, as if he were coming home.

Finally, the police demanded that Caesar be muzzled and they warned that if he committed any major crime again—they cited the case of the Olson man—he would be shot on sight. Mrs Placer, although she had no respect for the law, knowing as much as she did about its agents, obeyed. She obeyed, that is, in part; she put the muzzle on Caesar for a few hours a day, usually early in the morning when the traffic was light and before the deliveries had started, but the rest of the time his powerful jaws and dazzling white saber teeth were free and snapping. There was between these two such preternatural rapport, such an impressive conjugation of suspicion, that he, sensing the approach of a policeman, could convey instantly to her the immediate necessity of clapping his nose cage on. And the policeman, sent out on the complaint of a terrorized neighbor, would be greeted by this law-abiding pair at the door.

Daisy and I wished we were dead. We were divided between

hating Caesar and loving Laddy, and we could not give up the hope that something, some day, would change him back into the loving animal he had been before he was appointed vice-president of the Placerites. Now at the meetings after supper on the porch he took an active part, standing rigidly at Gran's side except when she sent him on an errand. He carried out these assignments not with the air of a servant but with that of an accomplice. 'Get me the paper, Caesar,' she would say to him, and he, dismayingly intelligent and a shade smart-alecky, would open the screen door by himself and in a minute come back with the *Bulletin*, from which Mrs Placer would then read an item, like the Gospel of the day, and then read between the lines of it, scandalized.

In the deepening of our woe and our bereavement and humiliation, we mutely appealed to Mr Murphy. We did not speak outright to him, for Mr Murphy lived in a state of indirection, and often when he used the pronoun 'I,' he seemed to be speaking of someone standing a little to the left of him, but we went to see him and his animals each day during the sad summer, taking what comfort we could from the cozy, quiet indolence of his back yard, where small black eyes encountered ours politely and everyone was half asleep. When Mr Murphy inquired about Laddy in his bland, inattentive way, looking for a stratagem whereby to shift the queen of hearts into position by the king, we would say, 'Oh, he's fine,' or 'Laddy is a nifty dog.' And Mr Murphy, reverently slaking the thirst that was his talent and his concubine, would murmur, 'I'm glad.'

We wanted to tell him, we wanted his help, or at least his sympathy, but how could we cloud his sunny world? It was awful to see Mr Murphy ruffled. Up in the calm clouds as he generally was, he could occasionally be brought to earth with a thud, as we had seen and heard one day. Not far from his house, there lived a bad, troublemaking boy of twelve, who was forever hanging over the fence trying to teach the parrot obscene words. He got nowhere, for she spoke no English and she would flabbergast him with her cold eye and sneer, '*Tant pis*.' One day, this boorish fellow went too far; he suddenly shot his head over the fence like a jack-in-the-box and aimed a water pistol at the skunk's face. Mr Murphy leaped to his feet in a scarlet rage; he picked up a stone and threw it accurately, hitting the boy square in the back, so hard that he fell right down in a mud puddle and lay there kicking and squalling and, as it turned out, quite badly hurt. 'If you ever come back here again, I'll kill you!'

roared Mr Murphy. I think he meant it, for I have seldom seen an anger so resolute, so brilliant, and so voluble. 'How dared he!' he cried, scrambling into Mallow's cage to hug and pet and soothe her. 'He must be absolutely mad! He must be the Devil!' He did not go back to his game after that but paced the yard, swearing a blue streak and only pausing to croon to his animals, now as frightened by him as they had been by the intruder, and to drink straight from the bottle, not bothering with fixings. We were fascinated by this unfamiliar side of Mr Murphy, but we did not want to see it ever again, for his face had grown so dangerously purple and the veins of his forehead seemed ready to burst and his eyes looked scorched. He was the closest thing to a maniac we had ever seen. So we did not tell him about Laddy; what he did not know would not hurt him, although it was hurting us, throbbing in us like a great, bleating wound.

But eventually Mr Murphy heard about our dog's conversion, one night at the pool hall, which he visited from time to time when he was seized with a rare but compelling garrulity, and the next afternoon when he asked us how Laddy was and we replied that he was fine, he tranquilly told us, as he deliberated whether to move the jack of clubs now or to bide his time, that we were sweet girls but we were lying in our teeth. He did not seem at all angry but only interested, and all the while he questioned us, he went on about his business with the gin and the hearts and spades and diamonds and clubs. It rarely happened that he won the particular game he was playing, but that day he did, and when he saw all the cards laid out in their ideal pattern, he leaned back, looking disappointed, and he said, 'I'm damned.' He then scooped up the cards, in a gesture unusually quick and tidy for him, stacked them together, and bound them with a rubber band. Then he began to tell us what he thought of Gran. He grew as loud and apoplectic as he had been that other time, and though he kept repeating that he knew *we* were innocent and he put not a shred of the blame on us, we were afraid he might suddenly change his mind, and, speechless, we cowered against the monkeys' cage. In dread, the monkeys clutched the fingers we offered to them and made soft, protesting noises, as if to say, 'Oh, stop it, Murphy! Our nerves!'

As quickly as it had started, the tantrum ended. Mr Murphy paled to his normal complexion and said calmly that the only practical thing was to go and have it out with Mrs Placer. 'At once,' he added, although he said he bitterly feared that it was too late and there would be no exorcising the fiend from Laddy's misused spirit. And because he had given the dog to us and not to her, he required that we go along with him, stick up for our rights, stand on our own mettle, get up our Irish, and give the old bitch something to put in her pipe and smoke.

Oh, it was hot that day! We walked in a kind of delirium through the simmer, where only the grasshoppers had the energy to move, and I remember wondering if ether smelled like the gin on Mr Murphy's breath. Daisy and I, in one way or another, were going to have our gizzards cut out along with our hearts and our souls and our pride, and I wished I were as drunk as Mr Murphy, who swam effortlessly through the heat, his lips parted comfortably, his eyes half closed. When we turned in to the path at Gran's house, my blood began to scald my veins. It was so futile and so dangerous and so absurd. Here we were on a high moral mission, two draggletailed, gumptionless little girls and a toper whom no one could take seriously, partly because he was little more than a gurgling bottle of booze and partly because of the clothes he wore. He was a sight, as he always was when he was out of his own yard. There, somehow, in the carefree disorder, his clothes did not look especially strange, but on the streets of the town, in the barbershop or the post office or on Gran's path, they were fantastic. He wore a pair of hound's-tooth pants, old but maintaining a vehement pattern, and with them he wore a collarless blue flannelette shirt. His hat was the silliest of all, because it was a derby three sizes too big. And as if Shannon, too, was a part of his funny-paper costume, the elder capuchin rode on his shoulder, tightly embracing his thin red neck.

Gran and Caesar were standing side by side behind the screen door, looking as if they had been expecting us all along. For a moment, Gran and Mr Murphy faced each other across the length of weedy brick between the gate and the front porch, and no one spoke. Gran took no notice of Daisy and me. She adjusted her eyeglasses, using both hands, and then looked down at Caesar and matter-of-factly asked, 'Do you want out?'

Caesar flung himself full-length upon the screen and it sprang open like a jaw. I ran to meet him and head him off, and Daisy threw a library book at his head, but he was on Mr Murphy in one split second and had his monkey off his shoulder and had broken

Shannon's neck in two shakes. He would have gone on nuzzling and mauling and growling over the corpse for hours if Gran had not marched out of the house and down the path and slapped him lightly on the flank and said, in a voice that could not have deceived an idiot, 'Why, Caesar, you scamp! You've hurt Mr Murphy's monkey! Aren't you ashamed?'

Hurt the monkey! In one final, apologetic shudder, the life was extinguished from the little fellow. Bloody and covered with slather, Shannon lay with his arms suppliantly stretched over his head, his leather fingers curled into loose, helpless fists. His hind legs and his tail lay limp and helter-skelter on the path. And Mr Murphy, all of a sudden reeling drunk, burst into the kind of tears that Daisy and I knew well—the kind that time alone could stop. We stood aghast in the dark-red sunset, killed by our horror and our grief for Shannon and our unforgivable disgrace. We stood upright in a dead faint, and an eon passed before Mr Murphy picked up Shannon's body and wove away, sobbing, 'I don't believe it! I don't *believe it!*'

The very next day, again at morbid, heavy sunset, Caesar died in violent convulsions, knocking down two tall hollyhocks in his throes. Long after his heart had stopped, his right hind leg continued to jerk in aimless reflex. Madly methodical, Mr Murphy had poisoned some meat for him, had thoroughly envenomed a whole pound of hamburger, and early in the morning, before sunup, when he must have been near collapse with his hangover, he had stolen up to Mrs Placer's house and put it by the kitchen door. He was so stealthy that Caesar never stirred in his fool's paradise there on the floor by Gran. We knew these to be the facts, for Mr Murphy made no bones about them. Afterward he had gone home and said a solemn Requiem for Shannon in so loud a voice that someone sent for the police, and they took him away in the Black Maria to sober him up on strong green tea. By the time he was in the lockup and had confessed what he had done, it was far too late, for Caesar had already gulped down the meat. He suffered an undreamed-of agony in Gran's flower garden, and Daisy and I, unable to bear the sight of it, hiked up to the red rocks and shook there, wretchedly ripping to shreds the sand lilies that grew in the cracks. Flight was the only thing we could think of, but where could we go? We stared west at the mountains and quailed at the look of the stern white glacier; we wildly scanned the prairies for escape. 'If only we were something besides kids! Besides girls!' mourned Daisy. I could not speak at all; I huddled in a niche of the

258

rocks and cried.

No one in the town, except, of course, her lodgers, had the slightest sympathy for Gran. The townsfolk allowed that Mr Murphy was a drunk and was fighting Irish, but he had a heart and this was something that could never be said of Mrs Placer. The neighbor who had called the police when he was chanting the *Dies Irae* before breakfast in that deafening monotone had said, 'The poor guy is having some kind of a spell, so don't be rough on him, hear?' Mr Murphy became, in fact, a kind of hero; some people, stretching a point, said he was a saint for the way that every day and twice on Sunday he sang a memorial mass over Shannon's grave, now marked with a chipped, cheap plaster figure of Saint Francis. He withdrew from the world more and more, seldom venturing into the streets at all, except when he went to the bootlegger to get a new bottle to snuggle into. All summer, all fall, we saw him as we passed by his yard, sitting at his dilapidated table, enfeebled with gin, graying, withering, turning his head ever and ever more slowly as he maneuvered the protocol of the kings and the queens and the knaves. Daisy and I could never stop to visit him again.

It went on like this, year after year. Daisy and I lived in a mesh of lies and evasions, battled and mean, like rats in a maze. When we were old enough for beaux, we connived like sluts to see them, but we would never admit to their existence until Gran caught us out by some trick. Like this one, for example: Once, at the end of a long interrogation, she said to me, 'I'm more relieved than I can tell you that you *don't* have anything to do with Jimmy Gilmore, because I happen to know that he is after only one thing in a girl,' and then, off guard in the loving memory of sitting in the movies the night before with Jimmy, not even holding hands, I defended him and defeated myself, and Gran, smiling with success, said, 'I *thought* you knew him. It's a pretty safe rule of thumb that where there's smoke there's fire.' That finished Jimmy and me, for afterward I was nervous with him and I confounded and alarmed and finally bored him by trying to convince him, although the subject had not come up, that I did not doubt his good intentions.

Daisy and I would come home from school, or, later, from our jobs, with a small triumph or an interesting piece of news, and if we forgot ourselves and, in our exuberance, told Gran, we were hustled into court at once for cross-examination. Once, I remember, while I was still in high school, I told her about getting a part in a play. How very nice for me, she said, if that kind of make-believe seemed to me worth while. But what was my role? An old woman! A widow woman believed to be a witch? She did not care a red cent, but she did have to laugh in view of the fact that Miss Eccles, in charge of dramatics, had almost run her down in her car. And I would forgive her, would I not, if she did not come to see the play, and would not think her eccentric for not wanting to see herself ridiculed in public?

My pleasure strangled, I crawled, joy-killed, to our third-floor room. The room was small and its monstrous furniture was too big and the rag rugs were repulsive, but it was bright. We would not hang a blind at the window, and on this day I stood there staring into the mountains that burned with the sun. I feared the mountains, but at times like this their massiveness consoled me; they, at least, could not be gossiped about.

Why did we stay until we were grown? Daisy and I ask ourselves this question as we sit here on the bench in the municipal zoo, reminded of Mr Murphy by the polar bear, reminded by the monkeys not of Shannon but of Mrs Placer's insatiable gossips at their post-prandial feast.

'But how could we have left?' says Daisy, wringing her buttery hands. 'It was the depression. We had no money. We had nowhere to go.'

'All the same, we could have gone,' I say, resentful still of the waste of all those years. 'We could have come here and got jobs as waitresses. Or prostitutes, for that matter.'

'I wouldn't have wanted to be a prostitute,' says Daisy.

We agree that under the circumstances it would have been impossible for us to run away. The physical act would have been simple, for the city was not far and we could have stolen the bus fare or hitched a ride. Later, when we began to work as salesgirls in Kress's, it would have been no trick at all to vanish on Saturday afternoon with our week's pay, without so much as going home to say goodbye. But it had been infinitely harder than that, for Gran, as we now see, held us trapped by our sense of guilt. We were vitiated, and we had no choice but to wait, flaccidly, for her to die.

You may be sure we did not unlearn those years as soon as we put her out of sight in the cemetery and sold her house for a song to the first boob who would buy it. Nor did we forget when we left the town for another one, where we had jobs at a dude camp—the town where Daisy now lives with a happy husband and two happy sons. The succubus did not relent for years, and I can still remember, in the beginning of our days at the Lazy S3, overhearing an edgy millionaire say to his wife, naming my name, 'That girl gives me the cold shivers. One would think she had just seen a murder.' Well, I had. For years, whenever I woke in the night in fear or pain or loneliness, I would increase my suffering by the memory of Shannon, and my tears were as bitter as poor Mr Murphy's.

We have never been back to Adams. But we see that house plainly, with the hopvines straggling over the porch. The windows are hung with the cheapest grade of marquisette, dipped into coffee to impart to it an unwilling color, neither white nor tan but individual and spitefully unattractive. We see the wicker rockers and the swing, and through the screen door we dimly make out the slightly veering corridor, along one wall of which stands a glass-doored bookcase; when we were children, it had contained not books but stale old cardboard boxes filled with such things as WCTU tracts and anti-cigarette literature and newspaper clippings relating to sexual sin in the Christianized islands of the Pacific.

Even if we were able to close our minds' eyes to the past, Mr Murphy would still be before us in the apotheosis of the polar bear. My pain becomes intolerable, and I am relieved when Daisy rescues us. 'We've got to go,' she says in a sudden panic. 'I've got asthma coming on.' We rush to the nearest exit of the city park and hail a cab, and, once inside it, Daisy gives herself an injection of adrenalin and then leans back. We are heartbroken and infuriated, and we cannot speak.

Two hours later, beside my train, we clutch each other as if we were drowning. We ought to go out to the nearest policeman and say, 'We are not responsible women. You will have to take care of us because we cannot take care of ourselves.' But gradually the storm begins to lull.

'You're sure you've got your ticket?' says Daisy. 'You'll surely be able to get a roomette once you're on.'

'I don't know about that,' I say. 'If there are any VIPs on board, I won't have a chance. "Spinsters and Orphans Last" is the motto of this line.'

Daisy smiles. 'I didn't care,' she says, 'but I had to laugh when I saw that woman nab the redcap you had signaled to. I had a good

261

notion to give her a piece of my mind.'

'It will be a miracle if I ever see my bags again,' I say, mounting the steps of the train. 'Do you suppose that blackguardly porter knows about the twenty-dollar gold piece in my little suitcase?'

'Anything's possible!' cries Daisy, and begins to laugh. She is so pretty, standing there in her bright-red linen suit and her black velvet hat. A solitary ray of sunshine comes through a broken pane in the domed vault of the train shed and lies on her shoulder like a silver arrow.

'So long, Daisy!' I call as the train begins to move.

She walks quickly along beside the train. 'Watch out for pickpockets!' she calls.

'You, too!' My voice is thin and lost in the increasing noise of the speeding train wheels. 'Goodbye, old dear!'

I go at once to the club car and I appropriate the writing table, to the vexation of a harried priest, who snatches up the telegraph pad and gives me a sharp look. I write Daisy approximately the same letter I always write her under this particular set of circumstances, the burden of which is that nothing for either of us can ever be as bad as the past before Gran mercifully died. In a postscript I add: 'There is a Roman Catholic priest (that is to say, he is *dressed* like one) sitting behind me although all the chairs on the opposite side of the car are empty. I can only conclude that he is looking over my shoulder, and while I do not want to cause you any alarm, I think you would be advised to be on the lookout for any appearance of miraculous medals, scapulars, papist booklets, etc., in the shops of your town. It really makes me laugh to see the way he is pretending that all he wants is for me to finish this letter so that he can have the table.'

I sign my name and address on the envelope, and I give up my place to the priest, who smiles nicely at me, and then I move across the car to watch the fields as they slip by. They are alfalfa fields, but you can bet your bottom dollar that they are chockablock with marijuana.

I begin to laugh. The fit is silent but it is devastating; it surges and rattles in my rib cage and I turn my face to the window to avoid the narrow gaze of the Filipino bar boy. I must think of something sad to stop this unholy giggle, and I think of the polar bear. But even his bleak tragedy does not sober me. Wildly I fling open the newspaper I have brought and I pretend to be reading something screamingly funny. The words I see are in a Hollywood gossip column: 'How a well-known starlet can get a divorce in Nevada without her crooner husband's consent, nobody knows. It won't be worth a plugged nickel here.'

1964

A POETICS FOR BULLIES

Stanley Elkin

I'm Push the bully, and what I hate are new kids and sissies, dumb kids and smart, rich kids, poor kids, kids who wear glasses, talk funny, show off, patrol boys and wise guys and kids who pass pencils and water the plants—and cripples, *especially* cripples. I love nobody loved.

One time I was pushing this red-haired kid (I'm a pusher, no hitter, no belter; an aggressor of marginal violence, I hate *real* force) and his mother stuck her head out the window and shouted something I've never forgotten. *'Push,'* she yelled. *'You, Push.* You pick on him because you wish you had his red hair!' It's true; I *did* wish I had his red hair. I wish I were tall, or fat, or thin. I wish I had different eyes, different hands, a mother in the supermarket. I wish I were a man, a small boy, a girl in the choir. I'm a coveter, a Boston Blackie of the heart, casing the world. Endlessly I covet and case. (Do you know what makes me cry? The Declaration of Independence. 'All men are created equal.' That's beautiful.)

If you're a bully like me, you use your head. Toughness isn't enough. You beat them up, they report you. Then where are you? I'm not even particularly strong. (I used to be strong. I used to do exercise, work out, but strength implicates you, and often isn't an advantage anyway—read the judo ads. Besides, your big bullies aren't bullies at all—they're *athletes.* With them, beating guys up is a sport.) But what I lose in size and strength I make up in courage. I'm very brave. That's a lie about bullies being cowards underneath. If you're a coward, get out of the business.

I'm best at torment.

A kid has a toy bow, toy arrows. 'Let Push look,' I tell him.

He's suspicious, he knows me. 'Go way, Push,' he says, this mama-warned Push doubter.

'Come on,' I say, 'come on.'

'No, Push. I can't. My mother said I can't.'

I raise my arms, I spread them. I'm a bird—slow, powerful, easy, free. I move my head offering profile like something beaked. I'm the

Thunderbird. 'In the school where I go I have a teacher who teaches me magic,' I say. 'Arnold Salamancy, give Push your arrows. Give him one, he gives back two. Push is the God of the Neighborhood.'

'Go way, Push,' the kid says, uncertain.

'Right,' Push says, himself again. 'Right. I'll disappear. First the fingers.' My fingers ball to fists. 'My forearms next.' They jackknife into my upper arms. 'The arms.' Quick as bird-blink they snap behind my back, fit between the shoulder blades like a small knapsack. (I am double-jointed, protean.) 'My head,' I say.

'No, Push,' the kid says, terrified. I shudder and everything comes back, falls into place from the stem of self like a shaken puppet.

'The arrow, the arrow. Two where was one.' He hands me an arrow.

'*Trouble, trouble, double rubble!*' I snap it and give back the pieces.

Well, sure. There *is* no magic. If there were I would learn it. I would find out the words, the slow turns and strange passes, drain the bloods and get the herbs, do the fires like a vestal. I would look for the main chants. *Then* I'd change things. *Push* would!

But there's only casuistical trick. Sleight-of-mouth, the bully's poetics.

You know the formulas:

'Did you ever see a match burn twice?' you ask. Strike. Extinguish. Jab his flesh with the hot stub.

'Play "Gestapo"?'

'How do you play?'

'What's your name?'

'It's Morton.'

I slap him. 'You're lying.'

'Adam and Eve and Pinch Me Hard went down to the lake for a swim. Adam and Eve fell in. Who was left?'

'Pinch Me Hard.'

I do.

Physical puns, conundrums. Push the punisher, the conundrummer! But there has to be more than tricks in a bag of tricks.

I don't know what it is. Sometimes I think I'*m* the only new kid. In a room, the school, the playground, the neighborhood, I get the feeling I've just moved in, no one knows me. You know what I like? To stand in crowds. To wait with them at the airport to meet a plane. Someone asks what time it is. I'm the first to answer. Or at the ball park when the vendor comes. He passes the hot dog down the long row. I want *my* hands on it, too. On the dollar going up, the change coming down.

I am ingenious, I am patient.

A kid is going downtown on the elevated train. He's got his little suit on, his shoes are shined, he wears a cap. This is a kid going to the travel bureaus, the foreign tourist offices to get brochures, maps, pictures of the mountains for a unit at his school—a kid looking for extra credit. I follow him. He comes out of the Italian Tourist Information Center. His arms are full. I move from my place at the window. I follow for two blocks and bump into him as he steps from a curb. It's a *collision*—The pamphlets fall from his arms. Pretending confusion, I walk on his paper Florence. I grind my heel in his Riviera. I climb Vesuvius and sack his Rome and dance on the Isle of Capri.

The Industrial Museum is a good place to find children. I cut somebody's five- or six-year-old kid brother out of the herd of eleven- and twelve-year-olds he's come with. '*Quick*,' I say. I pull him along the corridors, up the stairs, through the halls, down to a mezzanine landing. Breathless, I pause for a minute. 'I've got some gum. Do you want a stick?' He nods; I stick him. I rush him into an auditorium and abandon him. He'll be lost for hours.

I sidle up to a kid at the movies. 'You smacked my brother,' I tell him. 'After the show—I'll be outside.'

I break up games. I hold the ball above my head. 'You want it? take it.'

I go into barber shops. There's a kid waiting. 'I'm next,' I tell him, 'understand?'

One day Eugene Kraft rang my bell. Eugene is afraid of me, so he helps me. He's fifteen and there's something wrong with his saliva glands and he drools. His chin is always chapped. I tell him he has to drink a lot because he loses so much water.

'Push? Push,' he says. He's wiping his chin with his tissues. 'Push, there's this kid—'

'Better get a glass of water, Eugene.'

'No, Push, no fooling, there's this new kid—he just moved in. You've got to see this kid.'

'Eugene, get some water please. You're drying up. I've never seen you so bad. There are deserts in you, Eugene.'

'All right, Push, but then you've got to see—'

'Swallow, Eugene. You better swallow.'

He gulps hard.

'Push, this is a kid and a half. Wait, you'll see.'

'I'm very concerned about you, Eugene. You're dying of thirst, Eugene. Come into the kitchen with me.'

I push him through the door. He's very excited. I've never seen him so excited. He talks at me over his shoulder, his mouth flooding, his teeth like the little stone pebbles at the bottom of a fishbowl. 'He's got this sport coat with a patch over the heart. Like a king, Push. No kidding.'

'Be careful of the carpet, Eugene.'

I turn on the taps in the sink. I mix in hot water. 'Use your tissues, Eugene. Wipe your chin.'

He wipes himself and puts the Kleenex in his pocket. All of Eugene's pockets bulge. He looks, with his bulging pockets, like a clumsy smuggler.

'Wipe, Eugene. Swallow, you're drowning.'

'He's got this funny accent—you could die.' Excited, he tamps at his mouth like a diner, a tubercular.

'Drink some water, Eugene.'

'No, Push. I'm not thirsty—really.'

'Don't be foolish, kid. That's because your mouth's so wet. Inside where it counts you're drying up. It stands to reason. Drink some water.'

'He has this crazy haircut.'

'*Drink*,' I command. I shake him. '*Drink!*'

'Push, I've got no glass. Give me a glass at least.'

'I can't do that, Eugene. You've got a terrible sickness. How could I let you use our drinking glasses? Lean under the tap and open your mouth.'

He knows he'll have to do it, that I won't listen to him until he does. He bends into the sink.

'Push, it's *hot*,' he complains. The water splashes into his nose, it gets on his glasses and for a moment his eyes are magnified, enormous. He pulls away and scrapes his forehead on the faucet.

'Eugene, you touched it. Watch out, please. You're too close to the tap. Lean your head deeper into the sink.'

'It's *hot*, Push.'

'Warm water evaporates better. With your affliction you've got to evaporate fluids before they get into your glands.'

He feeds again from the tap.

'Do you think that's enough?' I ask after a while.

'I do, Push, I really do,' he says. He is breathless.

'Eugene,' I say seriously, 'I think you'd better get yourself a canteen.'

'A canteen, Push?'

'That's right. Then you'll always have water when you need it. Get one of those Boy Scout models. The two-quart kind with a canvas strap.'

'But you hate the Boy Scouts, Push.'

'They make very good canteens, Eugene. *And wear it!* I never want to see you without it. Buy it today.'

'All right, Push.'

'Promise!'

'All right, Push.'

'Say it out.'

He made the formal promise that I like to hear.

'Well then,' I said, 'let's go see this new kid of yours.'

He took me to the schoolyard. 'Wait,' he said, 'you'll see.' He skipped ahead.

'Eugene,' I said, calling him back. 'Let's understand something. No matter what this new kid is like, nothing changes as far as you and I are concerned.'

'Aw, Push,' he said.

'Nothing, Eugene. I mean it. You don't get out from under me.'

'Sure, Push, I know that.'

There were some kids in the far corner of the yard, sitting on the ground, leaning up against the wire fence. Bats and gloves and balls lay scattered around them. (It was where they told dirty jokes. Sometimes I'd come by during the little kids' recess and tell them all about what their daddies do to their mommies.)

'There. See? Do you see him?' Eugene, despite himself, seemed hoarse.

'Be quiet,' I said, checking him, freezing as a hunter might. I stared.

He was a *prince*, I tell you.

He was tall, tall, even sitting down. His long legs comfortable in expensive wool, the trousers of a boy who had been on ships, jets; who owned a horse, perhaps; who knew Latin—what *didn't* he know?—somebody made up, like a kid in a play with a beautiful mother and a handsome father; who took his breakfast from a sideboard, and picked, even at fourteen and fifteen and sixteen, his mail from a silver plate. He would have hobbies—stamps, stars, things lovely dead. He wore a sport coat, brown as wood, thick as heavy bark. The buttons were leather buds. His shoes seemed carved from horses' saddles, gunstocks. His clothes had once grown in nature. *What it must feel like inside those clothes*, I thought.

I looked at his face, his clear skin, and guessed at the bones, white as bleached wood. His eyes had skies in them. His yellow hair swirled on his head like a crayoned sun.

'Look, look at him,' Eugene said. 'The sissy. Get him, Push.'

He was talking to them and I moved closer to hear his voice. It was clear, beautiful but faintly foreign—like herb-seasoned meat.

When he saw me he paused, smiling. He waved. The others didn't look at me.

'Hello there,' he called. 'Come over if you'd like. I've been telling the boys about tigers.'

'Tigers,' I said.

'Give him the "match burn twice," Push,' Eugene whispered.

'Tigers, is it?' I said. 'What do you know about tigers?' My voice was high.

'The "match burn twice," Push.'

'Not so much as a Master *Tugjah*. I was telling the boys. In India there are men of high caste—*Tugjahs*, they're called. I was apprenticed to one once in the Southern Plains and might perhaps have earned my mastership, but the Red Chinese attacked the northern frontier and . . . well, let's just say I had to leave. At any rate, these *Tugjahs* are as intimate with the tiger as you are with dogs. I don't mean they keep them as pets. The relationship goes decper. Your dog is a service animal, as is your elephant.'

'Did you ever see a match burn twice?' I asked suddenly.

'Why no, can you do that? Is it a special match you use?'

'No,' Eugene said, 'it's an ordinary match. He uses an ordinary match.'

'Can you do it with one of mine, do you think?'

He took a matchbook from his pocket and handed it to me. The cover was exactly the material of his jacket, and in the center was a patch with a coat-of-arms identical to the one he wore over his heart.

I held the matchbook for a moment and then gave it back to him. 'I don't feel like it,' I said.

'Then some other time, perhaps,' he said.

Eugene whispered to me. 'His accent, Push, his funny *accent*.'

'Some other time, perhaps,' I said. I am a good mimic. I can duplicate a particular kid's lisp, his stutter, a thickness in his throat. There were two or three here whom I had brought close to tears by holding up my mirror to their voices. I can parody their limps, their waddles, their girlish runs, their clumsy jumps. I can throw as they throw, catch as they catch. I looked around. 'Some other time, perhaps,' I said again. No one would look at me.

'I'm *so* sorry,' the new one said, 'we don't know each other's names. You are?'

'I'm so sorry,' I said. 'You are?'

He seemed puzzled. Then he looked sad, disappointed. No one said anything.

'It don't sound the same,' Eugene whispered.

It was true. I sounded nothing like him. I could imitate only defects, only flaws.

A kid giggled.

'Sshh,' the prince said. He put one finger to his lips.

'Look at that,' Eugene said under his breath. 'He's a sissy.'

He had begun to talk to them again. I squatted, a few feet away. I ran gravel through my loose fists, one bowl in an hourglass feeding another.

He spoke of jungles, of deserts. He told of ancient trade routes traveled by strange beasts. He described lost cities and a lake deeper than the deepest level of the sea. There was a story about a boy who had been captured by bandits. A woman in the story—it wasn't clear whether she was the boy's mother—had been tortured. His eyes clouded for a moment when he came to this part and he had to pause before continuing. Then he told how the boy escaped—it was cleverly done—and found help, mountain tribesmen riding elephants. The elephants charged the cave in which the mo—the *woman*—was still a prisoner. It might have collapsed and killed her, but one old bull rushed in and, shielding her with his body, took the weight of the crashing rocks. Your elephant is a service animal.

I let a piece of gravel rest on my thumb and flicked it in a high arc above his head. Some of the others who had seen me stared, but the boy kept on talking. Gradually I reduced the range, allowing the chunks of gravel to come closer to his head.

'You see?' Eugene said quietly. 'He's afraid. He pretends not to notice.'

The arcs continued to diminish. The gravel went faster, straighter.

270

No one was listening to him now, but he kept talking.

'—of magic,' he said, 'what occidentals call "a witch doctor." There are spices that induce these effects. The *Bogdovii* was actually able to stimulate the growth of rocks with the powder. The Dutch traders were ready to go to war for the formula. Well, you can see what it could mean for the Low Countries. Without accessible quarries they've never been able to construct a permanent system of dikes. But with the *Bogdovii*'s powder'—he reached out and casually caught the speeding chip as if it had been a ping-pong ball—'they could turn a grain of sand into a pebble, use the pebbles to grow stones, the stones to grow rocks. This little piece of gravel, for example, could be changed into a mountain.' He dipped his thumb into his palm as I had and balanced the gravel on his nail. He flicked it; it rose from his nail like a missile and climbed an impossible arc. It disappeared. 'The *Bogdovii* never revealed how it was done.'

I stood up. Eugene tried to follow me.

'Listen,' he said, 'you'll get him.'

'Swallow,' I told him. 'Swallow, you pig!'

I have lived my life in pursuit of the vulnerable: Push the chink seeker, wheeler dealer in the flawed cement of the personality, a collapse maker. But what isn't vulnerable, *who* isn't? There is that which is unspeakable, so I speak it, that which is unthinkable, which I think. Me and the devil, we do God's dirty work, after all.

I went home after I left him. I turned once at the gate, and the boys were around him still. The useless Eugene had moved closer. *He* made room for him against the fence.

I ran into Frank the fat boy. He made a move to cross the street, but I had seen him and he went through a clumsy retractive motion. I could tell he thought I would get him for that, but I moved by, indifferent to a grossness in which I had once delighted. As I passed he seemed puzzled, a little hurt, a little—this was astonishing— guilty. *Sure* guilty. Why *not* guilty? The forgiven tire of their exemption. Nothing could ever be forgiven, and I forgave nothing. I held them to the mark. Who else cared about the fatties, about the dummies and slobs and clowns, about the gimps and squares and oafs and fools, the kids with a mouthful of mush, all those shut-ins of the mind and heart, all those losers? Frank the fat boy knew, and passed me shyly. His wide, fat body, stiffened, forced jokishly martial when he saw me, had already become flaccid as he moved by, had already made one more forgiven surrender. Who cared? The streets were full of failure. Let them. Let them be. There was a paragon, a paragon loose. What could he be doing here, why had he come, what did he want? It was impossible that this hero from India and everywhere had made his home here; that he lived, as Frank the fat boy did, as Eugene did, as *I* did, in an apartment; that he shared our lives.

In the afternoon I looked for Eugene. He was in the park, in a tree. There was a book in his lap. He leaned against the thick trunk.

'Eugene,' I called up to him.

'Push, they're closed. It's Sunday, Push. The stores are closed. I looked for the canteen. The stores are closed.'

'Where is he?'

'Who, Push? What do you want, Push?'

'*Him*. Your pal. The prince. Where? Tell me, Eugene, or I'll shake you out of that tree. I'll burn you down. I swear it. Where is he?'

'No, Push. I was wrong about that guy. He's nice. He's really nice. Push, he told me about a doctor who could help me. Leave him alone, Push.'

'Where, Eugene? *Where*? I count to three.'

Eugene shrugged and came down the tree.

I found the name Eugene gave me—funny, foreign—over the bell in the outer hall. The buzzer sounded and I pushed open the door. I stood inside and looked up the carpeted stairs, the angled banisters.

'What is it?' She sounded old, worried.

'The new kid,' I called, 'the new kid.'

'It's for you,' I heard her say.

'Yes?' His voice, the one I couldn't mimic. I mounted the first stair. I leaned back against the wall and looked up through the high, boxy banister poles. It was like standing inside a pipe organ.

'Yes?'

From where I stood at the bottom of the stairs I could see only a boot. He was wearing boots.

'Yes? What is it, please?'

'*You*,' I roared. 'Glass of fashion, mold of form, it's me! It's Push the bully!'

I heard his soft, rapid footsteps coming down the stairs—a springy, spongy urgency. He jingled, the bastard. He had coins—I could see them: rough, golden, imperfectly round; raised, massively gowned goddesses, their heads fingered smooth, their arms gone—and keys

272

to strange boxes, thick doors. I saw his boots. I backed away.

'I brought you down,' I said.

'Be quiet, please. There's a woman who's ill. A boy who must study. There's a man with bad bones. An old man needs sleep.'

'He'll get it,' I said.

'We'll go outside,' he said.

'No. Do you live here? What do you do? Will you be in our school? Were you telling the truth?'

'Shh. Please. You're very excited.'

'Tell me your name,' I said. It could be my campaign, I thought. His *name*. Scratched in new sidewalk, chalked onto walls, written on papers dropped in the street. To leave it behind like so many clues, to give him a fame, to take it away, to slash and cross it out, to erase and to smear—my kid's witchcraft. 'Tell me your name.'

'It's John,' he said softly.

'What?'

'It's John.'

'John what? Come on now. I'm Push the bully.'

'John Williams,' he said.

'John Williams? John Williams? Only that? Only John Williams?'

He smiled.

'Who's that on the bell? The name on the box?'

'She needs me,' he said.

'Cut it out.'

'I help her,' he said.

'You stop that.'

'There's a man that's in pain. A woman who's old. A husband that's worried. A wife that despairs.'

'You're the bully,' I said. 'Your John Williams is a service animal,' I yelled in the hall.

He turned and began to climb the stairs. His calves bloomed in their leather sheathing.

'*Lover*,' I whispered to him.

He turned to me at the landing. He shook his head sadly.

'We'll see,' I said.

'We'll see what we'll see,' he said.

That night I painted his name on the side of the gymnasium in enormous letters. In the morning it was still there, but it wasn't what I meant. There was nothing incantatory in the huge letters, no scream, no curse. I had never traveled with a gang, there had been no

273

togetherness in my tearing, but this thing on the wall seemed the act of vandals, the low production of ruffians. When you looked at it you were surprised they had gotten the spelling right.

Astonishingly, it was allowed to remain. And each day there was something more celebrational in the giant name, something of increased hospitality, lavish welcome. John Williams might have been a football hero, or someone back from the kidnappers. Finally I had to take it off myself.

Something had changed.

Eugene was not wearing his canteen. Boys didn't break off their conversations when I came up to them. One afternoon a girl winked at me. (Push has never picked on girls. *Their* submissiveness is part of their nature. They are ornamental. Don't get me wrong, please. There is a way in which they function as part of the landscape, like flowers at a funeral. They have a strange cheerfulness. They are the organizers of pep rallies and dances. They put out the Year Book. They are *born* Gray Ladies. I can't bully them.)

John Williams was in the school, but except for brief glimpses in the hall I never saw him. Teachers would repeat the things he had said in their other classes. They read from his papers. In the gym the coach described plays he had made, set shots he had taken. Everyone talked about him, and girls made a reference to him a sort of love signal. If it was suggested that he had smiled at one of them, the girl referred to would blush or, what was worse, look aloofly mysterious. (*Then* I could have punished her, *then* I could.) Gradually his name began to appear on all their notebooks, in the margins of their texts. (It annoyed me to remember what *I* had done on the wall.) The big canvas books, with their careful, elaborate J's and W's, took on the appearance of ancient, illuminated fables. It was the unconscious embroidery of love, hope's bright doodle. Even the administration was aware of him. In Assembly the principal announced that John Williams had broken all existing records in the school's charity drives. She had never seen good citizenship like his before, she said.

It's one thing to live with a bully, another to live with a hero.

Everyone's hatred I understand, no one's love; everyone's grievance, no one's content.

I saw Mimmer. Mimmer should have graduated years ago. I saw Mimmer the dummy.

'Mimmer,' I said, 'you're in his class.'

'He's very smart.'

274

'Yes, but is it fair? You work harder. I've seen you study. You spend hours. Nothing comes. He was born knowing. You could have used just a little of what he's got so much of. It's not fair.'

'He's very clever. It's wonderful,' Mimmer says.

Slud is crippled. He wears a shoe with a built-up heel to balance himself.

'Ah, Slud,' I say, 'I've seen him run.'

'He has beaten the horses in the park. It's very beautiful,' Slud says.

'He's handsome, isn't he, Clob?' Clob looks contagious, radioactive. He has severe acne. He is ugly *under* his acne.

'He gets the girls,' Clob says.

He gets *everything*, I think. But I'm alone in my envy, awash in my lust. It's as if I were a prophet to the deaf. Schnooks, schnooks, I want to scream, dopes and settlers. What good does his smile do you, of what use is his good heart?

The other day I did something very stupid. I went to the cafeteria and shoved a boy out of the way and took his place in the line. It was foolish, but their fear is almost all gone and I felt I had to show the flag. The boy only grinned and let me pass. Then someone called my name. It was *him*. I turned to face him. 'Push,' he said, 'you forgot your silver.' He handed it to a girl in front of him and she gave it to the boy in front of her and it came to me down the long line.

I plot, I scheme. Snares, I think; tricks and traps. I remember the old days when there were ways to snap fingers, crush toes, ways to pull noses, twist heads and punch arms—the old-timey Flinch Law I used to impose, the gone bully magic of deceit. But nothing works against him, I think. How does he know so much? He is bully-prepared, that one, not to be trusted.

It is worse and worse.

In the cafeteria he eats with Frank. 'You don't want those potatoes,' he tells him. 'Not the ice cream, Frank. One sandwich, remember. You lost three pounds last week.' The fat boy smiles his fat love at him. John Williams puts his arm around him. He seems to squeeze him thin.

He's helping Mimmer to study. He goes over his lessons and teaches him tricks, short cuts. 'I want you up there with me on the Honor Roll, Mimmer.'

I see him with Slud the cripple. They go to the gym. I watch from

275

the balcony. 'Let's develop those arms, my friend.' They work out with weights. Slud's muscles grow, they bloom from his bones.

I lean over the rail. I shout down, 'He can bend iron bars. Can he peddle a bike? Can he walk on rough ground? Can he climb up a hill? Can he wait on a line? Can he dance with a girl? Can he go up a ladder or jump from a chair?'

Beneath me the rapt Slud sits on a bench and raises a weight. He holds it at arm's length, level with his chest. He moves it high, higher. It rises above his shoulders, his throat, his head. He bends back his neck to see what he's done. If the weight should fall now it would crush his throat. I stare down into his smile.

I see Eugene in the halls. I stop him. 'Eugene, what's he done for you?' I ask. He smiles—he never did this—and I see his mouth's flood. 'High tide,' I say with satisfaction.

Williams has introduced Clob to a girl. They have double-dated.

A week ago John Williams came to my house to see me! I wouldn't let him in.

'Please open the door, Push. I'd like to chat with you. Will you open the door? Push? I think we ought to talk. I think I can help you be happier.'

I was furious. I didn't know what to say to him. 'I don't want to be happier. Go way.' It was what little kids used to say to me.

'*Please* let me help you.'

'*Please* let me—' I begin to echo. 'Please let me alone.'

'We ought to be friends, Push.'

'No deals.' I am choking, I am close to tears. What can I do? *What?* I want to kill him.

I double-lock the door and retreat to my room. He is still out there. I have tried to live my life so that I could keep always the lamb from my door.

He has gone too far this time; and I think sadly, I will have to fight him, I will have to fight him. Push pushed. I think sadly of the pain. Push pushed. I will have to fight him. Not to preserve honor but its opposite. Each time I see him I will have to fight him. And then I think—*of course!* And *I* smile. He has done *me* a favor. I know it at once. If he fights me he fails. He fails if he fights me. *Push pushed pushes!* It's physics! Natural law! I know he'll beat me, but I won't prepare, I won't train, I won't use the tricks I know. It's strength against strength, and my strength is as the strength of ten because my jaw is glass! *He doesn't know everything, not everything he doesn't.* And I think, I could go out now, he's still there, I could hit him in the hall, but I think, No, I want them to see, I want *them* to see!

The next day I am very excited. I look for Williams. He's not in the halls. I miss him in the cafeteria. Afterward I look for him in the schoolyard where I first saw him. (He has them organized now. He teaches them games of Tibet, games of Japan; he gets them to play lost sports of the dead.) He does not disappoint me. He is there in the yard, a circle around him, a ring of the loyal.

I join the ring. I shove in between two kids I have known. They try to change places; they murmur and fret.

Williams sees me and waves. His smile could grow flowers. 'Boys,' he says, 'boys, make room for Push. Join hands, boys.' They welcome me to the circle. One takes my hand, then another. I give to each calmly.

I wait. *He doesn't know everything.*

'Boys,' he begins, 'today we're going to learn a game that the knights of the lords and kings of old France used to play in another century. Now you may not realize it, boys, because today when we think of a knight we think, too, of his fine charger, but the fact is that a horse was a rare animal—not a domestic European animal at all, but Asian. In western Europe, for example, there was no such thing as a work horse until the eighth century. Your horse was just too expensive to be put to heavy labor in the fields. (This explains, incidentally, the prevalence of famine in western Europe, whereas famine is unrecorded in Asia until the ninth century, when Euro-Asian horse trading was at its height.) It wasn't only expensive to purchase a horse, it was expensive to keep one. A cheap fodder wasn't developed in Europe until the tenth century. Then, of course, when you consider the terrific risks that the warrior horse of a knight naturally had to run, you begin to appreciate how expensive it would have been for the lord—unless he was extremely rich—to provide all his knights with horses. He'd want to make pretty certain that the knights who got them knew how to handle a horse. (Only your knights errant—an elite, crack corps—ever had horses. We don't realize that most knights were *home* knights; *chevalier chez* they were called.)

'This game, then, was devised to let the lord, or king, see which of his knights had the skill and strength in his hands to control a horse. Without moving your feet, you must try to jerk the one next to you off balance. Each man has two opponents, so it's very difficult. If a man falls, or if his knee touches the ground, he's out. The circle is diminished but must close up again immediately. Now, once for practice only—'

'Just a minute,' I interrupt.

'Yes, Push?'

I leave the circle and walk forward and hit him as hard as I can in the face.

He stumbles backward. The boys groan. He recovers. He rubs his jaw and smiles. I think he is going to let me hit him again. I am prepared for this. He knows what I'm up to and will use his passivity. Either way I win, but I am determined he shall hit me. I am ready to kick him, but as my foot comes up he grabs my ankle and turn it forcefully. I spin in the air. He lets go and I fall heavily on my back. I am surprised at how easy it was, but am content if they understand. I get up and am walking away, but there is an arm on my shoulder. He pulls me around roughly. He hits me.

'*Sic semper tyrannus*,' he exults.

'Where's your other cheek?' I ask, falling backward.

'One cheek for tyrants,' he shouts. He pounces on me and raises his fist and I cringe. His anger is terrific. I do not want to be hit again.

'You see? You see?' I scream at the kids, but I have lost the train of my former reasoning. I have in no way beaten him. I can't remember now what I had intended.

He lowers his fist and gets off my chest and they cheer. 'Hurrah,' they yell. 'Hurrah, hurrah.' The word seems funny to me.

He offers his hand when I try to rise. It is so difficult to know what to do. Oh God, it is so difficult to know which gesture is the right one. I don't even know this. He knows everything, and I don't even know this. I am a fool on the ground, one hand behind me pushing up, the other not yet extended but itching in the palm where the need is. It is better to give than receive, surely. It is best not to need at all.

Appalled, guessing what I miss, I rise alone.

'Friends?' he asks. He offers to shake.

'Take it, Push.' It's Eugene's voice.

'Go ahead, Push.' Slud limps forward.

'Push, hatred's so ugly,' Clob says, his face shining.

'You'll feel better, Push,' Frank, thinner, taller, urges softly.

'Push, don't be foolish,' Mimmer says.

I shake my head. I may be wrong. I am probably wrong. All I know at last is what feels good. 'Nothing doing,' I growl. 'No deals.' I begin to talk, to spray my hatred at them. They are not an easy target even now. 'Only your knights errant—your crack corps—ever have horses. Slud may dance and Clob may kiss but they'll never be good at it. *Push is no service animal*. No. *No*. Can you hear that, Williams? There isn't any magic, but your no is still stronger than your yes, and distrust is where I put my faith.' I turn to the boys. 'What have you settled for? Only your knights errant ever have horses. *What have you settled for?* Will Mimmer do sums in his head? How do you like your lousy hunger, thin boy? Slud, you can break me but you can't catch me. And Clob will never shave without pain, and ugly, let me tell you, is *still* in the eye of the beholder!'

John Williams mourns for me. He grieves his gamy grief. No one has everything—not even John Williams. He doesn't have *me*. He'll never have me, I think. If my life were only to deny him that, it would almost be enough. I could do his voice now if I wanted. His corruption began when he lost me. 'You,' I shout, rubbing it in, *'indulger*, dispense me no dispensations. Push the bully hates your heart!'

'Shut him up, somebody,' Eugene cries. His saliva spills from his mouth when he speaks.

'Swallow! *Pig, swallow!*'

He rushes toward me.

Suddenly I raise my arms and he stops. I feel a power in me. I am Push, Push the bully, God of the Neighborhood, its incarnation of envy and jealousy and need. I vie, strive, emulate, compete, a contender in every event there is. I didn't make myself. I probably can't save myself, but maybe that's the only need I don't have. I taste my lack and that's how I win—by having nothing to lose. It's not good enough! I want and I want and I will die wanting, but first I will have something. This time I will have something. I say it aloud. 'This time I will have something.' I step toward them. The power makes me dizzy. It is enormous. They feel it. They back away. They crouch in the shadow of my outstretched wings. It isn't deceit this time but the real magic at last, the genuine thing: the cabala of my hate, of my irreconcilableness.

Logic is nothing. Desire is stronger.

I move toward Eugene. *'I will have something,'* I roar.

'Stand back,' he shrieks, 'I'll spit in your eye.'

'I will have something. I will have terror. I will have drought. I bring

279

the dearth. Famine's contagious. Also is thirst. Privation, privation, barrenness, void. I dry up your glands, I poison your well.'

He is choking, gasping, chewing furiously. He opens his mouth. It is dry. His throat is parched. There is sand on his tongue.

They moan. They are terrified, but they move up to see. We are thrown together. Slud, Frank, Clob, Mimmer, the others, John Williams, myself. I will not be reconciled, or halve my hate. *It's* what I have, all I can keep. My bully's sour solace. It's enough, I'll make do.

I can't stand them near me. I move against them. I shove them away. I force them off. I press them, thrust them aside. *I push through.*

1965

UPON THE SWEEPING FLOOD

Joyce Carol Oates

One day in Eden County, in the remote marsh and swamplands to the south, a man named Walter Stuart was stopped in the rain by a sheriff's deputy along a country road. Stuart was in a hurry to get home to his family—his wife and two daughters—after having endured a week at his father's old farm, arranging for his father's funeral, surrounded by aging relatives who had sucked at him for the strength of his youth. He was a stern, quiet man of thirty-nine, beginning now to lose some of the muscular hardness that had always baffled others, masking as it did Stuart's remoteness, his refinement, his faith in discipline and order that seem to have belonged, even in his youth, to a person already grown safely old. He was a district vice-president for one of the gypsum mining plants, a man to whom financial success and success in love had come naturally, without fuss. When only a child he had shifted his faith with little difficulty from the unreliable God of his family's tradition to the things and emotions of this world, which he had admired in his thoughtful, rather conservative way, and this faith had given him access, as if by magic, to a communion with persons vastly different from himself—with someone like the sheriff's deputy, for example, who approached him that day in the hard, cold rain. 'Is something wrong?' Stuart said. He rolled down the window and nearly opened the door when the deputy, an old man with gray eyebrows and a slack, sunburned face, began shouting against the wind. 'Just the weather, mister. You plan on going far? How far are you going?'

'Two hundred miles,' Stuart said. 'What about the weather? Is it a hurricane?'

'A hurricane—yes—a hurricane,' the man said, bending to shout at Stuart's face. 'You better go back to town and stay put. They're evacuating up there. We're not letting anyone through.'

A long line of cars and pickup trucks, tarnished and gloomy in the rain, passed them on the other side of the road. 'How bad is it?' said Stuart. 'Do you need help?'

'Back at town, maybe, they need help,' the man said. 'They're putting up folks at the school house and the churches, and different families—The eye was spost to come by here, but last word we got it's veered further south. Just the same, though—'

'Yes, it's good to evacuate them,' Stuart said. At the back window of an automobile passing them two children's faces peered out at the rain, white and blurred. 'The last hurricane here—'

'Ah, God, leave off of that!' the old man said, so harshly that Stuart felt, inexplicably, hurt. 'You better turn around now and get on back to town. You got money they can put you up somewheres good—not with these folks coming along here.'

This was said without contempt, but Stuart flinched at its assumptions and, years afterward, he was to remember the old man's remark as the beginning of his adventure. The man's twisted face and unsteady, jumping eyes, his wind-snatched voice, would reappear to Stuart when he puzzled for reasons—but along with the deputy's face there would be the sad line of cars, the children's faces turned toward him, and, beyond them in his memory, the face of his dead father with skin wrinkled and precise as a withered apple.

'I'm going in to see if anybody needs help,' Stuart said. He had the car going again before the deputy could even protest. 'I know what I'm doing! I know what I'm doing!' Stuart said.

The car lunged forward into the rain, drowning out the deputy's outraged shouts. The slashing of rain against Stuart's face excited him. Faces staring out of oncoming cars were pale and startled, and Stuart felt rising in him a strange compulsion to grin, to laugh madly at their alarm . . . He passed cars for some time. Houses looked deserted, yards bare. Things had the look of haste about them, even trees—in haste to rid themselves of their leaves, to be stripped bare. Grass was twisted and wild. A ditch by the road was overflowing and at spots the churning, muddy water stretched across the red clay road. Stuart drove, splashing, through it. After a while his enthusiasm slowed, his foot eased up on the gas pedal. He had not passed any cars or trucks for some time.

The sky had darkened and the storm had increased. Stuart thought of turning back when he saw, a short distance ahead, someone standing in the road. A car approached from the opposite direction. Stuart slowed, bearing to the right. He came upon a farm—a small run-down one with just a few barns and a small pasture in which a horse stood drooping in the rain. Behind the roofs of the buildings a shifting edge of foliage from the trees beyond curled in the wind, now dark, now silver. In a neat harsh line against the bottom of the buildings the wind had driven up dust and red clay. Rain streamed off roofs, plunged into fat, tilted rain barrels, and exploded back out of them. As Stuart watched, another figure appeared, running out of the house. Both persons—they looked like children—jumped about in the road, waving their arms. A spray of leaves was driven against them and against the muddy windshield of the car that approached and passed them. They turned: a girl and a boy, waving their fists in rage, their faces white and distorted. As the car sped past Stuart, water and mud splashed up in a vicious wave.

When Stuart stopped and opened the door the girl was already there, shouting, 'Going the wrong way! Wrong way!' Her face was coarse, pimply about her forehead and chin. The boy pounded up behind her, straining for air. 'Where the hell are you going, mister?' the girl cried. 'The storm's coming from this way. Did you see that bastard, going right by us? Did you see him? If I see him when I get to town—' A wall of rain struck. The girl lunged forward and tried to push her way into the car; Stuart had to hold her back. 'Where are your folks?' he shouted. 'Let me in,' cried the girl savagely. 'We're getting out of here!' 'Your folks,' said Stuart. He had to cup his mouth to make her hear. 'Your folks in there!' 'There ain't nobody there—*Goddamn* you,' she said, twisting about to slap her brother, who had been pushing at her from behind. She whirled upon Stuart again. 'You letting us in, mister? You letting us in?' she screamed, raising her hands as if to claw him. But Stuart's size must have calmed her, for she shouted hoarsely and mechanically: 'There ain't nobody in there. Our Pa's been gone the last two days. *Last two days*. Gone into town *by himself*. Gone drunk somewhere. He ain't here. He left us here. LEFT US HERE!' Again she rushed at Stuart, and he leaned forward against the steering wheel to let her get in back. The boy was about to follow when something caught his eye back at the farm. 'Get in,' said Stuart. 'Get in. Please. Get in.' 'My horse there,' the boy muttered. 'You little bastard! You get in here!' his sister screamed.

But once the boy got in, once the door was closed, Stuart knew that it was too late. Rain struck the car in solid walls and the road, when he could see it, had turned to mud. 'Let's go! Let's go!' cried the girl, pounding on the back of the seat. 'Turn it around! Go up on our drive and turn it around!' The engine and the wind roared together. 'Turn it! Get it going!' cried the girl. There was a scuffle and someone fell

283

against Stuart. 'It ain't no good,' the boy said. 'Let me out.' He lunged for the door and Stuart grabbed him. 'I'm going back to the house,' the boy cried appealing to Stuart with his frightened eyes, and his sister, giving up suddenly, pushed him violently forward. 'It's no use,' Stuart said. 'Goddamn fool,' the girl screamed, 'goddamn fool!'

The water was ankle deep as they ran to the house. The girl splashed ahead of Stuart, running with her head up and her eyes wide open in spite of the flying scud. When Stuart shouted to the boy, his voice was slammed back to him as if he were being mocked. 'Where are you going? Go to the house! Go to the house!' The boy had turned and was running toward the pasture. His sister took no notice but ran to the house. 'Come back, kid!' Stuart cried. Wind tore at him, pushing him back. 'What are you—'

The horse was undersized, skinny and brown. It ran to the boy as if it wanted to run him down but the boy, stooping through the fence, avoided the frightened hoofs and grabbed the rope that dangled from the horse's halter. 'That's it! That's it!' Stuart shouted as if the boy could hear. At the gate the boy stopped and looked around wildly, up to the sky—he might have been looking for someone who had just called him; then he shook the gate madly. Stuart reached the gate and opened it, pushing it back against the boy, who was now turned to gape at him. 'What? What are you doing here?' he said.

The thought crossed Stuart's mind that the child was insane. 'Bring the horse through!' he said. 'We don't have much time.'

'What are you doing here?' the boy shouted. The horse's eyes rolled, its mane lifted and haloed about its head. Suddenly it lunged through the gate and jerked the boy off the ground. The boy ran in the air, his legs kicking. 'Hang on and bring him around!' Stuart shouted. 'Let me take hold!' He grabbed the boy instead of the rope. They stumbled together against the horse. It had stopped now and was looking intently at something just to the right of Stuart's head. The boy pulled himself along the rope, hand over hand, and Stuart held onto him by the strap of his overalls. 'He's scairt of you!' the boy said. 'He's scairt of you!' Stuart reached over and took hold of the rope above the boy's fingers and tugged gently at it. His face was about a foot away from the horse's. 'Watch out for him,' said the boy. The horse reared and broke free, throwing Stuart back against the boy. 'Hey, hey,' screamed the boy, as if mad. The horse turned in mid-air as if whirled about by the wind, and Stuart looked up through his fingers to see its hoofs and a vicious flicking of its tail, and the face of the boy being yanked past him and away with incredible speed. The boy fell heavily on his side in the mud, arms outstretched above him, hands still gripping the rope with wooden fists. But he scrambled to his feet at once and ran alongside the horse. He flung one arm up around its neck as Stuart shouted, 'Let him go! Forget about him!' Horse and boy pivoted together back toward the fence, slashing wildly at the earth, feet and hoofs together. The ground erupted beneath them. But the boy landed upright, still holding the rope, still with his arm about the horse's neck. 'Let me help,' Stuart said. 'No,' said the boy, 'he's my horse, he knows me—' 'Have you got him good?' Stuart shouted. 'We got—we got each other here,' the boy cried, his eyes shut tight.

Stuart went to the barn to open the door. While he struggled with it, the boy led the horse forward. When the door was open far enough, Stuart threw himself against it and slammed it around to the side of the barn. A cloud of hay and scud filled the air. Stuart stretched out his arms, as if pleading with the boy to hurry, and he murmured, 'Come on. Please. Come on.' The boy did not hear him or even glance at him: his own lips were moving as he caressed the horse's neck and head. The horse's muddy hoof had just begun to grope about the step before the door when something like an explosion came against the back of Stuart's head, slammed his back, and sent him sprawling out at the horse.

'Damn you! Damn you!' the boy screamed. Stuart saw nothing except rain. Then something struck him, his shoulder and hand, and his fingers were driven down into the mud. Something slammed beside him in the mud and he seized it—the horse's foreleg—and tried to pull himself up, insanely, lurching to his knees. The horse threw him backwards. It seemed to emerge out of the air before and above him, coming into sight as though out of a cloud. The boy he did not see at all—only the hoofs—and then the boy appeared, inexplicably, under the horse, peering intently at Stuart, his face struck completely blank. 'Damn you!' Stuart heard, 'he's my horse! My horse! I hope he kills you!' Stuart crawled back in the water, crab fashion, watching the horse form and dissolve, hearing its vicious tattoo against the barn. The door, swinging madly back and forth, parodied the horse's rage, seemed to challenge its frenzy; then the door was all Stuart heard, and he got to his feet, gasping, to see that the horse was out of sight.

The boy ran bent against the wind, out toward nowhere, and

Stuart ran after him. 'Come in the house, kid! Come on! Forget about it, kid!' He grabbed the boy's arm. The boy struck at him with his elbow. 'He was my horse!' he cried.

In the kitchen of the house they pushed furniture against the door. Stuart had to stand between the boy and the girl to keep them from fighting. 'Goddamn sniffling fool,' said the girl. 'So your goddamn horse run off for the night!' The boy crouched down on the floor, crying steadily. He was about thirteen: small for his age, with bony wrists and face. 'We're all going to be blownt to hell, let alone your horse,' the girl said. She sat with one big thigh and leg outstretched on the table, watching Stuart. He thought her perhaps eighteen. 'Glad you come down to get us?' she said. 'Where are you from, mister?' Stuart's revulsion surprised him; he had not supposed there was room in his stunned mind for emotion of this sort. If the girl noticed it she gave no sign, but only grinned at him. 'I was—I was on my way home,' he said. 'My wife and daughters—' It occurred to him that he had forgotten about them entirely. He had not thought of them until now and, even now, no image came to his mind: no woman's face, no little girls' faces. Could he have imagined their lives, their love for him? For an instant he doubted everything. 'Wife and daughters,' said the girl, as if wondering whether to believe him. 'Are they in this storm too?' 'No—no,' Stuart said. To get away from her he went to the window. He could no longer see the road. Something struck the house and he flinched away. 'Them trees!' chortled the girl. 'I knew it! Pa always said how he ought to cut them down, so close to the house like they are! I knew it! I knew it! And the old bastard off safe now where they can't get him!'

'Trees?' said Stuart slowly.

'Them trees! Old oak trees!' said the girl.

The boy, struck with fear, stopped crying suddenly. He crawled on the floor to a woodbox beside the big old iron stove and got in, patting the disorderly pile of wood as if he were blind. The girl ran to him and pushed him. 'What are you doing?' Stuart cried in anguish. The girl took no notice of him. 'What am I doing?' he said aloud. 'What the hell am I doing here?' It seemed to him that the end would come in a minute or two, that the howling outside could get no louder, that the howling inside his mind could get no more intense, no more accusing. A goddamn fool! A goddamn fool! he thought. The deputy's face came to mind, and Stuart pictured himself groveling before the man, clutching at his knees, asking forgiveness and for time to be turned back . . . Then he saw himself back at the old farm, the farm of his childhood, listening to tales of his father's agonizing sickness, the old people's heads craning around, seeing how he took it, their eyes charged with horror and delight . . . 'My wife and daughters,' Stuart muttered.

The wind made a hollow, drumlike sound. It seemed to be tolling. The boy, crouching back in the woodbox, shouted: 'I ain't scairt! I ain't scairt!' The girl gave a shriek. 'Our chicken coop, I'll be gahdammed!' she cried. Try as he could, Stuart could see nothing out the window. 'Come away from the window,' Stuart said, pulling the girl's arm. She whirled upon him. 'Watch yourself, mister,' she said, 'you want to go out to your gahdamn bastardly worthless car?' Her body was strong and big in her men's clothing; her shoulders looked muscular beneath the filthy shirt. Cords in her young neck stood out. Her hair had been cut short and was now wet, plastered about her blemished face. She grinned at Stuart as if she were about to poke him in the stomach, for fun. 'I ain't scairt of what God can do!' the boy cried behind them.

When the water began to bubble up through the floor boards they decided to climb to the attic. 'There's an ax!' Stuart exclaimed, but the boy got on his hands and knees and crawled to the corner where the ax was propped before Stuart could reach it. The boy cradled it in his arms. 'What do you want with that?' Stuart said, and for an instant his heart was pierced with fear. 'Let me take it. I'll take it.' He grabbed it out of the boy's dazed fingers.

The attic was about half as large as the kitchen and the roof jutted down sharply on either side. Tree limbs rubbed and slammed against the roof on all sides. The three of them crouched on the middle beam, Stuart with the ax tight in his embrace, the boy pushing against him as if for warmth, and the girl kneeling, with her thighs straining her overalls. She watched the little paneless window at one end of the attic without much emotion or interest, like a large, wet turkey. The house trembled beneath them. 'I'm going to the window,' Stuart said, and was oddly relieved when the girl did not sneer at him. He crawled forward along the dirty beam, dragging the ax with him, and lay full length on the floor about a yard from the window. There was not much to see. At times the rain relaxed, and objects beneath in the water took shape: tree stumps, parts of buildings, junk whirling about in the water. The thumping on the roof was so loud at that end that he had to crawl backwards to the middle again. 'I ain't scairt, nothing God can do!' the boy cried. 'Listen to the sniveling baby,' said the girl. 'He thinks God pays him any mind! Hah!' Stuart crouched beside them, waiting for the boy to press against him again. 'As if God gives a good damn about him,' the girl said. Stuart looked at her. In the near dark her face did not seem so coarse; the set of her eyes was almost attractive. 'You don't think God cares about you?' Stuart said slowly. 'No, not specially,' the girl said, shrugging her shoulders. 'The hell with it. You seen the last one of these?' She tugged at Stuart's arm. 'Mister! It was something to see. Me an' Jackie was little then—him just a baby. We drove a far ways north to get out of it. When we come back the roads was so thick with sightseers from the cities! They took all the dead ones floating in the water and put them in one place, part of a swamp they cleared out. The families and things—they were mostly fruit pickers—had to come by on rafts and rowboats to look and see could they find the ones they knew. That was there for a day. The bodies would turn round and round in the wash from the boats. Then the faces all got alike and they wouldn't let anyone come any more and put oil on them and set them afire. We stood on top of the car and watched all that day. I wasn't but nine then.'

When the house began to shake, some time later, Stuart cried aloud: 'This is it!' He stumbled to his feet, waving the ax. He turned around and around as if he were in a daze. 'You goin' to chop somethin' with that?' the boy said, pulling at him. 'Hey, no, that ain't yours to—it ain't yours to chop—' They struggled for the ax. The boy sobbed, 'It ain't yours! It ain't yours!' and Stuart's rage at his own helplessness, at the folly of his being here, for an instant almost made him strike the boy with the ax. But the girl slapped him furiously. 'Get away from him! I swear I'll kill you!' she screamed.

Something exploded beneath them. 'That's the window,' the girl muttered, clinging to Stuart, 'and how am I to clean it again! The old bastard will want it clean, and mud over everything!' Stuart pushed her away so that he could swing the ax. Pieces of soft, rotted wood exploded back onto his face. The boy screamed insanely as the boards gave way to a deluge of wind and water, and even Stuart wondered if he had made a mistake. The three of them fell beneath the onslaught and Stuart lost the ax, felt the handle slam against his leg. 'You! You!' Stuart cried, pulling at the girl—for an instant, blinded by pain, he could not think who he was, what he was doing, whether he had any

288

life beyond this moment. The big-faced, husky girl made no effort to hide her fear and cried, 'Wait, wait!' But he dragged her to the hole and tried to force her out. 'My brother—' she gasped. She seized his wrists and tried to get away. 'Get out there! There isn't any time!' Stuart muttered. The house seemed about to collapse at any moment. He was pushing her through the hold, against the shattered wood, when she suddenly flinched back against him and he saw that her cheek was cut and she was choking. He snatched her hands away from her mouth as if he wanted to see something secret: blood welled out between her lips. She coughed and spat blood onto him. 'You're all right,' he said, oddly pleased. 'Now get out there and I'll get the kid. I'll take care of him.' This time she managed to crawl through the hole, with Stuart pushing her from behind; when he turned to seize the boy, the boy clung to his neck, sobbing something about God. 'God loves you!' Stuart yelled. 'Loves the least of you! The least of you!' The girl pulled her brother up in her great arms and Stuart was free to climb through himself.

It was actually quite a while—perhaps an hour—before the battering of the trees and the wind pushed the house in. The roof fell slowly and the section to which they clung was washed free. We're going somewheres!' shouted the girl. 'Look at the house! That gahdamn old shanty seen the last storm!'

The boy lay with his legs pushed in under Stuart's and had not spoken for some time. When the girl cried, 'Look at that!' he tried to burrow in farther. Stuart wiped his eyes to see the wall of darkness dissolve. The rain took on another look—a smooth, piercing, metallic glint, like nails driving against their faces and bodies. There was no horizon. They could see nothing except the rushing water and a thickening mist that must have been rain, miles and miles of rain, slammed by the wind into one great wall that moved remorselessly upon them. 'Hang on,' Stuart said, gripping the girl. 'Hang on to me.'

Waves washed over the roof, pushing objects at them with soft, muted thuds—pieces of fence, boards, branches heavy with foliage. Stuart tried to ward them off with his feet. Water swirled around them, sucking at them, sucking the roof, until they were pushed against one of the farm buildings. Something crashed against the roof—another section of the house—and splintered, flying up against the girl. She was thrown backwards, away from Stuart, who lunged after her. They fell into the water while the boy screamed. The girl's arms threshed wildly against Stuart. The water was cold, and its aliveness, its sinister energy, surprised him more than the thought that he would drown—that he would never endure the night. Struggling with the girl, he forced her back to the roof, pushed her up. Bare, twisted nails raked his hands. 'Gahdamn you, Jackie, you give a hand!' the girl said as Stuart crawled back up. He lay, exhausted, flat on his stomach and let the water and debris slosh over him.

His mind was calm beneath the surface buzzing. He liked to think that his mind was a clear, sane circle of quiet carefully preserved inside the chaos of the storm—that the three of them were safe within the sanctity of this circle, this was how man always conquered nature, how he subdued things greater than himself. But whenever he did speak to her it was in short grunts, in her own idiom: 'This ain't so bad!' or 'It'll let up pretty soon!' Now the girl held him in her arms as if he were a child, and he did not have the strength to pull away. Of his own free will he had given himself to the storm, or to the strange desire to save someone in it—but now he felt grateful for the girl, even for her brother, for they had saved him as much as he had saved them. Stuart thought of his wife at home, walking through the rooms, waiting for him; he thought of his daughters in their twin beds, two glasses of water on their bureau . . . But these people knew nothing of him: in his experience now he did not belong to them. Perhaps he had misunderstood his role, his life? Perhaps he had blundered out of his way, drawn into the wrong life, surrendered to the wrong role. What had blinded him to the possibility of many lives, many masks, many arms that might so embrace him? A word not heard one day, a gesture misinterpreted, a leveling of someone's eyes in a certain unmistakable manner, which he had mistaken just the same! The consequences of such errors might trail insanely into the future, across miles of land, across worlds. He only now sensed the incompleteness of his former life . . . 'Look! Look!' the girl cried, jostling him out of his stupor. 'Take a look at that, mister!'

He raised himself on one elbow. A streak of light broke out of the dark. Lanterns, he thought, a rescue party already . . . But the rain dissolved the light; then it reappeared with a beauty that startled him. 'What is it?' the boy screamed. 'How come it's here?' They watched it filter through the rain, rays knifing through and showing, now, how buildings and trees crouched close about them. 'It's the sun, the sun going down,' the girl said. 'The sun!' said Stuart, who had thought it was night. 'The sun!' They stared at it until it disappeared.

The waves calmed sometime before dawn. By then the roof had lost its peak and water ran unchecked over it, in generous waves and then in thin waves, alternately, as the roof bobbed up and down. The three huddled together with their backs to the wind. Water came now in slow drifts. 'It's just got to spread itself out far enough so's it will be even,' said the girl, 'then it'll go down.' She spoke without sounding tired, only a little disgusted—as if things weren't working fast enough to suit her. 'Soon as it goes down we'll start toward town and see if there ain't somebody coming out to get us in a boat,' she said, chattily and comfortably, into Stuart's ear. Her manner astonished Stuart, who had been thinking all night of the humiliation and pain he had suffered. 'Bet the old bastard will be glad to see us,' she said, 'even if he did go off like that. Well, he never knew a storm was coming. Me and him get along pretty well—he ain't so bad.' She wiped her face; it was filthy with dirt and blood. 'He'll buy you a drink, mister, for saving us how you did. That was something to have happen—a man just driving up to get us!' And she poked Stuart in the ribs.

The wind warmed as the sun rose. Rain turned to mist and back to rain again, still falling heavily, and now objects were clear about them. The roof had been shoved against the corner of the barn and a mound of dirt, and eddied there without much trouble. Right about them, in a kind of halo, a thick blanket of vegetation and filth bobbed. The fence had disappeared and the house had collapsed and been driven against a ridge of land. The barn itself had fallen in, but the stone support looked untouched, and it was against this they had been shoved. Stuart thought he could see his car—or something over there where the road used to be.

'I bet it ain't deep. Hell,' said the girl, sticking her foot into the water. The boy leaned over the edge and scooped up some of the filth in his hands. 'Lookit all the spiders,' he said. He wiped his face slowly. 'Leave them gahdamn spiders alone,' said the girl. 'You want me to shove them down your throat?' She slid to the edge and lowered her legs. 'Yah, I touched bottom. It ain't bad.' But then she began coughing and drew herself back. Her coughing made Stuart cough: his chest and throat were ravaged, shaken. He lay exhausted when the fit left him and realized, suddenly, that they were all sick— that something had happened to them. They had to get off the roof.

291

Now, with the sun up, things did not looks so bad: there was a ridge of trees a short distance away on a long, red clay hill. 'We'll go over there,' Stuart said. 'Do you think you can make it?'

The boy played in the filth, without looking up, but the girl gnawed at her lip to show she was thinking. 'I s'pose so,' she said. 'But him—I don't know about him.'

'Your brother? What's wrong?'

'Turn around. Hey, stupid. Turn around.' She prodded the boy, who jerked around, terrified, to stare at Stuart. His thin bony face gave way to a drooping mouth. 'Gone loony, it looks like,' the girl said with a touch of regret. 'Oh, he had times like this before. It might go away.'

Stuart was transfixed by the boy's stare. The realization of what had happened struck him like a blow, sickening his stomach. 'We'll get him over there,' he said, making his words sound good. 'We can wait there for someone to come. Someone in a boat. He'll be better there.'

'I s'pose so,' said the girl vaguely.

Stuart carried the boy while the girl splashed eagerly ahead. The water was sometimes up to his thighs. 'Hold on another minute,' he pleaded. The boy stared out at the water as if he thought he were taken somewhere to be drowned. 'Put your arms around my neck. Hold on,' Stuart said. He shut his eyes and every time he looked up the girl was still a few yards ahead and the hill looked no closer. The boy breathed hollowly, coughing into Stuart's face. His own face and neck were covered with small red bites. Ahead, the girl walked with her shoulders lunged forward as if to hurry her there, her great thighs straining against the water, more than a match for it. As Stuart watched her, something was on the side of his face—in his ear—and with a scream he slapped at it, nearly dropping the boy. The girl whirled around. Stuart slapped at his face and must have knocked it off—probably a spider. The boy, upset by Stuart's outcry, began sucking in air faster and faster as if he were dying. 'I'm all right, I'm all right,' Stuart whispered, 'just hold on another minute . . . '

When he finally got to the hill the girl helped pull him up. He set the boy down with a grunt, trying to put the boy's legs under him so he could stand. But the boy sank to the ground and turned over and vomited into the water; his body shook as if he were having convulsions. Again the thought that the night had poisoned them, their own breaths had sucked germs into their bodies, struck Stuart with an irresistible force. 'Let him lay down and rest,' the girl said, pulling tentatively at the back of her brother's belt, as if she were thinking of dragging him farther up the slope. 'We sure do thank you, mister,' she said.

Stuart climbed to the crest of the hill. His heart pounded madly, blood pounded in his ears. What was going to happen? Was anything going to happen? How disappointing it looked—ridges of land showing through the water and the healthy sunlight pushing back the mist. Who would believe him when he told of the night, of the times when death seemed certain . . . ? Anger welled up in him already as he imagined the tolerant faces of his friends, his children's faces ready to turn to other amusements, other oddities. His wife would believe him; she would shudder, holding him, burying her small face in his neck. But what could she understand of his experience, having had no part in it? . . . Stuart cried out; he had nearly stepped on a tangle of snakes. Were they alive? He backed away in terror. The snakes gleamed wetly in the morning light, heads together as if conspiring. Four . . . five of them—they too had swum for this land, they too had survived the night, they had as much reason to be proud of themselves as Stuart.

He gagged and turned away. Down by the water line the boy lay flat on his stomach and the girl squatted nearby, wringing out her denim jacket. The water behind them caught the sunlight and gleamed mightily, putting them into silhouette. The girl's arms moved slowly, hard with muscle. The boy lay coughing gently. Watching them, Stuart was beset by a strange desire: he wanted to run at them, demand their gratitude, their love. Why should they not love him, when he had saved their lives? When he had lost what he was just the day before, turned now into a different person, a stranger even to himself? Stuart stooped and picked up a rock. A broad hot hand seemed to press against his chest. He threw the rock out into the water and said, 'Hey!'

The girl glanced around but the boy did not move. Stuart sat down on the soggy ground and waited. After a while the girl looked away; she spread the jacket out to dry. Great banked clouds rose into the sky, reflected in the water—jagged and bent in the waves. Stuart waited as the sun took over the sky. Mist at the horizon glowed, thinned, gave way to solid shapes. Light did not strike cleanly across the land, but was marred by ridges of trees and parts of buildings, and around a corner at any time Stuart expected to see a rescuing

293

party—in a rowboat or something.

'Hey mister.' He woke; he must have been dozing. The girl had called him. 'Hey. Whyn't you come down here? There's all them snakes up there.'

Stuart scrambled to his feet. When he stumbled downhill, embarrassed and frightened, the girl said chattily, 'The sons of bitches are crawling all over here. He chast some away.' The boy was on his feet and looking around with an important air. His coming alive startled Stuart—indeed, the coming alive of the day, of the world, evoked alarm in him. All things came back to what they were. The sunlight had not changed, or the land, really; only Stuart had been changed. He wondered at it . . . and the girl must have seen something in his face that he himself did not yet know about, for her eyes narrowed, her throat gulped a big swallow, her arms moved slowly up to show her raw elbows. 'We'll get rid of them,' Stuart said, breaking the silence. 'Him and me. We'll do it.'

The boy was delighted. 'I got a stick,' he said, waving a thin whiplike branch. 'There's some over here.'

'We'll get them,' Stuart said. But when he started to walk, a rock slipped loose and he fell back into the mud. He laughed aloud. The girl, squatting a few feet away, watched him silently. Stuart got to his feet, still laughing. 'You know much about it, kid?' he said, cupping his hand on the boy's head.

'About what?' said the boy.

'Killing snakes,' said Stuart.

'I spose—I spose you just kill them.'

The boy hurried alongside Stuart. 'I need a stick,' Stuart said; they got him one from the water, about the size of an ax. 'Go by that bush,' Stuart said, 'there might be some there.'

The boy attacked the bush in a frenzy. He nearly fell into it. His enthusiasm somehow pleased Stuart, but there were no snakes in the bush. 'Go down that way,' Stuart ordered. He glanced back at the girl: she watched them. Stuart and the boy went on with their sticks held in mid-air. 'God put them here to keep us awake,' the boy said brightly. 'See we don't forget about Him.' Mud sucked at their feet. 'Last year we couldn't fire the woods on account of it so dry. This year can't either on account of the water. We got to get the snakes like this.'

Stuart hurried as if he had somewhere to go. The boy, matching his steps, went faster and faster, panting, waving his stick angrily in the air. The boy complained about snakes and, listening to him, fascinated by him, in that instant Stuart saw everything. He saw the conventional dawn that had mocked the night, had mocked his desire to help people in trouble; he saw, beyond that, his father's home emptied now even of ghosts. He realized that the God of these people had indeed arranged things, had breathed the order of chaos into forms, had animated them, had animated even Stuart himself forty years ago. The knowledge of this fact struck him about the same way as the nest of snakes had struck him—an image leaping right to the eye, pouncing upon the mind, joining itself with the perceiver. 'Hey, hey!' cried the boy, who had found a snake: the snake crawled noisily and not very quickly up the slope, a brown-speckled snake. The boy ran clumsily after it. Stuart was astonished at the boy's stupidity, at his inability to see, now, that the snake had vanished. Still he ran along the slope, waving his stick, shouting 'I'll get you! I'll get you!' This must have been the sign Stuart was waiting for. When the boy turned, Stuart was right behind him. 'It got away up there,' the boy said. 'We got to get it.' When Stuart lifted his stick the boy fell back a step but went on in mechanical excitement, 'It's up there, gotten hid in the weeds. It ain't me,' he said, 'it ain't me that—' Stuart's blow struck the boy on the side of the head, and the rotted limb shattered into soft wet pieces. The boy stumbled down toward the water. He was coughing when Stuart took hold of him and began shaking him madly, and he did nothing but cough, violently and with all his concentration, even when Stuart bent to grab a rock and brought it down on his head. Stuart let him fall into the water. He could hear him breathing and he could see, about the boy's lips, tiny flecks or bubbles of blood appearing and disappearing with his breath.

When the boy's eyes opened, Stuart fell upon him. They struggled savagely in the water. Again the boy went limp; Stuart stood, panting and waited. Nothing happened for a minute or so. But then he saw something—the boy's fingers moving up through the water, soaring to the surface! 'Will you quit it!' Stuart screamed. He was about to throw himself upon the boy again when the thought of the boy's life, bubbling out between his lips, moving his fingers, filled him with such outraged disgust that he backed away. He threw the rock out into the water and ran back, stumbling, to where the girl stood.

She had nothing to say: her jaw was hard, her mouth a narrow line, her thick nose oddly white against her dirty face. Only her eyes moved, and these were black, lustrous, at once demanding and terrified. She held a board in one hand. Stuart did not have time to think, but, as he lunged toward her, he could already see himself grappling with her in the mud, forcing her down, tearing her ugly clothing from her body—'Lookit!' she cried, the way a person might speak to a horse, cautious and coaxing, and pointed behind him. Stuart turned to see a white boat moving toward them, a half mile or so away. Immediately his hands dropped, his mouth opened in awe. The girl still pointed, breathing carefully, and Stuart, his mind shattered by the broken sunshine upon the water, turned to the boat, raised his hands, cried out, 'Save me! Save me!' He had waded out a short distance by the time the men arrived.

1966

THE INDIAN UPRISING

Donald Barthelme

We defended the city as best we could. The arrows of the Comanches came in clouds. The war clubs of the Comanches clattered on the soft, yellow pavements. There were earthworks along the Boulevard Mark Clark and the hedges had been laced with sparkling wire. People were trying to understand. I spoke to Sylvia. 'Do you think this is a good life?' The table held apples, books, long-playing records. She looked up. 'No.'

Patrols of paras and volunteers with armbands guarded the tall, flat buildings. We interrogated the captured Comanche. Two of us forced his head back while another poured water into his nostrils. His body jerked, he choked and wept. Not believing a hurried, careless and exaggerated report of the number of casualties in the outer districts where trees, lamps, swans had been reduced to clear fields of fire we issued entrenching tools to those who seemed trustworthy and turned the heavy-weapons companies so that we could not be surprised from that direction. And I sat there getting drunker and drunker and more in love and more in love. We talked.

'Do you know Fauré's "Dolly"?'

'Would that be Gabriel Fauré?'

'It would.'

'Then I know it,' she said. 'May I say that I play it at certain times, when I am sad, or happy, although it requires four hands.'

'How is that managed?'

'I accelerate,' she said, 'ignoring the time signature.'

And when they shot the scene in the bed I wondered how you felt under the eyes of the cameramen, grips, juicers, men in the mixing booth: excited? stimulated? And when they shot the scene in the shower I sanded a hollow-core door working carefully against the illustrations in texts and whispered instructions from one who had already solved the problem. I had made after all other tables, one while living with Nancy, one while living with Alice, one while living with Eunice, one while living with Marianne.

Red men in waves like people scattering in a square startled by something tragic or a sudden, loud noise accumulated against the barricades we had made of window dummies, silk, thoughtfully planned job descriptions (including scales for the orderly progress of other colors), wine in demijohns, and robes. I analyzed the composition of the barricade nearest me and found two ashtrays, ceramic, one dark brown and one dark brown with an orange blur at the lip; a tin frying pan; two-litre bottles of red wine; three-quarter-litre bottles of Black & White, aquavit, cognac, vodka, gin, Fad #6 sherry; a hollow-core door in birch veneer on black wrought-iron legs; a blanket, red-orange with faint blue stripes; a red pillow and a blue pillow; a woven straw wastebasket; two glass jars for flowers; corkscrews and can openers; two plates and two cups, ceramic, dark brown; a yellow-and-purple poster; a Yugoslavian carved flute, wood, dark brown; and other items. I decided I knew nothing.

The hospitals dusted wounds with powders the worth of which was not quite established, other supplies having been exhausted early in the first day. I decided I knew nothing. Friends put me in touch with a Miss R., a teacher, unorthodox they said, excellent they said, successful with difficult cases, steel shutters on the windows made the house safe. I had just learned via an International Distress Coupon that Jane had been beaten up by a dwarf in a bar on Tenerife but Miss R. did not allow me to speak of it. 'You know nothing,' she said, 'you feel nothing, you are locked in a most savage and terrible ignorance, I despise you, my boy, *mon cher*, my heart. You may attend but you must not attend now, you must attend later, a day or a week or an hour, you are making me ill . . . ' I nonevaluated these remarks as Korzybski instructed. But it was difficult. Then they pulled back in a feint near the river and we rushed into that sector with a reinforced battalion hastily formed among the Zouaves and cabdrivers. This unit was crushed in the afternoon of a day that began with spoons and letters in hallways and under windows where men tasted the history of the heart, cone-shaped muscular organ that maintains *circulation of the blood.*

But it is you I want now, here in the middle of this Uprising, with the streets yellow and threatening, short, ugly lances with fur at the throat and inexplicable shell money lying in the grass. It is when I am with you that I am happiest, and it is for you that I am making this hollow-core door table with black wrought-iron legs. I held Sylvia by her bear-claw necklace. 'Call off your braves,' I said. 'We have many years left to live.' There was a sort of muck running in the gutters, yellowish, filthy stream suggesting excrement, or nervousness, a city that does not know what it has done to deserve baldness, errors, infidelity. 'With luck you will survive until matins,' Sylvia said. She ran off down the Rue Chester Nimitz, uttering shrill cries.

Then it was learned that they had infiltrated our ghetto and that the people of the ghetto instead of resisting had joined the smooth, well-coordinated attack with zipguns, telegrams, lockets, causing that portion of the line held by the IRA to swell and collapse. We sent more heroin into the ghetto, and hyacinths, ordering another hundred thousand of the pale, delicate flowers. On the map we considered the situation with its strung-out inhabitants and merely personal emotions. Our parts were blue and their parts were green. I showed the blue-and-green map to Sylvia. 'Your parts are green,' I said. 'You gave me heroin first a year ago,' Sylvia said. She ran off down George C. Marshall Allée, uttering shrill cries. Miss R. pushed me into a large room painted white (jolting and dancing in the soft light, and I was excited! and there were people watching!) in which there were two chairs. I sat in one chair and Miss R. sat in the other. She wore a blue dress containing a red figure. There was nothing exceptional about her. I was disappointed by her plainness, by the bareness of the room, by the absence of books.

The girls of my quarter wore long blue mufflers that reached to their knees. Sometimes the girls hid Comanches in their rooms, the blue mufflers together in a room creating a great blue fog. Block opened the door. He was carrying weapons, flowers, loaves of bread. And he was friendly, kind, enthusiastic, so I related a little of the history of torture, reviewing the technical literature quoting the best modern sources, French, German, and American, and pointing out the flies which had gathered in anticipation of some new, cool color.

'What is the situation?' I asked.

'The situation is liquid,' he said. 'We hold the south quarter and they hold the north quarter. The rest is silence.'

'And Kenneth?'

'That girl is not in love with Kenneth,' Block said frankly. 'She is in love with his coat. When she is not wearing it she is huddling under it. Once I caught it going down the stairs by itself. I looked inside. Sylvia.'

Once I caught Kenneth's coat going down the stairs by itself but the coat was a trap and inside a Comanche who made a thrust with his short, ugly knife at my leg which buckled and tossed me over the

balustrade through a window and into another situation. Not
believing that your body brilliant as it was and your fat, liquid spirit
distinguished and angry as it was were stable quantities to which one
could return on wires more than once, twice, or another number of
times I said: 'See the table?'

In Skinny Wainwright Square the forces of green and blue swayed
and struggled. The referees ran out on the field trailing chains. And
then the blue part would be enlarged, the green diminished. Miss R.
began to speak. 'A former king of Spain, a Bonaparte, lived for a time
in Bordentown, New Jersey. But that's no good.' She paused. 'The
ardor aroused in men by the beauty of women can only be satisfied
by God. That is *very* good (it is Valéry) but it is not what I have to
teach you, goat, muck, filth, heart of my heart.' I showed the table to
Nancy. 'See the table?' She stuck out her tongue red as a cardinal's
hat. 'I made such a table once,' Block said frankly. 'People all over
America have made such tables. I doubt very much whether one can
enter an American home without finding at least one such table, or
traces of its having been there, such as faded places in the carpet.'
And afterward in the garden the men of the 7th Cavalry played
Gabrieli, Albinoni, Marcello, Vivaldi, Boccherini. I saw Sylvia. She
wore a yellow ribbon, under a long blue muffler. 'Which side are you
on,' I cried, 'after all?'

'The only form of discourse of which I approve,' Miss R. said in her
dry, tense voice, 'is the litany. I believe our masters and teachers as
well as plain citizens should confine themselves to what can safely be
said. Thus when I hear the words *pewter, snake, tea, Fad #6 sherry,
serviette, fenestration, crown, blue* coming from the mouth of some
public official, or some raw youth, I am not disappointed. Vertical
organization is also possible,' Miss R. said, 'as in

> pewter
> snake
> tea
> Fad #6 sherry
> serviette
> fenestration
> crown
> blue.

I run to liquids and colors,' she said, 'but you, you may run to
something else, my virgin, my darling, my thistle, my poppet, my

own. Young people,' Miss R. said, 'run to more and more unpleasant combinations as they sense the nature of our society. Some people,' Miss R. said, 'run to conceits or wisdom but I hold to the hard, brown, nutlike word. I might point out that there is enough aesthetic excitement here to satisfy anyone but a damned fool.' I sat in solemn silence.

Fire arrows lit my way to the post office in Patton Place where members of the Abraham Lincoln Brigade offered their last, exhausted letters, postcards, calendars. I opened a letter but inside was a Comanche flint arrowhead played by Frank Wedekind in an elegant gold chain and congratulations. Your earring rattled against my spectacles when I leaned forward to touch the soft, ruined place where the hearing aid had been. 'Pack it in! Pack it in!' I urged, but the men in charge of the Uprising refused to listen to reason or to understand that it was real and that our water supply had evaporated and that our credit was no longer what it had been, once.

We attached wires to the testicles of the captured Comanche. And I sat there getting drunker and drunker and more in love and more in love. When we threw the switch he spoke. His name, he said, was Gustave Aschenbach. He was born at L—, a country town in the province of Silesia. He was the son of an upper official in the judicature, and his forebears had all been officers, judges, departmental functionaries . . . And you can never touch a girl in the same way more than once, twice, or another number of times however much you may wish to hold, wrap, or otherwise fix her hand, or look, or some other quality, or incident, known to you previously. In Sweden the little Swedish children cheered when we managed nothing more remarkable than getting off a bus burdened with packages, bread and liver-paste and beer. We went to an old church and sat in the royal box. The organist was practising. And then into the graveyard next to the church. *Here lies Anna Pederson, a good woman.* I threw a mushroom on the grave. The officer commanding the garbage dump reported by radio that the garbage had begun to move.

Jane! I heard via an International Distress Coupon that you were beaten up by a dwarf in a bar on Tenerife. That doesn't sound like you, Jane. Mostly you kick the dwarf in his little dwarf groin before he can get his teeth into your tasty and nice-looking leg, don't you, Jane? Your affair with Harold is reprehensible, you know that, don't you, Jane? Harold is married to Nancy. And there is Paula to think about (Harold's kid), and Billy (Harold's other kid). I think your values are peculiar, Jane! Strings of language extend in every direction to bind the world into a rushing, ribald whole.

And you can never return to felicities in the same way, the brilliant body, the distinguished spirit recapitulating moments that occur once, twice, or another number of times in rebellions, or water. The rolling consensus of the Comanche nation smashed our inner defenses on three sides. Block was firing a greasegun from the upper floor of a building designed by Emery Roth & Sons. 'See the table?' 'Oh, pack it in with your bloody table!' The city officials were tied to trees. Dusky warriors padded with their forest tread into the mouth of the mayor. 'Who do you want to be?' I asked Kenneth and he said he wanted to be Jean-Luc Godard but later when time permitted conversations in large, lighted rooms, whispering galleries with black-and-white Spanish rugs and problematic sculpture on calm, red catafalques. The sickness of the quarrel lay thick in the bed. I touched your back, the white, raised scars.

We killed a great many in the south suddenly with helicopters and rockets but we found that those we had killed were children and more came from the north and from the east and from other places where there are children preparing to live. 'Skin,' Miss R. said softly in the white, yellow room. 'This is the Clemency Committee. And would you remove your belt and shoelaces.' I removed my belt and shoelaces and looked (rain shattering from a great height the prospects of silence and clear, neat rows of houses in the subdivisions) into their savage black eyes, paint, feathers, beads.

1968

IN THE HEART OF THE HEART
OF THE COUNTRY
William Gass

A PLACE

O I have sailed the seas and come . . .
                              to B . . .
a small town fastened to a field in Indiana. Twice there have been
twelve hundred people here to answer to the census. The town is
outstandingly neat and shady, and always puts its best side to the
highway. On one lawn there's even a wood or plastic iron deer.

You can reach us by crossing a creek. In the spring the lawns are
green, the forsythia is singing, and even the railroad that guts the
town has straight bright rails which hum when the train is coming,
and the train itself has a welcome horning sound.

Down the back streets the asphalt crumbles into gravel. There's
Westbrook's, with the geraniums, Horsefall's, Mott's. The sidewalk
shatters. Gravel dust rises like breath behind the wagons. And I am
in retirement from love.

WEATHER

In the Midwest, around the lower Lakes, the sky in the winter is
heavy and close, and it is a rare day, a day to remark on, when the
sky lifts and allows the heart up. I am keeping count, and as I write
this page, it is eleven days since I have seen the sun.

MY HOUSE

There's a row of headless maples behind my house, cut to free the
passage of electric wires. High stumps, ten feet tall, remain, and I
climb these like a boy to watch the country sail away from me. They
are ordinary fields, a little more uneven than they should be, since in
the spring they puddle. The topsoil's thin, but only moderately stony.
Corn is grown one year, soybeans another. At dusk starlings darken

303

the single tree—a larch—which stands in the middle. When the sky moves, fields move under it. I feel, on my perch, that I've lost my years. It's as though I were living at last in my eyes, as I have always dreamed of doing, and I think then I know why I've come here: to see, and so to go out against new things—oh god how easily—like air in a breeze. It's true there are moments—foolish moments, ecstasy on a tree stump—when I'm all but gone, scattered I like to think like seed, for I'm the sort now in the fool's position of having love left over which I'd like to lose; what good is it now to me, candy ungiven after Halloween?

A PERSON

There are vacant lots on either side of Billy Holsclaw's house. As the weather improves, they fill with hollyhocks. From spring through fall, Billy collects coal and wood and puts the lumps and pieces in piles near his door, for keeping warm is his one work. I see him most often on mild days sitting on his doorsill in the sun. I notice he's squinting a little, which is perhaps the reason he doesn't cackle as I pass. His house is the size of a single garage, and very old. It shed its paint with its youth, and its boards are a warped and weathered gray. So is Billy. He wears a short lumpy faded black coat when it's cold, otherwise he always goes about in the same loose, grease-spotted shirt and trousers. I suspect his galluses were yellow once, when they were new.

WIRES

These wires offend me. Three trees were maimed on their account, and now these wires deface the sky. They cross like a fence in front of me, enclosing the crows with the clouds. I can't reach in, but like a stick, I throw my feelings over. What is it that offends me? I am on my stump, I've built a platform there and the wires prevent my going out. The cut trees, the black wires, all the beyond birds therefore anger me. When I've wormed through a fence to reach a meadow, do I ever feel the same about the field?

THE CHURCH

The church has a steeple like the hat of a witch, and five birds, all doves, perch in its gutters.

304

MY HOUSE

Leaves move in the windows. I cannot tell you yet how beautiful it is, what it means. But they do move. They move in the glass.

POLITICS

. . . for all those not in love.

I've heard Batista described as a Mason. A farmer who'd seen him in Miami made this claim. He's as nice a fellow as you'd ever want to meet. Of Castro, of course, no one speaks.

For all those not in love there's law: to rule . . . to regulate . . . to rectify. I cannot write the poetry of such proposals, the poetry of politics, though sometimes—often—always now—I am in that uneasy peace of equal powers which makes a State; then I communicate by passing papers, proclamations, orders, through my bowels. Yet I was not a State with you, nor were we both together any Indiana. A squad of Pershing Rifles at the moment, I make myself Right Face! Legislation packs the screw of my intestines. Well, king of the classroom's king of the hill. You used to waddle when you walked because my sperm between your legs was draining to a towel. Teacher, poet, folded lover—like the politician, like those drunkards, ill, or those who faucet-off while pissing heartily to preach upon the force and fullness of that stream, or pause from vomiting to praise the purity and passion of their puke—I chant, I beg, I orate, I command, I sing—

> *Come back to Indiana—not too late!*
> *(Or will you be a ranger to the end?)*
> *Good-bye . . . Good-bye . . . oh, I shall always wait*
> *You, Larry, traveler—*
> > *stranger,*
> > > *son,*
> > > > *—my friend—*

my little girl, my poem by heart, my self, my childhood.

But I've heard Batista described as a Mason. That dries up my pity, melts my hate. Back from the garage where I have overheard it, I slap the mended fender of my car to laugh, and listen to the metal stinging tartly in my hand.

PEOPLE

Their hair in curlers and their heads wrapped in loud scarves, young mothers, faltish in trousers, lounge about in the speedwash, smoking cigarettes, eating candy, drinking pop, thumbing magazines, and screaming at their children above the whir and rumble of the machines.

At the bank a young man freshly pressed is letting himself in with a key. Along the street, delicately teetering, many grandfathers move in a dream. During the murderous heat of summer, they perch on window ledges, their feet dangling just inside the narrow shelf of shade the store has made, staring steadily into the street. Where their consciousness has gone I can't say. It's not in the eyes. Perhaps it's diffuse, all temperature and skin, like an infant's though more mild. Near the corner there are several large overalled men employed in standing. A truck turns to be weighed on the scales at the Feed and Grain. Images drift on the drugstore window. The wind has blown the smell of cattle into town. Our eyes have been driven in like the eyes of the old men. And there's no one to have mercy on us.

VITAL DATA

There are two restaurants here and a tearoom. two bars. one bank, three barbers, one with a green shade with which he blinds his window. two groceries. a dealer in Fords. one drug, one hardware, and one appliance store. several that sell feed, grain, and farm equipment. an antique shop. a poolroom. a laundromat. three doctors. a dentist. a plumber. a vet. a funeral home in elegant repair the color of a buttercup. numerous beauty parlors which open and shut like night-blooming plants. a tiny dime and department store of no width but several floors. a hutch, homemade, where you can order, after lying down or squirming in, furniture that's been fashioned from bent lengths of stainless tubing, glowing plastic, metallic thread, and clear shellac. an American Legion Post and a root beer stand. little agencies for this and that: cosmetics, brushes, insurance, greeting cards and garden produce—anything—sample shoes—which do their business out of hats and satchels, over coffee cups and dissolving sugar. a factory for making paper sacks and pasteboard boxes that's lodged in an old brick building bearing the legend OPERA HOUSE, still faintly golden, on its roof. a library given by Carnegie. a post office. a school. a railroad station. fire station.

lumberyard. telephone company. welding shop. garage . . . and spotted through the town from one end to the other in a line along the highway, gas stations to the number five.

EDUCATION

In 1833, Colin Goodykoontz, an itinerant preacher with a name from a fairytale, summed up the situation in one Indiana town this way:

> Ignorance and her squalid brood. A universal dearth of intellect. Total abstinence from literature is very generally practiced . . . There is not a scholar in grammar or geography, or a *teacher capable* of *instructing* in them, to my knowledge . . . Others are supplied a few months of the year with the most antiquated & unreasonable forms of teaching reading, writing & cyphering . . . Need I stop to remind you of the host of loathsome reptiles such a stagnant pool is fitted to breed! Croaking jealousy; bloated bigotry; coiling suspicion; wormish blindness; crocodile malice!

Things have changed since then, but in none of the respects mentioned.

BUSINESS

One side section of street is blocked off with sawhorses. Hard, thin, bitter men in blue jeans, cowboy boots and hats, untruck a dinky carnival. The merchants are promoting themselves. There will be free rides, raucous music, parades and coneys, pop, popcorn, candy, cones, awards and drawings, with all you can endure of pinch, push, bawl, shove, shout, scream, shriek, and bellow. Children pedal past on decorated bicycles, their wheels a blur of color, streaming crinkled paper and excited dogs. A little later there's a pet show for a prize— dogs, cats, birds, sheep, ponies, goats—none of which wins. The whirlabouts whirl about. The Ferris wheel climbs dizzily into the sky as far as a tall man on tiptoe might be persuaded to reach, and the irritated operators measure the height and width of every child with sour eyes to see if they are safe for the machines. An electrical megaphone repeatedly trumpets the names of the generous sponsors. The following day they do not allow the refuse to remain long in the street.

MY HOUSE, THIS PLACE AND BODY

I have met with some mischance, wings withering, as Plato says obscurely, and across the breadth of Ohio, like heaven on a table, I've fallen as far as the poet, to the sixth sort of body, this house in B, in Indiana, with its blue and gray bewitching windows, holy magical insides. Great thick evergreens protect its entry. And I live *in*.

Lost in the corn rows, I remember feeling just another stalk, and thus this country takes me over in the way I occupy myself when I am well . . . completely—to the edge of both my house and body. No one notices, when they walk by, that I am brimming in the doorways. My house, this place and body, I've come in mourning to be born in. To anybody else it's pretty silly: love. Why should I feel a loss? How am I bereft? She was never mine; she was a fiction, always a golden tomgirl, barefoot, with an adolescent's slouch and a boy's taste for sports and fishing, a figure out of Twain, or worse, in Riley. Age cannot be kind.

There's little hand-in-hand here . . . not in B. No one touches except in rage. Occasionally girls will twine their arms about each other and lurch along, school out, toward home and play. I dreamed my lips would drift down your back, like a skiff on a river. I'd follow a vein with the point of my finger, hold your bare feet in my naked hands.

THE SAME PERSON

Billy Holsclaw lives alone—how alone it is impossible to fathom. In the post office he talks greedily to me about the weather. His head bobs on a wild flood of words, and I take this violence to be a measure of his eagerness for speech. He badly needs a shave, coal dust has layered his face, he spits when he speaks, and his fingers pick at his tatters. He wobbles out in the wind when I leave him, a paper sack mashed in the fold of his arm, the leaves blowing past him, and our encounter drives me sadly home to poetry—where there's no answer. Billy closes his door and carries coal or wood to his fire and closes his eyes, and there's simply no way of knowing how lonely and empty he is or whether he's as vacant and barren and loveless as the rest of us are—here in the heart of the country.

WEATHER

For we're always out of luck here. That's just how it is—for instance in the winter. The sides of the buildings, the roofs, the limbs of the trees are gray. Streets, sidewalks, faces, feelings—they are gray. Speech is gray, and the grass when it shows. Every flank and front, each top is gray. Everything is gray: hair, eyes, window glass, the hawkers' bills and touters' posters, lips, teeth, poles and metal signs—they're gray, quite gray. Horses, sheep, and cows, cats killed in the road, squirrels in the same way, sparrows, doves, and pigeons, all are gray, everything is gray, and everyone is out of luck who lives here.

A similar haze turns the summer sky milky, and the air muffles your head and shoulders like a sweater you've got caught in. In the summer light, too, the sky darkens a moment when you open your eyes. The heat is pure distraction. Steeped in our fluids, miserable in the folds of our bodies, we can scarcely think of anything but our sticky parts. Hot cyclonic winds and storms of dust crisscross the country. In many places, given an indifferent push, the wind will still coast for miles, gathering resource and edge as it goes, cunning and force. According to the season, paper, leaves, field litter, seeds, snow, fill up the fences. Sometimes I think the land is flat because the winds have leveled it, they blow so constantly. In any case, a gale can grow in a field of corn that's as hot as a draft from hell, and to receive it is one of the most dismaying experiences of this life, though the smart of the same wind in winter is more humiliating, and in that sense even worse. But in the spring it rains as well, and the trees fill with ice.

PLACE

Many small Midwestern towns are nothing more than rural slums, and this community could easily become one. Principally during the first decade of the century, though there were many earlier instances, well-to-do farmers moved to town and built fine homes to contain them in their retirement. Others desired a more social life, and so lived in, driving to their fields like storekeepers to their businesses. These houses are now dying like the bereaved who inhabit them; they are slowly losing their senses—deafness, blindness, forgetfulness, mumbling, an insecure gait, an uncontrollable trembling has overcome them. Some kind of Northern Snopes will occupy them next: large-familied, Catholic, Democratic, scrambling, vigorous, poor; and since the parents will work in larger, nearby

309

towns, the children will be loosed upon themselves and upon the hapless neighbors much as the fabulous Khan loosed his legendary horde. These Snopes will undertake makeshift repairs with materials that other people have thrown away; paint halfway round their house, then quit; almost certainly maintain an ugly loud cantankerous dog and underfeed a pair of cats to keep the rodents down. They will collect piles of possibly useful junk in the back yard, park their cars in the front, live largely leaning over engines, give not a hoot for the land, the old community, the hallowed ways, the established clans. Weakening widow ladies have already begun to hire large rude youths from families such as these to rake and mow and tidy the grounds they will inherit.

PEOPLE

In the cinders at the station boys sit smoking steadily in darkened cars, their arms bent out the windows, white shirts glowing behind the glass. Nine o'clock is the best time. They sit in a line facing the highway—two or three or four of them—idling their engines. As you walk by a machine may growl at you or a pair of headlights flare up briefly. In a moment one will pull out, spinning cinders behind it, to stalk impatiently up and down the dark streets or roar half a mile into the country before returning to its place in line and pulling up.

MY HOUSE, MY CAT, MY COMPANY

I must organize myself. I must, as they say, pull myself together, dump this cat from my lap, stir—yes, resolve, move, do. But do what? My will is like the rosy dustlike light in this room: soft, diffuse, and gently comforting. It lets me do . . . anything . . . nothing. My ears hear what they happen to; I eat what's put before me; my eyes see what blunders into them; my thoughts are not thoughts, they are dreams. I'm empty or I'm full . . . depending; and I cannot choose. I sink my claws in Tick's fur and scratch the bones of his back until his rear rises amorously. Mr Tick, I murmur, I must organize myself. I must pull myself together. And Mr Tick rolls over on his belly, all ooze.

I spill Mr Tick when I've rubbed his stomach. Shoo. He steps away slowly, his long tail rhyming with his paws. How beautifully he moves, I think; how beautifully, like you, he commands his loving, how beautifully he accepts. So I rise and wander from room to room, up and down, gazing through most of my forty-one windows. How well this house receives its loving too. Let out like Mr Tick, my eyes sink in the shrubbery. I am not here; I've passed the glass, passed second-story spaces, flown by branches, brilliant berries, to the ground, grass high in seed and leafage every season; and it is the same as when I passed above you in my aged, ardent body; it's, in short, a kind of love; and I am learning to restore myself, my house, my body, by paying court to gardens, cats, and running water, and with neighbors keeping company.

Mrs Desmond is my right-hand friend; she's eighty-five. A thin white mist of hair, fine and tangled, manifests the climate of her mind. She is habitually suspicious, fretful, nervous. Burglars break in at noon. Children trespass. Even now they are shaking the pear tree, stealing rhubarb, denting lawn. Flies caught in the screens and numbed by frost awake in the heat to buzz and scrape the metal cloth and frighten her, though she is deaf to me, and consequently cannot hear them. Boards creak, the wind whistles across the chimney mouth, drafts cruise like fish through the hollow rooms. It is herself she hears, her own flesh failing, for only death will preserve her from those daily chores she climbs like stairs, and all that anxious waiting. Is it now, she wonders. No? Then: is it now?

We do not converse. She visits me to talk. My task to murmur. She talks about her grandsons, her daughter who lives in Delphi, her sister or her husband—both gone—obscure friends—dead—obscurer aunts and uncles—lost—ancient neighbors, members of her church or of her clubs—passed or passing on; and in this way she brings the ends of her life together with a terrifying rush: she is a girl, a wife, a mother, widow, all at once. All at once—appalling—but I believe it; I wince in expectation of the clap. Her talk's a fence—a shade drawn, window fastened, door that's locked—for no one dies taking tea in a kitchen; and as her years compress and begin to jumble, I really believe in the brevity of life; I sweat in my wonder; death is the dog down the street, the angry gander, bedroom spider, goblin who's come to get her; and it occurs to me that in my listening posture I'm the boy who suffered the winds of my grandfather with an exactly similar politeness, that I am, right now, all my ages, out in elbows, as angular as badly stacked cards. Thus was I, when I loved you, every man I could be, youth and child—far from enough—and you, so strangely ambiguous a being, met me, heart for spade, play after play, the whole run of our suits.

311

Mr Tick, you do me honor. You not only lie in my lap, but you remain alive there, coiled like a fetus. Through your deep nap, I feel you hum. You are, and are not, a machine. You are alive, alive exactly, and it means nothing to you—much to me. You are a cat— you cannot understand—you are a cat so easily. Your nature is not something you must rise to. You, not I, live in: in house, in skin, in shrubbery. Yes. I think I shall hat my head with a steeple; turn church; devour people. Mr Tick, though, has a tail he can twitch, he need not fly his Fancy. Claws, not metrical schema, poetry his paws; while smoothing . . . smoothing . . . smoothing roughly, his tongue laps its neatness. O Mr Tick, I know you; you are an electrical penis. Go on now, shoo. Mrs Desmond doesn't like you. She thinks you will tangle yourself in her legs and she will fall. You murder her birds, she knows, and walk upon her roof with death in your jaws. I must gather myself together for a bound. What age is it I'm at right now, I wonder. The heart, don't they always say, keeps the true time. Mrs Desmond is knocking. Faintly, you'd think, but she pounds. She's brought me a cucumber. I believe she believes I'm a woman. Come in, Mrs Desmond, thank you, be my company, it looks lovely, and have tea. I'll slice it, crisp, with cream, for luncheon, each slice as thin as me.

POLITICS

O all ye isolate and separate powers, Sing! Sing, and sing in such a way that from a distance it will seem a harmony, a Strindberg play, a friendship ring . . . so happy—happy, happy, happy—as here we go hand in handling, up and down. Our union was a singing, though we were silent in the songs we sang like single notes are silent in a symphony. In no sense sober, we barbershopped together and never heard the discords in our music or saw ourselves as dirty, cheap, or silly. Yet cats have worn out better shoes than those thrown through our love songs at us. Hush. Be patient—prudent—politic. Still, Cleveland killed you, Mr Crane. Were you not politic enough and fond of being beaten? Like a piece of sewage, the city shat you from its stern three hundred miles from history—beyond the loving reach of sailors. Well, I'm not a poet who puts Paris to his temple in his youth to blow himself from Idaho, or—fancy that—Missouri. My god, I said, this is my country, but must my country go so far as Terre Haute or Whiting, go so far as Gary?

When the Russians first announced the launching of their satellite, many people naturally refused to believe them. Later others were outraged that they had sent a dog around the earth. I wouldn't want to take that mutt from out that metal flying thing if he's still living when he lands, our own dog catcher said; anybody knows you shut a dog up by himself to toss around the first thing he'll be setting on to do you let him out is bite somebody.

This Midwest. A dissonance of parts and people, we are a consonance of Towns. Like a man grown fat in everything but heart, we overlabor; our outlook never really urban, never rural either, we enlarge and linger at the same time, as Alice both changed and remained in her story. You are blond. I put my hand upon your belly; feel it tremble from my trembling. We always drive large cars in my section of the country. How could you be a comfort to me now?

MORE VITAL DATA

The town is exactly fifty houses, trailer, stores, and miscellaneous buildings long, but in places no streets deep. It takes on width as you drive south, always adding to the east. Most of the dwellings are fairly spacious farm houses in the customary white, with wide wraparound porches and tall narrow windows, though there are many of the grander kind—fretted, scalloped, turreted, and decorated with clapboards set at angles or on end, with stained-glass windows at the stair landings and lots of wrought iron full of fancy curls—and a few of these look like castles in their rarer brick. Old stables serve as garages now, and the lots are large to contain them and the vegetable and flower gardens which, ultimately, widows plant and weed and then entirely disappear in. The shade is ample, the grass is good, the sky a glorious fall violet; the apple trees are heavy and red, the roads are calm and empty; corn has sifted from the chains of tractored wagons to speckle the streets with gold and with the russet fragments of the cob, and a man would be a fool who wanted, blessed with this, to live anywhere else in the world.

EDUCATION

Buses like great orange animals move through the early light to school. There the children will be taught to read and warned against Communism. By Miss Janet Jakes. That's not her name. Her name is Helen something—Scott or James. A teacher twenty years. She's now worn fine and smooth, and has a face, Wilfred says, like a mail-order

313

ax. Her voice is hoarse, and she has a cough. For she screams abuse.
The children stare, their faces blank. This is the thirteenth week. They
are used to it. You will all, she shouts, you will all draw pictures of
me. No. She is a Mrs—someone's missus. And in silence they set to
work while Miss Jakes jabs hairpins in her hair. Wilfred says an ax,
but she has those rimless tinted glasses, graying hair, an almost
dimpled chin. I must concentrate. I must stop making up things. I
must give myself to life; let it mold me: that's what they say in
Wisdom's Monthly Digest every day. Enough, enough—you've been at
it long enough; and the children rise formally a row at a time to
present their work to her desk. No, she wears rims; it's her chin that's
dimpleless. Well, it will take more than a tablespoon of features to
sweeten that face. So she grimly shuffles their sheets, examines her
reflection crayoned on them. I would not dare . . . allow a child . . . to
put a line around me. Though now and then she smiles like a nick in
the blade, in the end these drawings depress her. I could not bear it—
how can she ask?—that anyone . . . draw me. Her anger's lit. That's
why she does it: flame. There go her eyes; the pink in her glasses
brightens, dims. She is a pumpkin, and her rage is breathing like the
candle in. No, she shouts, no—the cartoon trembling—no, John
Mauck, John Stewart Mauck, this will not do. The picture flutters
from her fingers. You've made me too muscular.

I work on my poetry. I remember my friends, associates, my
students, by their names. Their names are Maypop, Dormouse,
Upsydaisy. Their names are Gladiolus, Callow Bladder, Prince and
Princess Oleo, Hieronymus, Cardinal Mummum, Mr Fitchew, The
Silken Howdah, Spot. Sometimes you're Tom Sawyer, Huckleberry
Finn; it is perpetually summer; your buttocks are my pillow; we are
adrift on a raft; your back is our river. Sometimes you are Major
Barbara, sometimes a goddess who kills men in battle, sometimes you
are soft like a shower of water; you are bread in my mouth.

I do not work on my poetry. I forget my friends, associates, my
students, and their names: Gramophone, Blowgun, Pickle, Serenade
. . . Marge the Barge, Arena, Uberhaupt . . . Doctor Dildoe, The Fog
Machine. For I am now in B, in Indiana: out of job and out of patience,
out of love and time and money, out of bread and out of body, in a
temper, Mrs Desmond, out of tea. So shut your fist up, bitch, you bag
of death; go bang another door; go die, my dearie. Die, life-deaf old
lady. Spill your breath. Fall over like a frozen board. Gray hair grown
from the nose of your mind. You are a skull already—*memento mori*—

the foreskin retracts from your teeth. Will your plastic gums last longer than your bones, and color their grinning? And is your twot still hazel-hairy, or are you bald as a ditch? . . . bitch . . . . . . bitch . . . . bitch. I wanted to be famous, but you bring me age—my emptiness. Was it *that* which I thought would balloon me above the rest? Love? where are you? . . . love me. I want to rise so high, I said, that when I shit I won't miss anybody.

BUSINESS

For most people, business is poor. Nearby cities have siphoned off all but a neighborhood trade. Except for feed and grain and farm supplies, you stand a chance to sell only what one runs out to buy. Chevrolet has quit, and Frigidaire. A locker plant has left its afterimage. The lumberyard has been, so far, six months about its going. Gas stations change hands clumsily, a restaurant becomes available, a grocery closes. One day they came and knocked the cornices from the watch repair and pasted campaign posters on the windows. Torn across, by now, by boys, they urge you still to vote for half an orange beblazoned man who as a whole one failed two years ago to win at his election. Everywhere, in this manner, the past speaks, and it mostly speaks of failure. The empty stores, the old signs and dusty fixtures, the debris in alleys, the flaking paint and rusty gutters, the heavy locks and sagging boards: they say the same disagreeable things. What do the sightless windows see, I wonder, when the sun throws a passerby against them? Here a stair unfolds toward the street—dark, rickety, and treacherous—and I always feel, as I pass it, that if I just went carefully up and turned the corner at the landing, I would find myself out of the world. But I've never had the courage.

THAT SAME PERSON

The weeds catch up with Billy. In pursuit of the hollyhocks, they rise in coarse clumps all around the front of his house. Billy has to stamp down a circle by his door like a dog or cat does turning round to nest up, they're so thick. What particularly troubles me is that winter will find the weeds still standing stiff and tindery to take the sparks which Billy's little mortarless chimney spouts. It's true that fires are fun here. The town whistle, which otherwise only blows for noon (and there's no noon on Sunday), signals the direction of the fire by

315

the length and number of its blasts, the volunteer firemen rush past in their cars and trucks, houses empty their owners along the street every time like an illustration in a children's book. There are many bikes, too, and barking dogs, and sometimes—halleluiah—the fire's right here in town—a vacant lot of weeds and stubble flaming up. But I'd rather it weren't Billy or Billy's lot or house. Quite selfishly I want him to remain the way he is—counting his sticks and logs, sitting on his sill in the soft early sun—though I'm not sure what his presence means to me . . . or to anyone. Nevertheless, I keep wondering whether, given time, I might not someday find a figure in our language which would serve him faithfully, and furnish his poverty and loneliness richly out.

WIRES

Where sparrows sit like fists. Doves fly the steeple. In mist the wires change perspective, rise and twist. If they led to you, I would know what they were. Thoughts passing often, like the starlings who flock these fields at evening to sleep in the trees beyond, would form a family of paths like this; they'd foot down the natural height of air to just about a bird's perch. But they do not lead to you.

> *Of whose beauty it was sung*
> *She shall make the old man young.*

They fasten me.

If I walked straight on, in my present mood, I would reach the Wabash. It's not a mood in which I'd choose to conjure you. Similes dangle like baubles from me. This time of year the river is slow and shallow, the clay banks crack in the sun, weeds surprise the sandbars. The air is moist and I am sweating. It's impossible to rhyme in this dust. Everything—sky, the cornfield, stump, wild daisies, my old clothes and pressless feelings—seem fabricated for installment purchase. Yes. Christ. I am suffering a summer Christmas; and I cannot walk under the wires. The sparrows scatter like handfuls of gravel. Really, wires are voices in thin strips. They are words wound in cables. Bars of connection.

WEATHER

I would rather it were the weather that was to blame for what I am and what my friends and neighbors are—we who live here in the

316

heart of the country. Better the weather, the wind, the pale dying snow . . . the snow—why not the snow? There's never much really, not around the lower Lakes anyway, not enough to boast about, not enough to be useful. My father tells how the snow in the Dakotas would sweep to the roofs of the barns in the old days, and he and his friends could sled on the crust that would form because the snow was so fiercely driven. In Bemidji trees have been known to explode. That would be something—if the trees in Davenport or Francisville or Carbondale or Niles were to go blam some winter—blam! blam! blam! all the way down the gray, cindery, snow-sick streets.

A cold fall rain is blackening the trees or the air is like lilac and full of parachuting seeds. Who cares to live in any season but his own? Still I suspect the secret's in this snow, the secret of our sickness, if we could only diagnose it, for we are all dying like the elms in Urbana. This snow—like our skin it covers the country. Later dust will do it. Right now—snow. Mud presently. But it is snow without any laughter in it, a pale gray pudding thinly spread on stiff toast, and if that seems a strange description, it's accurate all the same. Of course soot blackens everything, but apart from that, we are never sufficiently cold here. The flakes as they come, alive and burning, we cannot retain, for if our temperatures fall, they rise promptly again, just as, in the summer, they bob about in the same feckless way. Suppose though . . . suppose they were to rise some August, climb and rise, and then hang in the hundreds like a hawk through December, what a desert we could make of ourselves—from Chicago to Cairo, from Hammond to Columbus—what beautiful Death Valleys.

PLACE

I would rather it were the weather. It drives us in upon ourselves—an unlucky fate. Of course there is enough to stir our wonder anywhere; there's enough to love, anywhere, if one is strong enough, if one is diligent enough, if one is perceptive, patient, kind enough—whatever it takes; and surely it's better to live in the country, to live on a prairie by a drawing of rivers, in Iowa or Illinois or Indiana, say, than in any city, in any stinking fog of human beings, in any blooming orchard of machines. It ought to be. The cities are swollen and poisonous with people. It ought to be better. Man has never been a fit environment for man—for rats, maybe, rats do nicely, or for dogs or cats and the household beetle.

317

And how long the street is, nowadays. These endless walls are fallen to keep back the tides of earth. Brick could be beautiful but we have covered it gradually with gray industrial vomits. Age does not make concrete genial, and asphalt is always—like America—twenty-one, until it breaks up in crumbs like stale cake. The brick, the asphalt, the concrete, the dancing signs and garish posters, the feed and excrement of the automobile, the litter of its inhabitants: they compose, they decorate, they line our streets, and there is nowhere, nowadays, our streets can't reach.

A man in the city has no natural thing by which to measure himself. His parks are potted plants. Nothing can live and remain free where he resides but the pigeon, starling, sparrow, spider, cockroach, mouse, moth, fly and weed, and he laments the existence of even these and makes his plans to poison them. The zoo? There *is* the zoo. Through its bars the city man stares at the great cats and dully sucks his ice. Living, alas, among men and their marvels, the city man supposes that his happiness depends on establishing, somehow, a special kind of harmonious accord with others. The novelists of the city, of slums and crowds, they call it love—and break their pens.

Wordsworth feared the accumulation of men in cities. He foresaw their 'degrading thirst after outrageous stimulation,' and some of their hunger for love. Living in a city, among so many, dwelling in the heat and tumult of incessant movement, a man's affairs are touch and go—that's all. It's not surprising that the novelists of the slums, the cities, and the crowds, should find that sex is but a scratch to ease a tickle, that we're most human when we're sitting on the john, and that the justest image of our life is in full passage through the plumbing.

> That man, immur'd in cities, still retains
> His inborn inextinguishable thirst
> Of rural scenes, compensating his loss
> By supplemental shifts, the best he may.

Come into the country, then. The air nimbly and sweetly recommends itself unto our gentle senses. Here, growling tractors tear the earth. Dust roils up behind them. Drivers sit jouncing under bright umbrellas. They wear refrigerated hats and steer by looking at the tracks they've cut behind them, their transistors blaring. Close to the land, are they? good companions to the soil? Tell me: do they live in harmony with the alternating seasons?

It's a lie of old poetry. The modern husbandman uses chemicals from cylinders and sacks, spike-ball-and-claw machines, metal sheds, and cost accounting. Nature in the old sense does not matter. It does not exist. Our farmer's only mystical attachment is to parity. And if he does not realize that cows and corn are simply different kinds of chemical engine, he cannot expect to make a go of it.

It isn't necessary to suppose our cows have feelings; our neighbor hasn't as many as he used to have either; but think of it this way a moment, you can correct for the human imputations later: how would it feel to nurse those strange tentacled calves with their rubber, glass, and metal lips, their stainless eyes?

PEOPLE

Aunt Pet's still able to drive her car—a high square Ford—even though she walks with difficulty and a stout stick. She has a watery gaze, a smooth plump face despite her age, and jet black hair in a bun. She has the slowest smile of anyone I ever saw, but she hates dogs, and not very long ago cracked the back of one she cornered in her garden. To prove her vigor she will tell you this, her smile breaking gently while she raises the knob of her stick to the level of your eyes.

HOUSE, MY BREATH AND WINDOW

My window is a grave, and all that lies within it's dead. No snow is falling. There's no haze. It is not still, not silent. Its images are not an animal that waits, for movement is no demonstration. I have seen the sea slack, life bubble through a body without a trace, its spheres impervious as soda's. Downwound, the whore at wagtag clicks and clacks. Leaves wiggle. Grass sways. A bird chirps, pecks the ground. An auto wheel in penning circles keeps its rigid spokes. These images are stones; they are memorials. Beneath this sea lies sea: god rest it . . . rest the world beyond my window, me in front of my reflection, above this page, my shade. Death is not so still, so silent, since silence implies a falling quiet, stillness a stopping, containing, holding in; for death is time in a clock, like Mr Tick, electric . . . like wind through a windup poet. And my blear floats out to visible against the glass, befog its country and bespill myself. The mist lifts slowly from the fields in the morning. No one now would say: the Earth throws back its covers; it is rising from sleep. Why is the feeling foolish? The

319

image is too Greek. I used to gaze at you so wantonly your body blushed. Imagine: wonder: that my eyes could cause such flowering. Ah, my friend, your face is pale, the weather cloudy; a street has been felled through your chin, bare trees do nothing, houses take root in their rectangles, a steeple stands up in your head. You speak of loving; then give me a kiss. The pane is cold. On icy mornings the fog rises to greet me (as you always did); the barns and other buildings, rather than ghostly, seem all the more substantial for looming, as if they grew in themselves while I watched (as you always did). Oh my approach, I suppose, was like breath in a rubber monkey. Nevertheless, on the road along the Wabash in the morning, though the trees are sometimes obscured by fog, their reflection floats serenely on the river, reasoning the banks, the sycamores in French rows. Magically, the world tips. I'm led to think that only those who grow down live (which will scarcely win me twenty-five from *Wisdom's Monthly Digest*), but I find I write that only those who live down grow; and what I write, I hold, whatever I really know. My every word's inverted, or reversed—or I am. I held you, too, that way. You were so utterly provisional, subject to my change. I could inflate your bosom with a kiss, disperse your skin with gentleness, enter your vagina from within, and make my love emerge like a fresh sex. The pane is cold. Honesty is cold, my inside lover. The sun looks, through the mist, like a plum on the tree of heaven, or a bruise on the slope of your belly. Which? The grass crawls with frost. We meet on this window, the world and I, inelegantly, swimmers of the glass; and swung wrong way round to one another, the world seems in. The world—how grand, how monumental, grave and deadly, that word is: the world, my house and poetry. All poets have their inside lovers. Wee penis does not belong to me, or any of this foggery. It is *his* property which he's thrust through what's womanly of me to set down this. These wooden houses in their squares, gray streets and fallen sidewalks, standing trees, your name I've written sentimentally across my breath into the whitening air, pale birds: they exist in me now because of him. I gazed with what intensity . . . A bush in the excitement of its roses could not have bloomed so beautifully as you did then. It was a look I'd like to give this page. For that is poetry: to bring within about, to change.

POLITICS

Sports, politics, and religion are the three passions of the badly educated. They are the Midwest's open sores. Ugly to see, a source of constant discontent, they sap the body's strength. Appalling quantities of money, time, and energy are wasted on them. The rural mind is narrow, passionate, and reckless on these matters. Greed, however shortsighted and direct, will not alone account for it. I have known men, for instance, who for years have voted squarely against their interests. Nor have I ever noticed that their surly Christian views prevented them from urging forward the smithereening, say, of Russia, China, Cuba, or Korea. And they tend to back their country like they back their local team: they have a fanatical desire to win; yelling is their forte; and if things go badly, they are inclined to sack the coach. All in all, then, Birch is a good name. It stands for the bigot's stick, the wild-child-tamer's cane.

Forgetfulness—is that their object?

Oh, I was new, I thought. A fresh start: new cunt, new climate, and new country—there you were, and I was pioneer, and had no history. That language hurts me, too, my dear. You'll never hear it.

FINAL VITAL DATA

The Modern Homemaker's Demonstration Club. The Prairie Home Demonstration Club. The Night-outers' Home Demonstration Club. The IOOF, FFF, VFW, WCTU, WSCS, 4-H, 40 and 8, Psi Iota Chi, and PTA. The Boy and Girl Scouts, Rainbows, Masons, Indians and Rebekah Lodge. Also the Past Noble Grand Club of the Rebekah Lodge. As well as the Moose and the Ladies of the Moose. The Elks, the Eagles, the Jaynettes and the Eastern Star. The Women's Literary Club, the Hobby Club, the Art Club, the Sunshine Society, the Dorcas Society, the Pythian Sisters, the Pilgrim Youth Fellowship, the American Legion, the American Legion Auxiliary, the American Legion Junior Auxiliary, the Gardez Club, the Bridge for Fun Club, the What-can-you-do? Club, the Get Together Club, the Coterie Club, the Worthwhile Club, the Let's Help Our Town Club, the No Name Club, the Forget-me-not Club, the Merry-go-round Club . . .

EDUCATION

Had a quarter disappeared from Paula Frosty's pocket book? Imagine the landscape of that face: no crayon could engender it; soft wax is wrong; thin wire in trifling snips might do the trick. Paula Frosty and Christopher Roger accuse the pale and splotchy Cheryl

Pipes. But Miss Jakes, I *saw* her. Miss Jakes is so extremely vexed she snaps her pencil. What else is missing? I appoint you a detective, John: search her desk. Gum, candy, paper, pencils, marble, round eraser—whose? A thief. I can't watch her all the time, I'm here to teach. Poor pale fossetted Cheryl, it's determined, can't return the money because she took it home and spent it. Cindy, Janice, John, and Pete—you four who sit around her—you will be detectives this whole term to watch her. A thief. In all my time. Miss Jakes turns, unfists, and turns again. I'll handle you, she cries. To think. A thief. In all my years. Then she writes on the blackboard the name of Cheryl Pipes and beneath that the figure twenty-five with a large sign for cents. Now Cheryl, she says, this won't be taken off until you bring that money out of home, out of home straight up to here, Miss Jakes says, tapping her desk.

Which is three days.

ANOTHER PERSON

I was raking leaves when Uncle Halley introduced himself to me. He said his name came from the comet, and that his mother had borne him prematurely in her fright of it. I thought of Hobbes, whom fear of the Spanish Armada had hurried into birth, and so I believed Uncle Halley to honor the philosopher, though Uncle Halley is a liar, and neither the one hundred twenty-nine nor the fifty-three he ought to be. That fall the leaves had burned themselves out on the trees, the leaf lobes had curled, and now they flocked noisily down the street and were broken in the wires of my rake. Uncle Halley was himself (like Mrs Desmond and history generally) both deaf and implacable, and he shooed me down his basement stairs to a room set aside there for stacks of newspapers reaching to the ceiling, boxes of leaflets and letters and programs, racks of photo albums, scrapbooks, bundles of rolled-up posters and maps, flags and pennants and slanting piles of dusty magazines devoted mostly to motoring and the Christian ethic. I saw a bird cage, a tray of butterflies, a bugle, a stiff straw boater, and all kinds of tassels tied to a coat tree. He still possessed and had on display the steering lever from his first car, a linen duster, driving gloves and goggles, photographs along the wall of himself, his friend, and his various machines, a shell from the first war, a record of 'Ramona' nailed through its hole to a post, walking sticks and fanciful umbrellas, shoes of all sorts (his baby shoes, their counters broken, were held in sorrow beneath my nose—they had not been bronzed, but he might have them done someday before he died, he said), countless boxes of medals, pins, beads, trinkets, toys, and keys (I scarcely saw—they flowed like jewels from his palms), pictures of downtown when it was only a path by the railroad station, a brightly colored globe of the world with a dent in Poland, antique guns, belt buckles, buttons, souvenir plates and cups and saucers (I can't remember all of it—I won't), but I recall how shamefully, how rudely, how abruptly, I fled, a good story in my mouth but death in my nostrils; and how afterward I busily, righteously, burned my leaves as if I were purging the world of its years. I still wonder if this town—its life, and mine now—isn't really a record like the one of 'Ramona' that I used to crank around on my grandmother's mahogany Victrola through lonely rainy days as a kid.

THE FIRST PERSON

Billy's like the coal he's found: spilled, mislaid, discarded. The sky's no comfort. His house and his body are dying together. His windows are boarded. And now he's reduced to his hands. I suspect he has glaucoma. At any rate he can scarcely see, and weeds his yard of rubble on his hands and knees. Perhaps he's a surgeon cleansing a wound or an ardent and tactile lover. I watch, I must say, apprehensively. Like mine-war detectors, his hands graze in circles ahead of him. Your nipples were the color of your eyes. Pebble. Snarl of paper. Length of twine. He leans down closely, picks up something silvery, holds it near his nose. Foil? cap? coin? He has within him—what, I wonder? Does he know more now because he fingers everything and has to sniff to see? It would be romantic cruelty to think so. He bends the down on your arms like a breeze. You wrote me: something is strange when we don't understand. I write in return: I think when I loved you I fell to my death.

Billy, I could read to you from Beddoes; he's your man perhaps; he held with dying, freed his blood of its arteries; and he said that there were many wretched love-ill fools like me lying alongside the last bone of their former selves, as full of spirit and speech, nonetheless, as Mrs Desmond, Uncle Halley and the Ferris wheel, Aunt Pet, Miss Jakes, Ramona or the megaphone; yet I reverse him finally, Billy, on no evidence but braggadocio, and I declare that though my inner organs were devoured long ago, the worm which swallowed down my parts still throbs and glows like a crystal palace.

Yes, you were younger. I was Uncle Halley, the museum man and

323

infrequent meteor. Here is my first piece of ass. They weren't so flat in those days, had more round, more juice. And over here's the sperm I've spilled, nicely jarred and clearly labeled. Look at this tape like lengths of intestine where I've stored my spew, the endless worm of words I've written, a hundred million emissions or more: oh I was quite a man right from the start; even when unconscious in my cradle, from crotch to cranium, I was erectile tissue; though mostly, after the manner approved by Plato, I had intercourse by eye. Never mind, old Holsclaw, you are blind. We pull down darkness when we go to bed; put out like Oedipus the actually offending organ, and train our touch to lies. All cats are gray, says Mr Tick; so under cover of glaucoma you are sack gray too, and cannot be distinguished from a stallion.

I must pull myself together, get a grip, just as they say, but I feel spilled, bewildered, quite mislaid. I did not restore my house to its youth, but to its age. Hunting, you hitch through the hollyhocks. I'm inclined to say you aren't half the cripple I am, for there is nothing left of me but mouth. However, I resist the impulse. It is another lie of poetry. My organs are all there, though it's there where I fail—at the roots of my experience. Poet of the spiritual, Rilke, weren't you? yet that's what you said. Poetry, like love, is—in and out—a physical caress. I can't tolerate any more of my sophistries about spirit, mind, and breath. Body equals being, and if your weight goes down, you are the less.

HOUSEHOLD APPLES

I knew nothing about apples. Why should I? My country came in my childhood, and I dreamed of sitting among the blooms like the bees. I failed to spray the pear tree too. I doubled up under them at first, admiring the sturdy low branches I should have pruned, and later I acclaimed the blossoms. Shortly after the fruit formed there were falls—not many—apples the size of goodish stones which made me wobble on my ankles when I walked about the yard. Sometimes a piece crushed by a heel would cling on the shoe to track the house. I gathered a few and heaved them over the wires. A slingshot would have been splendid. Hard, an unattractive green, the worms had them. Before long I realized the worms had them all. Even as the apples reddened, lit their tree, they were being swallowed. The birds preferred the pears, which were small—sugar pears I think they're called—with thick skins of graying green that ripen on toward violet.

So the fruit fell, and once I made some applesauce by quartering and paring hundreds; but mostly I did nothing, left them, until suddenly, overnight it seemed, in that ugly late September heat we often have in Indiana, my problem was upon me.

My childhood came in the country. I remember, now, the flies on our snowy luncheon table. As we cleared away they would settle, fastidiously scrub themselves and stroll to the crumbs to feed where I would kill them in crowds with a swatter. It was quite a game to catch them taking off. I struck heavily since I didn't mind a few stains; they'd wash. The swatter was a square of screen bound down in red cloth. It drove no air ahead of it to give them warning. They might have thought they'd flown headlong into a summered window. The faint pink dot where they had died did not rub out as I'd supposed, and after years of use our luncheon linen would faintly, pinkly, speckle.

The country became my childhood. Flies braided themselves on the flypaper in my grandmother's house. I can smell the bakery and the grocery and the stables and the dairy in that small Dakota town I knew as a kid; knew as I dreamed I'd know your body, as I've known nothing, before or since; knew as the flies knew, in the honest, unchaste sense: the burned house, hose-wet, which drew a mist of insects like the blue smoke of its smolder, and gangs of boys, moist-lipped, destructive as its burning. Flies have always impressed me; they are so persistently alive. Now they were coating the ground beneath my trees. Some were ordinary flies; there were the large blue-green ones; there were swarms of fruit flies too, and the red-spotted scavenger beetle; there were a few wasps, several sorts of bees and butterflies—checkers, sulphurs, monarchs, commas, question marks—and delicate dragonflies . . . but principally houseflies and horseflies and bottleflies, flies and more flies in clusters around the rotting fruit. They loved the pears. Inside, they fed. If you picked up a pear, they flew, and the pear became skin and stem. They were everywhere the fruit was: in the tree still—apples like a hive for them—or where the fruit littered the ground, squashing itself as you stepped . . . there was no help for it. The flies droned, feasting on the sweet juice. No one could go near the trees; I could not climb; so I determined at last to labor like Hercules. There were fruit baskets in the barn. Collecting them and kneeling under the branches, I began to gather remains. Deep in the strong rich smell of the fruit, I began to hum myself. The fruit caved in at the touch. Glistening red apples, my lifting disclosed, had families of beetles, flies, and bugs, devouring their rotten undersides. There were streams of flies; there were lakes and cataracts and rivers of flies, seas and oceans. The hum was heavier, higher, then the hum of the bees when they came to the blooms in the spring, though the bees were there, among the flies, ignoring me—ignoring everyone. As my work went on and juice covered my hands and arms, they would form a sleeve, black and moving, like knotty wool. No caress could have been more indifferently complete. Still I rose fearfully, ramming my head in the branches, apples bumping against me before falling, bursting with bugs. I'd snap my hand sharply but the flies would cling to the sweet. I could toss a whole cluster into a basket from several feet. As the pear or apple lit, they would explosively rise, like monads for a moment, windowless, certainly, with respect to one another, sugar their harmony. I had to admit, though, despite my distaste, that my arm had never been more alive, oftener or more gently kissed. Those hundreds of feet were light. In washing them off, I pretended the hose was a pump. What have I missed? Childhood is a lie of poetry.

THE CHURCH

Friday night. Girls in dark skirts and white blouses sit in ranks and scream in concert. They carry funnels loosely stuffed with orange and black paper which they shake wildly, and small megaphones through which, as drilled, they direct and magnify their shouting. Their leaders, barely pubescent girls, prance and shake and whirl their skirts above their bloomers. The young men, leaping, extend their arms and race through puddles of amber light, their bodies glistening. In a lull, though it rarely occurs, you can hear the squeak of tennis shoes against the floor. Then the yelling begins again, and then continues; fathers, mothers, neighbors joining in to form a single pulsing ululation—a cry of the whole community—for in this gymnasium each body becomes the bodies beside it, pressed as they are together, thigh to thigh, and the same shudder runs through all of them, and runs toward the same release. Only the ball moves serenely through this dazzling din. Obedient to law it scarcely speaks but caroms quietly and lives at peace.

BUSINESS

It is the week of Christmas and the stores, to accommodate the rush they hope for, are remaining open in the evening. You can see snow falling in the cones of the street lamps. The roads are filling—undisturbed. Strings of red and green lights droop over the principal highway, and the water tower wears a star. The windows of the stores have been bedizened. Shamelessly they beckon. But I am alone, leaning against a pole—no . . . there is no one in sight. They're all at home, perhaps by their instruments, tuning in on their evenings, and like Ramona, tirelessly playing and replaying themselves. There's a speaker perched in the tower, and through the boughs of falling snow and over the vacant streets, it drapes the twisted and metallic strains of a tune that can barely be distinguished—yes, I believe it's one of the jolly ones, it's 'Joy to the World.' There's no one to hear the music but myself, and though I'm listening, I'm no longer certain. Perhaps the record's playing something else.

1968

A Solo Song: For Doc

James Alan McPherson

1

So you want to know this business, youngblood? So you want to be a Waiter's Waiter? The Commissary gives you a book with all the rules and tells you to learn them. And you do, and think that is all there is to it. A big, thick black book. Poor youngblood.

Look at me. *I* am a Waiter's Waiter. I know all the moves, all the pretty, fine moves that big book will never teach you. *I* built this railroad with my moves; and so did Sheik Beasley and Uncle T. Boone and Danny Jackson, and so did Doc Craft. That book they made you learn came from our moves and from our heads. There was a time when six of us, big men, danced at the same time in that little Pantry without touching and shouted orders to the sweating paddies in the kitchen. There was a time when they *had* to respect us because our sweat and our moves supported them. We knew the service and the paddies, even the green dishwashers, knew that we did and didn't give us the crap they pull on you.

Do you know how to sneak a Blackplate to a nasty cracker? Do you know how to rub asses with five other men in the Pantry getting their orders together and still know that you are a man, just like them? Do you know how to bullshit while you work and keep the paddies in their places with your bullshit? Do you know how to breathe down the back of an old lady's dress to hustle a bigger tip.

No. You are summer stuff, youngblood. I am old, my moves are not so good any more, but I know this business. The Commissary hires you for the summer because they don't want to let anyone get as old as me on them. I'm sixty-three, but they can't fire me: I'm in the Union. They can't lay me off for fucking up: I know this business too well. And so they hire you, youngblood, for the summer when the tourists come, and in September you go away with some tips in your pocket to buy pussy and they wait all winter for me to die. I *am* dying, youngblood, and so is this business. Both of us will die together. There'll always be summer stuff like you, but the big men, the big trains, are dying every day and everybody can see it. And nobody but us who are dying with them gives a damn.

Look at the big picture at the end of the car, youngblood. That's the man who built this road. He's in your history books. He's probably in that big black bible you read. He was a great man. He hated people. He didn't want to feed them but the government said he had to. He didn't want to hire me, but he needed me to feed the people. I know this, youngblood, and that is why that book is written for you and that is why I have never read it. That is why you get nervous and jump up to polish the pepper and salt shakers when the word comes down the line that an inspector is getting on at the next stop. That is why you warm the toast covers for every cheap old lady who wants to get coffee and toast and good service for sixty-five cents and a dime tip. You know that he needs you only for the summer and that hundreds of youngbloods like you want to work this summer to buy that pussy in Chicago and Portland and Seattle. The man uses you, but he doesn't need you. But me he needs for the winter, when you are gone, and to teach you something in the summer about this business you can't get from that big black book. He needs me and he knows it and I know it. That is why I am sitting here when there are tables to be cleaned and linen to be changed and silver to be washed and polished. He needs me to die. That is why I am taking my time. I know it. And I will take his service with me when I die, just like the Sheik did and like Percy Fields did, and like Doc.

Who are they? Why do I keep talking about them? Let me think about it. I guess it is because they were the last of the Old School, like me. We made this road. We got a million miles of walking up and down these cars under our feet. Doc Craft was the Old School, like me. He was a Waiter's Waiter. He danced down these aisles with us and swung his tray with the roll of the train, never spilling in all his trips a single cup of coffee. He could carry his tray on two fingers, or on one and a half if he wanted, and he knew all the tricks about hustling tips there are to know. He could work anybody. The girls at the Northland in Chicago knew Doc, and the girls at the Haverville in Seattle, and the girls at the Step-Inn in Portland and all the girls in Winnipeg knew Doc Craft.

But wait. It is just 1.30 and the first call for dinner is not until 5.00. You want to kill some time; you want to hear about the Old School and how it was in my day. If you look in that black book you would see that you should be polishing silver now. Look out the window; this is North Dakota, this is Jerry's territory. Jerry, the Unexpected

329

Inspector. Shouldn't you polish the shakers or clean out the Pantry or squeeze oranges, or maybe change the linen on the tables? Jerry Ewald is sly. The train may stop in the middle of this wheatfield and Jerry may get on. He lives by that book. He knows where to look for dirt and mistakes. Jerry Ewald, the Unexpected Inspector. He knows where to look; he knows how to get you. He got Doc.

Now you want to know about him, about the Old School. You have even put aside your book of rules. But see how you keep your finger in the pages as if the book was more important than what I tell you. That's a bad move, and it tells on you. You will be a waiter. But you will never be a Waiter's Waiter. The Old School died with Doc, and the very last of it is dying with me. What happened to Doc? Take your finger out of the pages, youngblood, and I will tell you about a kind of life these rails will never carry again.

When your father was a boy playing with himself behind the barn, Doc was already a man and knew what the thing was for. But he got tired of using it when he wasn't much older than you, and he set his mind on making money. He had no skills. He was black. He got hungry. On Christmas Day in 1916, the story goes, he wandered into the Chicago stockyards and over to a dining car waiting to be connected up to the main train for the Chicago-to-San Francisco run. He looked up through the kitchen door at the chef storing supplies for the kitchen and said: 'I'm hungry.'

'What do you want *me* to do about it?' the Swede chief said.

'I'll work,' said Doc.

That Swede was Chips Magnusson, fresh off the boat and lucky to be working himself. He did not know yet that he should save all extra work for other Swedes fresh off the boat. He later learned this by living. But at that time he considered a moment, bit into one of the fresh apples stocked for apple pie, chewed considerably, spit out the seeds and then waved the black on board the big train. 'You can eat all you want,' he told Doc. 'But you work all I tell you.'

He put Doc to rolling dough for the apple pies and the train began rolling for Doc. It never stopped. He fell in love with the feel of the wheels under his feet clicking against the track and he got the rhythm of the wheels in him and learned, like all of us, how to roll with them and move with them. After that first trip Doc was never at home on the ground. He worked everything in the kitchen from putting out dough to second cook, in six years. And then, when the commissary saw that he was good and would soon be going for one of the chef's spots they saved for the Swedes, they put him out of the kitchen and told him to learn this waiter business; and told him to learn how to bullshit on the other side of the Pantry. He was almost thirty, youngblood, when he crossed over to the black side of the Pantry. I wasn't there when he made his first trip as a waiter, but from what they tell me of that trip I know that he was broke in by good men. Pantryman was Sheik Beasley, who stayed high all the time and let the waiters steal anything they wanted as long as they didn't bother his reefers. Danny Jackson, who was black and knew Shakespeare before the world said he could work with it, was second man. Len Dickey was third, Reverend Hendricks was fourth, and Uncle T. Boone, who even in those early days could not straighten his back, ran fifth. Doc started in as sixth waiter, the 'mule.' They pulled some shit on him at first because they didn't want somebody fresh out of a paddy kitchen on the crew. They messed with his orders, stole his plates, picked up his tips on the sly, and made him do all the dirty work. But when they saw that he could take the shit without getting hot and when they saw that he was set on being a waiter, even though he was older than most of them, they settled down and began to teach him this business and all the words and moves and slickness that made it a good business.

His real name was Leroy Johnson, I think, but when Danny Jackson saw how cool and neat he was in his moves, and how he handled the plates, he began to call him 'the Doctor.' Then the Sheik, coming down from his high one day after missing the lunch and dinner service, saw how Doc had taken over his station and collected fat tips from his tables by telling the passengers that the Sheik had had to get off back along the line because of a heart attack. The Sheik liked that because he saw that Doc understood crackers and how they liked nothing better than knowing that a nigger had died on the job, giving them service. The Sheik was impressed. And he was not an easy man to impress because he knew too much about life and had to stay high most of the time. And when Doc would not split the tips with him, the Sheik got mad at first and called Doc a barrel of motherfuckers and some other words you would not recognize. But he was impressed. And later that night, in the crew car when the others were gambling and drinking and bullshitting about the women they had working the corners for them, the Sheik came over to Doc's bunk and said: 'You're a crafty motherfucker.'

'Yeah?' says Doc.

'Yeah,' says the Sheik, who did not say much. 'You're a crafty motherfucker but I like you.' Then he got into the first waiter's bunk and lit up again. But Reverend Hendricks, who always read his Bible before going to sleep and who always listened to anything the Sheik said because he knew the Sheik only said something when it was important, heard what was said and remembered it. After he put his Bible back in his locker, he walked over to Doc's bunk and looked down at him. 'Mister Doctor Craft,' the Reverend said. 'Youngblood Doctor Craft.'

'Yeah?' says Doc.

'Yeah,' says Reverend Hendricks. 'That's who you are.'

And that's who he was from then on.

2

I came to the road away from the war. This was after '41, when people at home were looking for Japs under their beds every night. I did not want to fight because there was no money in it and I didn't want to go overseas to work in a kitchen. The big war was on and a lot of soldiers crossed the country to get to it, and as long as a black man fed them on trains he did not have to go to that war. I could have got a job in a Chicago factory, but there was more money on the road and it was safer. And after a while it got into your blood so that you couldn't leave it for anything. The road got into my blood the way it got into everybody's; the way going to war got in the blood of redneck farm boys and the crazy Polacks from Chicago. It was all right for them to go to the war. They were young and stupid. And they died that way. I played it smart. I was almost thirty-five and I didn't want to go. But I took *them* and fed them and gave them good times on their way to the war, and for that I did not have to go. The soldiers had plenty of money and were afraid not to spend it all before they got to the ships on the Coast. And we gave them ways to spend it on the trains.

Now in those days there was plenty of money going around and everybody stole from everybody. The kitchen stole food from the company and the company knew it and wouldn't pay good wages. There were no rules in those days, there was no black book to go by and nobody said what you couldn't eat or steal. The paddy cooks used to toss boxes of steaks off the train in the Chicago yards for people at the restaurants there who paid them, cash. These were the days when ordinary people had to have red stamps or blue stamps to get powdered eggs and white lard to mix with red powder to make their own butter.

The stewards stole from the company and from the waiters; the waiters stole from the stewards and the company and from each other. I stole. Doc stole. Even Reverend Hendricks put his Bible far back in his locker and stole with us. You didn't want a man on your crew who didn't steal. He made it bad for everybody. And if the steward saw that he was a dummy and would never get to stealing, he wrote him up for something and got him off the crew so as not to slow down the rest of us. We had a redneck cracker steward from Alabama by the name of Casper who used to say: '*Jesus Christ!* I ain't got time to hate you niggers, I'm making so much money.' He used to keep all his cash at home under his bed in a cardboard box because he was afraid to put it in the bank.

Doc and Sheik Beasley and me were on the same crew together all during the war. Even in those days, as young as we were, we knew how to be Old Heads. We organized for the soldiers. We had to wear skullcaps all the time because the crackers said our hair was poison and didn't want any of it to fall in their food. The Sheik didn't mind wearing one. He kept reefers in his and used to sell them to the soldiers for double what he paid for them in Chicago and three times what he paid the Chinamen in Seattle. That's why we called him the Sheik. After every meal the Sheik would get in the linen closet and light up. Sometimes he wouldn't come out for days. Nobody gave a damn, though; we were all too busy stealing and working. And there was more for us to get as long as he didn't come out.

Doc used to sell bootlegged booze to the soldiers; that was his speciality. He had redcaps in the Chicago stations telling the soldiers who to ask for on the train. He was an open operator and had to give the steward a cut, but he still made a pile of money. That's why that old cracker always kept us together on his crew. We were the three best moneymakers he ever had. That's something you should learn, youngblood. They can't love you for being you. They only love you if you make money for them. All that talk these days about integration and brotherhood, that's a lot of bullshit. The man will love you as long as he can make money with you. I made money. And old Casper had to love me in the open although I knew he called me a nigger at home when he had put that money in his big cardboard box. I know he loved me on the road in the wartime because I used to

James Alan McPherson

bring in the biggest moneymakers. I used to handle the girls.

Look out that window. See all that grass and wheat? Look at that big farm boy cutting it. Look at that burnt cracker on that tractor. He probably has a wife who married him because she didn't know what else to do. Back during wartime the girls in this part of the country knew what to do. They got on the trains at night.

You can look out that window all day and run around all the stations when we stop, but you'll never see a black man in any of these towns. You know why, youngblood? These farmers hate you. They still remember when their girls came out of these towns and got on the trains at night. They've been running black men and dark Indians out of these towns for years. They hate anything dark that's not that way because of the sun. Right now there are big farm girls with hair under their arms on the corners in San Francisco, Chicago, Seattle and Minneapolis who got started on these cars back during wartime. The farmers still remember that and they hate you and me for it. But it wasn't for me they got on. Nobody wants a stiff, smelly farm girl when there are sporting women to be got for a dollar in the cities. It was for the soldiers they got on. It was just business to me. But they hate you and me anyway.

I got off in one of these towns once, a long time after the war, just to get a drink while the train changed engines. Everybody looked at me and by the time I got to a bar there were ten people on my trail. I was drinking a fast one when the sheriff came in the bar.

'What are you doing here?' he asks me.

'Just getting a shot,' I say.

He spit on the floor. 'How long you plan to be here?'

'I don't know,' I say, just to be nasty.

'There ain't no jobs here,' he says.

'I wasn't looking,' I say.

'We don't want you here.'

'I don't give a good goddamn,' I say.

He pulled his gun on me. 'All right, coon, back on the train,' he says.

'Wait a minute,' I tell him. 'Let me finish my drink.'

He knocked my glass over with his gun. 'You're finished *now*,' he says. 'Pull you ass out of here *now*!'

I didn't argue.

I was the night man. After dinner it was my job to pull the cloths off the tables and put paddings on. Then I cut out the lights and locked both doors. There was a big farm girl from Minot named Hilda who could take on eight or ten soldiers in one night, white soldiers. These white boys don't know how to last. I would stand by the door and when the soldiers came back from the club car they would pay me and I would let them in. Some of the girls could make as much as one hundred dollars in one night. And I always made twice as much. Soldiers don't care what they do with their money. They just have to spend it.

We never bothered with the girls ourselves. It was just business as far as we were concerned. But there was one dummy we had with us once, a boy from the South named Willie Joe something who handled the dice. He was really hot for one of these farm girls. He used to buy her good whiskey and he hated to see her go in the car at night to wait for the soldiers. He was a real dummy. One time I heard her tell him: 'It's all right. They can have my body. I know I'm black inside. *Jesus*, I'm so black inside I wish I was black all over!'

And this dummy Willie Joe said: 'Baby, *don't you ever change!*'

I knew we had to get rid of him before he started trouble. So we had the steward bump him off the crew as soon as we could find a good man to handle the gambling. That old redneck Casper was glad to do it. He saw what was going on.

But you want to hear about Doc, you say, so you can get back to your reading. What can I tell you? The road got into his blood? He liked being a waiter? You won't understand this, but he did. There were no Civil Rights or marches or riots for something better in those days. In those days a man found something he liked to do and liked it from then on because he couldn't help himself. What did he like about the road? He liked what I liked: the money, owning the car, running it, telling the soldiers what to do, hustling a bigger tip from some old maid by looking under her dress and laughing at her, having all the girls at the Haverville Hotel waiting for us to come in for stopover, the power we had to beat them up or lay them if we wanted. He liked running free and not being married to some bitch who would spend his money when he was out of town or give it to some stud. He liked getting drunk with the boys up at Andy's, setting up the house and then passing out from drinking too much, knowing that the boys would get him home.

I ran with that one crew all during wartime and they, Doc, the Sheik and Reverend Hendricks, had taken me under their wings. I was still a youngblood then, and Doc liked me a lot. But he never said that much to me; he was not a talker. The Sheik had taught him the value of silence in things that really matter. We roomed together in Chicago at Mrs Wright's place in those days. Mrs Wright didn't allow women in the room and Doc liked that, because after being out for a week and after stopping over in those hotels along the way, you get tired of women and bullshit and need your privacy. We weren't like you. We didn't need a woman every time we got hard. We knew when we had to have it and when we didn't. And we didn't spend all our money on it, either. You youngbloods think the way to get a woman is to let her see how you handle your money. That's stupid. The way to get a woman is to let her see how you handle other women. But you'll never believe that until it's too late to do you any good.

Doc knew how to handle women. I can remember a time in a Winnipeg hotel how he ran a bitch out of his room because he had had enough of it and did not need her any more. I was in the next room and heard everything.

'Come on, Doc,' the bitch said. 'Come on honey, let's do it one more time.'

'Hell no,' Doc said. 'I'm tired and I don't want to any more.'

'How can you say you're tired?' the bitch said. 'How can you say you're tired when you didn't go but two times?'

'I'm tired of it,' Doc said, 'because I'm tired of you. And I'm tired of you because I'm tired of it and bitches like you in all the towns I been in. You drain a man. And I know if I beat you, you'll still come back when I hit you again. *That's* why I'm tired. I'm tired of having things around I don't care about.'

'What *do* you care about, Doc?' the bitch said.

'I don't know,' Doc said. 'I guess I care about moving and being somewhere else when I want to be. I guess I care about going out, and coming in to wait for the time to go out again.'

'You crazy, Doc,' the bitch said.

'Yeah?' Doc said. 'I guess I'm crazy all right.'

Later that bitch knocked on my door and I did it for her because she was just a bitch and I knew Doc wouldn't want her again. I don't think he ever wanted a bitch again. I never saw him with one after that time. He was just a little over fifty then and could have still done whatever he wanted with women.

The war ended. The farm boys who got back from the war did not spend money on their way home. They did not want to spend any more money on women, and the girls did not get on at night any more. Some of them went into the cities and turned pro. Some of them stayed in the towns and married the farm boys who got back from the war. Things changed on the road. The Commissary started putting that book of rules together and told us to stop stealing. They were losing money on passengers now because of the airplanes and they began to really tighten up and started sending inspectors down along the line to check on us. They started sending in spotters, too. One of them caught that redneck Casper writing out a check for two dollars less than he had charged the spotter. The Commissary got him in on the rug for it. I wasn't there, but they told me he said to the General Superintendent: 'Why are you getting on me, a white man, for a lousy son-of-a-bitching two bucks? There's niggers out there been stealing for *years!*'

'Who?' the General Superintendent asked.

And Casper couldn't say anything because he had that cardboard box full of money still under his bed and knew he would have to tell how he got it if any of us was brought in. So he said nothing.

'Who?' the General Superintendent asked him again.

'Why, all them nigger waiters steal, *everybody knows that!*'

'And the cooks, what about them?' the Superintendent said.

'They're white,' said Casper.

They never got the story out of him and he was fired. He used the money to open a restaurant someplace in Indiana and I heard later that he started a branch of the Klan in his town. One day he showed up at the station and told Doc, Reverend Hendricks and me: 'I'll see you boys gets *yours*. Damn if I'm takin' the rap for you niggers.'

We just laughed in his face because we knew he could do nothing to us through the Commissary. But just to be safe we stopped stealing so much. But they did get the Sheik, though. One day an inspector got on in the mountains just outside of Whitefish and grabbed him right out of that linen closet. The Sheik had been smoking in there all day and he was high and laughing when they pulled him off the train.

That was the year we got in the Union. The crackers and Swedes finally let us in after we paid off. We really stopped stealing and got organized and there wasn't a damn thing the company could do about it, although it tried like hell to buy us out. And to get back at us, they put their heads together and began to make up that big book of rules you keep your finger in. Still, *we* knew the service and they had to write the book the way we gave the service and at first there was nothing for the Old School men to learn. We got seniority through the Union, and as long as we gave the service and didn't steal, they couldn't touch us. So they began changing the rules, and sending us notes about the service. Little changes at first, like how the initials on the doily should always face the customer, and how the silver should be taken off the tables between meals. But we were getting old and set in our old service, and it got harder and harder learning all those little changes. And we had to learn new stuff all the time because there was no telling when an inspector would get on and catch us giving bad service. It was hard as hell. It was hard because we knew that the company was out to break up the Old School. The Sheik was gone, and we knew that Reverend Hendricks or Uncle T. or Danny Jackson would go soon because they stood for the Old School, just like the Sheik. But what bothered us most was knowing that they would go for Doc first, before anyone else, because he loved the road so much.

Doc was over sixty-five then and had taken to drinking hard when we were off. But he never touched a drop when we were on the road. I used to wonder whether he drank because being a Waiter's Waiter was getting hard or because he had to do something until his next trip. I could never figure it. When we had our layovers he would spend all his time in Andy's, setting up the house. He had no wife, no relatives, not even a hobby. He just drank. Pretty soon the slicksters at Andy's got to using him for a good thing. They commenced putting the touch on him because they saw he was getting old and knew he didn't have far to go, and they would never have to pay him back. Those of us who were close to him tried to pull his coat, but it didn't help. He didn't talk about himself much, he didn't talk much about anything that wasn't related to the road; but when I tried to hip him once about the hustlers and how they were closing in on him, he just took another shot and said: 'I don't need no money. Nobody's jiving me. I'm jiving them. You know I can still pull in a hundred in tips in one trip. I *know* this business.'

'Yeah, I know, Doc,' I said. 'But how many more trips can you make before you have to stop?'

'I ain't never gonna stop. Trips are all I know and I'll be making them as long as these trains haul people.'

'That's just it,' I said. 'They don't *want* to haul people any more. The planes do that. The big roads want freight now. Look how they hire youngbloods just for the busy seasons just so they won't get any seniority in the winter. Look how all the Old School waiters are dropping out. They got the Sheik, Percy Field just lucked up and died before they got to *him*, they almost got Reverend Hendricks. Even *Uncle T.* is going to retire! And they'll get us too.'

'Not me,' said Doc. 'I know my moves. This old fox can still dance with a tray and handle four tables at the same time. I can still bait a queer and make the old ladies tip big. There's no waiter better than me and I know it.'

'Sure, Doc,' I said. 'I know it too. But please save your money. Don't be a dummy. There'll come a day when you just can't get up to go out and they'll put you on the ground for good.'

Doc looked at me like he had been shot. 'Who taught you the moves when you were just a raggedy-ass waiter?'

'You did, Doc,' I said.

'Who's always the first man down in the yard at train-time?' He threw down another shot. 'Who's there sitting in the car every tenth morning while you other old heads are still at home pulling on your longjohns?'

I couldn't say anything. He was right and we both knew it.

'I have to go out,' he told me. 'Going out is my whole life, I wait for that tenth morning. I ain't never missed a trip and I don't mean to.'

What could I say to him, youngblood? What can I say to you? He had to go out, not for the money; it was in his blood. You have to go out too, but it's for the money you go. You hate going out and you love coming in. He loved going out and he hated coming in. Would *you* listen if I told you to stop spending your money on pussy in Chicago? Would he listen if I told him to save *his* money? To stop setting up the bar at Andy's? No. Old men are just as bad as young men when it comes to money. They can't think. They always try to buy what they should have for free. And what they buy, after they have it, is nothing.

They called Doc into the Commissary and the doctors told him he had lumbago and a bad heart and was weak from drinking to much, and they wanted him to get down for his own good. He wouldn't do it. Tesdale, the General Superintendent, called him in and told him that he had enough years in the service to pull down a big pension and that the company would pay for a retirement party for him, since he was the oldest waiter working, and invite all the Old School waiters to see him off, if he would come down. Doc said no. He knew that the Union had to back him. He knew that he could ride as long as he made the trains on time and as long as he knew the service. And he knew that he could not leave the road.

The company called in its lawyers to go over the Union contract. I wasn't there, but Len Dickey was in on the meeting because of his office in the Union. He told me about it later. Those fat company lawyers took the contract apart and went through all their books. They took the seniority clause apart word by word, trying to figure a way to get at Doc. But they had written it airtight back in the days when the company *needed* waiters, and there was nothing in it about compulsory retirement. Not a word. The paddies in the Union must have figured that waiters didn't *need* a new contract when they let us in, and they had let us come in under the old one thinking that all waiters would die on the job, or drink themselves to death when they were still young, or die from buying too much pussy, or just quit when they had put in enough time to draw a pension. But *nothing* in the whole contract could help them get rid of Doc Craft. They were sweating, they were working so hard. And all the time Tesdale, the General Superintendent, was calling them sons-of-bitches for not earning their money. But there was nothing the company lawyers could do but turn the pages of their big books and sweat and promise Tesdale that they would find some way if he gave them more time.

The word went out from the Commissary: 'Get Doc.' The stewards got it from the assistant superintendents: 'Get Doc.' Since they could not get him to retire, they were determined to catch him giving bad service. He had more seniority than most other waiters, so they couldn't bump him off our crew. In fact, all the waiters with more seniority than Doc were on the crew with him. There were four of us from the Old School: me, Doc, Uncle T. Boone, and Danny Jackson. Reverend Hendricks wasn't running regular any more; he was spending all his Sundays preaching in his church on the South Side because he knew what was coming and wanted to have something steady going for him in Chicago when his time came. Fifth and sixth men on that crew were two hardheads who had read the book. The steward was Crouse, and he really didn't want to put the screws to Doc but he couldn't help himself. Everybody wants to work. So Crouse started in to riding Doc, sometimes about moving too fast, sometimes about not moving fast enough. I was on the crew, I saw it all. Crouse would seat four singles at the same table, on Doc's station, and Doc had to take care of all four different orders at the same time. He was seventy-three, but that didn't stop him, knowing this business the way he did. It just slowed him down some. But Crouse got on him even for that and would chew him out in front of the passengers, hoping that he'd start cursing and bother the passengers so that they would complain to the company. It never worked, though. Doc just played it cool. He'd look into Crouse's eyes and know what was going on. And then he'd lay on his good service, the only service he knew, and the passengers would see how good he was with all that age on his back and they would get mad at the steward, and leave Doc a bigger tip when they left.

The Commissary sent out spotters to catch him giving bad service. These were pale-white little men in glasses who never looked you in the eye, but who always felt the plate to see if it was warm. And there were the old maids, who like that kind of work, who would order shrimp or crabmeat cocktails or celery and olive plates because they knew how the rules said these things had to be made. And when they came, when Doc brought them out, they would look to see if the oyster fork was stuck into the thing, and look out the window a long time.

'Ain't no use trying to fight it,' Uncle T. Boone told Doc in the crew car one night, 'the black waiter is *doomed*. Look at all the good restaurants, the class restaurants in Chicago. *You* can't work in them. Them white waiters got those jobs sewed up fine.'

'I can be a waiter anywhere,' says Doc. 'I know the business and I like it and I can do it anywhere.'

'The black waiter is doomed,' Uncle T. says again. 'The whites is taking over the service in the good places. And when they run you off of here, you won't have no place to go.'

'They won't run me off of here,' says Doc. 'As long as I give the right service they can't touch me.'

'You're a goddamn *fool*!' says Uncle T. 'You're a nigger and you ain't got no rights except what the Union says you have. And that ain't worth a damn because when the Commissary finally gets you, those niggers won't lift a finger to help you.'

'Leave off him,' I say to Boone. 'If anybody ought to be put off it's you. You ain't had your back straight for thirty years. You even make the crackers sick the way you keep bowing and folding your hands and saying, 'Thank you, Mr Boss.' Fifty years ago that would of got you a bigger tip,' I say, 'but now it ain't worth a shit. And every time you do it the crackers hate you. And every time I see you serving with that skullcap on *I* hate you. The Union said we didn't have to wear them *eighteen years ago*! Why can't you take it off!'

Boone just sat on his bunk with his skullcap in his lap, leaning against his big belly. He knew I was telling the truth and he knew he wouldn't change. But he said: 'That's the trouble with the Negro waiter today. He ain't got no humility. And as long as he don't have humility, he keeps losing the good jobs.'

Doc had climbed into the first waiter's bunk in his longjohns and I got in the second waiter's bunk under him and lay there. I could hear him breathing. It had a hard sound. He wasn't well and all of us knew it.'

'Doc?' I said in the dark.

'Yeah?'

'Don't mind Boone, Doc. He's a dead man. He just don't know it.'

'We all are,' Doc said.

'Not you,' I said.

'What's the use? He's right. They'll get me in the end.'

'But they ain't done it yet.'

'They'll get me. And they know it and I know it. I can even see it in old Crouse's eyes. He knows they're gonna get me.'

'Why don't you get a woman?'

He was quiet. 'What can I do with a woman now, that I ain't already done too much?'

I thought for a while. 'If you're on the ground, being with one might not make it so bad.'

'I hate women,' he said.

'You ever try fishing?'

'No.'

'You want to?'

'No,' he said.

'You can't keep *drinking*.'

He did not answer.

'Maybe you could work in town. In the Commissary.'

I could hear the big wheels rolling and clicking along the tracks and I knew by the smooth way we were moving that we were almost out of the Dakota flatlands. Doc wasn't talking. 'Would you like that?' I thought he was asleep. 'Doc, would you like that?'

'Hell, no,' he said.

'You have to try *something*!'

He was quiet again. 'I know,' he finally said.

3

Jerry Ewald, the Unexpected Inspector, got on in Winachee that next day after lunch and we knew that he had the word from the Commissary. He was cool about it: he laughed with the steward and the waiters about the old days and his hard gray eyes and shining glasses kept looking over our faces as if to see if we knew why he had got on. The two hardheads were in the crew car stealing a nap on company time. Jerry noticed this and could have caught them, but he was after bigger game. We all knew that, and we kept talking to him about the days of the big trains and looking at his white hair and not into the eyes behind his glasses because we knew what was there. Jerry sat down on the first waiter's station and said to Crouse: 'Now I'll have some lunch. Steward, let the headwaiter bring me a menu.'

Crouse stood next to the table where Jerry sat, and looked at Doc, who had been waiting between the tables with his tray under his arm. The way the rules say. Crouse looked sad because he knew what was coming. Then Jerry looked directly at Doc and said: 'Headwaiter Doctor Craft, bring me a menu.'

Doc said nothing and he did not smile. He brought the menu. Danny Jackson and I moved back into the hall to watch. There was nothing we could do to help Doc and we knew it. He was the Waiter's Waiter, out there by himself, hustling the biggest tip he would ever get in his life. Or losing it.

'Goddamn,' Danny said to me, 'Now let's sit on the ground and talk about how *kings* are gonna get fucked.'

'Maybe not,' I said. But I did not believe it myself because Jerry is the kind of man who lies in bed all night, scheming. I knew he had a plan.

Doc passed us on his way to the kitchen for water and I wanted to say something to him. But what was the use? He brought the water to Jerry. Jerry looked him in the eye. 'Now, Headwaiter,' he said. 'I'll have a bowl of onion soup, a cold roast beef sandwich on white, rare, and a glass of iced tea.'

'Write it down,' said Doc. He was playing it right. He knew that the new rules had stopped waiters from taking verbal orders.

'Don't be so professional, Doc,' Jerry said. 'It's me, one of the *boys*.'

'You have to write it out,' said Doc, 'it's in the black book.'

Jerry clicked his pen and wrote the order out on the check. And handed it to Doc. Uncle T. followed Doc back into the Pantry.

'He's gonna get you, Doc,' Uncle T. said. 'I knew it all along. You know why? The Negro waiter ain't got no more humility.'

'Shut the fuck up, Boone!' I told him.

'You'll see,' Boone went on. 'You'll see I'm right. There ain't a thing Doc can do about it, either. We're gonna lose all the good jobs.'

We watched Jerry at the table. He saw us watching and smiled with his gray eyes. Then he poured some of the water from the glass on the linen cloth and picked up the silver sugar bowl and placed it right on the wet spot. Doc was still in the Pantry. Jerry turned the silver sugar bowl around and around on the linen. He pressed down on it some as he turned. But when he picked it up again, there was no dark ring on the wet cloth. We had polished the silver early that morning, according to the book, and there was not a dirty piece of silver to be found in the whole car. Jerry was drinking the rest of the water when Doc brought out the polished silver soup tureen, underlined with a doily and a breakfast plate, with a shining soup bowl underlined with a doily and a breakfast plate, and a bread-and-butter plate with six crackers; not four or five or seven, but six, the number the commissary had written in the black book. He swung down the aisle of the car between the two rows of white tables and you could not help but be proud of the way he moved with the roll of the train and the way that tray was like a part of his arm. It was good service. He placed everything neat, with all company initials showing, right where things should go.

'Shall I serve up the soup?' he asked Jerry.

'Please,' said Jerry.

Doc handled that silver soup ladle like one of those Chicago Jew tailors handles a needle. He ladled up three good-sized spoonfuls from the tureen and then laid the wet spoon on an extra bread-and-butter plate on the side of the table, so he would not stain the cloth. Then he put a napkin over the wet spot Jerry had made and changed the ashtray for a prayer-card because every good waiter knows that nobody wants to eat a good meal looking at an ashtray.

'You know about the spoon plate, I see,' Jerry said to Doc.

'I'm a waiter,' said Doc. 'I know.'

'You're a damn good waiter,' said Jerry.

Doc looked Jerry square in the eye. 'I know,' he said slowly.

Jerry ate a little of the soup and opened all six of the cracker packages. Then he stopped eating and began to look out the window. We were passing through his territory, Washington State, the country he loved because he was the only company inspector in the state and knew that once we got through Montana he would be the only man the waiters feared. He smiled and then waved for Doc to bring out the roast beef sandwich.

But Doc was into his service now and cleared the table completely. Then he got the silver crumb knife from the Pantry and gathered all the cracker crumbs, even the ones Jerry had managed to get in between the salt and pepper shakers.

'You want the tea with your sandwich, or later?' he asked Jerry.

'Now is fine,' said Jerry, smiling.

'You're going good,' I said to Doc when he passed us on his way to the Pantry. 'He can't touch you or nothing.'

He did not say anything.

Uncle T. Boone looked at Doc like he wanted to say something too, but he just frowned and shuffled out to stand next to Jerry. You could see that Jerry hated him. But Jerry knew how to smile at everybody, and so he smiled at Uncle T. while Uncle T. bent over the table with his hands together like he was praying, and moved his head up and bowed it down.

Doc brought out the roast beef, proper service. The crock of mustard was on a breakfast plate, underlined with a doily, initials facing Jerry. The lid was on the mustard and it was clean, like it says in the book, and the little silver service spoon was clean and polished on a bread-and-butter plate. He set it down. And then he served the tea. You think you know the service, youngblood, all of you do. But you don't. Anybody can serve, but not everybody can become a part of the service. When Doc poured that pot of hot tea into that glass of crushed ice, it was like he was pouring it through his own fingers; it was like he and the tray and the pot and the glass and all of it was the same body. It was a beautiful move. It was fine service. The iced tea glass sat in a shell dish, and the iced tea spoon lay straight in front of Jerry. The lemon wedge Doc put in a shell dish half-full of crushed ice with an oyster fork stuck into its skin. Not in the meat, mind you, but squarely under the skin of that lemon, and the whole thing lay in a pretty curve on top of that crushed ice.

Doc stood back and waited. Jerry had been watching his service and was impressed. He mixed the sugar in his glass and sipped. Danny Jackson and I were down the aisle in the hall. Uncle T. stood behind Jerry, bending over, his arms folded, waiting. And Doc stood next to the table, his tray under his arm looking straight ahead and

345

calm because he had given good service and knew it. Jerry sipped again.

'Good tea,' he said. 'Very good tea.'

Doc was silent.

Jerry took the lemon wedge off the oyster fork and squeezed it into the glass, and stirred, and sipped again. '*Very* good,' he said. Then he drained the glass. Doc reached over to pick it up for more ice but Jerry kept his hand on the glass. 'Very good service, Doc,' he said. 'But you served the lemon wrong.'

Everybody was quiet. Uncle T. folded his hands in the praying position.

'How's that?' said Doc.

'The service was wrong,' Jerry said. He was not smiling now.

'How could it be? I been giving that same service for years, right down to the crushed ice for the lemon wedge.'

'That's just it, Doc,' Jerry said. 'The lemon wedge. You served it wrong.'

'Yeah?' said Doc.

'Yes,' said Jerry, his jaws tight. 'Haven't you seen the new rule?'

Doc's face went loose. He knew now that they had got him.

'Haven't you *seen* it?' Jerry asked again.

Doc shook his head.

Jerry smiled that hard, gray smile of his, the kind of smile that says: 'I have always been the boss and I am smiling this way because I know it and can afford to give you something.' 'Steward Crouse,' he said. 'Steward Crouse, go get the black bible for the headwaiter.'

Crouse looked beaten too. He was sixty-three and waiting for his pension. He got the bible.

Jerry took it and turned directly to the very last page. He knew where to look. 'Now, Headwaiter,' he said, '*listen* to this.' And he read aloud: 'Memorandum Number 22416. From: Douglas A. Tesdale, General Superintendent of Dining Cars. To: Waiters, Stewards, Chefs of Dining Cars. Attention: As of 7/9/65 the proper service for iced tea will be (a) Fresh brewed tea in a teapot, poured over crushed ice at table; iced tea glass set in shell dish (b) Additional ice to be immediately available upon request after first glass of tea (c) Fresh lemon wedge will be served on bread-and-butter plate, no doily, with tines of oyster fork stuck into *meat* of lemon.' Jerry paused.

'Now you know, Headwaiter,' he said.

'Yeah,' said Doc.
'But why didn't you know before?'
No answer.
'This notice came out last week.'
'I didn't check the book yet,' said Doc.
'But that's a rule. Always check the book before each trip. *You* know that, Headwaiter.'
'Yeah,' said Doc.
'Then that's *two* rules you missed.'
Doc was quiet.
'Two rules you didn't read,' Jerry said. 'You're slowing down, Doc.'
'I know,' Doc mumbled.
'You want some time off to rest?'
Again Doc said nothing.
'I think you need some time on the ground to rest up, don't you?'
Doc put his tray on the table and sat down in the seat across from Jerry. This was the first time we had ever seen a waiter sit down with a customer, even an inspector. Uncle. T., behind Jerry's back, began waving his hands, trying to tell Doc to get up. Doc did not look at him.
'You *are* tired, aren't you?' said Jerry.
'I'm just resting my feet,' Doc said.
'Get up, Headwaiter,' Jerry said. 'You'll have plenty of time to do that. I'm writing you up.'
But Doc did not move and just continued there. And all Danny and I could do was watch him from the back of the car. For the first time I saw that his hair was almost gone and his legs were skinny in the baggy white uniform. I don't think Jerry expected Doc to move. I don't think he really cared. But then Uncle. T. moved around the table and stood next to Doc, trying to apologize for him to Jerry with his eyes and bowed head. Doc looked at Uncle T. and then got up and went back to the crew car. He left his tray on the table. It stayed there all that evening because none of us, not even Crouse or Jerry or Uncle T., would touch it. And Jerry didn't try to make any of us take it back to the Pantry. He understood at least that much. The steward closed down Doc's tables during dinner service, all three settings of it. And Jerry got off the train someplace along the way, quiet, like he had got on.
After closing down the car we went back to the crew quarters and

Doc was lying on his bunk with his hands behind his head and his eyes open. He looked old. No one knew what to say until Boone went over to his bunk and said: 'I feel bad for you, Doc, but all of us are gonna get it in the end. The railroad waiter is *doomed*.'

Doc did not even notice Boone.

'I could of told you about the lemon but he would of got you on something else. It wasn't no use. Any of it.'

'Shut the fuck up, Boone!' Danny said. 'The one thing that really hurts is that a crawling son-of-a-bitch like you will be riding when all the good men are gone. Dummies like you and these two hardheads will be working your asses off reading that damn bible and never know a goddamn thing about being a waiter. *That* hurts like a *motherfucker!*'

'It ain't my fault if the colored waiter is doomed,' said Boone. 'It's your fault for letting go your humility and letting the whites take over the good jobs.'

Danny grabbed the skullcap off Boone's head and took it into the bathroom and flushed it down the toilet. In a minute it was half a mile away and soaked in old piss on the tracks. Boone did not try to fight, he just sat on his bunk and mumbled. He had other skullcaps. No one said anything to Doc, because that's the way real men show that they care. You don't talk. Talking makes it worse.

4

What else is there to tell you, youngblood? They made him retire. He didn't try to fight it. He was beaten and he knew it; not by the service, but by a book. *That book*, that *bible* you keep your finger stuck in. That's not a good way for a man to go. He should die in service. He should die doing the things he likes. But not by a book.

All of us Old School men will be beaten by it. Danny Jackson is gone now, and Reverend Hendricks put in for his pension and took up preaching, full-time. But Uncle T. Boone is still riding. They'll get *me* soon enough, with that book. But it will never get you because you'll never be a waiter, or at least a Waiter's Waiter. You read too much.

Doc got a good pension and he took it directly to Andy's. And none of the boys who knew about it knew how to refuse a drink on Doc. But none of us knew how to drink with him knowing that we would be going out again in a few days, and he was on the ground.

So a lot of us, even the drunks and hustlers who usually hang around Andy's, avoided him whenever we could. There was nothing to talk about any more.

He died five months after he was put on the ground. He was seventy-three and it was winter. He froze to death wandering around the Chicago yards early one morning. He had been drunk, and was still steaming when the yard crew found him. Only the few of us left in the Old School know what he was doing there.

I am sixty-three now. And I haven't decided if I should take my pension when they ask me to go or continue to ride. I *want* to keep riding, but I know that if I do, Jerry Ewald or Harry Silk or Jack Tate will get me one of these days. I could get down if I wanted: I have a hobby and I am too old to get drunk by myself. I couldn't drink with you, youngblood. We have nothing to talk about. And after a while you would get mad at me for talking anyway, and keeping you from your pussy. You are tired already. I can see it in your eyes and in the way you play with the pages of your rule book.

I know it. And I wonder why I should keep talking to you when you could never see what I see or understand what I understand or know the real difference between my school and yours. I wonder why I have kept talking this long when all the time I have seen that you can hardly wait to hit the city to get off this thing and spend your money. You have a good story. But you will never remember it. Because all this time you have had pussy in your mind, and your fingers in the pages of that black bible.

1968

THE BABYSITTER

Robert Coover

She arrives at 7.40, ten minutes late, but the children, Jimmy and Bitsy, are still eating supper, and their parents are not ready to go yet. From other rooms come the sound of a baby screaming, water running, a television musical (no words: probably a dance number— patterns of gliding figures come to mind). Mrs Tucker sweeps into the kitchen, fussing with her hair, and snatches a baby bottle full of milk out of a pan of warm water, rushes out again. 'Harry!' she calls. 'The babysitter's here already!'

* * *

That's My Desire? I'll Be Around? He smiles toothily, beckons faintly with his head, rubs his fast balding pate. Bewitched, maybe? Or, What's the Reason? He pulls on his shorts, gives his hips a slap. The baby goes silent in mid-scream. Isn't this the one who used their tub last time? Who's Sorry Now, that's it.

* * *

Jack is wandering around town, not knowing what to do. His girlfriend is babysitting at the Tuckers', and later, when she's got the kids in bed, maybe he'll drop over there. Sometimes he watches TV with her when she's babysitting, it's about the only chance he gets to make out a little since he doesn't own wheels, but they have to be careful because most people don't like their sitters to have boyfriends over. Just kissing her makes her nervous. She won't close her eyes because she has to be watching the door all the time. Married people really have it good, he thinks.

* * *

'Hi,' the babysitter says to the children, and puts her books on top of the refrigerator. 'What's for supper?' The little girl, Bitsy, only stares at her obliquely. She joins them at the end of the kitchen table. 'I don't have to go to bed until nine,' the boy announces flatly, and stuffs his mouth full of potato chips. The babysitter catches a glimpse of Mr Tucker hurrying out of the bathroom in his underwear.

350

* * *

Her tummy. Under her arms. And her feet. Those are the best places. She'll spank him, she says sometimes. Let her.

* * *

That sweet odor that girls have. The softness of her blouse. He catches a glimpse of the gentle shadows amid her thighs, as she curls her legs up under her. He stares hard at her. He has a lot of meaning packed into that stare, but she's not even looking. She's popping her gum and watching television. She's sitting right there, inches away, soft, fragrant, and ready: but what's his next move? He notices his buddy Mark in the drugstore, playing the pinball machine, and joins him. 'Hey, this mama's cold, Jack baby! She needs your touch!'

* * *

Mrs Tucker appears at the kitchen doorway, holding a rolled-up diaper. 'Now, don't just eat potato chips, Jimmy! See that he eats his hamburger, dear.' She hurried away to the bathroom. The boy glares sullenly at the babysitter, silently daring her to carry out the order. 'How about a little of that good hamburger now, Jimmy?' she says perfunctorily. He lets half of it drop to the floor. The baby is silent and a man is singing a love song on the TV. The children crunch chips.

* * *

He loves her. She loves him. They whirl airily, stirring a light breeze, through a magical landscape of rose and emerald and deep blue. Her light brown hair coils and wisps softly in the breeze, and the soft folds of her white gown tug at her body and then float away. He smiles in a pulsing crescendo of sincerity and song.

* * *

'You mean she's alone?' Mark asks. 'Well, there's two or three kids,' Jack says. He slides the coin in. There's a rumble of steel balls tumbling, lining up. He pushes a plunger with his thumb, and one ball pops up in place, hard and glittering with promise. His stare? to say he loves her. That he cares for her and would protect her, would shield her, if need be, with his own body. Grinning, he bends over the ball to take careful aim: he and Mark have studied this machine and have it figured out, but still it's not that easy to beat.

* * *

On the drive to the party, his mind is partly on the girl, partly on his

351

own high-school days, long past. Sitting at the end of the kitchen table there with his children, she had seemed to be self-consciously arching her back, jutting her pert breasts, twitching her thighs: and for whom if not for him? So she'd seen him coming out of there, after all. He smiles. Yet what could he ever do about it? Those good times are gone, old man. He glances over at his wife, who, readjusting a garter, asks: 'What do you think of our babysitter?'

* * *

He loves her. She loves him. And then the babies come. And dirty diapers and one goddamn meal after another. Dishes. Noise. Clutter. And fat. Not just tight, her girdle actually hurts. Somewhere recently she's read about women getting heart attacks or cancer or something from too-tight girdles. Dolly pulls the car door shut with a grunt, strangely irritated, not knowing why. Party mood. Why is her husband humming, 'Who's Sorry Now?' Pulling out of the drive, she glances back at the lighted kitchen window. 'What do you think of our babysitter?' she asks. While her husband stumbles all over himself trying to answer, she pulls a stocking tight, biting deeper with the garters.

* * *

'Stop it!' she laughs. Bitsy is pulling on her skirt and he is tickling her in the ribs. 'Jimmy! Don't!' But she is laughing too much to stop him. He leaps on her, wrapping his legs around her waist, and they all fall to the carpet in front of the TV, where just now a man in a tuxedo and a little girl in a flouncy white dress are doing a tapdance together. The babysitter's blouse is pulling out of her skirt, showing a patch of bare tummy: the target. 'I'll spank!'

* * *

Jack pushes the plunger, thrusting up a steel ball, and bends studiously over the machine. 'You getting any off her?' Mark asks, and clears his throat, flicks ash from his cigarette. 'Well, not exactly, not yet,' Jack says, grinning awkwardly, but trying to suggest more than he admits to, and fires. He heaves his weight gently against the machine as the ball bounds off a rubber bumper. He can feel her warming up under his hands, the flippers suddenly coming alive, delicate rapid-fire patterns emerging in the flashing of the lights. 1000 WHEN LIT: *now!* 'Got my hand on it, that's about all.' Mark glances up from the machine, cigarette dangling from his lip. 'Maybe you need some help,' he suggests with a wry one-sided grin. 'Like maybe together, man, we could do it.'

* * *

She likes the big tub. She uses the Tucker's bath salts, and loves to sink into the hot fragrant suds. She can stretch out, submerged, up to her chin. It gives her a good sleepy tingly feeling.

* * *

'What do you think of our babysitter?' Dolly asks, adjusting a garter. 'Oh, I hardly noticed,' he says 'Cute girl. She seems to get along fine with the kids. Why?' 'I don't know.' His wife tugs her skirt down, glances at a lighted window they are passing, adding: 'I'm not sure I trust her completely, that's all. With the baby, I mean. She seems a little careless. And the other time, I'm almost sure she had a boyfriend over.' He grins, claps one hand on his wife's broad gartered thigh. 'What's wrong with that?' he asks. Still in anklets, too. Bare thighs, no girdles, nothing up there but a flimsy pair of panties and soft adolescent flesh. He's flooded with vague remembrances of football rallies and movie balconies.

* * *

How tiny and rubbery it is! she thinks, soaping between the boy's legs, giving him his bath. Just a funny jiggly little thing that looks like it shouldn't even be there at all. Is that what all the songs are about?

* * *

Jack watches Mark lunge and twist against the machine. Got her running now, racked them up. He's not too excited about the idea of Mark fooling around with his girlfriend, but Mark's a cooler operator than he is, and maybe, doing it together this once, he'd get over his own timidity. And if she didn't like it, there were other girls around. If Mark went too far, he could cut him off too. He feels his shoulders tense: enough's enough, man . . . but sees the flesh, too. 'Maybe I'll call her later,' he says.

* * *

'Hey, Harry! Dolly! Glad you could make it!' 'I hope we're not late.' 'No, no, you're one of the first, come on in! By golly, Dolly, you're looking younger every day! How do you do it? Give my wife your secret, will you?' He pats her on her girdled bottom behind Mr Tucker's back, leads them in for drinks.

* * *

8.00 The babysitter runs water in the tub, combs her hair in front of the bathroom mirror. There's a western on television, so she lets Jimmy watch it while she gives Bitsy her bath. But Bitsy doesn't want a bath. She's angry and crying because she has to be first. The babysitter tells her if she'll take her bath quickly, she'll let her watch television while Jimmy takes his bath, but it does no good. The little girl fights to get out of the bathroom, and the babysitter has to squat with her back against the door and forcibly undress the child. There are better places to babysit. Both children mind badly, and then, sooner or later, the baby is sure to wake up for a diaper change and more bottle. The Tuckers do have a good color TV, though, and she hopes things will be settled down enough to catch the 8.30 program. She thrusts the child into the tub, but she's still screaming and thrashing around. 'Stop it now, Bitsy, or you'll wake the baby!' 'I have to go potty!' the child wails, switching tactics. The babysitter sighs, lifts the girl out of the tub and onto the toilet, getting her skirt and blouse all wet in the process. She glances at herself in the mirror. Before she knows it, the girl is off the seat and out of the bathroom. 'Bitsy! Come back here!'

* * *

'OK, that's enough!' Her skirt is ripped and she's flushed and crying. 'Who says?' 'I do, man!' The bastard goes for her, but she tackles him. They roll and tumble. Tables tip, lights topple, the TV crashes to the floor. He slams a hard right to the guy's gut, clips his chin with a rolling left.

* * *

'We hope it's a girl.' That's hardly surprising, since they already have four boys. Dolly congratulates the woman like everybody else, but she doesn't envy her, not a bit. That's all she needs about now. She stares across the room at Harry, who is slapping backs and getting loud, as usual. He's spreading out through the middle, so why the hell does he have to complain about her all the time? 'Dolly, you're looking younger every day!' was the nice greeting she got tonight. 'What's your secret?' And Harry: 'It's all those calories. She's getting back her baby fat.' 'Haw haw! Harry, have a heart!'

* * *

'Get her feet!' he hollers at Bitsy, his fingers in her ribs, running over her naked tummy, tangling in the underbrush of straps and strange clothing. 'Get her shoes off!' He holds her pinned by pressing his head against her soft chest. 'No! No, Jimmy! Bitsy, stop!' But though she kicks and twists and rolls around, she doesn't get up, she can't get up, she's laughing too hard, and the shoes come off, and he grabs a stockinged foot and scratches the sole ruthlessly, and she raises up her legs, trying to pitch him off, she's wild, boy, but he hangs on, and she's laughing, and on the screen there's a rattle of hooves, and he and Bitsy are rolling around and around on the floor in a crazy rodeo of long bucking legs.

* * *

He slips the coin in. There's a metallic fall and a sharp click as the dial tone begins. 'I hope the Tuckers have gone,' he says. 'Don't worry, they're at our place,' Mark says. 'They're always the first ones to come and last ones to go home. My old man's always bitching about them.' Jack laughs nervously and dials the number. 'Tell her we're coming over to protect her from getting raped,' Mark suggests, and lights a cigarette. Jack grins, leaning casually against the door jamb of the phonebooth, chewing gum, one hand in his pocket. He's really pretty uneasy, though. He has the feeling he's somehow messing up a good thing.

* * *

Bitsy runs naked into the livingroom, keeping a hassock between herself and the babysitter. 'Bitsy . . . !' the babysitter threatens. Artificial reds and greens and purples flicker over the child's wet body, as hooves clatter, guns crackle, and stagecoach wheels thunder over rutted terrain. 'Get outa the way, Bitsy!' the boy complains. 'I can't see!' Bitsy streaks past and the babysitter chases, cornering the girl in the back bedroom. Bitsy throws something that hits her softly in the face: a pair of men's undershorts. She grabs the girl scampering by, carries her struggling to the bathroom, and with a smart crack on her glistening bottom, pops her back into the tub. In spite, Bitsy peepees in the bathwater.

* * *

Mr Tucker stirs a little water into his bourbon and kids with his host and another man, just arrived, about their golf games. They set up a match for the weekend, a threesome looking for a fourth. Holding his drink in his right hand, Mr Tucker swings his left through the motion of a tee-shot. 'You'll have to give me a stroke a hole,' he says. 'I'll give you a stroke!' says his host: 'Bend over!' Laughing, the other man asks: 'Where's your boy Mark tonight?' 'I don't know,' replies the host, gathering up a trayful of drinks. Then he adds in a low growl: 'Out chasing tail probably.' They chuckle loosely at that, then shrug in commiseration and return to the livingroom to join their women.

* * *

Shades pulled. Door locked. Watching the TV. Under a blanket maybe. Yes, that's right, under a blanket. Her eyes close when he kisses her. Her breasts, under both their hands, are soft and yielding.

* * *

A hard blow to the belly. The face. The dark beardy one staggers, the lean-jawed sheriff moves in, but gets a spurred boot in his face. The dark one hurls himself forward, drives his shoulder into the sheriff's hard midriff, her own tummy tightens, withstands, as the sheriff smashes the dark man's nose, slams him up against a wall, slugs him again! and again! The dark man grunts rhythmically, backs off, then plunges suicidally forward—her own knees draw up protectively— the sheriff staggers! caught low! but instead of following through, the other man steps back—a pistol! the dark one has a pistol! the sheriff draws! shoots from the hip! explosions! she clutches her hands between her thighs—no! the sheriff spins! wounded! the dark man hesitates, aims, her legs stiffen toward the set, the sheriff rolls desperately in the straw, fires: dead! the dark man is dead! groans, crumples, his pistol drooping in his collapsing hand, dropping, he drops. The sheriff, spent, nicked, watches weakly from the floor where he lies. Oh, to be whole! to be good and strong and right! to embrace and be embraced by harmony and wholeness! The sheriff, drawing himself painfully up on one elbow, rubs his bruised mouth with the back of his other hand.

* * *

'Well, we just sorta thought we'd drop over,' he says, and winks broadly at Mark. 'Who's we?' 'Oh, me and Mark here.' 'Tell her, good thing like her, gotta pass it around,' whispers Mark, dragging on his smoke, then flicking the butt over under the pinball machine. 'What's that?' she asks. 'Oh, Mark and I were just saying, like, two's company, three's an orgy,' Jack says and winks again. She giggles. 'Oh Jack!' Behind her, he can hear shouts and gunfire. 'Well, OK, for just a little while, if you'll both be good.' Way to go, man.

* * *

Probably some damn kid over there right now. Wrestling around on the couch in front of his TV. Maybe he should drop back to the house. Just to check. None of that stuff, she was there to do a job! Park the car a couple doors down, slip in the front door before she knows it. He sees the disarray of clothing, the young thighs exposed to the flickering television light, hears his baby crying. 'Hey, what's going on here! Get outa here, son, before I call the police!' Of course, they haven't really been doing anything. They probably don't even know how. He stares benignly down upon the girl, her skirt rumpled loosely around her thighs. Flushed, frightened, yet excited, she stares back at him. He smiles. His finger touches a knee, approaches the hem. Another couple arrives. Filling up here with people. He wouldn't be missed. Just slip out, stop back casually to pick up something or other he forgot, never mind what. He remembers that the other time they had this babysitter, she took a bath in their house. She had a date afterwards, and she'd come from cheerleading practice or something. Aspirin maybe. Just drop quietly and casually into the bathroom to pick up some aspirin. 'Oh, excuse me, dear! I only . . . !' She gazes back at him, astonished, yet strangely moved. Her soft wet breasts rise and fall in the water, and her tummy looks pale and ripply. He recalls that her pubic hairs, left in the tub, were brown. Light brown.

* * *

She's no more than stepped into the tub for a quick bath, when Jimmy announces from outside the door that he has to go to the bathroom. She sighs: just an excuse, she knows. 'You'll have to wait.' The little nuisance. 'I can't wait.' 'OK, then come ahead, but I'm taking a bath.' She supposes that will stop him, but it doesn't. In he comes. She slides down into the suds until she's eye-level with the edge of the tub. He hesitates. 'Go ahead, if you have to,' she says, a little awkwardly, 'but I'm not getting out.' 'Don't look,' he says. She: 'I will if I want to.'

* * *

She's crying. Mark is rubbing his jaw where he's just slugged him. A lamp lies shattered. 'Enough's enough, Mark! Now get outa here!' Her skirt is ripped to the waist, her bare hip bruised. Her panties lie on the floor like a broken balloon. Later, he'll wash her wounds, help her dress, he'll take care of her. Pity washes through him, giving him a sudden hard-on. Mark laughs at it, pointing. Jack crouches, waiting, ready for anything.

357

* * *

Laughing, they roll and tumble. Their little hands are all over her, digging and pinching. She struggles to her hands and knees, but Bitsy leaps astride her neck, bowing her head to the carpet. 'Spank her, Jimmy!' His swats sting: is her skirt up? The phone rings. 'The cavalry to the rescue!' she laughs, and throws them off to go answer.

* * *

Kissing Mark, her eyes closed, her hips nudge toward Jack. He stares at the TV screen, unsure of himself, one hand slipping cautious under her skirt. Her hand touches his arm as though to resist, then brushes on by to rub his leg. This blanket they're under was a good idea. 'Hi! This is Jack!'

* * *

Bitsy's out and the water's running. 'Come on, Jimmy, your turn!' Last time, he told her he took his own baths, but she came in anyway. 'I'm not gonna take a bath,' he announces, eyes glued on the set. He readies for the struggle. 'But I've already run your water. Come on, Jimmy, please!' He shakes his head. She can't make him, he's sure he's as strong as she is. She sighs. 'Well, it's up to you. I'll use the water myself then,' she says. He waits until he's pretty sure she's not going to change her mind, then sneaks in and peeks through the keyhole in the bathroom door: just in time to see her big bottom as she bends over to stir in the bubblebath. Then she disappears. Trying to see as far down as the keyhole will allow, he bumps his head on the knob. 'Jimmy, is that you?' 'I—I have to go to the bathroom!' he stammers.

* * *

Not actually in the tub, just getting in. One foot on the mat, the other in the water. Bent over slightly, buttocks flexed, teats swaying, holding on to the edge of the tub. 'Oh, excuse me! I only wanted . . . !' He passes over her astonishment, the awkward excuses, moves quickly to the part where he reaches out to—'What on earth are you doing, Harry?' his wife asks, staring at his hand. His host, passing, laughs. 'He's practising his swing for Sunday, Dolly, but it's not going to do him a damn bit of good!' Mr Tucker laughs, sweeps his right hand on through the air as though lifting a seven-iron shot onto the green. He makes a *dok*! sound with his tongue. 'In there!'

* * *

'No, Jack, I don't think you'd better.' 'Well, we just called, we just, uh, thought we'd, you know, stop by for a minute, watch television for thirty minutes, or, or something.' 'Who's we?' 'Well, Mark's here, I'm with him, and he said he'd like to, you know, like if it's all right, just—' 'Well, it's *not* all right. The Tuckers said no.' 'Yeah, but if we only—' 'And they seemed awfully suspicious about last time.' 'Why? We didn't—I mean, I just thought—' 'No, Jack, and that's period.' She hangs up. She returns to the TV, but the commercial is on. Anyway, she's missed most of the show. She decides maybe she'll take a quick bath. Jack might come by anyway, it'd make her mad, that'd be the end as far as he was concerned, but if he should, she doesn't want to be all sweaty. And besides, she likes the big tub the Tuckers have.

* * *

He is self-conscious and stands with his back to her, his little neck flushed. It takes him forever to get started, and when it finally does come, it's just a tiny trickle. 'See, it was just an excuse,' she scolds, but she's giggling inwardly at the boy's embarrassment. 'You're just a nuisance, Jimmy.' At the door, his hand on the knob, he hesitates, staring timidly down on his shoes. 'Jimmy?' She peeks at him over the edge of the tub, trying to keep a straight face, as he sneaks a nervous glance back over his shoulder 'As long as you bothered me,' she says, 'you might as well soap my back.'

* * *

'The aspirin . . . ' They embrace. She huddles in his arms like a child. Lovingly, paternally, knowledgeably, he wraps her nakedness. How compact, how tight and small her body is! Kissing her ear, he stares down past her rump at the still clear water. 'I'll join you,' he whispers hoarsely.

* * *

She picks up the shorts Bitsy threw at her. Men's underwear. She holds them in front of her, looks at herself in the bedroom mirror. About twenty sizes too big for her, of course. She runs her hand inside the opening in front, pulls out her thumb. How funny it must feel!

* * *

'Well, man, I say we just go rape her,' Mark says flatly, and swings his weight against the pinball machine. 'Uff! Ahh! Get in there, you mother! Look at that! Hah! Man, I'm gonna turn this baby over!' Jack is embarrassed about the phone conversation. Mark just snorted in disgust when he hung up. He cracks down hard on his gum, angry that he's such a chicken. 'Well, I'm game if you are,' he says coldly.

* * *

8.30. 'OK, come on, Jimmy, it's time.' He ignores her. The western gives way to a spy show. Bitsy, in pajamas, pads into the livingroom. 'No, Bitsy, it's time to go to bed.' 'You said I could watch!' the girl whines, and starts to throw another tantrum. 'But you were too slow and it's late. Jimmy, you get in that bathroom, and right now! Jimmy stares sullenly at the set, unmoving. The babysitter tries to catch the opening scene of the television program so she can follow it later, since Jimmy gives himself his own baths. When the commercial interrupts she turns off the sound, stands in front of the screen. 'OK, into the tub, Jimmy Tucker, or I'll take you in there and give you your bath myself!' 'Just try it,' he says, 'and see what happens.'

* * *

They stand outside, in the dark, crouched in the bushes, peeking in. She's on the floor, playing with the kids. Too early. They seem to be tickling her. She gets to her hands and knees, but the little girl leaps on her head, pressing her face to the floor. There's an obvious target, and the little boy proceeds to beat on it. 'Hey, look at that kid go!' whispers Mark, laughing and snapping his fingers softly. Jack feels uneasy out here. Too many neighbors, too many cars going by, too many people in the world. That little boy in there is one up on him, though: he's never thought about tickling her as a starter.

* * *

His little hand, clutching the bar of soap, lathers shyly a narrow space between her shoulderblades. She is doubled forward against her knees, buried in rich suds, peeking at him over the edge of her shoulder. The soap slithers out of his grip and plunks into the water. 'I . . . I dropped the soap,' he whispers. She: 'Find it.'

* * *

'I dream of Jeannie with the light brown pubic hair!' 'Harry! Stop that! You're drunk!' But they're laughing, they're all laughing, damn! he's feeling pretty goddamn good at that, and now he just knows he needs that aspirin. Watching her there, her thighs spread for him, on the couch, in the tub, hell, on the kitchen table for that matter, he tees off on Number Nine, and—*whap*!—swats his host's wife on the bottom. 'Hole in one!' he shouts. 'Harry!' Why can't his goddamn wife Dolly ever get happy-drunk instead of sour-drunk all the time? 'Gonna be tough Sunday, old buddy!' 'You're pretty tough right now, Harry,' says his host.

* * *

The babysitter lunges forward, grabs the boy by the arms and hauls him off the couch, pulling two cushions with him, and drags him toward the bathroom. He lashes out, knocking over an endtable full of magazines and ashtrays. 'You leave my brother alone!' Bitsy cries and grabs the sitter around the waist. Jimmy jumps on her and down they all go. On the silent screen, there's a fade-in to a dark passageway in an old apartment building in some foreign country. She kicks out and somebody falls between her legs. Somebody else is sitting on her face. 'Jimmy! Stop that!' the babysitter laughs, her voice muffled.

* * *

She's watching television. All alone. It seems like a good time to go in. Just remember: really, no matter what she says, she wants it. They're standing in the bushes, trying to get up the nerve. 'We'll tell her to be good,' Mark whispers, 'and if she's not good, we'll spank her.' Jack giggles softly, but his knees are weak. She stands. They freeze. She looks right at them. 'She can't see us.' Mark whispers tensely. 'Is she coming out?' 'No,' says Mark, 'She's going into—that must be the bathroom!' Jack takes a deep breath, his heart pounding. 'Hey, is there a window back there?' Mark asks.

* * *

The phone rings. She leaves the tub, wrapped in a towel. Bitsy give a tug on the towel. 'Hey, Jimmy, get the towel!' she squeals. 'Now stop that, Bitsy!' the babysitter hisses, but too late: with one hand on the phone, the other isn't enough to hang on to the towel. Her sudden nakedness awes them and it takes them a moment to remember about tickling her. By then, she's in the towel again. 'I hope you got a good look,' she says angrily. She feels chilled and oddly a little frightened. 'Hello?' No answer. She glances at the window—is somebody out there? Something, she saw something, and a rustling—footsteps?

* * *

'OK, I don't care, Jimmy, don't take a bath,' she says irritably. Her blouse is pulled out and wrinkled, her hair is all mussed, and she feels sweaty. There's about a million things she'd rather be doing than babysitting with these two. Three: at last the baby's sleeping. She knocks on the overturned endtable for luck, rights it, replaces the magazines and ashtrays. The one thing that really makes her sick is a dirty diaper. 'Just go on to bed.' 'I don't have to go to bed until nine,' he reminds her. Really, she couldn't care less. She turns up the volume on the TV, settles down on the couch, poking her blouse back into her skirt, pushing her hair out of her eyes. Jimmy and Bitsy watch from the floor. Maybe, once they're in bed, she'll take a quick bath. She wishes Jack would come by. The man, no doubt the spy, is following a woman, but she doesn't know why. The woman passes another man. Something seems to happen, but it's not clear what. She's probably already missed too much. The phone rings.

* * *

Mark is kissing her. Jack is under the blanket, easing her panties down over her squirming hips. Her hand is in his pants, pulling it out, pulling it toward her, pulling it hard. She knew just where it was! Mark is stripping, too. God, it's really happening! he thinks with a kind of pious joy, and notices the open door. 'Hey! What's going on here?'

* * *

He soaps her back, smooth and slippery under his hand. She is doubled over, against her knees, between his legs. Her light brown hair, reaching her gleaming shoulders, is wet at the edges. The soap slips, falls between his legs. He fishes for it, finds it, slips it behind him. 'Help me find it,' he whispers in her ear. 'Sure Harry,' says his host, going around behind him. 'What'd you lose?'

* * *

Soon be nine, time to pack the kids off to bed. She clears the table, dumps paper plates and leftover hamburgers into the garbage, puts glasses and silverware into the sink, and the mayonnaise, mustard, and ketchup in the refrigerator. Neither child has eaten much supper finally, mostly potato chips and ice cream, but it's really not her problem. She glances at the books on the refrigerator. Not much chance she'll get to them, she's already pretty worn out. Maybe she'd feel better if she had a quick bath. She runs water into the tub, tosses in bubblebath salts, undresses. Before pushing down her panties, she stares for a moment at the smooth silken panel across her tummy, fingers the place where the opening would be if there were one. Then she steps quickly out of them, feeling somehow ashamed, unhooks her brassiere. She weighs her breasts in the palms of her hands, watching herself in the bathroom mirror, where, in the open window behind her, she sees a face. She screams.

* * *

She screams: 'Jimmy! Give me that!' 'What's the matter?' asks Jack on the other end. 'Jimmy! Give me my towel! Right now!' 'Hello? Hey, are you still there?' 'I'm sorry, Jack,' she says, panting. 'You caught me in the tub. I'm just wrapped in a towel and these silly kids grabbed it away!' 'Gee, I wish I'd been there!' 'Jack—!' 'To protect you, I mean.' 'Oh, sure,' she says, giggling. 'Well, what do you think, can I come over and watch TV with you?' 'Well, not right this minute,' she says. He laughs lightly. He feels very cool. 'Jack?' 'Yeah?' 'Jack, I . . . I think there's somebody outside the window!'

* * *

She carries him, fighting all the way, to the tub, Bitsy pummeling her in the back and kicking her ankles. She can't hang on to him and undress him at the same time. 'I'll throw you in, clothes and all, Jimmy Tucker!' she gasps. 'You better not!' he cries. She sits on the toilet seat, locks her legs around him, whips his shirt up over his head before he knows what's happening. The pants are easier. Like all little boys his age, he has almost no hips at all. He hangs on desperately to his underpants, but when she succeeds in snapping these down out of his grip, too, he gives up, starts to bawl, and beats her wildly in the face with his fists. She ducks her head, laughing hysterically, oddly entranced by the spectacle of that pale little thing down there, bobbing and bouncing rubberlike about the boy's helpless fury and anguish.

* * *

'Aspirin? Whaddaya want aspirin for, Harry? I'm sure they got aspirin here, if you—' 'Did I say aspirin? I meant uh, my glasses. And, you know, I thought, well, I'd sorta check to see if everything was OK at home.' Why the hell is it his mouth feels like it's got about six sets of teeth packed in there, and a tongue the size of that liverwurst his host's wife is passing around? 'Whaddaya want your glasses for, Harry? I don't understand you at all!' 'Aw, well, honey, I was feeling kind of dizzy or something, and I thought—' 'Dizzy is right. If you want to check on the kids, why don't you just call on the phone?'

* * *

They can tell she's naked and about to get into the tub, but the bathroom window is frosted glass, and they can't see anything clearly. 'I got an idea,' Mark whispers. 'One of us goes and calls her on the phone, and the other watches when she comes out.' 'OK, but who calls?' 'Both of us, we'll do it twice. Or more.'

* * *

Down forbidden alleys. Into secret passageways. Unlocking the world's terrible secrets. Sudden shocks: a trapdoor! a fall! or the stunning report of a rifle shot, the *whaaii-ii-ing*! of the bullet biting concrete by your ear! Careful! Then edge forward once more, avoiding the light, inch at a time, now a quick dash for an open doorway—*look out*! there's a knife! a struggle! no! the long blade glistens! jerks! thrusts! *stabbed*! No, no, it missed! The assailant's down, yes! the spy's on top, pinning him, a terrific thrashing about, the spy rips off the assailant's mask: *a woman*!

* * *

Fumbling behind her, she finds it, wraps her hand around it, tugs. 'Oh!' she gasps, pulling her hand back quickly, her ears turning crimson. 'I . . . I thought it was the soap!' He squeezes her close between his thighs, pulls her back toward him, one hand sliding down her tummy between her legs. I Dream of Jeannie—'I have to go to the bathroom!' says someone outside the door.

* * *

She's combing her hair in the bathroom when the phone rings. She hurries to answer it before it wakes the baby. 'Hello, Tuckers.' There's no answer. 'Hello?' A soft click. Strange. She feels suddenly alone in the big house, and goes in to watch TV with the children.

* * *

'Stop it!' she screams, 'Please stop!' She's on her hands and knees, trying to get up, but they're too strong for her. Mark holds her head down. 'Now, baby, we're gonna teach you how to be a nice girl,' he says coldly, and nods at Jack. When she's doubled over like that, her skirt rides up her thighs to the leg bands of her panties. 'C'mon, man, go! This baby's cold! She needs your touch!'

* * *

Parks the car a couple blocks away. Slips up to the house, glances in his window. Just like he's expected. Her blouse is off and the kid's shirt is unbuttoned. He watches, while slowly, clumsily, childishly, they fumble with each other's clothes. My God, it takes them forever. 'Some party!' 'You said it!' When they're more or less naked, he walks in. 'Hey! What's going on here?' They go white as bleu cheese. Haw haw! 'What's the little thing you got sticking out there, boy?' 'Harry, behave yourself!' No, he doesn't let the kid get dressed, he sends him home bareassed. 'Bareassed!' He drinks to that. 'Promises, promises,' says his host's wife. 'I'll mail you your clothes, son!' He gazes down on the naked little girl on his couch. 'Looks like you and me, we got a little secret to keep, honey,' he says coolly. 'Less you wanna go home the same way your boyfriend did! He chuckles at his easy wit, leans down over her, and unbuckles his belt. 'Might as well make it two secrets, right?' 'What in God's name are you talking about, Harry?' He staggers out of there, drink in hand, and goes to look for his car.

* * *

'Hey! What's going on here?' They huddle half-naked under the blanket, caught utterly unawares. On television: the clickety-click of frightened running feet on foreign pavements. Jack is fumbling for his shorts, tangled somehow around his ankles. The blanket is snatched away. 'On your feet there!' Mr Tucker, Mrs Tucker, and Mark's mom and dad, the police, the neighbors, everybody comes crowding in. Hopelessly, he has a terrific erection. So hard it hurts. Everybody stares down at it.

* * *

Bitsy's sleeping on the floor. The babysitter is taking a bath. For more than an hour, he'd had to use the bathroom. He doesn't know how much longer he can wait. Finally, he goes to knock on the bathroom door. 'I have to use the bathroom.' 'Well, come ahead, if you have to.' 'Not while you're in there.' She sighs loudly. 'OK, OK, just a minute,' she says, 'but you're a real nuisance, Jimmy!' He's holding on, pinching it as tight as he can. '*Hurry!*' He holds his breath, squeezing shut his eyes. No. Too late. At last, she opens the door. 'Jimmy!' 'I *told* you to hurry!' he sobs. She drags him into the bathroom and pulls his pants down.

* * *

He arrives just in time to see her emerge from the bathroom, wrapped in a towel, to answer the phone. His two kids sneak up behind her and pull the towel away. She's trying to hang onto the phone and get the towel back at the same time. It's quite a picture. She's got a sweet ass. Standing there in the bushes, pawing himself with one hand, he lifts his glass with the other and toasts her sweet ass, which his son now swats. Haw haw, maybe that boy's gonna shape up, after all.

* * *

They're in the bushes, arguing about their next move, when she comes out of the bathroom, wrapped in a towel. They can hear the baby crying. Then it stops. They see her running, naked, back to the bathroom like she's scared or something. 'I'm going in after her, man, whether you're with me or not!' Mark whispers, and he starts out of the bushes. But just then, a light comes sweeping up through the yard, as a car swings in the drive. They hit the dirt, hearts pounding. 'Is it the cops?' 'I don't know!' 'Do you think they saw us?' 'Sshh!' A man comes staggering up the walk from the drive, a drink in his hand, stumbles on in the kitchen door and then straight into the bathroom. 'It's Mr Tucker!' Mark whispers. A scream. 'Let's get outa here, man!'

* * *

9.00. Having missed most of the spy show anyway and having little else to do, the babysitter has washed the dishes and cleaned the kitchen up a little. The books on the refrigerator remind her of her better intentions, but she decides that first she'll see what's next on TV. In the livingroom, she finds little Bitsy sound asleep on the floor. She lifts her gently, carries her into her bed, and tucks her in. 'OK, Jimmy, it's nine o'clock, I've let you stay up, now be a good boy.' Sullenly, his sleepy eyes glued still to the set, the boy backs out of the room toward his bedroom. A drama comes on. She switches channels. A ballgame and a murder mystery. She switches back to the drama. It's a love story of some kind. A man married to an aging invalid wife, but in love with a younger girl. 'Use the bathroom and brush your teeth before going to bed, Jimmy!' she calls, but as quickly regrets it, for she hears the baby stir in its crib.

* * *

Two of them are talking about mothers they've salted away in rest homes. Oh boy, that's just wonderful, this is one helluva party. She leaves them to use the john, takes advantage of the retreat to ease her girdle down awhile, get a few good deep breaths. She has this picture of her three kids carting her off to a rest home. In a wheelbarrow. That sure is something to look forward to, all right. When she pulls her girdle back up, she can't seem to squeeze into it. The host looks in. 'Hey, Dolly, are you all right?' 'Yeah, I just can't get into my damn girdle, that's all.' 'Here, let me help.'

* * *

She pulls them on, over her own, standing in front of the bedroom mirror, holding her skirt bundled up around the waist. About twenty sizes too big for her, of course. She pulls them tight from behind, runs her hand inside the opening in front, pulls out her thumb. 'And what a good boy am I!' She giggles: how funny it must feel! Then in the mirror, she sees him: in the doorway behind her, sullenly watching. 'Jimmy! You're supposed to be in bed!' 'Those are my daddy's!' the boy says. 'I'm gonna tell!'

* * *

'Jimmy!' She drags him into the bathroom and pulls his pants down. 'Even your shoes are wet! Get them off!' She soaps up a warm washcloth she's had with her in the bathtub, scrubs him from the waist down with it. Bitsy stands in the doorway, staring. 'Get out! Get out!' the boy screams at his sister. 'Go back to bed, Bitsy. It's just an accident.' 'Get out!' The baby wakes and starts to howl.

* * *

The young lover feels sorry for her rival, the invalid wife; she believes the man has a duty toward the poor woman and insists she is willing to wait. But the man argues that he also has a duty toward himself: his life, too, is short, and he could not love his wife now even were she well. He embraces the young girl feverishly; she twists away in anguish. The door opens. They stand there grinning, looking devilish, but pretty silly at the same time. 'Jack! I thought I told you not to come!' She's angry, but she's also glad in a way: she was beginning to feel a little too alone in the big house, with the children all sleeping. She should have taken that bath, after all. 'We just came by to see if you were being a good girl,' Jack says and blushes. The boys glance at each other nervously.

* * *

She's just sunk down into the tubful of warm fragrant suds, ready for a nice long soaking, when the phone rings. Wrapping a towel around her, she goes to answer: no one there. But now the baby's awake and bawling. She wonders if that's Jack bothering her all the time. If it is, brother, that's the end. Maybe it's the end anyway. She tries to calm the baby with the half-empty bottle, not wanting to change it until she's finished her bath. The bathroom's where the diapers go dirty, and they make it stink to high heaven. 'Shush, shush!' she whispers, rocking the crib. The towel slips away, leaving an airy empty tingle up and down her backside. Even before she stoops for the towel, even before she turns around, she knows there's somebody behind her.

* * *

'We just came by to see if you were being a good girl,' Jack says, grinning down at her. She's flushed and silent, her mouth half open. 'Lean over,' says Mark amiably. 'We'll soap your back, as long as we're here.' But she just huddles there, down in the suds, staring up at them with big eyes.

* * *

'Hey! What's going on here?' It's Mr Tucker, stumbling through the door with a drink in his hand. She looks up from the TV. 'What's the matter, Mr Tucker?' 'Oh, uh, I'm sorry, I got lost—no, I mean, I had to get some aspirin. Excuse me!' And he rushes past her into the bathroom, caroming off the livingroom door jamb on the way. The baby awakes.

* * *

'OK, get off her, Mr Tucker!' 'Jack!' she cries, 'what are *you* doing here?' He stares hard at them a moment: so that's where it goes. Then, as Mr Tucker swings heavily off, he leans into the bastard with a hard right to the belly. Next thing he knows, though, he's got a face full of an old man's fist. He's not sure, as the lights go out, if that's his girlfriend screaming or the baby . . .

* * *

Her host pushes down on her fat fanny and tugs with all his might on her girdle, while she bawls on his shoulder: 'I don't *wanna* go to a rest home!' 'Now, now, take it easy, Dolly, nobody's gonna make you—' 'Ouch! Hey, you're hurting!' 'You should buy a bigger girdle, Dolly.' 'You're telling me?' Some other guy pokes his head in. 'Whatsamatter? Dolly fall in?' 'No, she fell out. Give me a hand.'

* * *

By the time she's chased Jack and Mark out of there, she's lost track of the program she's been watching on television. There's another woman in the story now for some reason. That guy lives a very complicated life. Impatiently, she switches channels. She hates ballgames, so she settles for the murder mystery. She switches just in time, too: there's a dead man sprawled out on the floor of what looks like an office or a study or something. A heavyset detective gazes up from his crouch over the body: 'He's been strangled.' Maybe she'll take that bath, after all.

* * *

She drags him into the bathroom and pulls his pants down. She soaps up a warm washcloth she's had in the tub with her, but just as she reaches between his legs, it starts to spurt, spraying her arms and hands, 'Oh, Jimmy! I thought you were done!' she cries, pulling him toward the toilets and aiming it into the bowl. How moist and rubbery it is! And you can turn it every which way. How funny it must feel!

* * *

'Stop it!' she screams. 'Please stop!' She's on her hands and knees and Jack is holding her head down. 'Now we're gonna teach you how to be a nice girl,' Mark says and lifts her skirt. 'Well, I'll be damned!' 'What's the matter?' asks Jack, his heart pounding. 'Look at this big pair of men's underpants she's got on!' 'Those are my daddy's!' says Jimmy, watching them from the doorway. 'I'm gonna tell!'

* * *

People are shooting at each other in the murder mystery, but she's so mixed up, she doesn't know which ones are the good guys. She switches back to the love story. Something seems to have happened because now the man is kissing his invalid wife tenderly. Maybe she's finally dying. The baby wakes, begins to scream. Let it. She turns up the volume on the TV.

* * *

Leaning down over her, unbuckling his belt. It's all happening just like he's known it would. Beautiful! The kid is gone, though his pants, poor lad, remain. 'Looks like you and me, we got a secret to keep, child!' But he's cramped on the couch and everything is too slippery and small. 'Lift your legs up, honey. Put them around my back.' But instead, she screams. He rolls off, crashing to the floor. There they all come, through the front door. On television, somebody is saying: 'Am I a burden to you, darling?' 'Dolly! My God! Dolly, I can explain . . . !'

* * *

The game of the night is Get Dolly Tucker Back in Her Girdle Again. They've got her down on her belly in the livingroom and the whole damn crowd is working on her. Several of them are stretching the girdle, while others try to jam the fat inside. 'I think we made a couple inches on this side! Roll her over!' Harry?

* * *

She's just stepped into the tub, when the phone rings, waking the baby. She sinks down in the suds, trying not to hear. But that baby doesn't cry, it screams. Angrily, she wraps a towel around herself, stamps peevishly into the baby's room, just letting the phone jangle. She tosses the baby down on its back, unpins its diapers hastily, and gets yellowish baby stool all over her hands. Her towel drops away. She turns to find Jimmy staring at her like a little idiot. She slaps him in the face with her dirty hand, while the baby screams, the phone rings, and nagging voices argue on the TV. There are better things she might be doing.

* * *

What's happening? Now there's a young guy in it. Is he after the young girl or the old invalid? To tell the truth, it looks like he's after the same man the women are. In disgust, she switches channels. 'The strangler again,' growls the fat detective, hands on hips, staring down at the body of a half-naked girl. She's considering either switching back to the love story or taking a quick bath, when a hand suddenly clutches her mouth.

* * *

'You're both chicken,' she says, staring up at them. 'But what if Mr Tucker comes home?' Mark asks nervously.

* * *

How did he get here? He's standing pissing in his own goddamn bathroom, his wife is still back at the party, the three of them are, like good kids, sitting in there in the livingroom watching TV. One of them is his host's boy Mark. 'It's a good murder mystery, Mr Tucker,' Mark said, when he came staggering in on them a minute ago. 'Sit still!' he shouted, 'I am just home for a moment!' Then whump thump on into the bathroom. Long hike for a wee-wee, Mister. But

370

something keeps bothering him. Then it hits him: the girl's panties hanging like a broken balloon from the rabbit-ear antennae on the TV! He barges back in there, giving his shoulder a helluva crack on the livingroom door jamb on the way—but they're not hanging there any more. Maybe he only imagined it. 'Hey, Mr Tucker,' Mark says flatly. 'Your fly's open.'

* * *

The baby's dirty. Stinks to high heaven. She hurries back to the livingroom, hearing sirens and gunshots. The detective is crouched outside a house, peering in. Already, she's completely lost. The baby screams at the top of its lungs. She turns up the volume. But it's all confused. She hurries back in there, claps an angry hand to the baby's mouth. 'Shut up!' she cries. She throws the baby down on its back, starts to unpin the diaper, as the baby tunes up again. The phone rings. She answers it, one eye on the TV. '*What?*' The baby cries so hard it starts to choke. Let it. 'I said, hi, this is Jack!' Then it hits her: oh no! the diaper pin!

* * *

'The aspirin . . . ' But she's already in the tub. Way down in the tub. Staring at him through the water. Her tummy looks pale and ripply. He hears sirens, people on the porch.

* * *

Jimmy gets up to go to the bathroom and gets his face slapped and smeared with baby poop. Then she hauls him off to the bathroom, yanks off his pajamas, and throws him into the tub. That's OK, but next she gets naked and acts like she's gonna get in the tub, too. The baby's screaming and the phone's ringing like crazy and in walks his dad. Saved! he thinks, but, no, his dad grabs him right back out of the tub and whales the dickens out of him, no questions asked, while she watches, then sends him—*whack!*—back to bed. So he's lying there, wet and dirty and naked and sore, and he still has to go to the bathroom, and outside his window he hears two older guys talking. 'Listen, you know where to do it if we get her pinned?' 'No! Don't you?'

* * *

'Yo ho heave ho! *Ugh!*' Dolly's on her back and they're working on the belly side. Somebody got the great idea of buttering her down first. Not to lose the ground they've gained, they've shot it inside

371

with a basting syringe. But now suddenly there's this big tug-of-war under way between those who want to stuff her in and those who want to let her out. Something rips, but she feels better. The odor of hot butter makes her think of movie theaters and popcorn. 'Hey, has anybody seen Harry?' she asks. 'Where's Harry?'

* * *

Somebody's getting chased. She switches back to the love story, and now the man's back kissing the young lover again. What's going on? She gives it up, decides to take a quick, bath. She's just stepping into the tub, one foot in, one foot out, when Mr Tucker walks in. 'Oh, excuse me! I only wanted some aspirin . . . ' She grabs for a towel, but he yanks it away. 'Now, that's not how it's supposed to happen, child,' he scolds. 'Please! Mr Tucker . . . !' He embraces her savagely, his calloused old hands clutching roughly at her backside. 'Mr Tucker!' she cries, squirming. 'Your wife called—!' He's pushing something between her legs, hurting her. She slips, they both slip— something cold and hard slams her in the back, cracks her skull, she seems to be sinking into a sea . . .

* * *

They've got her over the hassock, skirt up and pants down. 'Give her a little lesson there, Jack baby!' The television lights flicker and flash over her glossy flesh, 1000 WHEN LIT. Whack! Slap! Bumper to bumper! He leans into her, feeling her come alive.

* * *

The phone rings, waking the baby. 'Jack, is that you? Now, you listen to me—' 'No, dear, this is Mrs Tucker. Isn't the TV awfully loud?' 'Oh, I'm sorry, Mrs Tucker! I've been getting—' 'I tried to call you before, but I couldn't hang on. To the phone, I mean. I'm sorry, dear.' 'Just a minute, Mrs Tucker, the baby's—' 'Honey, listen! Is Harry there? Is Mr Tucker there, dear?'

* * *

'Stop it!' she screams and claps a hand over the baby's mouth. 'Stop it! Stop it! *Stop it!*' Her other hand is full of baby stool and she's afraid she's going to be sick. The phone rings. 'No!' she cries. She's hanging on to the baby, leaning woozily away, listening to the phone ring. 'OK, OK,' she sighs, getting ahold of herself. But when she lets go of the baby, it isn't screaming any more. She shakes it. Oh no . . .

372

* * *

'Hello?' No answer. Strange. She hangs up and, wrapped only in a towel, stares out the window at the cold face staring in—she screams!

* * *

She screams, scaring the hell out of him. He leaps out of the tub, glances up at the window she's gaping at just in time to see two faces duck away, then slips on the bathroom tiles, and crashes to his ass, whacking his head on the sink on the way down. She stares down at him, trembling, a towel over her narrow shoulder. 'Mr Tucker! Mr Tucker, are you all right . . . ?' Who's Sorry Now? Yessir, who's back is breaking with each . . . He stares up at the little tufted locus of all his woes, and passes out, dreaming of Jeannie . . .

* * *

The phone rings. 'Dolly! It's for you!' 'Hello?' 'Hello, Mrs Tucker?' 'Yes, speaking.' 'Mrs Tucker, this is the police calling . . .'

* * *

It's cramped and awkward and slippery, but he's pretty sure he got it in her, once anyway. When he gets the suds out of his eyes, he sees her staring up at them. Through the water. 'Hey, Mark! Let her up!'

* * *

Down in the suds. Feeling sleepy. The phone rings, startling her. Wrapped in a towel, she goes to answer. 'No, he's not here, Mrs Tucker.' Strange. Married people act pretty funny sometimes. The baby is awake and screaming. Dirty, a real mess. Oh boy, there's a lot of things she'd rather be doing than babysitting in this madhouse. She decides to wash the baby off in her own bathwater. She removes her towel, unplugs the tub, lowers the water level so the baby can sit. Glancing back over her shoulder, she sees Jimmy staring at her. 'Go back to bed, Jimmy.' 'I have to go to the bathroom.' 'Good grief, Jimmy! It looks like you already have!' The phone rings. She doesn't bother with the towel—what can Jimmy see he hasn't already seen?—and goes to answer. 'No, Jack, and that's final.' Sirens, on the TV, as the police move in. But wasn't that the channel with the love story? Ambulance maybe. Get this over with so she can at least catch the news. 'Get those wet pajamas off, Jimmy, and I'll find clean ones. Maybe you better get in the tub, too.' 'I think something's wrong with the baby,' he says. 'It's down in the water and it's not swimming or anything.'

* * *

She's staring up at them from the rug. They slap her. Nothing happens. 'You just tilted her, man!' Mark says softly. 'We gotta get outa here!' Two little kids are standing wideeyed in the doorway. Mark looks hard at Jack. 'No, Mark, they're just little kids . . . !' 'We gotta, man, or we're dead.'

* * *

'Dolly! My God! Dolly, I can explain!' She glowers down at them, her ripped girdle around her ankles. 'What the four of you are doing in the bathtub with *my* babysitter?' she says sourly. 'I can hardly wait!'

* * *

Police sirens wail, lights flash. 'I heard the scream!' somebody shouts. 'There were two boys!' 'I saw a man!' 'She was running with the baby!' 'My God!' somebody screams 'they're *all* dead!' Crowds come running. Spotlights probe the bushes.

* * *

'Harry, where the hell you been?' his wife whines, glaring blearily up at him from the carpet. 'I can explain,' he says. 'Hey, whatsamatter, Harry?' his host asks, smeared with butter for some goddamn reason. 'you look like you just seen a ghost!' Where did he leave his drink? Everybody's laughing, everybody except Dolly, whose cheeks are streaked with tears. 'Hey, Harry, you won't let them take me to a rest home, will you, Harry?'

* * *

10.00. The dishes done, children to bed, her books read, she watches the news on television. Sleepy. The man's voice is gentle, soothing. She dozes—awakes with a start: a babysitter? Did the announcer say something about a babysitter?

* * *

'Just want to catch the weather,' the host says, switching on the TV. Most of the guests are leaving, but the Tuckers stay to watch the news. As it comes on, the announcer is saying something about a babysitter. The host switches channels. 'They got a better weatherman on four,' he explains. 'Wait!' says Mrs Tucker. 'There was something about a babysitter . . . !' The host switches back. 'Details have not yet been released by the police,' the announcer says. 'Harry, maybe we'd better go . . .'

* * *

They stroll casually out of the drugstore, run into a buddy of theirs. 'Hey! Did you hear about the babysitter?' the guy asks. Mark grunts, glances at Jack. 'Got a smoke?' he asks the guy.

* * *

'I think I hear the baby screaming!' Mrs Tucker cries, running across the lawn from the drive.

* * *

She wakes, startled, to find Mr Tucker hovering over her. 'I must have dozed off!' she exclaims. 'Did you hear the news about the babysitter?' Mr Tucker asks. 'Part of it,' she says, rising. 'Too bad, wasn't it?' Mr Tucker is watching the report of the ball scores and golf tournaments. 'I'll drive you home in just a minute, dear,' he says. 'Why, how nice!' Mrs Tucker exclaims from the kitchen. 'The dishes are all done!'

* * *

'What can I say, Dolly?' the host says with a sigh, twisting the buttered strands of her ripped girdle between his fingers. 'Your children are murdered, your husband gone, a corpse in your bathtub, and your house is wrecked. I'm sorry. But what can I say?' On the TV, the news is over, and they're selling aspirin. 'Hell, I don't know,' she says. 'Let's see what's on the late late movie.'

1969

CITY BOY

Leonard Michaels

'Phillip,' she said, 'this is crazy.'

I didn't agree or disagree. She wanted some answer. I bit her neck. She kissed my ear. It was nearly three in the morning. We had just returned. The apartment was dark and quiet. We were on the living room floor and she repeated, 'Phillip, this is crazy.' Her crinoline broke under us like cinders. Furniture loomed all around in the darkness—settee, chairs, a table with a lamp. Pictures were cloudy blotches drifting above. But no lights, no things to look at, no eyes in her head. She was underneath me and warm. The rug was warm, soft as mud, deep. Her crinoline cracked like sticks. Our naked bellies clapped together. Air fired out like farts. I took it as applause. The chairs smirked and spit between their feet. The chandelier clicked giddy teeth. The clock ticked as if to split its glass. 'Phillip,' she said, 'this is crazy.' A little voice against the grain and power. Not enough to stop me. Yet once I had been a man of feeling. We went to concerts, walked in the park, trembled in the maid's room. Now in the foyer, a flash of hair and claws. We stumbled to the living room floor. She said, 'Phillip, this is crazy.' Then silence, except in my head where a conference table was set up, ashtrays scattered about. Priests, ministers and rabbis were rushing to take seats. I wanted their opinion, but came. They vanished. A voice lingered, faintly crying, 'You could mess up the rug, Phillip, break something . . . ' Her fingers pinched my back like ants. I expected a remark to kill good death. She said nothing. The breath in her nostrils whipped mucus. It cracked in my ears like flags. I dreamed we were in her mother's Cadillac, trailing flags. I heard her voice before I heard the words. 'Phillip, this is crazy. My parents are in the next room.' Her cheek jerked against mine, her breasts were knuckles in my nipples. I burned. Good death was killed. I burned with hate. A rabbi shook his finger. 'You shouldn't hate.' I lifted on my elbows, sneering in pain. She wrenched her hips, tightened muscles in belly and neck. She said, 'Move.' It was imperative to move. Her parents were thirty feet away. Down the hall between Utrillos and Vlamincks, through the door, flick the light and

376

I'd see them. Maybe like us, Mr Cohen adrift on the missus. Hair sifted down my cheek. 'Let's go to the maid's room,' she whispered. I was reassured. She tried to move. I kissed her mouth. Her crinoline smashed like sugar. Pig that I was, I couldn't move. The clock ticked hysterically. Ticks piled up like insects. Muscles lapsed in her thighs. Her fingers scratched on my neck as if looking for buttons. She slept. I sprawled like a bludgeoned pig, eyes open, loose lips. I flopped into sleep, in her, in the rug, in our scattered clothes.

Dawn hadn't shown between the slats in the blinds. Her breathing sissed in my ear. I wanted to sleep more, but needed a cigarette. I thought of the cold avenue, the lonely subway ride. Where could I buy a newspaper, a cup of coffee? This was crazy, dangerous, a waste of time. The maid might arrive, her parents might wake. I had to get started. My hand pushed along the rug to find my shirt, touched a brass lion's paw, then a lamp cord.

A naked heel bumped wood.

She woke, her nails in my neck. 'Phillip, did you hear?' I whispered, 'Quiet.' My eyes rolled like Milton's. Furniture loomed, whirled. 'Dear God,' I prayed, 'save my ass.' The steps ceased. Neither of us breathed. The clock ticked. She trembled. I pressed my cheek against her mouth to keep her from talking. We heard pajamas rustle, phlegmy breathing, fingernails scratching hair. A voice, 'Veronica, don't you think it's time you sent Phillip home?'

A murmur of assent started in her throat, swept to my cheek, fell back drowned like a child in a well. Mr Cohen had spoken. He stood ten inches from our legs. Maybe less. It was impossible to tell. His fingernails grated through hair. His voice hung in the dark with the quintessential question. Mr Cohen, scratching his crotch, stood now as never in the light. Considerable. No tool of his wife, whose energy in business kept him eating, sleeping, overlooking the park. Pinochle change in his pocket four nights a week. But were they his words? Or was he the oracle of Mrs Cohen, lying sleepless, irritated, waiting for him to get me out? I didn't breathe. I didn't move. If he had come on his own he would leave without an answer. His eyes weren't adjusted to the dark. He couldn't see. We lay at his feet like worms. He scratched, made smacking noises with his mouth.

The question of authority is always with us. Who is responsible for the triggers pulled, buttons pressed, the gas, the fire? Doubt banged my brain. My heart lay in the fist of intellect, which squeezed out feeling like piss out of kidneys. Mrs Cohen's voice demolished doubt, feeling, intellect. It ripped from the bedroom.

'For God's sake, Morris, don't be banal. Tell the schmuck to go home and keep his own parents awake all night, if he has any.'

Veronica's tears slipped down my cheeks. Mr Cohen sighed, shuffled, made a strong voice. 'Veronica, tell Phillip . . . ' His foot came down on my ass. He drove me into his daughter. I drove her into his rug.

'I don't believe it,' he said.

He walked like an antelope, lifting hoof from knee, but stepped down hard. Sensitive to the danger of movement, yet finally impulsive, flinging his pot at the earth in order to cross it. His foot brought me his weight and character, a hundred fifty-five pounds of stomping *schlemiel*, in a mode of apprehension so primal we must share it with bugs. Let armies stomp me to insensate pulp—I'll yell 'Cohen' when he arrives.

Veronica squealed, had a contraction, fluttered, gagged a shriek, squeezed, and up like a frog out of the hand of a child I stood spread-legged, bolt naked, great with eyes. Mr Cohen's face was eyes in my eyes. A secret sharer. We faced each other like men accidentally met in hell. He retreated flapping, moaning, 'I will not believe it one bit.'

Veronica said, 'Daddy?'

'Who else you no good bum?'

The rug raced. I smacked against blinds, glass broke and I whirled. Veronica said, 'Phillip,' and I went off in streaks, a sparrow in the room, here, there, early American, baroque and rococo. Veronica wailed, 'Phillip.' Mr Cohen screamed, 'I'll kill him.' I stopped at the door, seized the knob. Mrs Cohen yelled from the bedroom, 'Morris, did something break? Answer me.'

'I'll kill that bastid.'

'Morris, if something broke you'll rot for a month.'

'Mother, stop it,' said Veronica. 'Phillip, come back.'

The door slammed. I was outside, naked as a wolf.

I needed poise. Without poise the street was impossible. Blood shot to my brain, thought blossomed. I'd walk on my hands. Beards were fashionable. I kicked up my feet, kicked the elevator button, faced the door and waited. I bent one elbow like a knee. The posture of a clothes model, easy, poised. Blood coiled down to my brain, weeds bourgeoned. I had made a bad impression. There was no other way to see it. But all right. We needed a new beginning. Everyone does. Yet how few of us know when it arrives. Mr Cohen had never spoken to

me before; this was a breakthrough. There had been a false element
in our relationship. It was wiped out. I wouldn't kid myself with the
idea that he had nothing to say. I'd had enough of his silent
treatment. It was worth being naked to see how mercilessly I could
think. I had his number. Mrs Cohen's, too. I was learning every
second. I was a city boy. No innocent shitkicker from Jersey. I was the
A train, the Fifth Avenue bus. I could be a cop. My name was Phillip,
my style New York City. I poked the elevator button with my toe. It
rang in the lobby, waking Ludwig. He'd come for me, rotten with
sleep. Not the first time. He always took me down, walked me
through the lobby and let me out on the avenue. Wires began tugging
him up the shaft. I moved back, conscious of my genitals hanging
upside down. Absurd consideration; we were both men one way or
another. There were social distinctions enforced by his uniform, but
they would vanish at the sight of me. 'The unaccommodated thing
itself.' 'Off ye lendings!' The greatest play is about a naked man. A
picture of Lear came to me, naked, racing through the wheat. I could
be cool. I thought of Ludwig's uniform, hat, whipcord collar. It
signified his authority. Perhaps he would be annoyed, in his
authority, by the sight of me naked. Few people woke him at such
hours. Worse, I never tipped him. Could I have been so indifferent
month after month? In a crisis you discover everything. Then it's too
late. Know yourself, indeed. You need a crisis every day. I refused to
think about it. I sent my mind after objects. It returned with the
chairs, settee, table and chandelier. Where were my clothes? I sent it
along the rug. It found buttons, eagles stamped in brass. I recognized
them as the buttons on Ludwig's coat. Eagles, beaks like knives,
shrieking for tips. Fuck'm, I thought. Who's Ludwig? A big coat, a
whistle, white gloves and a General MacArthur hat. I could
understand him completely. He couldn't begin to understand me. A
naked man is mysterious. But aside from that, what did he know? I
dated Veronica Cohen and went home late. Did he know I was out of
work? That I lived in a slum downtown? Of course not.

Possibly under his hat was a filthy mind. He imagined Veronica
and I might be having sexual intercourse. He resented it. Not that he
hoped for the privilege himself, in his coat and soldier hat, but he had
a proprietary interest in the building and its residents. I came from
another world. *The* other world against which Ludwig defended the
residents. Wasn't I like a burglar sneaking out late, making him my
accomplice? I undermined his authority, his dedication. He despised

me. It was obvious. But no one thinks such thoughts. It made me laugh to think them. My genitals jumped. The elevator door slid open. He didn't say a word. I padded inside like a seal. The door slid shut. Instantly, I was ashamed of myself, thinking as I had about him. I had no right. A better man than I. His profile was an etching by Dürer. Good peasant stock. How had he fallen to such work? Existence precedes essence. At the controls, silent, enduring, he gave me strength for the street. Perhaps the sun would be up, birds in the air. The door slid open. Ludwig walked ahead of me through the lobby. He needed new heels. The door of the lobby was half a ton of glass, encased in iron vines and leaves. Not too much for Ludwig. He turned, looked down into my eyes. I watched his lips move.

'I vun say sumding. Yur bisniss vot you do. Bud vy you mek her miserable? Nod led her slip. She has beks unter her eyes.'

Ludwig had feelings. They spoke to mine. Beneath the uniform, a man. Essence precedes existence. Even rotten with sleep, thick, dry bags under his eyes, he saw, he sympathized. The discretion demanded by his job forbade anything tangible, a sweater, a hat. 'Ludwig,' I whispered, 'you're all right.' It didn't matter if he heard me. He knew I said something. He knew it was something nice. He grinned, tugged the door open with both hands. I slapped out onto the avenue. I saw no one, dropped to my feet and glanced back through the door. Perhaps for the last time. I lingered, indulged a little melancholy. Ludwig walked to a couch in the rear of the lobby. He took off his coat, rolled it into a pillow and lay down. I had never stayed to see him do that before, but always rushed off to the subway. As if I were indifferent to the life of the building. Indeed, like a burglar. I seized the valuables and fled to the subway. I stayed another moment, watching good Ludwig, so I could hate myself. He assumed the modest, saintly posture of sleep. One leg here, the other there. His good head on his coat. A big arm across his stomach, the hand between his hips. He made a fist and punched up and down.

I went down the avenue, staying close to the buildings. Later I would work up a philosophy. Now I wanted to sleep, forget. I hadn't the energy for moral complexities: Ludwig cross-eyed, thumping his pelvis in such a nice lobby. Mirrors, glazed pots, rubber plants ten feet high. As if he were generating all of it. As if it were part of his job. I hurried. The buildings were on my left, the park on my right. There were doormen in all the buildings; God knows what was in the park. No cars were moving. No people in sight. Streetlights glowed in a receding sweep down to Fifty-ninth Street and beyond. A wind pressed my face like Mr Cohen's breath. Such hatred. Imponderable under any circumstances, a father cursing his daughter. Why? A fright in the dark? Freud said things about fathers and daughters. It was too obvious, too hideous. I shuddered and went more quickly. I began to run. In a few minutes I was at the spit-mottled steps of the subway. I had hoped for vomit. Spit is no challenge for bare feet. Still, I wouldn't complain. It was sufficiently disgusting to make me live in spirit. I went down the steps flatfooted, stamping, elevated by each declension. I was a city boy, no mincing creep from the sticks.

A Negro man sat in the change booth. He wore glasses, a white shirt, black knit tie and a silver tie clip. I saw a mole on his right cheek. His hair had spots of grey, as if strewn with ashes. He was reading a newspaper. He didn't hear me approach, didn't see my eyes take him in, figure him out. Shirt, glasses, tie—I knew how to address him. I coughed. He looked up.

'Sir, I don't have any money. Please let me through the turnstile. I come this way every week and will certainly pay you the next time.'

He merely looked at me. Then his eyes flashed like fangs. Instinctively, I guessed what he felt. He didn't owe favors to a white man. He didn't have to bring his allegiance to the transit authority into question for my sake.

'Hey, man, you naked?'

'Yes.'

'Step back a little.'

I stepped back. 'You're naked.'

I nodded.

'Get your naked ass the hell out of here.'

'Sir,' I said, 'I know these are difficult times, but can't we be reasonable? I know that . . . '

'Scat, mother, go home.'

I crouched as if to dash through the turnstile. He crouched, too. It proved he would come after me. I shrugged, turned back toward the steps. The city was infinite. There were many other subways. But why had he become so angry? Did he think I was a bigot? Maybe I was running around naked to get him upset. His anger was incomprehensible otherwise. It made me feel like a bigot. First a burglar, then a bigot. I needed a cigarette. I could hardly breathe. Air was too good for me. At the top of the steps, staring down, stood Veronica. She had my clothes.

'Poor, poor,' she said.

I said nothing. I snatched my underpants and put them on. She had my cigarettes ready. I tried to light one, but the match failed. I threw down the cigarette and the matchbook. She retrieved them as I dressed. She lit the cigarette for me and held my elbow to help me keep my balance. I finished dressing, took the cigarette. We walked back toward her building. The words 'thank you' sat in my brain like driven spikes. She nibbled her lip.

'How are things at home?' My voice was casual and morose, as if no answer could matter.

'All right,' she said, her voice the same as mine. She took her tone from me. I liked that sometimes, sometimes not. Now I didn't like it. I discovered I was angry. Until she said that I had no idea I was angry. I flicked the cigarette into the gutter and suddenly I knew why. I didn't love her. The cigarette sizzled in the gutter. Like truth. I didn't love her. Black hair, green eyes, I didn't love her. Slender legs. I didn't. Last night I had looked at her and said to myself, 'I hate communism.' Now I wanted to step on her head. Nothing less than that would do. If it was a perverted thought, then it was a perverted thought. I wasn't afraid to admit it to myself.

'All right? Really? Is that true?'

Blah, blah, blah. Who asked those questions? A zombie; not Phillip of the foyer and rug. He died in flight. I was sorry, sincerely sorry, but with clothes on my back I knew certain feelings would not survive humiliation. It was so clear it was thrilling. Perhaps she felt it, too. In any case she would have to accept it. The nature of the times. We are historical creatures. Veronica and I were finished. Before we reached her door I would say deadly words. They'd come in a natural way, kill her a little. Veronica, let me step on your head or we're through. Maybe we're through, anyway. It would deepen her looks, give philosophy to what was only charming in her face. The dawn was here. A new day. Cruel, but change is cruel. I could bear it. Love is infinite and one. Women are not. Neither are men. The human condition. Nearly unbearable.

'No, it's not true,' she said.

'What's not?'

'Things aren't all right at home.'

I nodded intelligently, sighed, 'Of course not. Tell me the truth, please. I don't want to hear anything else.'

'Daddy had a heart attack.'

'Oh God,' I yelled. 'Oh God, no.'

I seized her hand, dropped it. She let it fall. I seized it again. No use. I let it fall. She let it drift between us. We stared at one another. She said, 'What were you going to say? I can tell you were going to say something.'

I stared, said nothing

'Don't feel guilty, Phillip. Let's just go back to the apartment and have some coffee.'

'What can I say?'

'Don't say anything. He's in the hospital and my mother is there. Let's just go upstairs and not say anything.'

'Not say anything. Like moral imbeciles go slurp coffee and not say anything? What are we, nihilists or something? Assassins? Monsters?'

'Phillip, there's no one in the apartment. I'll make us coffee and eggs . . . '

'How about roast beef? Got a roast beef in the freezer?'

'Phillip, he's *my* father.'

We were at the door. I rattled. I was in a trance. This was life. Death!

'Indeed, your father. I'll accept that. I can do no less.'

'Phillip, shut up. Ludwig.'

The door opened. I nodded to Ludwig. What did he know about life and death? Give him a uniform and a quiet lobby—that's life and death. In the elevator he took the controls. 'Always got a hand on the controls, eh Ludwig?'

Veronica smiled in a feeble, grateful way. She liked to see me get along with the help. Ludwig said, 'Dot's right.'

'Ludwig has been our doorman for years, Phillip. Ever since I was a little girl.'

'Wow,' I said.

'Dots right.'

The door slid open. Veronica said, 'Thank you, Ludwig.' I said, 'Thank you, Ludwig.'

'Vulcum.'

'Vulcum? You mean, "welcome"? Hey, Ludwig, how long you been in this country?'

Veronica was driving her key into the door.

'How come you never learned to talk American, baby?'

'Phillip, come here.'

'I'm saying something to Ludwig.'

383

'Come here right now.'

'I have to go, Ludwig.'

'Vulcum.'

She went directly to the bathroom. I waited in the hallway between Vlamincks and Utrillos. The Utrillos were pale and flat. The Vlamincks were thick, twisted and red. Raw meat on one wall, dry stone on the other. Mrs Cohen had an eye for contrasts. I heard Veronica sob. She ran water in the sink, sobbed, sat down, peed. She saw me looking and kicked the door shut.

'At a time like this . . . '

'I don't like you looking.'

'Then why did you leave the door open? You obviously don't know your own mind.'

'Go away, Phillip. Wait in the living room.'

'Just tell me why you left the door open.'

'Phillip, you're going to drive me nuts. Go away. I can't do a damn thing if I know you're standing there.'

The living room made me feel better. The settee, the chandelier full of teeth and the rug were company. Mr Cohen was everywhere, a simple, diffuse presence. He jingled change in his pocket, looked out the window and was happy he could see the park. He took a little antelope step and tears came into my eyes. I sat among his mourners. A rabbi droned platitudes: Mr Cohen was generous, kind, beloved by his wife and daughter. 'How much did he weigh?' I shouted. The phone rang.

Veronica came running down the hall. I went and stood at her side when she picked up the phone. I stood dumb, stiff as a hatrack. She was whimpering, 'Yes, yes . . . ' I nodded my head yes, yes, thinking it was better than no, no. She put the phone down.

'It was my mother. Daddy's all right. Mother is staying with him in his room at the hospital and they'll come home together tomorrow.'

Her eyes looked at mine. At them as if they were as flat and opaque as hers. I said in a slow, stupid voice, 'You're allowed to do that? Stay overnight in a hospital with a patient? Sleep in his room?' She continued looking at my eyes. I shrugged, looked down. She took my shirt front in a fist like a bite. She whispered. I said, 'What?' She whispered again, 'Fuck me.' The clock ticked like crickets. The Vlamincks spilled blood. We sank into the rug as if it were quicksand.

1969

WHITE RAT

Gayl Jones

I learned where she was when Cousin Willie come down home and said Maggie sent for her but told her not to tell nobody where she was, especially me, but Cousin Willie come and told me anyway cause she said I was the lessen two evils and she didn't like to see Maggie stuck up in the room up there like she was. I asked her what she mean like she was. Willie said that she was pregnant by J.T. J.T. the man she run off with because she said I treat her like dirt. And now Willie say J.T. run off and left her after he got her knocked up. I asked Willie where she was. Willie said she was up in that room over Babe Lawson's. She told me not to be surprised when I saw her looking real bad. I said I wouldn't be least surprised. I asked Willie she think Maggie come back. Willie say she better.

The room was dirty and Maggie looked worser than Willie say she going to look. I knocked on the door and there weren't no answer so I just opened the door and went in and saw Maggie laying on the bed turned up against the wall. She turnt around when I came in but she didn't say nothing. I said Maggie we getting out a here. So I got the bag she brung when she run away and put all her loose things in it and just took her by the arm and brung her on home. You couldn't tell nothing was in her belly though.

I been taking care of little Henry since she been gone but he $3\frac{1}{2}$ years old and ain't no trouble since he can play hisself and know what it mean when you hit him on the ass when he do something wrong.

Maggie don't say nothing when we get in the house. She just go over to little Henry. He sleeping in the front room on the couch. She go over to little Henry and bend down an kiss him on the cheek and then she ask me have I had supper and when I say Naw she go back in the kitchen and start fixing it. We sitting at the table and nobody saying nothing but I feel I got to say something.

'You can go head and have the baby,' I say. 'I give him my name.'

I say it meaner than I want to. She just look up at me and don't say nothing. Then she say, 'He ain't yours.'

I say, 'I know he ain't mine. But don't nobody else have to know.

Even the baby. He don't even never have to know.'

She just keep looking at me with her big eyes that don't say nothing, and then she say, 'You know. I know.'

She look down at her plate and go on eating. We don't say nothing no more and then when she get through she clear up the dishes and I just go round front and sit out on the front porch. She don't come out like she used to before she start saying I treat her like dirt, and then when I go on in the house to go to bed, she hunched up on her side, with her back to me, so I just take my clothes off and get on in the bed on my side.

Maggie a light yeller woman with chicken scratch hair. That what my mama used to call it chicken scratch hair cause she say there weren't enough hair for a chicken to scratch around in. If it weren't for her hair she look like she was a white woman, a light yeller white woman though. Anyway, when we was coming up somebody say, 'Woman cover you hair if you ain't go'n' straightin' it. Look like chicken scratch.' Sometimes they say look like chicken shit, but they don't tell them to cover it no more, so they wear it like it is. Maggie wear hers like it is.

Me, I come from a family of white-looking niggers, some of 'em, my mama, my daddy musta been, my half daddy he weren't. Come down from the hills around Hazard, Kentucky most of them and claimed nigger cause somebody grandmammy way back there was. First people I know ever claim nigger, 'cept my mama say my daddy hate hoogies (up North I hear they call em honkies) worser than anybody. She say cause he look like he one hisself and then she laugh. I laugh too but I didn't know why she laugh. She say when I come, I look just like a little white rat, so that's why some a the people I hang aroun with call me 'White Rat.' When little Henry come he look just like a little white rabbit, but don't nobody call him 'White Rabbit' they just call him little Henry. I guess the other jus' ain't took. I tried to get them to call him little White Rabbit, but Maggie say naw, cause she say when he grow up he develop a complex, what with the problem he got already. I say what you come at me for with this a complex and then she say, Nothin, jus' something I heard on the radio on one of them edgecation morning shows. And then I say Aw. And then she say Anyway by the time he get seven or eight he probably get the pigment and be dark, cause some of her family was. So I say where I heard somewhere where the chil'ren couldn't be no darker'n the darkest of the two parent and bout the best he could do would be high yeller like she was. And then she say how her sister Lucky got the pigment when she was bout seven and come out real dark. I tell her Well y'all's daddy was dark. And she say, 'Yeah.' Anyway, I guess well she still think little Henry gonna get the pigment when he get to be seven or eight, and told me about all these people come out lighter'n I was and got the pigment fore they growed up.

Like I told you my relatives come down out of the hills and claimed nigger, but only people that believe 'em is people that got to know 'em and people that know 'em, so I usually just stay around with people I know and go in some joint over to Versailles or up to Lexington or down over in Midway where they know me cause I don't like to walk in no place where they say, 'What's that white man doing in here.' They probably say 'yap'—that the Kentucky word for honky. Or 'What that yap doing in here with that nigger woman.' So I jus' keep to the places where they know me. I member when I was young me and the other niggers used to ride around in these cars and when we go to some town where they don't know 'White Rat' everybody look at me like I'm some hoogie, but I don't pay them no mind. 'Cept sometime it hard not to pay em no mind cause I hate the hoogie much as they do, much as my daddy did. I drove up to this filling station one time and these other niggers drove up at the same time, they mighta even drove up a little ahead a me, but this filling station man come up to me first and bent down and said, 'I wait on you first, 'fore I wait on them niggers,' and then he laugh. And then I laugh and say, 'You can wait on them first. I'm a nigger too.' He don't say nothing. He just look at me like he thought I was crazy. I don't remember who he wait on first. But I guess he be careful next time who he say nigger to, even somebody got blonde hair like me, most which done passed over anyhow. That, or the way things been go'n, go'n be trying to pass back. I member once all of us was riding around one Saturday night, I must a been bout twenty-five then, close to forty now, but we was driving around, all us drunk cause it was Saturday, and Shotgun, he was driving and probably drunker'n a skunk and drunken the rest of us hit up on this police car and the police got out and by that time Shotgun done stop, and the police come over and told all us to get out the car, and he looked us over, he didn't have to do much looking because he probably smell it before he got there but he looked us all over and say he gonna haul us all in for being drunk and disord'ly. He say, 'I'm gone haul all y'all in.'

And I say, 'Haul y'all all.' Everybody laugh, but he don't hear me cause he over to his car ringing up the police station to have them send the wagon out. He turned his back to us cause he know we wasn goin nowhere. Didn't have to call but one man cause the only people in the whole Midway police station is Fat Dick and Skinny Dick, Buster Crab and Mr Willie. Sometime we call Buster Crab Face too, and Mr Willie is John Willie, but every body call him Mr Willie cause the name just took. So Skinny Dick come out with the wagon and hauled us all in. So they didn't know me well as I knew them. Thought I was some hoogie jus' run around with the niggers instead of be one of them. So they put my cousin Covington, cause he dark, in the cell with Shotgun and the other niggers and they put me in the cell with the white men. So I'm drunkern a skunk and I'm yellin' let me outa here I'm a nigger too. And Crab Face say, 'If you a nigger I'm a Chinee.' And I keep rattling the bars and saying 'Cov', they got me in here with the white men. Tell 'em I'm a nigger too.' And Cov' yell back, 'He a nigger too,' and then they all laugh, all the niggers laugh, the hoogies they laugh too, but for a different reason and Cov' say, 'Tha's what you get for being drunk and orderly.' And I say, 'Put me in there with the niggers too, I'm a nigger too.' And then one of the white men, he's sitting over in his corner say, 'I ain't never heard of a white man want to be a nigger. 'Cept maybe for the nigger women.' So I look around at him and haul off cause I'm goin hit him and then some man grab me and say, 'He keep a blade,' but that don't make me no difrent and I say, 'A spade don't need a blade.' But then he get his friend to help hole me and then he call Crab Face to come get me out a the cage. So Crab Face come and get me out a the cage and put me in a cage by myself and say, 'When you get out a here you can run around with the niggers all you want, but while you in here you ain't getting no niggers.' By now I'm more sober so I jus' say, 'My cousin's a nigger.' And he say, 'My cousin a monkey's uncle.'

By that time Grandy come. Cause Cov' took his free call but didn't nobody else. Grandy's Cov's grandmama. She my grandmama too on my stepdaddy's side. Anyway, Grandy come and she say, 'I want my *two* sons.' And he take her over to the nigger cage and say, 'Which two?' and she say, 'There one of them,' and points to Cov'ton. 'But I don't see t'other one.' And Crab Face say, 'Well, if you don't see him I don't see him.' Cov'ton just standing there grinning, and don't say nothing. I don't say nothing. I'm just waiting. Grandy ask, 'Cov', where Rat?' Sometime she just call me Rat and leave the 'White' off.

Cov' say, 'They put him in the cage with the white men.' Crab Face standing there looking funny now. His back to me, but I figure he looking funny now. Grandy says, 'Take me to my other boy, I want to see my other boy.' I don't think Crab Face want her to know he thought I was white so he don't say nothing. She just standing there looking up at him cause he tall and fat and she short and fat. Crab Face finally say, 'I put him in a cell by hisself cause he started a rucus.' He point over to me, and she turn and see me and frown. I'm just siting there. She look back at Crab Face and say, 'I want them both out.' 'That be about five dollars a piece for the both of them for disturbing the peace.' That what Crab Face say. I'm sitting there thinking he a poet and don't know it. He a bad poet and don't know it. Grandy say she pay it if it take all her money, which it probably did. So the police let Cov' and me out. And Shotgun waving. Some of the others already settled. Didn't care if they got out the next day. I wouldn't a cared neither, but Grandy say she didn like to see nobody in a cage, specially her own. I say I pay her back. Cov' say he pay her back too. She say we can both pay her back if we just stay out a trouble. So we got together and pay her next week's grocery bill.

Well, that was one 'sperience. I had others, but like I said, now I jus' about keep to the people I know and that know me. The only other big 'sperience was when me and Maggie tried to get married. We went down to the courthouse and fore I even said a word, the man behind the glass cage look up at us and say, 'Round here nigger don't marry white.' I don't say nothing just standing up there looking at him and he looking like a white toad, and I'm wondering if they call him 'white toad' more likely 'white turd.' But I just keep looking at him. Then he the one get tired a looking first and he say, 'Next.' I'm thinking I want to reach in that little winder and pull him right out of that little glass cage. but I don't. He say again, 'Around here nigger don't marry white.' I say, 'I'm a nigger. Nigger marry nigger, don't they?' He just look at me like he thinks I'm crazy. I say, 'I got rel'tives blacker'n your shit. Ain't you never heard a niggers what look like they white.' He just look at me like I'm a nigger too, and tell me where to sign.

Then we get married and I bring her over here to live in this house in Huntertown ain't got but three rooms and a outhouse that's where we always lived, seems like to me, all us Hawks, cept the ones come down from the mountains way back yonder, cept they don't count no more anyway. I kept telling Maggie it get harder and harder to be a white nigger now specially since it don't count no more how much white blood you got in you, in fact, it make you worser for it. I said nowadays sted a walking around like you something special people look at you, after they find out what you are if you like me, like you some kind a bad news that you had something to do with. I tell em I aint had nothing to do with the way I come out. They ack like they like you better if you go on ahead and try to pass, cause, least then they know how to feel about you. Cept nowadays everybody want to be a nigger, or it getting that way. I tell Maggie she got it made, cause at least she got that chicken shit hair, but all she answers is, 'That why you treat me like chicken shit.' But tha's only since we been having our troubles.

Little Henry the cause a our troubles. I tell Maggie I ain't changed since he was borned, but she say I have. I always say I been a hard man, kind of quick-tempered. A hard man to crack like one of them walnuts. She say all it take to crack a walnut is your teeth. She say she put a walnut between her teeth and it crack not even need a hammer. So I say I'm a nigger toe nut then. I ask her if she ever seen one of them nigger toe nuts they the toughest nuts to crack. She say, 'A nigger toe nut is black. A white nigger toe nut be easy to crack.' Then I don't say nothing and she keep saying I changed cause I took to drink. I tell her I drink before I married her. She say then I start up again. She say she don't like it when I drink cause I'm quicker tempered than when I ain't drunk. She say I come home drunk and say things and then go sleep and then the next morning forget what I say. She won't tell me what I say. I say, 'You a woman scart of words. Won't do nothing.' She say she ain't scart of words. She say one of these times I might not jus' say something. I might *do* something. Short time after she say that was when she run off with J.T.

Reason I took to drink again was because little Henry was borned club-footed. I tell the truth in the beginning I blamed Maggie, cause I herited all those hill man's superstitions and nigger superstitions too, and I said she didn't do something right when she was carrying him or she did something she shouldn't oughta did or looked at something she shouldn't oughta looked at like some cows fucking or something. I'm serious. I blamed her. Little Henry come out looking like a little club-footed rabbit. Or some rabbits being birthed or something. I said there weren't never nothing like that in my family ever since we been living on this earth. And they must have come from her side. And then I said cause she had more of whatever it was in her than I had in me. And then she said that brought it all out. All that stuff I been hiding up inside me cause she said I didn't hated them hoogies like my daddy did and I just been feeling I had to live up to something he set and the onliest reason I married her was because she was the lightest and brightest nigger woman I could get and still be nigger. Once that nigger start to lay it on me she jus' keep it up till I didn't feel nothing but start to feeling what she say, and then I even told her I was leaving and she say, 'What about little Henry?' And I say, 'He's your nigger.' And then it was like I didn't know no other word but nigger when I was going out that door.

I found some joint and went in it and just start pouring the stuff down. It weren't no nigger joint neither, it was a hoogie joint. First time in my life I ever been in a hoogie joint too, and I kept thinking a nigger woman did it. I wasn't drunk enough *not* to know what I was saying neither. I was sitting up to the bar talking to the tender. He just standing up there, wasn nothing special to him, he probably weren't even listen cept but with one ear. I say, 'I know this nigger. You know I know the niggers. (He just nod but don't say nothing.) Know them close. You know what I mean. Know them like they was my own. Know them where you s'pose to know them.' I grinned at him like he was s'pose to know them too. 'You know my family came down out of the hills, like they was some kind of rain gods, you know, miss'ology. What they teached you bout the Juicifer. Anyway, I knew this nigger that made hisself a priest, you know turned his white color I mean turned his white collar backwards and dressed up in a monkey suit—you get it?' He didn't get it. 'Well, he made hisself a priest, but after a while he didn't want to be no priest, so he pronounced hisself.' The bartender said, 'Renounced.' 'So he 'nounced hisself and took of his turned back collar and went back to just being a plain old ever day chi'lins and downhome and hamhocks and corn pone nigger. And you know what else he did? He got married. Yeah the nigger what once was a priest got married. Once took all them vows of cel'bacy come and got married. Got married so he could come.' I laugh. He don't. I got evil. 'Well, he come awight. He come and she come too. She come and had a baby. And you know what else? The baby come too. Ha. No ha? The baby come out clubfooted. So you know what he did? He didn't blame his wife. He blamed hisself. The nigger blamed hisself cause he said the God put a curse on him for goin' agin his vows. He said the God put a curse on him cause he took his vows of cel'bacy, which mean no fuckin', cept everybody know what *they* do, and went agin his vows of cel'bacy and married a nigger woman so he could do what every ord'narry onery person was doing and the Lord didn't just put a curse on him. He said he could a stood that. But the Lord carried the curse clear over to the next gen'ration and put a curse on his little baby boy who didn do nothing in his whole life . . . cept come.' I laugh and laugh. Then when I quit laughing I drink some more, and then when I quit drinking I talk some more. 'And you know something else?' I say. This time he say, 'No.' I say, 'I knew another priest that took the vows, only this priest was white. You wanta know what happen to him. He broke his vows same as the nigger and got married same as the nigger. And they had a baby too. Want to know what happen to him?' 'What?' 'He come out a nigger.'

Then I got so drunk I can't go no place but home. I'm thinking it's the Hawk's house, not hers. If anybody get throwed out it's her. She the nigger. I'm goin' fool her. Throw her right *out* the bed if she in it. But then when I get home I'm the one that's fool. Cause she gone *and* little Henry gone. So I guess I just badmouthed the walls like the devil till I jus' layed down and went to sleep. The next morning little Henry come back with a neighbor woman but Maggie don't come. The woman hand over little Henry, and I ask her, 'Where's Maggie?' She looked at me like she think I'm the devil and say, 'I don't know, but she lef' me this note to give to you.' So she jus' give me the note and went. I opened the note and read. She write like a chicken too, I'm thinking, chicken scratch. I read: 'I run off with J.T. cause he been wanting me to run off with him and I ain't been wanting to tell now. I'm send litle Henry back cause I just took him away last night cause I didn't want you to be doing nothing you regret in the morning.' So I figured she figured I got to stay sober if I got to take care of myself and little Henry. Little Henry didn't say nothing and I didn't say nothing. I just put him on in the house and let him play with hisself.

That was two months ago. I ain't take a drop since. But last night Cousin Willie come and say where Maggie was and now she moving around in the kitchen and feeding little Henry and I guess when I get up she feed me. I get up and get dressed and go in the kitchen. She say when the new baby come we see whose fault it was. J.T. blacker'n a lump of coal. Maggie keep saying 'When the baby come we see who fault it was.' It's two more months now that I been look at her, but I still don't see no belly change.

1971

ARE THESE ACTUAL MILES?

Raymond Carver

Fact is the car needs to be sold in a hurry, and Leo sends Toni out to do it. Toni is smart and has personality. She used to sell children's encyclopedias door to door. She signed him up, even though he didn't have kids. Afterward, Leo asked her for a date, and the date led to this. This deal has to be cash, and it has to be done tonight. Tomorrow somebody they owe might slap a lien on the car. Monday they'll be in court, home free—but word on them went out yesterday, when their lawyer mailed the letters of intention. The hearing on Monday is nothing to worry about, the lawyer has said. They'll be asked some questions, and they'll sign some papers, and that's it. But sell the convertible, he said—today, *tonight*. They can hold onto the little car, Leo's car, no problem. But they go into court with that big convertible, the court will take it, and that's that.

Toni dresses up. It's four o'clock in the afternoon. Leo worries the lots will close. But Toni takes her time dressing. She puts on a new white blouse, wide lacy cuffs, the new two-piece suit, new heels. She transfers the stuff from her straw purse into the new patent-leather handbag. She studies the lizard makeup pouch and puts that in too. Toni has been two hours on her hair and face. Leo stands in the bedroom doorway and taps his lips with his knuckles, watching.

'You're making me nervous,' she says. 'I wish you wouldn't just stand,' she says. 'So tell me how I look.'

'You look fine,' he says. 'You look great. I'd buy a car from you anytime.'

'But you don't have money,' she says, peering into the mirror. She pats her hair, frowns. 'And your credit's lousy. You're nothing,' she says. 'Teasing,' she says and looks at him in the mirror. 'Don't be serious,' she says. 'It has to be done, so I'll do it. You take it out, you'd be lucky to get three, four hundred and we both know it. Honey, you'd be lucky if you didn't have to pay *them*.' She gives her hair a final pat, gums her lips, blots the lipstick with a tissue. She turns away from the mirror and picks up her purse. 'I'll have to have dinner or something, I told you that already, that's the way they

393

work, I know them. But don't worry, I'll get out of it,' she says. 'I can handle it.'

'Jesus,' Leo says, 'did you have to say that?'

She looks at him steadily. 'Wish me luck,' she says.

'Luck,' he says. 'You have the pink slip?' he says.

She nods. He follows her through the house, a tall woman with a small high bust, broad hips and thighs. He scratches a pimple on his neck. 'You're sure?' he says. 'Make sure. You have to have the pink slip.'

'I have the pink slip,' she says.

'Make sure.'

She starts to say something, instead looks at herself in the front window and then shakes her head.

'At least call,' he says. 'Let me know what's going on.'

'I'll call,' she says. 'Kiss, kiss. Here,' she says and points to the corner of her mouth. 'Careful,' she says.

He holds the door for her. 'Where are you going to try first?' he says. She moves past him and onto the porch.

Ernest Williams looks from across the street. In his Bermuda shorts, stomach hanging, he looks at Leo and Toni as he directs a spray onto his begonias. Once, last winter, during the holidays, when Toni and the kids were visiting his mother's, Leo brought a woman home. Nine o'clock the next morning, a cold foggy Saturday, Leo walked the woman to the car, surprised Ernest Williams on the sidewalk with a newspaper in his hand. Fog drifted, Ernest Williams stared, then slapped the paper against his leg, hard.

Leo recalls that slap, hunches his shoulders, says, 'You have someplace in mind first?'

'I'll just go down the line,' she says. 'The first lot, then I'll just go down the line.'

'Open at nine hundred,' he says. 'Then come down. Nine hundred is low bluebook, even on a cash deal.'

'I know where to start,' she says.

Ernest Williams turns the hose in their direction. He stares at them through the spray of water. Leo has an urge to cry out a confession.

'Just making sure,' he says.

'OK, OK,' she says. 'I'm off.'

It's her car, they call it her car, and that makes it all the worse. They bought it new that summer three years ago. She wanted something to do after the kids started school, so she went back selling. He was working six days a week in the fiber-glass plant. For a while they didn't know how to spend the money. Then they put a thousand on the convertible and doubled and tripled the payments until in a year they had it paid. Earlier, while she was dressing, he took the jack and spare from the trunk and emptied the glove compartment of pencils, matchbooks, Blue Chip stamps. Then he washed it and vacuumed inside. The red hood and fenders shine.

'Good luck,' he says and touches her elbow.

She nods. He sees she is already gone, already negotiating.

'Things are going to be different!' he calls to her as she reaches the driveway. 'We start over Monday. I mean it.'

Ernest Williams looks at them and turns his head and spits. She gets into the car and lights a cigarette.

'This time next week!' Leo calls again. 'Ancient history!'

He waves as she backs into the street. She changes gear and starts ahead. She accelerates and the tires give a little scream.

In the kitchen Leo pours Scotch and carries the drink to the backyard. The kids are at his mother's. There was a letter three days ago, his name penciled on the outside of the dirty envelope, the only letter all summer not demanding payment in full. We are having fun, the letter said. We like Grandma. We have a new dog called Mr Six. He is nice. We love him. Good-bye.

He goes for another drink. He adds ice and sees that his hand trembles. He holds the hand over the sink. He looks at the hand for a while, sets down the glass, and holds out the other hand. Then he picks up the glass and goes back outside to sit on the steps. He recalls when he was a kid his dad pointing at a fine house, a tall white house surrounded by apple trees and a high white rail fence. 'That's Finch,' his dad said admiringly. 'He's been in bankruptcy at least twice. Look at that house.' But bankruptcy is a company collapsing utterly, executives cutting their wrists and throwing themselves from windows, thousands of men on the street.

Leo and Toni still had furniture. Leo and Toni had furniture and Toni and the kids had clothes. Those things were exempt. What else? Bicycles for the kids, but these he had sent to his mother's for safekeeping. The portable air-conditioner and the appliances, new washer and dryer, trucks came for those things weeks ago. What else did they have? This and that, nothing mainly, stuff that wore out or fell to pieces long ago. But there were some big parties back there,

395

some fine travel. To Reno and Tahoe, at eighty with the top down and the radio playing. Food, that was one of the big items. They gorged on food. He figures thousands on luxury items alone. Toni would go to the grocery and put in everything she saw. 'I had to do without when I was a kid,' she says. 'These kids are not going to do without,' as if he'd been insisting they should. She joins all the book clubs. 'We never had books around when I was a kid,' she says as she tears open the heavy packages. They enroll in the record clubs for something to play on the new stereo. They sign up for it all. Even a pedigreed terrier named Ginger. He paid two hundred and found her run over in the street a week later. They buy what they want. If they can't pay, they charge. They sign up.

His undershirt is wet; he can feel the sweat rolling from his underarms. He sits on the step with the empty glass in his hand and watches the shadows fill up the yard. He stretches, wipes his face. He listens to the traffic on the highway and considers whether he should go to the basement, stand on the utility sink, and hang himself with his belt. He understands he is willing to be dead.

Inside he makes a large drink and he turns the TV on and he fixes something to eat. He sits at the table with chili and crackers and watches something about a blind detective. He clears the table. He washes the pan and the bowl, dries these things and puts them away, then allows himself a look at the clock.

It's after nine. She's been gone nearly five hours.

He pours Scotch, adds water, carries the drink to the living room. He sits on the couch but finds his shoulders so stiff they won't let him lean back. He stares at the screen and sips, and soon he goes for another drink. He sits again. A news program begins—it's ten o'clock—and he says, 'God, what in God's name has gone wrong?' and goes to the kitchen to return with more Scotch. He sits, he closes his eyes, and opens them when he hears the telephone ringing.

'I wanted to call,' she says.

'Where are you?' he says. He hears piano music, and his heart moves.

'I don't know,' she says. 'Someplace. We're having a drink, then we're going someplace else for dinner. I'm with the sales manager. He's crude, but he's all right. He bought the car. I have to go now. I was on my way to the ladies and saw the phone.'

'Did somebody buy the car?' Leo says. He looks out the kitchen window to the place in the drive where she always parks.

'I told you,' she says. 'I have to go now.'

'Wait, wait a minute, for Christ's sake,' he says. 'Did somebody buy the car or not?'

'He had his checkbook out when I left,' she says. 'I have to go now. I have to go to the bathroom.'

'Wait!' he yells. The line goes dead. He listens to the dial tone. 'Jesus Christ,' he says as he stands with the receiver in his hand.

He circles the kitchen and goes back to the living room. He sits. He gets up. In the bathroom he brushes his teeth very carefully. Then he uses dental floss. He washes his face and goes back to the kitchen. He looks at the clock and takes a clean glass from a set that has a hand of playing cards painted on each glass. He fills the glass with ice. He stares for a while at the glass he left in the sink.

He sits against one end of the couch and puts his legs up at the other end. He looks at the screen, realizes he can't make out what the people are saying. He turns the empty glass in his hand and considers biting off the rim. He shivers for a time and thinks of going to bed, though he knows he will dream of a large woman with gray hair. In the dream he is always leaning over tying his shoelaces. When he straightens up, she looks at him, and he bends to tie again. He looks at his hand. It makes a fist as he watches. The telephone is ringing.

'Where are you, honey?' he says slowly, gently.

'We're at this restaurant,' she says, her voice strong, bright.

'Honey, which restaurant,' he says. He puts the heel of his hand against his eye and pushes.

'Downtown someplace,' she says. 'I think it's New Jimmy's. Excuse me,' she says to someone off the line, 'is this place New Jimmy's? This is New Jimmy's, Leo,' she says to him. 'Everything is all right, we're almost finished, then he's going to bring me home.'

'Honey?' he says. He holds the receiver against his ear and rocks back and forth, eyes closed. 'Honey?'

'I have to go,' she says. 'I wanted to call. Anyway, guess how much?'

'Honey,' he says.

'Six and a quarter,' she says. 'I have it in my purse. He said there's no market for convertibles. I guess we're born lucky,' she says and laughs. 'I told him everything. I think I had to.'

'Honey,' Leo says.

'He said he sympathizes,' she says. 'But he would have said anything.' She laughs again. 'He said personally he'd rather be classified a robber or a rapist than a bankrupt. He's nice enough, though,' she says.

'Come home,' Leo says. 'Take a cab and come home.'

'I can't,' she says. 'I told you, we're halfway through dinner.'

'I'll come for you,' he says.

'No,' she says. 'I said we're just finishing. I told you, it's part of the deal. They're out for all they can get. But don't worry, we're about to leave. I'll be home in a little while.' She hangs up.

In a few minutes he calls New Jimmy's. A man answers. 'New Jimmy's has closed for the evening,' the man says.

'I'd like to talk to my wife,' Leo says.

'Does she work here?' the man asks. 'Who is she?'

'She's a customer,' Leo says. 'She's with someone. A business person.'

'Would I know her?' the man says. 'What is her name?'

'I don't think you know her,' Leo says.

'That's all right,' Leo says. 'That's all right. I see her now.'

'Thank you for calling New Jimmy's,' the man says.

Leo hurries to the window. A car he doesn't recognize slows in front of the house, then picks up speed. He waits. Two, three hours later, the telephone rings again. There is no one at the other end when he picks up the receiver. There is only a dial tone.

'I'm right here!' Leo screams into the receiver.

Near dawn he hears footsteps on the porch. He gets up from the couch. The set hums, the screen glows. He opens the door. She bumps the wall coming in. She grins. Her face is puffy, as if she's been sleeping under sedation. She works her lips, ducks heavily and sways as he cocks his fist.

'Go ahead,' she says thickly. She stands there swaying. Then she makes a noise and lunges, catches his shirt, tears it down the front. 'Bankrupt!' she screams. She twists loose, grabs and tears his undershirt at the neck. 'You son of a bitch,' she says, clawing.

He squeezes her wrist, then lets go, steps back, looking for something heavy. She stumbles as she heads for the bedroom. 'Bankrupt,' she mutters. He hears her fall on the bed and groan.

He waits awhile, then splashes water on his face and goes to the bedroom. He turns the lights on, looks at her, and begins to take her clothes off. He pulls and pushes her from side to side undressing her. She says something in her sleep and moves her hand. He takes off her underpants, looks at them closely under the light, and throws them into a corner. He turns back the covers and rolls her in, naked. Then he opens her purse. He is reading the check when he hears the car come into the drive.

He looks through the front curtain and sees the convertible in the drive, its motor running smoothly, the headlamps burning, and he closes and opens his eyes. He sees a tall man come around in front of the car and up to the front porch. The man lays something on the porch and starts back to the car. He wears a white linen suit.

Leo turns on the porch light and opens the door cautiously. Her makeup pouch lies on the top step. The man looks at Leo across the front of the car, and then gets back inside and releases the handbrake.

'Wait!' Leo calls and starts down the steps. The man brakes the car as Leo walks in front of the lights. The car creaks against the brake. Leo tries to pull the two pieces of his shirt together, tries to bunch it all into his trousers.

'What is it you want?' the man says. 'Look,' the man says, 'I have to go. No offense. I buy and sell cars, right? The lady left her makeup. She's a fine lady, very refined. What is it?'

Leo leans against the door and looks at the man. The man takes his hands off the wheel and puts them back. He drops the gear into reverse and the car moves backward a little.

'I want to tell you,' Leo says and wets his lips.

The light in Ernest Williams' bedroom goes on. The shade rolls up.

Leo shakes his head, tucks in his shirt again. He steps back from the car. 'Monday,' he says.

'Monday,' the man says and watches for sudden movement.

Leo nods slowly.

'Well, goodnight,' the man says and coughs. 'Take it easy, hear? Monday, that's right. OK then.' He takes his foot off the brake, puts it on again after he has rolled back two or three feet. 'Hey, one question. Between friends, are these actual miles?' The man waits, then clears his throat. 'OK, look, it doesn't matter either way,' the man says. 'I have to go. Take it easy.' He backs into the street, pulls away quickly, and turns the corner without stopping.

Leo tucks at his shirt and goes back in the house. He locks the front door and checks it. Then he goes to the bedroom and locks that door and turns back the covers. He looks at her before he flicks the light. He takes off his clothes, folds them carefully on the floor, and gets in beside her. He lies on his back for a time and pulls the hair on his stomach, considering. He looks at the bedroom door, outlined now in the faint outside light. Presently he reaches out his hand and touches her hip. He runs his fingers over her hip and feels the stretch marks there. They are like roads, and he traces them in her flesh. He runs his fingers back and forth, first one, then another. They run everywhere in her flesh, dozens, perhaps hundreds of them. He remembers waking up the morning after they bought the car, seeing it, there in the drive, in the sun, gleaming.

1972

TRAIN

Joy Williams

Inside, the Auto-Train was violet. Both little girls were pleased because it was their favorite color. Violet was practically the only thing they agreed on. Danica Anderson and Jane Muirhead were both ten years old. They had traveled from Maine to Washington, DC, by car with Jane's parents and were now on the train with Jane's parents and one hundred nine other people and forty-two automobiles on the way to Florida where they lived. It was September. Danica had been with Jane since June. Danica's mother was getting married again and she had needed the summer months to settle down and have everything nice for Dan when she saw her in September. In August, her mother had written Dan and asked what she could do to make things nice for Dan when she got back. Dan replied that she would like a good wall-hung pencil sharpener and satin sheets. She would like cowboy bread for supper. Dan supposed that she would get none of these things. Her mother hadn't even asked her what cowboy bread was.

The girls explored the entire train, north to south. They saw everyone but the engineer. Then they sat down in their violet seats. Jane made faces at a cute little toddler holding a cloth rabbit until he started to cry. Dan took out her writing materials and began writing to Jim Anderson. She was writing him a postcard.

'Jim,' she wrote, 'I miss you and I will see you any minute. When I see you we will go swimming right away.'

'That is real messy writing,' Jane said. 'It's all scrunched together. If you were writing to anyone other than a dog, they wouldn't be able to read it at all.'

Dan printed her name on the bottom of the card and embellished it all with X's and O's.

'Your writing to Jim Anderson is dumb in about twelve different ways. He's a *golden retriever*, for Godssakes.'

Dan looked at her friend mildly. She was used to Jane yelling at her and expressing disgust and impatience. Jane had once lived in Manhattan. She had developed certain attitudes. Jane was a treasure

401

from the city of New York currently on loan to the state of Florida where her father, for the last two years, had been engaged in running down a perfectly good investment in a marina and dinner theater. Jane liked to wear scarves tied around her head. She claimed to enjoy grapes and brown sugar and sour cream for dessert more than ice cream and cookies. She liked artichokes. She *adored* artichokes. She *adored* the part in the New York City Ballet's *Nutcracker Suite* where the Dew Drops and the candied Petals of Roses dance to the 'Waltz of the Flowers.' Jane had seen the *Nutcracker* four *times*, for Godssakes.

Dan and Jane and Jane's mother and father had all lived with Jane's grandmother in her big house in Maine all summer. The girls hadn't seen that much of the Muirheads. The Muirheads were always 'cruising.' They were always 'gunk-holing' as they called it. Whatever that was, Jane said, for Godssakes. Jane's grandmother had a house on the ocean and knew how to make pizza and candy and sail a canoe. She called pizza 'za. She sang hymns in the shower. She sewed sequins on their jeans and made them say grace before dinner. After they said grace, Jane's grandmother would ask forgiveness for things done and left undone. She would, upon request, lie down and chat with them at night before they went to sleep. Jane was crazy about her grandmother and was quite a nice person in her presence. One night, at the end of the summer, Jane had had a dream in which men dressed in black suits and white bathing caps had broken into her grandmother's house and taken all her possessions and put them in the road. In Jane's dream, rain fell on all her grandmother's things. Jane woke up weeping. Dan had wept too. Jane and Dan were friends.

The train had not yet left the station even though it was two hours past the posted departure time. An announcement had just been made that said that a two-hour delay was built into the train's schedule.

'They make up the time at night,' Jane said. She plucked the postcard from Dan's hand. 'This is a good one,' she said. 'I think you're sending it to Jim Anderson just so you can save it yourself.' She read aloud, 'This is a photograph of the Phantom Dream Car crashing through a wall of burning television sets before a cheering crowd at the Cow Palace in San Francisco.'

At the beginning of summer, Dan's mother had given her one hundred dollars, four packages of new underwear and three dozen stamped postcards. Most of the cards were plain but there were a few with odd pictures on them. Dan's mother wanted to hear from her twice weekly throughout the summer. She had married a man named Jake, who was a carpenter. Jake had already built Dan three bookcases. This seemed to be the extent of what he knew how to do for Dan.

'I only have three left now,' Dan said, 'but when I get home, I'm going to start my own collection.'

'I've been through that phase,' Jane said. 'It's just a phase. I don't think you're much of a correspondent. You wrote, "I got sunburn. Love, Dan" . . . "I bought a green Frisbee. Love, Dan" . . . "Mrs Muirhead has swimmer's ear. Love, Dan" . . . "Mr Muirhead went water-skiing and cracked his rib. Love, Dan" . . . When you write to people you should have something to say.'

Dan didn't reply. She had been Jane's companion for a long time, and was wearying of what Jane's mother called her 'effervescence.'

Jane slapped Dan on the back and hollered, 'Danica Anderson, for Godssakes! What is a clod like yourself doing on this fabulous journey!'

Together, as the train began to move, the girls made their way to the Starlight Lounge in Car 7 where Mr and Mrs Muirhead told them they would be enjoying cocktails. They hesitated in the car where the train's magician was with his audience, watching him while he did the magic silks trick, the cut and restored handkerchief trick, the enchanted salt shaker trick, and the dissolving quarter trick. The audience, primarily retirees, screamed with pleasure.

'I don't mind the tricks,' Jane whispered to Dan, 'but the junk that gets said drives me crazy.'

The magician was a young man with a long spotted face. He did a lot of card forcing. Again and again, he called the card that people chose from a shuffled deck. Each time that the magician was successful, the audience participant yelled and smiled and in general acted thrilled. Jane and Dan passed on through.

'You don't really choose,' Jane said. 'He just makes you think you choose. He does it all with his pinky.' She pushed Dan forward into the Starlight Lounge where Mrs Muirhead was on a banquette staring out the window at a shed and an unkempt bush which was sliding slowly past. She was drinking a martini. Mr Muirhead was several tables away talking to a young man wearing jeans and a yellow jacket. Jane did not sit down. 'Mummy,' she said, 'can I have your olive?'

'Of course not,' Mrs Muirhead said, 'it's soaked in gin.'

Jane, Dan in tow, went to her father's table. 'Daddy,' Jane demanded, 'why aren't you sitting with Mummy? Are you and Mummy having a fight?'

Dan was astonished at this question. Mr and Mrs Muirhead fought continuously and as bitterly as vipers. Their arguments were baroque, stately, and although frequently extraordinary, never enlightening. At breakfast, they would be quarreling over an incident at a cocktail party the night before or a dumb remark made fifteen years ago. At dinner, they would be howling over the fate, which they called by many names, which had given them one another. Forgiveness, charity and cooperation were qualities unknown to them. They were opponents *pur sang*. Dan was sure that one morning, Jane would be called from her classroom and told as gently as possible by Mr Mooney, the school principal, that her parents had splattered one another's brains all over the lanai.

Mr Muirhead looked at the children sorrowfully and touched Jane's cheek.

'I am not sitting with your mother because I am sitting with this young man here. We are having a fascinating conversation.'

'Why are you always talking to young men?' Jane asked.

'Jane, honey,' Mr Muirhead said, 'I will answer that.' He took a swallow of his drink and sighed. He leaned forward and said earnestly, 'I talk to so many young men because your mother won't let me talk to young women.' He remained hunched over, patting Jane's cheek for a moment, and then leaned back.

The young man extracted a cigarette from his jacket and hesitated. Mr Muirhead gave him a book of matches. 'He does automobile illustrations,' Mr Muirhead said.

The young man nodded. 'Belly bands. Pearls and flakes. Flames. All custom work.'

Mr Muirhead smiled. He seemed happier now. Mr Muirhead loved conversation. He loved 'to bring people out.' Dan supposed that Jane had picked up this pleasant trait from her father and distorted it in some perversely personal way.

'I bet you have a Trans Am yourself,' Jane said.

'You are so-o-o right,' the young man said. 'It's ice-blue. You like ice-blue? Maybe you're too young.' He extended his hand showing a large gaudy stone in a setting that seemed to be gold. 'Same color as this ring,' he said.

Dan nodded. She could still be impressed by adults. Their mysterious, unreliable images still had the power to attract and confound her, but Jane was clearly not interested in the young man. She demanded much of life. She had very high standards when she wanted to. Mr Muirhead ordered the girls ginger ales and the young man and himself another round of drinks. Sometimes the train, in the mysterious way of trains, would stop, or even reverse, and they would pass unfamiliar scenes once more. The same green pasture filled with slanty light, the same row of clapboard houses, each with the shades of their windows drawn against the heat, the same boats on their trailers, waiting on dry land. The moon was rising beneath a spectacular lightning and thunder storm. People around them were commenting on it. Close to the train, a sheen of dark birds flew low across a dirt road.

'Birds are the only flying reptiles, I'm sure you're all aware,' Jane said suddenly.

'Oh my God, what a horrible thought!' Mr Muirhead said. His face had become a little slack and his hair had become somewhat disarranged.

'It's true, it's true,' Jane sang. 'Sad but true.'

'You mean like lizards and snakes?' the young man asked. He snorted and shook his head.

'*Glorified* reptiles, certainly,' Mr Muirhead said, recovering a bit of his sense of time and place.

Dan suddenly felt lonely. It was not homesickness, although she would have given anything at that moment to be poking around in her little aluminum boat with Jim Anderson. But she wouldn't be living any longer in the place she thought of as 'home.' The town was the same but the place was different. The house where she had been a little tiny baby and had lived her whole life belonged to someone else now. Over the summer, her mother and Jake had bought another house which Jake was going to fix up.

'Reptiles have scales,' the young man said, 'or else they are long and slimy.'

Dan felt like bawling. She could feel the back of her eyes swelling up like cupcakes. She was surrounded by strangers saying crazy things. Even her own mother often said crazy things in a reasonable way that made Dan know she was a stranger too. Dan's mother told Dan everything. Her mother told her she wouldn't have to worry about having brothers or sisters. Her mother discussed the particular

405

nature of the problem with her. Half the things Dan's mother told her, Dan didn't want to know. There would be no brothers and sisters. There would be Dan and her mother and Jake, sitting around the house together, caring deeply for one another, sharing a nice life together, not making any mistakes.

Dan excused herself and started toward the lavatory on the level below. Mrs Muirhead called to her as she approached and handed her a folded piece of paper. 'Would you be kind enough to give this to Mr Muirhead?' she asked. Dan returned to Mr Muirhead and gave him the note and then went down to the lavatory. She sat on the little toilet as the train rocked along and cried.

After a while, she heard Jane's voice saying, 'I hear you in there, Danica Anderson. What's the matter with you?'

Dan didn't say anything.

'I know it's you,' Jane said. 'I can see your stupid shoes and your stupid socks.'

Dan blew her nose, pushed the button on the toilet and said, 'What did the note say?'

'I don't know,' Jane said. 'Daddy ate it.'

'He ate it!' Dan exclaimed. She opened the door of the stall and went to the sink. She washed her hands and splashed her face with water. She giggled. 'He really ate it?'

'Everybody is looped in that Starlight Lounge,' Jane said. Jane patted her hair with a hairbrush. Jane's hair was full of tangles and she never brushed hard enough to get them out. She looked at Dan by looking in the mirror. 'Why were you crying?'

'I was thinking abut your grandma,' Dan said. 'She said that one year she left the Christmas tree up until Easter.'

'Why were you thinking about my grandma!' Jane yelled.

'I was thinking about her singing,' Dan said, startled. 'I like her singing.'

In her head, Dan could hear Jane's grandmother singing about Death's dark waters and sinking souls, about Mercy Seats and the Great Physician. She could hear the voice rising and falling through the thin walls of the Maine house, borne past the dark screens and into the night.

'I don't want you thinking about my grandma,' Jane said, pinching Dan's arm.

Dan tried not to think of Jane's grandma. Once, she had seen her fall coming out of the water. The beach was stony. The stones were round and smooth and slippery. Jane's grandmother had skinned her arm and bloodied her lip.

The girls went into the corridor and saw Mrs Muirhead standing there. Mrs Muirhead was deeply tanned. She had put her hair up in a twist and a wad of cotton was noticeable in her left ear. The three of them stood together, bouncing and nudging against one another with the motion of the train.

'My ear is killing me,' Mrs Muirhead said. 'I think there's something they're not telling me. It crackles and snaps in there. It's like a bird breaking seeds in there.' She touched the bone between cheekbone and ear. 'I think that doctor I was seeing should lose his license. He was handsome and competent, certainly, but on my last visit, he was vacuuming my ear and his secretary came in to ask him a question and she put her hand on his neck. She stroked his neck, his secretary! While I was sitting there having my ear vacuumed!' Mrs Muirhead's cheeks were flushed.

The three of them gazed out the window. The train must have been clipping along, but things outside, although gone in an instant, seemed to be moving slowly. Beneath a street light, a man was kicking his pickup truck.

'I dislike trains,' Mrs Muirhead said. 'I find them depressing.'

'It's the oxygen deprivation,' Jane said, 'coming from having to share the air with all these people.'

'You're such a snob, dear,' Mrs Muirhead sighed.

'We're going to supper now,' Jane said.

'Supper,' Mrs Muirhead said. 'Ugh.'

The children left her looking out the window, a disconsolate, pretty woman wearing a green dress with a line of frogs dancing around it.

The dining car was almost full. The windows reflected the eaters. The countryside was dim and the train pushed through it.

Jane steered them to a table where a man and woman silently labored over their meal.

'My name is Crystal,' Jane offered, 'and this is my twin sister, Clara.'

'Clara!' Dan exclaimed. Jane was always inventing drab names for her.

'We were triplets,' Jane went on, 'but the other died at birth. Cord got all twisted around his neck or something.'

The woman looked at Jane and smiled.

'What is your line of work?' Jane persisted brightly.

There was silence. The woman kept smiling, then the man said, 'I don't do anything, I don't have to do anything. I was injured in Vietnam and they brought me to the base hospital and worked on reviving me for forty-five minutes. Then they gave up. They thought I was dead. Four hours later, I woke up in the mortuary. The Army give me a good pension.' He pushed his chair away from the table and left.

Dan looked after him, astonished, a cold roll raised halfway to her mouth. 'Was your husband really dead for all that while?' she asked.

'My husband, ha!' the woman said. 'I'd never laid eyes on that man before the six-thirty seating.'

'I bet you're a professional woman who doesn't believe in men,' Jane said slyly.

'Crystal, how did you guess! It's true, men are a collective hallucination of women. It's like when a group of crackpots get together on a hilltop and see flying saucers.' The woman picked at her chicken.

Jane looked surprised, then said, 'My father went to a costume party once wrapped from head to foot in aluminum foil.'

'A casserole,' the woman offered.

'No! A spaceman, an alien astronaut!'

Dan giggled, remembering when Mr Muirhead had done that. She felt that Jane had met her match in this woman.

'What do you do!' Jane fairly screamed. 'You won't tell us!'

'I do drugs,' the woman said. The girls shrank back. 'Ha,' the woman said. 'Actually, I test drugs for pharmaceutical companies. And I do research for a perfume manufacturer. I am involved in the search for human pheromones.'

Jane looked levelly at the woman.

'I know you don't know what a pheromone is, Crystal. To put it grossly, a pheromone is a smell that a person has that can make another person do or feel a certain thing. It's an irresistible signal.'

Dan thought of mangrove roots and orange groves. Of the smell of gas when the pilot light blew out on Jane's grandmother's stove. She liked the smell of the Atlantic Ocean when it dried upon your skin and the smell of Jim Anderson's fur when he had been rained upon. There were smells that could make you follow them, certainly.

Jane stared at the woman, tipping forward slightly in her seat.

'Relax, will you, Crystal, you're just a child. You don't even *have* a smell yet,' the woman said. 'I test all sorts of things. Sometimes I'm part of a control group and sometimes I'm not. You never know. If you're part of the control group, you're just given a placebo. A placebo, Crystal, is something that is nothing, but you don't know it's nothing. You think you're getting something that will change you or make you feel better or healthier or more attractive or something, but you're not really.'

'I know what a placebo is,' Jane muttered.

'Well that's terrific, Crystal, you're a prodigy.' The woman removed a book from her handbag and began to read it. The book had a denim jacket on it which concealed its title.

'Ha!' Jane said, rising quickly and attempting to knock over a glass of water. 'My name's not Crystal!'

Dan grabbed the glass before it fell and hurried after her. They returned to the Starlight Lounge. Mr Muirhead was sitting with another young man. This young man had a blond beard and a studious manner.

'Oh, this is a wonderful trip!' Mr Muirhead said exuberantly. 'The wonderful people you meet on a trip like this! This is the most fascinating young man. He's a writer. Been everywhere. He's putting together a book on cemeteries of the world. It isn't that some subject? I told him anytime he's in our town, stop by our restaurant, be my guest for some stone crab claws.'

'Hullo,' the young man said to the girls.

'We were speaking of Père-Lachaise, the legendary Parisian cemetery,' Mr Muirhead said. 'So wistful. So grand and romantic. Your mother and I visited it, Jane, when we were in Paris. We strolled through it on a clear crisp autumn day. The desires of the human heart have no boundaries, girls. The mess of secrets in the human heart are without number. Witnessing Père-Lachaise was a very moving experience. As we strolled, your mother was screaming at me, Jane. Do you know why, honey-bunch? She was screaming at me because back in New York, I had garaged the car at the place on East 84th Street. Your mother said that the people in the place on East 84th Street never turned the ignition all the way off to the left and were always running down the battery. She said that there wasn't a soul in all of New York City who didn't know that the people running the garage on East 84th Street were idiots who were always ruining batteries. Before Père-Lachaise, girls, this young man and I were discussing the Panteón, just outside of Guanajuato in Mexico. It so happens that I am also familiar with the Panteón. Your

mother wanted some tiles for the foyer so we went to Mexico. You
stayed with Mrs Murphy, Jane. Remember? It was Mrs Murphy who
taught you how to make egg salad. In any case, the Panteón is a
walled cemetery, not unlike the Campo Santo in Genoa, Italy, but the
reason everybody goes there is to see the mummies. Something about
the exceptionally dry air in the mountains has preserved the bodies
and there's a little museum of mummies. It's grotesque of course, and
it certainly gave me pause. I mean it's one thing to think we will all
gather together in a paradise of fadeless splendor like your grandma
thinks, lamby-lettuce, and it's another thing to think as the Buddhists
do that latent possibilities withdraw into the heart at death, but do not
perish, thereby allowing the being to be reborn, and it's one more
thing, even, to believe like a Goddamn scientist in one of the essential
laws of physics which states that no energy is ever lost. It's one thing
to think any of those things, girls, but it's quite another to be standing
in that little museum looking at those miserable mummies. The horror
and indignation were in their faces still. I almost cried aloud, so vivid
was my sense of the fleetingness of this life. We made our way into the
fresh air of the courtyard and I bought a package of cigarettes at a little
stand which sold postcards and film and such. I reached into my
pocket for my lighter and it appeared that my lighter was not there. It
seemed that I had lost my lighter. The lighter was a very good one that
your mother had bought me the Christmas before, Jane, and your
mother started screaming at me. There was a very gentle, warm rain
falling, and there were bougainvillea petals on the walks. Your mother
grasped my arm and reminded me that the lighter had been a gift
from her. Your mother reminded me of the blazer she had brought for
me. I spilled buttered popcorn on it at the movies and you can still see
the spot. She reminded me of the hammock she bought for my fortieth
birthday, which I allowed to rot in the rain. She recalled the shoulder
bag she bought me, which I detested, it's true. It was somehow left out
in the yard and I mangled it with the lawnmower. Descending the
cobbled hill into Guanajuato, your mother recalled every one of her
gifts to me, offerings both monetary and of the heart. She pointed out
how I had mishandled and betrayed every one.'

No one said anything. 'Then,' Mr Muirhead continued, 'there was
the Modena Cemetery in Italy.'

'That hasn't been completed yet,' the young man said hurriedly.
'It's a visionary design by the architect Aldo Rossi. In our
conversation, I was just trying to describe the project to you.'

410

'You can be assured,' Mr Muirhead said, 'that when the project is finished and I take my little family on a vacation to Italy, as we walk, together and afraid, strolling through the hapless landscape of the Modena Cemetery, Jane's mother will be screaming at me.'

'Well, I must be going,' the young man said. He got up.

'So long,' Mr Muirhead said.

'Were they really selling postcards of the mummies in that place?' Dan asked.

'Yes they were, sweetie-pie,' Mr Muirhead said. 'In this world there is a postcard of everything. That's the kind of world this is.'

The crowd was getting boisterous in the Starlight Lounge. Mrs Muirhead made her way down the aisle toward them and with a deep sigh, sat beside her husband. Mr Muirhead gesticulated and formed words silently with his lips as though he was talking to the girls.

'What?' Mrs Muirhead said.

'I was just telling the girls some of the differences between men and women. Men are more adventurous and aggressive with greater spatial and mechanical abilities. Women are more consistent, nurturent and aesthetic. Men can see better than women, but women have better hearing,' Mr Muirhead said.

'Very funny,' Mrs Muirhead said.

The girls retired from the melancholy regard Mr and Mrs Muirhead had fixed upon one another, and wandered through the cars of the train, occasionally returning to their seats to fuss in the cluttered nests they had created there. Around midnight, they decided to revisit the game car where earlier, people had been playing backgammon, Diplomacy, anagrams, crazy eights and Clue. They were still at it, variously throwing down queens of diamonds, moving troops through Asia Minor and accusing Colonel Mustard of doing it in the conservatory with a wrench. Whenever there was a lull in the playing, they talked about the accident.

'What accident?' Jane demanded.

'Train hit a Buick,' a man said. 'Middle of the night.' The man had big ears and a tattoo on his forearm.

'There aren't any good new games,' a woman complained. 'Haven't been for years and years.'

'Did you fall asleep?' Jane said accusingly to Dan.

'When could that have happened?' Dan said.

'We didn't see it,' Jane said, disgusted.

411

'Two teenagers escaped without a scratch,' the man said. 'Lived to laugh about it. They are young and silly but it's no joke to the engineer. The engineer has a lot of paperwork to do after he hits something. The engineer will be filling out forms for a week.' The man's tattoo said MOM AND DAD.

'Rats,' Jane said.

The children returned to the darkened dining room where *Superman* was being shown on a small television set. Jane instantly fell asleep. Dan watched Superman spin the earth backward so he could prevent Lois Lane from being smothered in rock slide. The train shot past a group of old lighted buildings, SEWER KING, a sign said. When the movie ended, Jane woke up.

'When we lived in New York,' she said muzzily, 'I was sitting in the kitchen one afternoon doing my homework and this girl came in and sat down at the table. Did I ever tell you this? It was the middle of the winter and it was snowing. This person just came in with snow on her coat and sat right down at the table.'

'Who was she?' Dan asked.

'It was me, but I was old. I mean I was about thirty years old or something.'

'It was a dream,' Dan said.

'It was the middle of the afternoon, I tell you! I was doing my homework. She said, "You've never lifted a finger to help me." Then she asked me for a glass with some ice in it.'

After a moment, Dan said, 'It was probably the cleaning lady.'

'Cleaning lady! Cleaning lady for Godssakes, what do you know about cleaning ladies!'

Dan felt her hair bristle as though someone were running a comb through it back to front, and realized she was mad, madder than she'd been all summer, for all summer she'd only felt humiliated when Jane was nasty to her.

'Listen up,' Dan said, 'don't talk to me like that any more.'

'Like what,' Jane said coolly.

Dan stood up and walked away while Jane was saying, 'The thing I don't understand is how she ever got into that apartment. My father had about a dozen locks on the door.'

Dan sat in her seat in the quiet, dark coach and looked out at the dark night. She tried to recollect how it seemed dawn happened. Things just sort of rose out, she guessed she knew. There was nothing you could do about it. She thought of Jane's dream in which the men in white bathing caps were pushing all her grandma's things out of the house and into the street. The inside became empty and the outside became full. Dan was beginning to feel sorry for herself. She was alone, with no friends and no parents, sitting on a train between one place and another, scaring herself with someone else's dream in the middle of the night. She got up and walked through the rocking cars to the Starlight Lounge for a glass of water. After four a.m. it was no longer referred to as the Starlight Lounge. They stopped serving drinks and turned off the electric stars. It became just another place to sit. Mr Muirhead was sitting there, alone. He must have been on excellent terms with the stewards because he was drinking a Bloody Mary.

'Hi, Dan!' he said.

Dan sat opposite him. After a moment she said, 'I had a very nice summer. Thank you for inviting me.'

'Well, I hope you enjoyed your summer, sweetie,' Mr Muirhead said.

'Do you think Jane and I will be friends forever?' Dan asked.

Mr Muirhead looked surprised. 'Definitely not. Jane will not have friends. Jane will have husbands, enemies and lawyers.' He cracked ice noisily with his white teeth. 'I'm glad you enjoyed your summer, Dan, and I hope you're enjoying your childhood. When you grow up, a shadow falls. Everything's sunny and then this big Goddamn *wing* or something passes overhead.'

'Oh,' Dan said.

'Well, I've only heard that's the case actually,' Mr Muirhead said. 'Do you know what I want to be when I grow up?' He waited for her to smile. 'When I grow up I want to become an Indian so I can use my Indian name.'

'What is your Indian name?' Dan asked, smiling.

'My Indian name is "He Rides a Slow Enduring Heavy Horse."'

'That's a nice one,' Dan said.

'It is, isn't it?' Mr Muirhead said, gnawing ice.

Outside, the sky was lightening. Daylight was just beginning to flourish on the city of Jacksonville. It fell without prejudice on the slaughterhouses, Dairy Queens and courthouses, on the car lots, sabal palms and a billboard advertisement for pies.

The train went slowly around a long curve, and looking backward, past Mr Muirhead, Dan could see the entire length of it moving ahead. The bubble-topped cars were dark and sinister in the first flat and hopeful light of the morning.

Dan took the three postcards she had left out of her bookbag and looked at them. One showed Thomas Edison beneath a banyan tree. One showed a little tar-paper shack out in the middle of the desert in New Mexico where men were supposed to have invented the atomic bomb. One was a 'quicky' card showing a porpoise balancing a grapefruit on the top of his head.

'Oh, I remember those,' Mr Muirhead said, picking up the 'quicky' card. 'You just check off what you want.' He read aloud, *'How are you? I am fine ( ) lonesome ( ) happy ( ) sad ( ) broke ( ) flying high ( ).'* Mr Muirhead chuckled. He read, *'I have been good ( ) no good ( ). I saw The Gulf of Mexico ( ) The Atlantic Ocean ( ) The Orange Groves ( ) Interesting Attractions ( ) You in My Dreams ( ).'*

'I like this one,' Mr Muirhead said, chuckling.

'You can have it,' Dan said. 'I'd like you to have it.'

'You're a nice little girl,' Mr Muirhead said. He looked at his glass and then out the window. 'What do you think was on that note Mrs Muirhead had you give me?' he asked. 'Do you think there's something I've missed?'

1972

414

FUGUE IN A MINOR

William Kotzwinkle

Walking up the Bowery, man, carrying satchel and umbrella, through the bums. Bums, man, falling beaten broken crutches in the doorways sleeping, man. Bums creeping fall into doorway teeth dropping out lying down among the garbage cans. There's no place like home, man, and I feel like a nap myself, but I must proceed with my mission, to get all fifteen-year-old chicks singing Love Music. And after that, man, I am going to retire to Van Cortlandt Park and sing with the frogs at noon and midnight.

But now, man, here is St Nancy's Church on the Bowery, and here I am once again, Maestro Badorties, walking up the stone steps—which reminds me, man—always before doing music, it is necessary to vivify the corpuscles in the brain cage with the sacred smoke of the cultured herbal leaf. Let me just go around the corner, man, into a doorway here out of the wind, and stuff my Arabian camel-saddle-pipe with carefully-processed fig leaves, the smoke of which I am now drawing deeply into my system, and which I hold there for maximum benefit. Yes, man, all my brain cells are suddenly saying, *Hello, Horse,* and I have once more the power of a spaced-out camel. Across the desert sands, man, I am creeping out of this doorway. Numerous and incredible subtleties are now appearing to me, man, of rare and extraordinary design and the one I must select and concentrate on is that one which keeps me from being struck by the Bowery Avenue BUS, watch out, man!

Alright, man, up the church steps again, to perform the musical activity for which you were born and toward which all your training leads you—the conducting of fifteen-year-old chicks to the sublime heights of song and then later, still higher, to the ethereal regions of your fourth floor pad, where you will, in your capacity as Avatar of Song, screw them puce.

'Good evening, Horse,' says the priest, inside the door.

'Good evening, Father.'

'All of the chorus is here, and I think I see some new faces.'

'Yes, Father, I have been out recruiting more chicks and circulating leaflets in great number announcing the concert.'

The Super Hot Dog Mission of Horse Badorties, man, is slowly taking shape. For an entire year, man, I have held the Love Chorus together, dragging the valuable precious contents of my body here every night for rehearsal, and now, man, we are almost ready for our first performance. All we need is twenty-five fans, and I have ordered them, man, they are on the way.

Up the aisle, man, and up the stairs to the balcony where the Love Chorus is assembled—fifteen-year-old chicks, man, whom I have trained to sing the old church music, little known to the world, never heard in modern churches, but which I have uncovered from old vaults, locked drawers, and secret hiding places of old tombs. Most Church music, man, is enough to make me ill, man, make me shriek and feel awful, depressed rotten and piled-up with gloom, so lousy is it, man, so corny and terrible, written by old ladies and sung by zombies. But this church music, man, which I have found, is the white bird of reality, man, written by old cats in the Middle Ages, man, who were locked into wondrous harmonies, man, which make my hair stand on end, and that is why my hair is always sticking out in ninety different directions.

'Good evening, everyone.'

All the good little chiclets say *Good Evening, Horse.*

'I have a special announcement. Here in my hand you see a battery-powered fan, which makes a constant humming note, a drone around which we will all sing, strengthening our chords and opening our inner ear. I have ordered a fan for each of you, and we will sing, holding them in our hands. Nothing like it has ever been done before. All right, let us begin.'

'But I don't know how to read music!' A new chick, just joined the Love Chorus tonight.

'Dig, baby, the notes are in your soul. Just hold this sheet music in your hand and pretty soon you'll find your way. All right, Love Chorus, places, please. From the beginning, one, two . . . '

And we are into the music again. The new chick is spaced out, man, does not believe she can read music, but soon, man, soon the stream will carry her away, and she will dig that she knows exactly where the music is going because it couldn't go anywhere else. Dive in, baby, you wouldn't be here tonight if you didn't already know all about music. She's here, man, in the broken-down church in the fucked-up East Village because her soul said, go. The soul knows, man, and old Maestro Horse Badorties goes straight to the soul every time. It's no good, man, trying to teach music, the only way is to push the chick right into her soul-stream, man, where she'll learn immediately.

She's opening her mouth, man, she is making a musical note, there she is, man, I can see it lighting up her face. Instant recognition: *I know this music.* Smile. Spontaneous rapture of childhood recaptured. Another member of the Love Chorus has just been reborn, man. The ear hears, the heart knows, the voice sings out. You don't need music school, baby, you've got it made.

Maestro Badorties keeps the Love Chorus together, man, in supreme polyphonic harmony. This music, man, is from the angel of radiant joy in the central realm of the densely-packed, and when it is done right, it elevates my hot dog soul to the region of ecstasy. And it will sound a thousand times better, man, when everyone has a fan.

'Very good, that was terrible, the worst singing I ever heard except for one of two moments which were magnificent beyond belief. We will all meet again tomorrow night. Should for any reason I be retained, derailed, or deported, you all know how to continue practicing. Since this is the greatest music ever written, you will have no trouble. Father, we are all thankful to you for this wonderful church you gave us again tonight as a meeting place, see you tomorrow night.'

'It sounded wonderful,' says Father.

'Yes, it was terrible, and it will be even worse in time for our concert, unless my fans arrive, which are guaranteed to keep us resonating perfectly.' And now down the little winding steps of the balcony and out of the church into the night.

And standing on the street, man, is the beautiful Chinese chick, smiling.

'I listened to the music. It sounded beautiful.'

'Dig, baby, it will sound even better when we go back to my Fourth Street Academy pad and hear it played back at the wrong speed inside this worn-out tape recorder. Come on, baby, I'll give you a lesson in sight-reading.'

Quietly giving her delicate oriental assent to my suggestion, the Chinese chick walks beside me, man, through the picturesque Lower East Side streets, lined with wet thrown-out couches, on which little children are playing, jumping on the springs and sailing through the air.

417

'It's right here, baby, through this door falling off the hinges, and up the steps . . . ' A beautiful Chinese chick, man, returning with me to my Horse Badorties pad. In a few moments she will be experiencing the wonder of instantaneous sight-reading ability through the special Maestro Badorties thought-transference sex intercourse copulation fucky technique. 'Wait a second, baby, wait right here on this landing. I must run down to the store and get a box of teaballs, it'll only take two minutes.' Going down the steps, taking two at a time, as teaballs are a must, man, to simulate the oriental environment.

'Good ebening.'

'Two bottles of piña-colada to go, man . . . open the bottles, please, thank you . . . '

'Twenty-fi' cen', please.'

'All you need, man, is a fan to keep your bananas cool. Dig, man, the breeze from this little Japanese . . . EXCUSE ME, MAN, I have just remember an important engagement on the stairs . . . so long, man!' Go back up the steps quickly, man, overcoming the tendency to forget the main object at hand, which in this case is a Chinese chick on whom I must get my hands. There she is, man, still smiling, waiting for her music lesson.

'OK, baby, I've got the all-important piña-colada, and there are just two more flights to go to the top of the building.'

And up we go to the fourth floor, man, to where my wonderful Horse Badorties pad is located. How very odd, man. Someone seems to have clamped a huge padlock on the door to my pad.

'This is the work of the landlord, baby. He's trying to keep burglars out. See, here in the lock is a note explaining everything. It is in the form of an eviction notice, to make burglars think all the contents of the pad have been moved out.'

By merely taking out of my Horse Badorties survival satchel a handy ball-peen hammer, with one powerful blow of the tool, man, I have smashed the lock open.

'All right, baby, everything is in order now, step right through. As you can clearly see, the valuable precious contents of the pad have not been stolen.'

The pad, man. Incredible mountains of objects of moldy fig newtons and tuna fish cans confronting us, man, blurring the vision, fucking the mind up. How wonderful, man, to be home again. Man, I left the water running in the sink.

'Look at that water running all over the place, baby, flooding the pad, there must be a foot of water over everything, and dig, baby, this water is now COLD ENOUGH TO DRINK! If you were me, would you drink this filthy poisoned recirculated shit-water?'

'Is this where you live?'

'This is my study. You'll notice I am studying action painting, throwing modern art objects here and there, tin cans, paper bags. Don't step on anything if you can help it, it is all arranged according to number.'

'Jesus, you have a lot of stuff here.'

'It's a lifetime's work. If only I could get a frame around that splash of colored grease on the wall, mixed with old tomato paste. Do you think I should knock the whole wall down and take it to the Museum of Modern Art in my school bus?'

'I think you should shut off the water.'

'You're right, baby, there is no point in drinking this New York City water when we have in our hands a bottle each of piña-colada, the Puerto Rican soft drink to make your teeth fall out. And maybe we can find something to eat on the floor . . . WAIT A SECOND, MAN! I'VE GOT IT!' In my satchel, man, waiting there for me, synchronistically planned by my unconscious mind to coordinate with my meeting this Chinese chick is a long-forgotten but perfectly intact two containers of . . .

'Fried rice, baby, dig, and some chopsticks.'

I have scored, man, I have wigged the chick with fried rice. We were meant for each other, man, she knows it, I know it, we're happy with fried rice, if only we had a juicy steak to go with it.

And now, man, that we have eaten and drunk, there is the undeniable presence in my pants of a Horse Badorties hard-on. It has been such a long time, man, since I had time to fuck a chick, and here she is, man, smiling at me, giving me the fifteen-year-old power-wave of just awakened sexuality. I am going to her, going slowly over to where she is sitting on the arm of my stuffed chair, and I run my fingers through her jet-black hair and she turns her head up to me, man, her lips, eyes, the moment, man, has come, to make just one telephone call which I cannot postpone a moment longer.

'Just a second, baby, while we digest our rice I have just remembered to call my printer, who is working the night shift turning out thousands of sheets of publicity for the Love Concert.'

Here is the telephone, man, right by her foot, her little delicate oriental foot, which I caress with my sensitized dialing finger . . . dial . . . dial . . . dial.

'Hello, man, this is Horse Badorties, how's it going . . . great, man, run through another 5,000 sheets . . . I'll be in tomorrow with a school bus to pick it all up . . . right, man, and listen, there's just one more thing, man . . . hold on a moment, man . . . hold on . . . I . . . ' Have to touch this chick, man, run my hand up her legs, man, lift her skirt up to her black Chinese underwear with red dragons on it. Man, I must get a shipload of this underwear to give out with fans to the entire CHORUS!

'Where can I lay my skirt, I don't want to get it all greasy.'

'There must be a spot around here somewhere, baby . . . I don't know . . . you better keep it under your arm.'

'Take that scratchy old jacket off,' she says, playfully removing my jacket.

'Be careful where you lay that jacket down, baby. I might not be able to find it again.'

We struggle around in the junk, man, trying to find a place to lay down, but it is not safe on the floor, even the roaches are going around in little paper boats. 'We'll have to do it standing up, baby.'

She reaches for my Horse Badorties pants, man, and I am knocked off balance, and we topple, down into the unknown impossible-to-describe trash pile. We are rolling around in the dark contents, old loaf of bread, bicycle tire, bunch of string in peanut oil, bumping weird greasy things and slimey feelings and sand and water, lid of a tin can floating by on a sponge. There's my book on telepathy with a roach on page twelve reading about the Dalai Lama. I cannot get my prick into the chick yet, man, as I have just remembered another phone call which I must make, man. It should be made now, man, because one thing I don't dig is *coitus interruptus*, so I'd better make the call before we officially begin balling.

'This will just take a minute, baby, I have to call a junkyard in New Jersey, the owner is waiting for me to confirm a school bus, just relax, baby, while I dial.'

Direct dialing, man, straight to the junkyard. My complicated life, man. There are so many things to handle at once when you are head of the Fourth Street Music Academy and must purchase a school bus to carry fifteen-year-old chicks around in, from state to state. We're going to live in that school bus, man, and put beds in it and a washing machine.

'Hello? . . . Hello, Mr Thorne, how are you doing, man . . . This is Horse Badorties in New York City . . . yes, man, right . . . I wanted to tell you I will be over tomorrow to purchase the school bus, so please don't sell it to any other traveling artist. Yes, I'll be there about noontime . . . right . . . so long, man . . . '

'Maybe if we go in the other room,' says the chick, 'we could find a place to lay down.'

Possibly she is right, man, and so we fight our way across the abominable sea of trash . . . abominable, man, wait a second. 'Dig, baby, there is my rented typewriter, right there, under that pile of used noodles, and dig, baby, I am going to write an article IMMEDIATELY for *Argosy* magazine about an enormous footprint found in Central Asia.'

'There's even more junk in this room,' she says, looking into my Horse Badorties bedroom.

'Right, baby, but if we crawled up on top of these boxes of sheet music we could perform a fugue, come on, baby, let's try.'

It is the perfect place to screw, man, because it is better than a music lesson, the chick will assimilate directly through her ass cheeks the music of the Love Chorus.

'That's it, baby, just crawl up there, I'm right behind you.'

Crawling up from box to box, man, up to a platform of other boxes stuffed with sheet music, and now, man, NOW, high above the wet filthy floor, in our heavenly tower of sheet music, this fifteen-year-old Chinese chick is giving me her sweet little meatbun.

Man, what is that ripping sound, that collapsing wet cardboard tearing sound, it is the boxes, man, falling apart below us, man, and down, man, down once again into the darkness we are falling with sheet music flying in all directions, hitting other boxes we go falling through them breaking them apart and falling further down, into the water, splash, here, man, come the roaches with a lifeboat.

All right, man, we'll just have to screw on the floor in a pile of old dishrags and a rubber overshoe. Now is the time, man, to give her the downbeat.

'I have to go,' she says, standing up.

'Go? Baby, we just got here. Come on, baby, there's plenty of time.'

'I have to be home by ten o'clock,' she says, putting on her skirt. Fifteen-year-old chicks, man, do anything, fuck anybody, and be home by ten o'clock. I don't have the strength to protest, man, I've lost my suit jacket, I've wrecked fifteen boxes of sheet music, forgot to buy teaballs, and as a result am not getting balled. The gods, man, arrange everything. Maybe they will arrange for her to return tomorrow night, when I have my school bus and can drive her home. Man, I'm so tired from climbing up those boxes and falling down. I've got to find my bed, man, and get some zzzzzzz's.

1974

HERE COME THE MAPLES

John Updike

They had always been a lucky couple, and it was just their luck that, as they at last decided to part, the Puritan commonwealth in which they lived passed a no-fault amendment to its creaking, overworked body of divorce law. By its provision a joint affidavit had to be filed. It went, 'Now come Richard F. and Joan R. Maple and swear under the penalties of perjury that an irretrievable breakdown of the marriage exists.' For Richard, reading a copy of the document in his Boston apartment, the wording conjured up a vision of himself and Joan breezing into a party hand in hand while a liveried doorman trumpeted their names and a snow of confetti and champagne bubbles exploded in the room. In the many years of their marriage, they had gone together to a lot of parties, and always with a touch of excitement, a little hope, a little expectation of something lucky happening.

With the affidavit were enclosed various frightening financial forms and a request for a copy of their marriage license. Though they had lived in New York and London, on islands and farms and for one summer even in a log cabin, they had been married a few subway stops from where Richard now stood, reading his mail. He had not been in the Cambridge City Hall since the morning he had been granted the license, the morning of their wedding. His parents had driven him up from the Connecticut motel where they had all spent the night, on their way from West Virginia; they had risen at six, to get there on time and for much of the journey he had had his coat over his head, hoping to get back to sleep. He seemed in memory now a sea creature, boneless beneath the jellyfish bell of his own coat, rising helplessly along the coast as the air grew hotter and hotter. It was June, and steamy. When, toward noon, they got to Cambridge, and dragged their bodies and boxes of wedding clothes up the four flights to Joan's apartment, on Avon Street, the bride was taking a bath. Who else was in the apartment Richard could not remember; his recollection of the day was spotty—legible patches on a damp gray blotter. The day had no sky and no clouds, just a fog of shadowless sunlight enveloping the bricks on Brattle Street, and the white spires of Harvard, and the fat cars baking in the tarry streets. He was twenty-one, and Eisenhower was President, and the bride was behind the door, shouting that he mustn't come in, it would be bad luck for him to see her. Someone was in there with her, giggling and splashing. Who? Her sister? Her mother? Richard leaned against the bathroom door, and heard his parents heaving themselves up the stairs behind him, panting but still chattering, and pictured Joan as she was when in the bath, her toes pink, her neck tendrils flattened, her breasts floating and soapy and slick. Then the memory dried up, and the next blot showed her and him side by side, driving together into the shimmering noontime traffic jam of Central Square. She wore a summer dress of sun-faded cotton; he kept his eyes on the traffic, to minimize the bad luck of seeing her before the ceremony. Other couples, he thought at the time, must have arranged to have their papers in order more than two hours before the wedding. But then, no doubt, other grooms didn't travel to the ceremony with their coats over their heads like children hiding from a thunderstorm. Hand in hand, smaller than Hänsel and Gretel in his mind's eye, they ran up the long flight of stairs into a gingerbread-brown archway and disappeared.

Cambridge City Hall, in a changed world, was unchanged. The rounded Richardsonian castle, red sandstone and pink granite, loomed as a gentle giant in its crass neighborhood. Its interior was varnished oak, pale and gleaming. Richard seemed to remember receiving the license at a grated window downstairs with a brass plate, but an arrow on cardboard directed him upward. His knees trembled and his stomach churned at the enormity of what he was doing. He turned a corner. A grandmotherly woman reigned within a spacious, idle territory of green-topped desks and great ledgers in steel racks. 'Could I get a c-copy of a marriage license?' he asked her.

'Year?'

'Beg pardon?'

'What is the year of the marriage license, sir?'

'1954.' Enunciated, the year seemed distant as a star, yet here he was again, feeling not a minute older, and sweating in the same summer heat. Nevertheless, the lady, having taken down the names and the date, had to leave him and go to another chamber of the archives, so far away in truth was the event he wished to undo.

She returned with a limp he hadn't noticed before. The ledger she carried was three feet wide when opened, a sorcerer's tome. She turned the vast pages carefully, as if the chasm of lost life and forsaken time they represented might at a slip leap up and swallow them both. She must once have been a flaming redhead, but her hair had dulled to apricot and had stiffened to permanent curls, lifeless as dried paper. She smiled, a crimpy little smile. 'Yes,' she said. 'Here we are.'

And Richard could read, upside down, on a single long red line, Joan's maiden name and his own. Her profession was listed as 'Teacher' (she had been an apprentice art teacher; he had forgotten her splattered blue smock, the clayey smell of her fingers, the way she would bicycle to work on even the coldest days) and his own, inferiorly, as 'Student.' And their given addresses surprised him, in being different—the foyer on Avon Street, the entryway in Lowell House, forgotten doors opening on the corridor of shared addresses that stretched from then to now. Their signatures—He could not bear to study their signatures, even upside down. At a glance, Joan's seemed firmer, and bluer. 'You want one or more copies?'

'One should be enough.'

As fussily as if she had not done this thousands of times before, the former redhead, smoothing the paper and repeatedly dipping her antique pen, copied the information onto a standard form.

What else survived of that wedding day? There were a few slides, Richard remembered. A cousin of Joan's had posed the main members of the wedding on the sidewalk outside the church, all gathered around a parking meter. The meter, a slim silvery representative of the municipality, occupies the place of honor in the grouping, with his narrow head and scarlet tongue. Like the meter, the groom is very thin. He blinked simultaneously with the shutter, so the suggestion of death mask hovers about his face. The dimpled bride's pose, tense and graceful both, has something dancerlike about it, the feet pointed outward on the hot bricks; she might be about to pick up the organdie skirts of her bridal gown and vault herself into a tour jeté. The four parents, not yet transmogrified into grandparents, seem dim in the slide, half lost in the fog of light, benevolent and lumpy like the stones of the building in which Richard was shelling out the three-dollar fee for his copy, his anti-license.

Another image was captured by Richard's college roommate, who drove them to their honeymoon cottage in a seaside town an hour south of Cambridge. A croquet set had been left on the porch, and Richard, in one of those stunts he had developed to mask unease, picked up three of the balls and began to juggle. The roommate, perhaps also uneasy, snapped the moment up; the red ball hangs there forever, blurred, in the amber slant of the dying light, while the yellow and green glint in Richard's hands and his face concentrates upward in a slack-jawed ecstasy.

'I have another problem,' he told the grandmotherly clerk as she shut the vast ledger and prepared to shoulder it.

'What would that be?' she asked.

'I have an affidavit that should be notarized.'

'That wouldn't be my department, sir. First floor, to the left when you get off the elevator, to the right if you use the stairs. The stairs are quicker, if you ask me.'

He followed her directions and found a young black woman at a steel desk bristling with gold-framed images of fidelity and solidarity and stability, of children and parents, of a somber brown boy in a brown military uniform, of a family laughing by a lakeside; there was even a photograph of a house—an ordinary little ranch house somewhere, with a green lawn. She read Richard's affidavit without comment. He suppressed his urge to beg her pardon. She asked to see his driver's license and compared its face with his. She handed him a pen and set a seal of irrevocability beside his signature. The red ball still hung in the air, somewhere in a box of slides he would never see again, and the luminous hush of the cottage when they were left alone in it still traveled, a capsule of silence, outward to the stars; but what grieved Richard more, wincing as he stepped from the brown archway into the summer glare, was a suspended detail of the wedding. In his daze, his sleepiness, in his wonder at the white creature trembling beside him at the altar, on the edge of his awareness like a rainbow in a fog, he had forgotten to seal the vows with a kiss. Joan had glanced over at him, smiling, expectant; he had smiled back, not remembering. The moment passed, and they hurried down the aisle as now he hurried, ashamed, down the City Hall stairs to the street and the tunnel of the subway.

As the subway racketed through darkness, he read about the forces of nature. A scholarly extract had come in the mail, in the same mail as the affidavit. Before he lived alone, he would have thrown it away without a second look, but now, as he slowly took on the careful habits of a Boston codger, he read every scrap he was sent, and even stooped in the alleys to pick up a muddy fragment of newspaper and scan it for a message. *Thus, he read, it was already known in 1935 that the natural world was governed by four kinds of force: in order of increasing strength, they are the gravitational, the weak, the electromagnetic, and the strong.* Reading, he found himself rooting for the weak forces; he identified with them. Gravitation, though negligible at the microcosmic level, *begins to predominate with objects on the order of magnitude of a hundred kilometers, like large asteroids; it holds together the moon, the earth, the solar system, the stars, clusters of stars within galaxies, and the galaxies themselves.* To Richard it was as if a faint-hearted team overpowered at the start of the game was surging to triumph in the last, macrocosmic quarter; he inwardly cheered. The subway lurched to a stop at Kendall, and he remembered how, a few days after their wedding, he and Joan took a train north through New Hampshire, to summer jobs they had contracted for, as a couple. The train, long since discontinued, had wound its way north along the busy rivers sullied by sawmills and into evergreen mountains where ski lifts stood rusting. The seats had been purple plush, and the train incessantly, gently swayed. Her arms, pale against the plush, showed a pink shadowing of sunburn. Uncertain of how to have a honeymoon, yet certain that they must create memories to last till death did them part, they had played croquet naked, in the little yard that, amid the trees, seemed an eye of grass gazing upward at the sky. She beat him, every game. *The weak force,* Richard read, *does not appreciably affect the structure of the nucleus before the decay occurs; it is like a flaw in a bell of cast metal which has no effect on the ringing of the bell until it finally causes the bell to fall into pieces.*

The subway car climbed into light, to cross the Charles. Sailboats tilted on the glitter below. Across the river, Boston's smoke-colored skyscrapers hung like paralyzed fountains. The train had leaned around a bay of a lake and halted at The Weirs, a gritty summer place of ice cream dripped on asphalt, of a candy-apple scent wafted from the edge of childhood. After a wait of hours, they caught the mail boat to their island where they would work. The island was on the far side of Lake Winnipesaukee, with many other islands intervening, and many mail drops necessary. Before each docking, the boat blew its whistle—an immense noise. The Maples had sat on the prow, for the sun and scenery; once there, directly under the whistle, they felt they had to stay. The islands, the water, the mountains beyond the

shore did an adagio of shifting perspectives around them and then—
each time, astoundingly—the blast of the whistle would flatten their
hearts and crush the landscape into a wad of noise; these blows
assaulted their young marriage. He both blamed her and wished to
beg her forgiveness for what neither of them could control. After each
blast, the engine would be cut, the boat would sidle to a rickety dock,
and from the dappled soft paths of this or that evergreen island tan
children and counselors in bathing trunks and moccasins would spill
forth to receive their mail, their shouts ringing strangely in the
deafened ears of the newlyweds. By the time they reached their own
island, the Maples were exhausted.

Quantum mechanics and relativity, taken together, are extraordinarily
restrictive and they, therefore, provide us with a great logical engine.
Richard returned the pamphlet to his pocket and got off at Charles. He
walked across the overpass toward the hospital, to see his arthritis
man. His bones ached at night. He had friends who were dying, who
were dead; it no longer seemed incredible that he would follow them.
The first time he had visited this hospital, it had been to court Joan. He
had climbed this same ramp to the glass doors and inquired within,
stammering, for the whereabouts, in this grand maze of unhealth, of
the girl who had sat, with a rubber band around her ponytail, in the
front row of English 162b: 'The English Epic Tradition, Spenser to
Tennyson.' He had admired the tilt of the back of her head for three
hours a week all winter. He gathered up courage to talk in exam
period as, together at a library table, they were mulling over murky
photostats of Blake's illustrations to *Paradise Lost*. They agreed to meet
after the exam and have a beer. She didn't show. In that amphitheater
of desperately thinking heads, hers was absent. And, having put *The*
Faerie Queene and *The Idylls of the King* to rest together, he called her
dorm and learned that Joan had been taken to the hospital. A force of
nature drove him to brave the long corridors and the wrong turns and
the crowd of aunts and other suitors at the foot of the bed; he found
Joan in white, between white sheets, her hair loose about her
shoulders and a plastic tube feeding something transparent into the
underside of her arm. In later visits, he achieved the right to hold her
hand, trussed though it was with splints and tapes. Platelet deficiency
had been the diagnosis. The complaint had been she couldn't stop
bleeding. Blushing, she told him how the doctors and internes had
asked her when she had last had intercourse, and how embarrassing it
had been to confess, in the face of their polite disbelief, never.

The doctor removed the blood-pressure tourniquet from Richard's arm and smiled. 'Have you been under any stress lately?'

'I've been getting a divorce.'

'Arthritis, as you may know, belongs to a family of complaints with a psychosomatic component.'

'All I know is that I wake up at four in the morning and it's very depressing to think I'll never get over this, this pain'll be inside my shoulder for the rest of my life.'

'You will. It won't.'

'When?'

'When your brain stops sending out punishing signals.'

Her hand, in its little cradle of healing apparatus, its warmth unresisting and noncommittal as he held it at her bedside, rested high, nearly at the level of his eyes. On the island, the beds in the log cabin set aside for them were of different heights, and though Joan tried to make them into a double bed, there was a ledge where the mattresses met which either he or she had to cross, amid a discomfort of sheets pulling loose. But the cabin was in the woods and powerful moist scents of pine and fern swept through the screens with the morning chirrup of birds and the evening rustle of animals. There was a rumor there were deer on the island; they crossed the ice in the winter and were trapped when it melted in the spring. Though no one, neither camper nor counselor, ever saw the deer, the rumor persisted that they were there.

Why then has no one ever seen a quark? As he walked along Charles Street toward his apartment, Richard vaguely remembered some such sentence, and fished in his pockets for the pamphlet on the forces of nature, and came up instead with a new prescription for painkiller, a copy of his marriage license, and the signed affidavit. *Now come . . .* the pamphlet had got folded into it. He couldn't find the sentence, and instead read, *The theory that the strong force becomes stronger as the quarks are pulled apart is somewhat speculative; but its complement, the idea that the force gets weaker as the quarks are pushed closer to each other, is better established.* Yes, he thought, that had happened. In life there are four forces: love, habit, time, and boredom. Love and habit at short range are immensely powerful, but time, lacking a minus charge, accumulates inexorably, and with its brother boredom levels all. He was dying; that made him cruel. His heart flattened in horror at what he had just done. How could he tell Joan what he had done to their marriage license? The very quarks in the telephone circuits would rebel.

In the forest, there had been a green clearing, an eye of grass, a meadow starred with microcosmic white flowers, and here one dusk the deer had come, the female slightly in advance, the male larger and darker, his rump still in shadow as his mate nosed out the day's last sun, the silhouettes of both haloed by the same light that gilded the meadow grass. A fleet of blank-faced motorcyclists roared by, a rummy waved to Richard from a laundromat doorway, a girl in a seductive halter gave him a cold eye, the light changed from red to green, and he could not remember if he needed orange juice or bread, doubly annoyed because he could not remember if they had ever really seen the deer, or if he had imagined the memory, conjured it from the longing that it be so.

'I don't remember,' Joan said over the phone. 'I don't think we did, we just talked about it.'

'Wasn't there a kind of clearing beyond the cabin, if you followed the path?'

'We never went that way, it was too buggy.'

'A stag and a doe, just as it was getting dark. Don't you remember anything?'

'No. I honestly don't, Richard. How guilty do you want me to feel?'

'Not at all, if it didn't happen. Speaking of nostalgia—'

'Yes?'

'I went up to Cambridge City Hall this afternoon and got a copy of our marriage license.'

'Oh dear. How was it?'

'It wasn't bad. The place is remarkably the same. Did we get the license upstairs or downstairs?'

'Downstairs, to the left of the elevator as you go in.'

'That's where I got our affidavit notarized. You'll be getting a copy soon; it's a shocking document.'

'I did get it, yesterday. What was shocking about it? I thought it was funny, the way it was worded. Here we come, there we go.'

'Darley, you're so tough and brave.'

'I assume I must be. No?'

'Yes.'

Not for the first time in these two years did he feel an eggshell thinness behind which he crouched and which Joan needed only to raise her voice to break. But she declined to break it, either out of

430

ignorance of how thin the shell was, or because she was hatching on its other side, just as, on the other side of that bathroom door, she had been drawing near to marriage at the same rate as he, and with the same regressive impulses. 'What I don't understand,' she was saying, 'are we both supposed to sign the same statement, or do we each sign one, or what? And which one? My lawyer keeps sending me three of everything, and some of them are in blue covers. Are these the important ones or the unimportant ones that I can keep?'

In truth, the lawyers, so adroit in their accustomed adversary world of blame, of suit and countersuit, did seem confused by the no-fault provision. On the very morning of the divorce, Richard's greeted him on the courthouse steps with the possibility that he as plaintiff might be asked to specify what in the marriage had persuaded him of its irretrievable breakdown. 'But that's the whole point of no-fault,' Joan interposed, 'that you don't have to say anything.' She had climbed the courthouse steps beside Richard; indeed, they had come in the same car, because one of their children had taken her Volvo.

The proceeding was scheduled for early in the day. Picking her up at a quarter after seven, he had found her standing barefoot on the lawn in the circle of their driveway, up to her ankles in mist and dew. She was holding her high-heeled shoes in her hand. The sight made him laugh. Opening the car door, he said, 'So there *are* deer on the island!'

She was too preoccupied to make sense of his allusion. She asked him, 'Do you think the judge will mind if I don't wear stockings?'

'Keep your legs behind his bench,' he said. He was feeling fluttery, light-headed. He had scarcely slept, though his shoulder had not hurt, for a change. She got into the car, bringing with her her shoes and the moist smell of dawn. She had always been an early riser, and he a late one. 'Thanks for doing this,' she said, of the ride, adding, 'I guess.'

'My pleasure,' Richard said. As they drove to court, discussing their cars and their children, he marveled at how light Joan had become; she sat on the side of his vision as light as a feather, her voice tickling his ear, her familiar intonations and emphases thoroughly musical and half unheard, like the patterns of a concerto that sets us to daydreaming. He no longer blamed her: that was the reason for the lightness. All those years, he had blamed her for everything—for the traffic jam in Central Square, for the blasts of noise on the mail boat,

431

for the difference in the levels of their beds. No longer: he had set her adrift from omnipotence. He had set her free, free from fault. She was to him as Gretel to Hänsel, a kindred creature moving beside him down a path while birds behind them ate the bread crumbs.

Richard's lawyer eyed Joan lugubriously. 'I understand that, Mrs Maple,' he said. 'But perhaps I should have a word in private with my client.'

The lawyers they had chosen were oddly different. Richard's was a big rumpled Irishman, his beige summer suit baggy and his belly straining his shirt, a melancholic and comforting father-type. Joan's was small, natty, and flip; he dressed in checks and talked from the side of his mouth, like a racing tout. Twinkling, chipper even at this sleepy hour, he emerged from behind a pillar in the marble temple of justice and led Joan away. Her head, slightly higher than his, tilted to give him her ear; she dimpled, docile. Richard wondered in amazement, Could this sort of man have been, all these years, the secret type of her desire? His own lawyer, breathing heavily, asked him, 'If the judge does ask for a specific cause of the breakdown—and I don't say he will, we're all sailing uncharted waters here—what will you say?'

'I don't know,' Richard said. He studied the swirl of marble, like a tiny wave breaking, between his shoe tips. 'We had political differences. She used to make me go on peace marches.'

'Any physical violence?'

'Not much. Not enough, maybe. You really think he'll ask this sort of thing? Is this no-fault or what?'

'No-fault is a *tabula rasa* in this state. At this point, Dick, it's what we make of it. I don't know what he'll do. We should be prepared.'

'Well—aside from the politics, we didn't get along that well sexually.'

The air between them thickened; with his own father, too, sex had been a painful topic. His lawyer's breathing became grievously audible. 'So you'd be prepared to say there was personal and emotional incompatibility?'

It seemed profoundly untrue, but Richard nodded. 'If I have to.'

'Good enough.' The lawyer put his big hand on Richard's arm and squeezed. His closeness, his breathiness, his air of restless urgency and forced cheer, his old-fashioned suit and the folder of papers tucked under his arm like roster sheets all came into focus: he was a coach, and Richard was about to kick the winning field goal, do the high-difficulty dive, strike out the heart of the batting order with the bases already loaded. Go.

They entered the courtroom two by two. The chamber was chaste and empty; the carved trim was painted forest green. The windows gave on an ancient river blackened by industry. Dead judges gazed down from above. The two lawyers conferred, leaving Richard and Joan to stand awkwardly apart. He made his 'What now?' face at her. She made her 'Beats me' face back. 'Oyez, oyez,' a disembodied voice chanted, and the judge hurried in, smiling, his robes swinging. He was a little sharp-featured man with a polished pink face; his face declared that he was altogether good, and would never die. He stood and nodded at them. He seated himself. The lawyers went forward to confer in whispers. Richard inertly gravitated toward Joan, the only animate object in the room that did not repel him. 'It's a Daumier,' she whispered, of the tableau being enacted before them. The lawyers parted. The judge beckoned. He was so clean his smile squeaked. He showed Richard a piece of paper; it was the affidavit 'Is this your signature?' he asked him.

'It is,' Richard said.

'And do you believe, as this paper states, that your marriage has suffered an irretrievable breakdown?'

'I do.'

The judge turned his face toward Joan. His voice softened a notch. 'Is this *your* signature?'

'It is.' Her voice was a healing spray, full of tiny rainbows, in the corner of Richard's eye.

'And do you believe that your marriage has suffered an irretrievable breakdown?'

A pause. She did not believe that, Richard knew. She said, 'I do.'

The judge smiled and wished them both good luck. The lawyers sagged with relief, and a torrent of merry legal chitchat—speculations about the future of no-fault, reminiscences of the old days of Alabama quickies—excluded the Maples. Obsolete at their own ceremony, Joan and Richard stepped back from the bench in unison and stood side by side, uncertain of how to turn, until Richard at last remembered what to do; he kissed her.

1976

433

PRETTY ICE

Mary Robison

I was up the whole night before my fiancé was due to arrive from the East—drinking coffee, restless and pacing, my ears ringing. When the television signed off, I sat down with a packet of the month's bills and figured amounts on a lined tally sheet in my checkbook. Under the spray of a high-intensity lamp, my left hand moved rapidly over the touch tablets of my calculator.

Will, my fiancé, was coming from Boston on the six-fifty train—the dawn train, the only train that still stopped in the small Ohio city where I lived. At six-fifteen I was still at my accounts; I was getting some pleasure from transcribing the squarish green figures that appeared in the window of my calculator. 'Schwab Dental Clinic,' I printed in a raveled backhand. 'Thirty-eight and 50/100.'

A car horn interrupted me. I looked over my desktop and out the living-room window of my rented house. The saplings in my little yard were encased in ice. There had been snow all week, and then an ice storm. In the glimmering driveway in front of my garage, my mother was peering out of her car. I got up and turned off my lamp and capped my ivory Mont Blanc pen. I found a coat in the semidark in the hall, and wound a knitted muffler at my throat. Crossing the living room, I looked away from the big pine mirror; I didn't want to see how my face and hair looked after a night of accounting.

My yard was a frozen pond, and I was careful on the walkway. My mother hit her horn again. Frozen slush came through the toe of one of my chukka boots, and I stopped on the path and frowned at her. I could see her breath rolling away in clouds from the cranked-down window of her Mazda. I have never owned a car nor learned to drive, but I had a low opinion of my mother's compact. My father and I used to enjoy big cars, with tops that came down. We were both tall and we wanted what he called 'stretch room.' My father had been dead for fourteen years, but I resented my mother's buying a car in which he would not have fitted.

'Now what's wrong? Are you coming?' my mother said.

'Nothing's wrong except that my shoes are opening around the

434

soles,' I said. 'I just paid a lot of money for them.'

I got in on the passenger side. The car smelled of wet wool and Mother's hair spray. Someone had done her hair with a minty-white rinse, and the hair was held in place by a zebra-striped headband.

'I think you're getting a flat,' I said. 'That retread you bought for the left front is going.'

She backed the car out of the drive, using the rear-view mirror. 'I finally got a boy I can trust, at the Exxon station,' she said. 'He says that tire will last until hot weather.'

Out on the street, she accelerated too quickly and the rear of the car swung left. The tires whined for an instant on the old snow and then caught. We were knocked back in our seats a little, and an empty Kleenex box slipped off the dash and onto the floor carpet.

'This is going to be something,' my mother said. 'Will sure picked an awful day to come.'

My mother had never met him. My courtship with Will had all happened in Boston. I was getting my doctorate there, in musicology. Will was involved with his research at Boston U., and with teaching botany to undergraduates. 'You're sure he'll be at the station?' my mother said. 'Can the trains go in this weather? I don't see how they do.'

'I talked to him on the phone yesterday. He's coming.'

'How did he sound?' my mother said.

To my annoyance, she began to hum to herself.

I said, 'He's had rotten news about his work. Terrible, in fact.'

'Explain his work to me again,' she said.

'He's a plant taxonomist.'

'Yes?' my mother said. 'What does that mean?'

'It means he doesn't have a lot of money,' I said. 'He studies grasses. He said on the phone he's been turned down for a research grant that would have meant a great deal to us. Apparently the work he's been doing for the past seven or so years is irrelevant or outmoded. I guess "superficial" is what he told me.'

'I won't mention it to him, then,' my mother said.

We came to the expressway. Mother steered the car through some small windblown snow dunes and down the entrance ramp. She followed two yellow salt trucks with winking blue beacons that were moving side by side down the center and right-hand lanes.

'I think losing the grant means we should postpone the wedding,' I

435

said. 'I want Will to have his bearings before I step into his life for good.'

'Don't wait too much longer, though,' my mother said.

After a couple of miles, she swung off the expressway. We went past some tall high-tension towers with connecting cables that looked like staff lines on a sheet of music. We were in the decaying neighborhood near the tracks. 'Now I know this is right,' Mother said. 'There's our old sign.'

The sign was a tall billboard, black and white, that advertised my father's dance studio. The studio had been closed for years and the building it had been in was gone. The sign showed a man in a tuxedo waltzing with a woman in an evening gown. I was always sure it was a waltz. The dancers were nearly two stories high, and the weather had bleached them into phantoms. The lettering—the name of the studio, my father's name—had disappeared.

'They've changed everything,' my mother said, peering about. 'Can this be the station?'

We went up a little drive that wound past a cindery lot full of flatbed trucks and that ended up at the smudgy brownstone depot.

'Is that your Will?' Mother said.

Will was on the station platform, leaning against a baggage truck. He had a duffle bag between his shoes and a plastic cup of coffee in his mittened hand. He seemed to have put on weight, girlishly, through the hips, and his face looked thicker to me, from temple to temple. His gold-rimmed spectacles looked too small.

My mother stopped in an empty cab lane, and I got out and called to Will. It wasn't far from the platform to the car, and Will's pack wasn't a large one, but he seemed to be winded when he got to me. I let him kiss me, and then he stepped back and blew a cold breath and drank from the coffee cup, with his eyes on my face.

Mother was pretending to be busy with something in her handbag, not paying attention to me and Will.

'I look awful,' I said.

'No, no, but I probably do,' Will said. 'No sleep, and I'm fat. So this is your town?'

He tossed the coffee cup at an oil drum and glanced around at the cold train yards and low buildings. A brass foundry was throwing a yellowish column of smoke over a line of Canadian Pacific boxcars.

I said, 'The problem is you're looking at the wrong side of the tracks.'

A wind whipped Will's lank hair across his face. 'Does your mom smoke?' he said. 'I ran out in the middle of the night on the train, and the club car was closed. Eight hours across Pennsylvania without a cigarette.'

The car horn sounded as my mother climbed from behind the wheel. 'That was an accident,' she said, because I was frowning at her. 'Hello. Are you Will?' She came around the car and stood on tiptoes and kissed him. 'You picked a miserable day to come and visit us.'

She was using her young-girl voice, and I was embarrassed for her. 'He needs a cigarette,' I said.

Will got into the back of the car and I sat beside my mother again. After we started up, Mother said, 'Why doesn't Will stay at my place, in your old room, Belle? I'm all alone there, with plenty of space to kick around in.'

'We'll be able to get him a good motel,' I said quickly, before Will could answer. 'Let's try that Ramada, over near the new elementary school.' It was odd, after he had come all the way from Cambridge, but I didn't want him in my old room, in the house where I had been a child. 'I'd put you at my place,' I said, 'but there's mountains of tax stuff all over.'

'You've been busy,' he said.

'Yes,' I said. I sat sidewise, looking at each of them in turn. Will had some blackish spots around his mouth—ballpoint ink, maybe. I wished he had freshened up and put on a better shirt before leaving the train.

'It's up to you two, then,' my mother said.

I could tell she was disappointed in Will. I don't know what she expected. I was thirty-one when I met him. I had probably dated fewer men in my life than she had gone out with in a single year at her sorority. She had always been successful with men.

'William was my late husband's name,' my mother said. 'Did Belle ever tell you?'

'No,' Will said. He was smoking one of Mother's cigarettes.

'I always like the name,' she said. 'Did you know we ran a dance studio?'

I groaned.

'Oh, let me brag if I want to,' my mother said. 'He was such a handsome man.'

It was true. They were both handsome—mannequins, a pair of

437

dolls who had spent half their lives in evening clothes. But my father had looked old in the end, in a business in which you had to stay young. He had trouble with his eyes, which were bruised-looking and watery, and he had to wear glasses with thick lenses.

I said, 'It was in the dance studio that my father ended his life, you know. In the ballroom.'

'You told me,' Will said, at the same instant my mother said, 'Don't talk about it.'

My father killed himself with a service revolver. We never found out where he had bought it, or when. He was found in his warm-up clothes—a pullover sweater and pleated pants. He was wearing his tap shoes, and he had a short towel folded around his neck. He had aimed the gun barrel down his mouth, so the bullet would not shatter the wall of mirrors behind him. I was twenty then—old enough to find out how he did it.

My mother had made a wrong turn and we were on Buttles Avenue. 'Go there,' I said, pointing down a street beside Garfield Park. We passed a group of paper boys who were riding bikes with saddlebags. They were going slow, because of the ice.

'Are you very discouraged, Will?' my mother said. 'Belle tells me you are having a run of bad luck.'

'You could say so,' Will said. 'A little rough water.'

'I'm sorry,' Mother said. 'What seems to be the trouble?'

Will said, 'Well, this will be oversimplifying, but essentially what I do is take a weed and evaluate its structure and growth and habitat, and so forth.'

'What's wrong with that?' my mother said.

'Nothing. But it isn't enough.'

'I get it,' my mother said uncertainly.

I had taken a mirror and a comb from my handbag and I was trying for a clean center-part in my hair. I was thinking about finishing my bill paying.

Will said, 'What do you want to do after I check in, Belle? What about breakfast?'

'I've got to go home for a while and clean up that tax jazz, or I'll never rest,' I said. 'I'll just show up at your motel later. If we ever find it.'

'That'll be fine,' Will said.

Mother said, 'I'd offer to serve you two dinner tonight, but I think

438

you'll want to leave me out of it. I know how your father and I felt after he went away sometimes. Which way do I turn here?'

We had stopped at an intersection near the iron gates of the park. Behind the gates there was a frozen pond, where a single early-morning skater was skating backward, expertly crossing his blades.

I couldn't drive a car but, like my father, I have always enjoyed maps and atlases. During automobile trips, I liked comparing distances on maps. I liked the words *latitude, cartography, meridian.* It was extremely annoying to me that Mother had gotten us turned around and lost in our own city, and I was angry with Will all of a sudden, for wasting seven years on something superficial.

'What about up that way?' Will said to my mother, pointing to the left. 'There's some traffic up by that light, at least.'

I leaned forward in my seat and started combing my hair all over again.

'There's no hurry,' my mother said.

'How do you mean?' I asked her.

'To get William to the motel,' she said. 'I know everybody complains, but I think an ice storm is a beautiful thing. Let's enjoy it.'

She waved her cigarette at the windshield. The sun had burned through and was gleaming in the branches of all the maples and buckeye trees in the park. 'It's twinkling like a stage set,' Mother said.

'It is pretty,' I said.

Will said, 'It'll make a bad-looking spring. A lot of shrubs get damaged and turn brown, and the trees don't blossom right.'

For once I agreed with my mother. Everything was quiet and holding still. Everything was in place, the way it was supposed to be. I put my comb away and smiled back at Will—because I knew it was for the last time.

1977

TESTIMONY OF PILOT

Barry Hannah

When I was ten, eleven and twelve, I did a good bit of my play in the backyard of a three-story wooden house my father had bought and rented out, his first venture into real estate. We lived right across the street from it, but over here was the place to do your real play. Here there was a harrowed but overgrown garden, a vine-swallowed fence at the back end, and beyond the fence a cornfield which belonged to someone else. This was not the country. This was the town, Clinton, Mississippi, between Jackson on the east and Vicksburg on the west. On this lot stood a few water oaks, a few plum bushes, and much overgrowth of honeysuckle vine. At the very back end, at the fence, stood three strong nude chinaberry trees.

In Mississippi it is difficult to achieve a vista. But my friends and I had one here at the back corner of the garden. We could see across the cornfield, see the one lone tin-roofed house this side of the railroad tracks, then on across the tracks many other bleaker houses with rustier tin roofs, smoke coming out of the chimneys in the late fall. This was niggertown. We had binoculars and could see the colored children hustling about and perhaps a hopeless sow or two with her brood enclosed in a tiny boarded-up area. Through the binoculars one afternoon in October we watched some men corner and beat a large hog on the brain. They used an ax and the thing kept running around, head leaning toward the ground, for several minutes before it lay down. I thought I saw the men laughing when it finally did. One of them was staggering, plainly drunk to my sight from three hundred yards away. He had the long knife. Because of that scene I considered Negroes savage cowards for a good five more years of my life. Our maid brought some sausage to my mother and when it was put in the pan to fry, I made a point of running out of the house.

I went directly across the street and to the back end of the garden behind the apartment house we owned, without my breakfast. That was Saturday. Eventually, Radcleve saw me. His parents had him mowing the yard that ran alongside my dad's property. He clicked off the power mower and I went over to his fence, which was storm wire. His mother maintained handsome flowery grounds at all costs; she had a leaf-mold bin and St Augustine grass as solid as a rug.

Radcleve himself was a violent experimental chemist. When Radcleve was eight, he threw a whole package of .22 shells against the sidewalk in front of his house until one of them went off, driving lead fragments into his calf, most of them still deep in there where the surgeons never dared tamper. Radcleve knew about the sulfur, potassium nitrate and charcoal mixture for gunpowder when he was ten. He bought things through the mail when he ran out of ingredients in his chemistry sets. When he was an infant, his father, a quiet man who owned the Chevrolet agency in town, bought an entire bankrupt sporting-goods store, and in the middle of their backyard he built a house, plain-painted and neat, one room and a heater, where Radcleve's redundant toys forevermore were kept—all the possible toys he would need for boyhood. There were things in there that Radcleve and I were not mature enough for and did not know the real use of. When we were eleven, we uncrated the new Dunlop golf balls and went on up a shelf for the tennis rackets, went out in the middle of his yard, and served new golf ball after new golf ball with blasts of the rackets over into the cornfield, out of sight. When the strings busted we just went in and got another racket. We were absorbed by how a good smack would set the heavy little pills on an endless flight. Then Radcleve's father came down. He simply dismissed me. He took Radcleve into the house and covered his whole body with a belt. But within the week Radcleve had invented the mortar. It was a steel pipe into which a flashlight battery fit perfectly, like a bullet into a muzzle. He had drilled a hole for the fuse of an M-80 firecracker at the base, for the charge. It was a grand cannon, set up on a stack of bricks at the back of my dad's property, which was the free place to play. When it shot, it would back up violently with thick smoke and you could hear the flashlight battery whistling off. So that morning when I ran out of the house protesting the hog sausage, I told Radcleve to bring over the mortar. His ma and dad were in Jackson for the day, and he came right over with the pipe, the batteries and the M-80 explosives. He had two gross of them.

Before, we'd shot off toward the woods to the right of niggertown. I turned the bricks to the left; I made us a very fine cannon carriage pointing toward niggertown. When Radcleve appeared, he had two pairs of binoculars around his neck, one pair a newly plundered

German unit as big as a brace of whiskey bottles. I told him I wanted to shoot for that house where we saw them killing the pig. Radcleve loved the idea. We singled out the house with heavy use of the binoculars.

There were children in the yard. Then they all went in. Two men came out of the back door. I thought I recognized the drunkard from the other afternoon. I helped Radcleve fix the direction of the cannon. We estimated the altitude we needed to get down there. Radcleve put the M-80 in the breech with its fuse standing out of the hole. I dropped the flashlight battery in. I lit the fuse. We backed off. The M-80 blasted off deafeningly, smoke rose, but my concentration was on that particular house over there. I brought the binoculars up. We waited six or seven seconds. I heard a great joyful wallop on tin. 'We've hit him on the first try, the first try!' I yelled. Radcleve was ecstatic. 'Right on his roof!' We bolstered up the brick carriage. Radcleve remembered the correct height of the cannon exactly. So we fixed it, loaded it, lit it and backed off. The battery landed on the roof, blat, again, louder. I looked to see if there wasn't a great dent or hole in the roof. I could not understand why niggers weren't pouring out distraught from that house. We shot the mortar again and again and always our battery hit the tin roof. Sometimes there was only a dull thud, but other times there was a wild distress of tin. I was still looking through the binoculars, amazed that the niggers wouldn't even come out of their house to see what was hitting their roof. Radcleve was on to it better than me. I looked over at him and he had the huge German binocs much lower than I did. He was looking straight through the cornfield, which was all bare and open, with nothing left but rotten stalks. 'What we've been hitting is the roof of that house just this side of the tracks. White people live in there,' he said.

I took up my binoculars again. I looked around the yard of that white wooden house on this side of the tracks, almost next to the railroad. When I found the tin roof, I saw four significant dents in it. I saw one of our batteries lying in the middle of a sort of crater. I took the binoculars down into the yard and saw a blond middle-aged woman looking our way.

'Somebody's coming up toward us. He's from that house and he's got, I think, some sort of fancy gun with him. It might be an automatic weapon.'

I ran my binoculars all over the cornfield. Then, in a line with the house, I saw him. He was coming our way but having some trouble with the rows and dead stalks of the cornfield.

'That is just a boy like us. All he's got is a saxophone with him,' I told Radcleve. I had recently got in the school band, playing drums, and had seen all the weird horns that made up a band.

I watched this boy with the saxophone through the binoculars until he was ten feet from us. This was Quadberry. His name was Ard, short for Arden. His shoes were foot-square wads of mud from the cornfield. When he saw us across the fence and above him, he stuck out his arm in my direction.

'My dad says stop it!'

'We weren't doing anything,' says Radcleve.

'Mother saw the smoke puff up from here. Dad has a hangover.'

'A what?'

'It's a headache from indiscretion. You're lucky he does. He's picked up the poker to rap on you, but he can't move further the way his head is.'

'What's your name? You're not in the band,' I said, focusing on the saxophone.

'It's Ard Quadberry. Why do you keep looking at me through the binoculars?'

It was because he was odd, with his hair and its white ends, and his Arab nose, and now his name. Add to that the saxophone.

'My dad's a doctor at the college. Mother's a musician. You better quit what you're doing . . . I was out practicing in the garage. I saw one of those flashlight batteries roll off the roof. Could I see what you shoot 'em with?'

'No,' said Radcleve. Then he said: 'If you'll play that horn.'

Quadberry stood out there ten feet below us in the field, skinny, feet and pants booted with black mud, and at his chest the slung-on, very complex, radiant horn.

Quadberry began sucking and licking the reed. I didn't care much for this act, and there was too much desperate oralness in his face when he began playing. That was why I chose the drums. One had to engage himself like suck's revenge with a horn. But what Quadberry was playing was pleasant and intricate. I was sure it was advanced, and there was no squawking, as from the other eleven-year-olds on sax in the band room. He made the end with a clean upward riff, holding the final note high, pure and unwavering.

'Good!' I called to him.

Quadberry was trying to move out of the sunken row toward us, but his heavy shoes were impeding him.

'Sounded like a duck. Sounded like a girl duck,' said Radcleve, who was kneeling down and packing a mudball around one of the M-80s. I saw and I was an accomplice, because I did nothing. Radcleve lit the fuse and heaved the mudball over the fence. An M-80 is a very serious firecracker; it is like the charge they use to shoot up those sprays six hundred feet on July Fourth at country clubs. It went off, this one, even bigger than most M-80s.

When we looked over the fence, we saw Quadberry all muck specks and fragments of stalks. He was covering the mouthpiece of his horn with both hands. Then I saw there was blood pouring out of, it seemed, his right eye. I thought he was bleeding directly out of his eye.

'Quadberry?' I called.

He turned around and never said a word to me until I was eighteen. He walked back holding his eye and staggering through the cornstalks. Radcleve had him in the binoculars. Radcleve was trembling . . . but intrigued.

'His mother just screamed. She's running out in the field to get him.'

I thought we'd blinded him, but we hadn't. I thought the Quadberrys would get the police or call my father, but they didn't. The upshot of this is that Quadberry had a permanent white space next to his right eye, a spot that looked like a tiny upset crown.

I went from sixth through half of twelfth grade ignoring him and that wound. I was coming on as a drummer and a lover, but if Quadberry happened to appear within fifty feet of me and my most tender, intimate sweetheart, I would duck out. Quadberry grew up just like the rest of us. His father was still a doctor—professor of history—at the town college; his mother was still blond, and a musician. She was organist at an Episcopalian church in Jackson, the big capital city ten miles east of us.

As for Radcleve, he still had no ear for music, but he was there, my buddy. He was repentant about Quadberry, although not so much as I. He'd thrown the mud grenade over the fence only to see what would happen. He had not really wanted to maim. Quadberry had played his tune on the sax, Radcleve had played his tune on the mud grenade. It was just a shame they happened to cross talents.

Radcleve went into a long period of nearly nothing after he gave up violent explosives. Then he trained himself to copy the comic strips, *Steve Canyon* to *Major Hoople*, until he became quite a versatile cartoonist with some very provocative new faces and bodies that were gesturing intriguingly. He could never fill in the speech balloons with the smart words they needed. Sometimes he would pencil in 'Err' or 'What?' in the empty speech places. I saw him a great deal. Radcleve was not spooked by Quadberry. He even once asked Quadberry what his opinion was of his future as a cartoonist. Quadberry told Radcleve that if he took all his cartoons and stuffed himself with them, he would make an interesting dead man. After that, Radcleve was shy of him too.

When I was a senior we had an extraordinary band. Word was we had outplayed all the big AAA division bands last April in the state contest. Then came news that a new blazing saxophone player was coming into the band as first chair. This person had spent summers in Vermont in music camps, and he was coming in with us for the concert season. Our director, a lovable aesthete named Richard Prender, announced to us in a proud silent moment that the boy was joining us tomorrow night. The effect was that everybody should push over a seat or two and make room for this boy and his talent. I was annoyed. Here I'd been with the band and had kept hold of the taste among the whole percussion section. I could play rock and jazz drum and didn't even really need to be here. I could be in Vermont too, give me a piano and a bass. I looked at the kid on first sax, who was going to be supplanted tomorrow. For two years he had thought he was the star, then suddenly enters this boy who's three times better.

The new boy was Quadberry. He came in, but he was meek, and when he turned up he put his head almost on the floor, bending over trying to be inconspicuous. The girls in the band had wanted him to be handsome, but Quadberry refused and kept himself in such hiding among the sax section that he was neither handsome, ugly, cute or anything. What he was was pretty near invisible, except for the bell of his horn, the all-but-closed eyes, the Arabian nose, the brown hair with its halo of white ends, the desperate oralness, the giant reed punched into his face, and hazy Quadberry, loving the wound in a private dignified ecstasy.

I say dignified because of what came out of the end of his horn. He was more than what Prender had told us he would be. Because of

Quadberry, we could take the band arrangement of Ravel's *Bolero* with us to the state contest. Quadberry would do the saxophone solo. He would switch to alto sax, he would do the sly Moorish ride. When he played, I heard the sweetness, I heard the horn which finally brought human *talk* into the realm of music. It could sound like the mutterings of a field nigger, and then it could get up into inhumanly careless beauty, it could get among mutinous helium bursts around Saturn. I already loved *Bolero* for the constant drum part. The percussion was always there, driving along with the subtly increasing triplets, insistent, insistent, at last outraged and trying to steal the whole show from the horns and the others. I knew a large boy with dirty blond hair, name of Wyatt, who played viola in the Jackson Symphony and sousaphone in our band—one of the rare closet transmutations of my time—who was forever claiming to have discovered the central *Bolero* one Sunday afternoon over FM radio as he had seven distinct sexual moments with a certain B., girl flutist with black bangs and skin like mayonnaise, while the drums of Ravel carried them on and on in a ceremony of Spanish sex. It was agreed by all the canny in the band that *Bolero* was exactly the piece to make the band soar—now especially as we had Quadberry, who made his walk into the piece like an actual lean Spanish bandit. This boy could blow his horn. He was, as I had suspected, a genius. His solo was not quite the same as the New York Phil's saxophonist's, but it was better. It came in and was with us. It entered my spine and, I am sure, went up the skirts of the girls. I had almost deafened myself playing drums in the most famous rock and jazz band in the state, but I could hear the voice that went through and out that horn. It sounded like a very troubled forty-year-old man, a man who had had his brow in his hands a long time.

The next time I saw Quadberry up close, in fact the first time I had seen him up close since we were eleven and he was bleeding in the cornfield, was in late February. I had only three classes this last semester, and went up to the band room often, to loaf and complain and keep up my touch on the drums. Prender let me keep my set in one of the instrument rooms, with a tarpaulin thrown over it, and I would drag it out to the practice room and whale away. Sometimes a group of sophomores would come up and I would make them marvel, whaling away as if not only deaf but blind to them, although I wasn't at all. If I saw a sophomore girl with exceptional bod or face, I would do miracles of technique I never knew were in me. I would amaze myself. I would be threatening Buddy Rich and Sam Morello. But this time when I went into the instrument room, there was Quadberry on one side, and, back in a dark corner, a small ninth-grade euphonium player whose face was all red. The little boy was weeping and grinning at the same time.

'Queerberry,' the boy said softly.

Quadberry flew upon him like a demon. He grabbed the boy's collar, slapped his face, and yanked his arm behind him in a merciless wrestler's grip, the one that made them bawl on TV. Then the boy broke it and slugged Quadberry in the lips and ran across to my side of the room. He said 'Queerberry' softly again and jumped for the door. Quadberry plunged across the room and tackled him on the threshold. Now that the boy was under him, Quadberry pounded the top of his head with his fist made like a mallet. The boy kept calling him 'Queerberry' throughout this. He had not learned his lesson. The boy seemed to be going into concussion, so I stepped over and touched Quadberry, telling him to quit. Quadberry obeyed and stood up off the boy, who crawled on out into the band room. But once more the boy looked back with a bruised grin, saying 'Queerberry.' Quadberry made a move toward him, but I blocked it.

'Why are you beating up on this little guy?' I said. Quadberry was sweating and his eyes were wild with hate; he was a big fellow now, though lean. He was, at six feet tall, bigger than me.

'He kept calling me Queerberry.'

'What do you care?' I asked.

'I care,' Quadberry said, and left me standing there.

We were to play at Millsaps College Auditorium for the concert. It was April. We got on the buses, a few took their cars, and were a big tense crowd getting over there. To Jackson was only a twenty-minute trip. The director, Prender, followed the bus in his Volkswagen. There was a thick fog. A flashing ambulance, snaking the lanes, piled into him head on. Prender, who I would imagine was thinking of *Bolero* and hearing the young horn voices in his band—perhaps he was dwelling on Quadberry's spectacular gypsy entrance, or perhaps he was meditating on the percussion section, of which I was the king— passed into the airs of band-director heaven. We were told by the student director as we set up on the stage. The student director was a senior from the town college, very much afflicted, almost to the point of drooling, by a love and respect for Dick Prender, and now afflicted by a heartbreaking esteem for his ghost. As were we all.

I loved the tough and tender director awesomely and never knew it until I found myself bawling along with all the rest of the boys of the percussion. I told them to keep setting up, keep tuning, keep screwing the stands together, keep hauling in the kettledrums. To just quit and bawl seemed a betrayal to Prender. I caught some girl clarinetists trying to flee the stage and go have their cry. I told them to get the hell back to their section. They obeyed me. Then I found the student director. I had to have my say.

'Look. I say we just play *Bolero* and junk the rest. That's our horse. We can't play *Brighton Beach* and *Neptune's Daughter*. We'll never make it through them. And they're too happy.'

'We aren't going to play anything,' he said. 'Man, to play is filthy. Did you ever hear Prender play piano? Do you know what a cool man he was in all things?'

'We play. He got us ready, and we play.'

'Man, you can't play any more than I can direct. You're bawling your face off. Look out there at the rest of them. Man, it's a herd, it's a weeping herd.'

'What's wrong? Why aren't you pulling this crowd together?' This was Quadberry, who had come up urgently. 'I got those little brats in my section sitting down, but we've got people abandoning the stage, tearful little finks throwing their horns on the floor.'

'I'm not directing,' said the mustached college man.

'Then get out of here. You're weak, weak!'

'Man, we've got teenagers in ruin here, we got sorrowville. Nobody can—'

'Go ahead. Do your number. Weak out on us.'

'Man, I—'

Quadberry was already up on the podium, shaking his arms.

'We're right here! The band is right here! Tell your friends to get back in their seats. We're doing *Bolero*. Just put *Bolero* up and start tuning. *I'm* directing. I'll be right here in front of you. You look at *me*! Don't you dare quit on Prender. Don't you dare quit on me. You've got to be heard. *I've* got to be heard. Prender wanted me to be heard. I am the star, and I say we sit down and blow.'

And so we did. We all tuned and were burning low for the advent into *Bolero*, though we couldn't believe that Quadberry was going to remain with his saxophone strapped to him and conduct us as well as play his solo. The judges, who apparently hadn't heard about

Prender's death, walked down to their balcony desks.

One of them called out 'Ready' and Quadberry's hand was instantly up in the air, his fingers hard as if around the stem of something like a torch. This was not Prender's way, but it had to do. We went into the number cleanly and Quadberry one-armed it in the conducting. He kept his face, this look of hostility, at the reeds and the trumpets. I was glad he did not look toward me and the percussion boys like that. But he must have known we would be constant and tasteful because I was the king there. As for the others, the soloists especially, he was scaring them into excellence. Prender had never got quite this from them. Boys became men and girls became women as Quadberry directed us through *Bolero*. I even became a bit better of a man myself, though Quadberry did not look my way. When he turned around toward the people in the auditorium to enter on his solo, I knew it was my baby. I and the drums were the metronome. That was no trouble. It was talent to keep the metronome ticking amidst any given chaos of sound.

But this keeps one's mind occupied and I have no idea what Quadberry sounded like on his sax ride. All I know is that he looked grief-stricken and pale, and small. Sweat had popped out on his forehead. He bent over extremely. He was wearing the red brass-button jacket and black pants, black bow tie at the throat, just like the rest of us. In this outfit he bent over his horn almost out of sight. For a moment, before I caught the glint of his horn through the music stands, I thought he had pitched forward off the stage. He went down so far to do his deep oral thing, his conducting arm had disappeared so quickly, I didn't know but what he was having a seizure.

When *Bolero* was over, the audience stood up and made meat out of their hands applauding. The judges themselves applauded. The band stood up, bawling again, for Prender and because we had done so well. The student director rushed out crying to embrace Quadberry, who eluded him with his dipping shoulders. The crowd was still clapping insanely. I wanted to see Quadberry myself. I waded through the red backs, through the bow ties, over the white bucks. Here was the first-chair clarinetist, who had done his bit like an angel; he sat close to the podium and could hear Quadberry.

'Was Quadberry good?' I asked him.

'Are you kidding? These tears in my eyes, they're for how good he was. He was too good. I'll never touch my clarinet again.' The clarinetist slung the pieces of his horn into their case like underwear

449

and a toothbrush.

I found Quadberry fitting the sections of his alto in the velvet holds of his case.

'Hooray,' I said. 'Hip damn hooray for you.'

Arden was smiling too, showing a lot of teeth I had never seen. His smile was sly. He knew he had pulled off a monster unlikelihood.

'Hip hip hooray for me,' he said. 'Look at her. I had the bell of the horn almost smack in her face.'

There was a woman of about thirty sitting in the front row of the auditorium. She wore a sundress with a drastic cleavage up front; looked like something that hung around New Orleans and kneaded your heart to death with her feet. She was still mesmerized by Quadberry. She bore on him with a stare and there was moisture in her cleavage.

'You played well.'

'Well? Play well? Yes.'

He was trying not to look at her directly. Look at *me*, I beckoned to her with full face: I was the *drums*. She arose and left.

'I was walking downhill in a valley, is all I was doing,' said Quadberry. 'Another man, a wizard, was playing my horn.' He locked his sax case. 'I feel nasty for not being able to cry like the rest of them. Look at them. Look at them crying.'

True, the children of the band were still weeping, standing around the stage. Several moms and dads had come up among them, and they were misty-eyed too. The mixture of grief and superb music had been unbearable.

A girl in tears appeared next to Quadberry. She was a majorette in football season and played third-chair sax during the concert season. Not even her violent sorrow could take the beauty out of the face of this girl. I had watched her for a number of years—her alertness to her own beauty, the pride of her legs in the majorette outfit—and had taken out her younger sister, a second-rate version of her and a wayward overcompensating nymphomaniac whom several of us made a hobby out of pitying. Well, here was Lilian herself crying in Quadberry's face. She told him that she'd run off the stage when she heard about Prender, dropped her horn and everything, and had thrown herself into a tavern across the street and drunk two beers quickly for some kind of relief. But she had come back through the front doors of the auditorium and sat down, dizzy with beer, and seen Quadberry, the miraculous way he had gone on with *Bolero*. And now she was eaten up by feeling of guilt, weakness, cowardice.

'We didn't miss you,' said Quadberry.

'Please forgive me. Tell me to do something to make up for it.'

'Don't breathe my way, then. You've got beer all over your breath.'

'I want to talk to you.'

'Take my horn case and go out, get in my car, and wait for me. It's the ugly Plymouth in front of the school bus.'

'I know,' she said.

Lilian Field, this lovely teary thing, with the rather pious grace of her carriage, with the voice full of imminent swoon, picked up Quadberry's horn case and her own and walked off the stage.

I told the percussion boys to wrap up the packing. Into my suitcase I put my own gear and also managed to steal drum keys, two pairs of brushes, a twenty-inch Turkish cymbal, a Gretsch snare drum that I desired for my collection, a wood block, kettledrum mallets, a tuning harp and a score sheet of *Bolero* full of marginal notes I'd written down straight from the mouth of Dick Prender, thinking I might want to look at the score sheet sometime in the future when I was having a fit of nostalgia such as I am having right now as I write this. I had never done any serious stealing before, and I was stealing for my art. Prender was dead, the band had done its last thing of the year, I was a senior. Things were finished at the high school. I was just looting a sinking ship. I could hardly lift the suitcase. As I was pushing it across the stage, Quadberry was there again.

'You can ride back with me if you want to.'

'But you've got Lilian.'

'Please ride back with me . . . us. Please.'

'Why?'

'To help me get rid of her. Her breath is full of beer. My father always had that breath. Every time he was friendly, he had that breath. And she looks a great deal like my mother.' We were interrupted by the Tupelo band director. He put his baton against Quadberry's arm.

'You were big with *Bolero*, son, but that doesn't mean you own the stage.'

Quadberry caught the end of the suitcase and helped me with it out to the steps behind the auditorium. The buses were gone. There sat his ugly ocher Plymouth; it was a failed, gay, experimental shade from the Chrysler people. Lilian was sitting in the front wearing her shirt and bow tie, her coat off.

451

'Are you going to ride back with me?' Quadberry said to me.

'I think I would spoil something. You never saw her when she was a majorette. She's not stupid, either. She likes to show off a little, but she's not stupid. She's in the History Club.'

'My father has a doctorate in history. She smells of beer.'

I said, 'She drank two cans of beer when she heard about Prender.'

'There are a lot of other things to do when you hear about death. What I did, for example. She ran away. She fell to pieces.'

'She's waiting for us,' I said.

'One damned thing I am never going to do is drink.'

'I've never seen your mother up close, but Lilian doesn't look like your mother. She doesn't look like anybody's mother.'

I rode with them silently to Clinton. Lilian made no bones about being disappointed I was in the car, though she said nothing. I knew it would be like this and I hated it. Other girls in town would not be so unhappy that I was in the car with them. I looked for flaws in Lilian's face and neck and hair, but there weren't any. Couldn't there be a mole, an enlarged pore, too much gum on a tooth, a single awkward hair around the ear? No. Memory, the whole lying opera of it, is killing me now. Lilian was faultless beauty, even sweating, even and especially in the white man's shirt and the bow tie clamping together her collar, when one knew her uncomfortable bosoms, her poor nipples . . .

'Don't take me back to the band room. Turn off here and let me off at my house,' I said to Quadberry. He didn't turn off.

'Don't tell Arden what to do. He can do what he wants to,' said Lilian, ignoring me and speaking to me at the same time. I couldn't bear her hatred. I asked Quadberry to please just stop the car and let me out here, wherever he was: this front yard of the mobile home would do. I was so earnest that he stopped the car. He handed back the keys and I dragged my suitcase out of the trunk, then flung the keys back at him and kicked the car to get it going again.

My band came together in the summer. We were the Bop Fiends . . . that was our name. Two of them were from Ole Miss, our bass player was from Memphis State, but when we got together this time, I didn't call the tenor sax, who went to Mississippi Southern, because Quadberry wanted to play with us. During the school year the college boys and I fell into minor groups to pick up twenty dollars on a weekend, playing dances for the Moose Lodge, medical-student fraternities in Jackson, teenage recreation centers in Greenwood, and such as that: But come summer we were the Bop Fiends again, and the price for us went up to $1,200 a gig. Where they wanted the best rock and bop and they had some bread, we were called. The summer after I was a senior, we played in Alabama, Louisiana and Arkansas. Our fame was getting out there on the interstate route.

This was the summer that I made myself deaf.

Years ago Prender had invited down an old friend from a high school in Michigan. He asked me over to meet the friend, who had been a drummer with Stan Kenton at one time and was now a band director just like Prender. This fellow was almost totally deaf and he warned me very sincerely about deafing myself. He said there would come a point when you had to lean over and concentrate all your hearing on what the band was doing and that was the time to quit for a while, because if you didn't you would be irrevocably deaf like him in a month or two. I listened to him but could not take him seriously. Here was an oldish man who had his problems. My ears had ages of hearing left. Not so. I played the drums so loud the summer after I graduated from high school that I made myself, eventually, stone deaf.

We were at, say, the National Guard Armory in Lake Village, Arkansas, Quadberry out in front of us on the stage they'd built. Down on the floor were hundreds of sweaty teenagers. Four girls in sundresses, showing what they could, were leaning on the stage with broad ignorant lust on their minds. I'd play so loud for one particular chick, I'd get absolutely out of control. The guitar boys would have to turn the volume up full blast to compensate. Thus I went deaf. Anyhow, the dramatic idea was to release Quadberry on a very soft sweet ballad right in the middle of a long ear-piercing run of rock-and-roll tunes. I'd get out the brushes and we would astonish the crowd with our tenderness. By August, I was so deaf I had to watch Quadberry's fingers changing notes on the saxophone, had to use my eyes to keep time. The other members of the Bop Fiends told me I was hitting out of time. I pretended I was trying to do experimental things with rhythm when the truth was I simply could no longer hear. I was no longer a tasteful drummer, either. I had become deaf through lack of taste.

Which was—taste—exactly the quality that made Quadberry wicked on the saxophone. During the howling, during the churning, Quadberry had taste. The noise did not affect his personality; he was solid as a brick. He could blend. Oh, he could hoot through his horn when the right time came, but he could do supporting roles for an hour. Then, when we brought him out front for his solo on something like 'Take Five,' he would play with such light blissful technique that he even eclipsed Paul Desmond. The girls around the stage did not cause him to enter into excessive loudness or vibrato.

Quadberry had his own girl friend now, Lilian back at Clinton, who put all the sundressed things around the stage in the shade. In my mind I had congratulated him for getting up next to this beauty, but in June and July, when I was still hearing things a little, he never said a word about her. It was one night in August, when I could hear nothing and was driving him to his house, that he asked me to turn on the inside light and spoke in a retarded deliberate way. He knew I was deaf and counted on my being able to read lips.

'Don't . . . make . . . fun . . . of her . . . or me . . . We . . . think . . . she . . . is . . . in trouble.'

I wagged my head. Never would I make fun of him or her. She detested me because I had taken out her helpless little sister for a few weeks, but I would never think there was anything funny about Lilian, for all her haughtiness. I only thought of this event as monumentally curious.

'No one except you knows,' he said.

'Why did you tell me?'

'Because I'm going away and you have to take care of her. I wouldn't trust her with anybody but you.'

'She hates the sight of my face. Where are you going?'

'Annapolis.'

'You aren't going to any damned Annapolis.'

'That was the only school that wanted me.'

'You're going to play your saxophone on a boat?'

'I don't know what I'm going to do.'

'How . . . how can you just leave her?'

'She wants me to. She's very excited about me at Annapolis. William [this is my name], there is no girl I could imagine who has more inner sweetness than Lilian.'

I entered the town college, as did Lilian. She was in the same chemistry class I was. But she was rows away. It was difficult to learn anything, being deaf. The professor wasn't a pantomimer—but finally he went to the blackboard with the formulas and the algebra of problems, to my happiness. I hung in and made a B. At the end of the semester I was swaggering around the grade sheet he'd posted. I happened to see Lilian's grade. She'd only made a C. Beautiful Lilian got only a C while I, with my handicap, had made a B.

It had been a very difficult chemistry class. I had watched Lilian's stomach the whole way through. It was not growing. I wanted to see her look like a watermelon, make herself an amazing mother shape.

When I made the B and Lilian made the C, I got up my courage and finally went by to see her. She answered the door. Her parents weren't home. I'd never wanted this office of watching over her as Quadberry wanted me to, and this is what I told her. She asked me into the house. The rooms smelled of nail polish and pipe smoke. I was hoping her little sister wasn't in the house, and my wish came true. We were alone.

'You can quit watching over me.'

'Are you pregnant?'

'No.' Then she started crying. 'I wanted to be. But I'm not.'

'What do you hear from Quadberry?'

She said something but she had her back to me. She looked to me for an answer, but I had nothing to say. I knew she'd said something, but I hadn't heard it.

'He doesn't play the saxophone anymore,' she said.

This made me angry.

'Why not?'

'Too much math and science and navigation. He wants to fly. That's what his dream is now. He wants to get into an F-something jet.'

I asked her to say this over and she did. Lilian really was full of inner sweetness, as Quadberry had said. She understood that I was deaf. Perhaps Quadberry had told her.

The rest of the time in her house I simply witnessed her beauty and her mouth moving.

I went through college. To me it is interesting that I kept a B average and did it all deaf, though I know this isn't interesting to people who aren't deaf. I loved music, and never heard it. I loved poetry, and never heard a word that came out of the mouths of the visiting poets who read at the campus. I loved my mother and dad, but never heard a sound they made. One Christmas Eve, Radcleve was back from Ole Miss and threw an M-80 out in the street for old times' sake. I saw it

455

explode, but there was only a pressure in my ears. I was at parties when lusts were raging and I went home with two girls (I am medium handsome) who lived in apartments of the old two-story 1920 vintage, and I took my shirt off and made love to them. But I have no real idea what their reaction was. They were stunned and all smiles when I got up, but I have no idea whether I gave them the last pleasure or not. I hope I did. I've always been partial to women and have always wanted to see them satisfied till their eyes popped out.

Through Lilian I got the word that Quadberry was out of Annapolis and now flying jets off the *Bonhomme Richard*, an aircraft carrier headed for Vietnam. He telegrammed her that he would set down at the Jackson airport at ten o'clock one night. So Lilian and I were out there waiting. It was a familiar place to her. She was a stewardess and her loops were mainly in the South. She wore a beige raincoat, had red sandals on her feet; I was in a black turtleneck and corduroy jacket, feeling significant, so significant I could barely stand it. I'd already made myself the lead writer at Gordon-Marx Advertising in Jackson. I hadn't seen Lilian in a year. Her eyes were strained, no longer the bright blue things they were when she was a pious beauty. We drank coffee together. I loved her. As far as I knew, she'd been faithful to Quadberry.

He came down in an F-something Navy jet right on the dot of ten. She ran out on the airport pavement to meet him. I saw her crawl up the ladder. Quadberry never got out of the plane. I could see him in his blue helmet. Lilian backed down the ladder. Then Quadberry had the cockpit cover him again. He turned the plane around so its flaming red end was at us. He took it down the runway. We saw him leap out into the night at the middle of the runway going west, toward San Diego and the *Bonhomme Richard*. Lilian was crying.

'What did he say?' I asked.

'He said, "I am a dragon. America the beautiful, like you will never know." He wanted to give you a message. He was glad you were here.'

'What was the message?'

'The same thing. "I am a dragon. America the beautiful, like you will never know."'

'Did he say anything else?'

'Not a thing.'

'Did he express any love toward you?'

'He wasn't Ard. He was somebody with a sneer in a helmet.'

'He's going to war, Lilian.'

'I asked him to kiss me and he told me to get off the plane, he was firing up and it was dangerous.'

'Arden is going to war. He's just on his way to Vietnam and he wanted us to know that. It wasn't just him he wanted us to see. It was him in the jet he wanted us to see. He *is* that black jet. You can't kiss an airplane.'

'And what are we supposed to do?' cried sweet Lilian.

'We've just got to hang around. He didn't have to lift off and disappear straight up like that. That was to tell us how he isn't with us anymore.'

Lilian asked me what she was supposed to do now. I told her she was supposed to come with me to my apartment in the old 1920 Clinton place where I was. I was supposed to take care of her. Quadberry had said so. His six-year-old directive was still working.

She slept on the fold-out bed of the sofa for a while. This was the only bed in my place. I stood in the dark in the kitchen and drank a quarter bottle of gin on ice. I would not turn on the light and spoil her sleep. The prospect of Lilian asleep in my apartment made me feel like a chaplain on a visit to the Holy Land; I stood there getting drunk, biting my tongue when dreams of lust burst on me. That black jet Quadberry wanted us to see him in, its flaming rear end, his blasting straight up into the night at mid-runway—what precisely was he wanting to say in this stunt? Was he saying remember him forever or forget him forever? But I had my own life and was neither going to mother-hen it over his memory nor his old sweetheart. What did he mean, *America the beautiful, like you will never know*? I, William Howly, knew a goddamn good bit about America the beautiful, even as a deaf man. Being deaf had brought me up closer to people. There were only about five I knew, but I knew their mouth movements, the perspiration under their noses, their tongues moving over the crowns of their teeth, their fingers on their lips. Quadberry, I said, you don't have to get up next to the stars in your black jet to see America the beautiful.

I was deciding to lie down on the kitchen floor and sleep the night, when Lilian turned on the light and appeared in her panties and bra. Her body was perfect except for a tiny bit of fat on her upper thighs. She'd sunbathed herself so her limbs were brown, and her stomach, and the instinct was to rip off the white underwear and lick, suck, say

457

something terrific into the flesh that you discovered.

She was moving her mouth.

'Say it again slowly.'

'I'm lonely. When he took off in his jet, I think it meant he wasn't ever going to see me again. I think it meant he was laughing at both of us. He's an astronaut and he spits on us.'

'You want me on the bed with you?'

'I knew you're an intellectual. We could keep on the lights so you'd know what I said.'

'You want to say things? This isn't going to be just sex?'

'It could never be just sex.'

'I agree. Go to sleep. Let me make up my mind whether to come in there. Turn out the lights.'

Again the dark, and I thought I would cheat not only Quadberry but the entire Quadberry family if I did what was natural.

I fell asleep.

Quadberry escorted B-52s on bombing missions into North Vietnam. He was catapulted off the *Bonhomme Richard* in his suit at 100 degrees temperature, often at night, and put the F-8 on all it could get—the tiny cockpit, the immense long two-million-dollar fuselage, wings, tail and jet engine, Quadberry, the genius master of his dragon, going up to twenty thousand feet to be cool. He'd meet with the big B-52 turtle of the air and get in a position, his cockpit glowing with green and orange lights, and turn on his transistor radio. There was only one really good band, never mind the old American rock-and-roll from Cambodia, and that was Red Chinese opera. Quadberry loved it. He loved the nasal horde in the finale, when the peasants won over the old fat dilettante mayor. Then he'd turn the jet around when he saw the squatty abrupt little fires way down there after the B-52s had dropped their diet. It was a seven-hour trip. Sometimes he slept, but his body knew when to wake up. Another thirty minutes and there was his ship waiting for him out in the waves.

All his trips weren't this easy. He'd have to blast it out in daytime and get with the B-52s, and a SAM missile would come up among them. Two of his mates were taken down by these missiles. But Quadberry, as on saxophone, had endless learned technique. He'd put his jet perpendicular in the air and make the SAMs look silly. He even shot down two of them. Then, one day in daylight, an MIG came floating up level with him and his squadron. Quadberry couldn't believe it. Others in the squadron were shy, but Quadberry knew where and how the MIG could shoot. He flew below the cannons and then came in behind it. He knew the MIG wanted one of the B-52s and not mainly him. The MIG was so concentrated on the fat B-52 that he forgot about Quadberry. It was really an amateur suicide pilot in the MIG. Quadberry got on top of him and let down a missile, rising out of the way of it. The missile blew off the tail of the MIG. But then Quadberry wanted to see if the man got safely out of the cockpit. He thought it would be pleasant if the fellow got out with his parachute working. Then Quadberry saw that the fellow wanted to collide his wreckage with the B-52, so Quadberry turned himself over and cannoned, evaporated the pilot and cockpit. It was the first man he'd killed.

The next trip out, Quadberry was hit by a ground missile. But his jet kept flying. He flew it a hundred miles and got to the sea. There was the *Bonhomme Richard*, so he ejected. His back was snapped but, by God, he landed right on the deck. His mates caught him in their arms and cut the parachute off him. His back hurt for weeks, but he was all right. He rested and recuperated in Hawaii for a month.

Then he went off the front of the ship. Just like that, his F-6 plopped and sank like a rock. Quadberry saw the ship go over him. He knew he shouldn't eject just yet. If he ejected now he'd knock his head on the bottom and get chewed up in the motor blades. So Quadberry waited. His plane was sinking in the green and he could see the hull of the aircraft getting smaller, but he had oxygen through his mask and it didn't seem that urgent a decision. Just let the big ship get over. Down what later proved to be sixty feet, he pushed the ejection button. It fired him away, bless it, and he woke up ten feet under the surface swimming against an almost overwhelming body of underwater parachute. But two of his mates were in a helicopter, one of them on the ladder to lift him out.

Now Quadberry's back was really hurt. He was out of this war and all wars for good.

Lilian, the stewardess, was killed in a crash. Her jet exploded with a hijacker's bomb, an inept bomb which wasn't supposed to go off, fifteen miles out of Havana; the poor pilot, the poor passengers, the poor stewardesses were all splattered like flesh sparklers over the water just out of Cuba. A fisherman found one seat of the airplane. Castro expressed regrets.

Quadberry came back to Clinton two weeks after Lilian and the others bound for Tampa were dead. He hadn't heard about her. So I told him Lilian was dead when I met him at the airport. Quadberry was thin and rather meek in his civvies—a gray suit and an out-of-style tie. The white ends of his hair were not there—the halo had disappeared—because his hair was cut short. The Arab nose seemed a pitiable defect in an ash-whiskered face that was beyond anemic now. He looked shorter, stooped. The truth was he was sick, his back was killing him. His breath was heavy-laden with airplane martinis and in his limp right hand he held a wet cigar. I told him about Lilian. He mumbled something sideways that I could not possibly make out.

'You've got to speak right at me, remember? Remember me, Quadberry?'

'Mom and Dad of course aren't here.'

'No. Why aren't they?'

'He wrote me a letter after we bombed Hué. Said he hadn't sent me to Annapolis to bomb the architecture of Hué. He had been there once and had some important experience—French-kissed the queen of Hué or the like. Anyway, he said I'd have to do a hell of a lot of repentance for that. But he and Mom are separate people. Why isn't *she* here?'

'I don't know.'

'I'm not asking you the question. The question is to God.'

He shook his head. Then he sat down on the floor of the terminal. People had to walk around. I asked him to get up.

'No. How is old Clinton?'

'Horrible. Aluminum subdivisions, cigar boxes with four thin columns in front, thick as a hive. We got a turquoise water tank; got a shopping center, a monster Jitney Jungle, fifth-rate teenyboppers covering the place like ants.' Why was I being so frank just now, as Quadberry sat on the floor downcast, drooped over like a long weak candle? 'It's not our town anymore, Ard. It's going to hurt to drive back into it. Hurts me every day. Please get up.'

'And Lilian's not even over there now.'

'No. She's a cloud over the Gulf of Mexico. You flew out of Pensacola once. You know what beauty those pink and blue clouds are. That's how I think of her.'

'Was there a funeral?'

'Oh, yes. Her Methodist preacher and a big crowd over at Wright Ferguson funeral home. Your mother and father were there. Your father shouldn't have come. He could barely walk. Please get up.'

'Why? What am I going to do, where am I going?'

'You've got your saxophone.'

'Was there a coffin? Did you all go by and see the pink or blue cloud in it?' He was sneering now as he had done when he was eleven and fourteen and seventeen.

'Yes, they had a very ornate coffin.'

'Lilian was the Unknown Stewardess. I'm not getting up.'

'I said you still have your saxophone.'

'No, I don't. I tried to play it on the ship after the last time I hurt my back. No go. I can't bend my neck or spine to play it. The pain kills me.'

'Well, *don't* get up, then. Why am I asking you to get up? I'm just a deaf drummer, too vain to buy a hearing aid. Can't stand to write the ad copy I do. Wasn't I a good drummer?'

'Superb.'

'But we can't be in this condition forever. The police are going to come and make you get up if we do it much longer.'

The police didn't come. It was Quadberry's mother who came. She looked me in the face and grabbed my shoulders before she saw Ard on the floor. When she saw him she yanked him off the floor, hugging him passionately. She was shaking with sobs. Quadberry was gathered to her as if he were a rope she was trying to wrap around herself. Her mouth was all over him. Quadberry's mother was a good-looking woman of fifty. I simply held her purse. He cried out that his back was hurting. At last she let him go.

'So now we walk,' I said.

'Dad's in the car trying to quit crying,' said his mother.

'This is nice,' Quadberry said. 'I thought everything and everybody was dead around here.' He put his arms around his mother. 'Let's all go off and kill some time together.' His mother's hair was on his lips. 'You?' he asked me.

'Murder the devil out of it,' I said.

I pretended to follow their car back to their house in Clinton. But when we were going through Jackson, I took the North 55 exit and disappeared from them, exhibiting a great amount of taste, I thought. I would get in their way in this reunion. I had an unimprovable apartment on Old Canton Road in a huge plaster house, Spanish style, with a terrace and ferns and yucca plant, and a green door where I went in. When I woke up I didn't have to make my coffee or fry my egg. The girl who slept in my bed did that. She was Lilian's little sister, Esther Field. Esther was pretty in a minor way and I was proud how I had tamed her to clean and cook around the place. The Field family would appreciate how I lived with her. I showed her the broom and the skillet, and she loved them. She also learned to speak very slowly when she had to say something.

Esther answered the phone when Quadberry called me seven months later. She gave me his message. He wanted to know my opinion on a decision he had to make. There was this Dr Gordon, a surgeon at Emory Hospital in Atlanta, who said he could cure Quadberry's back problem. Quadberry's back was killing him. He was in torture even holding the phone to say this. The surgeon said there was a seventy-five/twenty-five chance. Seventy-five that it would be successful, twenty-five that it would be fatal. Esther waited for my opinion. I told her to tell Quadberry to go over to Emory. He'd got through with luck in Vietnam, and now he should ride it out in this petty back operation.

Esther delivered the message and hung up.

'He said the surgeon's just his age; he's some genius from John Hopkins Hospital. He said this Gordon guy has published a lot of articles on spinal operations,' said Esther.

'Fine and good. All is happy. Come to bed.'

I felt her mouth and her voice on my ears, but I could hear only a sort of loud pulse from the girl. All I could do was move toward moisture and nipples and hair.

Quadberry lost his gamble at Emory Hospital in Atlanta. The brilliant surgeon his age lost him. Quadberry died. He died with his Arabian nose up in the air.

That is why I told this story and will never tell another.

1978

GREENWICH TIME

Ann Beattie

'I 'm thinking about frogs,' Tom said to his secretary on the phone. 'Tell them I'll be in when I've come up with a serious approach to frogs.'

'I don't know what you're talking about,' she said.

'Doesn't matter. I'm the idea man, you're the message taker. Lucky you.'

'Lucky you,' his secretary said. 'I've got to have two wisdom teeth pulled this afternoon.'

'That's awful,' he said. 'I'm sorry.'

'Sorry enough to go with me?'

'I've got to think about frogs,' he said. 'Tell Metcalf I'm taking the day off to think about them, if he asks.'

'The health plan here doesn't cover dental work,' she said.

Tom worked at an ad agency on Madison Avenue. This week, he was trying to think of a way to market soap shaped like frogs—soap imported from France. He had other things on his mind. He hung up and turned to the man who was waiting behind him to use the phone.

'Did you hear that?' Tom said.

'Do what?' the man said.

'Christ,' Tom said. 'Frog soap.'

He walked away and went out to sit across the street from his favorite pizza restaurant. He read his horoscope in the paper (neutral), looked out the window of the coffee shop, and waited for the restaurant to open. At eleven-forty-five he crossed the street and ordered a slice of Sicilian pizza, with everything. He must have had a funny look on his face when he talked to the man behind the counter, because the man laughed and said, 'You sure? Everything? You even look surprised yourself.'

'I started out for work this morning and never made it there,' Tom said. 'After I wolf down a pizza I'm going to ask my ex-wife if my son can come back to live with me.'

The man averted his eyes and pulled a tray out from under the counter. When Tom realized that he was making the man nervous, he sat down. When the pizza was ready, he went to the counter and got it, and ordered a large glass of milk. He caught the man behind the counter looking at him one more time—unfortunately, just as he gulped his milk too fast and it was running down his chin. He wiped his chin with a napkin, but even as he did so he was preoccupied, thinking about the rest of his day. He was heading for Amanda's in Greenwich, and, as usual, he felt a mixture of relief (she had married another man, but she had given him a key to the back door) and anxiety (Shelby, her husband, was polite to him but obviously did not like to see him often).

When he had left the restaurant, he meant to get his car out of the garage and drive there immediately, to tell her that he wanted Ben— that somehow, in the confusion of the situation, he had lost Ben, and now he wanted him back. Instead, he found himself wandering around New York, to calm himself so that he could make a rational appeal. After an hour or so, he realized that he was becoming as interested in the city as a tourist—in the tall buildings; the mannequins with their pelvises thrust forward, almost touching the glass of the store windows; books piled into pyramids in bookstores. He passed a pet store; its front window space was full of shredded newspaper and sawdust. As he looked in, a teenage girl reached over the gate that blocked in the window area and lowered two brown puppies, one in each hand, into the sawdust. For a second, her eye met his, and she thrust one dog toward him with a smile. For a second, the dog's eye also met his. Neither looked at him again; the dog burrowed into a pile of paper, and the girl turned and went back to work. When he and the girl caught each other's attention, a few seconds before, he had been reminded of the moment, earlier in the week, when a very attractive prostitute had approached him as he was walking past the Sheraton Centre. He had hesitated when she spoke to him, but only because her eyes were very bright—wide-set eyes, the eyebrows invisible under thick blond bangs. When he said no, she blinked and the brightness went away. He could not imagine how such a thing was physically possible; even a fish's eye wouldn't cloud over that quickly, in death. But the prostitute's eyes had gone dim in the second it took him to say no.

He detoured now to go to the movies: *Singin' in the Rain*. He left after Debbie Reynolds and Gene Kelly and Donald O'Connor danced onto the sofa and tipped it over. Still smiling about that, he went to a bar. When the bar started to fill up, he checked his watch and was surprised to see that people were getting off work. Drunk enough now to wish for rain, because rain would be fun, he walked to his apartment and took a shower, and then headed for the garage. There was a movie house next to the garage, and before he realized what he was doing he was watching *Invasion of the Body Snatchers*. He was shocked by the dog with the human head, not for the obvious reason but because it reminded him of the brown puppy he had seen earlier. It seemed an omen—a nightmare vision of what a dog would become when it was not wanted.

Six o'clock in the morning: Greenwich, Connecticut. The house is now Amanda's, ever since her mother's death. The ashes of Tom's former mother-in-law are in a tin box on top of the mantel in the dining room. The box is sealed with wax. She has been dead for a year, and in that year Amanda has moved out of their apartment in New York, gotten a quickie divorce, remarried, and moved into the house in Greenwich. She has another life, and Tom feels that he should be careful in it. He puts the key she gave him into the lock and opens the door as gently as if he were disassembling a bomb. Her cat, Rocky, appears, and looks at him. Sometimes Rocky creeps around the house with him. Now, though, he jumps on the window seat as gently, as unnoticeably, as a feather blown across sand.

Tom looks around. She has painted the living-room walls white and the downstairs bathroom crimson. The beams in the dining room have been exposed; Tom met the carpenter once—a small, nervous Italian who must have wondered why people wanted to pare their houses down to the framework. In the front hall, Amanda has hung photographs of the wings of birds.

Driving out to Amanda's, Tom smashed up his car. It was still drivable, but only because he found a tire iron in the trunk and used it to pry the bent metal of the left front fender away from the tire, so that the wheel could turn. The second he veered off the road (he must have dozed off for an instant), the thought came to him that Amanda would use the accident as a reason for not trusting him with Ben. While he worked with the tire iron, a man stopped his car and got out and gave him drunken advice. 'Never buy a motorcycle,' he said. 'They spin out of control. You go with them—you don't have a chance.' Tom nodded. 'Did you know Doug's son?' the man asked. Tom said nothing. The man shook his head sadly and then went to the back of his car and opened the trunk. Tom watched him as he

465

took flares out of his trunk and began to light them and place them in the road. The man came forward with several flares still in hand. He looked confused that he had so many. Then he lit the extras, one by one, and placed them in a semicircle around the front of the car, where Tom was working. Tom felt like some saint, in a shrine.

When the wheel was freed, he drove the car to Amanda's, cursing himself for having skidded and slamming the car into somebody's mailbox. When he got into the house, he snapped on the floodlight in the back yard, and then went into the kitchen to make some coffee before he looked at the damage again.

In the city, making a last stop before he finally got his car out of the garage, he had eaten eggs and bagels at an all-night deli. Now it seems to him that his teeth still ache from chewing. The hot coffee in his mouth feels good. The weak early sunlight, nearly out of reach of where he can move his chair and still be said to be sitting at the table, feels good where it strikes him on one shoulder. When his teeth don't ache, he begins to notice that he feels nothing in his mouth; where the sun strikes him, he can feel the wool of his sweater warming him the way a sweater is supposed to, even without sun shining on it. The sweater was a Christmas present from his son. She, of course, picked it out and wrapped it: a box enclosed in shiny white paper, crayoned on by Ben. 'B E N,' in big letters. Scribbles that looked like the wings of birds.

Amanda and Shelby are upstairs. Through the doorway he can see a digital clock on the mantel in the next room, on the other side from the box of ashes. At seven, the alarm will go off and Shelby will come downstairs, his gray hair, in the sharpening morning light, looking like one of those cheap abalone lights they sell at the seashore. He will stumble around, look down to make sure his fly is closed; he will drink coffee from one of Amanda's mother's bone-china cups, which he holds in the palms of his hands. His hands are so big that you have to look to see that he is cradling a cup, that he is not gulping coffee from his hands the way you would drink water from a stream.

Once, when Shelby was leaving at eight o'clock to drive into the city, Amanda looked up from the dining-room table where the three of them had been having breakfast—having a friendly, normal time, Tom had thought—and said to Shelby, 'Please don't leave me alone with him.' Shelby looked perplexed and embarrassed when she got up and followed him into the kitchen. 'Who gave him the key, sweetheart?' Shelby whispered. Tom looked through the doorway.

Shelby's hand was low on her hip—partly a joking sexual gesture, partly a possessive one. 'Don't try to tell me there's anything you're afraid of,' Shelby said.

Ben sleeps and sleeps. He often sleeps until ten or eleven. Up there in his bed, sunlight washing over him.

Tom looks again at the box with the ashes in it on the mantel. If there is another life, what if something goes wrong and he is reincarnated as a camel and Ben as a cloud and there is just no way for the two of them to get together? He wants Ben. He wants him now.

The alarm is ringing, so loud it sounds like a million madmen beating tin. Shelby's feet on the floor. The sunlight shining a rectangle of light through the middle of the room. Shelby will walk through that patch of light as though it were a rug rolled out down the aisle of a church. Six months ago, seven, Tom went to Amanda and Shelby's wedding.

Shelby is naked, and startled to see him. He stumbles, grabs his brown robe from his shoulder and puts it on, asking Tom what he's doing there and saying good morning at the same time. 'Every goddam clock in the house is either two minutes slow or five minutes fast,' Shelby says. He hops around on the cold tile in the kitchen, putting water on to boil, pulling his robe tighter around him. 'I thought this floor would warm up in summer,' Shelby says, sighing. He shifts his weight from one side to the other, the way a fighter warms up, chafing his big hands.

Amanda comes down. She is wearing a pair of jeans, rolled at the ankles, black high-heeled sandals, a black silk blouse. She stumbles like Shelby. She does not look happy to see Tom. She looks, and doesn't say anything.

'I wanted to talk to you,' Tom says. He sounds lame. An animal in a trap, trying to keep its eyes calm.

'I'm going into the city,' she says. 'Claudia's having a cyst removed. It's all a mess. I have to meet her there, at nine. I don't feel like talking now. Let's talk tonight. Come back tonight. Or stay today.' Her hands through her auburn hair. She sits in a chair, accepts the coffee Shelby brings.

'More?' Shelby says to Tom. 'You want something more?'

Amanda looks at Tom through the steam rising from her coffee cup. 'I think that we are all dealing with this situation very well,' she says. 'I'm not sorry I gave you the key. Shelby and I discussed it, and we both felt that you should have access to the house. But in the back of my mind I assumed that you would use the key—I had in mind more . . . emergency situations.'

'I didn't sleep well last night,' Shelby says. 'Now I would like it if I didn't feel that there was going to be a scene to start things off this morning.'

Amanda sighs. She seems as perturbed with Shelby as she is with Tom. 'And if I can say something without being jumped on,' she says to Shelby, 'because, yes, you *told* me not to buy a Peugeot, and now the damned thing won't run—as long as you're here, Tom, it would be nice if you gave Inez a ride to the market.'

'We saw seven deer running through the woods yesterday,' Shelby says.

'Oh, cut it out, Shelby,' Amanda says.

'Your problems I'm trying to deal with, Amanda,' Shelby says. 'A little less of the rough tongue, don't you think?'

Inez has pinned a sprig of phlox in her hair, and she walks as though she feels pretty. The first time Tom saw Inez, she was working in her sister's garden—actually, standing in the garden in bare feet, with a long cotton skirt sweeping the ground. She was holding a basket heaped high with iris and daisies. She was nineteen years old and had just arrived in the United States. That year, she lived with her sister and her sister's husband, Metcalf—his friend Metcalf, the craziest man at the ad agency. Metcalf began to study photography, just to take pictures of Inez. Finally his wife got jealous and asked Inez to leave. She had trouble finding a job, and Amanda liked her and felt sorry for her, and she persuaded Tom to have her come live with them, after she had Ben. Inez came, bringing boxes of pictures of herself, one suitcase, and a pet gerbil that died her first night in the house. All the next day, Inez cried, and Amanda put her arms around her. Inez always seemed like a member of the family, from the first.

By the edge of the pond where Tom is walking with Inez, there is a black dog, panting, staring up at a Frisbee. Its master raises the Frisbee, and the dog stares as though transfixed by a beam of light from heaven. The Frisbee flies, curves, and the dog has it as it dips down.

'I'm going to ask Amanda if Ben can come live with me,' Tom says to Inez.

'She'll never say yes,' Inez says.

468

'What do you think Amanda would think if I kidnapped Ben?' Tom says.

'Ben's adjusting,' she says. 'That's a bad idea.'

'You think I'm putting you on? I'd kidnap you with him.'

'She's not a bad person,' Inez says. 'You think about upsetting her too much. She has problems, too.'

'Since when do you defend your cheap employer?'

His son has picked up a stick. The dog, in the distance, stares. The dog's owner calls its name: 'Sam!' The dog snaps his head around. He bounds through the grass, head raised, staring at the Frisbee.

'I should have gone to college,' Inez says.

'College?' Tom says. The dog is running and running. 'What would you have studied?'

Inez swoops down in back of Ben, picks him up and squeezes him. He struggles, as though he wants to be put down, but when Inez bends over he holds on to her. They come to where Tom parked the car, and Inez lowers Ben to the ground.

'Remember to stop at the market,' Inez says. 'I've got to get something for dinner.'

'She'll be full of sushi and Perrier. I'll bet they don't want dinner.'

'You'll want dinner,' she says. 'I should get something.'

He drives to the market. When they pull into the parking lot, Ben goes into the store with Inez, instead of to the liquor store next door with him. Tom gets a bottle of cognac and pockets the change. The clerk raises his eyebrows and drops them several times, like Groucho Marx, as he slips a flyer into the bag, with a picture on the front showing a blue-green drink in a champagne glass.

'Inez and I have secrets,' Ben says, while they are driving home. He is standing up to hug her around the neck from the back seat.

Ben is tired, and he taunts people when he is that way. Amanda does not think Ben should be condescended to: she reads him R. D. Laing, not fairy tales; she has him eat French food, and only indulges him by serving the sauce on the side. Amanda refused to send him to kindergarten. If she had, Tom believes, if he was around other children his age, he might get rid of some of his annoying mannerisms.

'For instance,' Inez says, 'I might get married.'

'Who?' he says, so surprised that his hands feel cold on the wheel.

'A man who lives in town. You don't know him.'

'You're dating someone?' he says.

He guns the car to get it up the driveway, which is slick with mud washed down by a lawn sprinkler. He steers hard, waiting for the instant when he will be able to feel that the car will make it. The car slithers a bit but then goes straight; they get to the top. He pulls onto the lawn, by the back door, leaving the way clear for Shelby and Amanda's car to pull into the garage.

'It would make sense that if I'm thinking of marrying somebody I would have been out on a date with him,' Inez says.

Inez has been with them since Ben was born, five years ago, and she has gestures and expressions now like Amanda's—Amanda's patient half-smile that lets him know she is half charmed and half at a loss that he is so unsophisticated. When Amanda divorced him, he went to Kennedy to pick her up when she returned, and her arms were loaded with pineapples when she came up the ramp. When he saw her, he gave her that same patient half-smile.

At eight, they aren't back, and Inez is worried. At nine, they still aren't back. 'She did say something about a play yesterday,' Inez whispers to Tom. Ben is playing with a puzzle in the other room. It is his bedtime—past it—and he has the concentration of Einstein. Inez goes into the room again, and he listens while she reasons with Ben. She is quieter than Amanda; she will get what she wants. Tom reads the newspaper from the market. It comes out once a week. There are articles about deer leaping across the road, lady artists who do batik who will give demonstrations at the library. He hears Ben running up the stairs, chased by Inez.

Water is turned on. He hears Ben laughing above the water. It makes him happy that Ben is so well adjusted; when he himself was five, no woman would have been allowed in the bathroom with him. Now that he is almost forty, he would like it very much if he were in the bathtub instead of Ben—if Inez were soaping his back, her fingers sliding down his skin.

For a long time, he has been thinking about water, about traveling somewhere so that he can walk on the beach, see the ocean. Every year he spends in New York he gets more and more restless. He often wakes up at night in his apartment, hears the air-conditioners roaring and the woman in the apartment above shuffling away her insomnia in satin slippers. (She has shown them to him, to explain that her walking cannot possibly be what is keeping him awake.) On nights when he can't sleep, he opens his eyes just a crack and pretends, as he

470

did when he was a child, that the furniture is something else. He squints the tall mahogany chest of drawers into the trunk of a palm tree; blinking his eyes quickly, he makes the night light pulse like a buoy bobbing in the water and tries to imagine that his bed is a boat, and that he is setting sail, as he and Amanda did years before, in Maine, where Perkins Cove widens into the choppy, ink-blue ocean.

Upstairs, the water is being turned off. It is silent. Silence for a long time. Inez laughs. Rocky jumps onto the stairs, and one board creaks as the cat pads upstairs. Amanda will not let him have Ben. He is sure of it. After a few minutes, he hears Inez laugh about making it snow as she holds the can of talcum powder high and lets it sift down on Ben in the tub.

Deciding that he wants at least a good night, Tom takes off his shoes and climbs the stairs; no need to disturb the quiet of the house. The door to Shelby and Amanda's bedroom is open. Ben and Inez are curled on the bed, and she has begun to read to him by the dim light. She lies next to him on the vast blue quilt spread over the bed, on her side with her back to the door, with one arm sweeping slowly through the air: *'Los soldados hicieron alto a la entrada del pueblo . . .'*

Ben sees him, and pretends not to. Ben loves Inez more than any of them. Tom goes away, so that she will not see him and stop reading.

He goes into the room where Shelby has his study. He turns on the light. There is a dimmer switch, and the light comes on very low. He leaves it that way.

He examines a photograph of the beak of a bird. A photograph next to it of a bird's wing. He moves in close to the picture and rests his cheek against the glass. He is worried. It isn't like Amanda not to come back, when she knows he is waiting to see her. He feels the coolness from the glass spreading down his body. There is no reason to think that Amanda is dead. When Shelby drives, he creeps along like an old man.

He goes into the bathroom and splashes water on his face, dries himself on what he thinks is Amanda's towel. He goes back to the study and stretches out on the daybed, under the open window, waiting for the car. He is lying very still on an unfamiliar bed, in a house he used to visit two or three times a year when he and Amanda were married—a house always decorated with flowers for Amanda's birthday, or smelling of newly cut pine at Christmas, when there was angel hair arranged into nests on the tabletops, with tiny Christmas balls glittering inside, like miraculously colored eggs. Amanda's mother is dead. He and Amanda are divorced. Amanda is married to Shelby. These events are unreal. What is real is the past, and the Amanda of years ago—that Amanda whose image he cannot get out of his mind, the scene he keeps remembering. It had happened on a day when he had not expected to discover anything; he was going along with his life with an ease he would never have again, and, in a way, what happened was so painful that even the pain of her leaving, and her going to Shelby, would later be dulled in comparison. Amanda—in her pretty underpants, in the bedroom of their city apartment, standing by the window—had crossed her hands at the wrists, covering her breasts, and said to Ben, 'It's gone now. The milk is gone.' Ben, in his diapers and T-shirt, lying on the bed and looking up at her. The mug of milk waiting for him on the bedside table— he'd drink it as surely as Hamlet would drink from the goblet of poison. Ben's little hand on the mug, her breasts revealed again, her hand overlapping his hand, the mug tilted, the first swallow. That night, Tom had moved his head from his pillow to hers, slipped down in the bed until his cheek came to the top of her breast. He had known he would never sleep, he was so amazed at the offhand way she had just done such a powerful thing. 'Baby—' he had said, beginning, and she had said, 'I'm not your baby.' Pulling away from him, from Ben. Who would have guessed that what she wanted was another man—a man with whom she would stretch into sleep on a vast ocean of blue quilted satin, a bed as wide as the ocean? The first time he came to Greenwich and saw that bed, with her watching him, he had cupped his hand to his brow and looked far across the room, as though he might see China.

The day he went to Greenwich to visit for the first time after the divorce, Ben and Shelby hadn't been there. Inez was there, though, and she had gone along on the tour of the redecorated house that Amanda had insisted on giving him. Tom knew that Inez had not wanted to walk around the house with them. She had done it because Amanda had asked her to, and she had also done it because she thought it might make it less awkward for him. In a way different from the way he loved Amanda, but still a very real way, he would always love Inez for that.

Now Inez is coming into the study, hesitating as her eyes accustom themselves to the dark. 'You're awake?' she whispers. 'Are you all right?' She walks to the bed slowly and sits down. His eyes are closed, and he is sure that he could sleep forever. Her hand is on his; he smiles as he begins to drift and dream. A bird extends its wing with the grace of a fan opening; *los soldados* are poised at the crest of the hill. About Inez he will always remember this: when she came to work on Monday, after the weekend when Amanda had told him about Shelby and said that she was getting a divorce, Inez whispered to him in the kitchen, 'I'm still your friend.' Inez had come close to him to whisper it, the way a bashful lover might move quietly forward to say 'I love you.' She had said that she was his friend, and he had told her that he never doubted that. Then they had stood there, still and quiet, as if the walls of the room were mountains and their words might fly against them.

1979

LECHERY

Jayne Anne Phillips

Though I have no money I must give myself what I need. Yes I know which lovers to call when the police have caught me peddling pictures, the store detectives twisting my wrists pull stockings out of my sleeves. And the butchers pummel the small of my back to dislodge their wrapped hocks; white bone and marbled tendon exposed as the paper tears and they push me against the wall. They curse me, I call my lovers. I'm nearly fifteen, my lovers get older and older. I know which ones will look at me delightedly, pay my bail, take me home to warm whiskey and bed. I might stay with them all day; I might run as the doors of their big cars swing open. Even as I run I can hear them behind me, laughing.

I go down by the schools with my pictures. The little boys smoke cigarettes, they're girlish as faggots, they try to act tough. Their Camels are wrinkled from pockets, a little chewed. I imagine them wet and stained pinkish at the tips, pink from their pouty lips. The boys have tight little chests, I see hard nipples in their T-shirts. Lines of smooth stomach, little penis tucked into jockey briefs. Already they're growing shaggy hair and quirky curves around their smiles. But no acne, I get them before they get pimples, I get them those first few times the eyes flutter and get strange. I show them what I do. Five or six surround me, jingling coins, tapping toes in tennis shoes. I know they've got some grade-school basketball coach, some ex-jock with a beer gut and a hard-on under his sweat pants in the locker room; that kills me. They come closer, I'm watching the ridged toes of their shoes. Now I do it with my eyes, I look up and pick the one I want. I tell him to collect the money and meet me at lunch in a park across the street, in a culvert, in a soft ditch, in a car parked under a bridge or somewhere shaded. Maybe I show them a few pills. One picture; blowsy redhead with a young blond girl, the girl a kneeling eunuch on white knees. The redhead has good legs, her muscles stand out tensed and she comes standing up. I tell them about it. Did you ever come standing up. I ask them, they shift their eyes at each

474

other. I know they've been in blankets in dark bedrooms, see who can beat off first. Slapping sounds and a dry urge. But they don't understand their soft little cocks all stiff when they wake up in daylight, how the bed can float around.

So at noon I wait for them. I don't smoke, it's filthy. I suck a smooth pebble and wait. I've brushed my teeth in a gas station. I press my lips with my teeth and suck them, make them soft. Press dots of oil to my neck, my hands. Ambergris or musk between my breasts, down in the shadowed place where hair starts in a line at my groin. Maybe I brush my hair. I let them see me do it, open a compact and tongue my lips real slow. They only see the soft tip of my tongue, I pretend it's not for them.

Usually just one of them comes, the one I chose, with a friend waiting out of sight where he can see us. If they came alone I can tell by looking at them. Sometimes they are high on something, I don't mind. Maybe I have them in an abandoned car down in a back lot, blankets on the seat or no back seat but an old mattress. Back windows covered up with paper sacks and speckled mud, sun through dirty windows or brown paper makes the light all patterns.

He is nervous. Right away he holds out the money. Or he is a little mean, he punches at me with his childish fist. A fine blond boy with a sweet neck and thin collarbones arched out like wings, or someone freckled whose ashen hair falls loose. A dark boy, thick lashes and cropped wooled hair, rose lips full and swelling a little in the darkened car. I give him a little whiskey, I rifle through the pictures and pretend to arrange them. I take a drink too, joke with him. This is my favorite time; he leans back against the seat with something like sleep in his eyes. I stroke his hard thighs, his chest, I comfort him.

I put the pictures beside us, some of them are smaller than postcards. We put our faces close to see them. A blond girl, a black girl, they like to see the girls. One bending back droops her white hair while the other arches over, holds her at the waist, puts her mouth to a breast so small only the nipple stands up. In the picture her mouth moves in and out, anyone can tell. A black hand nearly touching pale pubic hair, a forefinger almost tender curls just so, moves toward a slit barely visible just below the pelvic bone. I don't like pictures of shaven girls, it scares them to see so much. It makes them disappear.

I do things they've never seen, I could let them touch but no. I arrange their hands and feet, keep them here forever. Sometimes they tell me stories, they keep talking of baseball games and vicious battles with their friends. Lips pouty and soft, eyes a hard glass glitter. They lose the words and mumble like babies; I hold them just so, just tight, I sing the oldest songs. At times their smooth faces seem to grow smaller and smaller in my vision. I concentrate on their necks, their shoulders. Loosen their clothes and knead their scalps, pinching hard at the base of the head. Maybe that boy with dark hair and Spanish skin, his eyes flutter, I pull him across my legs and open his shirt. Push his pants down to just above his knees so his thin legs and smooth cock are exposed; our breathing is wavy and thick, we make a sound like music. He can't move his legs but stiffens in my lap, palms of his hands turned up. In a moment he will roll his eyes and come, I'll gently force my coated fingers into his mouth. I'll take off my shirt and rub my slick palms around my breasts until the nipples stand up hard and frothy. I force his mouth to them. I move my hand to the tight secret place between his buttocks. Sometimes they get tears in their eyes.

In the foster homes they used to give me dolls and I played the church game. At first I waited till everyone left the house. Then it didn't matter who was around. I lined up all the dolls on the couch, I sat them one after the other They were ugly, most of them had no clothes or backward arms. They were dolls from the trash, the Salvation Army at Christmas, junk-sale dolls. One of them was in a fire. The plastic hand was missing, melted into a bubbled fountain dribbling in nubs down the arm. We faced the front of the room. I made us sit for hours unmoving, listening to nothing at all and watching someone preach.

Uncle Wumpy gave me a doll. They call him that. Like his pocked face had rabbit ears and soft gray flesh. His face is pitted with tiny scars, his skin is flushed. We won at the carnival: cowboy hats, a rubber six-gun, a stuffed leopard with green diamond eyes for Kitty. We were on our way out between booths and machines, sawdust sticky with old candy and beer, to pick Kitty up at work. We passed the duckshoot. Wumpy was so drunk I had to help him with the gun and we drowned them all. Little yellow ducks with flipped up tail feathers and no eyeballs; they glided by hooked to a string. We hit them, knocked them back with a snap like something breaking. We hit twelve; the whole group popped up, started gliding by again as

476

eyeless as before. So we kept shooting and shooting . . . The barker came out from behind the counter with his fat long-ashed cigar. He held it pinched in two fingers like something dirty he respected. Then he sucked on it and took the gun away. The crowd behind us mumbled. He thrust the doll into my arms. She was nearly three feet tall, pearl earrings, patent leather heels. Long white dress and a veil fastened with a clear plastic bird. I took the bird, I lit it with Wumpy's lighter. Its neck melted down to a curve that that held its flat head molded to its wings. I liked to keep the bird where no one saw it. Finally I buried it in a hole, I took it to a place I knew I'd forget.

How I found Wumpy. I was twelve, I lived with Minnie. She made me work in the luncheonette, swab Formica tables with a rag. Bend over to wipe the aluminum legs, clotted ketchup. By the grill her frozen french fries thawed out limp and fishy. She threw them in sooty fat; they fizzled and jumped and came out shining. Her old face squinched like a rat's, she was forty. Wore thick glasses and a red handkerchief on her head, liked the gospel shows turned up loud. One hand was twisted. She had the arthritis, the rheumatism, the corns, the bunions on her knotted toes as she walked to the shower at home. Hunched in her long robe, she fixed her eyes on the bathroom door. Scuttled clinching herself at the waist and slammed the door.

After school I walked to the restaurant and helped her clear tables till seven. She cursed the miners under her breath. Slapped my butt if I was slow, moved her hard hand, its big twisted knuckles. Grabbed the curve of my ass and squeezed.

Wumpy came in every night for coffee. He cut brush for the State Road Commission. Watched Minnie and me. Kitty started coming in with him. Cellophane Baggie full of white crosses, cheap speed. She'd order a Pepsi, take a few pills, grind a few more to powder on the tabletop. She winked, gave me hair ribbons, said she'd like to take me to the movies. Wumpy told Minnie I needed some clothes, he and Kitty would take me to Pittsburgh to buy me some dresses. They gave her thirty dollars.

In the motel I stood in the bathroom and vomited. Sopors floated in the bowl, clumps of white undissolved powder in a clear mucus. I puked so easy, again and again, I almost laughed. Then they came in naked and took off my clothes. I couldn't stand up, they carried me to the bed. Wumpy got behind her and fucked her, she kept saying words but I couldn't keep my eyes open. She pulled me down She

477

said Honey Honey. In the bottom of something dark I rocked and rocked. His big arms put me there until he lifted me. Lifted me held my hips in the air and I felt her mouth on my legs, I felt bigger and bigger. The ceiling spun around like the lights at Children's Center spun in the dark halls when I woke up at night. Then a tight muscular flash, I curled up and hugged myself.

I stood by the window and fingered the flimsy curtains. I watched them sleeping, I didn't leave. I watched Wumpy's broad back rising and falling.

Wumpy would never do it to me, he gave me pictures to sell. I wanted to give him the money, he laughed at me. He had little stars in the flesh of his hands. He took me to bars. We took a man to some motel, Wumpy said he always had to watch . . . stood by the bed while I choked and gagged a little, salt exploding in my throat—

The dream is here again and again, the dream is still here. Natalie made the dream. I slept with her when I was eight, six months we slept together. She whimpered at night, she wet the bed. Both of us wards of the state, they got money for us. Cold in the bedroom, she wrapping her skinny arms around my chest. Asking can she look at me. But I fall asleep, I won't take off my clothes in bed with her. I fall asleep and the same dream comes.

Natalie is standing in the sand. Behind her the ocean spills over, the waves have thick black edges. Natalie in her shredded slip, knobbly knees, her pale blue eyes all watery. Natalie standing still as a dead thing spreads her legs and holds herself with her hand. Her fingers groping, her white face. She squeezes and pulls so hard she bleeds She calls for help She wants me. Faces all around us, big faces just teeth and lips to hold me down for Natalie. Natalie on top of me Natalie pressing down. Her watery eyes say nothing. She sighs with pleasure and her hot urine boils all around us.

I remember like this: Natalie watches me all the time. They're gone all day, we stay alone with the silent baby. Once there's no food but a box of salt. Bright blue box, the silver spout pops out. The girl with the umbrella dimples and swings her pony tails, flashes her white skin. I can eat it Natalie. I can eat it all. She looks out the window at the snow. I know she's scared. I sit down on the floor at her feet. The box is round like a tom-tom, I tip it up. Salt comes in my mouth so fast, fills me up but I can't quit pouring it . . . I start to strangle but

Natalie won't look, she screams and screams. She kicks at me with her bare blue feet, the box flies across the room throwing fans of salt. When it gets dark, salt gleams on the floor with a strange cool light. Natalie stays in her chair without moving and I get to sleep alone.

I got lavish cards at Children's Center, I think a jokester sent them. To Daughter From Mother At Christmas, scrolls of stand-up gold and velvet poinsettias. I used to think about the janitors, those high school boys with smirky eyes and beer breath, licking the envelopes . . . somehow mailing them from Wichita or Tucson. The agency moved me from home to home. Holidays I stayed at the center, they did paper work to place me again. Every time there was a different pasty-faced boy with ragged nails, dragging a dun-colored mop. The cards came, they were never quite right. When I was ten, For Baby's First Christmas—a fold-out hobbyhorse, a mommy with blond hair and popped eyes. I was seven, the card said Debutante in raised silver script, showed a girl in mink and heels. After I started getting arrested the psychiatrist told them to hold my mail. They said I might go to an asylum.

Baby Girl Approximately 14 Months Abandoned December 1960, Diagnosed As Mute. But when I was three I made sounds like trucks and wasps, I screamed and sang. They think I'm crazy, this is what happens—

I like to lock the bathroom door late at night. Stand in front of the mirrors, hold a candle under my chin. Stare at my shadowed face and see the white shape of a skull. I lay down on the cold tile floor and do it to myself by the stalls. I do it, I lay on my stomach. Hold my breath, riding on the heels of my hands I'm blind; I feel the hush hush of water pipes through the floor. Ride up over a hump into the heat the jangling it holds me. When I open my eyes and roll over, the ceiling is very high it is the color of bone, lamplight through the barred windows. I make myself good I do it. Lay on the cold floor, its tiny geometric blocks. My skin goes white as porcelain, I'm big as the old sinks and toilets, the empty white tubs. White glass, marble, rock, old pipes bubbling air. When those white streaks flash in my vision I run here. I watch her. I know she is me. She runs from stall to stall flushing toilets, she does it again and again. Slushing water louder and louder, then high-pitched wail of the tanks filling. Crash and wail. I crouch on the floor and listen. I don't let anyone in.

479

I think Natalie is dead, she said she would die when she was twelve. But only then. In August under trees we sat heaving rocks. She buried her feet in sand and said she was a stone. I could pinch her till my nails rimmed with red; if she didn't cry out I had to do what she said. She wanted to play house again: I'm a house I'm a giant house. Crawl through my legs Its the door. And she heaved herself onto my back, cupped my chin in her hands. Pulled my head back to see her face above me. She stroked my throat, pointed her pink tongue in my ear and hissed. Shhhh. Hissing. Shhhhhh. Purring, breathing deep in her belly. She pretended her voice was a man. I love you You're mine Eat your food. And I licked her hand all over, up and down between her fingers.

Once the man came after us. We were in the shed behind the house. Natalie liked that room with the tools and jugs, rusted rakes, wood in splintered piles and the squeaking rats. She took off her clothes, draped them on random nails to make an armless girl. A man's big black boots swallowed her ankles. She white and hairless, jingling the metal clasps. Natalie laughing and laughing. We held the blunt-nosed hammers, we threw them hard. Indented circles in the floor, piles of circles pressing down in the old wood like invisible coins. Natalie said we made money. More and more, on the wall, on the floor. Natalie at the windows crashing, glass in glittered piles on her shiny black rubber boots.

He opens the creaky door. What the hell are you doing. I hide by the workbench, back in the webs and spiders. The unbuckling, quick snaky swish of his belt against his pants. He catches her, throws her over the workbench. Natalie gets quiet, the big boots fall off her feet. Her feet almost have faces, dangling, alabaster, by my face; her thin white legs hanging down. Slaps of the belt and drawn-out breathing. You little bitch. He takes a penny and throws it to shadows in the dust. She knows She always knows She finds it. Handfuls of clattering coins. Natalie walks in her goose-pimpled skin, makes a pile of copper pennies by his shoes. He pushes her down on her knees, Natalie is laughing just a little. I see his back, his wide hips, the green work pants. Touch it, he says. Natalie says she can't, her hands are poison.

I'm pure, driven snow. I clean the house, make soup from a can. Wumpy drinks a beer. Squeezes cans till they buckle and fold, throws them in a corner. I want to touch him, squeeze him hard; he closes his eyes to make sounds in his scratchy voice. If I take off my shirt he hits me. Kitty hugs me, My Baby. She wants me to do what she wants. Wumpy does what she says. More and more, she wants what I want. We move around on the checkerboard floor.

Kitty is on probation. We give her lots of coffee and get her walking. Every Saturday the parole officer wants her to talk. Maybe she scores, comes back with smack in an envelope. Darker and darker, snow feathers down to wrap us up. Kitty nods out on the windowsill, curls up like a dormer mouse in her bulky red coat. She likes to lean out almost too far. Wumpy: I watch him through a lopsided hole in the bathroom door, he wants to be alone. Ties off, bulges a vein to hit. Hums and sighs. Pipes make watery yawns and wheezes, they come together in the tunneled walls. It's so quiet I hear the click of the neon sign before it changes and throws a splattered word across the floor. Rooms, it says, blue Rooms. When I see someone move, I'm afraid: If Natalie weren't dead she would find me.

1979

LIARS IN LOVE

Richard Yates

When Warren Mathews came to live in London, with his wife and their two-year-old daughter, he was afraid people might wonder at his apparent idleness. It didn't help much to say he was 'on a Fulbright' because only a few other Americans knew what that meant; most of the English would look blank or smile helpfully until he explained it, and even then they didn't understand.

'Why tell them anything at all?' his wife would say. 'Is it any of their business? What about all the Americans living here on *private* incomes?' And she'd go back to work at the stove, or the sink, or the ironing board, or at the rhythmic and graceful task of brushing her long brown hair.

She was a sharp-featured, pretty girl named Carol, married at an age she often said had been much too young, and it didn't take her long to discover that she hated London. It was big and drab and unwelcoming; you could walk or ride a bus for miles without seeing anything nice, and the coming of winter brought an evil-smelling sulphurous fog that stained everything yellow, that seeped through closed windows and doors to hang in your rooms and afflict your wincing, weeping eyes.

Besides, she and Warren hadn't been getting along well for a long time. They may both have hoped the adventure of moving to England might help set things right, but now it was hard to remember whether they'd hoped that or not. They didn't quarrel much— quarreling had belonged to an earlier phase of their marriage—but they hardly ever enjoyed each other's company, and there were whole days when they seemed unable to do anything at all in their small, tidy basement flat without getting in each other's way. 'Oh, sorry,' they would mutter after each clumsy little bump or jostle. 'Sorry . . . '

The basement flat had been their single stroke of luck: it cost them only a token rent because it belonged to Carol's English aunt, Judith, an elegant widow of seventy who lived alone in the apartment upstairs and who often told them, fondly, how 'charming' they were.

She was very charming too. The only inconvenience, carefully discussed in advance, was that Judith required the use of their bathtub because there wasn't one in her own place. She would knock shyly at their door in the mornings and come in, all smiles and apologies, wrapped in a regal floor-length robe. Later, emerging from her bath in billows of steam with her handsome old face as pink and fresh as a child's, she would make her way slowly into the front room. Sometimes she'd linger there to talk for a while, sometimes not. Once, pausing with her hand on the knob of the hallway door, she said 'Do you know, when we first made this living arrangement, when I agreed to sublet this floor, I remember thinking Oh, but what if I don't *like* them? And now it's all so marvelous, because I do like you both so very much.'

They managed to make pleased and affectionate replies; then, after she'd gone, Warren said 'That was nice, wasn't it.'

'Yes; very nice.' Carol was seated on the rug, struggling to sink their daughter's heel into a red rubber boot. 'Hold still, now, baby,' she said. 'Give Mommy a break, OK?'

The little girl, Cathy, attended a local nursery school called The Peter Pan Club every weekday. The original idea of this had been that it would free Carol to find work in London, to supplement the Fulbright income; then it turned out there was a law forbidding British employers to hire foreigners unless it could be established that the foreigner offered skills unavailable among British applicants, and Carol couldn't hope to establish anything like that. But they'd kept Cathy enrolled in the nursery school anyway because she seemed to like it, and also—though neither parent quite put it into words—because it was good to have her out of the house all day.

And on this particular morning Carol was especially glad of the prospect of the time alone with her husband: she had made up her mind last night that this was the day she would announce her decision to leave him. He must surely have come to agree, by now, that things weren't right. She would take the baby home to New York; once they were settled there she would get a job—secretary or receptionist or something—and make a life of her own. They would keep in touch by mail, of course, and when his Fulbright year was done they could—well, they could both think it over and discuss it then.

All the way to The Peter Pan Club with Cathy chattering and clinging to her hand, and all the way back, walking alone and faster,

Carol tried to rehearse her lines just under her breath; but when the time came it proved to be a much less difficult scene than she'd feared. Warren didn't even seem very surprised—not, at least, in ways that might have challenged or undermined her argument.

'OK,' he kept saying gloomily, without quite looking at her. 'OK...' Then after a while he asked a troubling question. 'What'll we tell Judith?'

'Well, yes, I've thought of that too,' she said, 'and it *would* be awkward to tell her the truth. Do you think we could just say there's an illness in my family, and that's why I have to go home?'

'Well, but your family is *her* family.'

'Oh, that's silly. My father was her brother, but he's dead. She's never even met my mother, and anyway they'd been divorced for God knows how many years. And there aren't any other lines of— you know—lines of communication, or anything. She'll never find out.'

Warren thought about it. 'OK,' he said at last, 'but I don't want to be the one to tell her. You tell her, OK?'

'Sure. Of course I'll tell her, if it's all right with you.'

And that seemed to settle it—what to tell Judith, as well as the larger matter of their separation. But late that night, after Warren had sat staring for a long time into the hot blue-and-pink glow of the clay filaments in their gas fireplace, he said 'Hey, Carol?'

'What?' She flapping and spreading clean sheets on the couch, where she planned to sleep alone.

'What do you suppose he'll be like, this man of yours?'

'What do you mean? *What* man of mine?'

'You know. The guy you're hoping to find in New York. Oh, I know he'll be better than me in about thirteen ways, and he'll certainly be an awful lot richer, but I mean what'll he be like? What'll he *look* like?'

'I'm not listening to any of this.'

'Well, OK, but tell me. What'll he look like?'

'I don't know,' she said impatiently. 'A dollar bill, I guess.'

Less than a week before Carol's ship was scheduled to sail, The Peter Pan Club held a party in honor of Cathy's third birthday. It was a fine occasion of ice cream and cake for 'tea,' as well as the usual fare of bread and meat paste, bread and jam, and cups of a bright fluid that was the English equivalent of Kool-Aid. Warren and Carol stood together on the sidelines, smiling at their happy daughter as if to promise her that one way or another they would always be her parents.

'So you'll be here alone with us for a while, Mr Mathews,' said Marjorie Blaine, who ran the nursery school. She was a trim, chain-smoking woman of forty or so, long divorced, and Warren had noticed a few times that she wasn't bad. 'You must come round to our pub,' she said. 'Do you know Finch's, in the Fulham Road? It's rather a scruffy little pub, actually, but all sorts of nice people go there.'

And he told her he would be sure to drop by.

Then it was the day of the sailing, and Warren accompanied his wife and child as far as the railroad station and the gate to the boat train.

'Isn't Daddy coming?' Cathy asked, looking frightened.

'It's all right, dear,' Carol told her. 'We have to leave Daddy here for now, but you'll see him again very soon.' And they walked quickly away into the enclosing crowd.

One of the presents given to Cathy at the party was a cardboard music box with a jolly yellow duck and a birthday-card message on the front, and with a little crank on one side: when you turned the crank it played a tinny rendition of 'Happy Birthday to You.' And when Warren came back to the flat that night he found it, among several other cheap, forgotten toys, on the floor beneath Cathy's stripped bed. He played it once or twice as he sat drinking whiskey over the strewn books and papers on his desk; then, with a child's sense of pointless experiment, he turned the crank the other way and played it backwards, slowly. And once he'd begun doing that he found he couldn't stop, or didn't want to, because the dim, rude little melody it made suggested all the loss and loneliness in the world.

> Dum *dee* dum da da-da
> Dum *dee* dum da da-da . . .

He was tall and very thin and always aware of how ungainly he must look, even when nobody was there to see—even when the whole of his life had come down to sitting alone and fooling with a cardboard toy, three thousand miles from home. It was March of 1953, and he was twenty-seven years old.

'Oh, you poor man,' Judith said when she came down for her bath in the morning. 'It's so *sad* to find you all alone here. You must miss them terribly.'

'Yeah, well, it'll only be a few months.'

'Well, but that's awful. Isn't there someone who could sort of look after you? Didn't you and Carol meet any young people who might be company for you?'

'Oh, sure, we met a few people,' he said, 'but nobody I'd want to—you know, nobody I'd especially want to have around or anything.'

'Well, then, you ought to get out and make *new* friends.'

Soon after the first of April, as was her custom, Judith went to live in her cottage in Sussex, where she would stay until September. She would make occasional visits back to town for a few days, she explained to Warren, but 'Don't worry; I'll always be sure to ring you up well in advance before I sort of *descend* on you again.'

And so he was truly alone. He went to the pub called Finch's one night with a vague idea of persuading Marjorie Blaine to come home with him and then of having her in his own and Carol's bed. And he found her alone at the crowded bar, but she looked old and fuddled with drink.

'Oh, I say, Mr Mathews,' she said. 'Do come and join me.'

'Warren,' he said.

'What?'

'People call me Warren.'

'Ah. Yes, well, this is England, you see; we're all dreadfully formal here.' And a little later she said 'I've never quite understood what it is you do, Mr Mathews.'

'Well, I'm on a Fulbright,' he said. 'It's an American scholarship program for students overseas. The government pays your way, and you—'

'Yes, well of course America *is* quite good about that sort of thing, isn't it. And I should imagine you must have a very clever mind.' She gave him a flickering glance. 'People who haven't lived often do.' Then she cringed, to pantomime evasion of a blow. 'Sorry,' she said quickly; 'sorry I said that.' But she brightened at once. 'Sarah!' she called. 'Sarah, do come and meet young Mr Mathews, who wants to be called Warren.'

A tall, pretty girl turned from a group of other drinkers to smile at him, extending her hand, but when Marjorie Blaine said 'He's an American,' the girl's smile froze and her hand fell.

'Oh,' she said. 'How nice.' And she turned away again.

It wasn't a good time to be an American in London. Eisenhower had been elected and the Rosenbergs killed; Joseph McCarthy was on the rise, and the war in Korea, with its reluctant contingent of British troops, had come to seem as if it might last forever. Still, Warren Mathews suspected that even in the best of times he would feel alien and homesick here. The very English language, as spoken by natives, bore so little relation to his own that there were far too many opportunites for missed points in every exchange. Nothing was clear.

He went on trying, but even on better nights, in happier pubs than Finch's and in the company of more agreeable strangers, he found only a slight lessening of discomfort—and he found no attractive, unattached girls. The girls, whether blandly or maddeningly pretty, were always fastened to the arms of men whose relentlessly witty talk could leave him smiling in bafflement. And he was dismayed to find how many of these people's innuendoes, winked or shouted, dwelt on the humorous aspects of homosexuality. Was all of England obsessed with that topic? Or did it haunt only this quiet, 'interesting' part of London where Chelsea met South Kensington along the Fulham Road?

Then one night he took a late bus for Piccadilly Circus. 'What do you want to go *there* for?' Carol would have said, and almost half the ride was over before he realized that he didn't have to answer questions like that anymore.

In 1945, as a boy on his first furlough from the Army after the war, he had been astonished at the nightly promenade of prostitutes then called Piccadilly Commandos, and there had been an unforgettable quickening of his blood as he watched them walk and turn, walk and turn again: girls for sale. They seemed to have become a laughingstock among more sophisticated soldiers, some of whom liked to slump against buildings and flip big English pennies onto the sidewalk at their feet as they passed, but Warren had longed for the courage to defy that mockery. He'd wanted to choose a girl and buy her and have her, however she might turn out to be, and he'd despised himself for letting the whole two weeks of his leave run out without doing so.

He knew that a modified version of that spectacle had still been going on as recently as last fall, because he and Carol had seen it on their way to some West End theater. 'Oh, I don't believe this,' Carol said. 'Are they really all whores? This is the saddest thing I've ever seen.'

487

There had lately been newspaper items about the pressing need to 'clean up Piccadilly' before the impending Coronation, but the police must have been lax in their efforts so far, because the girls were very much there.

Most of them were young, with heavily made-up faces; they wore bright clothes in the colors of candy and Easter eggs, and they either walked and turned or stood waiting in the shadows. It took him three straight whiskeys to work up the nerve, and even then he wasn't sure of himself. He knew he looked shabby—he was wearing a gray suit coat with old Army pants, and his shoes were almost ready to be thrown away—but no clothes in the world would have kept him from feeling naked as he made a quick choice among four girls standing along Shaftesbury Avenue and went up to her and said 'Are you free?'

'Am I free?' she said, meeting his eye for less than a second. 'Honey, I've been free all my life.'

The first thing she wanted him to agree on, before they'd walked half a block, was her price—steep, but within his means; then she asked if he would mind taking a short cab ride. And in the cab she explained that she never used the cheap hotels and rooming houses around here, as most of the other girls did, because she had a six-month-old daughter and didn't like to leave her for long.

'I don't blame you,' he said. 'I have a daughter too.'

And he instantly wondered why he'd felt it necessary to tell her that.

'Oh yeah? So where's your wife?'

'Back in New York.'

'You divorced then, or what?'

'Well, separated.'

'Oh yeah? That's too bad.'

They rode in awkward silence for a while until she said 'Listen, it's all right if you want to kiss me or anything, but no big feely-feely in the cab, OK? I really don't go for that.'

And only then, kissing her, did he begin to find out what she was like. She wore her bright yellow hair in ringlets around her face—it was illuminated and darkened again with each passing streetlamp; her eyes were pleasant despite all the mascara; her mouth was nice; and though he tried no big feely-feely his hands were quick to discover she was slender and firm.

It wasn't a short cab ride—it went on until Warren began to

wonder if it might stop only when they met a waiting group of hoodlums who would haul him out of the back seat and beat him up and rob him and take off in the cab with the girl—but it came to an end at last on a silent city block in what he guessed was the northeast of London. She took him into a house that looked rude but peaceful in the moonlight; then she said 'Shh,' and they tiptoed down a creaking linoleum corridor and into her room, where she switched on a light and closed the door behind them.

She checked the baby, who lay small and still and covered-up in the center of a big yellow crib against one wall. Along the facing wall, not six feet away, stood the reasonably fresh-looking double bed in which Warren was expected to take his pleasure.

'I just like to make sure she's breathing,' the girl explained, turning back from the crib; then she watched him count out the right number of pound and ten-shilling notes on the top of her dresser. She turned off the ceiling light but left a small one on at the bedside as she began to undress, and he managed to watch her while nervously taking off his own clothes. Except that her cotton-knit underpants looked pitifully cheap, that her brown pubic hair gave the lie to her blond head, that her legs were short and her knees a little thick, she was all right. And she was certainly young.

'Do you ever enjoy this?' he asked when they were clumsily in bed together.

'Huh? How do you mean?'

'Well, just—you know—after a while it must get so you can't really—' and he stopped there in a paralysis of embarrassment.

'Oh, no,' she assured him. 'Well, I mean it depends on the *guy* a lot, but I'm not—I'm not a block of ice or anything. You'll find out.'

And so, in wholly unexpected grace and nourishment, she became a real girl for him.

Her name was Christine Phillips and she was twenty-two. She came from Glasgow, and she'd been in London for four years. He knew it would be gullible to believe everything she told him when they sat up later that night over cigarettes and a warm quart bottle of beer; still, he wanted to keep an open mind. And if much of what she said was predictable stuff—she explained, for example, that she wouldn't have to be on the street at all if she were willing to take a job as a 'hostess' in a 'club,' but that she'd turned down many such offers because 'all those places are clip joints'—there were other, unguarded remarks that could make his arm tighten around her in tenderness, as when she said she had named her baby Laura 'because I've always thought that's the most beautiful girl's name in the world. Don't you?'

And he began to understand why there was scarcely a trace of Scotch or English accent in her speech: she must have known so many Americans, soldiers and sailors and random civilian strays, that they had invaded and plundered her language.

'So what do you do for a living, Warren?' she asked. 'You get money from home?'

'Well, sort of.' And he explained, once again, about the Fulbright program.

'Yeah?' she said. 'You have to be smart for that?'

'Oh, not necessarily. You don't have to be very smart for anything in America anymore.'

'You kidding me?'

'Not wholly.'

'Huh?'

'I mean I'm only kidding you a little.'

And after a thoughtful pause she said 'Well, I wish *I* could've had more schooling. I wish I was smart enough to write a book, because I'd have a hell of a book to write. Know what I'd call it?' She narrowed her eyes, and her fingers sketched a suggestion of formal lettering in the air. 'I'd call it *This is Piccadilly*. Because I mean people don't really *know* what goes on. Ah, Jesus, I could tell you things that'd make your—well, never mind. Skip it.'

' . . . Hey, Christine?' he said later still, when they were back in bed.

'Uh-huh?'

'Want to tell each other the stories of our lives?'

'OK,' she said with a child's eagerness, and so he had to explain again, shyly, that he was only kidding her a little.

The baby's cry woke them both at six in the morning, but Christine got up and told him he could go back to sleep for a while. When he awoke again he was alone in the room, which smelled faintly of cosmetics and piss. He could hear several women talking and laughing nearby, and he didn't know what he was expected to do but get up and dressed and find his way out of here.

Then Christine came to the door and asked if he would like a cup of tea. 'Whyn't you come on out, if you're ready,' she said as she carefully handed him the hot mug, 'and meet my friends, OK?'

And he followed her into a combination kitchen and living room whose windows overlooked a weed-grown vacant lot. A stubby woman in her thirties stood working at an ironing board with the electrical cord plugged into a ceiling fixture, and another girl of about Christine's age lay back in an easy chair, wearing a knee-length robe and slippers, with her bare, pretty legs ablaze in morning sunlight. A gas fireplace hissed beneath a framed oval mirror, and the good smells of steam and tea were everywhere.

'Warren, this is Grace Arnold,' Christine said of the woman at the ironing board, who looked up to say she was pleased to meet him, 'and this is Amy.' Amy licked her lips and smiled and said 'Hi.'

'You'll probably meet the kids in a minute,' Christine told him. 'Grace has six kids. Grace and *Alfred* do, I mean. Alfred's the man of the house.'

And very gradually, as he sipped and listened, mustering appropriate nods and smiles and inquiries, Warren was able to piece the facts together. Alfred Arnold was an interior housepainter, or rather a 'painter and decorator.' He and his wife, with all those children to raise, made ends meet by renting out rooms to Christine and Amy in full knowledge of how both girls earned their living, and so they had all become a kind of family.

How many polite, nervous men had sat on this sofa in the mornings, watching the whisk and glide of Grace Arnold's iron, helplessly intrigued with the sunny spectacle of Amy's legs, hearing the talk of these three women and wondering how soon it would be all right to leave? But Warren Mathews had nothing to go home to, so he began to hope this pleasant social occasion might last.

'You've a nice name, Warren,' Amy told him, crossing her legs. 'I've always liked that name.'

'Warren?' Christine said. 'Can you stay and have something to eat with us?'

Soon there was a fried egg on buttered toast for each of them, served with more tea around a clean kitchen table, and they all ate as daintily as if they were in a public place. Christine sat beside him, and once during the meal she gave his free hand a shy little squeeze.

'If you don't have to rush off,' she said, while Grace was stacking the dishes, 'we can get a beer. The pub'll be open in half an hour.'

'Good,' he said. 'Fine.' Because the last thing he wanted to do was rush off, even when all six children came clamoring in from their morning's play down the street, each of them in turn wanting to sit on his lap and poke fun at him and run jam-stained fingers through his hair. They were a shrill, rowdy crowd, and they all glowed with health. The oldest was a bright girl named Jane who looked oddly like a Negro—light-skinned, but with African features and hair—and who giggled as she backed away from him and said 'Are you Christine's fella?'

'I sure am,' he told her.

And he did feel very much like Christine's fella when he took her out alone to the pub around the corner. He liked the way she walked—she didn't look anything at all like a prostitute in her fresh tan raincoat with the collar turned up around her cheeks—and he liked her sitting close beside him on a leather bench against the wall of an old brown room where everything, even the mote-filled shafts of sunlight, seemed to be steeped in beer.

'Look, Warren,' she said after a while, turning her bright glass on the table. 'Do you want to stay over another night?'

'Well, no, I really—the thing is I can't afford it.'

'Oh, I didn't mean that,' she said, and squeezed his hand again. 'I didn't mean for money. I meant—just stay. Because I want you to.'

Nobody had to tell him what a triumph of masculinity it was to have a young whore offer herself to you free of charge. He didn't even need *From Here to Eternity* to tell him that, though he would always remember how that novel came quickly to mind as he drew her face up closer to his own. She had made him feel profoundly strong. 'Oh, that's nice,' he said huskily, and he kissed her. Then, just before kissing her again, he said 'Oh, that's awfully nice, Christine.'

And they both made frequent use of the word 'nice' all afternoon. Christine seemed unable to keep away from him except for brief intervals when she had to attend to the baby; once, when Warren was alone in the living room, she came dancing slowly and dreamily across the floor, as if to the sound of violins, and fell into his arms like a girl in the movies. Another time, curled fast against him on the sofa, she softly crooned a popular song called 'Unforgettable' to him, with a significant dipping of her eyelashes over the title word whenever the lyrics brought it around.

'Oh, you're nice, Warren,' she kept saying. 'You know that? You're really nice.'

And he would tell her, again and again, how nice she was too.

When Alfred Arnold came home from work—a compact and tired

and bashfully agreeable-looking man—his wife and young Amy were quick to busy themselves in the ritual of making him welcome: taking his coat, readying his chair, bringing his glass of gin. But Christine held back, clinging to Warren's arm, until the time came to take him up for a formal introduction to the man of the house.

'Pleased to meet you, Warren,' Alfred Arnold said. 'Make yourself at home.'

There was corned beef with boiled potatoes for supper, which everyone said was very good, and in the afterglow Alfred fell to reminiscing in a laconic way about his time as prisoner of war in Burma. 'Four years,' he said, displaying the fingers of one hand with only the thumb held down. 'Four years.'

And Warren said it must have been terrible.

'Alfred?' Grace said. 'Show Warren your citation.'

'Oh, no, love; nobody wants to bother with that.'

'Show him,' she insisted.

And Alfred gave in. A thick black wallet was shyly withdrawn from his hip pocket; then from one of its depths came a stained, much-folded piece of paper. It was almost falling apart at the creases, but the typewritten message was clear: it conveyed the British Army's recognition that Private A.J. Arnold, while a prisoner of war of the Japanese in Burma, had been commended by his captors as a good and steady worker on the construction of a railroad bridge in 1944.

'Well,' Warren said. 'That's fine.'

'Ah, you know the women,' Alfred confided, tucking the paper back where it came from. 'The women always want you to show this stuff around. I'd rather forget the whole bloody business.'

Christine and Warren managed to make an early escape, under Grace Arnold's winking smile, and as soon as the bedroom door was shut they were clasped and writhing and breathing heavily, eager and solemn in lust. The shedding of their clothes took no time at all but seemed a terrible hindrance and delay; then they were deep in bed and reveling in each other, and then they were joined again.

'Oh, Warren,' she said. 'Oh, God. Oh, Warren. Oh, I love you.'

And he heard himself saying more than once, more times than he cared to believe or remember, that he loved her too.

Sometime after midnight, as they lay quiet, he wondered how those words could have spilled so easily and often from his mouth. And at about the same time, when Christine began talking again, he became aware that she'd had a lot to drink. A quarter-full bottle of gin stood on the floor beside the bed, with two cloudy, fingerprinted glasses to prove they had both made ample use of it, but she seemed to be well ahead of him now. Pouring herself still another one, she sat back in comfort against the pillows and the wall and talked in a way that suggested she was carefully composing each sentence for dramatic effect, like a little girl pretending to be an actress.

'You know something, Warren? Everything I ever wanted was taken away from me. All my life. When I was eleven I wanted a bicycle more than anything in the world, and my father finally bought me one. Oh, it was only second-hand and cheap, but I loved it. And then that same summer he got mad and wanted to punish me for something—I can't even remember what—and he took it away. I never saw it again.'

'Yeah, well, that must've felt bad,' Warren said, but then he tried to steer the talk along less sentimental lines. 'What kind of work does your father do?'

'Oh, he's a pen-pusher. For the gas works. We don't get along at all, and I don't get along with my mother either. I never go home. No, but it's true what I said: everything I ever wanted was—you know—taken away from me.' She paused there, as if to bring her stage voice back under control, and when she began to speak again, with greater confidence, it was in the low, hushed tones appropriate for an intimate audience of one.

'Warren? Would you like to hear about Adrian? Laura's father? Because I'd really like to tell you, if you're interested.'

'Sure.'

'Well, Adrian's an American Army officer. A young major. Or maybe he's a lieutenant colonel by now, wherever he is. I don't even know where he is, and the funny part is I don't care, I really don't care at all anymore. But Adrian and I had a wonderful time until I told him I was pregnant; then he froze up. He just froze up. Oh, I suppose I didn't really think he'd ask me to marry him or anything— he had this rich society girl waiting for him back in the States; I knew that. But he got very cold and he told me to get an abortion, and I said no. I said "I'm going to have this baby, Adrian." And he said "All right." He said "All right, but you're on your own, Christine. You'll have to raise this child any way you can." That was when I decided to go and see his commanding officer.'

'His commanding officer?'

'Well, *somebody* had to help,' she said. '*Somebody* had to make him see his responsibility. And God, I'll never forget that day. The regimental commander was this very dignified man named Colonel Masters, and he just sat there behind his desk and looked at me and listened, and he nodded a few times. Adrian was there with me, not saying a word; there were just the three of us in the office. And in the end Colonel Masters said "Well, Miss Phillips, as far as I can see it comes down to this. You made a mistake. You made a mistake, and you'll have to live it."'

'Yeah,' Warren said uneasily. 'Yeah, well, that must've been—'

But he didn't have to finish that sentence, or to say anything else that might let her know he hadn't believed a word of the story, because she was crying. She had drawn up her knees and laid the side of her rumpled head on them as the sobs began; then she set her empty glass carefully on the floor, slid back into bed, and turned away from him, crying and crying.

'Hey, come on,' he said. 'Come on, baby, don't cry.' And there was nothing to do but turn her around and take her in his arms until she was still.

After a long time she said 'Is there any more gin?'

'Some.'

'Well, listen, let's finish it, OK? Grace won't mind, or if she wants me to pay her for it I'll *pay* her for it.'

In the morning, with her face so swollen from emotion and sleep that she tried to hide it with her fingers, she said 'Jesus. I guess I got pretty drunk last night.'

'That's OK; we both drank a lot.'

'Well, I'm sorry,' she said in the impatient, almost defiant way of people accustomed to making frequent apologies. 'I'm sorry.' She had taken care of the baby and was walking unsteadily around the little room in a drab green bathrobe. 'Anyway, listen. Will you come back, Warren?'

'Sure. I'll call you, OK?'

'No, there's no telephone here. But will you come back soon?' She followed him out to the front door, where he turned to see the limpid appeal in her eyes. 'If you come in the daytime,' she said, 'I'll always be home.'

For a few days, idling at his desk or wandering the streets and the park in the first real spring weather of the year, Warren found it impossible to keep his mind on anything but Christine. Nothing like this could ever have been expected to happen in his life: a young Scotch prostitute in love with him. With a high, fine confidence that wasn't at all characteristic of him, he had begun to see himself as a rare and privileged adventurer of the heart. Memories of Christine in his arms whispering 'Oh, I love you' made him smile like a fool in the sunshine, and at other moments he found a different, subtler pleasure in considering all the pathetic things about her—the humorless ignorance, the cheap, drooping underwear, the drunken crying. Even her story of 'Adrian' (a name almost certainly lifted from a women's magazine) was easy to forgive—or would be, once he'd found some wise and gentle way of letting her know he knew it wasn't true. He might eventually have to find a way of telling her he hadn't really meant to say he loved her, too, but all that could wait. There was no hurry, and the season was spring.

'Know what I like most about you, Warren?' she asked very late in their third or fourth night together. 'Know what I really love about you? It's that I feel I can trust you. All my life, that's all I ever wanted: somebody to trust. And you see I keep making mistakes and making mistakes because I trust people who turn out to be—'

'Shh, shh,' he said, 'it's OK, baby. Let's just sleep now.'

'Well, but wait a second. Listen a minute, OK? Because I really do want to tell you something, Warren. I knew this boy Jack. He kept saying he wanted to marry me and everything, but this was the trouble: Jack's a gambler. He'll always be a gambler. And I suppose you can guess what that meant.'

'What'd it mean?'

'It meant money, that's what it meant. Staking him, covering his losses, helping him get through the month until payday—ah, Christ, it makes me sick just to think of all that now. For almost a year. And do you know how much of it I ever got back? Well, you won't believe this, but I'll tell you. Or no, wait—I'll show you. Wait a second.'

She got up and stumbled and switched on the ceiling light in an explosion of brilliance that startled the baby, who whimpered in her sleep. 'It's OK, Laura,' Christine said softly as she rummaged in the top drawer of her dresser; then she found what she was looking for and brought it back to the bed. 'Here,' she said. 'Look. Read this.'

It was a single sheet of cheap ruled paper torn from a tablet of the kind meant for school children, and it bore no date.

Dear Miss Phillips:
Enclosed is the sum of two pounds ten shillings. This is all I can

496

afford now and there will be no more as I am being shipped back to the US next week for discharge and separation from the service.

My Commanding Officer says you telephoned him four times last month and three times this month and this must stop as he is a busy man and can not be bothered with calls of this kind. Do not call him again, or the 1st Sgt either, or anyone else in this organization.

Pfc. John F. Curtis

'Isn't that the damnedest thing?' Christine said. 'I mean really, Warren, isn't that the God damnedest thing?'

'Sure is.' And he read it over again. It was the sentence beginning 'My Commanding Officer' that seemed to give it all away, demolishing 'Adrian' at a glance and leaving little doubt in Warren's mind that John F. Curtis had fathered her child.

'Could you turn the light off now, Christine?' he said, handing the letter back to her.

'Sure, honey. I just wanted you to see that.' And she had undoubtedly wanted to see if he'd be dumb enough to swallow the story too.

When the room was dark again and she lay curled against his back, he silently prepared a quiet, reasonable speech. He would say Baby, don't get mad, but listen. You mustn't try to put these stories over on me anymore. I didn't believe the one about Adrian and I don't believe Jack the Gambler either, so how about cutting this stuff out? Wouldn't it be better if we could sort of try to tell each other the truth?

What stopped his mouth, on thinking it over, was that to say all that would humiliate her into wrath. She'd be out of bed and shouting in an instant, reviling him in the ugliest language of her trade until long after the baby woke up crying, and then there would be nothing but wreckage.

There might still be an appropriate moment for inquiring into her truthfulness—there would have to be, and soon—but whether it made him feel cowardly or not he had to acknowledge, as he lay facing the wall with her sweet arm around his ribs, that this wasn't the time.

A few nights later, at home, he answered the phone and was startled to hear her voice: 'Hi, honey.'

'Christine? Well, hi, but how'd you—how'd you get this number?'

'You gave it to me. Don't you remember? You wrote it down.'

'Oh, yeah, sure,' he said, smiling foolishly into the mouthpiece, but this was alarming. The phone here in the basement flat was only an extension of Judith's phone upstairs. They rang simultaneously, and when Judith was home she always picked up her receiver on the first or second ring.

'So listen,' Christine was saying. 'Can you come over Thursday instead of Friday? Because it's Jane's birthday and we're having a party. She'll be nine . . . '

After he'd hung up he sat hunched for a long time in the attitude of a man turning over grave and secret questions in his mind. How could he have been dumb enough to give her Judith's number? And soon he remembered something else, a second dumb thing that brought him to his feet for an intense, dramatic pacing of the floor: she knew his address too. Once in the pub he had run out of cash and been unable to pay for all the beer, so he'd given Christine a check to cover it.

'Most customers find it's a convenience to have their street addresses printed beneath their names on each check,' an assistant bank manager had explained when Warren and Carl opened their checking account last year. 'Shall I order them that way for you?'

'Sure, I guess so,' Carol had said. 'Why not?'

He was almost all the way to the Arnolds' house on Thursday before he realized he'd forgotten to buy a present for Jane. But he found a sweetshop and kept telling the girl at the counter to scoop more and more assorted hard candies into a paper bag until he had a heavy bundle of the stuff that he could only hope might be of passing interest to a nine-year-old.

And whether it was or not, Jane's party turned out to be a profound success. There were children all over that bright, ramshackle apartment, and when the time came for them to be seated at the table—three tables shoved together—Warren stood back smiling and watching with his arm around Christine, thinking of that other party at The Peter Pan Club. Alfred came home from work with a giant stuffed panda bear that he pressed into Jane's arms, laughing and then crouching to receive her long and heartfelt hug. But soon Jane was obliged to bring her delirium under control because the cake was set before her. She frowned, closed her eyes, made a wish, and blew out all nine candles in a single heroic breath as the room erupted into full-throated cheers.

There was plenty to drink for the grownups after that, even before the last of the party guests had gone home and all the Arnold children were in bed. Christine left the room to put her baby down for the night, carrying a drink along with her. Grace had begun fixing supper with apparent reluctance, and when Alfred excused himself to have a bit of a rest she turned the gas burners down very low and abandoned the stove to join him.

That left Warren alone with Amy, who stood meticulously applying her makeup at the oval mirror above the mantelpiece. She was really a lot better looking than Christine, he decided as he sat on the sofa with a drink in his hand, watching her. She was tall and long-legged and flawlessly graceful, with a firm slender ass that made you ache to clasp it and with plump, pointed little breasts. Her dark hair hung to her shoulderblades, and this evening she had chosen to wear a narrow black skirt with a peach-colored blouse. She was a proud and lovely girl, and he didn't want to think about the total stranger who would have her for money at the end of the night.

Amy had finished with her eyes and begun to work on her mouth, drawing the lipstick slowly along the yielding shape of each full lip until it glistened like marzipan, then pouting so that one lip could caress and rub the other, then parting them to inspect her perfect young teeth for possible traces of red. When she was finished, when she'd put all her implements back into a little plastic case and snapped it shut, she continued to stand at the mirror for what seemed at least half a minute, doing nothing, and that was when Warren realized she knew he'd been staring at her in all this privacy and silence, all this time. At last she turned around in such a quick, high-shouldered way, and with such a look of bravery conquering fear, that it was as if he might be halfway across the floor to make a grab for her.

'You look very nice, Amy,' he said from the sofa.

Her shoulders slackened then and she let out a breath of relief, but she didn't smile. 'Jesus,' she said. 'You scared the shit out of me.'

When she'd put on her coat and left the house, Christine came back into the room with the languorous, self-indulgent air of a girl who has found a good reason for staying home from work.

'Move over,' she said, and sat close beside him. 'How've you been?'

'Oh, OK. You?'

'OK.' She hesitated then, as if constrained by the difficulty of making small talk. 'Seen any good movies?'

'No.'

She took his hand and held it in both of her own. 'You miss me?'
'I sure did.'

'The hell you did.' And she flung down his hand as if it were
something vile. 'I went around to your place the other night, to
surprise you, and I saw you going in there with a girl.'

'No, you didn't,' he told her. 'Come on, Christine, you know you
didn't do that at all. Why do you always want to tell me these—'

Her eyes narrowed in menace and her lips went flat. 'You calling
me a liar?'

'Oh, Jesus,' he said, 'don't be like that. Why do you want to be like
that? Let's just drop it, OK?'

She seemed to be thinking it over. 'OK,' she said. 'Look: it was dark
and I was across the street; I could've had the wrong house; it
could've been somebody else I saw with the girl, so OK, we'll drop it.
But I want to tell you something: don't ever call me a liar, Warren.
I'm warning you. Because I swear to God'—and she pointed
emphatically toward her bedroom—'I swear on that baby's life I'm
not a liar.'

'Ah, look at the lovebirds,' Grace Arnold called, appearing in the
doorway with her arm around her husband. 'Well, you're not making
me jealous. Me and Alfred are lovebirds too, aren't we, love? Married
all these years and still lovebirds.'

There was supper then, much of it consisting of partly burned
beans, and Grace held forth at length on the unforgettable night when
she and Alfred had first met. There'd been a party; Alfred had come
alone, all shy and strange and still wearing his army uniform, and
from the moment Grace spotted him across the room she'd thought:
Oh, him. Oh, yes, he's the one. They had danced for a while to some
phonograph records, though Alfred wasn't much of a dancer; then
they'd gone outside and sat together on a low stone wall and talked.
Just talked.

'What'd we talk about, Alfred?' she asked, as if trying in vain to
remember.

'Oh, I don't know, love,' he said, pink with pleasure and
embarrassment as he pushed his fork around in his beans. 'Don't
suppose it could've been much.'

And Grace turned back to address her other listeners in a lowered,
intimate voice. 'We talked about—well, about everything and
nothing,' she said. 'You know how that can be? It was like we both
knew—you know?—like we both knew we were made for each

other.' This last statement seemed a little sentimental even for Grace's taste, and she broke off with a laugh. 'Oh, and the funny part,' she said, laughing, 'the funny part was, these friends of mine left the party a little after we did because they were going to the pictures? So they went up to the pictures and stayed for the whole show, then they went round to the pub afterwards and stayed there till closing time, and it was practically morning when they came back down that same road and found me and Alfred still sitting on the wall, still talking. Ah, God, they still tease me about that, my friends do when I see them, even now. They say "Whatever were you two *talking* about, Grace?" And I just laugh. I say "Oh, never mind. We were talking, that's all."'

A respectful hush fell around the table.

'Isn't that wonderful?' Christine asked quietly. 'Isn't it wonderful when two people can just—find each other that way?'

And Warren said it certainly was.

Later that night, when he and Christine sat naked on the edge of her bed to drink, she said 'Well, I'll tell you one thing, anyway: I wouldn't half mind having Grace's life. The part of it that came *after* she met Alfred, I mean; not the part before.' And after a pause she said 'I don't suppose you'd ever guess it, from the way she acts now—I don't suppose you'd ever guess she was a Piccadilly girl herself.'

'Was she?'

'Ha, "was she." You better bet she was. For years, back during the war. Got into it because she didn't know any better, like all the rest of us; then she had Jane and didn't know how to get out.' And Christine gave him a little glancing smile with a wink in it. 'Nobody knows where Jane came from.'

'Oh.' And if Jane was nine years old today it meant she had been conceived and born in a time when tens of thousands of American Negro soldiers were quartered in England and said to be having their way with English girls, provoking white troops into fights and riots that ended only when everything went under in the vast upheaval of the Normandy Invasion. Alfred Arnold would still have been a prisoner in Burma then, with well over a year to wait for his release.

'Oh, she's never tried to deny it,' Christine said. 'She's never lied about it; give her credit for that. Alfred knew what he was getting, right from the start. She probably even told him that first night they met, because she would've known she couldn't hide it—or maybe he

501

knew already because maybe that whole *party* was Piccadilly girls; I don't know. But I know he knew. He took her off the street and he married her, and he adopted her child. You don't find very many men like that. And I mean Grace is my best friend and she's done a lot for me, but sometimes she acts like she doesn't even know how lucky she is. Sometimes—oh, not tonight; she was showing off for you tonight—but sometimes she treats Alfred like dirt. Can you imagine that? A man like Alfred? That really pisses me off.'

She reached down to fill their glasses, and by the time she'd settled back to sip he knew what his own next move would have to be.

'Well, so I guess you're sort of looking for a husband too, aren't you, baby,' he said. 'That's certainly understandable, and I'd like you to know I wish I could—you know—ask you to marry me, but the fact is I can't. Just can't.'

'Sure,' she said quietly, looking down at an unlighted cigarette in her fingers. 'That's OK; forget it.'

And he was pleased with the way this last exchange had turned out—even with the whopping lie of the 'wish' in his part of it. His bewildering, hazardous advance into this strange girl's life was over, and now he could prepare for an orderly withdrawal. 'I know you'll find the right guy, Christine,' he told her, warm in the kindness of his own voice, 'and it's bound to happen soon because you're such a nice girl. In the meantime, I want you to know that I'll always—'

'Look, I said *forget* it, OK? Jesus Christ, do you think *I* care? You think I give a shit about you? Listen.' She was on her feet, naked and strong in the dim light, wagging one stiff forefinger an inch away from his wincing face. 'Listen, skinny. I can get anybody I want, any time, and you better get that straight. You're only here because I felt sorry for you, and you better get that straight too.'

'Felt sorry for me?'

'Well, *sure*, with all that sorrowful shit about your wife taking off, and your little girl. I felt sorry for you and I thought Well, why not? That's my trouble; I never learn. Sooner or later I always think Why not? and then I'm shit outa luck. Listen: Do you have any idea how much money I could've made all this time? Huh? No, you never even thought about that part of it, didja. Oh, no, you were all hearts and flowers and sweet-talk and bullshit, weren'tcha. Well, you know what I think you are? I think you're a ponce.'

'What's a "ponce"?'

'I don't know what it is where you come from,' she said, 'but in

502

this country it's a man who lives off the earnings of a—ah, never mind. The hell with it. Fuck it. I'm tired. Move over, OK? Because I mean if all we're gonna do is sleep, let's sleep.'

But instead of moving over he got up in the silent, trembling dignity of an insulted man and began to put his clothes on. She seemed either not to notice or not to care what he was doing as she went heavily back to bed, but before very long, when he was buttoning his shirt, he could tell she was watching him and ready to apologize.

'Warren?' she said in a small, fearful voice. 'Don't go. I'm sorry I called you that, and I'll never say it again. Just please come back and stay with me, OK?'

That was enough to make his fingers pause in the fastening of shirt buttons; then, soon, it was enough to make him begin unfastening them again. Leaving now, with nothing settled, might easily be worse than staying. Besides, there was an undeniable advantage in being seen as a man big enough to be capable of forgiveness.

' . . . Oh,' she said when he was back in bed. 'Oh, this is better. This is better. Oh, come closer and let me there. There. Oh. Oh, I don't think anybody in the whole world ever wants to be alone at night. Do you?'

It was a fragile, pleasant truce that lasted well into the morning, when he made an agreeable if nervous departure.

But all the way home on the Underground he regretted having made no final statement to her. He went over the opening of several final statements in his mind as he rode—'Look, Christine, I don't think this is working out at all . . . ' or 'Baby, if you're going to think of me as a ponce, and stuff like that, I think it's about time we . . .'— until he realized, from the uneasy, quickly averted glances of other passengers on the train, that he was moving his lips and making small, reasonable gestures with his hands.

'Warren?' said Judith's old, melodious voice on the telephone that afternoon, calling from Sussex. 'I thought I might run up to town on Tuesday and stay for a week or two. Would that be a terrible nuisance for you?'

He told her not to be silly and said he'd be looking forward to it, but he'd scarcely hung up the phone before it rang again and Christine said 'Hi, honey.'

'Oh, hi. How are you?'

'Well, OK, except I wasn't very nice to you last night. I get that way sometimes. I know it's awful, but I do. Can I make it up to you, though? Can you come over Tuesday night?'

'Well, I don't know, Christine, I've been thinking. Maybe we'd better sort of—'

Her voice changed. 'You coming or not?'

He let her wait through a second or two of silence before he agreed to go—and he agreed then only because he knew it would be better to make his final statement in person than on the phone.

He wouldn't spend the night. He would stay only as long as it took to make himself clear to her; if the house were crowded he would take her around to the pub, where they could talk privately. And he resolved not to rehearse any more speeches: he would find the right words when the time came, and the right tone.

But apart from its having to be final, the most important thing about his statement—the dizzyingly difficult thing—was that it would have to be nice. If it wasn't, if it left her resentful, there might be any amount of trouble later on the phone—a risk that could no longer be taken, with Judith home—and there might be worse events even than that. He could picture Christine and himself as Judith's guests at afternoon tea in her sitting room ('Do bring your young friend along, Warren.') just as Carol and he had often been in the past. He could see Christine waiting for a conversational lull, then setting down her cup and saucer firmly, for emphasis, and saying 'Listen, lady. I got news for you. You know what this big sweet nephew of yours is? Huh? Well, I'll tell you. He's a ponce.'

He had planned to arrive well after supper, but they must have gotten a late start tonight because they were all still at the table, and Grace Arnold offered him a plate.

'No thanks,' he said, but he sat down beside Christine anyway, with a drink, because it would have seemed rude not to.

'Christine?' he said. 'When you've finished eating, want to come around to the pub with me for a while?'

'What for?' she asked with her mouth full.

'Because I want to talk to you.'

'We can talk here.'

'No we can't.'

'So what's the big deal? We'll talk later, then.'

And Warren felt his plans begin to slide away like sand.

Amy seemed to be in a wonderful mood that night. She laughed generously at everything Alfred and Warren said; she sang a chorus of 'Unforgettable' with at least as much feeling as Christine had brought to it; she backed away into the middle of the room, stepped out of her shoes, and favored her audience with a neat, slow little hip-switching dance to the theme music of the movie *Moulin Rouge*.

'How come you're not going out tonight, Amy?' Christine inquired.

'Oh, I don't know; I don't feel like it. Sometimes all I want to do is stay home and be quiet.'

'Alfred?' Grace called. 'See if there's any lime juice, love, because if there's lime juice we can have gin and lime.'

They found dance music on the radio and Grace melted into Alfred's arms for an old-fashioned waltz. 'I love a waltz,' she explained. 'I've always loved a waltz'—but it stopped abruptly when they waltzed into the ironing board and knocked it over, which struck everyone as the funniest thing they had ever seen.

Christine wanted to prove she could jitterbug, perhaps in rivalry with Amy's dance, but Warren made a clumsy partner for her: he hopped and shuffled and worked up a sweat and didn't really know how to send her whirling out to their arms' length and bring her whirling back, the way it was supposed to be done, so their performance too dissolved into awkwardness and laughter.

' . . . Oh, isn't it nice that we're all such good friends,' Grace Arnold said, earnestly breaking the seal on a new bottle of gin. 'We can just be here and enjoy ourselves tonight and nothing else matters in the world as long as we're together, right?'

Right. Sometime later Alfred and Warren sat together on the sofa discussing points of difference and similarity in the British and American armies, a couple of old soldiers at peace; then Alfred excused himself to get another drink, and Amy sank smiling into the place he had left, lightly touching Warren's thigh with her fingertips to establish the opening of a new conversation.

'Amy,' Christine said from across the room. 'Take your hands off Warren or I'll kill you.'

And everything went bad after that. Amy sprang to her feet in heated denial of any wrongdoing, Christine's rebuttal was loud and foul, Grace and Alfred stood with the weak smiles of spectators at a street accident, and Warren wanted to evaporate.

'You're *always* doing that,' Christine shouted. 'Ever since I got you *in*to this house you've been waving it around and rubbing it up

505

against every man I bring home. You're cheap; you're a tart; you're a little slut.'

'And you're a *whore*,' Amy cried, just before bursting into tears. She lurched for the door then, but didn't make it: she was obliged to turn back with her fist in her mouth, her eyes bright with terror, in order to witness what Christine was saying to Grace Arnold.

'All right, Grace, listen.' Christine's voice was high and perilously steady. 'You're my best friend and you always will be, but you've got to make a choice. It's her or me. I mean it. Because I swear on that baby's life'—and one arm made a theatrical sweep in the direction of her bedroom—'I swear on that baby's life I'm not staying in this house another day if she stays too.'

'Oh,' Amy said, advancing on her. 'Oh, that was a rotten thing to do. Oh, you're a filthy—'

And the two girls were suddenly locked in combat, wrestling and punching, or trying to punch, tearing clothes and pulling hair. Grace tried to separate them, a shrill, quivering referee, but she only got pummeled and pushed around herself until she fell down, and that was when Alfred Arnold moved in.

'Shit,' he said. 'Break it up. Break it *up*.' He managed to pull Christine away from Amy's throat and shove her roughly aside, then he prevented Amy from any further action by throwing her down full-length on the sofa, where she covered her face and wept.

'Cows,' Alfred said as he stumbled and righted himself. 'Fucking cows.'

'Put some coffee on,' Grace suggested from the chair she had crawled to, and Alfred blundered to the stove and set a pan of water on the gas. He fumbled around for a bottle of instant-coffee syrup and put a spoonful of the stuff into each of five clean cups, breathing hard; then he began stalking the room with the wide and glittering eyes of a man who never thought his life would turn out like this.

'Fucking cows,' he said again. 'Cows.' And with all his strength he smashed his right fist against the wall.

'Well, I knew Alfred was upset,' Christine said later, when she and Warren were in bed, 'but I didn't think he'd go and hurt his hand that way. That was awful.'

'Can I come in?' Grace asked with a timid knock on the door, and she came in looking happy and disheveled. She was still wearing her dress but had evidently removed her garter belt, for her black nylon stockings had fallen into wrinkles around her ankles and her shoes. Her naked legs were pale and faintly hairy.

'How's Alfred's hand?' Christine inquired.

'Well, he's got it soaking in hot water,' Grace said, 'but he keeps taking it out and trying to put it in his mouth. He'll be all right. Anyway, listen, though, Christine. You're right about Amy. She's no good. I've known that ever since you brought her here. I didn't want to say anything because she was your friend, but that's the God's truth. And I just want you to know you're my favorite, Christine. You'll always be my favorite.'

Lying and listening, with the bedclothes pulled up to his chin, Warren longed for the silence of home.

' . . . Remember the time she lost all the dry-cleaning tickets and lied about it?'

'Oh, and remember when you and me were getting ready to go to the pictures that day?' Grace said. 'And there wasn't time to fix sandwiches so we had egg on toast instead because it was quicker? And she kept hanging around saying "What're you making *eggs* for?" She was so mad and jealous because we hadn't asked her to come along to the pictures she was acting like a little kid.'

'Well, she *is* a little kid. She doesn't have any—doesn't have any maturity at all.'

'Right. You're absolutely right about that, Christine. And I'll tell you what I've decided to do: I'll tell her first thing in the morning. I'll simply say "I'm sorry, Amy, but you're no longer welcome in my home . . ."'

Warren got out of the house before dawn and tried to sleep in his own place, though he couldn't hope for more than an hour or two because he had to be up and dressed and smiling when Judith came down for her bath.

'I must say you're certainly *looking* well, Warren,' Judith told him. 'You look as calm and fit as a man thoroughly in charge of his life. There isn't a *trace* of that haggard quality that used to worry me about you sometimes.'

'Oh?' he said. 'Well, thanks Judith. You're looking very well too, but then of course you always do.'

He knew the phone was going to ring, and he could only hope it would be silent until noon. That was when Judith went out to lunch—or, on days when she'd decided to economize, it was the time she went out to do her modest grocery shopping. She would carry a string bag around the neighborhood to be filled by deferential, admiring shopkeepers—Englishmen and women schooled for generations to know a lady when they saw one.

At noon, from the front windows, he watched her stately old figure descend the steps and move slowly down the street. And it seemed no more than a minute after that when the phone burst into ringing, his nerves making it sound much louder than it was.

'You sure took off in a hurry,' Christine said.

'Yeah. Well, I couldn't sleep. How'd it go with Amy this morning?'

'Oh, that's OK now. That's all over. The three of us had a long talk, and in the end I talked Grace into letting her stay.'

'Well, good. Still, I'm surprised she'd *want* to stay.'

'Are you kidding? Amy? You think she has anywhere else to go? Jesus, if you think *Amy* has anywhere else to go you're outa your mind. And I mean you know me, Warren: I get all upset sometimes, but I couldn't ever just turn somebody out on the street.' She paused, and he could hear the faint rhythmic click of her chewing gum. He hadn't known, until then, that she ever chewed gum.

For a moment it occurred to him that having her in this placid, rational, gum-chewing frame of mind might be his best opportunity yet for breaking off with her, over the telephone or not, but he hadn't quite organized his opening remarks before she was talking again.

'So listen, honey, I don't think I'll be able to see you for a while. Tonight's out, and tomorrow night too, and all through the weekend.' And she gave a quietly harsh little laugh. 'I've got to make *some* money, don't I?'

'Well, *sure*,' he said. '*Sure* you do; I know that.' And not until those agreeable words were out of his mouth did he realize they were exactly the kind of thing a ponce might say.

'I might be able to come around to your place some afternoon, though,' Christine suggested.

'No, don't do that,' he said quickly. 'I'm—I'm almost always out at the library in the afternoons.'

They settled on an evening in the following week, at her place, at five; but something in her voice made him suspect even then that she wouldn't be there—that intentionally failing to keep this appointment would be her inarticulate way of getting rid of him, or at least of making a start at it: nobody's ponce could expect to last forever. And so, when the day and the hour came, he wasn't surprised to find her gone.

'Christine's not here, Warren,' Grace Arnold explained, backing politely away from the door to let him come in. 'She said to tell you she'd call. She had to go up to Scotland for a few days.'

'Oh? Is there—trouble at home, then?'

'How do you mean "trouble"?'

'Well, I just mean is there an—' And Warren found himself mouthing the same lame alibi that Carol and he had once agreed would be good enough for Judith, in what now seemed another life. 'Is there an illness in her family, or something like that?'

'That's right, yes.' Grace was visibly grateful for his help. 'There's an illness in her family.'

And he said he was sorry to hear it.

'Can I get you something, Warren?'

'No thanks. I'll see you, Grace.' Turning to leave, he found that the words for a cool, final exit line were already forming themselves in his mind. But he hadn't yet reached the door when Alfred came in from work, looking embarrassed, with his forearm encased in a heavy plaster cast from the elbow to the tips of the splinted fingers and hung in a muslin sling.

'Jesus,' Warren said, 'that sure looks uncomfortable.'

'Ah, you get used to it,' Alfred said, 'like everything else.'

'Know how many bones he broke, Warren?' Grace asked, almost as if she were boasting. 'Three. Three bones.'

'Wow. Well, but how can you do any work, Alfred, with a hand like that?'

'Oh, well.' And Alfred managed a small, self-deprecating smile. 'They give me all the cushy jobs.'

At the door, holding the knob in readiness, Warren turned back and said 'Tell Christine I stopped by, Grace, OK? And you might tell her too that I don't believe a word of anything you said about Scotland. Oh, and if she wants to call me, tell her I said not to bother. So long.'

Riding home, he kept assuring himself that he would probably never hear from Christine again. He might have wished for a more satisfactory conclusion; still, perhaps no satisfactory conclusion would ever have been possible. And he was increasingly pleased with the last thing he'd said: 'If she wants to call me, tell her I said not to bother.' That, under the circumstances, had been just the right message, delivered in just the right way.

It was very late at night when the phone rang the next time; Judith

509

was almost certainly asleep, and Warren sprang to pick it up before it could wake her.

'Listen,' Christine said, her voice empty of all affection and even of all civility, like that of an informer in a crime movie. 'I'm just calling because this is something you ought to know. Alfred's mad at you. I mean really mad.'

'He is? Why?'

And he could almost see the narrowing of her eyes and lips. 'Because you called his wife a liar.'

'Oh, come on. I don't believe—'

'You don't believe me? All right, wait and see. I'm just telling you for your own good. When a man like Alfred feels his wife has been insulted, that's trouble.'

The next day was Sunday—the man of the house would be home—and it took Warren most of the morning to decide that he'd better go there and talk to him. It seemed a silly thing to do, and he dreaded meeting Christine; still, once it was done he could put all of them out of his mind.

But he didn't have to go near the house. Turning the corner into the last block he met Alfred and the six children walking up the street, all dressed up for some Sunday outing, possibly to the zoo. Jane seemed glad to see him: she was holding Alfred's good left hand and wearing a bright pink ribbon in her African hair. 'Hi, Warren,' she said as the younger ones came to a stop and clustered around.

'Hi, Jane. You look really nice.' And then he faced the man. 'Alfred, I understand I owe you an apology.'

'Apology? What for?'

'Well, Christine said you were angry with me for what I said to Grace.'

Alfred looked puzzled, as if contemplating issues too complex and subtle ever to be sorted out. 'No,' he said. 'No, there was nothing like that.'

'OK, then. Good. But I wanted to tell you I didn't mean any—you know.'

With a slight grimace, Alfred hitched his cast into a better position in the sling. 'Piece of advice for you, Warren,' he said. 'You don't ever want to listen to the women too much.' And he winked like an old comrade.

When Christine called him again it was in a rush of girlish ebullience, as if nothing had ever gone wrong between them—but Warren would never know what brought about the change, nor ever need to weigh its truth or falsehood.

'Honey, listen,' she said, 'I think it's mostly all blown over at home now—I mean he's all calmed down and everything—so if you want to come over tomorrow night, or the next night or whenever you can, we can have a nice—'

'Now, wait a minute,' he told her. 'You just listen to me a minute, sweetheart—oh, and by the way I think it's about time we cut out all the "honey" and the "sweetheart" stuff, don't you? Listen to me.'

He had gotten to his feet for emphasis, standing his ground, with the telephone cord snaked tight across his shirt and his free hand clenched into a fist that shook as rhythmically in the air as that of an impassioned public speaker as he made his final statement.

'Listen to me. Alfred didn't even know what the hell I meant when I tried to apologize. Didn't even know what the hell I was talking about, do you understand me? All right. That's one thing. Here's the other thing. I've had enough. Don't be calling me anymore, Christine, do you understand me? Don't be *calling* me anymore.'

'OK, honey,' she said in a quick, meek voice that was almost lost in the sound of her hanging up.

And he was still gripping the phone at his cheek, breathing hard, when he heard the slow and careful deposit of Judith's receiver into its cradle upstairs.

Well, all right, and who cared? He walked over to a heavy cardboard box full of books and kicked it hard enough to send it skidding three or four feet away and release a shuddering cloud of dust; then he looked around for other things to kick, or to punch, or to smash and break, but instead he went back and sat bouncingly on the couch again and socked one fist into the palm of the other hand. Yeah, yeah, well, the hell with it. So what? Who cared?

After a while, as his heart slowed down, he found he could think only of the way Christine's voice had flickered to nothingness with the words 'OK, honey.' There had never been anything to fear. All this time, if he had ever before taken a stern tone with her, she would have vanished from his life in an instant—'OK, honey'—even, perhaps, with an obliging, cowering smile. She was only a dumb little London streetwalker, after all.

A few days later there was a letter from his wife that changed

511

everything. She had mailed hasty, amicable letters once a week or so since she'd been back in New York, typed on the rattling stationery of the business office where she'd found her job, but this one was in handwriting, on soft blue paper, and gave every sign of having been carefully composed. It said she loved him, that she missed him terribly and wanted him to come home—though it added quickly that the choice would have to be entirely his own.

' . . . When I think back over our time together I know the trouble was more my fault than yours. I used to mistake your gentleness for weakness—that must have been my worst mistake because it's the most painful to remember, but oh there were so many others . . . '

Characteristically, she devoted a long paragraph to matters of real estate. The apartment shortage in New York was terrible, she explained, but she'd found a fairly decent place: three rooms on the second floor in a not-bad neighborhood, and the rent was surprisingly . . .

He hurried through the parts about the rent and the lease and the dimensions of the rooms and windows, and he lingered over the end of her letter.

'The Fulbright people won't object to your coming home early if you *want* to, will they? Oh, I do hope you will—that you'll want to, I mean. Cathy keeps asking me when her daddy is coming home, and I keep saying "Soon."'

'I have a terrible confession,' Judith said over tea in her sitting room that afternoon. 'I listened in to your talk on the phone the other night—and then of course I made the silly mistake of hanging up before you did, so you certainly must have known I was there. I'm frightfully sorry, Warren.'

'Oh,' he said. 'Well, that doesn't matter.'

'No, I don't suppose it does, really. If we're going to live in close quarters I suppose there'll always be these small invasions of privacy. But I did want you to know I'm—well, never mind. You know.' Then after a moment she gave him a sly, teasing look. 'I wouldn't have expected you to have such a temper, Warren. So harsh. So loud and domineering. Still, I must say I didn't much care for the girl's voice. She sounded a bit vulgar.'

'Yeah. Well, it's a long story.' And he looked down at his teacup, aware that he was blushing, until he felt it would be all right to look up again and change the subject. 'Judith, I think I'll be going home

512

pretty soon. Carol's found a place for us to live in New York, so as soon as I—'

'Oh, then you've settled it,' Judith said. 'Oh, that's marvelous.'

'Settled what?'

'Whatever it was that was making you both so miserable. Oh, I'm so glad. You didn't ever really think I believed the nonsense about the illness in the family, did you? Has any young wife ever crossed the ocean alone for a reason like that? I was even a little annoyed with Carol for *assuming* I'd believe it. I kept wanting to say Oh, tell me, dear. Tell me. Because you see when you're old, Warren—' Her eyes began to leak and she wiped them ineffectually with her hand. 'When you're old, you want so much for the people you love to be happy.'

On the night before his sailing, with his bags packed and with the basement flat as clean as a whole day's scrubbing could make it, Warren set to work on the final task of clearing his desk. Most of the books could be thrown away and all the necessary papers could be stacked and made to fit the last available suitcase space—Christ, he was getting out of here; Oh, Christ, he was going home—but when he gathered up the last handful of stuff it uncovered the little cardboard music box.

He took the time to play it backwards, slowly, as if to remind himself forever of its dim and melancholy song. He allowed it to call up a vision of Christine in his arms whispering 'Oh, I love you,' because he would want to remember that too, and then he let it fall into the trash.

1981

513

THE CIRCLING HAND

Jamaica Kincaid

During my holidays from school, I was allowed to stay in bed until long after my father had gone to work. He left our house every weekday at the stroke of seven by the Anglican church bell. I would lie in bed awake, and I could hear all the sounds my parents made as they prepared for the day ahead. As my mother made my father his breakfast, my father would shave, using his shaving brush that had an ivory handle and a razor that matched; then he would step outside to the little shed he had built for us as a bathroom, to quickly bathe in water that he had instructed my mother to leave outside overnight in the dew. That way, the water would be very cold, and he believed that cold water strengthened his back. If I had been a boy, I would have gotten the same treatment, but since I was a girl, and on top of that went to school only with other girls, my mother would always add some hot water to my bathwater to take off the chill. On Sunday afternoons, while I was in Sunday school, my father took a hot bath; the tub was half filled with plain water, and then my mother would add a large caldronful of water in which she had just boiled some bark and leaves from a bay-leaf tree. The bark and leaves were there for no reason other than that he liked the smell. He would then spend hours lying in this bath, studying his pool coupons or drawing examples of pieces of furniture he planned to make. When I came home from Sunday school, we would sit down to our Sunday dinner.

My mother and I often took a bath together. Sometimes it was just a plain bath, which didn't take very long. Other times, it was a special bath in which the barks and flowers of many different trees, together with all sorts of oils, were boiled in the same large caldron. We would then sit in this bath in a darkened room with a strange-smelling candle burning away. As we sat in this bath, my mother would bathe different parts of my body; then she would do the same to herself. We took these baths after my mother had consulted with her obeah woman, and with her mother and a trusted friend, and all three of them had confirmed that from the look of things around our house— the way a small scratch on my instep had turned into a small sore, then a large sore, and how long it had taken to heal; the way a dog she knew, and a friendly dog at that, suddenly turned and bit her; how a porcelain bowl she had carried from one eternity and hoped to carry into the next suddenly slipped out of her capable hands and broke into pieces the size of grains of sand; how words she spoke in jest to a friend had been completely misunderstood—one of the many women my father had loved, had never married, but with whom he had had children was trying to harm my mother and me by setting bad spirits on us.

When I got up, I placed my bedclothes and my nightie in the sun to air out, brushed my teeth, and washed and dressed myself. My mother would then give me my breakfast, but since, during my holidays, I was not going to school, I wasn't forced to eat an enormous breakfast of porridge, eggs, an orange or half a grapefruit, bread and butter, and cheese. I could get away with just some bread and butter and cheese and porridge and cocoa. I spent the day following my mother around and observing the way she did everything. When we went to the grocer's, she would point out to me the reason she bought each thing. I was shown a loaf of bread or a pound of butter from at least ten different angles. When we went to market, if that day she wanted to buy some crabs she would inquire from the person selling them if they came from near Parham, and if the person said yes my mother did not buy the crabs. In Parham was the leper colony, and my mother was convinced that the crabs ate nothing but the food from the lepers' own plates. If we were then to eat the crabs, it wouldn't be long before we were lepers ourselves and living unhappily in the leper colony.

How important I felt to be with my mother. For many people, their wares and provisions laid out in front of them, would brighten up when they saw her coming and would try hard to get her attention. They would dive underneath their stalls and bring out goods even better than what they had on display. They were disappointed when she held something up in the air, looked at it, turning it this way and that, and then, screwing up her face, said 'I don't think so,' and turned and walked away—off to another stall to see if someone who only last week had sold her some delicious christophine had something that was just as good. They would call out after her turned back that next week they expected to have eddoes or dasheen or whatever, and my mother would say, 'We'll see,' in a very disbelieving tone of voice. If then we went to Mr Kenneth, it would

515

be only for a few minutes, for he knew exactly what my mother wanted and always had it ready for her. Mr Kenneth had known me since I was a small child, and he would always remind me of little things I had done then as he fed me a piece of raw liver he had set aside for me. It was one of the few things I liked to eat, and, to boot, it pleased my mother to see me eat something that was so good for me, and she would tell me in great detail the effect it would have on my red blood corpuscles.

We walked home in the hot midmorning sun mostly without event. When I was much smaller, quite a few times while I was walking with my mother she would suddenly grab me and wrap me up in her skirt and drag me along with her as if in a great hurry. I would hear an angry voice saying angry things, and then, after we had passed the angry voice, my mother would release me. Neither my mother nor my father ever came straight out and told me anything, but I had put two and two together and I knew that it was one of the women that my father had loved and with whom he had had a child or children, and who never forgave him for marrying my mother and having me. It was one of those women who were always trying to harm my mother and me, and they must have loved my father very much, for not once did any of them ever try to hurt him, and whenever he passed them on the street it was as if he and these women had never met.

When we got home, my mother started to prepare our lunch (pumpkin soup with droppers, banana fritters with salt fish stewed in antroba and tomatoes, fungie with salt fish stewed in antroba and tomatoes, or pepper pot, all depending on what my mother had found at market that day). As my mother went about from pot to pot, stirring one, adding something to the other, I was ever in her wake. As she dipped into a pot of boiling something or other to taste for correct seasoning, she would give me a taste of it also, asking me what I thought. Not that she really wanted to know what I thought, for she had told me many times that my taste buds were not quite developed yet, but it was just to include me in everything. While she made our lunch, she would also keep an eye on her washing. If it was a Tuesday and the colored clothes had been starched, as she placed them on the line I would follow, carrying a basket of clothespins for her. While the starched colored clothes were being dried on the line, the white clothes were being whitened on the stone heap. It was a beautiful stone heap that my father had made for her: an enormous circle of stones, about six inches high, in the middle of our yard. On it the soapy white clothes were spread out; as the sun dried them, bleaching out all stains, they had to be made wet again by dousing them with buckets of water. On my holidays, I did this for my mother. As I watered the clothes, she would come up behind me, instructing me to get the clothes thoroughly wet, showing me a shirt that I should turn over so that the sleeves were exposed.

Over our lunch, my mother and father talked to each other about the houses my father had to build; how disgusted he had become with one of his apprentices, though sometimes it was how disgusted he was with Mr Oatie, his partner in housebuilding; what they thought of my schooling so far; what they thought of the noises Mr Smith and his friends made for so many days as they locked themselves up inside Mr Smith's house and drank rum and ate fish they had caught themselves and danced to the music of an accordion that they took turns playing. On and on they talked. As they talked, my head would move from side to side, looking at them. When my eyes rested on my father, I didn't think very much of the way he looked. But when my eyes rested on my mother, I found her beautiful. Her head looked as if it should be on a sixpence. What a beautiful long neck, and long plaited hair, which she pinned up around the crown of her head because when her hair hung down it made her too hot. Her nose was the shape of a flower on the brink of opening. Her mouth, moving up and down as she ate and talked at the same time, was such a beautiful mouth I could have looked at it forever if I had to and not mind. Her lips were wide and almost thin, and when she said certain words I could see small parts of big, white teeth—so big, and pearly, like some nice buttons on one of my dresses. I didn't much care about what she said when she was in this mood with my father. She made him laugh so. She could hardly say a word before he would burst out laughing. We ate our food and drank our lemonade, I cleared the table, we said goodbye to my father as he went back to work, I helped my mother with the dishes, and then we settled into the afternoon.

When my mother, at sixteen, after quarrelling with her father, left his house on Dominica and came to Antigua, she packed all her things in an enormous wooden trunk that she had bought in Roseau for almost six shillings. She painted the trunk yellow and green outside, and she lined the inside with wallpaper that had a cream background with

517

pink roses printed all over it. Two days after she left her father's house, she boarded a boat and sailed for Antigua. It was a small boat, and the trip would have taken a day and a half ordinarily, but a hurricane blew up and the boat was lost at sea for almost five days. By the time it got to Antigua, the boat was practically in splinters, and though two or three of the passengers were lost overboard, along with some of the cargo, my mother and her trunk were safe. Now, twenty-four years later, this trunk was kept under my bed, and in it were things that had belonged to me, starting from just before I was born. There was the chemise, made of white cotton, with scallop edging around the sleeves, neck, and hem, and white flowers embroidered on the front—the first garment I wore after being born. My mother had made that herself, and once, when we were passing by, I was even shown the tree under which she sat as she made this garment. There were some of my diapers, with their handkerchief hemstitch that she had also done herself. There was a pair of white wool booties with matching jacket and hat. There was a blanket in white wool and a blanket in white flannel cotton. There was a plain white linen hat with lace trimming. There was my christening outfit. There were two of my baby bottles: one in the shape of a normal baby bottle, and the other shaped like a boat, with a nipple on either end. There was a thermos in which my mother had kept a tea that was supposed to have a soothing effect on me. There was the dress I wore on my first birthday: a yellow cotton with green smocking on the front. There was the dress I wore on my second birthday: pink cotton with green smocking on the front. There was also a photograph of me on my second birthday wearing my pink dress and my first pair of earrings, a chain around my neck, and a pair of bracelets, all specially made of gold from British Guiana. There was the first pair of shoes I grew out of after I knew how to walk. There was the dress I wore when I first went to school, and the first notebook in which I wrote. There were the sheets for my crib and the sheets for my first bed. There was my first straw hat, my first straw basket—decorated with flowers—my grandmother had sent me from Dominica. There were my report cards, my certificates of merit from school, and my certificates of merit from Sunday school.

From time to time, my mother would fix on a certain place in our house and give it a good cleaning. If I was at home when she happened to do this, I was at her side, as usual. When she did this with the trunk, it was a tremendous pleasure, for after she had removed all the things from the trunk, and aired them out, and changed the camphor balls, and then refolded the things and put them back in their places in the trunk, as she held each thing in her hand she would tell me a story about myself. Sometimes I knew the story first hand, for I could remember the incident quite well; sometimes what she told me had happened when I was too young to know anything; and sometimes it happened before I was even born. Whichever way, I knew exactly what she would say, for I had heard it so many times before, but I never got tired of it. For instance, the flowers on the chemise, the first garment I wore after being born, were not put on correctly, and that is because when my mother was embroidering them I kicked so much that her hand was unsteady. My mother said that usually when I kicked around in her stomach and she told me to stop I would but on that day I paid no attention at all. When she told me this story, she would smile at me and say, 'You see, even then you were hard to manage.' It pleased me to think that even then, before she could see my face, my mother spoke to me in the same way she did now. On and on my mother would go. No small part of my life was so unimportant that she hadn't made a note of it, and now she would tell it to me over and over again. I would sit next to her and she would show me the very dress I wore on the day I bit another child my age with whom I was playing. 'Your biting phase,' she called it. Or the day she warned me not to play around the coal brazier, because I liked to sing to myself and dance around the fire. Two seconds later, I fell into the hot coals, burning my elbows. My mother cried when she saw that it wasn't serious, and now, as she told me about it, she often kissed the little black patches of scars on my elbows.

As she told me the stories, I sometimes sat at her side, leaning against her, or I would sit on my knees behind her back, leaning over her shoulder. As I did this, I would occasionally sniff at her neck, or behind her ears, or at her hair. She smelled sometimes of lemons, sometimes of sage, sometimes of roses, sometimes of bay leaf. Sometimes I would no longer hear what it was she was saying; I just liked to look at her mouth as it opened and closed over words, or as she laughed. How terrible it must be for all the people who had no one to love them so and no one whom they loved so, I thought. My father, for instance. When he was a little boy, his parents, after leaving him with his grandmother, boarded a boat and sailed to South America. He never saw them again, though they wrote to him and sent him presents—packages of clothes on his birthday and at Christmas. He then grew to love his grandmother, and she loved him, for she took care of him and worked hard at keeping him well fed and clothed. From the time he was a baby, they slept in the same bed, and as he became a young man they continued to do so. When he was no longer in school and had started working, every night, after he and his grandmother had eaten their dinner, my father would go off to visit his friends. He would then return home at around eleven and fall asleep next to his grandmother. In the morning, his grandmother would awake at half past five or so, a half hour before my father, and prepare his bath and breakfast and make everything proper and ready for him, so that at seven o'clock sharp he stepped out the door off to work. One morning, though, he overslept, because his grandmother didn't wake him up; she was still lying next to him. When he tried to wake her, he couldn't. She had died lying next to him sometime during the night. Even though he was overcome with grief, he built her coffin and made sure she had a nice funeral. He never slept in that bed again, and shortly afterward he moved out of that house.

When my father first told me this story, I threw myself at him at the end of it, and we both started to cry—he just a little, I quite a lot. It was a Sunday afternoon; he and my mother and I had gone for a walk in the botanical gardens. My mother had wandered off to look at some strange kind of thistle, and we could see her as she bent over the bushes to get a closer look and reach out to touch the leaves of the plant. When she returned to us and saw that we had both been crying, she started to get quite worked up, but my father quickly told her what had happened and she laughed at us and called us her little fools. But then she took me in her arms and kissed me, and she said that I needn't worry about such a thing as her sailing off or dying and leaving me all alone in the world. But if ever after that I saw my father sitting alone with a faraway look on his face, I was filled with pity for him. He had been alone in the world all that time, what with his mother sailing off on a boat with his father and his never seeing her again, and then his grandmother dying while lying next to him in the middle of the night. It was more than anyone should have to bear. I loved him so and wished that I had a mother to give him, for, no matter how much my own mother loved him, it could never be the same.

When my mother got through with the trunk, and I had heard

again and again just what I had been like and who had said what to
me at what point in my life, I was given my tea—a cup of cocoa and a
buttered bun. My father by then would return home from work, and
he was given his tea. As my mother went around preparing our
supper, picking up clothes from the stone heap, or taking clothes off
the clothesline, I would sit in a corner of our yard and watch her. She
never stood still. Her powerful legs carried her from one part of the
yard to the other, and in and out of the house. Sometimes she might
call out to me to go and get some thyme or basil or some other herb
for her, for she grew all her herbs in little pots that she kept in a
corner of our little garden. Sometimes when I gave her the herbs, she
might stoop down and kiss me on my lips and then on my neck. It
was in such a paradise that I lived.

The summer of the year I turned twelve, I could see that I had grown
taller; most of my clothes no longer fit. When I could get a dress over
my head, the waist then came up to just below my chest. My legs had
become more spindlelike, the hair on my head even more unruly
than usual, small tufts of hair had appeared under my arms, and
when I perspired the smell was strange, as if I had become an animal.
I didn't say anything about it, and my mother and father didn't seem
to notice, for they didn't say anything, either. Up to then, my mother
and I had many dresses made out of the same cloth, though hers had
a different, more grownup style, a boat neck or a sweetheart neckline,
and a pleated or gored skirt, while my dresses had high necks with
collars, a deep hemline, and, of course, a sash that tied in the back.
One day, my mother and I had gone to get some material for new
dresses to celebrate her birthday (the usual gift from my father),
when I came upon a piece of cloth—a yellow background, with
figures of men, dressed in a long-ago fashion, seated at pianos that
they were playing, and all around them musical notes flying off into
the air. I immediately said how much I loved this piece of cloth and
how nice I thought it would look on us both, but my mother replied,
'Oh, no. You are getting too old for that. It's time you had your own
clothes. You just cannot go around the rest of your life looking like a
little me.' To say that I felt the earth swept away from under me
would not be going too far. It wasn't just what she said, it was the
way she said it. No accompanying little laugh. No bending over and
kissing my little wet forehead (for suddenly I turned hot, then cold,
and all my pores must have opened up, for fluids just poured out of

521

me). In the end, I got my dress with the men playing their pianos, and my mother got a dress with red and yellow overgrown hibiscus, but I was never able to wear my own dress or see my mother in hers without feeling bitterness and hatred, directed not so much toward my mother as toward, I suppose, life in general.

As if that were not enough, my mother informed me that I was on the verge of becoming a young lady, so there were quite a few things I would have to do differently. She didn't say exactly just what it was that made me on the verge of becoming a young lady, and I was so glad of that, because I didn't want to know. Behind a closed door, I stood naked in front of a mirror and looked at myself from head to toe. I was so long and bony that I more than filled up the mirror—the same one in which my parents could comfortably observe their full selves—and my small ribs pressed out against my skin. I tried to push my unruly hair down against my head so that it would lie flat, but as soon as I let it go it bounced up again. I could see the small tufts of hair under my arms. And then I got a good look at my nose. It had suddenly spread across my face, almost blotting out my cheeks, taking up my whole face, so that if I didn't know I was me standing there I would have wondered about that strange girl—and to think that only so recently my nose had been a small thing, the size of a rosebud. But what could I do? I thought of begging my mother to ask my father if he could build for me a set of clamps into which I could screw myself at night before I went to sleep and which would surely cut back on my growing. I was about to ask her this when I remembered that a few days earlier I had asked in my most pleasing, winning way for a look through the trunk. A person I did not recognize answered in a voice I did not recognize, 'Absolutely not! You and I don't have time for that anymore.' Again, did the ground wash out from under me? Again, the answer would have to be yes, and I wouldn't be going too far.

Because of this young-lady business, instead of days spent in perfect harmony with my mother, I trailing in her footsteps, she showering down on me her kisses and affection and attention, I was now sent off to learn one thing and another. I was sent to an expert in embroidering. I was sent to someone who knew all about manners and how to meet and greet important people in the world. This woman soon asked me not to come again, since I could not resist making comical noises each time I had to practice a curtsy, it made the other girls laugh so. I was sent for piano lessons. The piano teacher, a shrivelled up old English spinster from Lancashire, soon asked me not to come back, since I seemed unable to resist eating from the bowl of plums she had placed on the piano purely for decoration. In the first case, I told my mother a lie—something I had hardly ever needed to do before. I told her that the manners teacher had found that my manners needed no improvement, so I needn't come anymore. This made her very pleased. In the second case, there was no getting around it—she had to find out. When the piano teacher told her of my misdeed, she turned and walked away from me, and I wasn't sure that if she had been asked who I was she wouldn't have said, 'I don't know,' right then and there. What a new thing this was for me: my mother's back turned on me in disgust. It was true that I didn't spend all my days at my mother's side before this, that I spent most of my days at school, but before this young-lady business I could sit and think of my mother, see her doing one thing or another, and always her face bore a smile for me. Now I often saw her with the corners of her mouth turned down in disapproval of me. And why was my mother carrying my new state so far? She took to pointing out that one day I would have my own house and I might want it to be a different house from the one she kept. Once, when showing me a way to store linen, she patted the folded sheets in place and said, 'Of course, in your own house you might choose another way.' That the day might actually come when we would live apart I had never believed. My eyes hurt from the tears I wanted to cry but didn't cry. Sometimes we would both forget the new order of things and would slip into our old ways. But that didn't last very long.

In the middle of all these new things, I had forgotten that I was to enter a new school that September. I had then a set of things to do, preparing for school. I had to go to the seamstress to be measured for new uniforms, since my body now made a mockery of the old measurements. I had to get shoes, a new school hat, and lots of new books. In my new school, I needed a different exercise book for each subject, and in addition to the usual—English, arithmetic, and so on—I now had to take Latin and French, and attend classes in a brand-new science building. I began to look forward to my new school. I hoped that everyone there would be new, that there would be no one I had ever met before. That way, I could put on a new set of airs; I could say I was something that I was not, and no one would ever know the difference. In my old school, all the girls knew me as the bright but frail, much protected Annie. I was very often unable to defend myself against their cruel taunts about my thin legs or against their actual fists. Many days, I had gone home with my clothes in shreds. One day, my mother walked me to school and asked my teacher to please try and protect me, since I was not used to such roughness. That only made things worse between me and the bullying girls. I was not such a bad girl, but I was stuckup and wasn't afraid to show that I knew all the answers. What a good opportunity, then, to wash the slate clean and be someone new. I was sure there was a way that I could still know all the answers, let my teacher know about my abilities, and be loved by my classmates.

On the Sunday before the Monday I started at my new school, my mother became cross over the way I had made my bed. In the center of my bedspread, my mother had embroidered a bowl overflowing with flowers, two lovebirds on either side of the bowl. I had placed the bedspread on my bed in a lopsided way so that the embroidery was not in the center of my bed, the way it should have been. My mother made a fuss about it, and I could see that she was right and I regretted very much not doing that one little thing that would have pleased her. I had lately become careless, she said, and I could only silently agree with her.

I came home from church, and my mother still seemed to hold the bedspread against me, so I kept out of her way. At half past two in the afternoon, I went off to Sunday school. At Sunday school, I was given a certificate for best student in my study-of-the-Bible group. It was a surprise that I would receive the certificate on that day, though we had known about the results of a test weeks before. I rushed home with my certificate in hand, feeling that with this prize I would reconquer my mother—a chance for her to smile on me again.

When I got to our house, I rushed into the yard and called out to her, but no answer came. I then walked into the house. At first, I didn't hear anything. Then I heard sounds coming from the direction of my parents' room. My mother must be in there, I thought. When I got to the door, I could see that my mother and father were lying in their bed. It didn't interest me what they were doing—only that my mother's hand was on the small of my father's back and that it was making a circular motion. But her hand! It was white and bony, as if it had long been dead and had been left out in the elements. It seemed not to be her hand, and yet it could only be her hand, so well did I know it. It went around and around in the same circular motion, and I looked at it as if I would never see anything else in my life again. If I were to forget everything else in the world, I could not forget her hand as it looked then. I could also make out that the sounds I had heard were her kissing my father's ears and his mouth and his face. I looked at them for I don't know how long.

When I next saw my mother, I was standing at the dinner table that I had just set, having made a tremendous commotion with knives and forks as I got them out of their drawer, letting my parents know that I was home. I had set the table and was now half standing near my chair, half draped over the table, staring at nothing in particular and trying to ignore my mother's presence. Though I couldn't remember our eyes' having met, I was quite sure that she had seen me in the bedroom, and I didn't know what I would say if she mentioned it. Instead, she said in a voice that was sort of cross and sort of something else, 'Are you going to just stand there doing nothing all day?' The something else was new; I had never heard it in her voice before. I couldn't say exactly what it was, but I know that it caused me to reply, 'And what if I do?' and at the same time to stare at her directly in the eyes. It must have been a shock to her, the way I spoke. I had never talked back to her before. She looked at me, and then, instead of saying some squelching thing that would put me back in my place, she dropped her eyes and walked away. From the back, she looked small and funny. She carried her hands limp at her sides. I was sure I could never let those hands touch me again; I was sure that I could never let her kiss me again. All that was finished.

I was amazed that I could eat my food, for all of it reminded me of things that had taken place between my mother and me. A long time ago, when I wouldn't eat my beef, complaining that it involved too much chewing, my mother would first chew up pieces of meat in her own mouth and then feed it to me. When I had hated carrots so much that even the sight of them would send me into a fit of tears, my mother would try to find all sorts of ways to make them palatable for me. All that was finished now. I didn't think that I would ever think of any of it again with fondness. I looked at my parents. My father was just the same, eating his food in the same old way, his two rows of false teeth clop-clopping like a horse being driven off to market. He was regaling us with another one of his stories about when he was a young man and played cricket on one island or the other. What he said now must have been funny, for my mother couldn't stop laughing. He didn't seem to notice that I was not entertained.

My father and I then went for our customary Sunday-afternoon walk. My mother did not come with us. I don't know what she stayed home to do. On our walk, my father tried to hold my hand, but I pulled myself away from him, doing it in such a way that he would think I felt too big for that now.

That Monday, I went to my new school. I was placed in a class with girls I had never seen before. Some of them had heard about me, though, for I was the youngest among them and was said to be very bright. I was amazed at the way they regarded me, seeking me out during recess for chats. I liked a girl named Albertine, and I liked a girl named Gweneth. At the end of the day, Gwen and I were in love, and so we walked home arm in arm together. Just before we parted, we drew hearts with arrows piercing through them in each other's books. Underneath the hearts we wrote our names. This was so that when we were apart and had a longing for each other we had only to look at the hearts and the names and the longing would cease.

When I got home, my mother greeted me with the customary kiss and inquiries. I told her in complete detail everything that had happened to me, leaving out, of course, Gwen and anything else that was really important.

1983

TERRITORY

David Leavitt

Neil's mother, Mrs Campbell, sits on her lawn chair behind a card table outside the food co-op. Every few minutes, as the sun shifts, she moves the chair and table several inches back so as to remain in the shade. It is a hundred degrees outside, and bright white. Each time someone goes in or out of the co-op a gust of air-conditioning flies out of the automatic doors, raising dust from the cement.

Neil stands just inside, poised over a water fountain, and watches her. She has on a sun hat, and a sweatshirt over her tennis dress; her legs are bare, and shiny with cocoa butter. In front of her, propped against the table, a sign proclaims: MOTHERS, FIGHT FOR YOUR CHILDREN'S RIGHTS—SUPPORT A NON-NUCLEAR FUTURE. Women dressed exactly like her pass by, notice the sign, listen to her brief spiel, finger pamphlets, sign petitions or don't sign petitions, never give money. Her weary eyes are masked by dark glasses. In the age of Reagan, she has declared, keeping up the causes of peace and justice is a futile, tiresome, and unrewarding effort; it is therefore an effort fit only for mothers to keep up. The sun bounces off the window glass through which Neil watches her. His own reflection lines up with her profile.

Later that afternoon, Neil spreads himself out alongside the pool and imagines he is being watched by the shirtless Chicano gardener. But the gardener, concentrating on his pruning, is neither seductive nor seducible. On the lawn, his mother's large Airedales—Abigail, Lucille, Fern—amble, sniff, urinate. Occasionally, they accost the gardener, who yells at them in Spanish.

After two years' absence, Neil reasons, he should feel nostalgia, regret, gladness upon returning home. He closes his eyes and tries to muster the proper background music for the cinematic scene of return. His rhapsody, however, is interrupted by the noises of his mother's trio—the scratchy cello, whining violin, stumbling piano—as she and Lillian Havalard and Charlotte Feder plunge through Mozart. The tune is cheery, in a Germanic sort of way, and utterly inappropriate to what Neil is trying to feel. Yet it *is* the music of his adolescence; they have played it for years, bent over the notes, their heads bobbing in silent time to the metronome.

It is getting darker. Every few minutes, he must move his towel so as to remain within the narrowing patch of sunlight. In four hours, Wayne, his love of ten months and the only person he has ever imagined he could spend his life with, will be in this house, where no love of his has ever set foot. The thought fills him with a sense of grand terror and curiosity. He stretches, tries to feel seductive, desirable. The gardener's shears whack at the ferns; the music above him rushes to a loud, premature conclusion. The women laugh and applaud themselves as they give up for the day. He hears Charlotte Feder's full nasal twang, the voice of a fat woman in a pink pants suit—odd, since she is a scrawny, arthritic old bird, rarely clad in anything other than tennis shorts and a blouse. Lillian is the fat woman in the pink pants suit; her voice is thin and warped by too much crying. Drink in hand, she calls out from the porch, 'Hot enough!' and waves. He lifts himself up and nods to her.

The women sit on the porch and chatter; their voices blend with the clink of ice in glasses. They belong to a small circle of ladies all of whom, with the exception of Neil's mother, are widows and divorcées. Lillian's husband left her twenty-two years ago, and sends her a check every month to live on; Charlotte has been divorced twice as long as she was married, and has a daughter serving a long sentence for terrorist acts committed when she was nineteen. Only Neil's mother has a husband, a distant sort of husband, away often on business. He is away on business now. All of them feel betrayed—by husbands, by children, by history.

Neil closes his eyes, tries to hear the words only as sounds. Soon, a new noise accosts him: his mother arguing with the gardener in Spanish. He leans on his elbows and watches them; the syllables are loud, heated, and compressed, and seem on the verge of explosion. But the argument ends happily; they shake hands. The gardener collects his check and walks out the gate without so much as looking at Neil.

He does not know the gardener's name; as his mother has reminded him, he does not know most of what has gone on since he moved away. Her life has gone on, unaffected by his absence. He flinches at his own egoism, the egoism of sons.

'Neil! Did you call the airport to make sure the plane's coming in on time?'

'Yes,' he shouts to her. 'It is.'

'Good. Well, I'll have dinner ready when you get back.'

'Mom—'

'What?' The word comes out in a weary wail that is more of an answer than a question.

'What's wrong?' he says, forgetting his original question.

'Nothing's wrong,' she declares in a tone that indicates that everything is wrong. 'The dogs have to be fed, dinner has to be made, and I've got people here. Nothing's wrong.'

'I hope things will be as comfortable as possible when Wayne gets here.'

'Is that a request or a threat?'

'Mom—'

Behind her sunglasses, her eyes are inscrutable. 'I'm tired,' she says. 'It's been a long day. I . . . I'm anxious to meet Wayne. I'm sure he'll be wonderful, and we'll all have a wonderful, wonderful time. I'm sorry. I'm just tired.'

She heads up the stairs. He suddenly feels an urge to cover himself; his body embarrasses him, as it has in her presence since the day she saw him shirtless and said with delight, 'Neil! You're growing hair under your arms!'

Before he can get up, the dogs gather round him and begin to sniff and lick at him. He wriggles to get away from them, but Abigail, the largest and stupidest, straddles his stomach and nuzzles his mouth. He splutters and, laughing, throws her off. 'Get away from me, you goddamn dogs,' he shouts, and swats at them. They are new dogs, not the dog of his childhood, not dogs he trusts.

He stands, and the dogs circle him, looking up at his face expectantly. He feels renewed terror at the thought that Wayne will be here so soon: Will they sleep in the same room? Will they make love? He has never had sex in his parents' house. How can he be expected to be a lover here, in this place of his childhood, of his earliest shame, in this household of mothers and dogs?

'Dinnertime! Abbylucyferny, Abbylucyferny, dinnertime!' His mother's litany disperses the dogs, and they run for the door.

'Do you realize,' he shouts to her, 'that no matter how much those dogs love you they'd probably kill you for the leg of lamb in the freezer?'

Neil was twelve the first time he recognized in himself something like sexuality. He was lying outside, on the grass, when Rasputin—the dog, long dead, of his childhood—began licking his face. He felt a tingle he did not recognize, pulled off his shirt to give the dog access to more of him. Rasputin's tongue tickled coolly. A wet nose started to sniff down his body, toward his bathing suit. What he felt frightened him, but he couldn't bring himself to push the dog away. Then his mother called out, 'Dinner,' and Rasputin was gone, more interested in food than in him.

It was the day after Rasputin was put to sleep, years later, that Neil finally stood in the kitchen, his back turned to his parents, and said, with unexpected ease, 'I'm a homosexual.' The words seemed insufficient, reductive. For years, he had believed his sexuality to be detachable from the essential him, but now he realized that it was part of him. He had the sudden, despairing sensation that though the words had been easy to say, the fact of their having been aired was incurably damning. Only then, for the first time, did he admit that they were true, and he shook and wept in regret for what he would not be for his mother, for having failed her. His father hung back, silent; he was absent for that moment as he was mostly absent—a strong absence. Neil always thought of him sitting on the edge of the bed in his underwear, captivated by something on television. He said, 'It's OK, Neil.' But his mother was resolute; her lower lip didn't quaver. She had enormous reserves of strength to which she only gained access at moments like this one. She hugged him from behind, wrapped him in the childhood smells of perfume and brownies, and whispered, 'It's OK, honey.' For once, her words seemed as inadequate as his. Neil felt himself shrunk to an embarrassed adolescent, hating her sympathy, not wanting her to touch him. It was the way he would feel from then on whenever he was in her presence—even now, at twenty-three, bringing home his lover to meet her.

All through his childhood, she had packed only the most nutritious lunches, had served on the PTA, had volunteered at the children's library and at his school, had organized a successful campaign to ban a racist history textbook. The day after he told her, she located and got in touch with an organization called the Coalition of Parents of Lesbians and Gays. Within a year, she was president of it. On weekends, she and the other mothers drove their station wagons to San Francisco, set up their card tables in front of the Bulldog Baths, the Liberty Baths, passed out literature to men in leather and denim who were loath to admit they even had mothers. These men, who would habitually do violence to each other, were strangely cowed by the suburban ladies with their informational booklets, and bent their heads. Neil was a sophomore in college then, and lived in San Francisco. She brought him pamphlets detailing the dangers of bathhouses and back rooms, enemas and poppers, wordless sex in alleyways. His excursion into that world had been brief and lamentable, and was over. He winced at the thought that she knew all his sexual secrets, and vowed to move to the East Coast to escape her. It was not very different from the days when she had campaigned for a better playground, or tutored the Hispanic children in the audiovisual room. Those days, as well, he had run away from her concern. Even today, perched in front of the co-op, collecting signatures for nuclear disarmament, she was quintessentially a mother. And if the lot of mothers was to expect nothing in return, was the lot of sons to return nothing?

Driving across the Dumbarton Bridge on his way to the airport, Neil thinks, I have returned nothing; I have simply returned. He wonders if she would have given birth to him had she known what he would grow up to be.

Then he berates himself: Why should he assume himself to be the cause of her sorrow? She has told him that her life is full of secrets. She has changed since he left home—grown thinner, more rigid, harder to hug. She has given up baking, taken up tennis; her skin has browned and tightened. She is no longer the woman who hugged him and kissed him, who said, 'As long as you're happy, that's all that's important to us.'

The flats spread out around him; the bridge floats on purple and green silt, and spongy bay fill, not water at all. Only ten miles north, a whole city has been built on gunk dredged up from the bay.

He arrives at the airport ten minutes early, to discover that the plane has landed twenty minutes early. His first view of Wayne is from behind, by the baggage belt. Wayne looks as he always looks— slightly windblown—and is wearing the ratty leather jacket he was wearing the night they met. Neil sneaks up on him and puts his hands on his shoulders; when Wayne turns around, he looks relieved to see him.

They hug like brothers; only in the safety of Neil's mother's car do they dare to kiss. They recognize each other's smells, and grow comfortable again. 'I never imagined I'd actually see you out here,' Neil says, 'but you're exactly the same here as there.'

'It's only been a week.'

They kiss again. Neil wants to go to a motel, but Wayne insists on being pragmatic. 'We'll be there soon. Don't worry.'

'We could go to one of the bathhouses in the city and take a room for a couple of aeons,' Neil says. 'Christ, I'm hard up. I don't even know if we're going to be in the same bedroom.'

'Well, if we're not,' Wayne says, 'we'll sneak around. It'll be romantic.'

They cling to each other for a few more minutes, until they realize that people are looking in the car window. Reluctantly, they pull apart. Neil reminds himself that he loves this man, that there is a reason for him to bring this man home.

He takes the scenic route on the way back. The car careers over foothills, through forests, along white four-lane highways high in the mountains. Wayne tells Neil that he sat next to a woman on the plane who was once Marilyn Monroe's psychiatrist's nurse. He slips his foot out of his shoe and nudges Neil's ankle, pulling Neil's sock down with his toe.

'I have to drive,' Neil says. 'I'm very glad you're here.'

There is a comfort in the privacy of the car. They have a common fear of walking hand in hand, of publicly showing physical affection, even in the permissive West Seventies of New York—a fear that they have admitted only to one another. They slip through a pass between two hills, and are suddenly in residential Northern California, the land of expensive ranch-style houses.

As they pull into Neil's mother's driveway, the dogs run barking toward the car. When Wayne opens the door, they jump and lap at him, and he tries to close it again. 'Don't worry. Abbylucyferny! Get in the house, damn it!'

His mother descends from the porch. She has changed into a blue flower-print dress, which Neil doesn't recognize. He gets out of the car and halfheartedly chastises the dogs. Crickets chirp in the trees. His mother looks radiant, even beautiful, illuminated by the headlights, surrounded by the now quiet dogs, like a Circe with her slaves. When she walks over to Wayne, offering her hand, and says, 'Wayne, I'm Barbara,' Neil forgets that she is his mother.

'Good to meet you, Barbara,' Wayne says, and reaches out his hand. Craftier than she, he whirls her around to kiss her cheek.

Barbara! He is calling his mother Barbara! Then he remembers that Wayne is five years older than he is. They chat by the open car door, and Neil shrinks back—the embarrassed adolescent, uncomfortable, unwanted.

So the dreaded moment passes and he might as well not have been there. At dinner, Wayne keeps the conversation smooth, like a captivated courtier seeking Neil's other's hand. A faggot son's sodomist—such words spit into Neil's head. She has prepared tiny meatballs with fresh coriander, fettucine with pesto. Wayne talks about the street people in New York; El Salvador is a tragedy; if only Sadat had lived; Phyllis Schlafly—what can you do?

'It's a losing battle,' she tells him. 'Every day I'm out there with my card table, me and the other mothers, but I tell you, Wayne, it's a losing battle. Sometimes I think us old ladies are the only ones with enough patience to fight.'

Occasionally, Neil says something, but his comments seem stupid and clumsy. Wayne continues to call her Barbara. No one under forty has ever called her Barbara as long as Neil can remember. They drink wine; he does not.

Now is the time for drastic action. He contemplates taking Wayne's hand, then checks himself. He has never done anything in her presence to indicate that the sexuality he confessed to five years ago was a reality and not an invention. Even now, he and Wayne might as well be friends, college roommates. Then Wayne, his savior, with a single, sweeping gesture, reaches for his hand, and clasps it, in the midst of a joke he is telling about Saudi Arabians. By the time he is laughing, their hands are joined. Neil's throat contracts; his heart begins to beat violently. He notices his mother's eyes flicker, glance downward; she never breaks the stride of her sentence. The dinner goes on, and every taboo nurtured since childhood falls quietly away.

She removes the dishes. Their hands grow sticky; he cannot tell which fingers are his and which Wayne's. She clears the rest of the table and rounds up the dogs.

'Well, boys, I'm very tired, and I've got a long day ahead of me tomorrow, so I think I'll hit the sack. There are extra towels for you in Neil's bathroom, Wayne. Sleep well.'

'Good night, Barbara,' Wayne calls out. 'It's been wonderful meeting you.'

533

David Leavitt

They are alone. Now they can disentangle their hands.

'No problem about where we sleep, is there?'

'No,' Neil says. 'I just can't imagine sleeping with someone in this house.'

His leg shakes violently. Wayne takes Neil's hand in a firm grasp and hauls him up.

Later that night, they lie outside, under redwood trees, listening to the hysteria of the crickets, the hum of the pool cleaning itself. Redwood leaves prick their skin. They fell in love in bars and apartments, and this is the first time that they have made love outdoors. Neil is not sure he has enjoyed the experience. He kept sensing eyes, imagined that the neighborhood cats were staring at them from behind a fence of brambles. He remembers he once hid in this spot when he and some of the children from the neighborhood were playing sardines, remembers the intoxication of small bodies packed together, the warm breath of suppressed laughter on his neck. 'The loser had to go through the spanking machine,' he tells Wayne.

'Did you lose often?'

'Most of the time. The spanking machine never really hurt—just a whirl of hands. If you moved fast enough, no one could actually get you. Sometimes, though, late in the afternoon, we'd get naughty. We'd chase each other and pull each other's pants down. That was all. Boys and girls together!'

'Listen to the insects,' Wayne says, and closes his eyes.

Neil turns to examine Wayne's face, notices a single, small pimple. Their lovemaking usually begins in a wrestle, a struggle for dominance, and ends with a somewhat confusing loss of identity—as now, when Neil sees a foot on the grass resting against his leg, and tries to determine if it is his own or Wayne's.

From inside the house, the dogs begin to bark. Their yelps grow into alarmed falsettos. Neil lifts himself up. 'I wonder if they smell something,' he says.

'Probably just us,' says Wayne.

'My mother will wake up. She hates getting waked up.'

Lights go on in the house; the door to the porch opens.

'What's wrong, Abby? What's wrong?' his mother's voice calls softly.

Wayne clamps his hand over Neil's mouth. 'Don't say anything,' he whispers.

534

'I can't just—' Neil begins to say, but Wayne's hand closes over his mouth again. He bites it, and Wayne starts laughing.

'What was that?' Her voice projects into the garden. 'Hello?' she says.

The dogs yelp louder. 'Abbylucyferny, it's OK, it's OK.' Her voice is soft and panicked. 'Is anyone there?' she asks loudly.

The brambles shake. She takes a flashlight, shines it around the garden. Wayne and Neil duck down; the light lands on them and hovers for a few seconds. Then it clicks off and they are in the dark— a new dark, a darker dark, which their eyes must readjust to.

'Let's go to bed, Abbylucyferny,' she says gently. Neil and Wayne hear her pad into the house. The dogs whimper as they follow her, and the lights go off.

Once before, Neil and his mother had stared at each other in the glare of bright lights. Four years ago, they stood in the arena created by the headlights of her car, waiting for the train. He was on his way back to San Francisco, where he was marching in a Gay Pride Parade the next day. The train station was next door to the food co-op and shared its parking lot. The co-op, familiar and boring by day, took on a certain mystery in the night. Neil recognized the spot where he had skidded on his bicycle and broken his leg. Through the glass doors, the brightly lit interior of the store glowed, its rows and rows of cans and boxes forming their own horizon, each can illuminated so that even from outside Neil could read the labels. All that was missing was the ladies in tennis dresses and sweatshirts, pushing their carts past bins of nuts and dried fruits.

'Your train is late,' his mother said. Her hair fell loosely on her shoulders, and her legs were tanned. Neil looked at her and tried to imagine her in labor with him—bucking and struggling with his birth. He felt then the strange, sexless love for women which through his whole adolescence he had mistaken for heterosexual desire.

A single bright light approached them; it preceded the low, haunting sound of the whistle. Neil kissed his mother, and waved goodbye as he ran to meet the train. It was an old train, with windows tinted a sort of horrible lemon-lime. It stopped only long enough for him to hoist himself on board, and then it was moving again. He hurried to a window, hoping to see her drive off, but the tint of the window made it possible for him to make out only vague patches of light—street lamps, cars, the co-op.

He sank into the hard, green seat. The train was almost entirely empty; the only other passenger was a dark-skinned man wearing bluejeans and a leather jacket. He sat directly across the aisle from Neil, next to the window. He had rough skin and a thick mustache. Neil discovered that by pretending to look out the window he could study the man's reflection in the lemon-lime glass. It was only slightly hazy—the quality of a bad photograph. Neil felt his mouth open, felt sleep closing in on him. Hazy red and gold flashes through the glass pulsed in the face of the man in the window, giving the curious impression of muscle spasms. It took Neil a few minutes to realize that the man was staring at him, or, rather, staring at the back of his head—staring at his staring. The man smiled as though to say, I know exactly what you're staring at, and Neil felt the sickening sensation of desire rise in his throat.

Right before they reached the city, the man stood up and sat down in the seat next to Neil's. The man's thigh brushed deliberately against his own. Neil's eyes were watering; he felt sick to his stomach. Taking Neil's hand, the man said, 'Why so nervous, honey? Relax.'

Neil woke up the next morning with the taste of ashes in his mouth. He was lying on the floor, without blankets or sheets or pillows. Instinctively, he reached for his pants, and as he pulled them on came face to face with the man from the train. His name was Luis; he turned out to be a dog groomer. His apartment smelled of dog.

'Why such a hurry?' Luis said.

'The parade. The Gay Pride Parade. I'm meeting some friends to march.'

'I'll come with you,' Luis said. 'I think I'm too old for these things, but why not?'

Neil did not want Luis to come with him, but he found it impossible to say so. Luis looked older by day, more likely to carry diseases. He dressed again in a torn T-shirt, leather jacket, bluejeans. 'It's my everyday apparel,' he said, and laughed. Neil buttoned his pants, aware that they had been washed by his mother the day before. Luis possessed the peculiar combination of hypermasculinity and effeminacy which exemplifies faggotry. Neil wanted to be rid of him, but Luis's mark was on him, he could see that much. They would become lovers whether Neil liked it or not.

They joined the parade midway. Neil hoped he wouldn't meet anyone he knew; he did not want to have to explain Luis, who clung to him. The parade was full of shirtless men with oiled, muscular shoulders. Neil's back ached. There were floats carrying garishly dressed prom queens and cheerleaders, some with beards, some actually looking like women. Luis said, 'It makes me proud, makes me glad to be what I am.' Neil supposed that by darting into the crowd ahead of him he might be able to lose Luis forever, but he found it difficult to let him go; the prospect of being alone seemed unbearable.

Neil was startled to see his mother watching the parade, holding up a sign. She was with the Coalition of Parents of Lesbians and Gays; they had posted a huge banner on the wall behind them proclaiming: OUR SONS AND DAUGHTERS, WE ARE PROUD OF YOU. She spotted him; she waved, and jumped up and down.

'Who's that woman?' Luis asked.

'My mother. I should go say hello to her.'

'OK,' Luis said. He followed Neil to the side of the parade. Neil kissed his mother. Luis took off his shirt, wiped his face with it, smiled.

'I'm glad you came,' Neil said.

'I wouldn't have missed it, Neil. I wanted to show you I cared.'

He smiled, and kissed her again. He showed no intention of introducing Luis, so Luis introduced himself.

'Hello, Luis,' Mrs Campbell said. Neil looked away. Luis shook her hand, and Neil wanted to warn his mother to wash it, warned himself to check with a VD clinic first thing Monday.

'Neil, this is Carmen Bologna, another one of the mothers,' Mrs Campbell said. She introduced him to a fat Italian woman with flushed cheeks, and hair arranged in the shape of a clamshell.

'Good to meet you, Neil, good to meet you,' said Carmen Bologna. 'You know my son, Michael? I'm so proud of Michael! He's doing so well now. I'm proud of him, proud to be his mother I am, and your mother's proud, too!'

The woman smiled at him, and Neil could think of nothing to say but 'Thank you.' He looked uncomfortably toward his mother, who stood listening to Luis. It occured to him that the worst period of his life was probably about to begin and he had no way to stop it.

A group of drag queens ambled over to where the mothers were standing. 'Michael! Michael!' shouted Carmen Bologna, and embraced a sticklike man wrapped in green satin. Michael's eyes were heavily dosed with green eyeshadow, and his lips were painted pink.

Neil turned and saw his mother staring, her mouth open. He marched over to where Luis was standing, and they moved back into the parade. He turned and waved to her. She waved back; he saw pain in her face, and then, briefly, regret. That day, he felt she would have traded him for any other son. Later, she said to him, 'Carmen Bologna really was proud, and, speaking as a mother, let me tell you, you have to be brave to feel such pride.'

Neil was never proud. It took him a year to dump Luis, another year to leave California. The sick taste of ashes was still in his mouth. On the plane, he envisioned his mother sitting alone in the dark, smoking. She did not leave his mind until he was circling New York, staring down at the dawn rising over Queens. The song playing in his earphones would remain hovering on the edges of his memory, always associated with her absence. After collecting his baggage, he took a bus into the city. Boys were selling newspapers in the middle of highways, through the windows of stopped cars. It was seven in the morning when he reached Manhattan. He stood for ten minutes on East Thirty-fourth Street, breathed the cold air, and felt bubbles rising in his blood.

Neil got a job as a paralegal—a temporary job, he told himself. When he met Wayne a year later, the sensations of that first morning returned to him. They'd been up all night, and at six they walked across the park to Wayne's apartment with the nervous, deliberate gait of people aching to make love for the first time. Joggers ran by with their dogs. None of them knew what Wayne and he were about to do, and the secrecy excited him. His mother came to mind, and the song, and the whirling vision of Queens coming alive below him. His breath solidified into clouds, and he felt happier than he had ever felt before in his life.

The second day of Wayne's visit, he and Neil go with Mrs Campbell to pick up the dogs at the dog parlor. The grooming establishment is decorated with pink ribbons and photographs of the owner's champion pit bulls. A fat, middle-aged woman appears from the back, leading the newly trimmed and fluffed Abigail, Lucille, and Fern by three leashes. The dogs struggle frantically when they see Neil's mother, tangling the woman up in their leashes. 'Ladies, behave!' Mrs Campbell commands, and collects the dogs. She gives Fern to Neil and Abigail to Wayne. In the car on the way back, Abigail begins pawing to get on Wayne's lap.

'Just push her off,' Mrs Campbell says 'She knows she's not supposed to do that.'

'You never groomed Rasputin,' Neil complains.

'Rasputin was a mutt.'

'Rasputin was a beautiful dog, even if he did smell.'

'Do you remember when you were a little kid, Neil, you used to make Rasputin dance with you? Once you tried to dress him up in one of my blouses.'

'I don't remember that,' Neil says.

'Yes. I remember,' says Mrs Campbell. 'Then you tried to organize a dog beauty contest in the neighborhood. You wanted to have runners-up—everything.'

'A dog beauty contest?' Wayne says.

'Mother, do we have to—'

'I think it's a mother's privilege to embarrass her son,' Mrs Campbell says, and smiles.

When they are about to pull into the driveway, Wayne starts screaming, and pushes Abigail off his lap. 'Oh, my God' he says. 'The dog just pissed all over me.'

Neil turns around and sees a puddle seeping into Wayne's slacks. He suppresses his laughter, and Mrs Campbell hands him a rag.

'I'm sorry, Wayne,' she says. 'It goes with the territory.'

'This is really disgusting,' Wayne says, swatting at himself with the rag.

Neil keeps his eyes on his own reflection in the rearview mirror and smiles.

At home, while Wayne cleans himself in the bathroom, Neil watches his mother cook lunch—Japanese noodles in soup. 'When you went off to college,' she says, 'I went to the grocery store. I was going to buy you ramen noodles, and I suddenly realized you weren't going to be around to eat them. I started crying right then, blubbering like an idiot.'

Neil clenches his fists inside his pockets. She has a way of telling him little sad stories when he doesn't want to hear them—stories of dolls broken by her brothers, lunches stolen by neighborhood boys on the way to school. Now he has joined the ranks of male children who have made her cry.

'Mama, I'm sorry,' he says.

She is bent over the noodles, which steam in her face. 'I didn't want to say anything in front of Wayne, but I wish you had answered

539

me last night. I was very frightened—and worried.'

'I'm sorry,' he says, but it's not convincing. His fingers prickle. He senses a great sorrow about to be born.

'I lead a quiet life,' she says. 'I don't want to be a disciplinarian. I just don't have the energy for these—shenanigans. Please don't frighten me that way again.'

'If you were so upset, why didn't you say something?'

'I'd rather not discuss it. I lead a quiet life. I'm not used to getting woken up late at night. I'm not used—'

'To my having a lover?'

'No, I'm not used to having other people around, that's all. Wayne is charming. A wonderful young man.'

'He likes you, too.'

'I'm sure we'll get along fine.'

She scoops the steaming noodles into ceramic bowls. Wayne returns, wearing shorts. His white, hairy legs are a shocking contrast to hers, which are brown and sleek.

'I'll wash those pants, Wayne,' Mrs Campbell says. 'I have a special detergent that'll take out the stain.'

She gives Neil a look to indicate that the subject should be dropped. He looks at Wayne, looks at his mother; his initial embarrassment gives way to a fierce pride—the arrogance of mastery. He is glad his mother knows that he is desired, glad it makes her flinch.

Later, he steps into the back yard; the gardener is back, whacking at the bushes with his shears. Neil walks by him in his bathing suit, imagining he is on parade.

That afternoon, he finds his mother's daily list on the kitchen table:

TUESDAY

7.00—breakfast
Take dogs to groomer
Groceries (?)

Campaign against Draft—4–7

Buy underwear
Trios—2.00
Spaghetti
Fruit

Asparagus if sale
Peanuts
Milk

Doctor's Appointment (make)
Write Cranston/Hayakawa
re disarmament

Handi-Wraps
Mozart
Abigail
Top Ramen
Pedro

Her desk and trash can are full of such lists; he remember them from the earliest days of his childhood. He had learned to read from them. In his own life, too, there have been endless lists—covered with check marks and arrows, at least one item always spilling over onto the next day's agenda. From September to November, 'Buy plane ticket for Christmas' floated from list to list to list.

The last item puzzles him: Pedro. Pedro must be the gardener. He observes the accretion of names, the arbitrary specifics that give a sense of his mother's life. He could make a list of his own selves: the child, the adolescent, the promiscuous faggot son, and finally the good son, settled, relatively successful. But the divisions wouldn't work; he is today and will always be the child being licked by the dog, the boy on the floor with Luis; he will still be everything he is ashamed of. The other lists—the lists of things done and undone— tell their own truth: that his life is measured more properly in objects than in stages. He knows himself as 'jump rope,' 'book,' 'sunglasses,' 'underwear.'

'Tell me about your family, Wayne,' Mrs Campbell says that night, as they drive toward town. They are going to see an Esther Williams movie at the local revival house: an underwater musical, populated by mermaids, underwater Rockettes.

'My father was a lawyer,' Wayne says. 'He had an office in Queens, with a neon sign. I think he's probably the only lawyer in the world who had a neon sign. Anyway, he died when I was ten. My mother never remarried. She lives in Queens. Her great claim to fame is that when she was twenty-two she went on "The $64,000 Question." Her category was mystery novels. She made it to sixteen thousand before she got tripped up.'

541

'When I was about ten, I wanted you to go on "Jeopardy,"' Neil says to his mother. 'You really should have, you know. You would have won.'

'You certainly loved "Jeopardy,"' Mrs Campbell says. 'You used to watch it during dinner. Wayne, does your mother work?'

'No,' he says. 'She lives off investments.'

'You're both only children,' Mrs Campbell says. Neil wonders if she is ruminating on the possible connection between that coincidence and their 'alternative life style.'

The movie theater is nearly empty. Neil sits between Wayne and his mother. There are pillows on the floor at the front of the theater, and a cat is prowling over them. It casts a monstrous shadow every now and then on the screen, disturbing the sedative effect of water ballet. Like a teen-ager, Neil cautiously reaches his arm around Wayne's shoulder. Wayne takes his hand immediately. Next to them, Neil's mother breathes in, out, in, out. Neil timorously moves his other arm and lifts it behind his mother's neck. He does not look at her, but he can tell from her breathing that she senses what he is doing. Slowly, carefully, he lets his hand drop on her shoulder; it twitches spasmodically, and he jumps, as if he had received an electric shock. His mother's quiet breathing is broken by a gasp; even Wayne notices. A sudden brightness on the screen illuminates the panic in her eyes, Neil's arm frozen above her, about to fall again. Slowly, he lowers his arm until his fingertips touch her skin, the fabric of her dress. He has gone too far to go back now; they are all too far.

Wayne and Mrs Campbell sink into their seats, but Neil remains stiff, holding up his arms, which rest on nothing. The movie ends, and they go on sitting just like that.

'I'm old,' Mrs Campbell says later, as they drive back home. 'I remember when those films were new. Your father and I went to one on our first date. I loved them, because I could pretend that those women underwater were flying—they were so graceful. They really took advantage of Technicolor in those days. Color was something to appreciate. You can't know what it was like to see a color movie for the first time, after years of black-and-white. It's like trying to explain the surprise of snow to an East Coaster. Very little is new anymore, I fear.'

Neil would like to tell her about his own nostalgia, but how can he explain that all of it revolves around her? The idea of her life before he was born pleases him. 'Tell Wayne how you used to look like Esther Williams,' he asks her.

She blushes. 'I was told I looked like Esther Williams, but really more like Gene Tierney,' she says. 'Not beautiful, but interesting. I like to think I had a certain magnetism.'

'You still do,' Wayne says, and instantly recognizes the wrongness of his comment. Silence and a nervous laugh indicate that he has not yet mastered the family vocabulary.

When they get home, the night is once again full of the sound of crickets. Mrs Campbell picks up a flashlight and calls the dogs. 'Abbylucyferny, Abbylucyferny,' she shouts, and the dogs amble from their various corners. She pushes them out the door to the back yard and follows them. Neil follows her. Wayne follows Neil, but hovers on the porch. Neil walks behind her as she tramps through the garden. She hold out her flashlight, and snails slide from behind bushes, from under rocks, to where she stands. When the snails become visible, she crushes them underfoot. They make a wet, cracking noise, like eggs being broken.

'Nights like this,' she says, 'I think of children without pants on, in hot South American countries. I have nightmares about tanks rolling down our street.'

'The weather's never like this in New York,' Neil says. 'When it's hot, it's humid and sticky. You don't want to go outdoors.'

'I could never live anywhere else but here. I think I'd die. I'm too used to the climate.'

'Don't be silly.'

'No, I mean it,' she says. 'I have adjusted too well to the weather.'

The dogs bark and howl by the fence. 'A cat, I suspect,' she says. She aims her flashlight at a rock, and more snails emerge—uncountable numbers, too stupid to have learned not to trust light.

'I know what you were doing at the movie,' she says.

'What?'

'I know what you were doing.'

'What? I put my arm around you.'

'I'm sorry, Neil,' she says. 'I can only take so much. Just so much.'

'What do you mean?' he says. 'I was only trying to show affection.'

'Oh, affection—I know about affection.'

He looks up at the porch, sees Wayne moving toward the door, trying not to listen.

'What do you mean?' Neil says to her.

543

She puts down the flashlight and wraps her arms around herself. 'I remember when you were a little boy,' she says. 'I remember, and I have to stop remembering. I wanted you to grow up happy. And I'm very tolerant, very understanding. But I can only take so much.'

His heart seems to have risen into his throat. 'Mother,' he says, 'I think you know my life isn't your fault. But for God's sake, don't say that your life is my fault.'

'It's not a question of fault,' she says. She extracts a Kleenex from her pocket and blows her nose. 'I'm sorry, Neil. I guess I'm just an old woman with too much on her mind and not enough to do.' She laughs halfheartedly. 'Don't worry. Don't say anything,' she says. 'Abbylucyferny, Abbylucyferny, time for bed!'

He watches her as she walks toward the porch, silent and regal. There is the pad of feet, the clinking of dog tags as the dogs run for the house.

He was twelve the first time she saw him march in a parade. He played the tuba, and as his elementary-school band lumbered down the streets of their then small town she stood on the sidelines and waved. Afterward, she had taken him out for ice cream. He spilled some on his red uniform, and she swiped at it with a napkin. She had been there for him that day, as well as years later, at that more memorable parade; she had been there for him every day.

Somewhere over Iowa, a week later, Neil remembers this scene, remembers other days, when he would find her sitting in the dark, crying. She had to take time out of her own private sorrow to appease his anxiety. 'It was part of it,' she told him later. 'Part of being a mother.'

'The scariest thing in the world is the thought that you could unknowingly ruin someone's life,' Neil tells Wayne. 'Or even change someone's life. I hate the thought of having such control. I'd make a rotten mother.'

'You're crazy,' Wayne says. 'You have this great mother, and all you do is complain. I know people whose mothers have disowned them.'

'Guilt goes with the territory,' Neil says.

'Why?' Wayne asks, perfectly seriously.

Neil doesn't answer. He lies back in his seat, closes his eyes, imagines he grew up in a house in the mountains of Colorado, surrounded by snow—endless white snow on hills. No flat places, and no trees; just white hills. Every time he has flown away, she has come into his mind, usually sitting alone in the dark, smoking. Today she is outside at dusk, skimming leaves from the pool.

'I want to get a dog,' Neil says.

Wayne laughs. 'In the city? It'd suffocate.'

The hum of the airplane is druglike, dazing. 'I want to stay with you a long time,' Neil says.

'I know.' Imperceptibly, Wayne takes his hand.

'It's very hot there in the summer, too. You know, I'm not thinking about my mother now.'

'It's OK.'

For a moment, Neil wonders what the stewardess or the old woman on the way to the bathroom will think, but then he laughs and relaxes.

Later, the plane makes a slow circle over New York City, and on it two men hold hands, eyes closed, and breathe in unison.

1983

BRIDGING

Max Apple

1

At the Astrodome, Nolan Ryan is shaving the corners. He's going through the Giants in order. The radio announcer is not even mentioning that by the sixth the Giants haven't had a hit. The K's mount on the scoreboard. Tonight Nolan passes the Big Train and is now the all-time strikeout king. He's almost as old as I am and he still throws nothing but smoke. His fastball is an aspirin; batters tear their tendons lunging for his curve. Jessica and I have season tickets, but tonight she's home listening and I'm in the basement of St Anne's Church watching Kay Randall's fingertips. Kay is holding her hands out from her chest, her fingertips on each other. Her fingers move a little as she talks and I can hear her nails click when they meet. That's how close I'm sitting.

Kay is talking about 'bridging'; that's what her arched fingers represent.

'Bridging,' she says, 'is the way Brownies become Girl Scouts. It's a slow steady process. It's not easy, but we allow a whole year for bridging.'

Eleven girls in brown shirts with red bandannas at their neck are imitating Kay as she talks. They hold their stumpy chewed fingertips out and bridge them. So do I.

I brought the paste tonight and the stick-on gold stars and the thread for sewing buttonholes.

'I feel a little awkward,' Kay Randall said on the phone, 'asking a man to do these errands . . . but that's my problem, not yours. Just bring the supplies and try to be at the church meeting room a few minutes before seven.'

I arrive a half hour early.

'You're off your rocker,' Jessica says. She begs me to drop her at the Astrodome on my way to the Girl Scout meeting. 'After the game, I'll meet you at the main souvenir stand on the first level. They stay open an hour after the game. I'll be all right. There are cops and ushers every five yards.'

She can't believe that I am missing this game to perform my

546

functions as an assistant Girl Scout leader. Our Girl Scout battle has been going on for two months.

'Girl Scouts is stupid,' Jessica says. 'Who wants to sell cookies and sew buttons and walk around wearing stupid old badges?'

When she agreed to go to the first meeting, I was so happy I volunteered to become an assistant leader. After the meeting, Jessica went directly to the car the way she does after school, after a birthday party, after a ball game, after anything. A straight line to the car. No jabbering with girlfriends, no smiles, no dallying, just right to the car. She slides into the back seat, belts in, and braces herself for destruction. It has already happened once.

I swoop past five thousand years of stereotypes and accept my assistant leader's packet and credentials.

'I'm sure there have been other men in the movement,' Kay says, 'we just haven't had any in our district. It will be good for the girls.'

Not for my Jessica. She won't bridge, she won't budge.

'I know why you're doing this,' she says. 'You think that because I don't have a mother, Kay Randall and the Girl Scouts will help me. That's crazy. And I know that Sharon is supposed to be like a mother too. Why don't you just leave me alone.'

Sharon is Jessica's therapist. Jessica sees her twice a week. Sharon and I have a meeting once a month.

'We have a lot of shy girls,' Kay Randall tells me. 'Scouting brings them out. Believe me, it's hard to stay shy when you're nine years old and you're sharing a tent with six other girls. You have to count on each other, you have to communicate.'

I imagine Jessica zipping up in her sleeping bag, mumbling good night to anyone who first says it to her, then closing her eyes and hating me for sending her out among the happy.

'She likes all sports, especially baseball,' I tell my leader.

'There's room for baseball in scouting,' Kay says. 'Once a year the whole district goes to a game. They mention us on the big scoreboard.'

'Jessica and I go to all the home games. We're real fans.'

Kay smiles

'That's why I want her in Girl Scouts. You know, I want her to go to things with her girlfriends instead of always hanging around with me at ball games.'

'I understand,' Kay says. 'It's part of bridging.'

With Sharon the term is 'separation anxiety.' That's the fastball, 'bridging' is the curve. Amid all their magic words I feel as if Jessica and I are standing at home plate blindfolded.

While I await Kay and the members of Troop 111, District 6, I eye St Anne in her grotto and St Gregory and St Thomas. Their hands are folded as if they started out bridging, ended up praying.

In October the principal sent Jessica home from school because Mrs Simmons caught her in spelling class listening to the World Series through an earphone.

'It's against the school policy,' Mrs Simmons said. 'Jessica understands school policy. We confiscate radios and send the child home.'

'I'm glad,' Jessica said. 'It was a cheap-o radio. Now I can watch the TV with you.'

They sent her home in the middle of the sixth game. I let her stay home for the seventh too.

The Brewers are her favorite American League team. She likes Rollie Fingers, and especially Robin Yount.

'Does Yount go in the hole better than Harvey Kuenn used to?'

'You bet,' I tell her. 'Kuenn was never a great fielder but he could hit three hundred with his eyes closed.'

Kuenn is the Brewers' manager. He has an artificial leg and can barely make it up the dugout steps, but when I was Jessica's age and the Tigers were my team, Kuenn used to stand at the plate, tap the corners with his bat, spit some tobacco juice, and knock liners up the alley.

She took the Brewers' loss hard.

'If Fingers wasn't hurt they would have squashed the Cards, wouldn't they?'

I agreed.

'But I'm glad for Andujar.'

We had Andujar's autograph. Once we met him at a McDonald's. He was a relief pitcher then, an erratic right-hander. In St Louis he improved. I was happy to get his name on a napkin. Jessica shook his hand.

One night after I read her a story, she said, 'Daddy, if we were rich could we go to the away games too? I mean, if you didn't have to be at work every day.'

'Probably we could,' I said, 'but wouldn't it get boring? We'd have to stay at hotels and eat in restaurants. Even the players get sick of it.'

'Are you kidding?' she said. 'I'd never get sick of it.'

'Jessica has fantasies of being with you forever, following baseball or whatever,' Sharon says. 'All she's trying to do is please you. Since she lost her mother she feels that you and she are alone in the world. She doesn't want to let anyone or anything else into that unit, the two of you. She's afraid of any more losses. And, of course, her greatest worry is about losing you.'

'You know,' I tell Sharon, 'that's pretty much how I feel too.'

'Of course it is,' she says. 'I'm glad to hear you say it.'

Sharon is glad to hear me say almost anything. When I complain that her $100-a-week fee would buy a lot of peanut butter sandwiches, she says she is 'glad to hear me expressing my anger.'

'Sharon's not fooling me,' Jessica says. 'I know that she thinks drawing those pictures is supposed to make me feel better or something. You're just wasting your money. There's nothing wrong with me.'

'It's a long, difficult, expensive process,' Sharon says. 'You and Jessica have lost a lot. Jessica is going to have to learn to trust the world again. It would help if you could do it too.'

So I decide to trust Girl Scouts. First Girl Scouts, then the world. I make my stand at the meeting of Kay Randall's fingertips. While Nolan Ryan breaks Walter Johnson's strikeout record and pitches a two-hit shutout, I pass out paste and thread to nine-year-olds who are sticking and sewing their lives together in ways Jessica and I can't.

2

Scouting is not altogether new to me. I was a Cub Scout. I owned a blue beanie and I remember very well my den mother, Mrs Clark. A den mother made perfect sense to me then and still does. Maybe that's why I don't feel uncomfortable being a Girl Scout assistant leader.

We had no den father. Mr Clark was only a photograph on the living room wall, the tiny living room where we held our monthly meetings. Mr Clark was killed in the Korean War. His son John was in the troop. John was stocky but Mrs Clark was huge. She couldn't sit on a regular chair, only on a couch or a stool without sides. She was the cashier in the convenience store beneath their apartment. The story we heard was that Walt, the old man who owned the store, felt sorry for her and gave her the job. He was her landlord too. She sat on a swivel stool and rang up the purchases.

We met at the store and watched while she locked the door; then we followed her up the steep staircase to her three-room apartment. She carried two wet glass bottles of milk. Her body took up the entire width of the staircase. She passed the banisters the way semi trucks pass each other on a narrow highway.

We were ten years old, a time when everything is funny, especially fat people. But I don't remember anyone ever laughing about Mrs Clark. She had great dignity and character. So did John. I didn't know what to call it then, but I knew John was someone you could always trust.

She passed out milk and cookies, then John collected the cups and washed them. They didn't even have a TV set. The only decoration in the room that barely held all of us was Mr Clark's picture on the wall. We saw him in his uniform and we knew he died in Korea defending his country. We were little boys in blue beanies drinking milk in the apartment of a hero. Through that aura I came to scouting. I wanted Kay Randall to have all of Mrs Clark's dignity.

When she took a deep breath and then bridged, Kay Randall had noticeable armpits. Her wide shoulders slithered into a tiny rib cage. Her armpits were like bridges. She said 'bridging' like a mantra, holding her hands before her for about thirty seconds at the start of each meeting.

'A promise is a promise,' I told Jessica. 'I signed up to be a leader, and I'm going to do it with you or without you.'

'But you didn't even ask me if I liked it. You just signed up without talking it over.'

'That's true; that's why I'm not going to force you to go along. It was my choice.'

'What can you like about it? I hate Melissa Randall. She always has a cold.'

'Her mother is a good leader.'

'How do you know?'

'She's my boss. I've got to like her, don't I?' I hugged Jessica. 'C'mon, honey, give it a chance. What do you have to lose?'

'If you make me go I'll do it, but if I have a choice I won't.'

Every other Tuesday, Karen, the fifteen-year-old Greek girl who lives on the corner, babysits Jessica while I go to the Scout meetings. We talk about field trips and how to earn merit badges. The girls giggle when Kay pins a promptness badge on me, my first.

Jessica think it's hilarious. She tells me to wear it to work.

Sometimes when I watch Jessica brush her hair and tie her ponytail and make up her lunch kit I start to think that maybe I should just relax and stop the therapy and the scouting and all my not-so-subtle attempts to get her to invite friends over. I start to think that, in spite of everything, she's a good student and she's got a sense of humor. She's barely nine years old. She'll grow up like everyone else does. John Clark did it without a father; she'll do it without a mother. I start to wonder if Jessica seems to the girls in her class the way John Clark seemed to me: dignified, serious, almost an adult even while we were playing. I admired him. Maybe the girls in her class admire her. But John had that hero on the wall, his father in a uniform, dead for reasons John and all the rest of us understood.

My Jessica had to explain a neurologic disease she couldn't even pronounce. 'I hate it when people ask me about Mom,' she says. 'I just tell them she fell off the Empire State Building.'

3

Before our first field trip I go to Kay's house for a planning session. We're going to collect wildflowers in East Texas. It's a one-day trip. I arranged to rent the school bus.

I told Jessica that she could go on the trip even though she wasn't a troop member, but she refused.

We sit on colonial furniture in Kay's den. She brings in coffee and we go over the supply list. Another troop is joining ours so there will be twenty-two girls, three women, and me, a busload among the bluebonnets.

'We have to be sure the girls understand that the bluebonnets they pick are on private land and that we have permission to pick them. Otherwise they might pick them along the roadside, which is against the law.'

I imagine all twenty-two of them behind bars for picking bluebonnets and Jessica laughing while I scramble for bail money.

I keep noticing Kay's hands. I notice them as she pours coffee, as she checks off the items on the list, as she gestures. I keep expecting her to bridge. She has large, solid, confident hands. When she finishes bridging I sometimes feel like clapping the way people do after the national anthem.

'I admire you,' she tells me. 'I admire you for going ahead with Scouts even though your daughter rejects it. She'll get a lot out of it indirectly from you.'

Kay Randall is thirty-three, divorced, and has a Bluebird too. Her older daughter is one of the stubby-fingered girls, Melissa. Jessica is right; Melissa always has a cold.

Kay teaches fifth grade and has been divorced for three years. I am the first assistant she's ever had.

'My husband, Bill, never helped with Scouts,' Kay says. 'He was pretty much turned off to everything except his business and drinking. When we separated I can't honestly say I missed him; he'd never been there. I don't think the girls miss him either. He only sees them about once a month. He has girlfriends, and his business is doing very well. I guess he has what he wants.'

'And you?'

She uses one of those wonderful hands to move the hair away from her eyes, a gesture that makes her seem very young.

'I guess I do too. I've got the girls and my job. I'm lonesome, though. It's not exactly what I wanted.'

We both think about what might have been as we sit beside her glass coffeepot with our lists of sachet supplies. If she was Barbra Streisand and I Robert Redford and the music started playing in the background to give us a clue and there was a long close-up of our lips, we might just fade into middle age together. But Melissa called for Mom because her mosquito bite was bleeding where she scratched it. And I had an angry daughter waiting for me. And all Kay and I had in common was Girl Scouts. We were both smart enough to know it. When Kay looked at me before going to put alcohol on the mosquito bite, our mutual sadness dripped from us like the last drops of coffee through the grinds.

'You really missed something tonight,' Jessica tells me. 'The Astros did a double steal. I've never seen one before. In the fourth they sent Thon and Moreno together, and Moreno stole home.'

She knows batting averages and won-lost percentages too, just like the older boys, only they go out to play. Jessica stays in and waits for me.

During the field trip, while the girls pick flowers to dry and then manufacture into sachets, I think about Jessica at home, probably beside the radio. Juana, our once-a-week cleaning lady, agreed to work on Saturday so she could stay with Jessica while I took the all-day field trip.

It was no small event. In the eight months since Vicki died I had not gone away for an entire day.

I made waffles in the waffle iron for her before I left, but she hardly ate.

'If you want anything, just ask Juana.'

'Juana doesn't speak English.'

'She understands, that's enough.'

'Maybe for you it's enough.'

'Honey, I told you, you can come; there's plenty of room on the bus. It's not too late for you to change your mind.'

'It's not too late for you either. There's going to be plenty of other leaders there. You don't have to go. You're just doing this to be mean to me.'

I'm ready for this. I spent an hour with Sharon steeling myself. 'Before she can leave you,' Sharon said, 'you'll have to show her that you can leave. Nothing's going to happen to her. And don't let her be sick that day either.'

Jessica is too smart to pull the 'I-don't-feel-good' routine. Instead she becomes more silent, more unhappy looking than usual. She stays in her pajamas while I wash the dishes and get ready to leave.

I didn't notice the sadness as it was coming upon Jessica. It must have happened gradually in the years of Vicki's decline, the years in which I paid so little attention to my daughter. There were times when Jessica seemed to recognize the truth more than I did.

As my Scouts picked their wildflowers, I remembered the last outing I had planned for us. It was going to be a Fourth of July picnic with some friends in Austin. It stopped at the bank and got $200 in cash for the long weekend. But when I came home Vicki was too sick to move and the air conditioner had broken. I called our friends to cancel the picnic; then I took Jessica to the mall with me to buy a fan. I bought the biggest one they had, a 8-inch oscillating model that sounded like a hurricane. It could cool 10,000 square feet, but it wasn't enough.

Vicki was home sitting blankly in front of the TV set. The fan could move eight tons of air an hour, but I wanted it to save my wife. I wanted a fan that would blow the whole earth out of its orbit.

I had $50 left. I gave it Jessica and told her to buy anything she wanted.

'Whenever you're sad, Daddy, you want to buy me things.' She put the money back in my pocket. 'It won't help.' She was seven years old, holding my hand tightly in the appliance department at J.C. Penney's.

I watched Melissa sniffle even more among the wildflowers, and I pointed out the names of various flowers to Carol and JoAnne and Sue and Linda and Rebecca, who were by now used to me and treated me pretty much as they treated Kay. I noticed that the Girl Scout flower book had very accurate photographs that made it easy to identify the bluebonnets and buttercups and poppies. There were also several varieties of wild grasses.

We were only 70 miles from home on some land a wealthy rancher long ago donated to the Girl Scouts. The girls bending among the flowers seemed to have been quickly transformed by the colorful meadow. The gigglers and monotonous singers on the bus were now, like the bees, sucking strength from the beauty around them. Kay was in the midst of them and so, I realized, was I, not watching and keeping score and admiring from the distance but a participant, a player.

JoAnne and Carol sneaked up from behind me and dropped some dandelions down my back. I chased them; then I helped the other leaders pour the Kool-Aid and distribute the Baggies and the name tags for each girl's flowers.

My daughter is home listening to a ball game, I thought, and I'm out here having fun with nine-year-olds. It's upside down.

When I came home with dandelion fragments still on my back, Juana had cleaned the house and I could smell the taco sauce in the kitchen. Jessica was in her room. I suspected that she had spent the day listless and tearful, although I had asked her to invite a friend over.

'I had a lot of fun, honey, but I missed you.'

She hugged me and cried against my shoulder. I felt like holding her the way I used to when she was an infant, the way I rocked her to sleep. But she was a big girl now and needed not sleep but wakefulness.

'I heard on the news that the Rockets signed Ralph Sampson,' she sobbed, 'and you hardly ever take me to any pro basketball games.'

'But if they have a new center things will be different. With Sampson we'll be contenders. Sure I'll take you.'

'Promise?'

'Promise.' I promise to take you everywhere, my lovely child, and then to leave you. I'm learning to be a leader.

1984

GREASY LAKE

T. Coraghessan Boyle

It's about a mile down on the dark side of Route 88

Bruce Springsteen

There was a time when courtesy and winning ways went out of style, when it was good to be bad, when you cultivated decadence like a taste. We were all dangerous characters then. We wore torn-up leather jackets, slouched around with toothpicks in our mouths, sniffed glue and ether and what somebody claimed was cocaine. When we wheeled our parents' whining station wagons out into the street we left a patch of rubber half a block long. We drank gin and grape juice, Tango, Thunderbird, and Bali Hai. We were nineteen. We were bad. We read André Gide and struck elaborate poses to show that we didn't give a shit about anything. At night, we went up to Greasy Lake.

Through the center of town, up the strip, past the housing developments and shopping malls, street lights giving way to the thin streaming illumination of the headlights, trees crowding the asphalt in a black unbroken wall: that was the way out to Greasy Lake. The Indians had called it Wakan, a reference to the clarity of its waters. Now it was fetid and murky, the mud banks glittering with broken glass and strewn with beer cans and the charred remains of bonfires. There was a single ravaged island a hundred yards from shore, so stripped of vegetation it looked as if the air force had strafed it. We went up to the lake because everyone went there, because we wanted to snuff the rich scent of possibility on the breeze, watch a girl take off her clothes and plunge into the festering murk, drink beer, smoke pot, howl at the stars, savor the incongruous full-throated roar of rock and roll against the primeval susurrus of frogs and crickets. This was nature.

I was there one night, late, in the company of two dangerous characters. Digby wore a gold star in his right ear and allowed his father to pay his tuition at Cornell; Jeff was thinking of quitting school to become a painter/musician/head-shop proprietor. They were both expert in the social graces, quick with a sneer, able to manage a Ford with lousy shocks over a rutted and gutted blacktop road at eighty-five while rolling a joint as compact as a Tootsie Roll Pop stick. They could lounge against a bank of booming speakers and trade 'man's with the best of them or roll out across the dance floor as if their joints worked on bearings. They were slick and quick and they wore their mirror shades at breakfast and dinner, in the shower, in closets and caves. In short, they were bad.

I drove. Digby pounded the dashboard and shouted along with Toots & the Maytals while Jeff hung his head out the window and streaked the side of my mother's Bel Air with vomit. It was early June, the air soft as a hand on your cheek, the third night of summer vacation. The first two nights we'd been out till dawn, looking for something we never found. On this, the third night, we'd cruised the strip sixty-seven times, been in and out of every bar and club we could think of in a twenty-mile radius, stopped twice for bucket chicken and forty-cent hamburgers, debated going to a party at the house of a girl Jeff's sister knew, and chucked two dozen raw eggs at mailboxes and hitchhikers. It was 2.00 a.m.; the bars were closing. There was nothing to do but take a bottle of lemon-flavored gin up to Greasy Lake.

The taillights of a single car winked at us as we swung into the dirt lot with its tufts of weed and washboard corrugations; '57 Chevy, mint, metallic blue. On the far side of the lot, like the exoskeleton of some gaunt chrome insect, a chopper leaned against its kickstand. And that was it for excitement: some junkie half-wit biker and a car freak pumping his girlfriend. Whatever it was we were looking for, we weren't about to find it at Greasy Lake. Not that night.

But then all of a sudden Digby was fighting for the wheel. 'Hey, that's Tony Lovett's car! Hey!' he shouted, while I stabbed at the brake pedal and the Bel Air nosed up to the gleaming bumper of the parked Chevy. Digby leaned on the horn, laughing, and instructed me to put my brights on. I flicked on the brights. This was hilarious. A joke. Tony would experience premature withdrawal and expect to be confronted by grim-looking state troopers with flashlights. We hit the horn, strobed the lights, and then jumped out of the car to press our witty faces to Tony's windows; for all we knew we might even catch a glimpse of some little fox's tit, and then we could slap backs with red-faced Tony, roughhouse a little, and go on to new heights of adventure and daring.

The first mistake, the one that opened the whole floodgate, was losing my grip on the keys. In the excitement, leaping from the car with the gin in one hand and a roach clip in the other, I spilled them in the grass—in the dark, rank, mysterious nighttime grass of Greasy Lake. This was a tactical error, as damaging and irreversible in its way as Westmoreland's decision to dig in at Khe Sanh. I felt it like a jab of intuition, and I stopped there by the open door, peering vaguely into the night that puddled up round my feet.

The second mistake—and this was inextricably bound up with the first—was identifying the car as Tony Lovett's. Even before the very bad character in greasy jeans and engineer boots ripped out of the driver's door, I began to realize that this chrome blue was much lighter than the robin's-egg of Tony's car, and that Tony's car didn't have rear-mounted speakers. Judging from their expressions, Digby and Jeff were privately groping toward the same inevitable and unsettling conclusion as I was.

In any case, there was no reasoning with this bad greasy character—clearly he was a man of action. The first lusty Rockette kick of his steel-toed boot caught me under the chin, chipped my favorite tooth, and left me sprawled in the dirt. Like a fool, I'd gone down on one knee to comb the stiff hacked grass for the keys, my mind making connections in the most dragged-out, testudineous way, knowing that things had gone wrong, that I was in a lot of trouble, and that the lost ignition key was my grail and my salvation. The three or four succeeding blows were mainly absorbed by my right buttock and the tough piece of bone at the base of my spine.

Meanwhile, Digby vaulted the kissing bumpers and delivered a savage kung-fu blow to the greasy character's collarbone. Digby had just finished a course in martial arts for phys-ed credit and had spent the better part of the past two nights telling up apocryphal tales of Bruce Lee types and of the raw power invested in lightning blows shot from coiled wrists, ankles, and elbows. The greasy character was unimpressed. He merely backed off a step, his face like a Toltecmask, and laid Digby out with a single whistling roundhouse blow . . . but by now Jeff had got into the act, and I was beginning to extricate myself from the dirt, a tinny compound of shock, rage, and impotence wadded in my throat.

Jeff was on the guy's back, biting at his ear. Digby was on the ground, cursing. I went for the tire iron I kept under the driver's seat. I kept it there because bad characters always keep tire irons under the driver's seat, for just such an occasion as this. Never mind that I hadn't been involved in a fight since sixth grade, when a kid with a sleepy eye and two streams of mucus depending from his nostrils hit me in the knee with a Louisville slugger; never mind that I'd touched the tire iron exactly twice before, to change tires: it was there. And I went for it.

I was terrified. Blood was beating in my ears, my hands were shaking, my heart turning over like a dirtbike in the wrong gear. My antagonist was shirtless, and a single cord of muscle flashed across his chest as he bent forward to peel Jeff from his back like a wet overcoat. 'Motherfucker,' he spat, over and over, and I was aware in that instant that all four of us—Digby, Jeff, and myself included—were chanting 'motherfucker, motherfucker,' as if it were a battle cry. (What happened next? the detective asks the murderer from beneath the turned-down brim of his porkpie hat. I don't know, the murderer says, something came over me. Exactly.)

Digby poked the flat of his hand in the bad character's face and I came at him like a kamikaze, mindless, raging, stung with humiliation—the whole thing, from the initial boot in the chin to this murderous primal instant involving no more than sixty hyperventilating, gland-flooding seconds—I came at him and brought the tire iron down across his ear. The effect was instantaneous, astonishing. He was a stunt man and this was Hollywood, he was a big grimacing toothy balloon and I was a man with a straight pin. He collapsed. Wet his pants. Went loose in his boots.

A single second, big as a zeppelin, floated by. We were standing over him in a circle, gritting our teeth, jerking our necks, our limbs and hands and feet twitching with glandular discharges. No one said anything. We just stared down at the guy, the car freak, the lover, the bad greasy character laid low. Digby looked at me; so did Jeff. I was still holding the tire iron, a tuft of hair clinging to the crook like dandelion fluff, like down. Rattled, I dropped it in the dirt, already envisioning the headlines, the pitted faces of the police inquisitors, the gleam of handcuffs, clank of bars, the big black shadows rising from the back of the cell . . . when suddenly a raw torn shriek cut through me like all the juice in all the electric chairs in the country.

It was the fox. She was short, barefoot, dressed in panties and a man's shirt. 'Animals!' she screamed, running at us with her fists clenched and wisps of blow-dried hair in her face. There was a silver chain round her ankle, and her toenails flashed in the glare of the headlights. I think it was the toenails that did it. Sure, the gin and the cannabis and even the Kentucky Fried may have had a hand in it, but it was the sight of those flaming toes that set us off—the toad emerging from the loaf in *Virgin Spring*, lipstick smeared on a child: she was already tainted. We were on her like Bergman's deranged brothers—see no evil, hear none, speak none—panting, wheezing, tearing at her clothes, grabbing for flesh. We were bad characters, and we were scared and hot and three steps over the line—anything could have happened.

It didn't.

Before we could pin her to the hood of the car, our eyes masked with lust and greed and the purest primal badness, a pair of headlights swung into the lot. There we were, dirty, bloody, guilty, dissociated from humanity and civilization, the first of the Ur-crimes behind us, the second in progress, shreds of nylon panty and spandex brassiere dangling from our fingers, our flies open, lips licked—there we were, caught in the spotlight. Nailed.

We bolted. First for the car, and then, realizing we had no way of starting it, for the woods. I thought nothing. I thought escape. The headlights came at me like accusing fingers. I was gone.

Ram-bam-bam, across the parking lot, past the chopper and into the feculent undergrowth at the lake's edge, insects flying up in my face, weeds whipping, frogs and snakes and red-eyed turtles splashing off into the night: I was already ankle-deep in muck and tepid water and still going strong. Behind me, the girl's screams rose in intensity, disconsolate, incriminating, the screams of the Sabine women, the Christian martyrs, Anne Frank dragged from the garret. I kept going, pursued by those cries, imagining cops and bloodhounds. The water was up to my knees when I realized what I was doing: I was going to swim for it. Swim the breadth of Greasy Lake and hide myself in the thick clot of woods on the far side. They'd never find me there.

I was breathing in sobs, in gasps. The water lapped at my waist as I looked out over the moon-burnished ripples, the mats of algae that clung to the surface like scabs. Digby and Jeff had vanished. I paused. Listened. The girl was quieter now, screams tapering to sobs, but there were male voices, angry, excited, and the high-pitched ticking of the second car's engine. I waded deeper, stealthy, hunted, the ooze sucking at my sneakers. As I was about to take the plunge—at the very instant I dropped my shoulder for the first slashing stroke—I blundered into something. Something unspeakable, obscene, something soft, wet, moss-grown. A patch of weed? A log? When I reached out to touch it, it gave like a rubber duck, it gave like flesh.

In one of those nasty little epiphanies for which we are prepared by films and TV and childhood visits to the funeral home to ponder the shrunken painted forms of dead grandparents, I understood what it was that bobbed there so inadmissibly in the dark. Understood, and stumbled back in horror and revulsion, my mind yanked in six different directions (I was nineteen, a mere child, an infant, and here in the space of five minutes I'd struck down one greasy character and blundered into the waterlogged carcass of a second), thinking, The keys, the keys, why did I have to go and lose the keys? I stumbled back, but the muck took hold of my feet—a sneaker snagged, balance lost—and suddenly I was pitching face forward into the buoyant black mass, throwing out my hands in desperation while simultaneously conjuring the image of reeking frogs and muskrats revolving in slicks of their own deliquescing juices. AAAAArrrgh! I shot from the water like a torpedo, the dead man rotating to expose a mossy beard and eyes cold as the moon. I must have shouted out, thrashing around in the weeds, because the voices behind me suddenly became animated.

'What was that?'

'It's them, it's them: they tried to ... *rape* me!' Sobs.

A man's voice, flat Midwestern accent. 'You sons a bitches, we'll kill you!'

Frogs, crickets.

Then another voice, harsh, r-less, Lower East Side: 'Motherfucker!' I recognized the verbal virtuosity of the bad greasy character in the engineer boots. Tooth chipped, sneakers gone, coated in mud and slime and worse, crouching breathless in the weeds waiting to have my ass thoroughly and definitively kicked and fresh from the hideous stinking embrace of a three-days-dead-corpse, I suddenly felt a rush of joy and vindication: the son of a bitch was alive! Just as quickly, my bowels turned to ice. 'Come on out of there, you pansy motherfuckers!' the bad greasy character was screaming. He shouted curses till he was out of breath.

The crickets started up again, then the frogs. I held my breath. All at once there was a sound in the reeds, a swishing, a splash: thunk-a-thunk. They were throwing rocks. The frogs fell silent. I cradled my head. Swish, swish, thunk-a-thunk. A wedge of feldspar the size of a

560

cue ball glanced off my knee. I bit my finger.

It was then that they turned to the car. I heard a door slam, a curse, and then the sound of the headlights shattering—almost a good-natured sound, celebratory, like corks popping from the necks of bottles. This was succeeded by the dull booming of the fenders, metal on metal, and then the icy crash of the windshield. I inched forward, elbows and knees, my belly pressed to the muck, thinking of guerrillas and commandos and *The Naked and the Dead*. I parted the weeds and squinted the length of the parking lot.

The second car—it was a Trans-Am—was still running, its high beams washing the scene in a lurid stagy light. Tire iron flailing, the greasy bad character was laying into the side of my mother's Bel Air like an avenging demon, his shadow riding up the trunks of the trees. Whomp. Whomp. Whomp-whomp. The other two guys—blond types, in fraternity jackets—were helping out with tree branches and skull-sized boulders. One of them was gathering up bottles, rocks, muck, candy wrappers, used condoms, poptops, and other refuse and pitching it through the window on the driver's side. I could see the fox, a white bulb behind the windshield of the '57 Chevy. 'Bobbie,' she whined over the thumping, 'come *on*.' The greasy character paused a moment, took one good swipe at the left taillight, and then heaved the tire iron halfway across the lake. Then he fired up the '57 and was gone.

Blond head nodded at blond head. One said something to the other, too low for me to catch. They were no doubt thinking that in helping to annihilate my mother's car they'd committed a fairly rash act, and thinking too that there were three bad characters connected with that very car watching them from the woods. Perhaps other possibilities occurred to them as well—police, jail cells, justices of the peace, reparations, lawyers, irate parents, fraternal censure. Whatever they were thinking, they suddenly dropped branches, bottles, and rocks and sprang for their car in unison, as if they'd choreographed it. Five seconds. That's all it took. The engine shrieked, the tires squealed, a cloud of dust rose from the rutted lot and then settled back on darkness.

I don't know how long I lay there, the bad breath of decay all around me, my jacket heavy as a bear, the primordial ooze subtly reconstituting itself to accommodate my upper thighs and testicles. My jaws ached, my knee throbbed, my coccyx was on fire. I contemplated suicide, wondered if I'd need bridgework, scraped the recesses of my brain for some sort of excuse to give my parents—a tree had fallen on the car, I was blindsided by a bread truck, hit and run, vandals had got to it while we were playing chess at Digby's. Then I thought of the dead man. He was probably the only person on the planet worse off than I was. I thought about him, fog on the lake, insects chirring eerily, and felt the tug of fear, felt the darkness opening up inside me like a set of jaws. Who was he, I wondered, this victim of time and circumstance bobbing sorrowfully in the lake at my back. The owner of the chopper, no doubt, a bad older character come to this. Shot during a murky drug deal, drowned while drunkenly frolicking in the lake. Another headline. My car was wrecked; he was dead.

When the eastern half of the sky went from black to cobalt and the trees began to separate themselves from the shadows, I pushed myself up from the mud and stepped out into the open. By now the birds had begun to take over for the crickets, and dew lay slick on the leaves. There was a smell in the air, raw and sweet at the same time, the smell of the sun firing buds and opening blossoms. I contemplated the car. It lay there like a wreck along the highway, like a steel sculpture left over from a vanished civilization. Everything was still. This was nature.

I was circling the car, as dazed and bedraggled as the sole survivor of an air blitz, when Digby and Jeff emerged from the trees behind me. Digby's face was crosshatched with smears of dirt; Jeff's jacket was gone and his shirt was torn across the shoulder. They slouched across the lot, looking sheepish, and silently came up beside me to gape at the ravaged automobile. No one said a word. After a while Jeff swung open the driver's door and began to scoop the broken glass and garbage off the seat. I looked at Digby. He shrugged. 'At least they didn't slash the tires,' he said.

It was true: the tires were intact. There was no windshield, the headlights were staved in, and the body looked as if it had been sledge-hammered for a quarter a shot at the countyfair, but the tires were inflated to regulation pressure. The car was drivable. In silence, all three of us bent to scrape the mud and shattered glass from the interior. I said nothing about the biker. When we were finished, I reached in my pocket for the keys, experienced a nasty stab of recollection, cursed myself, and turned to search the grass. I spotted them almost immediately, no more than five feet from the open door, glinting like jewels in the first tapering shaft of sunlight. There was no reason to get philosophical about it: I eased into the seat and turned the engine over.

It was at that precise moment that the silver Mustang with the flame decals rumbled into the lot. All three of us froze; then Digby and Jeff slid into the car and slammed the door. We watched as the Mustang rocked and bobbed across the ruts and finally jerked to a halt beside the forlorn chopper at the far end of the lot. 'Let's go,' Digby said. I hesitated, the Bel Air wheezing beneath me.

Two girls emerged from the Mustang. Tight jeans, stiletto heels, hair like frozen fur. They bent over the motorcycle, paced back and forth aimlessly, glanced once or twice at us, and then ambled over to where the reeds sprang up in a green fence around the perimeter of the lake. One of them cupped her hands to her mouth. 'Al,' she called. 'Hey, Al!'

'Come on,' Digby hissed. 'Let's get out of here.'

But it was too late. The second girl was picking her way across the lot, unsteady on her heels, looking up at us and then away. She was older—twenty-five or -six—and as she came closer we could see there was something wrong with her: she was stoned or drunk, lurching now and waving her arms for balance. I gripped the steering wheel as if it were the ejection lever of a flaming jet, and Digby spat out my name, twice, terse and impatient.

'Hi,' the girl said.

We looked at her like zombies, like war veterans, like deaf-and-dumb pencil peddlers.

She smiled, her lips cracked and dry. 'Listen,' she said, bending from the waist to look in the window, 'you guys seen Al?' Her pupils were pinpoints, her eyes glass. She jerked her neck. 'That's his bike over there—Al's. You seen him?'

Al. I didn't know what to say. I wanted to get out of the car and retch. I wanted to go home to my parents' house and crawl into bed. Digby poked me in the ribs. 'We haven't seen anybody,' I said.

The girl seemed to consider this, reaching out a slim veiny arm to brace herself against the car. 'No matter,' she said, slurring the T's, 'he'll turn up.' And then, as if she'd just taken stock of the whole scene—the ravaged car and our battered faces, the desolation of the place—she said: 'Hey, you guys look like some pretty bad characters—been fightin', huh?' We stared straight ahead, rigid as catatonics. She was fumbling in her pocket and muttering something. Finally she held out a handful of tablets in glassine wrappers: 'Hey, you want to party, you want to do some of these with me and Sarah?'

I just looked at her. I thought I was going to cry. Digby broke the silence. 'No thanks,' he said, leaning over me. 'Some other time.'

I put the car in gear and it inched forward with a groan, shaking off pellets of glass like an old dog shedding water after a bath, heaving over the ruts on its worn springs, creeping toward the highway. There was a sheen of sun on the lake. I looked back. The girl was still standing there, watching us, her shoulder slumped, hand outstretched.

1985

THE RICH BROTHER

Tobias Wolff

T here were two brothers, Pete and Donald.

Pete, the older brother, was in real estate. He and his wife had a Century 21 franchise in Santa Cruz. Pete worked hard and made a lot of money, but not any more than he thought he deserved. He had two daughters, a sailboat, a house from which he could see a thin slice of the ocean, and friends doing well enough in their own lives not to wish bad luck on him. Donald, the younger brother, was still single. He lived alone, painted houses when he found the work and got deeper in debt to Pete when he didn't.

No one would have taken them for brothers. Where Pete was stout and hearty and at home in the world, Donald was bony, grave, and obsessed with the fate of his soul. Over the years Donald had worn the images of two different Perfect Masters around his neck. Out of devotion to the second of these he entered an ashram in Berkeley, where he nearly died of undiagnosed hepatitis. By the time Pete ;finished paying the medical bills Donald had become a Christian. He drifted from church to church, then joined a pentecostal community that met somewhere in the Mission District to sing in tongues and swap prophecies.

Pete couldn't make sense of it. Their parents were both dead, but while they were alive neither of them had found it necessary to believe in anything. They managed to be decent people without making fools of themselves, and Pete had the same ambition. He thought that the whole thing was an excuse for Donald to take himself seriously.

The trouble was that Donald couldn't content himself with worrying about his own soul. He had to worry about everyone else's, and especially Pete's. He handed down his judgments in ways that he seemed to consider subtle: through significant silence, innuendo, looks of mild despair that said, *Brother, what have you come to?* What Pete had come to, as far as he could tell, was prosperity and Donald did not prosper.

At the age of forty Pete took up sky diving. He made his first jump with two friends who'd started only a few months earlier and were already doing stunts. They were both coked to the gills when they jumped but Pete wanted to do it straight, at least the first time, and he was glad that he did. He would never have used the word *mystical*, but that was how Pete felt about the experience. Later he made the mistake of trying to describe it to Donald, who kept asking how much it cost and then acted appalled when Pete told him.

'At least I'm trying something new,' Pete said. 'At least I'm breaking the pattern.'

Not long after that conversation Donald also broke the pattern, by going to live on a farm outside of Paso Robles. The farm was owned by several members of Donald's community, who had bought it and moved there with the idea of forming a family of faith. That was how Donald explained it in the first letter he sent. Every week Pete heard how happy Donald was, how 'in the Lord.' He told Pete he was praying for him, he and the rest of Pete's brothers and sisters on the farm.

'I only have one brother,' Pete wanted to answer, 'and that's enough.' But he kept this thought to himself.

In November the letters stopped. Pete didn't worry about this at first, but when he called Donald at Thanksgiving Donald was grim. He tried to sound upbeat but he didn't try hard enough to make it convincing. 'Now listen,' Pete said, 'you don't have to stay in that place if you don't want to.'

'I'll be all right,' Donald answered.

'That's not the point. Being all right is not the point. If you don't like what's going on up there, then get out.'

'I'm all right,' Donald said again, more firmly. 'I'm doing fine.'

But he called Pete a week later and said that he was quitting the farm. When Pete asked him where he intended to go, Donald admitted that he had no plan. His car had been repossessed just before he left the city, and he was flat broke.

'I guess you'll have to stay with us,' Pete said.

Donald put up a show of resistance. Then he gave in. 'Just until I get my feet on the ground,' he said.

'Right,' Pete said. 'Check out your options.' He told Donald he'd send him money for a bus ticket, but as they were about to hang up Pete changed his mind. He knew that Donald would try hitchhiking to save the fare. Pete didn't want him out on the road all alone where some head case could pick him up, where anything could happen to him.

'Better yet, he said, 'I'll come and get you.'

'You don't have to do that. I didn't expect you to do that,' Donald said. He added, 'It's a pretty long drive.'

'Just tell me how to get there.'

But Donald wouldn't give him directions. He said that the farm was too depressing, that Pete wouldn't like it. Instead, he insisted on meeting Pete at a service station called Jonathan's Mechanical Emporium.

'You must be kidding,' Pete said.

'It's close to the highway,' Donald said. 'I didn't name it.'

'That's one for the collection,' Pete said.

The day before he left to bring Donald home, Pete received a letter from a man who described himself as 'head of household' at the farm where Donald had been living. From this letter Pete learned that Donald had not quit the farm, but had been asked to leave. The letter was written on the back of a mimeographed survey form asking people to record their response to a ceremony of some kind. The last question said:

What did you feel during the liturgy?
a) *Being*
b) *Becoming*
c) *Being and Becoming*
d) *None of the Above*
e) *All of the Above*

Pete tried to forget the letter. But of course he couldn't. Each time he thought of it he felt crowded and breathless, a feeling that came over him again when he drove into the service station and saw Donald sitting against a wall with his head on his knees. It was late afternoon. A paper cup tumbled slowly past Donald's feet, pushed by the damp wind.

Pete honked and Donald raised his head. He smiled at Pete, then stood and stretched. His arms were long and thin and white. He wore a red bandanna across his forehead, a T-shirt with a couple of words on the front. Pete couldn't read them because the letters were inverted.

'Grow up,' Pete yelled. 'Get a Mercedes.'

Donald came up to the window. He bent down and said, 'Thanks for coming. You must be totally whipped.'

'I'll make it.' Pete pointed at Donald's T-shirt. 'What's that supposed to say?'

Donald looked down at his shirt front. 'Try God. I guess I put it on backwards. Pete, could I borrow a couple of dollars? I owe these people for coffee and sandwiches.'

Pete took five twenties from his wallet and held them out the window.

Donald stepped back as if horrified. 'I don't need that much.'

'I can't keep track of all these nickels and dimes,' Pete said. 'Just pay me back when your ship comes in.' He waved the bills impatiently. 'Go on—take it.'

'Only for now.' Donald took the money and went into the service station office. He came out carrying two orange sodas, one of which he gave to Pete as he got into the car. 'My treat,' he said.

'No bags?'

'Wow, thanks for reminding me,' Donald said. He balanced his drink on the dashboard, but the slight rocking of the car as he got out tipped it onto the passenger's seat, where half its contents foamed over before Pete could snatch it up again. Donald looked on while Pete held the bottle out the window, soda running down his fingers.

'Wipe it up,' Pete told him. 'Quick!'

'With what?'

Pete stared at Donald. 'That shirt. Use the shirt.'

Donald pulled a long face but did as he was told, his pale skin puckering against the wind.

'Great, just great,' Pete said. 'We haven't even left the gas station yet.'

Afterwards on the highway, Donald said, 'This is a new car, isn't it?'

'Yes. This is a new car.'

'Is that why you're so upset about the seat?'

'Forget it, OK? Let's just forget about it.'

'I said I was sorry.'

Pete said, 'I just wish you'd be more careful. These seats are made of leather. That stain won't come out, not to mention the smell. I don't see why I can't have leather seats that smell like leather instead of orange pop.'

'What was wrong with the other car?'

Pete glanced over at Donald. Donald had raised the hood of the blue sweatshirt he'd put on. The peaked hood above his gaunt, watchful face gave him the look of an inquisitor.

'There wasn't anything wrong with it,' Pete said. 'I just happened to like this one better.'

Donald nodded.

There was a long silence between them as Pete drove on and the day darkened toward evening. On either side of the road lay stubble-covered fields. A line of low hills ran along the horizon, topped here and there with trees black against the grey sky. In the approaching line of cars a driver turned on his headlights. Pete did the same.

'So what happened? he asked. 'Farm life not your bag?'

Donald took some time to answer, and at last he said, simply, 'It was my fault.'

'What was your fault?'

'The whole thing. Don't play dumb, Pete. I know they wrote to you.' Donald looked at Pete, then stared out the windshield again.

'I'm not playing dumb.'

Donald shrugged.

'All I really know is they asked you to leave,' Pete went on. 'I don't know any of the particulars.'

'I blew it,' Donald said. 'Believe me, you don't want to hear the gory details.'

'Sure I do,' Pete said. He added, 'Everybody likes the gory details.'

'You mean everybody likes to hear how someone messed up.'

'Right,' Pete said. 'That's the way it is here on Spaceship Earth.'

Donald bent one knee onto the front seat and leaned against the door so that he was facing Pete instead of the windshield. Pete was aware of Donald's scrutiny. He waited. Night was coming on in a rush now, filling the hollows of the land. Donald's long cheeks and deep-set eyes were dark with shadow. His brow was white. 'Do you ever dream about me?' Donald asked.

'Do I ever dream about you? What kind of a question is that? Of course I don't dream about you,' Pete said, untruthfully.

'What do you dream about?'

'Sex and money. Mostly money. A nightmare is when I dream I don't have any.'

'You're just making that up,' Donald said.

Pete smiled.

'Sometimes I wake up at night,' Donald went on, 'and I can tell you're dreaming about me.'

'We were talking about the farm,' Pete said. 'Let's finish that conversation and then we can talk about our various out-of-body experiences and the interesting things we did during previous incarnations.'

For a moment Donald looked like a grinning skull; then he turned serious again. 'There's not that much to tell,' he said. 'I just didn't do anything right.'

'That's a little vague,' Pete said.

'Well, like the groceries. Whenever it was my turn to get the groceries I'd blow it somehow. I'd bring the groceries home and half of them would be missing, or I'd have all the wrong things, the wrong kind of flour or the wrong kind of chocolate or whatever. One time I gave them away. It's not funny, Pete.'

Pete said, 'Who did you give the groceries to?'

'Just some people I picked up on the way home. Some fieldworkers. They had about eight kids with them and they didn't even speak English—just nodded their heads. Still, I shouldn't have given away the groceries. Not all of them, anyway. I really learned my lesson about that. You have to be practical. You have to be fair to yourself.' Donald leaned forward, and Pete could sense his excitement. 'There's nothing actually wrong with being in business,' he said. 'As long as you're fair to other people you can still be fair to yourself. I'm thinking of going into business, Pete.'

'We'll talk about it,' Pete said. 'So, that's the story? There isn't any more to it than that?'

'What did they tell you?' Donald asked.

'Nothing.'

'They must have told you something.'

Pete shook his head.

'They didn't tell you about the fire?' When Pete shook his head again Donald regarded him for a time, then said, 'I don't know. It was stupid. I just completely lost it.' He folded his arms across his chest and slumped back into the corner. 'Everybody had to take turns cooking dinner. I usually did tuna casserole or spaghetti with garlic bread. But this one night I thought I'd do something different, something really interesting.' Donald looked sharply at Pete. 'It's all a big laugh to you, isn't it?'

'I'm sorry,' Pete said.

'You don't know when to quit. You just keep hitting away.'

'Tell me about the fire, Donald.'

Donald kept watching him. 'You have this compulsion to make me look foolish.'

'Come off it, Donald. Don't make a big thing out of this.'

'I know why you do it. It's because you don't have any purpose in life. You're afraid to relate to people who do, so you make fun of them.'

'Relate,' Pete said softly.

'You're basically a very frightened individual,' Donald said. 'Very threatened. You've always been like that. Do you remember when you used to try to kill me?'

'I don't have any compulsion to make you look foolish, Donald— you do it yourself. You're doing it right now.'

'You can't tell me you don't remember,' Donald said. 'It was after my operation. You remember that.'

'Sort of.' Pete shrugged. 'Not really.'

'Oh yes,' Donald said. 'Do you want to see the scar?'

'I remember you had an operation. I don't remember the specifics, that's all. And I sure as hell don't remember trying to kill you.'

'Oh yes,' Donald repeated, maddeningly. 'You bet your life you did. All the time. The thing was, I couldn't have anything happen to me where they sewed me up because then my intestines would come apart again and poison me. That was a big issue, Pete. Mom was always in a state about me climbing trees and so on. And you used to hit me there every chance you got.'

'Mom was in a state every time you burped,' Pete said. 'I don't know. Maybe I bumped into you accidentally once or twice. I never did it deliberately.'

'Every chance you got,' Donald said. 'Like when the folks went out at night and left you to baby-sit. I'd hear them say good night, and then I'd hear the car start up, and when they were gone I'd lie there and listen. After a while I would hear you coming down the hall, and I would close my eyes and pretend to be asleep. There were nights when you would stand outside the door, just stand there, and then go away again. But most nights you'd open the door and I would hear you in the room with me, breathing. You'd come over and sit next to me on the bed—you remember, Pete, you have to—you'd sit next to me on the bed and pull the sheets back. If I was on my stomach you'd roll me over. Then you would lift up my pajama shirt and start hitting me on my stitches. You'd hit me as hard as you

571

could, over and over. And I would just keep lying there with my eyes closed. I was afraid that you'd get mad if you knew I was awake. Is that strange or what? I was afraid that you'd get mad if you found out that I knew you were trying to kill me.' Donald laughed. 'Come on, you can't tell me you don't remember that.'

'It might have happened once or twice. Kids do those things. I can't get all excited about something I maybe did twenty-five years ago.'

'No maybe about it. You did it.'

Pete said, 'You're wearing me out with this stuff. We've got a long drive ahead of us and if you don't back off pretty soon we aren't going to make it. You aren't, anyway.'

Donald turned way.

'I'm doing my best,' Pete said. The self-pity in his own voice made the words sound like a lie. But they weren't a lie! He was doing his best.

The car topped a rise. In the distance Pete saw a cluster of lights that blinked out when he started downhill. There was no moon. The sky was low and black.

'Come to think of it,' Pete said, 'I did have a dream about you the other night.' Then he added, impatiently, as if Donald were badgering him, 'A couple of other nights too. I'm getting hungry,' he said.

'The same dream?'

'Different dreams. I only remember one of them well. There was something wrong with me, and you were helping out. Taking care of me. Just the two of us. I don't know where everyone else was supposed to be.'

Pete left it at that. He didn't tell Donald that in this dream he was blind.

'I wonder if that was when I woke up,' Donald said. He added, 'I'm sorry I got into that thing about my scar. I keep trying to forget it but I guess I never will. Not really. It was pretty strange, having someone around all the time who wanted to get rid of me.'

'Kid stuff,' Pete said. 'Ancient history.'

They ate dinner at Denny's on the other side of King City. As Pete was paying the check he heard a man behind him say, 'Excuse me, but I wonder if I might ask which way you're going?' and Donald answer, 'Santa Cruz.'

'Perfect,' the man said.

Pete could see him in the fish-eye mirror above the cash register: a red blazer with some kind of crest on the pocket, little black moustache, glossy black hair combed down on his forehead like a Roman emperor's. A rug, Pete thought. Definitely a rug.

Pete got his change and turned. 'Why is that perfect?' he asked.

The man looked at Pete. He had a soft ruddy face that was doing its best to express pleasant surprise, as if this new wrinkle were all he could have wished for, but the eyes behind the aviator glasses showed signs of regret. His lips were moist and shiny. 'I take it you're together,' he said.

'You got it,' Pete told him.

'All the better, then,' the man went on. 'It so happens I'm going to Santa Cruz myself. Had a spot of car trouble down the road. The old Caddy let me down.'

'What kind of trouble?' Pete asked.

'Engine trouble,' the man said. 'I'm afraid it's a bit urgent. My daughter is sick. Urgently sick. I've got a telegram here.' He patted the breast pocket of his blazer.

Pete grinned. Amazing, he thought, the old sick daughter ploy, but before he could say anything Donald got into the act again. 'No problem,' Donald said, 'We've got tons of room.'

'Not that much room,' Pete said.

Donald nodded. 'I'll put my things in the trunk.'

'The trunk's full,' Pete told him.

'It so happens I'm traveling light,' the man said. 'This leg of the trip anyway. In fact I don't have any luggage at this particular time.'

Pete said, 'Left it in the old Caddy, did you?'

'Exactly,' the man said.

'No problem,' Donald repeated. He walked outside and the man went with him. Together they strolled across the parking lot, Pete following at a distance. When they reached Pete's car Donald raised his face to the sky, and the man did the same. They stood there looking up. 'Dark night,' Donald said.

'Stygian,' the man said.

Pete still had it in mind to brush him off, but he didn't do that. Instead he unlocked the door for him. He wanted to see what would happen. It was an adventure, but not a dangerous adventure. The man might steal Pete's ashtrays but he wouldn't kill him. If Pete got killed on the road it would be by some spiritual person in a sweatsuit, someone with his eyes on the far horizon and a wet Try

God T-shirt in his duffel bag.

As soon as they left the parking lot the man lit a cigar. He blew a cloud of smoke over Pete's shoulder and sighed with pleasure. 'Put it out,' Pete told him.

'Of course,' the man said. Pete looked into the rear-view mirror and saw the man take another long puff before dropping the cigar out the window. 'Forgive me,' he said. 'I should have asked. Name's Webster, by the way.'

Donald turned and looked back at him. 'First name or last.'

The man hesitated. 'Last,' he said finally.

'I know a Webster,' Donald said. 'Mick Webster.'

'There are many of us,' Webster said.

'Big fellow, wooden leg,' Pete said.

Donald gave Pete a look.

Webster shook his head. 'Doesn't ring a bell. Still, I wouldn't deny the connection. Might be one of the cousinry.'

'What's your daughter got?' Pete asked.

'That isn't clear,' Webster answered. 'It appears to be a female complaint of some nature. Then again it may be tropical.' He was quiet for a moment, and added: 'If indeed it *is* tropical, I will have to assume some of the blame myself. It was my own vaulting ambition that first led us to the tropics and kept us in the tropics all those many years, exposed to every evil. Truly I have much to answer for. I left my wife there.'

Donald said quietly, 'You mean she died?'

'I buried her with these hands. The earth will be repaid, gold for gold.'

'Which tropics?' Pete asked.

'The tropics of Peru.'

'What part of Peru are they in?'

'The lowlands,' Webster said.

Pete nodded. 'What's it like down there?'

'Another world,' Webster said. His tone was sepulchral. 'A world far better imagined than described.'

'Far out,' Pete said.

The three men rode in silence for a time. A line of trucks went past in the other direction, trailers festooned with running lights, engines roaring.

'Yes,' Webster said at last, 'I have much to answer for.'

Pete smiled at Donald, but Donald had turned in his seat again and was gazing at Webster. 'I'm sorry about your wife,' Donald said.

'What did she die of?' Pete asked.

'A wasting illness,' Webster said. 'The doctors have no name for it, but I do.' He leaned forward and said, fiercely, '*Greed*.' Then he slumped back against his seat. 'My greed, not hers. She wanted no part of it.'

Pete bit his lip. Webster was a find and Pete didn't want to scare him off by hooting at him. In a voice low and innocent of knowingness, he asked, 'What took you there?'

'It's difficult for me to talk about.'

'Try,' Pete told him.

'A cigar would make it easier.'

Donald turned to Pete and said, 'It's OK with me.'

'All right,' Pete said. 'Go ahead. Just keep the window rolled down.'

'Much obliged.' A match flared. There were eager sucking sounds.

'Let's hear it,' Pete said.

'I am by training an engineer,' Webster began. 'My work has exposed me to all but one of the continents, to desert and alp and forest, to every terrain and season of the earth. Some years ago I was hired by the Peruvian government to search for tungsten in the tropics. My wife and daughter accompanied me. We were the only white people for a thousand miles in any direction, and we had no choice but to live as the Indians lived—to share their food and drink and even their culture.'

Pete said, 'You knew the lingo, did you?'

'We picked it up.' The ember of the cigar bobbed up and down. 'We were used to learning as necessity decreed. At any rate, it became evident after a couple of years that there was no tungsten to be found. My wife had fallen ill and was pleading to be taken home. But I was deaf to her pleas, because by then I was on the trail of another metal—a metal far more valuable than tungsten.'

'Let me guess,' Pete said. 'Gold?'

Donald looked at Pete, then back at Webster.

'Gold,' Webster said. 'A vein of gold greater than the Mother Lode itself. After I found the first traces of it nothing could tear me away from my search—not the sickness of my wife nor anything else. I was determined to uncover the vein, and so I did—but not before I laid my wife to rest. As I say, the earth will be repaid.'

Webster was quiet. Then he said, 'But life must go on. In the years since my wife's death I have been making the arrangements necessary to open the mine. I could have done it immediately, of course, enriching myself beyond measure, but I knew what that would mean—the exploitation of our beloved Indians, the brutal destruction of their environment. I felt I had too much to atone for already.' Webster paused, and when he spoke again his voice was dull and rushed, as if he had used up all the interest he had in his own words. 'Instead I drew up a program for returning the bulk of the wealth to the Indians themselves. A kind of trust fund. The interest alone will allow them to secure their ancient lands and rights in perpetuity. At the same time, our investors will be rewarded a thousandfold. Two-thousandfold. Everyone will prosper together.'

'That's great,' Donald said. 'That's the way it ought to be.'

Pete said, 'I'm willing to bet that you just happen to have a few shares left. Am I right?'

Webster made no reply.

'Well?' Pete knew that Webster was on to him now, but he didn't care. The story had bored him. He'd expected something different, something original, and Webster had let him down. He hadn't even tried. Pete felt sour and stale. His eyes burned from cigar smoke and the high beams of road-hogging truckers. 'Douse the stogie,' he said to Webster. 'I told you to keep the window down.'

'Got a little nippy back here.'

Donald said, 'Hey, Pete. Lighten up.'

'Douse it!'

Webster sighed. He got rid of the cigar.

'I'm a wreck,' Pete said to Donald. 'You want to drive for a while?'

Donald nodded.

Pete pulled over and they changed places.

Webster kept his counsel in the back seat. Donald hummed while he drove, until Pete told him to stop. Then everything was quiet.

Donald was humming again when Pete woke up. Pete stared sullenly at the road, at the white lines sliding past the car. After a few moments of this he turned and said, 'How long have I been out?'

Donald glanced at him. 'Twenty, twenty-five minutes.'

Pete looked behind him and saw that Webster was gone. 'Where's our friend?'

'You just missed him. He got out in Soledad. He told me to say thanks and good-bye.'

'Soledad? What about his sick daughter? How did he explain her away?' Pete leaned over the seat. Both ashtrays were still in place. Floor mats. Door handles.

'He has a brother living there. He's going to borrow a car from him and drive the rest of the way in the morning.'

'I'll bet his brother's living there,' Pete said. 'Doing fifty concurrent life sentences. His brother and his sister and his mom and his dad.'

'I kind of liked him,' Donald said.

'I'm sure you did,' Pete said wearily.

'He was interesting. He'd been places.'

'His cigars had been places, I'll give you that.'

'Come on, Pete.'

'Come on yourself. What a phony.'

'You don't know that.'

'Sure I do.'

'How? How do you know?'

Pete stretched. 'Brother, there are some things you're just born knowing. What's the gas situation?'

'We're a little low.'

'Then why didn't you get some more?'

'I wish you wouldn't snap at me like that,' Donald said.

'Then why don't you use your head? What if we run out?'

'We'll make it,' Donald said. 'I'm pretty sure we've got enough to make it. You didn't have to be so rude to him,' Donald added.

Pete took a deep breath. 'I don't feel like running out of gas tonight, OK?'

Donald pulled in at the next station they came to and filled the tank while Pete went to the men's room. When Pete came back, Donald was sitting in the passenger's seat. The attendant came up to the driver's window as Pete got in behind the wheel. He bent down and said, 'Twelve fifty-five.'

'You heard the man,' Pete said to Donald.

Donald looked straight ahead. He didn't move.

'Cough up,' Pete said. 'This trip's on you.'

Donald said, softly, 'I can't.'

'Sure you can. Break out that wad.'

Donald glanced up at the attendant, then at Pete. 'Please,' he said. 'Pete, I don't have it anymore.'

Pete took this in. He nodded, and paid the attendant.

Donald began to speak when they left the station but Pete cut him

577

off. He said, 'I don't want to hear from you right now. You just keep quiet or I swear to God I won't be responsible.'

They left the fields and entered a tunnel of tall trees. The trees went on and on. 'Let me get this straight,' Pete said at last. 'You don't have the money I gave you.'

'You treated him like a bug or something,' Donald said.

'You don't have the money,' Pete said again.

Donald shook his head.

'Since I bought dinner, and since we didn't stop anywhere in between, I assume you gave it to Webster. Is that right? Is that what you did with it?'

'Yes.'

Pete looked at Donald. His face was dark under the hood but he still managed to convey a sense of remove, as if none of this had anything to do with him.

'Why?' Pete asked. 'Why did you give it to him?' When Donald didn't answer, Pete said, 'A hundred dollars. Gone. Just like that. I *worked* for that money, Donald.'

'I know, I know,' Donald said.

'You don't know! How could you? You get money by holding out your hand.'

'I work too,' Donald said.

'You work too. Don't kid yourself, brother.'

Donald leaned toward Pete, about to say something, but Pete cut him off again.

'You're not the only one on the payroll, Donald. I don't think you understand that. I have a family.'

'Pete, I'll pay you back.'

'Like hell you will. A hundred dollars!' Pete hit the steering wheel with the palm of his hand. 'Just because you think I hurt some goofball's feelings. Jesus, Donald.'

'That's not the reason,' Donald said. 'And I didn't just *give* him the money.'

'What do you call it, then? What do you call what you did?'

'I *invested* it. I wanted a share, Pete.' When Pete looked over at him Donald nodded and said again, 'I wanted a share.'

Pete said 'I take it you're referring to the gold mine in Peru.'

'Yes,' Donald said.

'You believe that such a gold mine exists?'

Donald looked at Pete, and Pete could see him just beginning to catch on. 'You'll believe anything,' Pete said. 'Won't you? You really will believe anything at all.'

'I'm sorry,' Donald said, and turned away.

Pete drove on between the trees and considered the truth of what he had just said—that Donald would believe anything at all. And it came to him that it would be just like this unfair life for Donald to come out ahead in the end, by believing in some outrageous promise that would turn out to be true and that he, Pete, would reject out of hand because he was too wised up to listen to anybody's pitch anymore except for laughs. What a joke. What a joke if there really was a blessing to be had, and the blessing didn't come to the one who deserved it, the one who did all the work, but to the other.

And as if this had already happened Pete felt a shadow move upon him, darkening his thoughts. After a time he said, 'I can see where all this is going, Donald.'

'I'll pay you back,' Donald said.

'No,' Pete said. 'You won't pay me back. You can't. You don't know how. All you've ever done is take. All your life.'

Donald shook his head.

'I see exactly where this is going,' Pete went on. 'You can't work, you can't take care of yourself, you believe anything anyone tells you. I'm stuck with you, aren't I?' He looked over at Donald. 'I've got you on my hands for good.'

Donald pressed his fingers against the dashboard as if to brace himself. 'I'll get out,' he said.

Pete kept driving.

'Let me out,' Donald said. 'I mean it, Pete.'

'Do you?'

Donald hesitated. 'Yes,' he said.

'Be sure,' Pete told him. 'This is it. This is for keeps.'

'I mean it.'

'All right. You made the choice.' Pete braked the car sharply and swung it to the shoulder of the road. He turned off the engine and got out. Trees loomed on both sides, shutting out the sky. The air was cold and musty. Pete took Donald's duffel bag from the back seat and set it down behind the car. He stood there, facing Donald in the red glow of the taillights. 'It's better this way,' Pete said.

Donald just looked at him.

'Better for you,' Pete said.

Donald hugged himself. He was shaking. 'You don't have to say all that,' he told Pete. 'I don't blame you.'

'Blame me? What the hell are you talking about? Blame me for what?'

'For anything,' Donald said.

'I want to know what you mean by blame me.'

'Nothing. Nothing, Pete. You'd better get going. God bless you.'

'That's it,' Pete said. He dropped to one knee, searching the packed dirt with his hands. He didn't know what he was looked for; his hands would know when they found it.

Donald touched Pete's shoulder. 'You'd better go,' he said,

Somewhere in the trees Pete heard a branch snap. He stood up. He looked at Donald, then went back to the car and drove away. He drove fast, hunched over the wheel, conscious of the way he was hunched and the shallowness of his breathing, refusing to look at the mirror above his head until there was nothing behind him but darkness.

Then he said, 'A hundred dollars,' as if there were someone to hear.

The trees gave way to fields. Metal fences ran beside the road, plastered with windblown scraps of paper. Tule fog hung above the ditches, spilling into the road, dimming the ghostly halogen lights that burned in the yards of the farms Pete passed. The fog left beads of water rolling up the windshield.

Pete rummaged among his cassettes. He found Pachelbel's Canon and pushed it into the tape deck. When the violins began to play he leaned back and assumed an attentive expression as if he were really listening to them. He smiled to himself like a man at liberty to enjoy music, a man who has finished his work and settled his debts, done all things meet and due.

And in this way, smiling, nodding to the music, he went another mile or so and pretended that he was not already slowing down, that he was not going to turn back, that he would be able to drive on like this, alone, and have the right answer when his wife stood before him in the doorway of his home and asked, Where is he? Where is your brother?

1985

AMERICAN EXPRESS

James Salter

It's hard now to think of all the places and nights. Nicola's like a railway car, deep and gleaming, the crowd at the *Un, Deux, Trois,* Billy's. Unknown brilliant faces jammed at the bar. The dark, dramatic eye that blazes for a moment and disappears.

In those days they were living in apartments with funny furniture and on Sundays sleeping until noon. They were in the last rank of the armies of law. Clever junior partners were above them, partners, associates, men in fine suits who had lunch at the Four Seasons. Frank's father went there three or four times a week, or else to the Century Club or the Union where there were men even older than he. Half of the members can't urinate, he used to say, and the other half can't stop.

Alan, on the other hand, was from Cleveland where his father was well known, if not detested. No defendant was too guilty, no case too clear-cut. Once in another part of the state he was defending a murderer, a black man. He knew what the jury was thinking, he knew what he looked like to them. He stood up slowly. It could be they had heard certain things, he began. They may have heard, for instance, that he was a big-time lawyer from the city. They may have heard that he wore three-hundred-dollar suits, that he drove a Cadillac and smoked expensive cigars. He was walking along as if looking for something on the floor. They may have heard that he was Jewish.

He stopped and looked up. Well, he was from the city, he said. He wore three-hundred-dollar suits, he drove a Cadillac, smoked big cigars, and he was Jewish. 'Now that we have that settled, let's talk about this case.'

Lawyers and sons of lawyers. Days of youth. In the morning in stale darkness the subways shrieked.

'Have you noticed the new girl at the reception desk?'

'What about her?' Frank asked.

They were surrounded by noise like the launch of a rocket. 'She's hot,' Alan confided.

'How do you know?'
'I know.'
'What do you mean, you know?'
'Intuition.'
'Int*ui*tion?' Frank said.
'What's wrong?'
'That doesn't count.'

Which was what made them inseparable, the hours of work, the lyric, the dreams. As it happened, they never knew the girl at the reception desk with her nearsightedness and wild, full hair. They knew various others, they knew Julie, they knew Catherine, they knew Ames. The best, for nearly two years, was Brenda who had somehow managed to graduate from Marymount and had a walk-through apartment on West Fourth. In a smooth, thin, silver frame was the photograph of her father with his two daughters at the Plaza, Brenda, thirteen, with an odd little smile.

'I wish I'd known you then,' Frank told her.

Brenda said, 'I bet you do.'

It was her voice he liked, the city voice, scornful and warm. They were two of a kind, she liked to say, and in a way it was true. They drank in her favorite places where the owner played the piano and everyone seemed to know her. Still, she counted on him. The city has its incomparable moments—rolling along the wall of the apartment, kissing, bumping like stones. Five in the afternoon, the vanishing light. 'No,' she was commanding. 'No, no, no.'

He was kissing her throat. 'What are you going to do with that beautiful struma of yours?'

'You won't take me to dinner,' she said.

'Sure I will.'

'Beautiful what?'

She was like a huge dog, leaping from his arms.

'Come here,' he coaxed.

She went into the bathroom and began combing her hair. 'Which restaurant are we going to?' she called.

She would give herself but it was mostly unpredictable. She would do anything her mother hadn't done and would live as her mother lived, in the same kind of apartment, in the same soft chairs. Christmas and the envelopes for the doormen, the snow sweeping past the awning, her children coming home from school. She adored her father. She went on a trip to Hawaii with him and sent back postcards, two or three scorching lines in a large, scrawled hand. It was summer.

'Anybody here?' Frank called.

He rapped on the door which was ajar. He was carrying his jacket, it was hot.

'All right,' he said in a loud voice, 'come out with your hands over your head. Alan, cover the back.'

The party, it seemed, was over. He pushed the door open. There was one lamp on, the room was dark.

'Hey, Bren, are we too late?' he called. She appeared mysteriously in the doorway, barelegged but in heels. 'We'd have come earlier but we were working. We couldn't get out of the office. Where is everybody? Where's all the food? Hey, Alan, we're late. There's no food, nothing.'

She was leaning against the doorway.

'We tried to get down here,' Alan said. 'We couldn't get a cab.'

Frank had fallen onto the couch. 'Bren, don't be mad,' he said. 'We were working, that's the truth. I should have called. Can you put some music on or something? Is there anything to drink?'

'There's about that much vodka,' she finally said.

'Any ice?'

'About two cubes.' She pushed off the wall without much enthusiasm. He watched her walk into the kitchen and heard the refrigerator door open.

'So, what do you think, Alan?' he said. 'What are you going to do?'

'Me?'

'Where's Louise?' Frank called.

'Asleep,' Brenda said.

'Did she really go home?'

'She goes to work in the morning.'

'So does Alan.'

Brenda came out of the kitchen with the drinks.

'I'm sorry we're late,' he said. He was looking in the glass. 'Was it a good party?' He stirred the contents with one finger. 'This is the ice?'

'Jane Harrah got fired,' Brenda said.

'That's too bad. Who is she?'

'She does big campaigns. Ross wants me to take her place.'

'Great.'

'I'm not sure if I want to,' she said lazily.

'Why not?'

'She was sleeping with him.'

'And she got fired?'

'Doesn't say much for him, does it?'

'It doesn't say much for her.'

'That's just like a man. God.'

'What does she look like? Does she look like Louise?'

The smile of the thirteen-year-old came across Brenda's face. 'No one looks like Louise,' she said. Her voice squeezed the name whose legs Alan dreamed of. 'Jane has these thin lips.'

'Is that all?'

'Thin-lipped women are always cold.'

'Let me see yours,' he said.

'Burn up.'

'Yours aren't thin. Alan, these aren't thin, are they? Hey, Brenda, don't cover them up.'

'Where were you? You weren't really working.'

He'd pulled down her hand. 'Come on, let them be natural,' he said. 'They're not thin, they're nice. I just never noticed them before.' He leaned back. 'Alan, how're you doing? You getting sleepy?'

'I was thinking. How much the city has changed,' Alan said.

'In five years?'

'I've been here almost six years.'

'Sure, it's changing. They're coming down, we're going up.'

Alan was thinking of the vanished Louise who had left him only a jolting ride home through the endless streets. 'I know.'

That year they sat in the steam room on limp towels, breathing the eucalyptus and talking about Hardmann Roe. They walked to the showers like champions. Their flesh still had firmness. Their haunches were solid and young.

Hardmann Roe was a small drug company in Connecticut that had strayed slightly outside of its field and found itself suing a large manufacturer for infringement of an obscure patent. The case was highly technical with little chance of success. The opposing lawyers had thrown up a barricade of motions and delays and the case had made its way downwards, to Frik and Frak whose offices were near the copying machines, who had time for such things, and who pondered it amid the hiss of steam. No one else wanted it and this also made it appealing.

So they worked. They were students again, sitting around in polo shirts with their feet on the desk, throwing off hopeless ideas, crumpling wads of paper, staying late in the library and having the words blur in books.

They stayed on through vacations and weekends sometimes sleeping in the office and making coffee long before anyone came to work. After a late dinner they were still talking about it, its complexities, where elements somehow fit in, the sequence of letters, articles in journals, meetings, the limits of meaning. Brenda met a handsome Dutchman who worked for a bank. Alan met Hopie. Still there was this infinite forest, the trunks and vines blocking out the light, the roots of distant things joined. With every month that passed they were deeper into it, less certain of where they had been or if it could end. They had become like the old partners whose existence had been slowly sealed off, fewer calls, fewer consultations, lives that had become lunch. It was known they were swallowed up by the case with knowledge of little else. The opposite was true—no one else understood its details. Three years had passed. The length of time alone made it important. The reputation of the firm, at least in irony, was riding on them.

Two months before the case was to come to trial they quit Weyland, Braun. Frank sat down at the polished table for Sunday lunch. His father was one of the best men in the city. There is a kind of lawyer you trust and who becomes your friend. 'What happened?' he wanted to know.

'We're starting our own firm,' Frank said.

'What about the case you've been working on? You can't leave them with a litigation you've spent years preparing.'

'We're not. We're taking it with us,' Frank said.

There was a moment of dreadful silence.

'Taking it with you? You can't. You went to one of the best schools, Frank. They'll sue you. You'll ruin yourself.'

'We thought of that.'

'Listen to me,' his father said.

Everyone said that, his mother, his Uncle Cook, friends. It was worse than ruin, it was dishonor. His father said that.

Hardmann Roe never went to trial, as it turned out. Six weeks later there was a settlement. It was for thirty-eight million, a third of it their fee.

His father had been wrong, which was something you could not hope for. They weren't sued either. That was settled, too. In place of ruin there were new offices overlooking Bryant Park which from above seemed like a garden behind a dark château, young clients, opera tickets, dinners in apartments with divorced hostesses, surrendered apartments with books and big, tiled kitchens.

The city was divided, as he had said, into those going up and those coming down, those in crowded restaurants and those on the street, those who waited and those who did not, those with three locks on the door and those rising in an elevator from a lobby with silver mirrors and walnut paneling.

And those like Mrs Christie who was in the intermediate state though looking assured. She wanted to renegotiate the settlement with her ex-husband. Frank had leafed through the papers. 'What do you think?' she asked candidly.

'I think it would be easier for you to get married again.'

She was in her fur coat, the dark lining displayed. She gave a little puff of disbelief. 'It's not that easy,' she said.

He didn't know what it was like, she told him. Not long ago she'd been introduced to someone by a couple she knew very well. 'We'll go to dinner,' they said, 'you'll love him, you're perfect for him, he likes to talk about books.'

They arrived at the apartment and the two women immediately went into the kitchen and began cooking. What did she think of him? She'd only had a glimpse, she said, but she liked him very much, his beautiful bald head, his dressing gown. She had begun to plan what she would do with the apartment which had too much blue in it. The man—Warren was his name—was silent all evening. He'd lost his job, her friend explained in the kitchen. Money was no problem, but he was depressed. 'He's had a shock,' she said. 'He likes you.' And in fact he'd asked if he could see her again.

'Why don't you come for tea, tomorrow?' he said.

'I could do that,' she said. 'Of course. I'll be in the neighborhood,' she added.

The next day she arrived at four with a bag filled with books, at least a hundred dollars worth which she'd bought as a present. He was in pajamas. There was no tea. He hardly seemed to know who she was or why she was there. She said she remembered she had to meet someone and left the books. Going down in the elevator she felt suddenly sick to her stomach.

'Well,' said Frank, 'there might be a chance of getting the settlement overturned, Mrs Christie, but it would mean a lot of expense.'

'I see.' Her voice was smaller. 'Couldn't you do it as one of those things where you got a percentage?'

'Not on this kind of case,' he said.

It was dusk. He offered her a drink. She worked her lips, in contemplation, one against the other. 'Well, then, what can I do?'

Her life had been made up of disappointments, she told him, looking into her glass, most of them the result of foolishly falling in love. Going out with an older man just because he was wearing a white suit in Nashville which was where she was from. Agreeing to marry George Christie while they were sailing off the coast of Maine. 'I don't know where to get the money,' she said, 'or how.'

She glanced up. She found him looking at her, without haste. The lights were coming on in buildings surrounding the park, in the streets, on homeward bound cars. They talked as evening fell. They went out to dinner.

At Christmas that year Alan and his wife broke up. 'You're kidding,' Frank said. He'd moved into a new place with thick towels and fine carpets. In the foyer was a Biedermeier desk, black, tan, and gold. Across the street was a private school.

Alan was staring out the window which was as cold as the side of a ship. 'I don't know what to do,' he said in despair. 'I don't want to get divorced. I don't want to lose my daughter.' Her name was Camille. She was two.

'I know how you feel,' Frank said.

'If you had a kid, you'd know.'

'Have you seen this?' Frank asked. He held up the alumni magazine. It was the fifteenth anniversary of their graduation. 'Know any of these guys?'

Five members of the class had been cited for achievement. Alan recognized two or three of them. 'Cummings,' he said, 'he was a zero—elected to Congress. Oh, God, I don't know what to do.'

'Just don't let her take the apartment,' Frank said.

Of course, it wasn't that easy. It was easy when it was someone else. Nan Christie had decided to get married. She brought it up one evening.

'I just don't think so,' he finally said.

'You love me, don't you?'

'This isn't a good time to ask.'

They lay silently. She was staring at something across the room.

She was making him feel uncomfortable. 'It wouldn't work. It's the attraction of opposites,' he said.

'We're not opposites.'

'I don't mean just you and me. Women fall in love when they get to know you. Men are just the opposite. When they finally know you they're ready to leave.'

She got up without saying anything and began gathering her clothes. He watched her dress in silence. There was nothing interesting about it. The funny thing was that he had meant to go on with her.

'I'll get you a cab,' he said.

'I used to think that you were intelligent,' she said, half to herself. Exhausted, he was searching for a number. 'I don't want a cab. I'm going to walk.'

'Across the park?'

'Yes.' She had an instant glimpse of herself in the next day's paper. She paused at the door for a moment. 'Good-bye,' she said coolly.

She wrote him a letter which he read several times. *Of all the loves I have known, none has touched me so. Of all the men, no one has given me more.* He showed it to Alan who did not comment.

'Let's go out and have a drink,' Frank said.

They walked up Lexington. Frank looked carefree, the scarf around his neck, the open topcoat, the thinning hair. 'Well, you know . . . ' he managed to say.

They went into a place called Jack's. Light was gleaming from the dark wood and the lines of glasses on narrow shelves. The young bartender stood with his hands on the edge of the bar. 'How are you this evening?' he said with a smile. 'Nice to see you again.'

'Do you know me?' Frank asked.

'You look familiar,' the bartender smiled.

'Do I? What's the name of this place, anyway? Remind me not to come in here again.'

There were several other people at the bar. The nearest of them carefully looked away. After a while the manager came over. He had emerged from the brown-curtained back. 'Anything wrong, sir?' he asked politely.

Frank looked at him. 'No,' he said, 'everything's fine.'

'We've had a big day,' Alan explained. 'We're just unwinding.'

'We have a dining room upstairs,' the manager said. Behind him was an iron staircase winding past framed drawings of dogs—borzois they looked like. 'We serve from six to eleven every night.'

'I bet you do,' Frank said. 'Look, your bartender doesn't know me.'

'He made a mistake,' the manager said.

'He doesn't know me and he never will.'

'It's nothing, it's nothing,' Alan said, waving his hands.

They sat at a table by the window. 'I can't stand these out-of-work actors who think they're everybody's friend,' Frank commented.

At dinner they talked about Nan Christie. Alan thought of her silk dresses, her devotion. The trouble, he said after a while, was that he never seemed to meet that kind of woman, the ones who sometimes walked by outside Jack's. The women he met were too human, he complained. Ever since his separation he'd been trying to find the right one.

'You shouldn't have any trouble,' Frank said. 'They're all looking for someone like you.'

'They're looking for you.'

'They think they are.'

Frank paid the check without looking at it. 'Once you've been married,' Alan was explaining, 'you want to be married again.'

'I don't trust anyone enough to marry them,' Frank said.

'What do you want then?'

'This is all right,' Frank said.

Something was missing in him and women had always done anything to find out what it was. They always would. Perhaps it was simpler, Alan thought. Perhaps nothing was missing.

The car, which was a big Renault, a tourer, slowed down and pulled off the *autostrada* with Brenda asleep in back, her mouth a bit open and the daylight gleaming off her cheekbones. It was near Como, they had just crossed, the border police had glanced in at her.

'Come on, Bren, wake up,' they said, 'we're stopping for coffee.'

She came back from the ladies' room with her hair combed and fresh lipstick on. The boy in the white jacket behind the counter was rinsing spoons.

'Hey, Brenda, I forget. Is it *espresso* or *expresso*?' Frank asked her.

'*Espresso*,' she said.

'How do you know?'

'I'm from New York,' she said.

'That's right,' he remembered. 'The Italians don't have an *x*, do they?'

'They don't have a *j* either,' Alan said.

'Why is that?'

'They're such careless people,' Brenda said. 'They just lost them.'

It was like old times. She was divorced from Doop or Boos or whoever. Her two little girls were with her mother. She had that quirky smile.

In Paris Frank had taken them to the Crazy Horse. In blackness like velvet the music struck up and six girls in unison kicked their legs in the brilliant light. They wore high heels and a little strapping. The nudity that is immortal. He was leaning on one elbow in the darkness. He glanced at Brenda. 'Still studying, eh?' she said.

They were over for three weeks. Frank wasn't sure, maybe they would stay longer, take a house in the south of France or something. Their clients would have to struggle along without them. There comes a time, he said, when you have to get away for a while.

They had breakfast together in hotels with the sound of workmen chipping at the stone of the fountain outside. They listened to the angry woman shouting in the kitchen, drove to little towns, and drank every night. They had separate rooms, like staterooms, like passengers on a fading boat.

At noon the light shifted along the curve of buildings and people were walking far off. A wave of pigeons rose before a trotting dog. The man at the table in front of them had a pair of binoculars and was looking here and there. Two Swedish girls strolled past.

'Now they're turning dark,' the man said.

'What is?' said his wife.

'The pigeons.'

'Alan,' Frank confided.

'What?'

'The pigeons are turning dark.'

'That's too bad.'

There was silence for a moment.

'Why don't you just take a photograph?' the woman said.

'A photograph?'

'Of those women. You're looking at them so much.'

He put down the binoculars.

'You know, the curve is so graceful,' she said. 'It's what makes this square perfect.'

'Isn't the weather glorious?' Frank said in the same tone of voice.

'And the pigeons,' Alan said.

'The pigeons, too.'

After a while the couple got up and left. The pigeons leapt up for a running child and hissed overhead. 'I see you're still playing games,' Brenda said. Frank smiled.

'We ought to get together in New York,' she said that evening. They were waiting for Alan to come down. She reached across the table to pick up a magazine. 'You've never met my kids, have you?' she said.

'No.'

'They're terrific kids.' She leafed through the pages not paying attention to them. Her forearms were tanned. She was not wearing a wedding band. The first act was over or rather the first five minutes. Now came the plot. 'Do you remember those nights at Goldie's?' she said.

'Things were different then, weren't they?'

'Not so different.'

'What do you mean?'

She wiggled her bare third finger and glanced at him. Just then Alan appeared. He sat down and looked from one of them to the other. 'What's wrong?' he asked. 'Did I interrupt something?'

When the time came for her to leave she wanted them to drive to Rome. They could spend a couple of days and she would catch the plane. They weren't going that way, Frank said.

'It's only a three-hour drive.'

'I know, but we're going the other way,' he said.

'For God's sake. Why won't you drive me?'

'Let's do it,' Alan said.

'Go ahead. I'll stay here.'

'You should have gone into politics,' Brenda said. 'You have a real gift.'

After she was gone the mood of things changed. They were by themselves. They drove through the sleepy country to the north. The green water slapped as darkness fell on Venice. The lights in some *palazzos* were on. On the curtained upper floors the legs of countesses uncoiled, slithering on the sheets like a serpent.

In Harry's, Frank held up a dense, icy glass and murmured his fathers line, 'Good night, nurse.' He talked to some people at the next table, a German who was manager of a hotel in Düsseldorf and his girlfriend. She'd been looking at him. 'Want a taste?' he asked her. It was his second. She drank looking directly at him. 'Looks like you finished it,' he said.

'Yes. I like to do that.'

He smiled. When he was drinking he was strangely calm. In Lugano in the park that time a bird had sat on his shoe.

In the morning across the canal, wide as a river, the buildings of the Giudecca lay in their soft colors, a great sunken barge with roofs and the crowns of hidden trees. The first winds of autumn were blowing, ruffling the water.

Leaving Venice, Frank drove. He couldn't ride in a car unless he was driving. Alan sat back, looking out the window, sunlight falling on the hillsides of antiquity. European days, the silence, the needle floating at a hundred.

In Padua, Alan woke early. The stands were being set up in the market. It was before daylight and cool. A man was laying out boards on the pavement, eight of them like doors to set bags of grain on. He was wearing the jacket from a suit. Searching in the truck he found some small pieces of wood and used them to shim the boards, testing with his foot.

The sky became violet. Under the colonnade the butchers had hung out chickens and roosters, spurred legs bound together. Two men sat trimming artichokes. The blue car of the *carabiniere* lazed past. The bags of rice and dry beans were set out now, the tops folded back like cuffs. A girl in a tailored coat with a scarf around her head called, '*Signore*,' then arrogantly, '*dica!*'

He saw the world afresh, its pavements and architecture, the names that had lasted for a thousand years. It seemed that his life was being clarified, the sediment was drifting down. Across the street in a jeweler's shop a girl was laying things out in the window. She was wearing white gloves and arranging the pieces with great care. She glanced up as he stood watching. For a moment their eyes met, separated by the lighted glass. She was holding a lapis lazuli bracelet, the blue of the police car. Emboldened, he formed the silent words, *Quanto costa? Tre cento settante mille*, her lips said. It was eight in the morning when he got back to the hotel. A taxi pulled up and rattled the narrow street. A woman dressed for dinner got out and went inside.

The days passed. In Verona the points of the steeples and then its domes rose from the mist. The white-coated waiters appeared from the kitchen. *Primi, secondi, dolce.* They stopped in Arezzo. Frank came back to the table. He had some postcards. Alan was trying to write to his daughter once a week. He never knew what to say: where they were and what they'd seen. Giotto—what would that mean to her? They sat in the car. Frank was wearing a soft tweed jacket. It was like cashmere—he'd been shopping in Missoni and everywhere, windbreakers, shoes. Schoolgirls in dark skirts were coming through an arch across the street. After a while one came through alone. She stood as if waiting for someone. Alan was studying the map. He felt the engine start. Very slowly they moved forward. The window glided down.

'*Scusi, signorina,*' he heard Frank say.

She turned. She had pure features and her face was without expression, as if a bird had turned to look, a bird which might suddenly fly away.

Which way, Frank asked her, was the *centro,* the center of town? She looked one way and then the other. 'There,' she said.

'Are you sure?' he said. He turned his head unhurriedly to look more or less in the direction she was pointing.

'*Si,*' she said.

They were going to Siena, Frank said. There was silence. Did she know which road went to Siena?

She pointed the other way.

'Alan, you want to give her a ride?' he asked.

'What are you talking about?'

Two men in white smocks like doctors were working on the wooden doors of the church. They were up on top of some scaffolding. Frank reached back and opened the rear door.

'Do you want to go for a ride?' he asked. He made a little circular motion with his finger.

They drove through the streets in silence. The radio was playing. Nothing was said. Frank glanced at her in the rearview mirror once or twice. It was at the time of a famous murder in Poland, the killing of a priest. Dusk was falling. The lights were coming on in shop windows and evening papers were in the kiosks. The body of the murdered man lay in a long coffin in the upper right corner of the *Corriere Della Sera.* It was in clean clothes like a worker after a terrible accident.

'Would you like an *aperitivo*?' Frank asked over his shoulder.

'No,' she said.

They drove back to the church. He got out for a few minutes with her. His hair was very thin, Alan noticed. Strangely, it made him look younger. They stood talking, then she turned and walked down the street.

'What did you say to her?' Alan asked. He was nervous.

'I asked if she wanted a taxi.'

'We're headed for trouble.'

'There's not going to be any trouble,' Frank said.

His room was on the corner. It was large, with a sitting area near the windows. On the wooden floor there were two worn oriental carpets. On a glass cabinet in the bathroom were his hairbrush, lotions, cologne. The towels were a pale green with the name of the hotel in white. She didn't look at any of that. He had given the *portiere* forty thousand lire. In Italy the laws were very strict. It was nearly the same hour of the afternoon. He kneeled to take off her shoes.

He had drawn the curtains but light came in around them. At one point she seemed to tremble, her body shuddered. 'Are you all right?' he said.

She had closed her eyes.

Later, standing, he saw himself in the mirror. He seemed to have thickened around the waist. He turned so that it was less noticeable. He got into bed again but was too hasty. '*Basta*,' she finally said.

They went down later and met Alan in a café. It was hard for him to look at them. He began to talk in a foolish way. What was she studying at school, he asked. For God's sake, Frank said. Well, what did her father do? She didn't understand.

'What work does he do?'

'Furniture,' she said.

'He sells it?'

'*Restauro*.'

'In our country, no *restauro*,' Alan explained. He made a gesture. 'Throw it away.'

'I've got to start running again,' Frank decided.

The next day was Saturday. He had the *portiere* call her number and hand him the phone.

'Hello, Eda? It's Frank.'

'I know.'

'What are you doing?'

He didn't understand her reply.

'We're going to Florence. You want to come to Florence?' he said. There was a silence. 'Why don't you come and spend a few days?'

'No,' she said.

'Why not?'

In a quieter voice she said, 'How do I explain?'

'You can think of something.'

At a table across the room children were playing cards while three well-dressed women, their mothers, sat and talked. There were cries of excitement as the cards were thrown down.

'Eda?'

She was still there. '*Si*,' she said.

In the hills they were burning leaves. The smoke was invisible but they could smell it as they passed through, like the smell from a restaurant or paper mill. It made Frank suddenly remember childhood and country houses, raking the lawn with his father long ago. The green signs began to say Firenze. It started to rain. The wipers swept silently across the glass. Everything was beautiful and dim.

They had dinner in a restaurant of plain rooms, whitewashed, like vaults in a cellar. She looked very young. She looked like a young dog, the white of her eyes was that pure. She said very little and played with a strip of pink paper that had come off the menu.

In the morning they walked aimlessly. The windows displayed things for women who were older, in their thirties at least, silk dresses, bracelets, scarves. In Fendi's was a beautiful coat, the price beneath in small metal numbers.

'Do you like it?' he asked. 'Come on, I'll buy it for you.'

He wanted to see the coat in the window, he told them inside.

'For the *signorina*?'

'Yes.'

She seemed uncomprehending. Her face was lost in the fur. He touched her cheek through it.

'You know how much that is?' Alan said. 'Four million five hundred thousand.'

'Do you like it?' Frank asked her.

She wore it continually. She watched the football matches on television in it, her legs curled beneath her. The room was in disorder, they hadn't been out all day.

'What do you say to leaving here?' Alan asked unexpectedly. The announcers were shouting in Italian. 'I thought I'd like to see Spoleto.'

'Sure. Where is it?' Frank said. He had his hand on her knee and was rubbing it with the barest movement, as one might a dozing cat.

The countryside was flat and misty. They were leaving the past behind them, unwashed glasses, towels on the bathroom floor. There was a stain on his lapel, Frank noticed in the dining room. He tried to get it off as the headwaiter grated fresh Parmesan over each plate. He dipped the corner of his napkin in water and rubbed the spot. The table was near the doorway, visible from the desk. Eda was fixing an earring.

'Cover it with your napkin,' Alan told him.

'Here, get this off, will you?' he asked Eda.

She scratched at it quickly with her fingernail.

'What am I going to do without her?' Frank said.

'What do you mean, without her?'

'So this is Spoleto,' he said. The spot was gone. 'Let's have some more wine.' He called the waiter. '*Senta*. Tell him,' he said to Eda.

They laughed and talked about old times, the days when they were getting eight hundred dollars a week and working ten, twelve hours a day. They remembered Weyland and the veins in his nose. The word he always used was 'vivid,' testimony a bit too vivid, far too vivid, a rather vivid decor.

They left talking loudly. Eda was close between them in her huge coat. '*Alla rovina*,' the clerk at the front desk muttered as they reached the street, '*alle macerie*,' he said, the girl at the switchboard looked over at him, '*alla polvere*.' It was something about rubbish and dust.

The mornings grew cold. In the garden there were leaves piled against the table legs. Alan sat alone in the bar. A waitress, the one with the mole on her lip, came in and began to work the coffee machine. Frank came down. He had an overcoat across his shoulders. In his shirt without a tie he looked like a rich patient in some hospital. He looked like a man who owned a produce business and had been playing cards all night.

'So, what do you think?' Alan said.

Frank sat down. 'Beautiful day,' he commented. 'Maybe we ought to go somewhere.'

In the room, perhaps in the entire hotel, their voices were the only sound, irregular and low, like the soft strokes of someone sweeping. One muted sound, then another.

'Where's Eda?'

'She's taking a bath.'

'I thought I'd say good-bye to her.'

'Why? What's wrong?'

'I think I'm going home.'

'What happened?' Frank said.

Alan could see himself in the mirror behind the bar, his sandy hair. He looked pale somehow, nonexistent. 'Nothing happened,' he said. She had come into the bar and was sitting at the other end of the room. He felt a tightness in his chest. 'Europe depresses me.'

Frank was looking at him. 'Is it Eda?'

'No. I don't know.' It seemed terribly quiet. Alan put his hands in his lap. They were trembling.

'Is that all it is? We can share her,' Frank said.

'What do you mean?' He was too nervous to say it right. He stole a glance at Eda. She was looking at something outside in the garden.

'Eda,' Frank called, 'do you want something to drink? *Cosa vuoi?*' He made a motion of glass raised to the mouth. In college he had been a great favorite. Shuford had been shortened to Shuf and then Shoes. He had run in the Penn Relays. His mother could trace her family back for six generations.

'Orange juice,' she said.

They sat there talking quietly. That was often the case, Eda had noticed. They talked about business or things in New York.

When they came back to the hotel that night, Frank explained it. She understood in an instant. No. She shook her head. Alan was sitting alone in the bar. He was drinking some kind of sweet liqueur. It wouldn't happen, he knew. It didn't matter anyway. Still, he felt shamed. The hotel above his head, its corridors and quiet rooms, what else were they for?

Frank and Eda came in. He managed to turn to them. She seemed impassive—he could not tell. What was this he was drinking, he finally asked? She didn't understand the question. He saw Frank nod once slightly, as if in agreement. They were like thieves.

In the morning the first light was blue on the window glass. There was the sound of rain. It was leaves blowing in the garden, shifting across the gravel. Alan slipped from the bed to fasten the loose shutter. Below, half hidden in the hedges, a statue gleamed white. The few parked cars shone faintly. She was asleep, the soft, heavy pillow beneath her head. He was afraid to wake her. 'Eda,' he whispered, 'Eda.'

Her eyes opened a bit and closed. She was young and could stay asleep. He was afraid to touch her. She was unhappy, he knew, her bare neck, her hair, things he could not see. It would be a while before they were used to it. He didn't know what to do. Apart from that, it was perfect. It was the most natural thing in the world. He would buy her something himself, something beautiful.

In the bathroom he lingered at the window. He was thinking of the first day they had come to work at Weyland, Braun—he and Frank. They would become inseparable. Autumn in the gardens of the Veneto. It was barely dawn. He would always remember meeting Frank. He couldn't have done these things himself. A young man in a cap suddenly came out of a doorway below. He crossed the driveway and jumped onto a motorbike. The engine started, a faint blur. The headlight appeared and off he went, delivery basket in back. He was going to get the rolls for breakfast. His life was simple. The air was pure and cool. He was part of that great, unchanging order of those who live by wages, whose world is unlit and who do not realize what is above.

1988

THE JOY LUCK CLUB
Amy Tan

My father has asked me to be the fourth corner at the Joy Luck Club. I am to replace my mother, whose seat at the mah jong table has been empty since she died two months ago. My father thinks she was killed by her own thoughts.

'She had a new idea inside her head,' said my father. 'But before it could come out of her mouth, the thought grew too big and burst. It must have been a very bad idea.'

The doctor said she died of a cerebral aneurysm. And her friends at the Joy Luck Club said she died just like a rabbit: quickly and with unfinished business left behind. My mother was supposed to host the next meeting of the Joy Luck Club.

The week before she died, she called me, full of pride, full of life: 'Auntie Lin cooked red bean soup for Joy Luck. I'm going to cook black sesame-seed soup.'

'Don't show off,' I said.

'It's not showoff.' She said the two soups were almost the same, *chabudwo*. Or maybe she said *butong*, not the same thing at all. It was one of those Chinese expressions that means the better half of mixed intentions. I can never remember things I didn't understand in the first place.

My mother started the San Francisco version of the Joy Luck Club in 1949, two years before I was born. This was the year my mother and father left China with one stiff leather trunk filled only with fancy silk dresses. There was no time to pack anything else, my mother had explained to my father after they boarded the boat. Still his hands swam frantically between the slippery silks, looking for his cotton shirts and wool pants.

When they arrived in San Francisco, my father made her hide those shiny clothes. She wore the same brown-checked Chinese dress until the Refugee Welcome Society gave her two hand-me-down dresses, all too large in sizes for American women. The society was composed of a group of white-haired American missionary ladies from the First Chinese Baptist Church. And because of their gifts, my parents could not refuse their invitation to join the church. Nor could they ignore the old ladies' practical advice to improve their English through Bible study class on Wednesday nights and, later, through choir practice on Saturday mornings. This was how my parents met the Hsus, the Jongs, and the St. Clairs. My mother could sense that the women of these families also had unspeakable tragedies they had left behind in China and hopes they couldn't begin to express in their fragile English. Or at least, my mother recognized the numbness in these women's faces. And she saw how quickly their eyes moved when she told them her idea for the Joy Luck Club.

Joy Luck was an idea my mother remembered from the days of her first marriage in Kweilin, before the Japanese came. That's why I think of Joy Luck as her Kweilin story. It was the story she would always tell me when she was bored, when there was nothing to do, when every bowl had been washed and the Formica table had been wiped down twice, when my father sat reading the newspaper and smoking one Pall Mall cigarette after another, a warning not to disturb him. This is when my mother would take out a box of old ski sweaters sent to us by unseen relatives from Vancouver. She would snip the bottom of a sweater and pull out a kinky thread of yarn, anchoring it to a piece of cardboard. And as she began to roll with one sweeping rhythm, she would start her story. Over the years, she told me the same story, except for the ending, which grew darker, casting long shadows into her life, and eventually into mine.

'I dreamed about Kweilin before I ever saw it,' my mother began, speaking Chinese. 'I dreamed of jagged peaks lining a curving river, with magic moss greening the banks. At the tops of these peaks were white mists. And if you could float down this river and eat the moss for food, you would be strong enough to climb the peak. If you slipped, you would only fall into a bed of soft moss and laugh. And once you reached the top, you would be able to see everything and feel such happiness it would be enough to never have worries in your life ever again.

'In China, everybody dreamed about Kweilin. And when I arrived, I realized how shabby my dreams were, how poor my thoughts. When I saw the hills, I laughed and shuddered at the same time. The peaks looked like giant fried fish heads trying to jump out of a vat of oil. Behind each hill, I could see shadows of another fish, and then another and another. And then the clouds would move just a little

600

and the hills would suddenly become monstrous elephants marching slowly toward me! Can you see this? And at the root of the hill were secret caves. Inside grew hanging rock gardens in the shapes and colors of cabbage, winter melons, turnips, and onions. These were things so strange and beautiful you can't ever imagine them.

'But I didn't come to Kweilin to see how beautiful it was. The man who was my husband brought me and our two babies to Kweilin because he thought we would be safe. He was an officer with the Kuomintang, and after he put us down in a small room in a two-story house, he went off to the northwest, to Chungking.

'We knew the Japanese were winning, even when the newspapers said they were not. Every day, every hour, thousands of people poured into the city, crowding the sidewalks, looking for places to live. They came from the East, West, North, and South. They were rich and poor, Shanghainese, Cantonese, northerners, and not just Chinese, but foreigners and missionaries of every religion. And there was, of course, the Kuomintang and their army officers who thought they were top level to everyone else.

'We were a city of leftovers mixed together. If it hadn't been for the Japanese, there would have been plenty of reason for fighting to break out among these different people. Can you see it? Shanghai people with north-water peasants, bankers with barbers, rickshaw pullers with Burma refugees. Everybody looked down on someone else. It didn't matter that everybody shared the same sidewalk to spit on and suffered the same fast-moving diarrhea. We all had the same stink, but everybody complained someone else smelled the worst. Me? Oh, I hated the American air force officers who said habba-habba sounds to make my face turn red. But the worst were the northern peasants who emptied their noses into their hands and pushed people around and gave everybody their dirty diseases.

'So you can see how quickly Kweilin lost its beauty for me. I no longer climbed the peaks to say, How lovely are these hills! I only wondered which hills the Japanese had reached. I sat in the dark corners of my house with a baby under each arm, waiting with nervous feet. When the sirens cried out to warn us of bombers, my neighbors and I jumped to our feet and scurried to the deep caves to hide like wild animals. But you can't stay in the dark for so long. Something inside of you starts to fade and you become like a starving person, crazy-hungry for light. Outside I could hear the bombing. Boom! Boom! And then the sound of raining rocks. And inside I was no longer hungry for the cabbage or the turnips of the hanging rock garden. I could only see the dripping bowels of an ancient hill that might collapse on top of me. Can you imagine how it is, to want to be neither inside nor outside, to want to be nowhere and disappear?

'So when the bombing sounds grew farther away, we would come back out like newborn kittens scratching our way back to the city. And always, I would be amazed to find the hills against the burning sky had not been torn apart.

'I thought up Joy Luck on a summer night that was so hot even the moths fainted to the ground, their wings were so heavy with the damp heat. Every place was so crowded there was no room for fresh air. Unbearable smells from the sewers rose up to my second-story window and the stink had nowhere else to go but into my nose. At all hours of the night and day, I heard screaming sounds. I didn't know if it was a peasant slitting the throat of a runaway pig or an officer beating a half-dead peasant for lying in his way on the sidewalk. I didn't go to the window to find out. What use would it have been? And that's when I thought I needed something to do to help me move.

'My idea was to have a gathering of four women, one for each corner of my mah jong table. I knew which women I wanted to ask. They were all young like me, with wishful faces. One was an army officer's wife, like myself. Another was a girl with very fine manners from a rich family in Shanghai. She had escaped with only a little money. And there was a girl from Nanking who had the blackest hair I have ever seen. She came from a low-class family, but she was pretty and pleasant and had married well, to an old man who died and left her with a better life.

'Each week one of us would host a party to raise money and to raise our spirits. The hostess had to serve special *dyansyin* foods to bring good fortune of all kinds—dumplings shaped like silver money ingots, long rice noodles for long life, boiled peanuts for conceiving sons, and of course, many good-luck oranges for a plentiful, sweet life.

'What fine food we treated ourselves to with our meager allowances! We didn't notice that the dumplings were stuffed mostly with stringy squash and that the oranges were spotted with wormy holes. We ate sparingly, not as if we didn't have enough, but to protest how we could not eat another bite, we had already bloated ourselves from earlier in the day. We knew we had luxuries few people could afford. We were the lucky ones.

'After filling our stomachs, we would then fill a bowl with money and put it where everyone could see. Then we would sit down at the mah jong table. My table was from my family and was of a very fragrant red wood, not what you call rosewood, but *hong mu*, which is so fine there's no English word for it. The table had a very thick pad, so that when the mah jong *pai* were spilled onto the table the only sound was of ivory tiles washing against one another.

'Once we started to play, nobody could speak, except to say *"Pung!"* or *"Chr!"* when taking a tile. We had to play with seriousness and think of nothing else but adding to our happiness through winning. But after sixteen rounds, we would again feast, this time to celebrate our good fortune. And then we would talk into the night until the morning, saying stories about good times in the past and good times yet to come.

'Oh, what good stories! Stories spilling out all over the place! We almost laughed to death. A rooster that ran into the house screeching on top of dinner bowls, the same bowls that held him quietly in pieces the next day! And one about a girl who wrote love letters for two friends who loved the same man. And a silly foreign lady who fainted on a toilet when firecrackers went off next to her.

'People thought we were wrong to serve banquets every week while many people in the city were starving, eating rats and, later, the garbage that the poorest rats used to feed on. Others thought we were possessed by demons—to celebrate when even within our own families we had lost generations, had lost homes and fortunes, and were separated, husband from wife, brother from sister, daughter from mother. Hnnnh! How could we laugh, people asked.

'It's not that we had no heart or eyes for pain. We were all afraid. We all had our miseries. But to despair was to wish back for something already lost. Or to prolong what was already unbearable. How much can you wish for a favorite warm coat that hangs in the closet of a house that burned down with your mother and father inside of it? How long can you see in your mind arms and legs hanging from telephone wires and starving dogs running down the streets with half-chewed hands dangling from their jaws? What was worse, we asked among ourselves, to sit and wait for our own deaths with proper somber faces? Or to choose our own happiness?

'So we decided to hold parties and pretend each week had become the new year. Each week we could forget past wrongs done to us. We weren't allowed to think a bad thought. We feasted, we laughed, we played games, lost and won, we told the best stories. And each week, we could hope to be lucky. That hope was our only joy. And that's how we came to call our little parties Joy Luck.'

My mother used to end the story on a happy note, bragging about her skill at the game. 'I won many times and was so lucky the others teased that I had learned the trick of a clever thief,' she said. 'I won tens of thousands of *yuan*. But I wasn't rich. No. By then paper money had become worthless. Even toilet paper was worth more. And that made us laugh harder, to think a thousand-*yuan* note wasn't even good enough to rub on our bottoms.'

I never thought my mother's Kweilin story was anything but a Chinese fairy tale. The endings always changed. Sometimes she said she used that worthless thousand-*yuan* note to buy a half-cup of rice. She turned that rice into a pot of porridge. She traded that gruel for two feet from a pig. Those two feet became six eggs, those eggs six chickens. The story always grew and grew.

And then one evening, after I had begged her to buy me a transistor radio, after she refused and I had sulked in silence for an hour, she said, 'Why do you think you are missing something you never had?' And then she told me a completely different ending to the story.

'An army officer came to my house early one morning,' she said, 'and told me to go quickly to my husband in Chungking. And I knew he was telling me to run away from Kweilin. I knew what happened to officers and their families when the Japanese arrived. How could I go? There were no trains leaving Kweilin. My friend from Nanking, she was so good to me. She bribed a man to steal a wheelbarrow used to haul coal. She promised to warn our other friends.

'I packed my things and my two babies into this wheelbarrow and began pushing to Chungking four days before the Japanese marched into Kweilin. On the road I heard news of the slaughter from people running past me. It was terrible. Up to the last day, the Kuomintang insisted that Kweilin was safe, protected by the Chinese army. But later that day, the streets of Kweilin were strewn with newspapers reporting great Kuomintang victories, and on top of these papers, like fresh fish from a butcher, lay rows of people—men, women, and children who had never lost hope, but had lost their lives instead. When I heard this news, I walked faster and faster, asking myself at each step, Were they foolish? Were they brave?

'I pushed toward Chungking, until my wheel broke. I abandoned my beautiful mah jong table of *hong mu*. By then I didn't have enough feeling left in my body to cry. I tied scarves into slings and put a baby on each side of my shoulder. I carried a bag in each hand, one with clothes, the other with food. I carried these things until deep grooves grew in my hands. And I finally dropped one bag after the other when my hands began to bleed and became too slippery to hold onto anything.

'Along the way, I saw others had done the same, gradually given up hope. It was like a pathway inlaid with treasures that grew in value along the way. Bolts of fine fabric and books. Paintings of ancestors and carpenter tools. Until one could see cages of ducklings now quiet with thirst and, later still, silver urns lying in the road, where people had been too tired to carry them for any kind of future hope. By the time I arrived in Chungking I had lost everything except for three fancy silk dresses which I wore one on top of the other.'

'What do you mean by "everything"?' I gasped at the end. I was stunned to realize the story had been true all along. 'What happened to the babies?'

She didn't even pause to think. She simply said in a way that made it clear there was no more to the story: 'Your father is not my first husband. You are not those babies.'

When I arrive at the Hsus' house, where the Joy Luck Club is meeting tonight, the first person I see is my father. 'There she is! Never on time!' he announces. And it's true. Everybody's already here, seven family friends in their sixties and seventies. They look up and laugh at me, always tardy, a child still at thirty-six.

I'm shaking, trying to hold something inside. The last time I saw them, at the funeral, I had broken down and cried big gulping sobs. They must wonder now how someone like me can take my mother's place. A friend once told me that my mother and I were alike, that we had the same wispy hand gestures, the same girlish laugh and sideways look. When I shyly told my mother this, she seemed insulted and said, 'You don't even know little percent of me! How can you be me?' And she's right. How can I be my mother at Joy Luck?

'Auntie, Uncle,' I say repeatedly, nodding to each person there. I have always called these old family friends Auntie and Uncle. And then I walk over and stand next to my father.

He's looking at the Jongs' pictures from their recent China trip. 'Look at that,' he says politely, pointing to a photo of the Jongs} tour group standing on wide slab steps. There is nothing in this picture that shows it was taken in China rather than San Francisco, or any other city for that matter. But my father doesn't seem to be looking at the picture anyway. It's as though everything were the same to him, nothing stands out. He has always been politely indifferent. But what's the Chinese word that means indifferent because you can't *see* any differences? That's how troubled I think he is by my mother's death.

'Will you look at that,' he says, pointing to another nondescript picture.

The Hsus' house feels heavy with greasy odors. Too many Chinese meals cooked in a too small kitchen, too many once fragrant smells compressed onto a thin layer of invisible grease. I remember how my mother used to go into other people's houses and restaurants and wrinkle her nose, then whisper very loudly: 'I can see and feel the stickiness with my nose.'

I have not been to the Hsus' house in many years, but the living room is exactly the same as I remember it. When Aunti An-mei and Uncle George moved to the Sunset district from Chinatown twenty-five years ago, they bought new furniture. It's all there, still looking mostly new under yellowed plastic. The same turquoise couch shaped in a semicircle of nubby tweed. The colonial end tables made out of heavy maple. A lamp of fake cracked porcelain. Only the scroll-length calendar, free from the Bank of Canton, changes every year.

I remember this stuff, because when we were children, Aunti An-mei didn't let us touch any of her new furniture except through the clear plastic coverings. On Joy Luck nights, my parents brought me to the Hsus'. Since I was the guest, I had to take care of all the younger children, so many children it seemed as if there were always one baby who was crying from having bumped its head on a table-leg.

'You are responsible,' said my mother, which meant I was in trouble if anything was spilled, burned, lost, broken, or dirty. I was responsible, no matter who did it. She and Auntie An-mei were dressed up in funny Chinese dresses with stiff stand-up collars and blooming branches of embroidered silk sewn over their breasts. These clothes were too fancy for real Chinese people, I thought, and too strange for American parties. In those days, before my mother told me her Kweilin story, I imagined Joy Luck was a shameful Chinese custom, like the secret gathering of the Ku Klux Klan or the tom-tom dances of TV Indians preparing for war.

But tonight, there's no mystery. The Joy Luck aunties are all wearing slacks, bright print blouses, and different versions of sturdy walking shoes. We are all seated around the dining room table under a lamp that looks like a Spanish candelabra. Uncle George puts on his bifocals and starts the meeting by reading the minutes:

'Our capital account is $24,825, or about $6,206 a couple, $3,103 per person. We sold Subaru for a loss at six and three-quarters. We bought a hundred shares of Smith International at seven. Our thanks to Lindo and Tin Jong for the goodies. The red bean soup was especially delicious. The March meeting had to be canceled until further notice. We were sorry to have to bid a fond farewell to our dear friend Suyuan and extended our sympathy to the Canning Woo family. Respectfully submitted, George Hsu, president and secretary.'

That's it. I keep thinking the others will start talking about my mother, the wonderful friendship they shared, and why I am here in her spirit, to be the fourth corner and carry on the idea my mother came up with on a hot day in Kweilin.

But everybody just nods to approve the minutes. Even my father's head bobs up and down routinely. And it seems to me my mother's life has been shelved for new business.

Auntie An-mei heaves herself up from the table and moves slowly to the kitchen to prepare the food. And Auntie Lin, my mother's best friend, moves to the turquoise sofa, crosses her arms, and watches the men still seated at the table. Auntie Ying, who seems to shrink even more every time I see her, reaches into her knitting bag and pulls out the start of a tiny blue sweater.

The Joy Luck uncles begin to talk about stocks they are interested in buying. Uncle Jack, who is Auntie Ying's younger brother, is very keen on a company that mines gold in Canada.

'It's a great hedge on inflation,' he says with authority. He speaks the best English, almost accentless. I think my mother's English was the worst, but she always thought her Chinese was the best. She spoke Mandarin slightly blurred with a Shanghai dialect.

'Weren't we going to play mah jong tonight?' I whisper loudly to

607

Aunti Ying, who's slightly deaf.

'Later,' she says, 'after midnight.'

'Ladies, are you at this meeting or not?' says Uncle George.

After everybody votes unanimously for the Canada gold stock, I go into the kitchen to ask Auntie An-mei why the Joy Luck Club started investing in stocks.

'We used to play mah jong, winner take all. But the same people were always winning, the same people always losing,' she says. She is stuffing wonton, one chopstick jab of gingery meat dabbed onto a thin skin and then a single fluid turn with her hand that seals the skin into the shape of a tiny nurse's cap. 'You can't have luck when someone else has skill. So long time ago, we decided to invest in the stock market. There's no skill in that. Even your mother agreed.'

Auntie An-mei takes count of the tray in front of her. She's already made five rows of eight wonton each. 'Forty wonton, eight people, ten each, five row more,' she says aloud to herself, and then continues stuffing. 'We got smart. Now we can all win and lose equally. We can have stock market luck. And we can play mah jong for fun, just for a few dollars, winner take all. Losers take home leftovers! So everyone can have some joy. Smart-hanh?'

I watch Auntie An-mei make more wonton. She has quick, expert fingers. She doesn't have to think about what she is doing. That's what my mother used to complain about, that Auntie An-mei never thought about what she was doing.

'She's not stupid,' said my mother on one occasion, 'but she has no spine. Last week, I had a good idea for her. I said to her, Let's go to the consulate and ask for papers for your brother. And she almost wanted to drop her things and go right then. But later she talked to someone. Who knows who? And that person told her she can get her brother in bad trouble in China. That person said FBI will put her on a list and give her trouble in the U.S. the rest of her life. That person said, You ask for a house loan and they say no loan, because your brother is a communist. I said, You already have a house! But still she was scared.

'Auntie An-mei runs this way and that,' said my mother, 'and she doesn't know why.'

As I watch Auntie An-mei, I see a short bent woman in her seventies, with a heavy bosom and thin, shapeless legs. She has the flattened soft fingertips of an old woman. I wonder what Auntie An-mei did to inspire a lifelong stream of criticism from my mother. Then again, it seemed my mother was always displeased with all her friends, with me, and even with my father. Something was always missing. Something always needed improving. Something was not in balance. This one or that had too much of one element, not enough of another.

The elements were from my mother's own version of organic chemistry. Each person is made of five elements, she told me.

Too much fire and you had a bad temper. That was like my father, whom my mother always criticized for his cigarette habit and who always shouted back that she should keep her thoughts to herself. I think he now feels guilty that he didn't let my mother speak her mind.

Too little wood and you bent too quickly to listen to other people's ideas, unable to stand on your own. This was like my Auntie An-mei.

Too much water and you flowed in too many directions, like myself, for having started half a degree in biology, then half a degree in art, and then finishing neither when I went off to work for a small ad agency as a secretary, later becoming a copywriter.

I used to dismiss her criticisms as just more of her Chinese superstitions, beliefs that conveniently fit the circumstances. In my twenties, while taking Introduction to Psychology, I tried to tell her why she shouldn't criticize so much, why it didn't lead to a healthy learning environment.

'There's a school of thought,' I said, 'that parents shouldn't criticize children. They should encourage instead. You know, people rise to other people's expectations. And when you criticize, it just means you're expecting failure.'

'That's the trouble,' my mother said. 'You never rise. Lazy to get up. Lazy to rise to expectations.'

'Time to eat,' Auntie An-mei happily announces, bringing out a steaming pot of the wonton she was just wrapping. There are piles of food on the table, served buffet style, just like at the Kweilin feasts. My father is digging into the chow mein, which still sits in an oversize aluminum pan surrounded by little plastic packets of soy sauce. Auntie An-mei must have bought this on Clement Street. The wonton soup smells wonderful with delicate sprigs of cilantro floating on top. I'm drawn first to a large platter of *chaswei*, sweet barbecued pork cut into coin-sized slices, and then to a whole assortment of what I've always called finger goodies—thin-skinned pastries filled with chopped pork, beef, shrimp, and unknown stuffings that my mother used to describe as 'nutritious things.'

Eating is not a gracious event here. It's as though everybody had been starving. They push large forkfuls into their mouths, jab at more pieces of pork, one right after the other. They are not like the ladies of Kweilin, who I always imagined savored their food with a certain detached delicacy.

And then, almost as quickly as they started, the men get up and leave the table. As if on cue, the women peck at last morsels and then carry plates and bowls to the kitchen and dump them in the sink. The women take turns washing their hands, scrubbing them vigorously. Who started this ritual? I too put my plate in the sink and wash my hands. The women are talking about the Jongs' China trip, then they move toward a room in the back of the apartment. We pass another room, what used to be the bedroom shared by the four Hsu sons. The bunk beds with their scuffed, splintery ladders are still there. The Joy Luck uncles are already seated at the card table. Uncle George is dealing out cards, fast, as though he learned this technique in a casino. My father is passing out Pall Mall cigarettes, with one already dangling from his lips.

And then we get to the room in the back, which was once shared by the three Hsu girls. We were all childhood friends. And now they've all grown and married and I'm here to play in their room again. Except for the smell of camphor, it feels the same—as if Rose, Ruth, and Janice might soon walk in with their hair rolled up in big orange-juice cans and plop down on their identical narrow beds. the white chenille bedspreads are so worn they are almost translucent. Rose and I used to pluck the nubs out while talking about our boy problems. Everything is the same, except now a mahogany-colored mah jong table sits in the center. And next to it is a floor lamp, a long black pole with three oval spotlights attached like the broad leaves of a rubber plant.

Nobody says to me, 'Sit here, this is where your mother used to sit.' But I can tell even before everyone sits down. The chair closest to the door has an emptiness to it. But the feeling doesn't really have to do with the chair. It's her place on the table. Without having anyone tell me, I know her corner on the table was the East.

The East is where things begin, my mother once told me, the direction from which the sun rises, where the wind comes from.

Auntie An-mei, who is sitting on my left, spills the tiles onto the green felt tabletop and then says to me, 'Now we wash tiles.' We

610

swirl them with our hands in a circular motion. They make a cool swishing sound as they bump into one another.

'Do you win like your mother?' asks Auntie Lin across from me. She is not smiling.

'I only played a little in college with some Jewish friends.'

'Annh! Jewish mah jong,' she says in disgusted tones. 'Not the same thing.' This is what my mother used to say, although she could never explain exactly why.

'Maybe I shouldn't play tonight, I'll just watch,' I offer.

Auntie Lin looks exasperated, as though I were a simple child: 'How can we play with just three people? Like a table with three legs, no balance. When Auntie Ying's husband died, she asked her brother to join. Your father asked you. So it's decided.'

'What's the difference between Jewish and Chinese mah jong?' I once asked my mother. I couldn't tell by her answer if the games were different or just her attitude toward Chinese and Jewish people.

'Entirely different kind of playing,' she said in her English explanation voice. 'Jewish mah jong, they watch only for their own tile, play only with their eyes.'

Then she switched to Chinese: 'Chinese mah jong, you must play using your head, very tricky. You must watch what everybody else throws away and keep that in your head as well. And if nobody plays well, then the game becomes like Jewish mah jong. Why play? There's no strategy. You're just watching people make mistakes.'

These kinds of explanations made me feel my mother and I spoke two different languages, which we did. I talked to her in English, she answered back in Chinese.

'So what's the difference between Chinese and Jewish mah jong?' I ask Auntie Lin.

'Aii-ya,' she exclaims in a mock scolding voice. 'Your mother did not teach you anything?'

Auntie Ying pats my hand. 'You a smart girl. You watch us, do the same. Help us stack the tiles and make four walls.'

I follow Auntie Ying, but mostly I watch Auntie Lin. She is the fastest, which means I can almost keep up with the others by watching what she does first. Auntie Ying throws the dice and I'm told that Auntie Lin has become the East wind. I've become the North wind, the last hand to play. Auntie Ying is the South and Auntie An-mei is the West. And then we start taking tiles, throwing the dice, counting back on the wall to the right number of spots where our chosen tiles lie. I rearrange my tiles, sequences of bamboo and balls, doubles of colored number tiles, odd tiles that do not fit anywhere.

'Your mother was the best, like a pro,' says Auntie An-mei while slowly sorting her tiles, considering each piece carefully.

Now we begin to play, looking at our hands, casting tiles, picking up others at an easy, comfortable pace. The Joy Luck aunties begin to make small talk, not really listening to each other. They speak in their special language, half in broken English, half in their own Chinese dialect. Auntie Ying mentions she bought yarn at half price, somewhere out in the avenues. Aunti An-mei brags about a sweater she made for her daughter Ruth's new baby. 'She thought it was store-bought,' she says proudly.

Auntie Lin explains how mad she got at a store clerk who refused to let her return a skirt with a broken zipper. 'I was *chiszle*,' she says, still fuming, 'mad to death.'

'But Lindo, you are still with us. You didn't die,' teases Auntie Ying, and then as she laughs Auntie Lin says '*Pung!*' and '*Mah jong!*' and then spreads her tiles out, laughing back at Auntie Ying while counting up her points. We start washing tiles again and it grows quiet. I'm getting bored and sleepy.

'Oh, I have a story,' says Auntie Ying loudly, startling everybody. Auntie Ying has always been the weird auntie, someone lost in her own world. My mother used to say, 'Auntie Ying is not hard of hearing. She is hard of listening.'

'Police arrested Mrs Emerson's son last weekend,' Auntie Ying says in a way that sounds as if she were proud to be the first with this big news. 'Mrs Chan told me at church. Too many TV set found in his car.'

Auntie Lin quickly says, 'Aii-ya, Mrs Emerson good lady,' meaning Mrs Emerson didn't deserve such a terrible son. But now I see this is also said for the benefit of Auntie An-mei, whose own youngest son was arrested two years ago for selling stolen car stereos. Auntie An-mei is rubbing her tile carefully before discarding it. She looks pained.

'Everybody has TVs in China now,' says Auntie Lin, changing the subject. 'Our family there all has TV sets—not just black-and-white, but color and remote! They have everything. So when we asked them what we should buy them, they said nothing, it was enough that we would come to visit them. But we bought them different things anyway, VCR and Sony Walkman for the kids. They said, No, don't give it to us, but I think they liked it.'

Poor Auntie An-mei rubs her tiles ever harder. I remember my mother telling me about the Hsus' trip to China three years ago. Auntie An-mei had saved two thousand dollars, all to spend on her brother's family. She had shown my mother the insides of her heavy suitcases. One was crammed with See's Nuts & Chews, M & M's, candy-coated cashews, instant hot chocolate with miniature marshmallows. My mother told me the other bag contained the most ridiculous clothes, all new: bright California-style beachwear, baseball caps, cotton pants with elastic waists, bomber jackets, Stanford sweatshirts, crew socks.

My mother had told her, 'Who wants those useless things? They just want money.' But Auntie An-mei said her brother was so poor and they were so rich by comparison. So she ignored my mother's advice and took the heavy bags and their two thousand dollars to China. And when their China tour finally arrived in Hangzhou, the whole family from Ningbo was there to meet them. It wasn't just Auntie An-mei's little brother, but also his wife's stepbrothers and stepsisters, and a distant cousin, and that cousin's husband and that husband's uncle. They had all brought their mothers-in-law and children, and even their village friends who were not lucky enough to have overseas Chinese relatives to show off.

As my mother told it, 'Auntie An-mei had cried before she left for China, thinking she would make her brother very rich and happy by communist standards. But when she got home, she cried to me that everyone had a palm out and she was the only one who left with an empty hand.'

My mother confirmed her suspicions. Nobody wanted the sweatshirts, those useless clothes. The M & M's were thrown in the air, gone. And when the suitcases were emptied, the relatives asked what else the Hsus had brought.

Auntie An-mei and Uncle George were shaken down, not just for two thousand dollars' worth of TVs and refrigerators but also for a night's lodging for twenty-six people in the Overlooking the Lake Hotel, for three banquet tables at a restaurant that catered to rich foreigners, for three special gifts for each relative, and finally, for a loan of five thousand *yuan* in foreign exchange to a cousin's so-called uncle who wanted to buy a motorcycle but who later disappeared for good along with the money. When the train pulled out of Hangzhou the next day, the Hsus found themselves depleted of some nine thousand dollars' worth of goodwill. Months later, after an inspiring Christmastime service at the First Chinese Baptist Church, Auntie An-mei tried to recoup her loss by saying it truly was more blessed to give than to receive, and my mother agreed, her longtime friend had blessings for at least several lifetimes.

Listening now to Auntie Lin bragging about the virtues of her family in China, I realize that Auntie Lin is oblivious to Auntie An-mei's pain. Is Auntie Lin being mean, or is it that my mother never told anybody but me the shameful story of Auntie An-mei's greedy family?

'So, Jing-mei, you go to school now?' says Auntie Lin.

'Her name is June. They all go by their American names,' says Auntie Ying.

'That's okay,' I say, and I really mean it. In fact, it's even becoming fashionable for American-born Chinese to use their Chinese names.

'I'm not in school anymore, though,' I say. 'That was more than ten years ago.'

Auntie Lin's eyebrows arch. 'Maybe I'm thinking of someone else daughter,' she says, but I know right away she's lying. I know my mother probably told her I was going back to school to finish my degree, because somewhere back, maybe just six months ago, we were again having this argument about my being a failure, a 'college drop-off,' about my going back to finish.

Once again I had told my mother what she wanted to hear: 'You're right. I'll look into it.'

I had always assumed we had an unspoken understanding about these things: that she didn't really mean I was a failure, and I really meant I would try to respect her opinions more. But listening to Auntie Lin tonight reminds me once again: My mother and I never really understood one another. We translated each other's meanings and I seemed to hear less than what was said, while my mother heard more. No doubt she told Auntie Lin I was going back to school to get a doctorate.

Auntie Lin and my mother were both best friends and arch enemies who spent a lifetime comparing their children. I was one month older than Waverly Jong, Auntie Lin's prized daughter. From the time we were babies, our mothers compared the creases in our belly buttons, how shapely our earlobes were, how fast we healed when we scraped our knees, how thick and dark our hair, how many shoes we wore out in one year, and later, how smart Waverly was at playing chess, how many trophies she had won last month, how many newspapers had printed her name, how many cities she had visited.

I know my mother resented listening to Auntie Lin talk about Waverly when she had nothing to come back with. At first my mother tried to cultivate some hidden genius in me. She did housework for an old retired piano teacher down the hall who gave me lessons and free use of a piano to practice on in exchange. When I failed to become a concert pianist, or even an accompanist for the church youth choir, she finally explained that I was late-blooming, like Einstein, who everyone thought was retarded until he discovered a bomb.

Now it is Auntie Ying who wins this hand of mah jong, so we count points and begin again.

'Did you know Lena move to Woodside?' asks Auntie Ying with obvious pride, looking down at the tiles, talking to no one in particular. She quickly erases her smile and tries for some modesty. 'Of course, it's not best house in neighborhood, not million-dollar house, not yet. But it's good investment. Better than paying rent. Better than somebody putting you under their thumb to rub you out.'

So now I know Auntie Ying's daughter, Lena, told her about my being evicted from my apartment on lower Russian Hill. Even though Lena and I are still friends, we have grown naturally cautious about telling each other too much. Still, what little we say to one another often comes back in another guise. It's the same old game, everybody talking in circles.

'It's getting late,' I say after we finish the round. I start to stand up, but Auntie Lin pushes me back down into the chair.

'Stay, stay. We talk awhile, get to know you again,' she says. 'Been a long time.'

I know this is a polite gesture on the Joy Luck aunties' part—a protest when actually they are just as eager to see me go as I am to leave. 'No, I really must go now, thank you, thank you,' I say, glad I remembered how the pretense goes.

'But you must stay! We have something important to tell you, from your mother,' Auntie Ying blurts out in her too-loud voice. The others look uncomfortable, as if this were not how they intended to break some sort of bad news to me.

I sit down. Auntie An-mei leaves the room quickly and returns with a bowl of peanuts, then quietly shuts the door. Everybody is quiet, as if nobody knew where to begin.

It is Auntie Ying who finally speaks. 'I think your mother die with an important thought on her mind,' she says in halting English. And then she begins to speak in Chinese, calmly, softly.

'Your mother was a very strong woman, a good mother. She loved you very much, more than her own life. And that's why you can understand why a mother like this could never forget her other daughters. She knew they were alive, and before she died she wanted to find her daughters in China.'

The babies in Kweilin, I think. I was not those babies. The babies in a sling on her shoulder. Her other daughters. And now I feel as if I were in Kweilin amidst the bombing and I can see these babies lying on the side of the road, their red thumbs popped out of their mouths, screaming to be reclaimed. Somebody took them away. They're safe. And now my mother's left me forever, gone back to China to get these babies. I can barely hear Auntie Ying's voice.

'She had searched for years, written letters back and forth,' says Auntie Ying. 'And last year she got an address. She was going to tell your father soon. Aii-ya, what a shame. A lifetime of waiting.'

Auntie An-mei interrupts with an excited voice: 'So your aunties and I, we wrote to this address,' she says. 'We say that a certain party, your mother, want to meet another certain party. And this party write back to us. They are your sisters, Jing-mei.'

My sisters, I repeat to myself, saying those two words together for the first time.

Auntie An-mei is holding a sheet of paper as thin as wrapping tissue. In perfectly straight vertical rows I see Chinese characters written in blue fountain-pen ink. A word is smudged. A tear? I take the letter with shaking hands, marveling at how smart my sisters must be to able to read and write Chinese.

The aunties are all smiling at me, as though I had been a dying person who has now miraculously recovered. Auntie Ying is handing me another envelope. Inside is a check made out to June Woo for $1,200. I can't believe it.

'My sisters are sending *me* money?' I ask.

'No, no,' says Auntie Lin with her mock exasperated voice. 'Every year we save our mah jong winnings for big banquet at fancy restaurant. Most times your mother win, so most is her money. We add just a little, so you can go Hong Kong, take a train to Shanghai, see your sisters. Besides, we all getting too rich, too fat.' She pats her stomach for proof.

'See my sisters,' I say numbly. I am awed by this prospect, trying to imagine what I would see. And I am embarrassed by the end-of-the-year-banquet lie my aunties have told to mask their generosity. I am crying now, sobbing and laughing at the same time, seeing but not understanding this loyalty to my mother.

'You must see your sisters and tell them about your mother's death,' says Auntie Ying. 'But most important, you must tell them about her life. The mother they did not know, they must now know.'

'See my sisters, tell them about my mother,' I say, nodding. 'What will I say? What can I tell them about my mother? I don't know anything. She was my mother.'

The aunties are looking at me as if I had become crazy right before their eyes.

'Not know your own mother?' says Auntie An-mei with disbelief. 'How can you say? Your mother is in your bones!'

'Tell them stories of your family here. How she became success,' offers Auntie Lin.

'Tell them stories she told you, lessons she taught, what you know about her mind that has become your mind,' says Auntie Ying. 'Your mother very smart lady.'

I hear more choruses of 'Tell them, tell them' as each Auntie frantically tries to think what should be passed on.

'Her kindness.'

'Her smartness.'

'Her dutiful nature to family.'

'Her hopes, things that matter to her.'

'The excellent dishes she cooked.'

'Imagine, a daughter not knowing her own mother!'

And then it occurs to me. They are frightened. In me, they see their own daughters, just as ignorant, just as unmindful of all the truths and hopes they have brought to America. They see daughters who grow impatient when their mothers talk in Chinese, who think they are stupid when they explain things in fractured English. They see that joy and luck do not mean the same to their daughters, that to these closed American-born minds 'joy luck' is not a word, it does not exist. They see daughters who will bear grandchildren born without any connecting hope passed from generation to generation.

'I will tell them everything,' I say simply, and the aunties look at me with doubtful faces.

'I will remember everything about her and tell them,' I say more firmly. And gradually, one by one, they smile and pat my hand. They still look troubled, as if something were out of balance. But they also look hopeful that what I say will become true. What more can they ask? What more can I promise?

They go back to eating their soft boiled peanuts, saying stories among themselves. They are young girls again, dreaming of good times in the past and good times yet to come. A brother from Ningbo who makes his sister cry with joy when he returns nine thousand dollars plus interest. A youngest son whose stereo and TV repair business is so good he sends leftovers to China. A daughter whose babies are able to swim like fish in a fancy pool in Woodside. Such good stories. The best. They are the lucky ones.

And I am sitting at my mother's place at the mah jong table, on the East, where things begin.

1989

THE FIREMAN'S WIFE

Richard Bausch

Jane's husband, Martin, works for the fire department. He's on four days, off three; on three, off four. It's the kind of shift work that allows plenty of time for sustained recreation, and during the off times Martin likes to do a lot of socializing with his two shift mates, Wally Harmon and Teddy Lynch. The three of them are like brothers: they bicker and squabble and compete in a friendly way about everything, including their common hobby, which is the making and flying of model airplanes. Martin is fanatical about it—spends way too much money on the two planes he owns, which are on the worktable in the garage, and which seem to require as much maintenance as the real article. Among the arguments between Jane and her husband—about money, lack of time alone together, and housework—there have been some about the model planes, but Jane can't say or do much without sounding like a poor sport: Wally's wife, Milly, loves watching the boys, as she calls them, fly their planes, and Teddy Lynch's ex-wife, before they were divorced, had loved the model planes too. In a way, Jane is the outsider here: Milly Harmon has known Martin most of his life, and Teddy Lynch was once point guard to Martin's power forward on their high school basketball team. Jane is relatively new, having come to Illinois from Virginia only two years ago, when Martin brought her back with him from his reserve training there.

This evening, a hot September twilight, they're sitting on lawn chairs in the dim light of the coals in Martin's portable grill, talking about games. Martin and Teddy want to play Risk, though they're already arguing about the rules. Teddy says that a European version of the game contains a wrinkle that makes it more interesting, and Martin is arguing that the game itself was derived from some French game.

'Well, go get it' Teddy says, 'and I'll show you. I'll bet it's in the instructions.'

'Don't get that out now,' Jane says to Martin.

'It's too long,' Wally Harmon says.

'What if we play cards,' Martin says.

'Martin doesn't want to lose his bet,' Teddy says.

'We don't have any bets, Teddy.'

'OK, so let's bet.'

'Let's play cards,' Martin says. 'Wally's right. Risk takes too long.'

'I feel like conquering the world,' Teddy says.

'Oh, Teddy,' Milly Harmon says. 'Please shut up.'

She's expecting. She sits with her legs out, holding her belly as though it were unattached, separate from her. The child will be her first, and she's excited and happy; she glows, as if she knows everyone's admiring her.

Jane thinks Milly is spreading it on a little thick at times: lately all she wants to talk about is her body and what it's doing.

'I had a dream last night,' Milly says now. 'I dreamed that I was pregnant. Big as a house. And I woke up and I was. What I want to know is, was that a nightmare?'

'How did you feel in the dream?' Teddy asks her.

'I said. Big as a house.'

'Right, but was it bad or good?'

'How would you feel if you were big as a house?'

'Well, that would depend on what the situation was.'

'The situation is, you're big as a house.'

'Yeah, but what if somebody was chasing me? I'd want to be big, right?'

'Oh, Teddy, please shut up.'

'I had a dream,' Wally says. 'A bad dream. I dreamed I died. I mean, you know, I was dead—and what was weird was that I was also the one who had to call Milly to tell her about it.'

'Oh, God,' Milly says. 'Don't talk about this.'

'It was weird. I got killed out at sea or something. Drowned, I guess. I remember I was standing on the deck of this ship talking to somebody about how it went down. And then I was calling Milly to tell her. And the thing is, I talked like a stranger would—you know, "I'm sorry to inform you that your husband went down at sea." It was weird.'

'How did you feel when you woke up?' Martin says.

'I was scared. I didn't know who I was for a couple of seconds.'

'Look,' Milly says, 'I don't want to talk about dreams.'

'Let's talk about good dreams,' Jane says. 'I had a good dream. I

620

was fishing with my father out at a creek—some creek that felt like a real place. Like if I ever really did go fishing with my father, this is where we would have fished when I was small.'

'What?' Martin says after a pause, and everyone laughs.

'Well,' Jane says, feeling the blood rise in her face and neck, 'I never—my father died when I was a baby.'

'I dreamed I got shot once,' Teddy says. 'Guy shot me with a forty-five automatic as I was running downstairs. I fell and hit bottom, too. I could feel the cold concrete on the side of my face before I woke up.'

Milly Harmon sits forward a little and says to Wally, 'Honey, why did you have to tell about having a dream like that? Now I'm going to dream about it, I just know it.'

'I think we all ought to call it a night,' Jane says. 'You guys have to get up at six o'clock in the morning.'

'What're you talking about?' Martin says. 'We're going to play cards, aren't we?'

'I thought we were going to play Risk,' Teddy says.

'All right,' Martin says, getting out of his chair. 'Risk it is.'

Milly groans, and Jane gets up and follows Martin into the house. 'Honey,' she says. 'Not Risk. Come on. We'd need four hours at least.'

He says over his shoulder, 'So then we need four hours.'

'Martin, I'm tired.'

He's leaning up into the hall closet, where the games are stacked. He brings the Risk game down and turns, holding it in both hands like a tray. 'Look, where do you get off, telling everybody to go home the way you did?'

She stands there staring at him.

'These people are our friends, Jane.'

'I just said I thought we ought to call it a night.'

'Well don't say—all right? It's embarrassing.'

He goes around her and back out to the patio. The screen door slaps twice in the jamb. She waits a moment and then moves through the house to the bedroom. She brushes her hair, thinks about getting out of her clothes. Martin's uniforms are lying across the foot of the bed. She picks them up, walks into the living room with them and drapes them over the back of the easy chair.

'Jane,' Martin calls from the patio. 'Are you playing or not?'

'Come on, Jane,' Milly says. 'Don't leave me alone out here.'

'What color armies do you want?' Martin asks.

She goes to the patio door and looks out at them. Martin has
lighted the tiki lamps; everyone's sitting at the picnic table in the
moving firelight. 'Come on,' Martin says, barely concealing his
irritation. She can hear it, and she wants to react to it—wants to let
him know that she is hurt. But they're all waiting for her, so she steps
out and takes her place at the table. she chooses green for her armies,
and she plays the game to lose, attacking in all directions until her
forces are so badly depleted that when Wally begins to make his own
move she's the first to lose all her armies. This takes more than an
hour. When she's out of the game, she sits for a while, cheering
Teddy on against Martin, who is clearly going to win; finally she
excuses herself and goes back into the house. The glow from the tiki
lamps makes weird patterns on the kitchen wall. She pours herself a
glass of water and drinks it down; then she pours more and swallows
some aspirin. Teddy sees this as he comes in for more beer, and he
grasps her by the elbow and asks if she wants something a little better
than aspirin for a headache.

'Like what?' she says, smiling at him. She's decided a smile is what
one offers under such circumstances; one laughs things off, pretends
not to notice the glazed look in the other person's eyes.

Teddy is staring at her, not quite smiling. Finally he puts his hands
on her shoulders and says, 'What's the matter, lady?'

'Nothing,' she says. 'I have a headache. I took some aspirin.'

'I've got some stuff,' he says. 'It makes America beautiful. Want
some?'

She says, 'Teddy.'

'No problem,' he says. He holds both hands up and backs away
from her. Then he turns and is gone. She hears him begin to tease
Martin about the French rules of the game. Martin is winning. He
wants Wally Harmon to keep playing, and Wally wants to quit. Milly
and Teddy are talking about flying the model airplanes. They know
about an air show in Danville on Saturday. They all keep playing and
talking, and for a long time Jane watches them from the screen door.
She smokes half a pack of cigarettes, and she paces a little. She drinks
three glasses of orange juice, and finally she walks into the bedroom
and lies down with her face in her hands. Her forehead feels hot.
She's thinking about the next four days, when Martin will be gone
and she can have the house to herself. She hasn't been married even
two years, and she feels crowded; she's depressed and tired every
day. She never has enough time to herself. And yet when she's alone,

she feels weak and afraid. Now she hears someone in the hallway and she sits up, smooths her hair back from her face. Milly Harmon comes in with her hands cradling her belly.

'Ah,' Milly says. 'A bed.' She sits down next to Jane and then leans back on her hands. 'I'm beat,' she says.

'I have a headache,' Jane says.

Milly nods. Her expression seems to indicate how unimportant she finds this, as if Jane had told her she'd already got over a cold or something. 'They're in the garage now,' she says.'

'Who?'

'Teddy, Wally, Martin. Martin conquered the world.'

'What're they doing?' Jane asks. 'It's almost midnight.'

'Everybody's going to be miserable in the morning,' Milly says.

Jane is quiet.

'Oh,' Milly says, looking down at herself. 'He kicked. Want to feel it?'

She takes Jane's hand and puts it on her belly. Jane feels movement under her fingers,something very slight, like one heartbeat.

'Wow,' she says. She pulls her hand away.

'Listen,' Milly says. 'I know we can all be overbearing sometimes. Martin doesn't realize some of his responsibilities yet. Wally was the same way.'

'I just have this headache,' Jane says. She doesn't want to talk about it, doesn't want to get into it. Even when she talks to her mother on the phone and her mother asks how things are, she says it's all fine. She has nothing she wants to confide.

'You feel trapped, don't you,' Milly says.

Jane looks at her.

'Don't you?'

'No.'

'OK—you just have a headache.'

'I do,' Jane says.

Milly sits forward a little, folds her hands over the roundness of her belly. 'This baby's jumping all over the place.'

Jane is silent.

'Do you believe my husband and that awful dream? I wish he hadn't told us about it—now I know I'm going to dream something like it. You know pregnant women and dreams. I begin to shake just thinking of it.'

'Try not to think of it,' Jane says.

623

Milly waits for a moment and then clears her throat and says, 'You know, for a while there after Wally and I were married, I thought maybe I'd made a mistake. I remember realizing that I didn't like the way he laughed. I mean, let's face it, Wally laughs like a hyena. And somehow that took on all kinds of importance—you know, I had to absolutely like everything about him or I couldn't like anything. Have you ever noticed the way he laughs?'

Jane has never really thought about it. But she says nothing now. She simply nods.

'But you know,' Milly goes on, 'all I had to do was wait. Just—you know, wait for love to come around and surprise me again.'

'Milly, I have a headache. I mean, what do you think is wrong, anyway?'

'OK,' Milly says, rising.

Then Jane wonders whether the other woman has been put up to this conversation. 'Hey,' she says, 'did Martin say something to you?'

'What would Martin say?'

'I don't know. I mean, I really don't know, Milly. Jesus Christ, can't a person have a simple headache?'

'OK,' Milly says. 'OK.'

'I like the way everyone talks around me here, you know it?'

'Nobody's talking around you—'

'I think it's wonderful how close you all are.'

'All right,' Milly says, standing there with her hands folded under the bulge of her belly. 'You just look so unhappy these days.'

'Look,' Jane says, 'I have a headache, all right? I'm going to go to bed. I mean, the only way I can get rid of it is to lie down in the dark and be very quiet—OK?'

'Sure, honey,' Milly says.

'So—goodnight, then.'

'Right,' Milly says. 'Goodnight.' She steps toward Jane and kisses her on the cheek. 'I'll tell Martin to call it a night. I know Wally'll be miserable tomorrow.'

'It's because they can take turns sleeping on shift,' Jane says.

'I'll tell them,' Milly says, going down the hall.

Jane steps out of her jeans, pulls her blouse over her head and crawls under the sheets, which are cool and fresh and crisp. She turns the light off and closes her eyes. She can't believe how bad it is. She hears them all saying goodnight, and she hears Martin shutting the doors and turning off the lights. In the dark she waits for him to get to her. She's very still, lying on her back with her hands at her sides. He goes into the bathroom at the end of the hall. She hears him cough, clear his throat. He's cleaning his teeth. Then he comes to the entrance of the bedroom and stands in the light of the hall.

'I know you're awake,' he says.

She doesn't answer.

'Jane,' he says.

She says, 'What?'

'Are you mad at me?'

'No.'

'Then what's wrong?'

'I have a headache.'

'You always have a headache.'

'I'm not going to argue now, Martin. So you can say what you want.'

He moves toward her, is standing by the bed. He's looming above her in the dark. 'Teddy had some dope.'

She says, 'I know. He offered me some.'

'I'm flying,' Martin says.

She says nothing.

'Let's make love.'

'Martin,' she says. Her heart is beating fast. He moves a little, staggers taking off his shirt. He's so big and quick and powerful; nothing fazes him. When he's like this, the feeling she has is that he might do anything. 'Martin,' she says.

'All right,' he says. 'I won't. OK? You don't have to worry your little self about it.'

'Look,' she says.

But he's already headed into the hall.

'Martin,' she says.

He's in the living room. He turns the television on loud. A rerun of *Kojak*. She hears Theo calling someone sweetheart. 'Sweetheart,' Martin says. When she goes to him, she finds that he's opened a beer and is sitting on the couch with his legs out. The beer is balanced on his stomach.

'Martin,' she says. 'You have to start your shift in less than five hours.'

He holds the beer up. 'Baby,' he says.

In the morning he's sheepish, obviously in pain. He sits at the kitchen table with his hands up to his head while she makes coffee and hard-boiled eggs. She has to go to work, too, at a car dealership in town. All day she sits behind a window with a circular hole in the glass, where people line up to pay for whatever the dealer sells or provides, including mechanical work, parts, license plates, used cars, rental cars and, of course, new cars. Her day is long and exhausting, and she's already feeling as though she worked all night. The booth she has to sit in is right off the service bay area, and the smell of exhaust and grease is everywhere. Everything seems coated with a film of grime. She's standing at her sink, looking at the sun coming up past the trees beyond her street, and without thinking about it she puts the water on and washes her hands. The idea of the car dealership is like something clinging to her skin.

'Jesus,' Martin says. He can't eat much.

She's drying her hands on a paper towel.

'Listen,' he says, 'I'm sorry, OK?'

'Sorry?' she says.

'Don't press it, all right? You know what I mean.'

'OK,' she says, and when he gets up and comes over to put his arms around her, she feels his difference from her. She kisses him. They stand there.

'Four days,' he says.

When Teddy and Wally pull up in Wally's new pickup, she stands in the kitchen door and waves at them. Martin walks down the driveway, carrying his tote bag of uniforms and books to read. He turns around and blows her a kiss. This morning is like so many other mornings. They drive off. She goes back into the bedroom and makes the bed, and puts his dirty uniforms in the wash. She showers and chooses something to wear. It's quiet. She puts the radio on and then decides she'd rather have the silence. After she's dressed, she stands at the back door and looks out at the street. Children are walking to school in little groups of friends. She thinks about the four days ahead. What she needs is to get into the routine and stop thinking so much. She knows that problems in a marriage are worked out over time.

Before she leaves for work she goes out into the garage to look for signs of Teddy's dope. She doesn't want someone stumbling on incriminating evidence. On the worktable along the back wall are Martin's model planes. She walks over and stands staring at them. She stands very still, as if waiting for something to move.

At work her friend Eveline smokes one cigarette after another, apologizing for each one. During Martin's shifts Jane spends a lot of time with Eveline, who is twenty-nine and single and wants very much to be married. The problem is she can't find anyone. Last year, when Jane was first working at the dealership, she got Eveline a date with Teddy Lynch. Teddy took Eveline to Lum's for hot dogs and beer, and they had fun at first. But then Eveline got drunk and passed out—put her head down on her arms and went to sleep like a child asked to take a nap in school. Teddy put her in a cab for home and then called Martin to laugh about the whole thing. Eveline was so humiliated by the experience that she goes out of her way to avoid Teddy—doesn't want anything to do with him or with any of Martin's friends, or with Martin, for that matter. She will come over to the house only when she knows Martin is away at work. And when Martin calls the dealership and she answers the phone, she's very stiff and formal, and she hands the phone quickly to Jane.

Today things aren't very busy, and they work a crossword together, making sure to keep it out of sight of the salesmen, who occasionally wander in to waste time with them. Eveline plays her radio and hums along with some of the songs. It's a long, slow day, and when Martin calls Jane feels herself growing anxious— something is moving in the pit of her stomach.

'Are you still mad at me?' he says.

'No,' she tells him.

'Say you love me.'

'I love you.'

'Everybody's asleep here,' he says. 'I wish you were with me.'

She says, 'Right.'

'I do,' he says.

'OK.'

'You don't believe me?'

'I said *OK.*'

'Is it busy today?' he asks.

'Not too.'

'You're bored, then.'

'A little,' she says.

'How's the headache?'

'Just the edge of one.'

'I'm sorry,' he says.

'It's not your fault.'

'Sometimes I feel like it is.'

'How's *your* head?' she says.

'Terrible.'

'Poor boy.'

'I wish something would happen around here,' he says. 'A lot of guys snoring.'

'Martin,' she says, 'I've got to go.'

'OK.'

'You want me to stop by tonight?' she asks.

'If you want to.'

'Maybe I will.'

'You don't have to.'

She thinks about him where he is: she imagines him, comfortable, sitting on a couch in front of a television. Sometimes, when nothing's going on, he watches all the soaps. He was hooked on *General Hospital* for a while. That he's her husband seems strange, and she thinks of the nights she's lain in his arms, whispering his name over and over, putting her hands in his hair and rocking with him in the dark. She tells him she loves him, and hangs the phone up. Eveline makes a gesture of frustration and envy.

'Nuts,' Eveline says. 'Nuts to you and your lovey-dovey stuff.'

Jane is sitting in a bath of cold inner light, trying to think of her husband as someone she recognizes.

'Let's do something tonight,' Eveline says. 'Maybe I'll get lucky.'

'I'm not going with you if you're going to be giving strange men the eye,' Jane says. She hasn't quite heard herself. She's surprised when Eveline reacts.

'How dare you say a nasty thing like that? I don't know if I want to go out with someone who doesn't think any more of me than *that*.'

'I'm sorry,' Jane says, patting the other woman's wrist. 'I didn't mean anything by it, really. I was just teasing.'

'Well, don't tease that way. It hurts my feelings.'

'I'm sorry,' Jane says again. 'Please—really.' She feels near crying.

'Well, OK,' Eveline says. 'Don't get upset. I'm half teasing myself.'

Jane sniffles, wipes her eyes with the back of one hand.

'What's wrong, anyway?' Eveline says.

'Nothing,' Jane says. 'I hurt your feelings.'

That evening they ride in Eveline's car over to Shakey's for a pizza, and then stroll down to the end of the block to the new mini-mall on

Lincoln Avenue. The night is breezy and warm. A storm is building over the town square. They window-shop for a while, and finally they stop at a new corner café, to sit in a booth by the windows, drinking beer. Across the street one of the movies has ended, and people are filing out, or waiting around. A few of them head this way.

'They don't look like they enjoyed the movie very much,' Eveline says.

'Maybe they did, and they're just depressed to be back in the real world.'

'Look, what is it?' Eveline asks suddenly.

Jane returns her gaze.

'What's wrong?'

'Nothing.'

'Something's wrong,' Eveline says.

Two boys from the high school come past, and one of them winks at Jane. She remembers how it was in high school—the games of flirtation and pursuit, of ignoring some people and noticing others. That seemed like such an unbearable time, and it's already years ago. She watches Eveline light yet another cigarette and feels very much older than her own memory of herself. She sees the person she is now, with Martin, somewhere years away, happy, with children, and with different worries. It's a vivid daydream. She sits there fabricating it, feeling it for what it is and feeling, too, that nothing will change: the Martin she sees in the daydream is nothing like the man she lives with. She thinks of Milly Harmon, pregnant and talking about waiting to be surprised by love.

'I think I'd like to have a baby,' she says. She hadn't known she would say it.

Eveline says, 'Yuck,' blowing smoke.

'Yuck,' Jane says. 'That's great. Great response, Evie.'

They're quiet awhile. Beyond the square the clouds break up into tatters, and lightning strikes out. They hear thunder, and the smell of rain is in the air. The trees in the little park across from the theater move in the wind, and leaves blow out of them.

'Wouldn't you like to have a family?' Jane says.

'Sure.'

'Well, the last time I checked, that meant having babies.'

'Yuck,' Eveline says again.

'Oh, all right—you just mean because of the pain and all.'

'I mean yuck.'

'Well, what does "yuck" mean, OK?'

'What *is* the matter with you?' Eveline says. 'What difference does it make?'

'I'm trying to have a normal conversation,' Jane says, 'and I'm getting these weird one-word answers, that's all. I mean what's "yuck," anyway? What's it mean?'

'Let's say it means I don't want to talk about having babies.'

'I wasn't talking about you.'

Each is now a little annoyed with the other. Jane has noticed that whenever she talks about anything that might border on plans for the future, the other woman becomes irritatingly sardonic and closemouthed. Eveline sits there smoking her cigarette and watching the storm come. From beyond the square they hear sirens, which seem to multiply. The whole city seems to be mobilizing. Jane thinks of Martin out there where all those alarms are converging. How odd to know where your husband is by a sound everyone hears. She remembers lying awake nights early in the marriage, hearing sirens and worrying about what might happen. And now, through a slanting sheet of rain, as though something in these thoughts has produced her, Milly Harmon comes, holding an open magazine above her head. She sees Jane and Eveline in the window and waves at them. 'Oh, God,' Eveline says. 'Isn't that Milly Harmon?'

Milly comes into the café and stands for a moment, shaking water from herself. Her hair is wet, as are her shoulders. She pushes her hair away from her forehead, and wipes the rain away with the back of one hand. Then she walks over and says, 'Hi, honey,' to Jane, bending down to kiss her on the side of the face. Jane manages to seem glad to see her. 'You remember my friend Eveline from work,' she says.

'I think I do, sure,' Milly says.

'Maybe not,' Eveline says.

'No, I think I do.'

'I have one of those faces that remind you of somebody you never met,' Eveline says.

Jane covers this with a laugh as Milly settles on her side of the booth.

Milly is breathless, all bustle and worry, arranging herself, getting comfortable. 'Do you hear that?' she says about the sirens. 'I swear, it must be a big one. I wish I didn't hear the sirens. It makes me so jumpy and scared. Wally would never forgive me if I did, but I wish I could get up the nerve to go see what it is.'

'So,' Eveline says, blowing smoke, 'how's the baby coming along?'

Milly looks down at herself. 'Sleeping now, I think.'

'Wally—is it Wally?'

'Wally, yes.'

'Wally doesn't let you chase ambulances.'

'I don't chase ambulances.'

'Well, I mean—you aren't allowed to go see what's what when you hear sirens?'

'I don't want to see.'

'I guess not.'

'He's seen some terrible things. They all have. It must be terrible sometimes.'

'Right,' Eveline says. 'It must be terrible.'

Milly waves her hand in front of her face. 'I wish you wouldn't smoke.'

'I was smoking before you came,' Eveline says. 'I didn't know you were coming.'

Milly looks confused for a second. Then she sits back a little and folds her hands on the table. She's chosen to ignore Eveline. She looks at Jane and says, 'I had that dream last night.'

Jane says, 'What dream?'

'That Wally was gone.'

Jane says nothing.

'But it wasn't the same, really. He'd left me, you know—the baby was born and he'd just gone off. I was so mad at him. And I had this crying little baby in my lap.'

Eveline swallows the last of her beer and then gets up and goes out to stand near the line of wet pavement at the edge of the awninged sidewalk.

'What's the matter with her?' Milly asks.

'She's just unhappy.'

'Did I say something wrong?'

'No—really. It's nothing,' Jane says.

She pays for the beer. Milly talks to her for a while, but Jane has a hard time concentrating on much of anything now, with sirens going and Eveline standing out there at the edge of the sidewalk. Milly goes on, talking nervously about Wally's leaving her in her dream and how funny it is that she woke up mad at him, that she had to wait a few minutes and get her head clear before she could kiss him good morning.

'I've got to go,' Jane says. 'I came in Eveline's car.'

'Oh, I'm sorry—sure. I just stepped in out of the rain myself.'

They join Eveline outside, and Milly says she's got to go get her nephews before they knock down the ice-cream parlor. Jane and Eveline watch her walk away in the rain, and Eveline says, 'Jesus.'

'She's just scared,' Jane says. 'God, leave her alone.'

'I don't mean anything by it,' Eveline says. 'A little malice, maybe.'

Jane says nothing. They stand there watching the rain and lightning, and soon they're talking about people at work, the salesmen and the boys in the parts shop. They're relaxed now; the sirens have stopped and the tension between them has lifted. They laugh about one salesman who's apparently interested in Eveline. He's a married man—an overweight, balding, middle-aged Texan who wears snakeskin boots and a string tie, and who has an enormous fake-diamond ring on the little finger of his left hand. Eveline calls him Disco Bill. And yet Jane thinks her friend may be secretly attracted to him. She teases her about this, or begins to, and then a clap of thunder so frightens them both that they laugh about it, off and on, through the rest of the evening. They wind up visiting Eveline's parents, who live only a block from the café. Eveline's parents have been married almost thirty years, and, sitting in their living room, Jane looks at their things—the love seat and the antique chairs, the handsome grandfather clock in the hall, the paintings. The place has a lovely *tended* look about it. Everything seems to stand for the kind of life she wants for herself: an attentive, loving husband; children; and a quiet house with a clock that chimes. She knows this is all very dreamy and childish, and yet she looks at Eveline's parents, those people with their almost thirty years' love, and her heart aches. She drinks four glasses of white wine and realizes near the end of the visit that she's talking too much, laughing too loudly.

It's very late when she gets home. She lets herself in the side door of the house and walks through the rooms, turning on all the lights, as is her custom—she wants to be sure no one is hiding in any of the nooks and crannies. Tonight she looks at everything and feels demeaned by it. Martin's clean uniforms are lying across the back of the lounge chair in the living room. The television and the television trays are in one corner, next to the coffee table, which is a gift from Martin's parents, something they bought back in the fifties, before Martin was born. Martin's parents live on a farm ten miles outside town, and for the past year Jane has had to spend Sundays out there, sitting in that living room with its sparse, starved look, listening to Martin's father talk about the weather, or what he had to eat for lunch, or the wrestling matches he watches on television. He's a kindly man but he has nothing whatever of interest to say, and he seems to know it—his own voice always seems to surprise him at first, as if some profound inner silence had been broken; he pauses, seems to gather himself, and then continues with the considered, slow cadences of oration. He's tall and lean and powerful looking; he wears coveralls, and he reminds Jane of those pictures of hungry, bewildered men in the Dust Bowl thirties—with their sad, straight, combed hair and their desperation. Yet he's a man who seems quite certain about things, quite calm and satisfied. His wife fusses around him, making sure of his comfort, and he speaks to her in exactly the same soft, sure tones he uses with Jane.

Now, sitting in her own living room, thinking about this man, her father-in-law, Jane realizes that she can't stand another Sunday afternoon listening to him talk. It comes to her like a chilly premonition and quite suddenly, with a kind of tidal shifting inside her, she feels the full weight of her unhappiness. For the first time it seems unbearable, like something that might drive her out of her mind. She breathes, swallows, closes her eyes and opens them. She looks at her own reflection in one of the darkened windows of the kitchen, and then she finds herself in the bedroom, pulling her things out of the closet and throwing them on the bed. Something about this is a little frantic, as though each motion fed some impulse to go further, go through with it—use this night, make her way somewhere else. For a long time she works, getting the clothes out where she can see them. She's lost herself in the practical matter of getting packed. She can't decide what to take, and then she can't find a suitcase or an overnight bag. Finally she settles on one of Martin's travel bags, from when he was in the reserves. She's hurrying, stuffing everything into the bag, and when the bag is almost full she stops, feeling spent and out of breath. She sits down at her dressing table for a moment, and now she wonders if perhaps this is all the result of what she's had to drink. The alcohol is wearing off. She has the beginning of a headache. But she knows that whatever she decides to do should be done in the light of day, not now, at night. At last she gets up from the chair and lies down on the bed to think. She's dizzy. Her mind swims. She can't think, so she remains where she is, lying in the tangle of clothes she hasn't packed yet. Perhaps half an hour goes by. She wonders how long this will go on. And then she's asleep. She's nowhere, not even dreaming.

She wakes to the sound of voices. She sits up and tries to get her eyes to focus, tries to open them wide enough to see in the light. The imprint of the wrinkled clothes is in the skin of her face; she can feel it with her fingers. And then she's watching as two men bring Martin in through the front door and help him lie down on the couch. It's all framed in the perspective of the hallway and the open bedroom door, and she's not certain that it's actually happening.

'Martin?' she murmurs, getting up, moving toward them. She stands in the doorway of the living room, rubbing her eyes and trying to clear her head. The two men are standing over her husband, who says something in a pleading voice to one of them. He's lying on his side on the couch, both hands bandaged, a bruise on the side of his face as if something had spilled there.

'Martin,' Jane says.

And the two men move, as if startled by her voice. She realizes she's never seen them before. One of them, the younger one, is already explaining. They're from another company. 'We were headed back this way,' he says, 'and we thought it'd be better if you didn't hear anything over the phone.' While he talks, the older one is leaning over Martin, going on about insurance. He's a big square-shouldered man with an extremely rubbery look to his face. Jane notices this, notices the masklike quality of it, and she begins to tremble. Everything is oddly exaggerated—something is being said, they're telling her that Martin burned his hands, and another voice is murmuring something. Both men go on talking, apologizing, getting ready to leave her there. She's not fully awake. The lights in the room hurt her eyes; she feels a little sick to her stomach. The two men go out on the porch and then look back through the screen. 'You take it easy, now,' the younger one says to Jane. She closes the door, understands that what she's been hearing under the flow of the past few moments is Martin's voice muttering her name, saying something. She walks over to him.

'Jesus,' he says. 'It's awful. I burned my hands and I didn't even know it. I didn't even feel it.'

She says, 'Tell me what happened.'

'God,' he says. 'Wally Harmon's dead. God. I saw it happen.'

'Milly—' she begins. She can't speak.

He's crying. She moves to the entrance of the kitchen and turns to look at him. 'I saw Milly tonight.' The room seems terribly small to her.

'The Van Pickel Lumberyard went up. The warehouse. Jesus.'

She goes into the kitchen and runs water. Outside the window above the sink she sees the dim street, the shadows of houses without light. She drinks part of a glass of water and then pours the rest down the sink. Her throat is still very dry. When she goes back into the living room, she finds him lying on his side, facing the wall.

'Martin?' she says.

'What?'

But she can't find anything to tell him. She says, 'God—poor Milly.' Then she makes her way into the bedroom and begins putting away the clothes. She doesn't hear him get up and she's startled to find him standing in the doorway, staring at her.

'What're you doing?' he asks.

She faces him, at a loss—and it's her hesitation that gives him his answer.

'Jane?' he says, looking at the travel bag.

'Look,' she tells him, 'I had a little too much to drink tonight.'

He just stares at her.

'Oh, this,' she manages. 'I—I was just going through what I have to wear.'

But it's too late. 'Jesus,' he says, turning from her a little.

'Martin,' she says.

'What.'

'Does—did somebody tell Milly?'

He nods. 'Teddy. Teddy stayed with her. She was crazy. Crazy.'

He looks at his hands. It's as if he just remembered them. They're wrapped tight; they look like two white clubs. 'Jesus, Jane, are you—' He stops, shakes his head. 'Jesus.'

'Don't,' she says.

'Without even talking to me about it—'

'Martin, this is not the time to talk about anything.'

He's quiet a moment, standing there in the doorway. 'I keep seeing it,' he says. 'I keep seeing Wally's face. The—the way his foot jerked. His foot jerked like with electricity and he was—oh, Christ, he was already dead.'

'Oh, don't,' she says. 'Please. Don't talk. Stop picturing it.'

'They gave me something to make me sleep,' he says. 'And I won't sleep.' He wanders back into the living room. A few minutes later she goes to him there and finds that whatever the doctors gave him has worked. He's lying on his back, and he looks smaller somehow, his bandaged hands on his chest, his face pinched with grief, with whatever he's dreaming. He twitches and mutters something and moans. She turns the light off and tiptoes back to the bedroom. She's the one who won't sleep. She gets into the bed and huddles there, leaving the light on. Outside the wind gets up—another storm rolls in off the plains. She listens as the rain begins, and hears the far-off drumming of thunder. The whole night seems deranged. She thinks of Wally Harmon, dead out in the blowing, rainy dark. And then she remembers Milly and her bad dreams, how she looked coming from the downpour, the wet street, with the magazine held over her head—her body so rounded, so weighted down with her baby, her love, the love she had waited for, that she said had surprised her. These events are too much to think about, too awful to imagine. The world seems cruelly immense now, and remorselessly itself. When Martin groans in the other room, she wishes he'd stop, and then she imagines that it's another time, that she's just awakened from a dream and is trying to sleep while they all sit in her living room and talk the hours of the night away.

In the morning she's awake first. She gets up and wraps herself in a robe and then shuffles into the kitchen and puts coffee on. For a minute it's like any other morning. She sits at the table to wait for the coffee water to boil. He comes in like someone entering a stranger's kitchen—his movements are tentative, almost shy. She's surprised to see that he's still in his uniform. He says, 'I need you to help me go to the bathroom. I can't get my pants undone.' He starts trying to work his belt loose.

'Wait,' she says. 'Here, hold on.'

'I have to get out of these clothes, Jane. I think they smell like smoke.'

'Let me do it,' she says.

'Milly's in the hospital—they had to put her under sedation.'

'Move your hands out of the way,' Jane says to him.

She has to help with everything, and when the time comes for him to eat, she has to feed him. She spoons scrambled eggs into his mouth and holds the coffee cup to his lips, and when that's over with, she wipes his mouth and chin with a damp napkin. Then she starts bathwater running and helps him out of his underclothes. They work silently, and with a kind of embarrassment, until he's sitting down and the water is right. When she begins to run a soapy rag over his back, he utters a small sound of satisfaction and comfort. But then he's crying again. He wants to talk about Wally Harmon's death. He says he has to. He tells her that a piece of hot metal the size of an arrow dropped from the roof of the Van Pickel warehouse and hit poor Wally Harmon in the top of the back.

'It didn't kill him right away,' he says, sniffling. 'Oh, Jesus. He looked right at me and asked if I thought he'd be all right. We were talking about it, honey. He reached up—he—over his shoulder. He took ahold of it for a second. Then he—then he looked at me and said he could feel it down in his stomach.'

'Don't think about it,' Jane says.

'Oh, God.' He's sobbing. 'God.'

'Martin, honey—'

'I've done the best I could,' he says. 'Haven't I?'

'Shhh,' she says, bringing the warm rag over his shoulders and wringing it, so that the water runs down his back.

They're quiet again. Together they get him out of the tub, and then she dries him off, helps him into a pair of jeans.

'Thanks,' he says, not looking at her. Then he says, 'Jane.'

She's holding his shirt out for him, waiting for him to turn and put his arms into the sleeves. She looks at him.

'Honey,' he says.

'I'm calling in,' she tells him. 'I'll call Eveline. We'll go be with Milly.'

'Last night,' he says.

She looks straight at him.

He hesitates, glances down. 'I—I'll try and do better.' He seems about to cry again. For some reason this makes her feel abruptly very irritable and nervous. She turns from him, walks into the living room and begins putting the sofa back in order. When he comes to the doorway and says her name, she doesn't answer, and he walks through to the kitchen door.

'What're you doing?' she says to him.

'Can you give me some water?'

637

She moves into the kitchen and he follows her. She runs water, to get it cold, and he stands at her side. When the glass is filled, she holds it to his mouth. He swallows, and she takes the glass away. 'If you want to talk about anything—' he says.

'Why don't you try to sleep awhile?' she says.

He says, 'I know I've been talking about Wally—'

'Just please—go lie down or something.'

'When I woke up this morning, I remembered everything, and I thought you might be gone.'

'Well, I'm not gone.'

'I knew we were having some trouble, Jane—'

'Just let's not talk about it now,' she says. 'All right? I have to go call Eveline.' She walks into the bedroom, and when he comes in behind her she tells him very gently to please go get off his feet. He backs off, makes his way into the living room. 'Can you turn on the television?' he calls to her.

She does so. 'What channel do you want?'

'Can you just go through them a little?'

She's patient. She waits for him to get a good look at each channel. There isn't any news coverage; it's all commercials and cartoons and children's shows. Finally he settles on a rerun of *The Andy Griffith Show*, and she leaves him there. She fills the dishwasher and wipes off the kitchen table. Then she calls Eveline to tell her what's happened.

'You poor thing,' Eveline says. 'You must be so relieved. And I said all that bad stuff about Wally's wife.'

Jane says, 'You didn't mean it,' and suddenly she's crying.

'You poor thing,' Eveline says. 'You want me to come over there?'

'No, it's all right—I'm all right.'

'Poor Martin. Is he hurt bad?'

'It's his hands.'

'Is it very painful?'

'Yes,' Jane says.

Later, while he sleeps on the sofa, she wanders outside and walks down to the end of the driveway. The day is sunny and cool, with little cottony clouds—the kind of clear day that comes after a storm. She looks up and down the street. Nothing is moving. A few houses away someone has put up a flag, and it flutters in a stray breeze. This is the way it was, she remembers, when she first lived here—when she first stood on this sidewalk and marveled at how flat the land was, how far it stretched in all directions. Now she turns and makes her way back to the house, and then she finds herself in the garage. It's almost as if she's saying good-bye to everything, and as this thought occurs to her, she feels a little stir of sadness. Here on the worktable, side by side under the light from the one window, are Martin's model airplanes. He won't be able to work on them again for weeks. The light reveals the miniature details, the crevices and curves on which he lavished such care, gluing and sanding and painting. The little engines are lying on a paper towel at one end of the table; they smell just like real engines, and they're shiny with lubrication. She picks one of them up and turns it in the light, trying to understand what he might see in it that could require such time and attention. She wants to understand him. She remembers that when they dated, he liked to tell her about flying these planes, and his eyes would widen with excitement. She remembers that she liked him best when he was glad that way. She puts the little engine down, thinking how people change. She knows she's going to leave him, but just for this moment, standing among these things, she feels almost peaceful about it. There's no need to hurry. As she steps out on the lawn, she realizes she can take the time to think clearly about when and where; she can even change her mind. But she doesn't think she will.

He's up. He's in the hallway—he had apparently wakened and found her gone. 'Jesus,' he says. 'I woke up and you weren't here.'

'I didn't go anywhere,' she says, and she smiles at him.

'I'm sorry,' he says, starting to cry. 'God, Janey, I'm so sorry. I'm all messed up here. I've got to go to the bathroom again.'

She helps him. The two of them stand over the bowl. He's stopped crying now, though he says his hands hurt something awful. When he's finished he thanks her, and then tries a bawdy joke. 'You don't have to let go so soon.'

She ignores this, and when she has him tucked safely away, he says quietly, 'I guess I better just go to bed and sleep some more if I can.'

She's trying to hold on to the feeling of peace and certainty she had in the garage. It's not even noon, and she's exhausted. She's very tired of thinking about everything. He's talking about his parents; later she'll have to call them. But then he says he wants his mother to hear his voice first, to know he's all right. He goes on—something about Milly and her unborn baby, and Teddy Lynch—but Jane can't

639

quite hear him: he's a little unsteady on his feet, and they have trouble negotiating the hallway together.

In their bedroom she helps him out of his jeans and shirt, and she actually tucks him into the bed. Again he thanks her. She kisses his forehead, feels a sudden, sick-swooning sense of having wronged him somehow. It makes her stand straighter, makes her stiffen slightly.

'Jane?' he says.

She breathes. 'Try to rest some more. You just need to rest now.' He closes his eyes and she waits a little. He's not asleep. She sits at the foot of the bed and watches him. Perhaps ten minutes go by. Then he opens his eyes.

'Janey?'

'Shhh,' she says.

He closes them again. It's as if he were her child. She thinks of him as he was when she first saw him, tall and sure of himself in his uniform, and the image makes her throat constrict.

At last he's asleep. When she's certain of this, she lifts herself from the bed and carefully, quietly withdraws. As she closes the door, something in the flow of her own mind appalls her, and she stops, stands in the dim hallway, frozen in a kind of wonder: she had been thinking in an abstract way, almost idly, as though it had nothing at all to do with her, about how people will go to such lengths leaving a room—wishing not to disturb, not to awaken, a loved one.

1990

HOT ICE

Stuart Dybek

The saint, a virgin, was uncorrupted. She had been frozen in a block of ice many years ago.

Her father had found her half-naked body floating facedown among water lilies, her blond hair fanning at the marshy edge of the overgrown duck pond people still referred to as the Douglas Park Lagoon.

That's how Eddie Kapusta had heard it.

Douglas Park was a black park now, the lagoon curdled in milky green scum as if it had soured, and Kapusta didn't doubt that were he to go there they'd find his body floating in the lily pads too. But sometimes in winter, riding by on the California Avenue bus, the park flocked white, deserted, and the lagoon frozen over, Eddie could almost picture what it had been back then: swans gliding around the small, wooded island at the center, and rowboats plying into sunlight from the gaping stone tunnels of the haunted-looking boathouse.

The girl had gone rowing with a couple of guys—some said they were sailors, neighborhood kids going off to the war—nobody ever said who exactly or why she went with them, as if it didn't matter. They rowed her around to the blind side of the little island. Nobody knew what happened there either. It was necessary for each person to imagine it for himself.

They were only joking at first was how Kapusta imagined it, laughing at her broken English, telling her to be friendly or swim home. One of them stroked her hair, gently, undid her bun, and as her hair fell cascading over her shoulders surprising them all, the other reached too suddenly for the buttons on her blouse; she tore away so hard the boat rocked violently, her slip and bra split, breasts sprung loose, she dove.

Even the suddenness was slow motion the way Kapusta imagined it. But once they were in the water the rest went through his mind in

641

a flash—the boat capsizing, the sailors thrashing for the little island, and the girl struggling alone in that sepia water too warm from summer, just barely deep enough for bullheads, with a mud bottom kids said was quicksand exploding into darkness with each kick. He didn't want to wonder what she remembered as she held her last breath underwater. His mind raced over that to her father wading out into cattails, scooping her half-naked and still limp from the resisting water lilies, and running with her in his arms, across the park crying in Polish or Slovak or Bohemian, whatever they were, and then riding with her on the streetcar he wouldn't let stop until it reached the icehouse he owned, where crazy with grief he sealed her in ice.

'I believe it up to the part about the streetcar,' Manny Santora said that summer when they told each other such stories, talking often about things Manny called *weirdness* while pitching quarters in front of Buddy's Bar. 'I don't believe he hijacked no streetcar, man.'

'What do you think, man, he called a cab?' Pancho, Manny's older brother, asked, winking at Eddie as if he'd scored.

Every time they talked like this Manny and Pancho argued. Pancho believed in everything—ghosts, astrology, legends. His nickname was Padrecito, which went back to his days as an altar boy when he would dress up as a priest and hold mass in the backyard with hosts punched with bottle caps from stale tortillas and real wine he'd collected from bottles the winos had left on door stoops. Eddie's nickname was Eduardo, though the only person who called him that was Manny, who had made it up. Manny wasn't the kind of guy to have a nickname—he was Manny or Santora.

Pancho believed if you played certain rock songs backward you'd hear secret messages from the devil. He believed in devils and angels. He still believed he had a guardian angel. It was something like being lucky, like making the sign of the cross before you stepped into the batter's box. 'It's why I don't get caught even when I'm caught,' he'd say when the cops would catch him dealing and not take him in. Pancho believed in saints. For a while he had even belonged to a gang called the Saints. They'd tried to recruit Manny too, who, though younger, was tougher than Pancho, but Manny had no use for gangs. 'I already belong to the Loners,' he said.

Pancho believed in the girl in ice. In sixth grade, Sister Joachim, the ancient nun in charge of the altar boys, had told him the girl should be canonized and that she'd secretly written to the pope informing him that already there had been miracles and cures. 'All the martyrs didn't die in Rome,' she'd told Pancho. 'They're still suffering today in China and Russia and Korea and even here in your own neighborhood.' Like all nuns she loved Pancho. Dressed in his surplice and cassock he looked as if he should be beatified himself, a young St Sebastian or Juan de la Cruz, the only altar boy in the history of the parish to spend his money on different-colored gym shoes so they would match the priest's vestments—red for martyrs, white for feast days, black for requiems. The nuns knew he punished himself during Lent, offering up his pain for the poor souls in purgatory.

Their love for Pancho had made things impossible for Manny in the Catholic school. He seemed Pancho's opposite in almost every way and dropped out after they'd held him back in sixth grade. He switched to public school, but mostly he hung out on the streets.

'I believe she worked miracles right in this neighborhood, man,' Pancho said.

'Bullshit, man. Like what miracles?' Manny wanted to know.

'OK, man, you know Big Antek,' Pancho said.

'Big Antek the wino?'

They all knew Big Antek. He bought them beer. He'd been a butcher in every meat market in the neighborhood, but drunkenly kept hacking off pieces of his hands, and finally quit completely to become a full-time alky.

Big Antek had told Pancho about working on Kedzie Avenue when it was still mostly people from the old country and he had found a job at a Czech meat market with sawdust on the floor and skinned rabbits in the window. He wasn't there a week when he got so drunk he passed out in the freezer and when he woke the door was locked and everyone was gone. It was Saturday and he knew they wouldn't open again until Monday and by then he'd be stiff as a two-by-four. He was already shivering so badly he couldn't stand still or he'd fall over. He figured he'd be dead already except that his blood was half alcohol. Parts of him were going numb and he started staggering around, bumping past hanging sides of meat, singing, praying out loud, trying to let the fear out before it became panic. He knew it was hopeless, but he was looking anyway for some place to smash out, some plug to pull, something to stop the cold. At the back of the freezer, behind racks of meat, he found a cooler. It was an old one, the kind that used to stand packed with blocks of ice and bottles of beer in taverns during the war. And seeing it, Big Antek suddenly

643

remembered a moment from his first summer back from the Pacific, discharged from the hospital in Manila and back in Buddy's lounge on Twenty-fourth Street, kitty-corner from a victory garden where a plaque erroneously listed his name among the parish war dead. It was an ordinary moment, nothing dramatic like his life flashing before his eyes, but the memory filled him with such clarity that the freezer became dreamlike beside it. The ball game was on the radio over at Buddy's, DiMaggio in center again, while Bing Crosby crooned from the jukebox, which was playing at the same time. Antek was reaching into Buddy's cooler, up to his elbow in ice water feeling for a beer, while looking out through the open tavern door that framed Twenty-fourth Street as if it were a movie full of girls blurred in brightness, slightly over-exposed blondes, a movie he could step into any time he chose now that he was home; but right at this moment he was taking his time, stretching it out until it encompassed his entire life, the cold bottles bobbing away from his fingertips, clunking against the ice, until finally he grabbed one, hauled it up dripping, wondering what he'd grabbed—a Monarch or Yusay Pilsner or Fox Head 400—then popped the cork in the opener on the side of the cooler, the foam rising as he tilted his head back and let it pour down his throat, privately celebrating being alive. That moment was what drinking had once been about. It was a good thing to be remembering now when he was dying with nothing else to do about it. He had the funny idea of climbing inside the cooler and going to sleep to continue the memory like a dream. The cooler was thick with frost, so white it seemed to glow. Its lid had been replaced with a slab of dry ice that smoked even within the cold of the freezer, reminding Antek that as kids they'd always called it hot ice. He nudged it aside. Beneath it was a block of ice as clear as if the icemen had just delivered it. There was something frozen inside. He glanced away but knew already, immediately, it was a body. He couldn't move away. He looked again. The longer he stared, the calmer he felt. It was a girl. He could make out her hair, not just blonde but radiating gold like a candle flame behind a window in winter. Her breasts were bare. The ice seemed even clearer. She was beautiful and dreamy looking, not dreamy like sleeping, but the dreamy look DPs sometimes get when they first come to the city. As long as he stayed beside her he didn't shiver. He could feel the blood return; he was warm as if the smoldering dry ice really was hot. He spent the weekend huddled against her, and early Monday morning when the Czech opened the freezer he said to Antek, 'Get out . . . you're fired.' That's all either one of them said.

'You know what I think,' Pancho said. 'They moved her body from the icehouse to the butcher shop because the cops checked, man.'

'You know what I think,' Manny said, 'I think you're doing so much shit that even the winos can bullshit you.'

They looked hard at one another, Manny especially looking bad because of a beard he was trying to grow that was mostly stubble except for a black knot of hair frizzing from the cleft under his lower lip—a little lip beard like a jazz musician's—and Pancho covered in crosses, a wooden one dangling from a leather thong over his open shirt, and small gold cross on a fine gold chain tight about his throat, and a tiny platinum cross in his right earlobe, and a faded India-ink cross tattooed on his wrist where one would feel for a pulse.

'He's got a cross-shaped dick,' Manny said.

'Only when I got a hard-on, man,' Pancho said, grinning, and they busted up.

'Hey, Eddie, man,' Pancho said, 'what you think of all this, man?'

Kapusta just shrugged as he always did. Not that he didn't have any ideas exactly, or that he didn't care. That shrug *was* what Kapusta believed.

'Yeah. Well, man,' Pancho said, 'I believe there's saints, and miracles happening everywhere only everybody's afraid to admit it. I mean like Ralph's little brother, the blue baby who died when he was eight. He knew he was dying all his life, man, and never complained. He was a saint. Or Big Antek who everybody says is a wino, man. But he treats everybody as human beings. Who you think's more of a saint—him or the president, man? And Mrs Corillo who everybody thought was crazy because she was praying loud all the time. Remember? She kneeled all day praying for Puerto Rico during that earthquake—the one Roberto Clemente crashed on the way to, going to help. Remember that, man? Mrs Corillo prayed all day and they thought she was still praying at night, and she was kneeling there dead. She was a saint, man, and so's Roberto Clemente. There should be like a church, St Roberto Clemente. With a statue of him in his batting stance by the altar. Kids could pray to him at night. That would mean something to them.'

'The earthquake wasn't in Puerto Rico, man,' Manny told him, 'and I don't believe no streetcar'd stop for somebody carrying a dead person.'

645

AMNESIA

It was hard to believe there ever were streetcars. The city back then, the city of their fathers, which was as far back as a family memory extended, even the city of their childhoods, seemed as remote to Eddie and Manny as the capital of some foreign country.

The past collapsed about them—decayed, bulldozed, obliterated. They walked past block-length gutted factories, past walls of peeling, multicolored doors hammered up around flooded excavation pits, hung out in half-boarded storefronts of groceries that had shut down when they were kids, dusty cans still stacked on the shelves. Broken glass collected everywhere, mounding like sand in the little, sunken front yards and gutters. Even the church's stained-glass windows were patched with plywood.

They could vaguely remember something different before the cranes and wrecking balls gradually moved in, not order exactly, but rhythms: five o'clock whistles, air-raid sirens on Tuesdays, Thursdays when the stockyards blew over like a brown wind of boiling hooves and bone, at least that's what people said, screwing up their faces: 'Phew! They're making glue today!'

Streetcar tracks were long paved over; black webs of trolley wires vanished. So did the victory gardens that had become weed beds taking the corroded plaques with the names of neighborhood dead with them.

Things were gone they couldn't remember but missed; and things were gone they weren't sure ever were there—the pickle factory by the railroad tracks where a DP with a net worked scooping rats out of the open vats, troughs for ragmen's horses, ragmen and their wooden wagons, knife sharpeners pushing screeching whetstones up alleys hollering 'Scissors! Knives!', hermits living in cardboard shacks behind billboards.

At times, walking past the gaps, they felt as if they were no longer quite there themselves, half-lost despite familiar street signs, shadows of themselves superimposed on the present, except there was no present—everything either rubbled past or promised future—and they were walking as if floating, getting nowhere as if they'd smoked too much grass.

That's how it felt those windy nights that fall when Manny and Eddie circled the county jail. They'd float down California past the courthouse, Bridwell Correctional, the auto pound, Communicable

Disease Hospital, and then follow the long, curving concrete wall of the prison back toward Twenty-sixth Street, sharing a joint, passing it with cupped hands, ready to flip it if a cop should cruise by, but one place you could count on not to see cops was outside the prison.

Nobody was there; just the wall, railroad tracks, the river, and the factories that lined it—boundaries that remained intact while neighborhoods came and went.

Eddie had never noticed any trees, but swirls of leaves scuffed past their shoes. It was Kapusta's favorite weather, wild, blowing nights that made him feel free, flagpoles knocking in the wind, his clothes flapping like flags. He felt both tight and loose, and totally alive even walking down a street that always made him sad. It was the street that followed the curve of the prison wall, and it didn't have a name. It was hardly a street at all, more a shadow of the wall, potholed, puddled, half-paved, rutted with rusted railroad tracks.

'Trains used to go down this street.' Manny said.

'I seen tanks going down this street.'

'Tank cars?'

'No, army tanks,' Kapusta said.

'Battleships too, Eduardo?' Manny asked seriously. Then the wind ripped a laugh from his mouth that was loud enough to carry over the prison wall.

Kapusta laughed loud too. But he *could* remember tanks, camouflaged with netting, rumbling on flatcars, their cannons outlined by the red lanterns of the dinging crossing gates that were down all along Twenty-sixth Street. It was one of the first things he remembered. He must have been very small. The train seemed endless. He could see the guards in the turrets on the prison wall watching it, the only time he'd ever seen them facing the street. 'Still sending them to Korea or someplace,' his father had said, and for years after Eddie believed you could get to Korea by train. For years after, he would wake in the middle of the night when it was quiet enough to hear the trains passing blocks away, and lie in bed listening, wondering if the tanks were rumbling past the prison, if not to Korea then to some other war that tanks went to at night; and he would think of the prisoners in their cells locked up for their violence with knives and clubs and cleavers and pistols, and wonder if they were lying awake, listening too as the netted cannons rolled by their barred windows. Even as a child Eddie knew the names of men inside there: Milo Hermanski, who had stabbed some guy in the eye in a fight at Andy's Tap; Billy Gomez, who set the housing project on fire every time his sister Gina got gang-banged; Ziggy's uncle, the war hero, who one day blew off the side of Ziggy's mother's face while she stood ironing her slip during an argument over a will; and other names of people he didn't know but had heard about—Benny Bedwell, with his 'Elvis' sideburns, who may have killed the Grimes sister; Mafia hit men; bank robbers; junkies; perverts; murderers on death row—he could sense them lying awake listening, could feel the tension of their sleeplessness, and Pancho lay among them now as Eddie and Manny walked outside the wall.

They stopped again as they'd been stopping and yelled together: 'Pancho, Panchoooooooo,' dragging out the last vowel the way they had as kids standing on the sidewalk calling up at one another's windows, as if knocking at the door were not allowed.

'Pancho, we're out here, brother, me and Eddie,' Manny shouted. 'Hang tough, man, we ain't forgetting you.'

Nobody answered. They kept walking, stopping to shout at intervals the way they had been doing almost every night.

'If only we knew what building he was in,' Eddie said.

They could see the upper stories of the brick buildings rising over the wall, their grated windows low lit, never dark, floodlights on the roof glaring down.

'Looks like a factory, man,' Eddie said. 'Looks like the same guy who planned the Harvester foundry on Western did the jail.'

'You rather be in the army or in there?' Manny asked.

'No way they're getting me in there,' Eddie said.

That was when Eddie knew Pancho was crazy, when the judge had given Pancho a choice at the end of his trial.

'You're a nice-looking kid,' the judge had said, 'too nice for prison. What do you want to do with your life?'

'Pose for holy cards,' Pancho said, 'St Joseph is my specialty.' Pancho was standing there wearing the tie they had brought him wound around his head like an Indian headband. He was wearing a black satin jacket with the signs of the zodiac on the back.

'I'm going to give you a chance to straighten out, to gain some self-respect. The court's attitude would be very sympathetic to any signs of self-direction and patriotism, joining the army, for instance.'

'I'm a captain,' Pancho told him.

'The army or jail, which is it?'

'I'm a captain, man, *soy capitán, capitán,*' Pancho insisted, humming

648

'La Bamba' under his breath.

'You're a misfit.'

Manny was able to visit Pancho every three weeks. Each time it got worse. Sometimes Pancho seemed hardly to recognize him, looking away, refusing to meet Manny's eyes the whole visit. Sometimes he'd cry. For a while at first he wanted to know how things were in the neighborhood. Then he stopped asking, and when Manny tried to tell him the news Pancho would get jumpy, irritable, and lapse into total silence. 'I don't wanna talk about out there, man,' he told Manny. 'I don't wanna remember that world until I'm ready to step into it again. You remember too much in here you go crazy, man. I wanna forget everything, like I never existed.'

'His fingernails are gone, man,' Manny told Eddie. 'He's gnawing on himself like a rat, and when I ask him what's going down all he'll say is "I'm locked in hell, my angel's gone, I've lost my luck"— bullshit like that, you know? Last time I seen him he says, "I'm gonna kill myself, man, if they don't stop hitting on me."'

'I can't fucking believe it. I can't fucking believe he's in there,' Eddie said. 'He should be in a monastery somewhere; he should've been a priest. He had a vocation.'

'He had a vocation to be an altar boy, man,' Manny said, spitting it out as if he was disgusted by what he was saying, talking down about his own brother. 'It was that nuns-and-priests crap that messed up his head. He was happy being an altar boy, man, if they'd've let him be an altar boy all his life he'd still be happy.'

By the time they were halfway down the nameless street it was drizzling a fine, misty spray, and Manny was yelling in Spanish, '*Estamos contigo, hermano! San Roberto Clemente te ayudará!*'

They broke into 'La Bamba,' Eddie singing in Spanish too, not sure exactly what he was singing, but it sounded good: '*Yo no soy marinero, soy capitán, capitán, ay, ay, Bamba! ay, ay, Bamba!*' He had lived beside Spanish in the neighborhood all his life, and every so often a word got through, like *juilota*, which was what Manny called pigeons when they used to hunt them with slingshots under the railroad bridges. It seemed a perfect word to Eddie, one in which he could hear both their cooing and the whistling rush of their wings. He didn't remember any words like that in Polish, which his grandma had spoken to him when he was little, and which, Eddie had been told, he could once speak too.

By midnight they were at the end of their circuit, emerging from the unlighted, nameless street, stepping over tracks that continued to curve past blinded switches. Under the streetlights on Twenty-sixth the prison wall appeared rust stained, oozing at the cracks. The wire spooled at the top of the wall looked rusty in the wet light, as did the tracks as if the rain were rusting everything overnight.

They stopped on the corner of Twenty-sixth where the old icehouse stood across the nameless street from the prison. One could still buy ice from a vending machine in front. Without realizing it, Eddie guarded his breathing as if still able to detect the faintest stab of ammonia, although it had been a dozen years since the louvered fans on the icehouse roof had clacked through clouds of vapor.

'Padrecitooooo!' they both hollered.

Their voices bounced back off the wall.

They stood on the corner by the icehouse as if waiting around for someone. From there they could stare down Twenty-sixth—five dark blocks, then an explosion of neon at Kedzie Avenue: taco places, bars, a street plugged in, winking festive as a pinball machine, traffic from it coming toward them in the rain.

The streetlights surged and flickered.

'You see that?' Eddie asked. 'They used to say when the streetlights flickered it meant they just fried somebody in the electric chair.'

'So much bullshit,' Manny said. '*Compadre, no te rajes!*' he yelled at the wall.

'Whatcha tell him?'

'It sounds different in English,' Manny said. '"Godfather, do not give up." It's words from an old song.'

Kapusta stepped out into the middle of Twenty-sixth and stood in the misting drizzle squinting at Kedzie through cupped hands, as if he held binoculars. He could make out the traffic light way down there changing to green. He could almost hear the music from the bars that would serve them without asking for IDs so long as Manny was there. 'You thirsty by any chance, man?' he asked.

'You buyin' by any chance, man?' Manny said, grinning.

'*Buenas noches*, Pancho,' they hollered. 'Catch you tomorrow, man.'

'Good night, guys,' a falsetto voice echoed back from over the wall.

'That ain't Pancho,' Manny said.

'Sounds like the singer on old Platters' records,' Eddie said. 'Ask him if he knows Pancho, man.'

'Hey, you know a guy named Pancho Santora?' Manny called.

'Oh, Pancho?' the voice inquired.

'Yeah, Pancho.'
'Oh, Cisco!' the voice shouted. They could hear him cackling. 'Hey, baby, I don't know no Pancho. Is that rain I smell?'
'It's raining,' Eddie hollered.
'Hey, baby, tell me something. What's it like out there tonight?'
Manny and Eddie looked at each other. 'Beautiful!' they yelled together.

Grief

There was never a requiem, but by Lent everyone knew that one way or another Pancho was gone. No wreaths, but plenty of rumors: Pancho had hung himself in his cell; his throat had been slashed in the showers; he'd killed another inmate and was under heavy sedation in a psycho ward at Kankakee. And there was talk he'd made a deal and was in the army, shipped off to a war he had sworn he'd never fight; that he had turned snitch and had been secretly relocated with a new identity; or that he had become a trustee and had simply walked away while mowing the grass in front of the courthouse, escaped maybe to Mexico, or maybe just across town to the North Side around Diversey where, if one made the rounds of the leather bars, they might see someone with Pancho's altar-boy eyes staring out from the makeup of a girl.

Some saw him late at night like a ghost haunting the neighborhood, collar up, in the back of the church lighting a vigil candle or veiled in a black mantilla, speeding past, face floating by on a greasy El window.

Rumors were becoming legends, but there was never a wake, never an obituary, and no one knew how to mourn a person who had just disappeared.

For a while Manny disappeared too. He wasn't talking, and Kapusta didn't ask. They had quit walking around the prison wall months before, around Christmas when Pancho refused to let anyone, even Manny, visit. But their night walks had been tapering off before that.

Eddie remembered the very last time they had walked beside the wall together. It was in December, and he was frozen from standing around a burning garbage can on Kedzie, selling Christmas trees. About ten, when the lot closed, Manny came by and they stopped to thaw out at the Carta Blanca. A guy named José kept buying them whiskeys, and they staggered out after midnight into a blizzard.

'Look at this white bullshit,' Manny said.

Walking down Twenty-sixth they stopped to fling snowballs over the wall. Then they decided to stand there singing Christmas carols. Snow was drifting against the wall, erasing the street that had hardly been there. Eddie could tell Manny was starting to go silent. Manny would get the first few words into a carol, singing at the top of his voice, then stop as if choked by the song. His eyes stayed angry when he laughed. Everything was bullshit to him, and finally Eddie couldn't talk to him anymore. Stomping away from the prison through fresh snow, Eddie had said, 'If this keeps up, man, I'll need boots.'

'It don't *have* to *keep up*, man,' Manny snapped. 'Nobody's making you come, man. It ain't your brother.'

'All I said is I'll need boots, man,' Eddie said.

'You said it's hopeless, man; things are always fucking hopeless to you.'

'Hey, you're the big realist, man,' Eddie told him.

'I never said I was no realist,' Manny mumbled.

Kapusta hadn't had a lot of time since then. He had dropped out of school again and was loading trucks at night for UPS. One more semester didn't matter, he figured, and he needed some new clothes, cowboy boots, a green leather jacket. The weather had turned drizzly and mild—a late Easter but an early spring. Eddie had heard Manny was hanging around by himself, still finding bullshit everywhere, only worse. Now he muttered as he walked like some crazy, bitter old man, or one of those black guys reciting the gospel to buildings, telling off posters and billboards, neon signs, stoplights, passing traffic—bullshit, all of it bullshit.

It was Tuesday in Holy Week, the statues inside the church shrouded in violet, when Eddie slipped on his green leather jacket and walked over to Manny's before going to work. He rang the doorbell, then stepped outside in the rain and stood on the sidewalk under Manny's windows, watching cars pass.

After a while Manny came down the stairs and slammed out the door.

'How you doin', man?' Eddie said as if they'd just run into each other by accident.

Manny stared at him. 'How far'd you have to chase him for that jacket, man?' he said.

'I knew you'd dig it.' Eddie smiled.

They went out for a few beers later that night, after midnight, when Eddie was through working, but instead of going to a bar they ended up just walking. Manny had rolled a couple bombers and they walked down the boulevard along California watching the headlights flash by like a procession of candles. Manny still wasn't saying much, but they were passing the reefer like having a conversation. At Thirty-first, by the Communicable Disease Hospital, Eddie figured they would follow the curve of the boulevard toward the bridge on Western, but Manny turned as if out of habit toward the prison.

They were back walking along the wall. There was still old ice from winter at the base of it.

'The only street in Chicago where it's still winter,' Eddie mumbled.

'Remember yelling?' Manny said, almost in a whisper.

'Sure,' Eddie nodded.

'Called, joked, prayed, sang Christmas songs, remember that night, how cold we were, man?'

'Yeah.'

'What a bunch of stupid bullshit, huh?'

Eddie was afraid Manny was going to start the bullshit stuff again. Manny had stopped and stood looking at the wall.

Then he cupped his hands over his mouth and yelled, 'Hey! You dumb fuckers in there! We're back! Can you hear me? Hey, wake up, niggers, hey, spics, hey, honkies, you buncha fuckin' monkeys in cages, hey! We're out here *free*!'

'Hey, Manny, come on, man,' Eddie said.

Manny uncupped his hands, shook his head, and smiled. They took a few steps, then Manny whirled back again. 'We're out here free, man! We're smokin' reefer, drinking cold beer while you're in there, you assholes! We're on our way to fuck your wives, man, your girlfriends are giving us blow jobs while you jack-offs flog it. Hey, man, I'm pumping your old lady out here right now. She likes it in the ass like you!'

'What are you doing, man?' Eddie was pleading. 'Take it easy.'

Manny was screaming his lungs out, almost incoherent, shouting every filthy thing he could think of, and voices, the voices they'd never heard before, had begun shouting back from the other side of the wall.

'Shadup! Shadup! Shadup out there, you crazy fuck!' came the voices.

'She's out here licking my balls while you're punking each other through the bars of your cage!'

'Shadup!' they were yelling, and then a voice howling over the others, 'I'll kill you, motherfucker! When I get out you're dead!'

'Come on out,' Manny was yelling. 'Come and get me, you pieces of shit, you sleazeballs, you scumbag cocksuckers, you creeps are missing it all, your lives are wasted garbage!'

Now there were too many voices to distinguish, whole tiers, whole buildings yelling and cursing and threatening, *shadup, shadup, shadup,* almost a chant, and then the searchlight from the guardhouse slowly turned and swept the street.

'We gotta get outa here,' Eddie said, pulling Manny away. He dragged him to the wall, right up against it where the light couldn't follow, and they started to run, stumbling along the banked strip of filthy ice, dodging stunted trees that grew out at odd angles, running toward Twenty-sixth until Eddie heard the sirens.

'This way, man,' he panted, yanking Manny back across the nameless street, jumping puddles and tracks, cutting down a narrow corridor between abandoned truck docks seconds before a squad car, blue dome light revolving, sped past.

They jogged behind the truck docks, not stopping until they came up behind the icehouse. Manny's panting sounded almost like laughing, the way people laugh after they've hurt themselves.

'I hate those motherfuckers,' Manny gasped, 'all of them, the fucking cops and guards and fucking wall and the bastards behind it. All of them. That must be what makes me a realist, huh, Eddie? I fucking hate them all.'

They went back the next night.

Sometimes a thing wasn't a sin—if there was such a thing as sin—Eddie thought, until it's done a second time. There were accidents, mistakes that could be forgiven once; it was repeating them that made them terribly wrong. That was how Eddie felt about going back the next night.

Manny said he was going whether Eddie came or not, so Eddie went, afraid to leave Manny on his own, even though he'd already had trouble trying to get some sleep before going to work. Eddie could still hear the voices yelling from behind the wall and dreamed they were all being electrocuted, electrocuted slowly, by degrees of their crimes, screaming with each surge of current and flicker of streetlights as if in a hell where electricity had replaced fire.

Standing on the dark street Wednesday night, outside the wall again, felt like an extension of his nightmare: Manny raging almost out of control, shouting curses and insults, baiting them over the wall the way a child tortures penned watchdogs, until he had what seemed like the entire west side of the prison howling back, the guards sweeping the street with searchlights, sirens wailing toward them from both Thirty-first and Twenty-sixth.

This time they raced down the tracks that curved toward the river, picking their way in the dark along the junkyard bank, flipping rusted cables of moored barges, running through the fire truck graveyard, following the tracks across the blackened trestles where they'd once shot pigeons and from which they could gaze across the industrial prairie that stretched behind factories all the way to the skyline of downtown. The skyscrapers glowed like luminescent peaks in the misty spring night. Manny and Eddie stopped in the middle of the trestle and leaned over the railing catching their breath.

'Downtown ain't as far away as I used to think when I was a kid.' Manny panted.

'These tracks'll take you right there,' Eddie said quietly, 'to railroad yards under the street, right by the lake.'

'How do you know, man?'

'A bunch of us used to hitch rides on the boxcars in seventh grade.' Eddie was talking very quietly, looking away.

'I usually take the bus, you know?' Manny tried joking.

'I ain't goin' back there with you tomorrow,' Eddie said. 'I ain't goin' back with you ever.'

Manny kept staring off toward the light downtown as if he hadn't heard. 'OK,' he finally said, more to himself, as if surrendering. 'OK, how about tomorrow we do something else, man?'

NOSTALGIA

They didn't go back.

The next night, Thursday, Eddie overslept and called in sick for work. He tried to get back to sleep but kept falling into half-dreams in which he could hear the voices shouting behind the prison wall. Finally he got up and opened a window. It was dark out. A day had passed almost unnoticed, and now the night felt as if it were a part of the night before, and the night before a part of the night before that,

655

all connected by his restless dreams, fragments of the same continuous night.

Eddie had said that at some point: 'It's like one long night,' and later Manny had said the same thing as if it had suddenly occurred to him.

They were strung out almost from the start, drifting stoned under the El tracks before Eddie even realized they weren't still sitting on the stairs in front of Manny's house. That was where Eddie had found him, watching traffic, taking sips out of a bottle of Gallo into which Manny had dropped several hits of speed.

Cars gunned by with their windows rolled down and radios playing loud. It sounded like a summer night.

'Ain't you hot wearin' that jacket, man?' Manny asked him.

'Now that you mention it,' Eddie said. He was sweating.

Eddie took his leather jacket off and they knotted a handkerchief around one of the cuffs, then slipped the Gallo bottle down the sleeve. They walked along under the El tracks passing a joint. A train, only two cars long, rattled overhead.

'So what we doing, Eduardo?' Manny kept repeating.

'Walking,' Eddie said.

'I feel like doing *something*, you know?'

'We are doing something,' Eddie insisted.

Eddie led them over to the Coconut Club on Twenty-second. They couldn't get in, but Eddie wanted to look at the window with its neon-green palm tree and winking blue coconuts.

'That's maybe my favorite window,' he said.

'You drag me all the way here to see your favorite window, man?!' Manny said.

'It's those blue coconuts,' Eddie tried explaining. His mouth was dry, but he couldn't stop talking. He started telling Manny how he had collected windows from the time he was a little kid, even though talking about it made it sound as if windows were more important to him than they actually were. Half the time he was only vaguely aware of collecting them. He would see a window from a bus, like the Greek butcher shop on Halsted with its pyramid of lamb skulls, and make a mental photograph of it. He had special windows all over the city. It was how he held the city together in his mind.

'I'd see all those windows from the El,' Eddie said, 'when I'd visit my *busha*, my grandma. Like I remember we'd pass this one building where the curtains were all slips hanging by their straps—black ones,

656

white ones, red ones. At night you could see the light bulbs shining through the lace tops. My *busha* said Gypsies lived there.' Eddie was walking down the middle of the street, jacket flung over his shoulder, staring up at the windows as if looking for the Gypsies as he talked.

'Someday they're gonna get you as a peeper, man.' Manny laughed. 'And when they do, don't try explaining to them about this thing of yours for windows, Eduardo.'

They were walking down Spaulding back toward Twenty-sixth. The streetlights beamed brighter and brighter, and Manny put his sunglasses on. A breeze was blowing that felt warmer than the air, and they took their shirts off. They saw rats darting along the curb into the sewer on the other side of the street and put their shirts back on.

'The rats get crazy where they start wrecking these old buildings,' Manny said.

The cranes and wrecking balls and urban-renewal signs were back with the early spring. They walked around a barricaded site. Water trickled along the gutters from an open hydrant, washing brick dust and debris toward the sewers.

'Can you smell that, man?' Manny asked him, suddenly excited. 'I can smell the lake through the hydrant.'

'Smells like rust to me,' Eddie said.

'I can smell fish! Smelt—the smelt are in! I can smell them right through the hydrant!'

'Smelt?' Eddie said.

'You ain't ever had smelt?' Manny asked. 'Little silver fish!'

They caught the Twenty-sixth Street bus—the Polish Zephyr, people called it—going east toward the lake. The back of the bus was empty. They sat in the swaying, long backseat, taking hits out of the bottle in Eddie's sleeve.

'It's usually too early for them yet, but they're out there, Eduardo,' Manny kept reassuring him, as if they were actually going fishing.

Eddie nodded. He didn't know anything about smelt. The only fish he ate was canned tuna, but it felt good to be riding somewhere with the windows open and Manny acting more like his old self—sure of himself, laughing easily. Eddie still felt like talking, but his molars were grinding on speed.

The bus jolted down the dark block past Kedzie and was flying when it passed the narrow street between the ice house and the prison, but Eddie and Manny caught a glimpse out the back window of the railroad tracks that curved down the nameless street. The tracks were lined with fuming red flares that threw a red reflection off the concrete walls. Eddie was sure the flares had been set there for them.

Eddie closed his eyes and sank into the rocking of the bus. Even with his eyes closed he could see the reddish glare of the walls. The glare was ineradicable, at the back of his sockets. The wall had looked the same way it had looked in his dreams. They rode in silence.

'It's like one long night,' Eddie said somewhere along the way.

His jaws were really grinding and his legs had forgotten gravity by the time they got to the lakefront. They didn't know the time, but it must have been around 3.00 or 4.00 a.m. and the smelt fishers were still out. The lights of their kerosene lanterns reflected along the breakwater over the glossy black lake. Eddie and Manny could hear the water lapping under the pier and the fishermen talking in low voices in different languages.

'My uncle Carlos would talk to the fish,' Manny said. 'No shit. He'd talk to them in Spanish. He didn't have no choice. Whole time here he couldn't speak English. Said it made his brain stuck. We used to come fishing here all the time—smelt, perch, everything. I'd come instead of going to school. If they weren't hitting, he'd start talking to them, singing them songs.'

'Like what?' Eddie said.

'He'd make them up. They were funny, man. It don't come across in English: 'Little silver ones fill up my shoes. My heart is lonesome for the fish of the sea.' It was like very formal how he'd say it. He'd always call this the sea. I'd tell him it's a lake, but he couldn't be talked out of it. He was very stubborn—too stubborn to learn English. I ain't been fishing since he went back to Mexico.'

They walked to the end of the pier, then back past the fishermen. A lot of them were old men gently tugging lines between their fingers, lifting nets as if flying underwater kites, plucking the wriggling silver fish from the netting, the yellow light of their lamps glinting off the bright scales.

'I told you they were out here,' Manny said.

They sat on a concrete ledge, staring at the dark water, which rocked hypnotically below the soles of their dangling feet.

'Feel like diving in?' Manny asked.

Eddie had just raised the bottle to his lips and paused as if actually considering Manny's question, then shook his head no and took a swallow.

'One time right before my uncle went back to Mexico we came fishing at night for perch,' Manny said. 'It was a real hot night, you know? And all these old guys fishing off the pier. No one getting a bite, man, and I started thinking how cool and peaceful it would be to just dive in the water with the fish, and then, like I just did it without even deciding to, clothes and all. Sometimes, man, I still remember that feeling underwater—like I could just keep swimming out, didn't need air, never had to come up. When I couldn't hold my breath no more and came up I could hear my uncle calling my name, and then all the old guys on the pier start calling my name to come back. What I really felt like doing was to keep swimming out until I couldn't hear them, until I couldn't even see their lanterns, man. I wanted to be way the fuck out alone in the middle of the lake when the sun came up. But then I thought about my uncle standing on the pier calling me, so I turned around.'

They killed the bottle sitting on a concrete ledge and dropped it into the lake. Then they rode the El back. It was getting lighter without a dawn. The El windows were streaked with rain, the Douglas Avenue station smelled wet. It was a dark morning. They should have ended it then. Instead they sat at Manny's kitchen table drinking instant coffee with canned milk. Eddie kept getting lost in the designs the milk would make, swirls and thunderclouds in his mug of coffee. He was numb and shaky. His jaw ached.

'I'm really crashin',' he told Manny.

'Here,' Manny said. 'Bring us down easier, man.'

'I don't like doing downers, man,' Eddie said.

"Ludes,' Manny said, 'from Pancho's stash.'

They sat across the table from each other for a long time—talking, telling their memories and secrets—only Eddie was too numb to remember exactly what they said. Their voices—his own as well as Manny's—seemed *outside*, removed from the center of his mind.

At one point Manny looked out at the dark morning and said, 'It still seems like last night.'

'That's right,' Eddie agreed. He wanted to say more but couldn't express it. He didn't try. Eddie didn't believe it was what they said that was important. Manny could be talking Spanish; I could be talking Polish, Eddie thought. It didn't matter. What meant something was sitting at the table together, wrecked together, still awake watching the rainy light spatter the window, walking out again, to the Prague bakery for bismarcks, past people under dripping umbrellas

659

on their way to church.

'Looks like Sunday,' Manny said.

'Today's Friday,' Eddie said. 'It's Good Friday.'

'I seen ladies with ashes on their heads waiting for the bus a couple days ago,' Manny told him.

They stood in the doorway of the Prague, out of the rain, eating their bismarcks. Just down from the church, the bakery was a place people crowded into after mass. Its windows displayed colored eggs and little frosted Easter lambs.

'One time on Ash Wednesday I was eating a bismarck and Pancho made a cross on my forehead with the powdered sugar like it was ashes. When I went to church the priest wouldn't give me real ashes,' Manny said with a grin.

It was one of the few times Eddie had heard Manny mention Pancho. Now that they were outside, Eddie's head felt clearer than it had in the kitchen.

'I used to try and keep my ashes on until Good Friday,' he told Manny, 'but they'd make me wash.'

The church bells were ringing, echoes bouncing off the sidewalks as if deflected by the ceiling of clouds. The neighborhood felt narrower, compressed from above.

'I wonder if it still looks the same in there,' Manny said as they passed the church.

They stepped in and stood in the vestibule. The saints of their childhood stood shrouded in purple. The altar was bare, stripped for Good Friday. Old ladies, ignoring the new liturgy, chanted a litany in Polish.

'Same as ever,' Eddie whispered as they backed out.

The rain had almost let up. They could hear its accumulated weight in the wing-flaps of pigeons.

'Good Friday was Pancho's favorite holiday, man,' Manny said. 'Everybody else always picked Christmas or Thanksgiving or Fourth of July. He hadda be different, man. I remember he used to drag me along visiting churches. You ever do that?'

'Hell, yeah,' Eddie said. 'Every Good Friday we'd go on our bikes. You hadda visit seven of them.'

Without agreeing to it they walked from St Roman's to St Michael's, a little wooden Franciscan church in an Italian neighborhood; and from there to St Casimir's, a towering, mournful church with twin copper-green towers. Then, as if following an invisible trail, they walked north up Twenty-second toward St Anne's, St Puis's, St Adalbert's. At first they merely entered and left immediately, as if touching base, but their familiarity with small rituals quickly returned: dipping their fingers in the holy water font by the door, making the automatic sign of the cross as they passed the life-size crucified Christs that hung in the vestibules where old women and school kids clustered to kiss the spikes in the bronze or bloody plaster feet. By St Anne's, Manny removed his sunglasses, out of respect, the way one removes a hat. Eddie put them on. His eyes felt hard-boiled. The surge of energy he had felt at the bakery had burned out fast. While Manny genuflected to the altar, Eddie slumped in the back pew pretending to pray, drowsing off behind the dark glasses. It never occurred to Eddie to simply go home. His head ached, he could feel his heart racing, and would suddenly jolt awake wondering where Manny was. Manny would be off—jumpy, frazzled, still popping speed on the sly—exploring the church as if searching for something, standing among lines of parishioners waiting to kiss relics the priest wiped repeatedly clean with a rag of silk. Then Manny would be shaking Eddie awake. 'How you holding up, man?'

'I'm cool,' he'd say, and they would be back on the streets heading for another parish under the overcast sky. Clouds, a shade between slate and lilac, smoked over the spires and roofs; lights flashed on in the bars and *taquerías*. On Eighteenth Street a great blue neon fish leapt in the storefront window of a tiny *ostenaria*. Eddie tried to note the exact location to add to his window collection. They headed along a wall of viaducts to St Procopius, where, Manny said, both he and Pancho had been baptized. The viaduct walls had been painted by schoolchildren into a mural that seemed to go for miles.

'I don't think we're gonna make seven churches, man,' Eddie said. He was walking without lifting his feet, his hair plastered by a sweatlike drizzle. It was around 3.00 p.m. It had been 3.00 p.m.— Christ's dark hour on the cross—inside the churches all day, but now it was turning 3.00 p.m. outside too. They could hear the ancient-sounding hymn *'Tantum Ergo,'* carrying from down the block.

Eddie sunk into the last pew, kneeling in the red glow of vigil lights that brought back the red flicker of the flares they had seen from the window of the bus as it sped by the prison. Manny had already faded into the procession making the stations of the cross—a shuffling crowd circling the church, kneeling before each station

Stuart Dybek

while altar boys censed incense and the priest recited Christ's agony. Old women answered with prayers like moans.

Old women were walking on their knees up the marble aisle to kiss the relics. A few were crying, and Eddie remembered how back in grade school he had heard old women cry sometimes after confession, crying as if their hearts would break, and even as a child he had wondered how such old women could possibly have committed sins terrible enough to demand such bitter weeping. Most everything from that world had changed or disappeared, but the old women had endured—Polish, Bohemian, Spanish, he knew it didn't matter; they were the same, dressed in black coats and babushkas the way holy statues wore violet, in constant mourning. A common pain of loss seemed to burn at the core of their lives, though Eddie had never understood exactly what it was they mourned. Nor how day after day they had sustained the intensity of their grief. He would have given up long ago. In a way he *had* given up, and the ache left behind couldn't be called grief. He had no name for it. He had felt it before Pancho or anyone was lost, almost from the start of memory. If it was grief; it was grief for the living. The hymns, with their ancient, keening melodies and mysterious words, had brought the feeling back, but when he tried to discover the source, to give the feeling a name, it eluded him as always, leaving in its place nostalgia and triggered nerves.

Oh God, he prayed, I'm really crashing.

He was too shaky to kneel, so he stretched out on the pew, lying on his back, eyes shut behind sunglasses, until the church began to whirl. To control it he tried concentrating on the stained-glass window overhead. None of the windows that had ever been special for him were from a church. This one was an angel, its colors like jewels and coals. Afternoon seemed to be dying behind it, becoming part of the night, part of the private history that he and Manny continued between them like a pact. He could see night shining through the colors of the angel, dividing into bands as if the angel were a prism for darkness; the neon and wet streetlights illuminated its wingspread.

LEGENDS

It started with ice.

That's how Big Antek sometimes began the story.

662

At dusk a gang of little Mexican kids appeared with a few lumps of dry ice covered in a shoe box, as if they had caught a bird. *Hot ice,* they called it, though the way they said it sounded to Antek like *hot eyes.* Kids always have a way of finding stuff like that. One boy touched his tongue to a piece and screamed *'Aye!'* when it stuck. They watched the ice boil and fume in a rain puddle along the curb, and finally they filled a bottle part way with water, inserted the fragments of ice they had left, capped the bottle, and set it in the mouth of an alley waiting for an explosion. When it popped they scattered.

Manny Santora and Eddie Kapusta came walking up the alley, wanting Antek to buy them a bottle of rum at Buddy's. Rum instead of beer. They were celebrating, Kapusta said, but he didn't say what. Maybe one of them had found a job or had just been fired, or graduated, or joined the army instead of waiting around to get drafted. It could be anything. They were always celebrating. Behind their sunglasses Antek could see they were high as usual, even before Manny offered him a drag off a reefer the size of a cigar.

Probably nobody was hired or fired or had joined anything; probably it was just so hot they had a good excuse to act crazy. They each had a bottle of Coke they were fizzing up, squirting. Eddie had limes stuffed in his pockets and was pretending they were his balls. Manny had a plastic bag of the little ice cubes they sell at gas stations. It was half-melted, and they were scooping handfuls of cubes over each other's heads, stuffing them down their jeans and yowling, rubbing ice on their chests and under their arms as if taking a cold shower. They looked like wild men—shirts hanging from their back pockets, handkerchiefs knotted around their heads, wearing sunglasses, their bodies slick with melted ice water and sweat; two guys in the prime of life going nowhere, both lean, Kapusta almost as tan as Santora, Santora with that frizzy beard under his lip, and Kapusta trying to juggle limes.

They were drinking rum using a method Antek had never seen before, and he had seen his share of drinking—not just in the neighborhood—all over the world when he was in the navy, and not the Bohemian navy either like somebody would always say when he would start telling navy stories.

They claimed they were drinking cuba libres, only they didn't have glasses, so they were mixing the drinks in their mouths, starting with some little cubes, then pouring in rum, coke, a squeeze of lime, and swallowing. Swallowing if one or the other didn't suddenly bust up over some private joke, spraying the whole mouthful out, and both of them choking and coughing and laughing.

'Hey, Antek, lemme build you a drink,' Manny kept saying, but Antek shook his head no thanks, and he wasn't known for passing up too many.

This was all going on in front of Buddy's, everyone catching a blast of music and air-conditioning whenever the door opened. It was hot. The moths sizzled as soon as they hit Buddy's buzzing orange sign. A steady beat of moths dropped like cinders on the blinking orange sidewalk where the kids were pitching pennies. Manny passed around what was left in the plastic bag of ice, and the kids stood sucking and crunching the cubes between their teeth.

It reminded Antek of summers when the ice trucks still delivered to Buddy's—flatbeds covered with canvas, the icemen, mainly DPs, wearing leather aprons. Their Popeye forearms, even in August, looked ruddy with cold. They would slide the huge, clear blocks off the tailgate so the whump reverberated through the hollow under the sidewalks, and deep in the ice the clarity shattered. Then with their ice hooks they'd lug the blocks across the sidewalk, trailing a slick, and boot them skidding down the chute into Buddy's beery-smelling cellar. And after the truck pulled away, kids would pick the splinters from the curb and suck them as if they were ice-flavored Popsicles.

Nobody seemed too interested when Antek tried to tell them about the ice trucks, or anything else about how the world had been, for that matter. Antek had been sick and had only recently returned from the VA hospital. Of all his wounds, sickness was the worst. He could examine his hacked butcher's hands almost as kids from the neighborhood did, inspecting the stubs where his fingers had been as if they belonged to someone else, but there were places deep within himself that he couldn't examine, yet where he could feel that something of himself far more essential than fingers was missing. He returned from the VA feeling old and as if the neighborhood had changed in the weeks he had been gone. People had changed. He couldn't be sure, but they treated him differently, colder, as if he were becoming a stranger in the place he had grown up in, now, just when he most needed to belong.

'Hey, Antek,' Manny said, 'you know what you can tell me? That girl that saved your life in the meat freezer, did she have good tits?'

'I tell you about a miracle and you ask me about tits?' Antek said. 'I don't talk about that anymore because now somebody always asks me did she have good tits. Go see.'

Kids had been trying for years to sneak into the icehouse to see her. It was what the neighborhood had instead of a haunted house. Each generation had grown up with the story of how her father had ridden with her half-naked body on the streetcar. Even the nuns had heard Antek's story about finding the girl still frozen in the meat freezer. The butcher shop in Kedzie had closed long ago, and the legend was that after the cops had stopped checking, her body had been moved at night back into the icehouse. But the icehouse wasn't easy to break into. It had stood padlocked and heavily boarded for years.

'They're gonna wreck it,' Eddie said. 'I went by on the bus and they got the crane out in front.'

'Uh-oh, last chance, Antek,' Manny said. 'If you're sure she's in there, maybe we oughta go save her.'

'She's in there,' Antek said. He noticed the little kids had stopped pitching pennies and were listening.

'Well, you owe her something after what she done for you—don't he, Eduardo?'

The kids who were listening chuckled, then started to go back to their pennies.

'You wanna go, I'll go!' Antek said loudly.

'All right, let's go.'

Antek got up unsteadily. He stared at Eddie and Manny. 'You guys couldn't loan me enough for a taste of wine just until I get my disability check?'

The little kids tagged after them to the end of the block, then turned back bored. Manny and Eddie kept going, picking the pace up a step or two ahead of Antek, exchanging looks and grinning. But Antek knew that no matter how much they joked or what excuses they gave, they were going, like him, for one last look. They were just old enough to have seen the icehouse before it shut down. It was a special building, the kind a child couldn't help but notice and remember—there, on the corner across the street from the prison, a factory that made ice, humming with fans, its louvered roof dripping and clacking, lost in acrid clouds of its own escaping vapor.

The automatic ice machine in front had already been carted away. The doors were still padlocked, but the way the crane was parked it was possible for Manny and Eddie to climb the boom onto the roof.

Stuart Dybek

Antek waited below. He gazed up at the new Plexiglas guard turrets on the prison wall. From his angle all he could see was the bluish fluorescence of their lighting. He watched Manny and Eddie jump from the boom to the roof, high enough to stare across at the turrets like snipers, to draw a level bead on the backs of the guards, high enough to gaze over the wall at the dim, barred windows of the buildings that resembled foundries more than ever in the sweltering heat.

Below, Antek stood swallowing wine, expecting more from the night than a condemned building. He didn't know exactly what else he expected. Perhaps only a scent, like the stab of remembered ammonia he might have detected if he were still young enough to climb the boom. Perhaps the secret isolation he imagined Manny and Eddie feeling now, alone on the roof, as if lost in clouds of vapor. At street level, passing traffic drowned out the tick of a single cricket keeping time on the roof—a cricket so loud and insistent that Manny didn't stop to worry about the noise when he kicked in the louvers. And Antek, though he had once awakened in a freezer, couldn't imagine the shock of cold that Manny and Eddie felt as they dropped out of the summer night to the floor below.

Earlier, on their way down Twenty-sixth, Manny had stopped to pick up an unused flare from along the tracks, and Antek pictured them inside now, Manny, his hand wrapped in a handkerchief, holding the flare away from him like a Roman candle, its red glare sputtering off the beams and walls.

There wasn't much to see—empty corners, insulated pipes. Their breaths steamed. They tugged on their shirts. Instinctively, they traced the cold down a metal staircase. Cold was rising from the ground floor through the soles of their gym shoes.

The ground floor was stacked to the ceiling with junked ice machines. A wind as from an enormous air conditioner was blowing down a narrow aisle between the machines. At the end of the aisle a concrete ramp slanted down to the basement.

That was where Antek suspected they would end up, the basement, a cavernous space extending under the nameless street, slowly collapsing as if the thick, melting pillars of ice along its walls had served as its foundation. The floor was spongy with waterlogged sawdust. An echoing rain plipped from the ceiling. The air smelled thawed, and ached clammy in the lungs.

'It's fuckin' freezing,' Eddie whispered.

Manny swung the flare in a slow arc, its reflections glancing as if they stood among cracked mirrors. Blocks of ice, framed in defrosted freezer coils, glowed back faintly, like aquarium windows, from niches along the walls. They were melting unevenly and leaned at precarious angles. Several had already tottered to the sawdust, where they lay like quarry stones from a wrecked cathedral. Manny and Eddie picked their way among them, pausing to wipe the slick of water from their surfaces and peer into the ice, but deep networks of cracks refracted the light. They could see only frozen shadows and had to guess at the forms: fish, birds, shanks of meat, a dog, a cat, a chair, what appeared to be a bicycle.

But Antek knew they would recognize her when they found her. There would be no mistaking the light. In the smoky, phosphorous glare her hair would reflect gold like a candle behind a frosted pane. He was waiting for them to bring her out. He had finished the wine and flung the pint bottle onto the street so that it shattered. The streets were empty. He was waiting patiently, and though he had nowhere else to be it was still a long wait. He would wait as long as it might take, but even so he wondered if there was time enough left to him for another miracle in his life. He could hear the cricket now, composing time instead of music, working its way headfirst from the roof down the brick wall. Listening to it, Antek became acutely aware of the silence of the prison across the street. He thought of all the men on the other side of the wall and wondered how many were still awake, listening to the cricket, waiting patiently as they sweated in the heavy night.

Manny and Eddie, shivering, their hands burning numb from grappling with ice, unbarred the rear door that opened onto the loading platform behind the icehouse. They pushed out an old handcar and rolled it onto the tracks that came right up to the dock. They had already slid the block of ice onto the handcar and draped it with a canvas tarp. Even gently inching it on they had heard the ice cracking. The block of ice had felt too light for its size, fragile, ready to break apart.

'It feels like we're kidnapping somebody,' Eddie whispered.

'Just think of it as ice.'

'I can't.'

'We can't just leave her here, Eduardo.'

'What'll we do with her?'

'We'll think of something.'

667

'What about Antek?'
'Forget him.'

They pushed off. Rust slowed them at first, but as the tracks inclined toward the river they gained momentum. It was like learning to row. By the trestle they hit their rhythm. Speed became wind—hair blowing, shirts flapping open, the tarp billowing up off the ice. The skyline gleamed ahead, and though Manny couldn't see the lake, he could feel it stretching beyond the skyscrapers; he could recall the sudden lightness of freedom he'd felt once when he had speared out underwater and glided effortlessly away, one moment expanding into another, while the flow of water cleansed him of memory, and not even the sound of his own breath disrupted the silence. The smelt would have disappeared to wherever they disappeared to, but the fishermen would still be sitting at the edge of the breakwater, their backs to the city, dreaming up fish. And if the fishermen still remembered his name, they might call it repeatedly in a chorus of voices echoing out over the dark surface of the water, but this time, Manny knew, there would be no turning back. He knew now where they were taking her, where she would finally be released. They were rushing through waist-deep weeds, crossing the vast tracts of prairie behind the factories, clattering over bridges and viaducts. Below, streetlights shimmered watery in the old industrial neighborhoods. Shiny with sweat, the girl already melting free between them, they forced themselves faster, rowing like a couple of sailors.

1990

YOU'RE UGLY, TOO

Lorrie Moore

You had to get out of them occasionally, those Illinois towns with the funny names: Paris, Oblong, Normal. Once, when the Dow-Jones dipped two hundred points, the Paris paper boasted a banner headline: NORMAL MAN MARRIES OBLONG WOMAN. They knew what was important. They did! But you had to get out once in a while, even if it was just across the border to Terre Haute, for a movie.

Outside of Paris, in the middle of a large field, was a scatter of brick buildings, a small liberal arts college with the improbable name of Hilldale-Versailles. Zoë Hendricks had been teaching American History there for three years. She taught 'The Revolution and Beyond' to freshmen and sophomores, and every third semester she had the Senior Seminar for Majors, and although her student evaluations had been slipping in the last year and a half—*Professor Hendricks is often late for class and usually arrives with a cup of hot chocolate, which she offers the class sips of*—generally, the department of nine men was pleased to have her. They felt she added some needed feminine touch to the corridors—that faint trace of Obsession and sweat, the light, fast clicking of heels. Plus they had had a sex-discrimination suit, and the dean had said, well, it was time.

The situation was not easy for her, they knew. Once, at the start of last semester, she had skipped into her lecture hall singing 'Getting to Know You'—both verses. At the request of the dean, the chairman had called her into his office, but did not ask her for an explanation, not really. He asked her how she was and then smiled in an avuncular way. She said, 'Fine,' and he studied the way she said it, her front teeth catching on the inside of her lower lip. She was almost pretty, but her face showed the strain and ambition of always having been close but not quite. There was too much effort with the eyeliner, and her earrings, worn no doubt for the drama her features lacked, were a little frightening, jutting out from the side of her head like antennae.

'I'm going out of my mind,' said Zoë to her younger sister, Evan, in Manhattan. *Professor Hendricks seems to know the entire sound track to The King and I. Is this history?* Zoë phoned her every Tuesday.

669

'You always say that,' said Evan, 'but then you go on your trips and vacations and then you settle back into things and then you're quiet for a while and then you say you're fine, you're busy, and then after a while you say you're going crazy again, and you start all over.' Evan was a part-time food-designer for photo shoots. She cooked vegetables in green dye. She propped up beef stew with a bed of marbles and shopped for new kinds of silicone sprays and plastic ice cubes. She thought her life was 'OK.' She was living with her boyfriend of many years, who was independently wealthy and had an amusing little job in book publishing. They were five years out of college, and they lived in a luxury midtown high-rise with a balcony and access to a pool. 'It's not the same as having your own pool,' Evan was always sighing, as if to let Zoë know that, as with Zoë, there were still things she, Evan, had to do without.

'Illinois. It makes me sarcastic to be here,' said Zoë on the phone. She used to insist it was irony, something gently layered and sophisticated, something alien to the Midwest, but her students kept calling it sarcasm, something they felt qualified to recognize, and now she had to agree. It wasn't irony. *What is your perfume?* a student once asked her. *Room freshener*, she said. She smiled, but he looked at her, unnerved.

Her students were by and large good Midwesterners, spacey with estrogen from large quantities of meat and cheese. They shared their parents' suburban values; their parents had given them things, things, things. They were complacent. They had been purchased. They were armed with a healthy vagueness about anything historical or geographic. They seemed actually to know very little about anything, but they were extremely good-natured about it. 'All those states in the East are so tiny and jagged and bunched up,' complained one of her undergraduates the week she was lecturing on 'The Turning Point of Independence: The Battle at Saratoga.' 'Professor Hendricks, you're from Delaware originally, right?' the student asked her.

'Maryland,' corrected Zoë.

'Aw,' he said, waving his hand dismissively. 'New England.'

Her articles—chapters toward a book called *Hearing the One About: Uses of Humour in the American Presidency*—were generally well received, though they came slowly for her. She liked her pieces to have something from every time of day in them—she didn't trust things written in the morning only—so she reread and rewrote painstakingly. No part of a day, its moods, its light, was allowed to dominate. She hung on to a piece for over a year sometimes, revising at all hours, until the entirety of a day had registered there.

The job she'd had before the one at Hilldale-Versailles had been at a small college in New Geneva, Minnesota, Land of the Dying Shopping Mall. Everyone was so blond there that brunettes were often presumed to be from foreign countries. *Just because Professor Hendricks is from Spain doesn't give her the right to be so negative about our country.* There was a general emphasis on cheerfulness. In New Geneva you weren't supposed to be critical or complain. You weren't supposed to notice that the town had overextended and that its shopping malls were raggedy and going under. You were never to say you weren't fine thank you and yourself. You were supposed to be Heidi. You were supposed to lug goat milk up the hills and not think twice. Heidi did not complain. Heidi did not do things like stand in front of the new IBM photocopier, saying, 'If this fucking Xerox machine breaks on me one more time, I'm going to slit my wrists.'

But now, in her second job, in her fourth year of teaching in the Midwest, Zoë was discovering something she never suspected she had: a crusty edge, brittle and pointed. Once she had pampered her students, singing them songs, letting them call her at home, even, and ask personal questions. Now she was losing sympathy. They were beginning to seem different. They were beginning to seem demanding and spoiled.

'You act,' said one of the Senior Seminar students at a scheduled conference, 'like your opinion is worth more than everybody else's in the class.'

Zoë's eyes widened. 'I *am* the teacher,' she said. 'I *do* get paid to act like that.' She narrowed her gaze at the student, who was wearing a big leather bow in her hair, like a cowgirl in a TV ranch show. 'I mean, otherwise *everybody* in the class would have little offices and office hours.' *Sometimes Professor Hendricks will take up the class's time just talking about movies she's seen.* She stared at the student some more, then added, 'I bet you'd like that.'

'Maybe I sound whiny to you,' said the girl, 'but I simply want my history major to mean something.'

'Well, there's your problem,' said Zoë, and with a smile, she showed the student to the door. 'I like your bow,' she added.

Zoë lived for the mail, for the postman, that handsome blue jay, and when she got a real letter, with a real full-price stamp from

671

someplace else, she took it to bed with her and read it over and over. She also watched television until all hours and had her set in the bedroom, a bad sign. *Professor Hendricks has said critical things about Fawn Hall, the Catholic religion, and the whole state of Illinois. It is unbelievable.* At Christmastime she gave twenty-dollar tips to the mailman and to Jerry, the only cabbie in town, whom she had gotten to know from all her rides to and from the Terre Haute airport, and who, since he realized such rides were an extravagance, often gave her cut rates.

'I'm flying in to visit you this weekend,' announced Zoë.

'I was hoping you would,' said Evan. 'Charlie and I are having a party for Halloween. It'll be fun.'

'I have a costume already. It's a bonehead. It's this thing that looks like a giant bone going through your head.'

'Great,' said Evan.

'It is, it's great.'

'All I have is my moon mask from last year and the year before. I'll probably end up getting married in it.'

'Are you and Charlie getting *married*?' Foreboding filled her voice.

'Hmmmmmmnnnno, not immediately.'

'Don't get married.'

'Why?'

'Just not yet. You're too young.'

'You're only saying that because you're five years older than I am and *you're* not married.'

'*I'm* not married? Oh, my God,' said Zoë. 'I forgot to get married.'

Zoë had been out with three men since she'd come to Hilldale-Versailles. One of them was a man in the Paris municipal bureaucracy who had fixed a parking ticket she'd brought in to protest and who then asked her to coffee. At first she thought he was amazing—at last, someone who did not want Heidi! But soon she came to realize that all men, deep down, wanted Heidi. Heidi with cleavage. Heidi with outfits. The parking ticket bureaucrat soon became tired and intermittent. One cool fall day, in his snazzy, impractical convertible, when she asked him what was wrong, he said, 'You would not be ill-served by new clothes, you know.' She wore a lot of gray-green corduroy. She had been under the impression that it brought out her eyes, those shy stars. She flicked an ant from her sleeve.

'Did you have to brush that off in the car?' he said, driving. He glanced down at his own pectorals, giving first the left, then the right, a quick survey. He was wearing a tight shirt.

'Excuse me?'

He slowed down at a yellow light and frowned. 'Couldn't you have picked it up and thrown it outside?'

'The ant? It might have bitten me. I mean, what difference does it make?'

'It might have bitten you! Ha! How ridiculous! Now it's going to lay eggs in my car!'

The second guy was sweeter, lunkier, though not insensitive to certain paintings and songs, but too often, too, things he'd do or say would startle her. Once, in a restaurant, he stole the garnishes off her dinner plate and waited for her to notice. When she didn't, he finally thrust his fist across the table and said, 'Look,' and when he opened it, there was her parsley sprig and her orange slice, crumpled to a wad. Another time he described to her his recent trip to the Louvre. 'And there I was in front of Géricault's *Raft of the Medusa*, and everyone else had wandered off, so I had my own private audience with it, all those painted, drowning bodies splayed in every direction, and there's this motion in that painting that starts at the bottom left, swirling and building, and building, and building, and going up to the right-hand corner, where there's this guy waving a flag, and on the horizon in the distance you could see this teeny tiny boat . . . ' He was breathless in the telling. She found this touching and smiled in encouragement. 'A painting like that,' he said, shaking his head. 'It just makes you shit.'

'I have to ask you something,' said Evan. 'I know every woman complains about not meeting men, but really, on my shoots, I meet a lot of men. And they're not all gay, either.' She paused. 'Not anymore.'

'What are you asking?'

The third guy was a political science professor named Murray Peterson, who liked to go out on double dates with colleagues whose wives he was attracted to. Usually the wives would consent to flirt with him. Under the table sometimes there was footsie, and once there was even kneesie. Zoë and the husband would be left to their food, staring into their water glasses, chewing like goats. 'Oh, Murray,' said one wife, who had never finished her master's in physical therapy and wore great clothes. 'You know, I know everything about you: your birthday, your license plate number. I have everything memorized. But then that's the kind of mind I have. Once at a dinner party I amazed the host by getting up and saying good-bye to every single person there, first *and* last names.'

673

'I knew a dog who could do that,' said Zoë, with her mouth full. Murray and the wife looked at her with vexed and rebuking expressions, but the husband seemed suddenly twinkling and amused. Zoë swallowed. 'It was a Talking Lab, and after about ten minutes of listening to the dinner conversation this dog knew everyone's name. You could say, "Bring this knife to Murray Peterson," and it would.'

'Really,' said the wife, frowning, and Murray Peterson never called again.

'Are you seeing anyone?' said Evan. 'I'm asking for a particular reason, I'm not just being like mom.'

'I'm seeing my house. I'm tending to it when it wets, when it cries, when it throws up.' Zoë had bought a mint-green ranch house near campus, though now she was thinking that maybe she shouldn't have. It was hard to live in a house. She kept wandering in and out of the rooms, wondering where she had put things. She went downstairs into the basement for no reason at all except that it amused her to own a basement. It also amused her to own a tree. The day she moved in, she had tacked to her tree a small paper sign that said *Zöe's Tree.*

Her parents, in Maryland, had been very pleased that one of their children had at last been able to afford real estate, and when she closed on the house they sent her flowers with a Congratulations card. Her mother had even UPS'd a box of old decorating magazines saved over the years, photographs of beautiful rooms her mother had used to moon over, since there never had been any money to redecorate. It was like getting her mother's pornography, that box, inheriting her drooled-upon fantasies, the endless wish and tease that had been her life. But to her mother it was a rite of passage that pleased her. 'Maybe you will get some ideas from these,' she had written. And when Zoë looked at the photographs, at the bold and beautiful living rooms, she was filled with longing. Ideas and ideas of longing.

Right now Zoë's house was rather empty. The previous owner had wallpapered around the furniture, leaving strange gaps and silhouettes on the walls, and Zoë hadn't done much about that yet. She had bought furniture, then taken it back, furnishing and unfurnishing, preparing and shedding, like a womb. She had bought several plain pine chests to use as love seats or boot boxes, but they came to look to her more and more like children's coffins, so she returned them. And she had recently bought an Oriental rug for the living room, with Chinese symbols on it she didn't understand. The salesgirl had kept saying she was sure they meant *Peace* and *Eternal Life*, but when Zoë got the rug home, she worried. What if they didn't mean *Peace* and *Eternal Life*? What if they meant, say, *Bruce Springsteen*. And the more she thought about it, the more she became convinced she had a rug that said *Bruce Springsteen*, and so she returned that, too.

She had also bought a little baroque mirror for the front entryway, which she had been told, by Murray Peterson, would keep away evil spirits. The mirror, however, tended to frighten *her*, startling her with an image of a woman she never recognized. Sometimes she looked puffier and plainer than she remembered. Sometimes shifty and dark. Most times she just looked vague. *You look like someone I know*, she had been told twice in the last year by strangers in restaurants in Terre Haute. In fact, sometimes she seemed not to have a look of her own, or any look whatsoever, and it began to amaze her that her students and colleagues were able to recognize her at all. How did they know? When she walked into a room, how did she look so that they knew it was her? Like this? Did she look like this? And so she returned the mirror.

'The reason I'm asking is that I know a man I think you should meet,' said Evan. 'He's fun. He's straight. He's single. That's all I'm going to say.'

'I think I'm too old for fun,' said Zoë. She had a dark bristly hair in her chin, and she could feel it now with her finger. Perhaps when you had been without the opposite sex for too long, you began to resemble them. In an act of desperate invention, you began to grow your own. 'I just want to come, wear my bonehead, visit with Charlie's tropical fish, ask you about your food shoots.'

She thought about all the papers on 'Our Constitution: How It Affects Us' she was going to have to correct. She thought about how she was going in for ultrasound tests on Friday, because, according to her doctor and her doctor's assistant, she had a large, mysterious growth in her abdomen. Gallbladder, they kept saying. Or ovaries or colon. 'You guys practice medicine?' asked Zoë, aloud, after they had left the room. Once, as a girl, she brought her dog to a vet, who had told her, 'Well, either your dog has worms or cancer or else it was hit by a car.'

She was looking forward to New York.

'Well, whatever. We'll just play it cool. I can't wait to see you, hon.

Don't forget your bonehead,' said Evan.
'A bonehead you don't forget,' said Zoë.
'I suppose so,' said Evan.
The ultrasound Zoë was keeping a secret, even from Evan. 'I feel like I'm dying,' Zoë had hinted just once on the phone.
'You're not dying,' said Evan. 'You're just annoyed.'
'Ultrasound,' Zoë now said jokingly to the technician who put the cold jelly on her bare stomach. 'Does that sound like a really great stereo system, or what?' She had not had anyone make this much fuss over her bare stomach since her boyfriend in graduate school, who had hovered over her whenever she felt ill, waved his arms, pressed his hands upon her navel, and drawled evangelically, 'Heal! Heal for thy Baby Jesus' sake!' Zoë would laugh and they would make love, both secretly hoping she would get pregnant. Later they would worry together, and he would sink a cheek to her belly and ask whether she was late, was she late, was she sure, she might be late, and when after two years she had not gotten pregnant, they took to quarreling and drifted apart.
'OK,' said the technician absently.
The monitor was in place, and Zoë's insides came on the screen in all their gray and ribbony hollowness. They were marbled in the finest gradations of black and white, like stone in an old church or a picture of the moon. 'Do you suppose,' she babbled at the technician, 'that the rise in infertility among so many couples in this country is due to completely different species trying to reproduce?' The technician moved the scanner around and took more pictures. On one view in particular, on Zoë's right side, the technician became suddenly alert, the machine he was operating clicking away.
Zoë stared at the screen. 'That must be the growth you found there,' suggested Zoë.
'I can't tell you anything,' said the technician rigidly. 'Your doctor will get the radiologist's report this afternoon and will phone you then.'
'I'll be out of town,' said Zoë.
'I'm sorry,' said the technician.
Driving home, Zoë looked in the rearview mirror and decided she looked—well, how would one describe it? A little wan. She thought of the joke about the guy who visits his doctor and the doctor says, 'Well, I'm sorry to say you've got six weeks to live.'
'I want a second opinion,' says the guy. *You act like your opinion is*

worth more than everyone else's in the class.

'You want a second opinion? OK,' says the doctor. 'You're ugly, too.' She liked that joke. She thought it was terribly, terribly funny.

She took a cab to the airport, Jerry the cabbie happy to see her.

'Have fun in New York,' he said, getting her bag out of the trunk. He liked her, or at least he always acted as if he did. She called him 'Jare.'

'Thanks, Jare.'

'You know, I'll tell you a secret: I've never been to New York. I'll tell you two secrets: I've never been on a plane.' And he waved at her sadly as she pushed her way in through the terminal door. 'Or an escalator!' he shouted.

The trick to flying safe, Zoë always said, was never to buy a discount ticket and to tell yourself you had nothing to live for anyway, so that when the plane crashed it was no big deal. Then, when it didn't crash, when you had succeeded in keeping it aloft with your own worthlessness, all you had to do was stagger off, locate your luggage, and, by the time a cab arrived, come up with a persuasive reason to go on living.

'You're here!' shrieked Evan over the doorbell, before she even opened the door. Then she opened it wide. Zoë set her bags on the hall floor and hugged Evan hard. When she was little, Evan had always been affectionate and devoted. Zoë had always taken care of her, advising, reassuring, until recently, when it seemed Evan had started advising and reassuring *her*. It startled Zoë. She suspected it had something to do with Zoë's being alone. It made people uncomfortable. 'How *are* you?'

'I threw up on the plane. Besides that, I'm OK.'

'Can I get you something? Here, let me take your suitcase. Sick on the plane. Eeeyew.'

'It was into one of those sickness bags,' said Zoë, just in case Evan thought she'd lost it in the aisle. 'I was very quiet.'

The apartment was spacious and bright, with a view all the way downtown along the East Side. There was a balcony and sliding glass doors. 'I keep forgetting how nice this apartment is. Twentieth floor, doorman . . . ' Zoë could work her whole life and never have an apartment like this. So could Evan. It was Charlie's apartment. He and Evan lived in it like two kids in a dorm, beer cans and clothes strewn around. Evan put Zoë's bag away from the mess, over by the fish tank. 'I'm so glad you're here,' she said. 'Now what can I get you?'

Evan made them a snack—soup from a can, and saltines.

'I don't know about Charlie,' she said, after they had finished. 'I feel like we've gone all sexless and middle-aged already.'

'Hmmm,' said Zoë. She leaned back into Evan's sofa and stared out the window at the dark tops of the buildings. It seemed a little unnatural to live up in the sky like this, like birds that out of some wrongheaded derring-do had nested too high. She nodded toward the lighted fish tanks and giggled. 'I feel like a bird,' she said, 'with my own personal supply of fish.'

Evan sighed. 'He comes home and just sacks out on the sofa, watching fuzzy football. He's wearing the psychic cold cream and curlers, if you know what I mean.'

Zoë sat up, readjusted the sofa cushions. 'What's fuzzy football?'

'We haven't gotten cable yet. Everything comes in fuzzy. Charlie just watches it that way.'

'Hmmm, yeah, that's a little depressing,' Zoë said. She looked at her hands. 'Especially the part about not having cable.'

'This is how he gets into bed at night.' Evan stood up to demonstrate. 'He whips all his clothes off, and when he gets to his underwear, he lets it drop to one ankle. Then he kicks up his leg and flips the underwear in the air and catches it. I, of course, watch from the bed. There's nothing else. There's just that.'

'Maybe you should just get it over with and get married.'

'Really?'

'Yeah. I mean, you guys probably think living together like this is the best of both worlds, but . . . ' Zoë tried to sound like an older sister; an older sister was supposed to be the parent you could never have, the hip, cool mom. '. . . I've always found that as soon as you think you've got the best of both worlds'—she thought now of herself, alone in her house; of the toad-faced cicadas that flew around like little caped men at night, landing on her screens, staring; of the size fourteen shoes she placed at the doorstep, to scare off intruders; of the ridiculous inflatable blow-up doll someone had told her to keep propped at the breakfast table—'it can suddenly twist and become the worst of both worlds.'

'Really?' Evan was beaming. 'Oh, Zoë. I have something to tell you. Charlie and I *are* getting married.'

'Really.' Zoë felt confused.

'I didn't know how to tell you.'

'Yes, well, I guess the part about fuzzy football misled me a little.'

'I was hoping you'd be my maid of honor,' said Evan, waiting. 'Aren't you happy for me?'

'Yes,' said Zoë, and she began to tell Evan a story about an award-winning violinist at Hilldale-Versailles, how the violinist had come home from a competition in Europe and taken up with a local man, who made her go to all his summer softball games, made her cheer for him in the stands, with the wives, until she later killed herself. But when she got halfway through, to the part about cheering at the softball games, Zoë stopped.

'What?' said Evan. 'So what happened?'

'Actually, nothing,' said Zoë lightly. 'She just really got into softball. I mean, really. You should have seen her.'

Zoë decided to go to a late-afternoon movie, leaving Evan to chores she needed to do before the party—*I have to do them alone*, she'd said, a little tense after the violinist story. Zoë thought about going to an art museum, but women alone in art museums had to look good. They always did. Chic and serious, moving languidly, with a great handbag. Instead, she walked over and down through Kips Bay, past an earring boutique called Stick It in Your Ear, past a beauty salon called Dorian Gray's. That was the funny thing about *beauty*, thought Zoë. Look it up in the yellow pages, and you found a hundred entries, hostile with wit, cutesy with warning. But look up *truth*—ha! There was nothing at all.

Zoë thought about Evan getting married. Would Evan turn into Peter Pumpkin Eater's wife? Mrs Eater? At the wedding would she make Zoë wear some flouncy lavender dress, identical with the other maids'? Zoë hated uniforms, had even, in the first grade, refused to join Elf Girls, because she didn't want to wear the same dress as everyone else. Now she might have to. But maybe she could distinguish it. Hitch it up on one side with a clothespin. Wear surgical gauze at the waist. Clip to her bodice one of those pins that said in loud letters, SHIT HAPPENS.

At the movie—*Death by Number*—she bought strands of red licorice to tug and chew. She took a seat off to one side in the theater. She felt strangely self-conscious sitting alone and hoped for the place to darken fast. When it did, and the coming attractions came on, she reached inside her purse for her glasses. They were in a Baggie. Her

Kleenex was also in a Baggie. So were her pen and her aspirin and her mints. Everything was in Baggies. This was what she'd become: *a woman alone at the movies with everything in a Baggie.*

At the Halloween party, there were about two dozen people. There were people with ape heads and large hairy hands. There was someone dressed as a leprechaun. There was someone dressed as a frozen dinner. Some man had brought his two small daughters: a ballerina and a ballerina's sister, also dressed as a ballerina. There was a gaggle of sexy witches—women dressed entirely in black, beautifully made up and jeweled. 'I hate those sexy witches. It's not in the spirit of Halloween,' said Evan. Evan had abandoned the moon mask and dolled herself up as a hausfrau, in curlers and an apron, a decision she now regretted. Charlie because he liked fish, had decided to go as a fish. He had fins and eyes on the side of his head. 'Zoë! How are you! I'm sorry I wasn't there when you first arrived!' He spent the rest of his time chatting up the sexy witches.

'Isn't there something I can help you with here?' Zoë asked her sister. 'You've been running yourself ragged.' She rubbed her sister's arm, gently, as if she wished they were alone.

'Oh, God, not at all,' said Evan, arranging stuffed mushrooms on a plate. The timer went off, and she pulled another sheetful out of the oven. 'Actually, you know what you can do?'

'What!' Zoë put on her bonehead.

'Meet Earl. He's the guy I had in mind for you. When he gets here, just talk to him a little. He's nice. He's fun. He's going through a divorce.'

'I'll try.' Zoë groaned. 'OK? I'll try.' She looked at her watch.

When Earl arrived, he was dressed as a naked woman, steel wool glued strategically to a body stocking, and large rubber breasts protruding like hams.

'Zoë, this is Earl,' said Evan.

'Good to meet you,' said Earl, circling Evan to shake Zoë's hand. He stared at the top of Zoë's head. 'Great bone.'

Zoë nodded. 'Great tits,' she said. She looked past him, out the window at the city thrown glitteringly up against the sky; people were saying the usual things: how it looked like jewels, like bracelets and necklaces unstrung. You could see Grand Central station, the clock of the Con Ed building, the red-and-gold-capped Empire State, the Chrysler like a rocket ship dreamed up in a depression. Far west you could glimpse the Astor Plaza, its flying white roof like a nun's habit. 'There's beer out on the balcony, Earl—can I get you one?' Zoë asked.

'Sure, uh, I'll come along. Hey, Charlie, how's it going?'

Charlie grinned and whistled. People turned to look. 'Hey, Earl,' someone called, from across the room. 'Va-va-va-voom.'

They squeezed their way past the other guests, past the apes and the sexy witches. The suction of the sliding door gave way in a whoosh, and Zoë and Earl stepped out onto the balcony, a bonehead and a naked woman, the night air roaring and smoky cool. Another couple was out here, too, murmuring privately. They were not wearing costumes. They smiled at Zoë and Earl. 'Hi,' said Zoë. She found the plastic-foam cooler, dug into it, and retrieved two beers.

'Thanks,' said Earl. His rubber breasts folded inward, dimpled and dented, as he twisted open the bottle.

'Well,' sighed Zoë anxiously. She had to learn not to be afraid of a man, the way, in your childhood, you learned not to be afraid of an earthworm or a bug. Often, when she spoke to men at parties, she rushed things in her mind. As the man politely blathered on, she would fall in love, marry, then find herself in a bitter custody battle with him for the kids and hoping for a reconciliation, so that despite all his betrayals she might no longer despise him, and in the few minutes remaining, learn, perhaps, what his last name was and what he did for a living, though probably there was already too much history between them. She would nod, blush, turn away.

'Evan tells me you're a professor. Where do you teach?'

'Just over the Indiana border into Illinois.'

He looked a little shocked. 'I guess Evan didn't tell me that part.'

'She didn't?'

'No.'

'Well, that's Evan for you. When we were kids we both had speech impediments.'

'That can be tough,' said Earl. One of his breasts was hidden behind his drinking arm, but the other shone low and pink, full as a strawberry moon.

'Yes, well, it wasn't a total loss. We used to go to what we called peach pearapy. For about ten years of my life I had to map out every sentence in my mind, way ahead, before I said it. That was the only way I could get a coherent sentence out.'

Earl drank from his beer. 'How did you do that? I mean, how did you get through?'

'I told a lot of jokes. Jokes you know the lines to already—you can just say them. I love jokes. Jokes and songs.'

Earl smiled. He had on lipstick, a deep shade of red, but it was wearing off from the beer. 'What's your favourite joke?'

'Uh, my favourite joke is probably . . . OK, all right. This guy goes into a doctor's office and—'

'I think I know this one,' interrupted Earl, eagerly. He wanted to tell it himself. 'A guy goes into a doctor's office, and the doctor tells him he's got some good news and some bad news—that one, right?'

'I'm not sure,' said Zoë. 'This might be a different version.'

'So the guy says, "Give me the bad news first," and the doctor says, "OK. You've got three weeks to live." And the guy cries, "Three weeks to live! Doctor, what is the good news?" And the doctor says, "Did you see that secretary out front? I finally fucked her."'

Zoë frowned.

'That's not the one you were thinking of?'

'No.' There was accusation in her voice. 'Mine was different.'

'Oh,' said Earl. He looked away and then back again. 'You teach history, right? What kind of history do you teach?'

'I teach American, mostly—eighteenth and nineteenth century.' In graduate school, at bars, the pickup line was always: 'So, what's your century?'

'Occasionally I teach a special theme course,' she added, 'say, "Humour and Personality in the White House." That's what my book's on.' She thought of something someone once told her about bowerbirds, how they build elaborate structures before mating.

'Your book's on *humor*?'

'Yeah, and, well, when I teach a theme course like that, I do all the centuries.' *So what's your century?*

'All three of them.'

'Pardon?' The breeze glistened her eyes. Traffic revved beneath them. She felt high and puny, like someone lifted into heaven by mistake and then spurned.

'Three. There's only three.'

'Well, four, really.' She was thinking of Jamestown, and of the Pilgrims coming here with buckles and witch hats to say their prayers.

'I'm a photographer,' said Earl. His face was starting to gleam, his rouge smearing in a sunset beneath his eyes.

'Do you like that?'

'Well, actually I'm starting to feel it's a little dangerous.'

'Really?'

'Spending all your time in a darkroom with that red light and all those chemicals. There's links with Parkinson's, you know.'

'No, I didn't.'

'I suppose I should wear rubber gloves, but I don't like to. Unless I'm touching it directly, I don't think of it as real.'

'Hmmm,' said Zoë. Alarm buzzed through her, mildly, like a tea.

'Sometimes, when I have a cut or something, I feel the sting and think, *Shit*. I wash constantly and just hope. I don't like rubber over skin like that.'

'Really.'

'I mean, the physical contact. That's what you want, or why bother?'

'I guess,' said Zoë. She wishes she could think of a joke, something slow and deliberate, with the end in sight. She thought of gorillas, how when they had been kept too long alone in cages, they would smack each other in the head instead of mating.

'Are you . . . in a relationship?' Earl suddenly blurted.

'Now? As we speak?'

'Well, I mean, I'm sure you have a relationship to your *work*.' A smile, a weird one, nestled in his mouth like an egg. She thought of zoos in parks, how when cities were under siege, during world wars, people ate animals. 'But I mean, with a *man*.'

'No, I'm not in a relationship with a *man*.' She rubbed her chin with her hand and could feel the one bristly hair there. 'But my last relationship was with a very sweet man,' she said. She made something up. 'From Switzerland. He was a botanist—a weed expert. His name was Jerry. I called him "Jare." He was so funny. You'd go to the movies with him and all he would notice were the plants. He would never pay attention to the plot. Once, in a jungle movie, he started rattling off all these Latin names, out loud. It was very exciting for him.' She paused, caught her breath. 'Eventually he went back to Europe to, uh, study the edelweiss.' She looked at Earl. 'Are you involved in a relationship? With a *woman*?'

Earl shifted his weight, and the creases in his body stocking changed, splintering outward like something broken. His pubic hair slid over to one hip, like a corsage on a saloon girl. 'No,' he said, clearing his throat. The steel wool in his underarms was inching toward his biceps. 'I've just gotten out of a marriage that was full of bad dialogue, like "You want more *space*? I'll give you more space!" *Clonk*. Your basic Three Stooges.'

Zoë looked at him sympathetically. 'I suppose it's hard for love to recover after that.'

His eyes lit up. He wanted to talk about love. 'But *I* keep thinking love should be like a tree. You look at trees and they've got bumps and scars from tumors, infestations, what have you, but they're still growing. Despite the bumps and bruises, they're . . . straight.'

'Yeah, well,' said Zoë, 'where I'm from, they're all married or gay. Did you see that movie *Death by Number*?'

Earl looked at her, a little lost. She was getting away from him. 'No,' he said.

One of his breasts had slipped under his arm, tucked there like a baguette. She kept thinking of trees, of gorillas and parks, of people in wartime eating the zebras. She felt a stabbing pain in her abdomen.

'Want some hors d'oeuvres?' Evan came pushing through the sliding door. She was smiling, though her curlers were coming out, hanging bedraggled at the ends of her hair like Christmas decorations, like food put out for the birds. She thrust forward a plate of stuffed mushrooms.

'Are you asking for donations or giving them away,' said Earl, wittily. He liked Evan, and he put his arm around her.

'You know, I'll be right back,' said Zoë.

'Oh,' said Evan, looking concerned.

'Right back. I promise.'

Zoë hurried inside, across the living room, into the bedroom, to the adjoining bath. It was empty; most of the guests were using the half bath near the kitchen. She flicked on the light and closed the door. The pain had stopped and she didn't really have to go to the bathroom, but she stayed there anyway, resting. In the mirror above the sink she looked haggard beneath her bonehead, violet grays showing under the skin like a plucked and pocky bird. She leaned closer, raising her chin a little to find the bristly hair. It was there, at the end of the jaw, sharp and dark as a wire. She opened the medicine cabinet, pawed through it until she found some tweezers. She lifted her head again and poked at her face with the metal tips, grasping and pinching and missing. Outside the door she could hear two people talking low. They had come into the bedroom and were discussing something. They were sitting on the bed. One of them

684

giggled in a false way. She stabbed again at her chin, and it started to bleed a little. She pulled the skin tight along the jawbone, gripped the tweezers hard around what she hoped was the hair, and tugged. A tiny square of skin came away with it, but the hair remained, blood bright at the root of it. Zoë clenched her teeth. 'Come on,' she whispered. The couple outside in the bedroom were now telling stories, softly, and laughing. There was a bounce and squeak of mattress, and the sound of a chair being moved out of the way. Zoë aimed the tweezers carefully, pinched, then pulled gently away, and this time the hair came too, with a slight twinge of pain and then a great flood of relief. 'Yeah!' breathed Zoë. She grabbed some toilet paper and dabbed at her chin. It came away spotted with blood, and so she tore off some more and pressed hard until it stopped. Then she turned off the light and opened the door, to return to the party. 'Excuse me,' she said to the couple in the bedroom. They were the couple from the balcony, and they looked at her, a bit surprised. They had their arms around each other, and they were eating candy bars.

Earl was still out on the balcony, alone, and Zoë rejoined him there.

'Hi,' she said. He turned around and smiled. He had straightened his costume out a bit, though all the secondary sex characteristics seemed slightly doomed, destined to shift and flip and zip around again any moment.

'Are you OK?' he asked. He had opened another beer and was chugging.

'Oh, yeah. I just had to go to the bathroom.' She paused. 'Actually I have been going to a lot of doctors recently.'

'What's wrong?' asked Earl.

'Oh, probably nothing. But they're putting me through tests.' She sighed. 'I've had sonograms. I've had mammograms. Next week I'm going in for a candygram.' He looked at her worriedly. 'I've had too many gram words,' she said.

'Here, I saved you these.' He held out a napkin with two stuffed mushroom caps. They were cold and leaving oil marks on the napkin.

'Thanks,' said Zoë, and pushed them both in her mouth. 'Watch,' she said with her mouth full. 'With my luck, it'll be a gallbladder operation.'

Earl made a face. 'So your sister's getting married,' he said, changing the subject. 'Tell me, really, what you think about love.'

'*Love?*' Hadn't they done this already? 'I don't know.' She chewed thoughtfully and swallowed. 'All right. I'll tell you what I think about love. Here is a love story. This friend of mine—'

'You've got something on your chin,' said Earl, and he reached over to touch it.

'*What?*' said Zoë, stepping back. She turned her face away and grabbed at her chin. A piece of toilet paper peeled off it, like tape. 'It's nothing,' she said. 'It's just—it's nothing.'

Earl stared at her.

'At any rate,' she continued, 'this friend of mine was this award-winning violinist. She traveled all over Europe and won competitions; she made records, she gave concerts, she got famous. But she had no social life. So one day she threw herself at the feet of this conductor she had a terrible crush on. He picked her up, scolded her gently, and sent her back to her hotel room. After that she came home from Europe. She went back to her old hometown, stopped playing the violin, and took up with a local boy. This was in Illinois. He took her to some Big Ten bar every night to drink with his buddies from the team. He used to say things like "Katrina here likes to play the violin," and then he'd pinch her cheek. When she once suggested that they go home, he said, "What, you think you're too famous for a place like this? Well, let me tell you something. You may think you're famous, but you're not *famous* famous." Two famouses. "No one here's ever heard of you." Then he went up and bought a round of drinks for everyone but her. She got her coat, went home, and shot a gun through her head.'

Earl was silent.

'That's the end of my love story,' said Zoë.

'You're not at all like your sister,' said Earl.

'Ho, really,' said Zoë. The air had gotten colder, the wind singing minor and thick as a dirge.

'No.' He didn't want to talk about love anymore. 'You know, you should wear a lot of blue—blue and white—around your face. It would bring out your coloring.' He reached an arm out to show her how the blue bracelet he was wearing might look against her skin, but she swatted it away.

'Tell me, Earl. Does the word *fag* mean anything to you?'

He stepped back, away from her. He shook his head in disbelief. 'You know, I just shouldn't try to go out with career women. You're all stricken. A guy can really tell what life has done to you. I do better

686

with women who have part-time jobs.'

'Oh, yes?' said Zoë. She had once read an article entitled 'Professional Women and the Demographics of Grief.' Or no, it was a poem: *If there were a lake, the moonlight would dance across it in conniptions.* She remembered that line. But perhaps the title was 'The Empty House; Aesthetics of Barrenness.' Or maybe 'Space Gypsies: Girls in Academe.' She had forgotten.

Earl turned and leaned on the railing of the balcony. It was getting late. Inside, the party guests were beginning to leave. The sexy witches were already gone. 'Live and learn,' Earl murmured.

'Live and get dumb,' replied Zoë. Beneath them on Lexington there were no cars, just the gold rush of an occasional cab. He leaned hard on his elbows, brooding.

'Look at those few people down there,' he said. 'They look like bugs. You know how bugs are kept under control? They're sprayed with bug hormones, female bug hormones. The male bugs get so crazy in the presence of this hormone, they're screwing everything in sight: trees, rocks—everything but female bugs. Population control. That's what's happening in this country,' he said drunkenly. 'Hormones sprayed around, and now men are screwing rocks. Rocks!'

In the back the Magic Marker line of his buttocks spread wide, a sketchy black on pink like a funnies page. Zoë came up, slow, from behind and gave him a shove. His arms slipped forward, off the railing, out over the street. Beer spilled out of his bottle, raining twenty stories down to the street.

'Hey, what are you doing?!' he said, whipping around. He stood straight and readied and moved away from the railing, sidestepping Zoë. 'What the *hell* are you doing?'

'Just kidding,' she said. 'I was just kidding.' But he gazed at her, appalled and frightened, his Magic Marker buttocks turned away now toward all of downtown, a naked pseudo-woman with a blue bracelet at the wrist, trapped out on a balcony with—with *what*? '*Really, I was just kidding!*' Zoë shouted. The wind lifted the hair up off her head, skyward in spines behind the bone. If there were a lake, the moonlight would dance across it in conniptions. She smiled at him, and wondered how she looked.

1990

687

THE THINGS THEY CARRIED

Tim O'Brien

First Lieutenant Jimmy Cross carried letters from a girl named Martha, a junior at Mount Sebastian College in New Jersey. They were not love letters, but Lieutenant Cross was hoping, so he kept them folded in plastic at the bottom of his rucksack. In the late afternoon, after a day's march, he would dig his foxhole, wash his hands under a canteen, unwrap the letters, hold them with the tips of his fingers, and spend the last hour of light pretending. He would imagine romantic camping trips into the White Mountains in New Hampshire. He would sometimes taste the envelope flaps, knowing her tongue had been there. More than anything, he wanted Martha to love him as he loved her, but the letters were mostly chatty, elusive on the matter of love. She was a virgin, he was almost sure. She was an English major at Mount Sebastian, and she wrote beautifully about her professors and roommates and mid-term exams, about her respect for Chaucer and her great affection for Virginia Woolf. She often quoted lines of poetry; she never mentioned the war, except to say, Jimmy, take care of yourself. The letters weighed 10 ounces. They were signed Love, Martha, but Lieutenant Cross understood that Love was only a way of signing and did not mean what he sometimes pretended it meant. At dusk, he would carefully return the letters to his rucksack. Slowly, a bit distracted, he would get up and move among his men, checking the perimeter, then at full dark he would return to his hole and watch the night and wonder if Martha was a virgin.

The things they carried were largely determined by necessity. Among the necessities or near-necessities were P-38 can openers, pocket knives, heat tabs, wristwatches, dog tags, mosquito repellent, chewing gum, candy, cigarettes, salt tablets, packets of Kool-Aid, lighters, matches, sewing kits, Military Payment Certificates, C rations, and two or three canteens of water. Together, these items weighed between 15 and 20 pounds, depending upon a man's habits or rate of metabolism. Henry Dobbins, who was a big man, carried extra rations; he was especially fond of canned peaches in heavy syrup over pound cake. Dave Jensen, who practiced field hygiene, carried a toothbrush, dental floss, and several hotel-sized bars of soap he'd stolen on R&R in Sydney, Australia. Ted Lavender, who was scared, carried tranquilizers until he was shot in the head outside the village of Than Khe in mid-April. By necessity, and because it was SOP, they all carried steel helmets that weighed 5 pounds including the liner and camouflage cover. They carried the standard fatigue jackets and trousers. Very few carried underwear. On their feet they carried jungle boots—2.1 pounds—and Dave Jensen carried three pairs of socks and a can of Dr Scholl's foot powder as a precaution against trench foot. Until he was shot, Ted Lavender carried six or seven ounces of premium dope, which for him was a necessity. Mitchell Sanders, the RTO, carried condoms. Norman Bowker carried a diary. Rat Kiley carried comic books. Kiowa, a devout Baptist, carried an illustrated New Testament that had been presented to him by his father, who taught school in Oklahoma City, Oklahoma. As a hedge against bad times, however, Kiowa also carried his grandmother's distrust of the white man, his grandfather's old hunting hatchet. Necessity dictated. Because the land was mined and booby-trapped, it was SOP for each man to carry a steel-centered, nylon-covered flak jacket, which weighed 6.7 pounds, but which on hot days seemed much heavier. Because you could die so quickly, each man carried at least one large compress bandage, usually in the helmet band for easy access. Because the nights were cold, and because the monsoons were wet, each carried a green plastic poncho that could be used as a raincoat or groundsheet or makeshift tent. With its quilted liner, the poncho weighed almost two pounds, but it was worth every ounce. In April, for instance, when Ted Lavender was shot, they used his poncho to wrap him up, then to carry him across the paddy, then to lift him into the chopper that took him away.

They were called legs or grunts.

To carry something was to hump it, as when Lieutenant Jimmy Cross humped his love for Martha up the hills and through the swamps. In its intransitive form, to hump meant to walk, or to march, but it implied burdens far beyond the intransitive.

Almost everyone humped photographs. In his wallet, Lieutenant Cross carried two photographs of Martha. The first was a Kodacolor

snapshot signed Love, though he knew better. She stood against a
brick wall. Her eyes were gray and neutral, her lips slightly open as
she stared straight-on at the camera. At night, sometimes, Lieutenant
Cross wondered who had taken the picture, because he knew she had
boyfriends, because he loved her so much, and because he could see
the shadow of the picture-taker spreading out against the brick wall.
The second photograph had been clipped from the 1968 Mount
Sebastian yearbook. It was an action shot—women's volleyball—and
Martha was bent horizontal to the floor, reaching, the palms of her
hands in sharp focus, the tongue taut, the expression frank and
competitive. There was no visible sweat. She wore white gym shorts.
Her legs, he thought, were almost certainly the legs of a virgin, dry
and without hair, the left knee cocked and carrying her entire weight,
which was just over one hundred pounds. Lieutenant Cross
remembered touching that left knee. A dark theater, he remembered,
and the movie was *Bonnie and Clyde*, and Martha wore a tweed skirt,
and during the final scene, when he touched her knee, she turned and
looked at him in a sad, sober way that made him pull his hand back,
but he would always remember the feel of the tweed skirt and the
knee beneath it and the sound of the gunfire that killed Bonnie and
Clyde, how embarrassing it was, how slow and oppressive. He
remembered kissing her good night at the dorm door. Right then, he
thought, he should've done something brave. He should've carried
her up the stairs to her room and tied her to the bed and touched that
left knee all night long. He should've risked it. Whenever he looked at
the photographs, he thought of new things he should've done.

What they carried was partly a function of rank, partly of field
specialty.

As a first lieutenant and platoon leader, Jimmy Cross carried a
compass, maps, code books, binoculars, and a .45-caliber pistol that
weighed 2.9 pounds fully loaded. He carried a strobe light and the
responsibility for the lives of his men.

As an RTO, Mitchell Sanders carried the PRC-25 radio, a killer, 26
pounds with its battery.

As a medic, Rat Kiley carried a canvas satchel filled with morphine
and plasma and malaria tablets and surgical tape and comic books
and all the things a medic must carry, including M&Ms for especially
bad wounds, for a total weight of nearly 20 pounds.

As a big man, therefore a machine gunner, Henry Dobbins carried the M-60, which weighed 23 pounds unloaded, but which was almost always loaded. In addition, Dobbins carried between 10 and 15 pounds of ammunition draped in belts across his chest and shoulders.

As PFCs or Spec 4s, most of them were common grunts and carried the standard M-16 gas-operated assault rifle. The weapon weighed 7.5 pounds unloaded, 8.2 pounds with its full 20-round magazine. Depending on numerous factors, such as topography and psychology, the riflemen carried anywhere from 12 to 20 magazines, usually in cloth bandoliers, adding on another 8.4 pounds at minimum, 14 pounds at maximum. When it was available, they also carried M-16 maintenance gear—rods and steel brushes and swabs and tubes of LSA oil—all of which weighed about a pound. Among the grunts, some carried the M-79 grenade launcher, 5.9 pounds unloaded, a reasonably light weapon except for the ammunition, which was heavy. A single round weighed 10 ounces. The typical load was 25 rounds. But Ted Lavender, who was scared, carried 34 rounds when he was shot and killed outside Than Khe, and he went down under an exceptional burden, more than 20 pounds of ammunition, plus the flak jacket and helmet and rations and water and toilet paper and tranquilizers and all the rest, plus the unweighed fear. He was dead weight. There was no twitching or flopping. Kiowa, who saw it happen, said it was like watching a rock fall, or a big sandbag or something—just boom, then down—not like the movies where the dead guy rolls around and does fancy spins and goes ass over teakettle—not like that, Kiowa said, the poor bastard just flat-fuck fell. Boom. Down. Nothing else. It was a bright morning in mid-April. Lieutenant Cross felt the pain. He blamed himself. They stripped off Lavender's canteens and ammo, all the heavy things, and Rat Kiley said the obvious, the guy's dead, and Mitchell Sanders used his radio to report one US KIA and to request a chopper. Then they wrapped Lavender in his poncho. They carried him out to a dry paddy, established security, and sat smoking the dead man's dope until the chopper came. Lieutenant Cross kept to himself. He pictured Martha's smooth young face, thinking he loved her more than anything, more than his men, and now Ted Lavender was dead because he loved her so much and could not stop thinking about her. When the dustoff arrived, they carried Lavender aboard. Afterward they burned Than Khe. They marched until dusk, then dug their holes, and that night Kiowa kept explaining how you had to be there, how fast it was, how the poor guy just dropped like so much concrete. Boom-down, he said. Like cement.

In addition to the three standard weapons—the M-60, M-16, and M-79—they carried whatever presented itself, or whatever seemed appropriate as a means of killing or staying alive. They carried catch-as-catch-can. At various times, in various situations, they carried M-14s and CAR-15s and Swedish Ks and grease guns and captured AK-47s and Chi-Coms and RPGs and Simonov carbines and black market Uzis and .38 caliber Smith & Wesson handguns and 66 mm LAWs and shotguns and silencers and blackjacks and bayonets and C-4 plastic explosives. Lee Strunk carried a slingshot; a weapon of last resort, he called it. Mitchell Sanders carried brass knuckles. Kiowa carried his grandfather's feathered hatchet. Every third or fourth man carried a Claymore antipersonnel mine—3.5 pounds with its firing device. They all carried fragmentation grenades—14 ounces each. They all carried at least one M-18 colored smoke grenade—24 ounces. Some carried CS or tear gas grenades. Some carried white phosphorus grenades. They carried all they could bear, and then some, including a silent awe for the terrible power of the things they carried.

In the first week of April, before Lavender died, Lieutenant Jimmy Cross received a good-luck charm from Martha. It was a simple pebble, an ounce at most. Smooth to the touch, it was a milky white color with flecks of orange and violet, oval shaped, like a miniature egg. In the accompanying letter, Martha wrote that she had found the pebble on the Jersey shoreline, precisely where the land touched water at high tide, where things came together but also separated. It was this separate-but-together quality, she wrote, that had inspired her to pick up the pebble and to carry it in her breast pocket for several days, where it seemed weightless, and then to send it through the mail, by air, as a token of her truest feelings for him. Lieutenant Cross found this romantic. But he wondered what her truest feelings were, exactly, and what she meant by separate-but-together. He wondered how the tides and waves had come into play on that afternoon along the Jersey shoreline when Martha saw the pebble and bent down to rescue it from geology. He imagined bare feet. Martha was a poet, with the poet's sensibilities, and her feet would be brown and bare, the toenails unpainted, the eyes chilly and somber like the ocean in March, and though it was painful, he wondered who had been with her that afternoon. He imagined a pair of shadows moving along the strip of sand where things came together but also separated. It was phantom jealousy, he knew, but he couldn't help himself. He loved her so much. On the march, through the hot days of early April, he carried the pebble in his mouth, turning it with his tongue, tasting sea salt and moisture. His mind wandered. He had difficulty keeping his attention on the war. On occasion he would yell at his men to spread out the column, to keep their eyes open, but then he would slip away into daydreams, just pretending, walking barefoot along the Jersey shore, with Martha, carrying nothing. He would feel himself rising. Sun and waves and gentle winds, all love and lightness.

What they carried varied by mission.

When a mission took them to the mountains, they carried mosquito netting, machetes, canvas tarps, and extra bug juice.

If a mission seemed especially hazardous, or if it involved a place they knew to be bad, they carried everything they could. In certain heavily mined AOs, where the land was dense with Toe Poppers and Bouncing Betties, they took turns humping a 28-pound mine detector. With its headphones and big sensing plate, the equipment was a stress on the lower back and shoulders, awkward to handle, often useless because of the shrapnel in the earth, but they carried it anyway, partly for safety, partly for the illusion of safety.

On ambush, or other night missions, they carried peculiar little odds and ends. Kiowa always took along his New Testament and a pair of moccasins for silence. Dave Jensen carried night-sight vitamins high in carotene. Lee Strunk carried his slingshot; ammo, he claimed, would never be a problem. Rat Kiley carried brandy and M&Ms candy. Until he was shot, Ted Lavender carried the starlight scope, which weighed 6.3 pounds with its aluminum carrying case. Henry Dobbins carried his girlfriend's pantyhose wrapped around his neck as a comforter. They all carried ghosts. When dark came, they would move out single file across the meadows and paddies to their ambush coordinates, where they would quietly set up the Claymores and lie down and spend the night waiting.

Other missions were more complicated and required special equipment. In mid-April, it was their mission to search out and destroy the elaborate tunnel complexes in the Than Khe area south of

Chu Lai. To blow the tunnels, they carried one-pound blocks of pentrite high explosives, four blocks to a man, 68 pounds in all. They carried wiring, detonators, and battery-powered clackers. Dave Jensen carried earplugs. Most often, before blowing the tunnels, they were ordered by higher command to search them, which was considered bad news, but by and large they just shrugged and carried out orders. Because he was a big man, Henry Dobbins was excused from tunnel duty. The others would draw numbers. Before Lavender died there were 17 men in the platoon, and whoever drew the number 17 would strip off his gear and crawl in headfirst with a flashlight and Lieutenant Cross's .45-caliber pistol. The rest of them would fan out as security. They would sit down or kneel, not facing the hole, listening to the ground beneath them, imagining cobwebs and ghosts, whatever was down there—the tunnel walls squeezing in—how the flashlight seemed impossibly heavy in the hand and how it was tunnel vision in the very strictest sense, compression in all ways, even time, and how you had to wiggle in—ass and elbows—a swallowed-up feeling—and how you found yourself worrying about odd things: Will your flashlight go dead? Do rats carry rabies? If you screamed, how far would the sound carry? Would your buddies hear it? Would they have the courage to drag you out? In some respects, though not many, the waiting was worse than the tunnel itself. Imagination was a killer.

On April 16, when Lee Strunk drew the number 17, he laughed and muttered something and went down quickly. The morning was hot and very still. Not good, Kiowa said. He looked at the tunnel opening, then out across a dry paddy toward the village of Than Khe. Nothing moved. No clouds or birds or people. As they waited, the men smoked and drank Kool-Aid, not talking much, feeling sympathy for Lee Strunk but also feeling the luck of the draw. You win some, you lose some, said Mitchell Sanders, and sometimes you settle for a rain check. It was a tired line and no one laughed.

Henry Dobbins ate a tropical chocolate bar. Ted Lavender popped a tranquilizer and went off to pee.

After five minutes, Lieutenant Jimmy Cross moved to the tunnel, leaned down, and examined the darkness. Trouble, he thought—a cave-in maybe. And then suddenly, without willing it, he was thinking about Martha. The stresses and fractures, the quick collapse, the two of them buried alive under all that weight. Dense, crushing love. Kneeling, watching the hole, he tried to concentrate on Lee

Strunk and the war, all the dangers, but his love was too much for him, he felt paralyzed, he wanted to sleep inside her lungs and breathe her blood and be smothered. He wanted her to be a virgin and not a virgin, all at once. He wanted to know her. Intimate secrets: Why poetry? Why so sad? Why that grayness in her eyes? Why so alone? Not lonely, just alone—riding her bike across campus or sitting off by herself in the cafeteria—even dancing, she danced alone—and it was the aloneness that filled him with love. He remembered telling her that one evening. How she nodded and looked away. And how, later, when he kissed her, she received the kiss without returning it, her eyes wide open, not afraid, not a virgin's eyes, just flat and uninvolved.

Lieutenant Cross gazed at the tunnel. But he was not there. He was buried with Martha under the white sand at the Jersey shore. They were pressed together, and the pebble in his mouth was her tongue. He was smiling. Vaguely, he was aware of how quiet the day was, the sullen paddies, yet he could not bring himself to worry about matters of security. He was beyond that. He was just a kid at war, in love. He was twenty-four years old. He couldn't help it.

A few moment later Lee Strunk crawled out of the tunnel. He came up grinning, filthy but alive. Lieutenant Cross nodded and closed his eyes while the others clapped Strunk on the back and made jokes about rising from the dead.

Worms, Rat Kiley said. Right out of the grave. Fuckin' zombie.

The men laughed. They all felt great relief.

Spook city, said Mitchell Sanders.

Lee Strunk made a funny ghost sound, a kind of moaning, yet very happy, and right then, when Strunk made that high happy moaning sound, when he went Ahhooooo, right then Ted Lavender was shot in the head on his way back from peeing. He lay with his mouth open. The teeth were broken. There was a swollen black bruise under his left eye. The cheekbone was gone. Oh shit, Rat Kiley said, the guy's dead. The guy's dead, he kept saying, which seemed profound—the guy's dead. I mean really.

The things they carried were determined to some extent by superstition. Lieutenant Cross carried his good-luck pebble. Dave Jensen carried a rabbit's foot. Norman Bowker, otherwise a very gentle person, carried a thumb that had been presented to him as a gift by Mitchell Sanders. The thumb was dark brown, rubbery to the touch, and weighed four ounces at most. It had been cut from a VC corpse, a boy of fifteen or sixteen. They'd found him at the bottom of an irrigation ditch, badly burned, flies in his mouth and eyes. The boy wore black shorts and sandals. At the time of his death he had been carrying a pouch of rice, a rifle, and three magazines of ammunition.

You want my opinion, Mitchell Sanders said, there's a definite moral here.

He put his hand on the dead boy's wrist. He was quiet for a time, as if counting a pulse, then he patted the stomach, almost affectionately, and used Kiowa's hunting hatchet to remove the thumb.

Henry Dobbins asked what the moral was.

Moral?

You know. *Moral*.

Sanders wrapped the thumb in toilet paper and handed it across to Norman Bowker. There was no blood. Smiling, he kicked the boy's head, watched the flies scatter, and said, It's like with that old TV show—Paladin. Have gun, will travel.

Henry Dobbins thought about it.

Yeah, well, he finally said. I don't see no moral.

There it *is*, man.

Fuck off.

They carried USO stationery and pencils and pens. They carried Sterno, safety pins, trip flares, signal flares, spools of wire, razor blades, chewing tobacco, liberated joss sticks and statuettes of the smiling Buddha, candles, grease pencils, *The Stars and Stripes*, fingernail clippers, Psy Ops leaflets, bush hats, bolos, and much more. Twice a week, when the resupply choppers came in, they carried hot chow in green mermite cans and large canvas bags filled with iced beer and soda pop. They carried plastic water containers, each with a two-gallon capacity. Mitchell Sanders carried a set of starched tiger fatigues for special occasions. Henry Dobbins carried Black Flag insecticide. Dave Jensen carried empty sandbags that could be filled at night for added protection. Lee Strunk carried tanning lotion. Some things they carried in common. Taking turns, they carried the big PRC-77 scrambler radio, which weighed 30 pounds with its battery. They shared the weight of memory. They took up what others could no longer bear. Often, they carried each other, the wounded or weak. They carried infections. They carried chess sets, basketballs, Vietnamese–English dictionaries, insignias of rank, Bronze Stars and

Purple Hearts, plastic cards imprinted with the Code of Conduct. They carried diseases, among them malaria and dysentery. They carried lice and ringworm and leeches and paddy algae and various rots and molds. They carried the land itself—Vietnam, the place, the soil—a powdery orange-red dust that covered their boots and fatigues and faces. They carried the sky. The whole atmosphere, they carried it, the humidity, the monsoons, the stink of fungus and decay, all of it, they carried gravity. They moved like mules. By daylight they took sniper fire, at night they were mortared, but it was not battle, it was just the endless march, village to village, without purpose, nothing won or lost. They marched for the sake of the march. They plodded along slowly, dumbly, leaning forward against the heat, unthinking, all blood and bone, simple grunts, soldiering with their legs, toiling up the hills and down into the paddies and across the rivers and up again and down, just humping, one step and then the next and then another, but no volition, no will, because it was automatic, it was anatomy, and the war was entirely a matter of posture and carriage, the hump was everything, a kind of inertia, a kind of emptiness, a dullness of desire and intellect and conscience and hope and human sensibility. Their principles were in their feet. Their calculations were biological. They had no sense of strategy or mission. They searched the villages without knowing what to look for, not caring, kicking over jars of rice, frisking children and old men, blowing tunnels, sometimes setting fires and sometimes not, then forming up and moving on to the next village, then other villages, where it would always be the same. They carried their own lives. The pressures were enormous. In the heat of early afternoon, they would remove their helmets and flak jackets, walking bare, which was dangerous but which helped ease the strain. They would often discard things along the route of march. Purely for comfort, they would throw away rations, blow their Claymores and grenades, no matter, because by nightfall the resupply choppers would arrive with more of the same, then a day or two later still more, fresh watermelons and crates of ammunition and sunglasses and woolen sweaters—the resources were stunning—sparklers for the Fourth of July, colored eggs for Easter—it was the great American war chest— the fruits of science, the smokestacks, the canneries, the arsenals at Hartford, the Minnesota forests, the machine shops, the vast fields of corn and wheat—they carried like freight trains; they carried it on their backs and shoulders—and for all the ambiguities of Vietnam, all the mysteries and unknowns, there was at least the single abiding certainty that they would never be at a loss for things to carry.

After the chopper took Lavender away, Lieutenant Jimmy Cross led his men into the village of Than Khe. They burned everything. They shot chickens and dogs, they trashed the village well, they called in artillery and watched the wreckage, then they marched for several hours through the hot afternoon, and then at dusk, while Kiowa explained how Lavender died, Lieutenant Cross found himself trembling.

He tried not to cry. With his entrenching tool, which weighed five pounds, he began digging a hole in the earth.

He felt shame. He hated himself. He had loved Martha more than his men, and as a consequence Lavender was now dead, and this was something he would have to carry like a stone in his stomach for the rest of the war.

All he could do was dig. He used his entrenching tool like an ax, slashing, feeling both love and hate, and then later, when it was full dark, he sat at the bottom of his foxhole and wept. It went on for a long while. In part, he was grieving for Ted Lavender, but mostly it was for Martha, and for himself, because she belonged to another world, which was not quite real, and because she was a junior at Mount Sebastian College in New Jersey, a poet and a virgin and uninvolved, and because he realized she did not love him and never would.

Like cement, Kiowa whispered in the dark. I swear to God—boom, down. Not a word.

I've heard this, said Norman Bowker.

A pisser, you know? Still zipping himself up. Zapped while zipping.

All right, fine. That's enough.

Yeah, but you had to see it, the guy just—

I *heard*, man. Cement. So why not shut the fuck *up*?

Kiowa shook his head sadly and glanced over at the hole where Lieutenant Jimmy Cross sat watching the night. The air was thick and wet. A warm dense fog had settled over the paddies and there was the stillness that precedes rain.

After a time Kiowa sighed.

One thing for use, he said. The lieutenant's in some deep hurt. I mean that crying jag—the way he was carrying on—it wasn't fake or anything, it was real heavy-duty hurt. The man cares.

Sure, Norman Bowker said.

Say what you want, the man does care.

We all got problems.

Not Lavender.

No, I guess not, Bowker said. Do me a favor, though.

Shut up?

That's a smart Indian. Shut up.

Shrugging, Kiowa pulled off his boots. He wanted to say more, just to lighten up his sleep, but instead he opened his New Testament and arranged it beneath his head as a pillow. The fog made things seem hollow and unattached. He tried not to think about Ted Lavender, but then he was thinking how fast it was, no drama, down and dead, and how it was hard to feel anything except surprise. It seemed unchristian. He wished he could find some great sadness, or even anger, but the emotion wasn't there and he couldn't make it happen. Mostly he felt pleased to be alive. He liked the smell of the New Testament under his cheek, the leather and ink and paper and glue, whatever the chemicals were. He liked hearing the sounds of night. Even his fatigue, it felt fine, the stiff muscles and the prickly awareness of his own body, a floating feeling. He enjoyed not being dead. Lying there, Kiowa admired Lieutenant Jimmy Cross's capacity for grief. He wanted to share the man's pain, he wanted to care as Jimmy Cross cared. And yet when he closed his eyes all he could think was Boom-down, and all he could feel was the pleasure of having his boots off and the fog curling in around him and the damp soil and the Bible smells and the plush comfort of night.

After a moment Norman Bowker sat up in the dark.

What the hell, he said. You want to talk, *talk*. Tell it to me.

Forget it.

No, man, go on. One thing I hate, it's a silent Indian.

For the most part they carried themselves with poise, a kind of dignity. Now and then, however, there were times of panic, when they squealed or wanted to squeal but couldn't, when they twitched and made moaning sounds and covered their heads and said Dear Jesus and flopped around on the earth and fired their weapons blindly and cringed and sobbed and begged for the noise to stop and went wild and made stupid promises to themselves and to God and to their mothers and fathers, hoping not to die. In different ways, it happened to all of them. Afterward, when the firing ended, they would blink and peek up. They would touch their bodies, feeling shame, then quickly hiding it. They would force themselves to stand. As if in slow motion, frame by frame, the world would take on the old logic—absolute silence, then the wind, then sunlight, then voices. It was the burden of being alive. Awkwardly, the men would reassemble themselves, first in private, then in groups, becoming soldiers again. They would repair the leaks in their eyes. They would check for casualties, call in dustoffs, light cigarettes, try to smile, clear their throats and spit and begin cleaning their weapons. After a time someone would shake his head and say, No lie, I almost shit my pants, and someone else would laugh, which meant it was bad, yes, but the guy had obviously not shit his pants, it wasn't that bad, and in any case nobody would ever do such a thing and then go ahead and talk about it. They would squint into the dense, oppressive sunlight. For a few moments, perhaps, they would fall silent, lighting a joint and tracking its passage from man to man, inhaling, holding in the humiliation. Scary stuff, one of them might say. But then someone else would grin or flick his eyebrows and say, Roger-dodger, almost cut me a new asshole, *almost*.

There were numerous such poses. Some carried themselves with a sort of wistful resignation, others with pride or stiff soldierly discipline or good humor or macho zeal. They were afraid of dying but they were even more afraid to show it.

They found jokes to tell.

They used a hard vocabulary to contain the terrible softness. *Greased* they'd say. *Offed, lit up, zapped while zipping*. It wasn't cruelty, just stage presence. They were actors. When someone died, it wasn't quite dying, because in a curious way it seemed scripted, and because they had their lines mostly memorized, irony mixed with tragedy, and because they called it by other names, as if to encyst and destroy the reality of death itself. They kicked corpses. They cut off thumbs. They talked grunt lingo. They told stories about Ted Lavender's supply of tranquilizers, how the poor guy didn't feel a thing, how incredibly tranquil he was.

There's a moral here, said Mitchell Sanders.

They were waiting for Lavender's chopper, smoking the dead man's dope. The moral's pretty obvious, Sanders said, and winked. Stay away from drugs. No joke, they'll ruin your day every time.

700

Cute, said Henry Dobbins.

Mind blower, get it? Talk about wiggy. Nothing left, just blood and brains.

They made themselves laugh.

There it is, they'd say. Over and over—there it is, my friend, there it is—as if the repetition itself were an act of poise, a balance between crazy and almost crazy, knowing without going, there it is, which meant be cool, let it ride, because Oh yeah, man, you can't change what can't be changed, there it is, there it absolutely and positively and fucking well *is*.

They were tough.

They carried all the emotional baggage of men who might die. Grief, terror, love, longing—these were intangibles, but the intangibles had their own mass and specific gravity, they had tangible weight. They carried shameful memories. They carried the common secret of cowardice barely restrained, the instinct to run or freeze or hide, and in many respects this was the heaviest burden of all, for it could never be put down, it required perfect balance and perfect posture. They carried their reputations. They carried the soldier's greatest fear, which was the fear of blushing. Men killed, and died, because they were embarrassed not to. It was what had brought them to the war in the first place, nothing positive, no dreams of glory or honor, just to avoid the blush of dishonor. They died so as not to die of embarrassment. They crawled into tunnels and walked point and advanced under fire. Each morning, despite the unknowns, they made their legs move. They endured. They kept humping. They did not submit to the obvious alternative, which was simply to close the eyes and fall. So easy, really. Go limp and tumble to the ground and let the muscles unwind and not speak and not budge until your buddies picked you up and lifted you into the chopper that would roar and dip its nose and carry you off to the world. A mere matter of falling, yet no one ever fell. It was not courage, exactly; the object was not valor. Rather, they were too frightened to be cowards.

By and large they carried these things inside, maintaining the masks of composure. They sneered at sick call. They spoke bitterly about guys who had found release by shooting off their own toes or fingers. Pussies, they'd say. Candy-asses. It was fierce, mocking talk, with only a trace of envy or awe, but even so the image played itself out behind their eyes.

They imagined the muzzle against flesh. So easy: squeeze the trigger and blow away a toe. They imagined it. They imagined the quick, sweet pain, then the evacuation to Japan, then a hospital with warm beds and cute geisha nurses.

And they dreamed of freedom birds.

At night, on guard, staring into the dark, they were carried away by jumbo jets. They felt the rush of takeoff. *Gone!* they yelled. And then velocity—wings and engines—a smiling stewardess—but it was more than a plane, it was a real bird, a big sleek silver bird with feathers and talons and high screeching. They were flying. The weights fell off; there was nothing to bear. They laughed and held on tight, feeling the cold slap of wind and altitude, soaring, thinking *It's over, I'm gone!*—they were naked, they were light and free—it was all lightness, bright and fast and buoyant, light as light, a helium buzz in the brain, a giddy bubbling in the lungs as they were taken up over the clouds and the war, beyond duty, beyond gravity and mortification and global entanglements—*Sin loi!* they yelled. *I'm sorry, motherfuckers, but I'm out of it, I'm goofed, I'm on a space cruise, I'm gone!*—and it was a restful, unencumbered sensation, just riding the light waves, sailing that big silver freedom bird over the mountains and oceans, over America, over the farms and great sleeping cities and cemeteries and highways and the golden arches of McDonald's, it was flight, a kind of fleeing, a kind of falling, falling higher and higher, spinning off the edge of the earth and beyond the sun and through the vast, silent vacuum where there were no burdens and where everything weighed exactly nothing—*Gone!* they screamed, *I'm sorry but I'm gone!*—and so at night, not quite dreaming, they gave themselves over to lightness, they were carried, they were purely borne.

On the morning after Ted Lavender died, First Lieutenant Jimmy Cross crouched at the bottom of his foxhole and burned Martha's letters. Then he burned the two photographs. There was a steady rain falling, which made it difficult, but he used heat tabs and Sterno to build a small fire, screening it with his body, holding the photographs over the tight blue flame with the tips of his finger.

He realized it was only a gesture. Stupid, he thought. Sentimental, too, but mostly just stupid.

Lavender was dead. You couldn't burn the blame.

Besides, the letters were in his head. And even now, without photographs, Lieutenant Cross could see Martha playing volleyball in her white gym shorts and yellow T-shirt. He could see her moving in the rain.

When the fire died out, Lieutenant Cross pulled his poncho over his shoulders and ate breakfast from a can.

There was no great mystery, he decided.

In those burned letters Martha had never mentioned the war, except to say, Jimmy, take care of yourself. She wasn't involved. She signed the letters Love, but it wasn't love, and all the fine lines and technicalities did not matter. Virginity was no longer an issue. He hated her. Yes, he did. He hated her. Love, too, but it was a hard, hating kind of love.

The morning came up wet and blurry. Everything seemed part of everything else, the fog and Martha and the deepening rain.

He was a soldier, after all.

Half smiling, Lieutenant Jimmy Cross took out his maps. He shook his head hard, as if to clear it, then bent forward and began planning the day's march. In ten minutes, or maybe twenty, he would rouse the men and they would pack up and head west, where the maps showed the country to be green and inviting. They would do what they had always done. The rain might add some weight, but otherwise it would be one more day layered upon all the other days.

He was realistic about it. There was that new hardness in his stomach. He loved her but he hated her.

No more fantasies, he told himself.

Henceforth, when he thought about Martha, it would be only to think that she belonged elsewhere. He would shut down the daydreams. This was not Mount Sebastian, it was another world, where there were no pretty poems or mid-term exams, a place where men died because of carelessness and gross stupidity. Kiowa was right. Boom-down, and you were dead, never partly dead.

Briefly, in the rain, Lieutenant Cross saw Martha's gray eyes gazing back at him.

He understood.

It was very sad, he thought. The things men carried inside. The things men did or felt they had to do.

He almost nodded at her, but didn't.

Instead he went back to his maps. He was now determined to perform his duties firmly and without negligence. It wouldn't help Lavender, he knew that, but from this point on he would comport himself as an officer. He would dispose of his good-luck pebble.

Swallow it, maybe, or use Lee Strunk's slingshot, or just drop it along the trail. On the march he would impose strict field discipline. He would be careful to send out flank security, to prevent straggling or bunching up, to keep his troops moving at the proper pace and at the proper interval. He would insist on clean weapons. He would confiscate the remainder of Lavender's dope. Later in the day, perhaps, he would call the men together and speak to them plainly. He would accept the blame for what had happened to Ted Lavender. He would be a man about it. He would look them in the eyes, keeping his chin level, and he would issue the new SOPs in a calm, impersonal tone of voice, a lieutenant's voice, leaving no room for argument or discussion. Commencing immediately, he'd tell them, they would no longer abandon equipment along the route of the march. They would police up their acts. They would get their shit together, and keep it together, and maintain it neatly and in good working order.

He would not tolerate laxity. He would show strength, distancing himself.

Among the men there would be grumbling, of course, and maybe worse, because their days would seem longer and their loads heavier, but Lieutenant Jimmy Cross reminded himself that his obligation was not to be loved but to lead. He would dispense with love; it was not now a factor. And if anyone quarreled or complained, he would simply tighten his lips and arrange his shoulders in the correct command posture. He might give a curt little nod. Or he might not. He might just shrug and say, Carry on, then they would saddle up and form into a column and move out toward the villages west of Than Khe.

1990

ACKNOWLEDGMENTS

'A Day in the Open' from *Plain Pleasures* by Jane Bowles and *The Collected Works of Jane Bowles*. Copyright © 1945 by Jane Bowles. Reprinted in the UK by permission of Peter Owen Ltd. Reprinted in the US by permission of Farrar, Straus & Giroux, Inc.

'A Distant Episode' from *A Thousand Days for Mokhtar* by Paul Bowles and *Collected Stories 1939–1976* by Paul Bowles. Reprinted in the UK by permission of Peter Owen Ltd. Reprinted in the US by permission of Black Sparrow Press.

'Blackberry Winter' from *The Circus in the Attic and Other Stories*, copyright © 1947 and renewed 1975 by Robert Penn Warren, reprinted in the UK and the US by permission of Harcourt Brace Jovanovich, Inc.

'O City of Broken Dreams' from *The Stories of John Cheever*. Copyright © 1948 by John Cheever. Reprinted in the UK by permission of Jonathan Cape. Reprinted in the US by permission of Alfred A. Knopf, Inc.

'The Lottery' from *The Lottery* by Shirley Jackson. Copyright © 1948, 1949 by Shirley Jackson. Renewal copyright © 1976, 1977 by Laurence Hyman, Barry Hyman, Mrs Sarah Webster and Mrs Joanne Schnurer.

'The View from the Balcony' from *The Collected Stories of Wallace Stegner*. Copyright © 1948 by Wallace Stegner. Renewal copyright © 1960 by Wallace Stegner. Reprinted in the UK by permission of Random House Inc. Reprinted in the US by permission of Brandt & Brandt Literary Agents, Inc.

'No Place For You, My Love' from *The Collected Stories of Eudora Welty* and *The Bride of the Innisfallen and Other Stories* by Eudora Welty. Copyright © 1952 and renewed 1980 by Eudora Welty. Reprinted in the UK by permission of Marion Boyars Publishers Ltd. Reprinted in the US by permission of Harcourt Brace Jovanovich, Inc.

'The State of Grace' from *First Love and Other Sorrows* by Harold Brodkey. Copyright © 1954 by Harold Brodkey. Reprinted in the UK and the US by permission of Wylie Aitken & Stone, Inc.

'The Magic Barrel' from *The Magic Barrel* by Bernard Malamud. Copyright © 1954 and renewal copyright © 1982 by Bernard Malamud. Reprinted in the UK by permission of Chatto & Windus. Reprinted in the US by permission of Farrar, Straus & Giroux, Inc.

'Good Country People' from *A Good Man is Hard to Find and Other Stories*, copyright © 1955 by Flannery O'Connor and renewed 1983 by Regina O'Connor. Reprinted in the UK by permission of Harold Matson Co., Inc. Reprinted in the US by permission of Harcourt Brace Jovanovich, Inc.

709